Unaccounted For

A. E. Dooland

Unaccounted For
Ebook edition ISBN: 978-0-9941779-7-1
Print edition ISBN: 978-0-9941779-8-8

For permission requests and licensing inquiries, write to the publisher via aedooland.com.

This is a work of fiction. Names, characters, businesses, organisations, places, events, and incidents are either the product of the author's imagination or are used fictitiously. Any resemblance to actual persons, living or dead, or actual events is entirely coincidental.

Edited by Martina Vesela

Cover Art by Yue Li

For Ghostywind, who got me writing again

For all my Rynnlings in the Spire: thank you for the energy and hype (but not the gifs)

And for my children:

may they grow up never once feeling lost.

Contents

Chapter 1: The Ravine

Allegra had driven 30 minutes into the bush to get away from people. She should have known one of them would wander in and need rescuing anyway.

For the moment, though, she was still pretending the plan had worked.

She was perched on the bonnet of her beat-up old LandCruiser, gazing out at what should have been a beautiful, tranquil sunset over Nattai National Park, complete with birdsong and technicolour sky.

Unfortunately, the Hume—loudest highway in the fucking world—hadn't got the memo that she'd driven 30 minutes to escape it. She'd thought the slope and the gumtrees might have swallowed the sound of the B-Doubles and motorbikes. Well, apparently not. Either that, or Google Maps had re-routed all the traffic between Sydney and Melbourne down the road just over the hill.

She drew a slow, deep breath and released it, eyes on the horizon—only to have someone lean on their horn in what sounded like a long and drawn-out slur. There was a much smaller and more nasal honk in reply.

Fuck it, Allegra thought, pressing her lips into a thin line. This was hopeless. She should just risk it and drive further in, even if her spare tyre was already fitted to one of her wheels. If she got another flat, she could hike out; she'd spent half her career finding people in worse terrain.

Then again, if she got caught out of mobile range... She exhaled audibly. Timothy.

At the thought of him, she found herself peeking at her phone: three notifications. Her eyes narrowed. He might have been her ex-husband and the father of their now-adult son, but from the *"Lasagna tonight, what do you say?* :)" texts, anyone would think she was expected home for dinner.

'Home' being generous, given most of her life was currently packed into the back of her LandCruiser. Timothy's place was where she kept the rest of it, where he kept feeding her, and where she kept pretending that it didn't make things complicated. It also meant she didn't have to pay for storage units, or worse, rent a flat she hardly ever needed.

She slipped her phone back into her pocket. *Sorry, Timothy, but lasagna won't be happening tonight*. She didn't bother reading the other notifications from him; if it was important, he'd call. So would work.

Her phone wasn't going to ring, though—it was a mild, still evening, and no one was going to need her to scale anything to find anyone.

On that—who was she kidding? She could definitely drive another 10 or 20km into the mountains and find somewhere that was sheltered from the noise pollution. What was the worst thing that could happen?

She pushed off the bonnet and hopped into the worn and dusty driver's seat, clicking her belt with one hand and twisting the key with the other. Then, ignoring the rattling engine, she reversed back onto the road and started the slow roll downhill on the unfenced, ungravelled, and unridged dirt road into the valley.

The sunlight vanished as she headed down below the tree canopy, and the temperature dropped as sharply as the edge of the road beside her. It may have been a mild evening 300 metres uphill, but it was a chilly night in the bushland. That suited Allegra just fine; it was easier to sleep when she was cool, anyway.

She was busy trying to decide what she was going to cook for dinner (or, more aptly, what she *could* cook with the few ingredients she had in the boot), when her headlights bounced off a brightly coloured item on the narrow verge.

At first, she thought it might just be a rubbish bag some wanker had tossed out of their car. But as she approached it, she realised it wasn't plastic but neon polyester: a high-vis backpack. The owner was nowhere to be seen.

Her stomach dropped. That was *not* a good sign.

She pulled up to it and turned off the engine, and her finger hovered over the 'area lights' button on her car's central console. *Come on Allegra, it could just have fallen off someone's roof racks,* she told herself. She found herself flicking the button anyway, and the entire bush around her was immediately struck with daylight-level floodlights. Instead of second-guessing herself, she slid out of the car and went to inspect the bag.

It was a typical large daypack—an expensive brand that didn't look very used. She hadn't really settled on a hypothesis about what had happened until she noticed a water bottle and a half-eaten sandwich close by. The person had been on foot, had been halfway through their dinner, and was now missing.

Across the road, the narrow verge ended in a steep, jagged fall into the dark.

Taking a deep breath to quiet the immediate adrenaline surge, she kept herself in the present and ducked back into her car for the torch. It was possible the person had decided on a quick scramble down towards the creek below. They might have been drunk—though a quick sniff of the bottle suggested only water, so probably not. Or they might be a tourist with no idea how dangerous the area was.

The drop was shielded from the car floodlights, so Allegra beamed her torch down into it. "Hello!" she called, pushing the words out with her diaphragm to make sure they carried as much as possible. "Are you alright down there?" The only thing she heard in reply was her own voice echoing off the rockface opposite.

The torchlight wasn't reflecting off glasses, watches or shoes. She couldn't see anything unusual, only the drop itself: near-vertical in places, jagged with rock and scrub. Not safe to descend on foot. While it might be possible for an amateur to scramble up it safely enough, there was very little chance anyone with no training or equipment could get down it. Judging by the pack and the little servo dinner left on the road, she was not dealing with a seasoned professional.

"Hello!" she called again, walking down the road a little further to get a better angle for her torchlight. "Welfare check! Can you hear me?"

Silence, except for the echoing ripples of her own voice.

Shit. Perhaps it was time for the big guns? "Search and Rescue, can you hear me?"

Still nothing. Announcing herself as SES usually prompted a response from anyone conscious enough to be embarrassed, evasive, or doing something they shouldn't. Silence was always a concern. She lowered the torch for a moment, considering her options.

There were probably many explanations that did not involve the owner of the pack falling into the ravine. She ran through them in her mind, her eyes resting on the backpack and half-eaten dinner. While less serious options *did* exist and *were* possible, she felt uneasy about them. She knew what the most likely explanation was. After all, she did this for a living.

She sighed; better safe than sorry. Jogging back over to the car, she leant into the cabin to activate her GPS beacon and unhook the radio handset. "Control, this is BSAR 118."

A scratchy voice buzzed through the receiver. "BSAR 118, go ahead." Allegra briefly explained the situation, trying to stress that it was just a precaution. Control listened, their silence speaking volumes.

"I'm not too keen on you going over the edge on a hunch without support," Control said. "Peter G's got a drone in the area on a private job.

You want a flyover if you don't radio in 15?" There was a pause. "Also, aren't you supposed to be off until after Christmas, Allegra?"

She groaned audibly. "*Yes*." There was a chuckle in response. "Tell Peter that would be great. I'll light a beacon if we need a team here."

"Okay. Standing by. Hopefully it turns out to be nothing and you can finally take your annual leave."

Hopefully. Allegra's hands and body knew the next steps in the process by heart. She backed her LandCruiser to the edge and pulled on her oh-so flattering orange high-vis jumpsuit. Then came the harnesses and protective gear, fitted by muscle memory while she tied up her thick blond mop of hair so it fit under her helmet. Finally kitted out, she turned back towards the drop and set the balls of her feet at the lip of the rock face.

Here we go, she told herself, and pushed off.

The bank was steep—vertical rescue steep—and worse, it was a shifting mess of soil, rock, and scrub. In the dark, every step was a guess: loose dirt, solid stone, sudden overhang. Branches caught at her ropes and straps, and without her brush knife she had to break them off by hand as she descended.

It was a slog, even for someone who'd spent decades moving through terrain like this. Every few metres, she twisted to shine the torch below her, checking for new sightlines as the bottom kept failing to appear.

She'd been going for probably the full 15 minutes she'd told Control she'd need and was considering radioing an update when her torchlight hit something.

Her breath caught.

She swung the torch back towards it. There it was again—red. And blue. And the reflective strap of a sneaker. Then, holding the light steady, she could make out the shape of a body against the grey of the rock.

I knew it, she realised, adjusting her hold of the torch. *I knew it.* "Hello?" she called out. "Bush Search and Rescue! Can you hear me?"

The figure didn't move.

God, I hope this doesn't turn into a recovery rather than a rescue, she thought, noting the solid rock the figure was sprawled on. She finished the descent as quickly as the slope allowed. Once her boots were stable on the rock, she unclipped from the rope, took the marker beacon from her chest, and switched it on. Red light pulsed across the rock and scrub. She placed it on bare stone for the drone to find, then rushed to the figure.

She dropped down beside him. A man, she thought. Young, white, probably in his 20s. About her son's age—she pushed that thought away.

There was no obvious blood splatter from his head or pooling on the rock. "Hello? Can you hear me?" She turned him over to assess him. No fluid foaming around his mouth, but there was a large laceration on his forehead partially absorbed by his long hair. Her fingers dipped into his neck for a pulse, and to her relief, she found one. Quick and shallow; he might have internal bleeding. It could just be from the head injury, though—he was completely unconscious.

She was feeling the length of his limbs for fractures that needed splinting when she heard the hornet-like buzz of a drone approaching. Looking up, she saw the tell-tale six-point shape hanging above her. While she was watching, it switched from low-profile lighting to the bright incident response flashes. *Good*, she thought, *they'd better hurry*.

She found what felt like a clean break in one of the boy's legs. She'd barely splinted it and rolled him into the recovery position before three (*three*?!) choppers rolled overhead. Even behind the floodlights, she could see the paramedic uniforms on the chopper unit crew as they slid the doors open.

Not that she wasn't grateful for the quick and powerful response, but even getting a *single* chopper out on site was sometimes an exercise in beating one's head against the wall. Three was completely insane, especially since the drone had cameras and Peter would have clearly been able to see there was only one casualty. Maybe it had something to do with that private job he'd been flying nearby?

She couldn't dwell on the thought, however, as two paramedics zipped down the line in the billowing downwash from the chopper, touching down on the rockface with their bags and various gear. No one she recognised.

"I found him here about 10 minutes ago," she said after they'd introduced themselves and got started. "I dressed his head wound—if his skull is fractured, no distortion. He's got a tib-fib in his left leg, splinted. Pulse is 120ish. Breathing's been okay."

Hair and clothes blowing about them, they were already cutting off his jumper and pulling out the mobile ECG to check if he needed to be stabilised before a lift.

Allegra wasn't needed much from this point. The chopper team usually took over immediately, sweeping in and sweeping out in a few minutes with the casualty strapped to a rescue stretcher. She watched them do exactly that: securing him, clipping in, and lifting him out with a paramedic riding the line beside him to keep the stretcher steady.

In what felt like a flash, this poor boy had been lifted into one of the choppers. It hovered for a moment to allow secure transfer inside, and then spun and tilted towards Sydney, powering off. The other two helicopters switched off their spotlights and followed suit.

Just as quickly as they'd arrived, they'd left—and the patient was en route to Westmead, the top trauma hospital in Sydney. If it was possible to survive his injuries, he now had the best chance to. Finding someone in time was the part that mattered.

Right place at the right time, Allegra realised, smiling briefly. With the wind and bluster from the choppers gone, she only noticed the drone was still there once her eyes adjusted enough to the lower light. She waved thanks at it. Peter obviously took that as 'operation over' because it lifted off into the sky.

Then, she was alone again in the quiet space of the ravine—ironically what she'd originally been seeking. After a rescue, though, the silence was oddly oppressive.

During operations, time sped up, her muscles sang, and her mind felt razor sharp. Afterwards, that all faded. Time slowed and her brain was still racing. It was a pity she didn't know any of the paramedics and couldn't catch up with them afterwards to follow up on the outcome.

She clipped on and was about to start retracting the winch when something reflected off her headlamp. Curious, she crossed to it and found a surprisingly intact mobile phone. The boy's, obviously.

She picked it up and slipped it into the deep thigh pocket of her jumpsuit. A phone could be a lifeline when the people you loved were somewhere else. She knew that better than most. Maybe he did, too.

The winch did most of the work on the way back up. All Allegra had to do was steer herself around trees and jutting rock, but her muscles were shaking badly enough that she hooked her wrist straps to the rope for support.

She was already thinking about unclipping, washing off the dirt, and finding somewhere nearby to let her body come down when she rose over the road edge and saw the boy's neon bag sitting in her floodlights.

She stood there for a moment, winch tight, grappling with her own feelings as much as the rope. She was immediately conscious of the weight of his mobile against her thigh. She should really return his things as promptly as possible; if he was still unconscious, the hospital might need them to identify him. If he woke up, he might want to call his family. And if someone was out there not knowing what had happened to him, they deserved an answer.

She unhooked and went to switch off the floodlights. Unfortunately, handing his possessions back meant driving into Sydney traffic and trying to find a park near Westmead Hospital; two of the worst possible ways she could imagine spending a Saturday night. But what could she do?

Once she was in her car and on the Hume, the traffic was worse than she expected for a Saturday night. It felt personal, like the universe knew how much she bloody hated the city and was making sure she experienced as much of it as possible.

She jabbed through the radio presets looking for traffic updates, but Saturday night radio was all sport, ads, and a Vale family-owned news station running a panel on youth crime that sounded like it had been assembled from Facebook comments. Allegra gave it 10 seconds, then switched it off.

Around Westmead itself was total gridlock, and she ended up parking illegally in Parramatta (fuck it), and just full on trekking the rest of the way to the hospital on foot with the man's pack slung over a shoulder.

Under the streetlights, she could see how dirty and cut up her hands and forearms were. That, with her faded tattoos and unbrushed helmet hair made her realise she probably should have had a shower *before* returning his bag, or people were going to think she'd straight up stolen it herself. It was too late to worry about those details now, though. She'd arrived.

Around Emergency there was rather more commotion than usual, even for Westmead. When she got closer, she spotted part of it roped off with police tape, and what could only be described as an absolute horde of media camped behind it. Every single station—TV and radio—was represented, including the Vale-owned ones Timothy liked to rant about and a few Allegra had never heard of. There were reporters, too.

Odd, she thought, but not odd enough to be her problem. She kept walking towards the doors. Two huge men stepped in front of her. "Sorry, no visitors at the moment." Taken aback, her eyes dipped down to their waists: they were wearing *guns*. Obviously something was going on in there.

Oh well, it wasn't like she needed to actually visit the boy, did she? "Well, can I ask someone to pass this to a recent chopper transfer?" She indicated the bag. "It was left on scene."

Noting her language, their demeanour changed. "You police?"

She shook her head. "SES."

Suddenly, the media circus beside them fell curiously quiet. It made her uneasy. The two guards looked at each other, and then one of them said more subduedly, "Let me check with security." He walked a small distance away and put his phone to his ear.

Beside her, she heard the smooth voice of a reporter call out to her, "You're SES?" Allegra turned a little suspiciously towards the woman, who was a walking advertisement for Sephora. Wondering if she was going to regret answering, she nodded.

The reporter's face lit up brighter than Allegra's floodlights. "Were you at the scene of the *terrible accident* in Nattai National Park?" She leant heavily into the words 'terrible accident' as every camera behind the rope swung towards Allegra.

She felt like a deer in headlights. "I'm not sure I should comment on it."

It wasn't like she could have anyway, because in an instant she was *mobbed*. Ropes or no ropes, suddenly she was surrounded by a ring of cameras and microphones and people crowding and shouting and calling and yelling for her attention and pushing her backwards towards the hospital while she struggled to catch a breath or a word of what any of them were—

"Right this way," a booming voice said behind her and the double-doors swung open to engulf her as she was pulled inside by a large tree-trunk arm.

The doors shut immediately behind her, sealing the noise on the other side.

Frozen, Allegra stared at the halo of light pushing through the door frame, jaw open.

The security guard laughed nervously. "Jesus Christ, what the fuck?" he said, perfectly voicing Allegra's inner thoughts. "Absolute fucking psychos, the lot of them." He touched Allegra's arm to indicate she should follow him. "Anyway, security says you're clear to go up to ORs, if you want. The Vale kid is still in surgery, though."

At that name, she stopped in place. "Vale?"

The media Vales?

"Yeah?" the security guard said, looking over his shoulder, confused. "The guy they pulled out of a ravine tonight, that's who you wanted to give the bag to, yeah?"

Allegra felt all the blood drain out of her face. "Yes."

Chapter 2: The Waiting Room

There were matching pairs of those black-suited, gun-toting security guards on every door inside the eerily quiet hospital. The usual hospital bustle was absent—only medical staff moving quickly between wards, and no visitors anywhere. She was walking down a corridor in what she believed was the right direction when she was stopped by another suit.

"OR 4 is that way, ma'am," the black suit said, gesturing back behind her. He had an American accent.

Uneasy, she gave him a searching look as she retraced her steps. In the end, the correct door was the one with *four* goons on it. They hardly even looked at her as they stepped aside to let her through. It was all very odd.

Inside, there was at least some semblance of normality. A group of people had assembled there, lounging, chatting, scrolling on their phones. They were an assorted bunch; several fashionably dressed teenagers and young adults, three or four older adults in very neat and clearly well-chosen clothes, and someone's toddler who was pulling all the plastic cups out of the water dispenser.

They all looked up as she entered. Someone already had a phone pointed at her. "Oh, she's here! Hey!" Several of them jumped up and started towards her, glossy and well-groomed enough that Allegra immediately pegged them as Vales, Vale-adjacent, or otherwise important enough to be unbearable.

Allegra spoke before they could get too close to her. "Yes. I wanted to return—" She realised she didn't even know who she'd rescued. "His bag and his personal belongings. Who should I leave them with?"

One of the security guards stepped out from behind her and received them. "You can leave them with me."

Allegra relaxed slightly. "Thank you." She forced a polite smile at the family and turned to leave.

"Wait!"

She turned, her pulse beginning to quicken. "You saved my brother and you're just going to walk out?" The man speaking looked mid-20s with too-white teeth and he was watching the screen of his iPhone as he pointed it at her, grinning—not at her, but at his own performance.

While she was watching him, he gave the phone to a man standing beside him who was roughly his age. "Hold this at us for a sec." His friend complied.

Then, to Allegra's panic, he rushed over and threw his arms around her, pretending to cry.

Families of casualties hugged her all the time. Usually, she could manage a back pat and a few kind words. But this man's tears were so obviously manufactured that she stood rigid in his arms, wondering if any part of him was real.

"God, can you fucking stop that, Beau? You're so fucking embarrassing." A young woman's voice. A glance at the owner suggested it was probably his sister. "Literally no one's going to watch it anyway."

"I have more followers than *you* do," 'Beau' said, immediately ceasing his act, straightening his clothes, and patting Allegra twice on the arm like one might do to an obedient busboy. "Thanks." Then, he gave her the once-over. "Did they not let you shower before you brought that stuff back or what?"

She bristled. "I thought he might wake up and want his phone."

At that, the whole room *laughed openly*. Her eyes narrowed.

"Oh, lady, did you get that part right," Beau told her, smacking her arm again. "Alright, you go have your shower. You're going to want to be cleaned up for tomorrow."

Allegra wasn't sure what to say to that, so she gave Beau a neutral nod and escaped as soon as the guards opened the door. Every single person in that room was someone she would have crossed a road to avoid.

Fortunately, security showed her out through a small side door, away from the media circus. She cut across the parklands towards her car, grateful for the grass under her boots and the trees overhead. With every step away from the hospital, the evening began to feel more like something she could leave behind.

As far as she was concerned, the night could end here.

Ordinarily, if she was this far from a public national park, she'd find whatever cheap motel had space. But she was in Sydney... and she *could* do a couple of loads of washing, maybe switch over to some more summery clothes. Plus, Timothy would be happy to see her. After the evening she'd had, being around someone familiar was an unexpectedly appealing prospect. Even if he was him.

The drive to his house in Point Piper through central Sydney was, predictably, fucking awful. Her petrol-guzzler of an old LandCruiser was nearly empty, which made every kilometre of traffic feel like a step closer to breaking down on a main road. By the time she crawled through the eastern suburbs, she was half prepared to put on her hazards, abandon the car, and walk.

In the end, she made it. She buzzed open the gate and pulled in beside Timothy's equally beat-up white Ford Transit, close enough to almost scrape the *Light of the Redeemer Mission* logo off its door.

She took only her phone and wallet to the front door—the tangle of unwashed clothes in her boot could wait until morning. Right now, all she cared about was food and a warm shower.

Timothy met her at the door in a dressing gown, his greying hair flat on one side. He'd clearly been in bed, but that hadn't stopped him getting to the door in under 20 seconds and looking far brighter than Allegra would have in the same situation.

"Allegra!" he said cheerfully, pulling her into a tight hug despite the half of Nattai still attached to her. "It's so wonderful to see you! Come in. I saved some lasagna for you in case you decided you'd like some after all."

Allegra let herself be led inside, into the stark, palatial central room overlooking the harbour. It was all white marble and glass, and the lights of the North Shore shone brighter through the floor-to-ceiling windows than the internal lights did. It was very impressive. Unfortunately, it was also wildly impractical and more or less stuck that way. Timothy still hadn't figured out how to reprogram the house settings, and his nephew Sebastian had disappeared on some spiritual retreat more than three years ago and become wholly uncontactable.

Timothy was certain Sebastian would eventually return, so he was dutifully minding the monster alone: cleaning it himself, maintaining the elaborate gardens himself, and emailing his missing nephew once a week with the minutiae of his life, just in case he wanted updates. He undertook each task with the same sacred duty he brought to his charity work.

It was either horribly tiresome or somewhat endearing, depending on Allegra's mood. This evening, it was endearing.

Timothy pulled a chair out for Allegra at the table. "Sit down, you look exhausted. Would you like me to zap you that lasagna first? I can run a bath while you're eating it."

Allegra normally balked at being taken care of, but he had that earnest look in his eyes again, and she *was* exhausted. Oh well, it would make him very happy. "Thanks, that would be amazing, actually."

His eyes lit up. "Great. Put your feet up. I'll get you a drink." Over at the fridge, he held up a Stone & Wood Pacific Ale in one hand and a reusable bottle of chilled tap water in the other. "What will it be?"

By the look on his face, he already knew what she would choose.

Of *course* he had her favourite beer in the fridge. She couldn't say no to that. "Thank you."

He opened it with his bare hands (something she'd once found very attractive), popped the lid in the recycling and brought the bottle over to her. She smiled at him and drank deeply while he busied himself around the kitchen, updating her on what Aaron was up to at uni, his own plans for the morning, and where they might eat the following night.

She half-listened; the beer kicked in quickly because she'd had nothing to eat. She felt herself start to relax.

Finishing the lasagna Timothy zapped for her and having a warm rinse in the shower helped, but it was sinking into the spa-sized bath that finished the job. It was *hot*, just as she liked it. God, it was just so *nice* to be here sometimes.

Finally clean again, she leant back, staring at her reflection in the marble ceiling. Her long blond hair trailed down the tub and fanned around her in the water, curling around her like the faded black tendrils of her tattoos. The angle was flattering, and she admired herself for a moment; her shoulders looked more ripped than they actually were. She tested one by flexing it and winced. They were unexpectedly sore.

She was just feeling around on the edge of the tub for her phone when some quiet *Ocean Alley* started to play over the speakers in the bathroom. Her phone buzzed, which helped her find it. *"Hope the song choice is okay! :)"*

She wasn't sure whether to groan or laugh. The song choice was fine, but Timothy having even heard of *Ocean Alley* suggested he'd either been snooping through her playlists or, worse, researching music she might like in his free time. He was lucky she was too tired to judge him for it; they'd been separated for years.

Anyway, Timothy had been hovering somewhere between old friend and pining ex for years, and she was sick of thinking about it. He'd picked a song for her, he was taking care of her, and she was certain he didn't want anything in return except her company. Case closed.

Pushing the heavier thoughts aside, she went back to mouthing lyrics and planning which summer clothes to take out into the field with her, until a sudden knock on the bathroom door cut through the music.

"Allegra?" There was a note of concern in his voice. "Did you know you're all over the news?"

She sat straight up out of the water, hair adhering to her body. "What?"

"Channel 7." He paused. "And 10. ABC has your face on their website."

"They don't..." she said darkly, grabbing her phone to check.

They did.

Chapter 3: The Morning Visitor

Allegra tabbed through the news websites, watching the same footage play over and over: herself unclipping from the harness on the rockface and rushing over to assess the casualty they'd winched out, then handing him over to paramedics, then standing back as they transferred him to the helicopter. Finally, there was the shot of her dirty and dishevelled, smiling with relief as she waved up at the camera—and that was when she realised it had come from Peter's drone. Had it been leaked?

She looked up from her screen for a second, deep in thought. The SES did often release footage from newsworthy rescues, so it might be official. Actually, it probably was. *Oh, God.* She went back to her phone. *Let's see what people are saying about it.*

She checked some headlines and news tickers.

'Sheer coincidence saves Vale grandchild' she scoffed; that pun could only have come from a commercial station. It had: Channel 9.

'Breaking: Isaiah Vale pulled from ravine unconscious in joint operation by SES and Westpac Rescue Helicopter Service', *'Vale heir rescued from bushland near Sydney'*, and various other iterations of the same message were plastered across every news station and page in the state.

There wasn't much detail there—specifically, she wasn't identified personally—and the focus was on Isaiah: who he was, how badly he'd been hurt, and speculation about how he'd got into trouble. A couple of the stations, however, mentioned that *'an SES specialist happened to be in the area off duty and was able to alert authorities'*.

She read that carefully a few times. Hopefully that was as much detail as they'd give.

She always hoped the people she rescued survived and recovered, but she *specifically* hoped this boy would. If he didn't, she would almost certainly end up in the firing line of some very, very powerful people. She was biting her lip, considering the implications of that, when her phone buzzed again.

The notification was a screenshot of her waving at the drone, captioned: *'That's my mum right there'* and a little sticker of a pulsing heart.

Allegra gripped the phone tighter: *Aaron*. She read it several times, feeling the warmth spread in her chest; she'd do it 1000 more times just to get a text like this from him.

She was still smiling as she hoisted her still-sore body out of the tub, carefully dried it with shaking arms and put on one of those ridiculous dressing gowns Timothy always had fluffed and folded beside the towel rack.

She rounded the couch and dropped her unlocked phone into Timothy's lap before sinking down beside him. He looked quizzically at her for a moment, then down at the screen. His face softened, too. "Well, he loves you."

It was nice to see it, even if she often felt she didn't deserve it after all those years away from him. She accepted her phone and settled back into the white leather couch (awful) to watch ABC News Live with Timothy. He gestured at the TV. "When were you planning on telling me you saved a Vale?"

She laughed once. "Would you have been happy if I had?"

"Well, all life is sacred," he said automatically, and then made a face. "Despite what that family is doing to democracy and the wealth gap, that's not Isaiah's fault. He's barely older than Aaron."

"Maybe he'll be a *good* Vale," Allegra said, hoping her sarcasm was very audible.

It apparently was. "Yes, I'm sure he'll rise to power and use his position to dismantle the media empire and devote his life to charity."

"You did," Allegra pointed out.

Timothy laughed. "If my family ever had the wealth his did, famine and preventable disease wouldn't exist anymore, which is why I will never forgive him or anyone like him. The money in any one of those mega corporations and empires could save everyone in the world. We could be living in utopia. Instead, we have war, famine, and greed." He took a deep breath, deliberately de-escalating himself. "Again, not Isaiah's fault."

Grinning, she reached between them to warmly rub his shoulder. "It's okay. Maybe he won't survive after all."

Timothy sighed at her. "Allegra..."

She was about to shoot something back at him when she heard her own voice on television. They both looked up at the screen. It was a shaky video of her in the hospital room with Beau rushing over to hug her. A voice off-screen said, "You came straight here from the mountains?"

Allegra watched herself say, "Well, I thought he might wake up and want his phone." The video was cut and it showed her handing his bag to security and then smiling at everyone and leaving. Beau faced the camera, lips quivering and eyes red from apparently crying with relief. "That woman just saved my brother."

Allegra felt deeply uneasy. "That's—not exactly what happened. It's been cut and edited."

Timothy looked impressed anyway. "I mean, it's a flattering edit. Why complain?"

Because it's not real, Allegra thought, feeling uncomfortable.

The video replayed multiple times—every time they aired an update on Isaiah—and by the fourth or fifth time, Allegra shook her head and stood up. "Bedtime for me."

Timothy indicated the TV with the hand holding his civilised glass of wine. "I want to see if they're going to canonise you by midnight." He was grinning.

She made a disgusted noise. *"Goodnight."*

Sleep came easily to her, thanks to the combination of exercise and ale. The utter hedonism of the enormous bed was a nice treat after weeks in bedrolls, and she rolled around in the doona before finding a comfortable position folded up in the corner.

The sun was peeking under the blinds before she knew it. She could hear Timothy was already up and in the kitchen, which made her think of breakfast. No sooner had she thought it, she could smell eggs. That man *did* know how to make a home, that was for sure.

She put the fluffy robe back on and wandered out to see what he was making, only to notice he still had the TV on. The ticker along the bottom advised viewers Isaiah Vale had been released from the ICU, and it was less than 15 seconds before that damn video of her in the ward played again.

"Can we turn that off?" she said flatly, sitting on a bar stool across the counter from him as he cooked.

"You know how." His eyes were twinkling; he knew how self-conscious she felt about verbally ordering the house to do things. "Besides, I think it's nice to hear everyone continuously praise someone I love." He slid a plate of eggs, salmon, and toast across to her. "Enjoy! The salmon isn't Tasmanian; it's wild-caught."

It smelt amazing. She was checking her phone before tucking in when she noticed the barrage of messages and several missed calls.

Taking a bite of salmon, she tabbed through them. Various people from work were letting her know she was on the news; some were complimenting her. Her younger sister Vanessa had also seen fit to descend from her extremely busy life as a North Shore soccer mum to message: *'Nice to see what you're up to, even if it is on breakfast TV. PS. The boys are insisting you take them rock climbing again.'*

Allegra replied with a thumbs up rather than argue about whose fault it was that Vanessa never bloody replied to messages.

The missed calls were from an unknown number. Or several. Allegra toyed with the idea of calling them from Timothy's phone just to see who answered. Instead, she decided to have breakfast and scroll through the news first.

Timothy hadn't been exaggerating about how complimentary everyone was being. It was as frustrating as it was unnerving; she'd saved hundreds, if not thousands, of people in her career, and she'd certainly done much more dangerous and miraculous lifts than Isaiah's. The only remarkable thing about this one was that Isaiah Vale was criminally wealthy. She didn't feel like last night warranted anywhere near this much attention. She'd sooner forget about it and be a nobody aga—

The gate buzzer sounded.

Allegra and Timothy looked up from their breakfast at each other, faces blank.

"You're not expecting anyone?" he asked, and she shook her head. "A delivery?" She shook her head again.

Frowning, he picked up his phone to check the camera app, holding it farther from his face so he could see without his glasses. His frown deepened. "Odd," he said, tapping the screen to activate the speaker. "Can we help you?"

The voice that answered was a woman's—and from her smooth manner, Allegra immediately thought, *sales*. "Oh, you certainly can. I'm looking to speak with the owner of the LandCruiser parked in your driveway."

Timothy gave Allegra a curious look. "May I ask why?"

"You can certainly ask, but I can really only discuss the matter at length with her. Is she available?"

Timothy's brow had lowered as he watched Allegra for her reaction. She presumed he was about to tell the woman to wait while he checked, but her curiosity had already got the better of her.

She stood. "It's fine, I'll go." Breakfast forgotten, she headed out the front door towards the gate in a fluffy gown, with Timothy hot on her heels.

Standing by the gate in front of the blackest, sportiest car Allegra had ever seen was an equally sleek woman. She had pale skin, black hair cut in a dead-straight bob, and a black suit meticulously tailored to hug all the important parts of her—a detail Allegra noticed before making herself look at the woman's face. Her eyeshadow was smoky and deep purple against the black of her outfit, and her stiletto heels were so high and sharp they looked like they might break NSW weapon carry laws. She had them crossed at the ankle as she leant one shoulder against the white render of the gate, waiting for them. She oozed confidence, and she didn't break eye contact as Allegra approached, increasingly suspicious.

A perfectly manicured hand extended through the rungs in an invitation to shake. The polished nails were short—a detail Allegra clocked with unnecessary speed. "Allegra, it's a pleasure to meet you."

"Likewise," she replied automatically, and shook the hand rather than be impolite before she knew exactly who this person was. A Vale, maybe? She had the same confident eccentricity as the family in the hospital from last night. Perhaps she was Isaiah's mother or something. "Mrs...?"

The woman laughed. "Please. 'Ms' is fine, but you can call me Sal. Sal Lategan."

Allegra glanced at Timothy; he shook his head minutely to indicate he hadn't heard of her. Allegra pressed her lips together. She hadn't either.

Timothy spoke first. "You... wanted to speak with Allegra about her LandCruiser?"

"Yes." Sal locked eyes with Allegra again. "It must be difficult to get around in a car that constantly needs fixing. And with the important work you do, I imagine a reliable car is paramount. Can't rescue anyone if you break down."

Allegra didn't bother hiding her disgust. "Are you trying to *sell me a new car*?"

Not at all insulted, Sal laughed. It seemed predatory, somehow. "Oh, no, Allegra. I'm doing consulting for a bank that takes its corporate responsibility very seriously. We're looking for a professional who really knows their stuff to do some pre-survey work and on-site safety for an orienteering fundraiser. And Allegra," she added, as if sharing a naughty secret with her, "after your success last night, your participation will mean the world to the charity. Think how much money they'll raise."

Timothy was getting more and more agitated as she spoke. "What is this? You call us out of our house at 7 o'clock in the morning, onto the street, to—"

Allegra quieted him by putting a hand on his arm. She wasn't above helping a charity, even for *this* woman. "What's the fundraiser for?"

Sal ignored Timothy. "The Homeward Foundation," she said, watching Allegra carefully. "Have you heard of it? It's a fabulous organisation that supports foster children and helps them feel safe and loved when their parents have to spend time away. Such a worthy cause; you should hear all the laughter during the events the foundation runs. Those sweet children forget how lonely they feel without mum and dad."

She could have stabbed Allegra in the chest to less effect. *Aaron*, Allegra immediately thought, keenly remembering his little face sobbing in Vanessa's arms as she'd walked through the departure gates at the airport. Aaron had had to manage with no idea when his mum and dad would be back—if they would be back. No one had organised events for him to feel less lonely. For a moment, she was breathless.

Timothy was not as breathless. In fact, he'd rather found his. "Who have you been speaking to?" he began, raising his voice. "It had better not be Aaron! Who sent you to—"

"Timothy." Allegra didn't need to yell over him; one word was enough to quiet him again.

"I don't like this, Allegra. I don't think that—"

"I know," she said, and then looked back at this Lategan woman, 'Sal' or whatever her stupid name was. There was no harm in hearing her out; it sounded like a good charity, regardless of how hugely obnoxious the woman trying to poach her for it was. "Send me more information," she told the woman coolly. "I gather you have my email address if you have my physical address."

Sal inclined her head, her perfectly straightened hair brushing a crisp shoulder pad. "I'll send you the prospectus."

Timothy was practically popping a vein, but he said no more, very obviously sizing Sal up before marching inside.

Allegra would have done the same, given how the conversation was ending, but something occurred to her. "Wait, did you just mention my LandCruiser as a trick to get us out here?"

Sal chuckled, that half-smile almost permanently on her face. "No tricks. The social media presence you'll build from the rescue and your charitable work will pay for a replacement." She paused. "Just think: no more rattle. No more flat tyre when you've already used the spare."

She looked pointedly over Allegra's shoulder.

Flat tyre when I've—Allegra looked behind her to see her LandCruiser leaning precariously to one side. She must have run over something yesterday, and the air had leaked out overnight. Fuck.

"Goodbye, Allegra," Sal told her in a knowing voice, her eyes dipping very obviously to the fluffy bathrobe Allegra had completely forgotten she was wearing.

Feeling her cheeks grow hot, Allegra listened to the staccato click of Sal's heels on the pavement as she unlocked her car with a double-blip and left.

Chapter 4: Paperwork and Aftermath

Having Corporate Australia's Pushiest Consultant paying them a home visit during breakfast had definitely ruined Timothy's day.

When Allegra walked back inside, Timothy was very aggressively clearing his nearly full plate into the bin with enough force that the muscles in his arms were bulging as much as the vein in his temple. His lips were pressed into a thin line against everything he clearly wanted to say.

He was going to give himself a stroke. "Don't worry, she's gone," Allegra told him, returning to her own half-eaten breakfast.

He couldn't hold it any longer. "Is she?" The words exploded out of his mouth. "Is she really, though? Because you just said *yes* to her!"

Allegra considered that for a moment. "I suppose I did."

He looked at her like she might genuinely be completely crazy. "*Why*? She's just going to use you for whatever profit-generating exploitation she can squeeze out of you before the last footage of your face disappears from the evening news! Why are you *letting that happen*?"

Granted, the visit from Sal had been wholly unwelcome, but Allegra really didn't see any reason to get as angry at her as Timothy was.

Sal had definitely knocked her off balance with the choice of charity, but the more Allegra thought about it, the less creepy and more rational it seemed. After all, it wasn't exactly a secret that she and Timothy had been posted overseas on and off for years while Aaron was young. Timothy himself had done interviews for various Christian publications about the pain of needing to choose between saving hundreds of people and spending time with his son.

And they did need someone with her very specific, very narrow skillset. The foster charity was a good fit for her. It took no soul-searching to decide she could ignore the eccentric millionaire waving fame and fortune at her if it meant participating in such a worthy event. "I'm agreeing to do it because it's for charity. You yourself tell me all the time how hard it is to raise money these days."

"She could sell her damn sports car and pay that foundation's costs for the entire year, if she really cared! She doesn't. She's just going to use you instead!"

That much, Allegra had gathered. It simply didn't bother her. That was how the world worked, and if a charity got money out of it, she was content enough. What she didn't understand was why Timothy, of all people, was so upset about it. Fundraising was half his job.

She sat back on her stool and folded her arms, considering him. "This is really getting to you."

He dropped his dishes in the sink with a loud clatter. "You think?" At her expression, he groaned and leaned heavily forward on the bench, running one weathered hand through his grey-blond hair before checking the dishes. "That was a bit much. I could have broken them."

"Sebastian wouldn't notice."

"That's not the point," he told her, chewing his lip as he looked towards the door. "That was all just so—" He searched for the right description. "It's so sleazy to show up at someone's house at 7am. Invading their privacy because you've decided you personally want an answer immediately, and then seeing you *reward* that..." He shook his head. "You deserve better."

She reached across the island bench to lightly rub his arm. "My hero," she said, mirth in her voice.

He scoffed at her. "Stop it. I mean it. She should have been upfront about what she wanted as soon as she rang the buzzer, and she should respect you enough to make the offer through ordinary channels." He sighed again, shaking his head and waving a hand in apparent dismissal of the topic. "Anyway, I'm going to wash that corporate sleaze off me before I head off to church. Do you need anything?"

"Got any spare Ridge Grapplers lying around?" He looked blankly at her. He wasn't a car person. "Off-road tyres. Both my spare and one of the tyres I have fitted are flat and I need to replace them."

He made an 'ah' shape with his mouth. "So that's why *that woman* hooked onto the idea of a new LandCruiser. Typical. Corporate vampires will latch onto anything they think they can get a grip on." He paused. "Also, I gather you're joking because my Transit just takes the standard size." Another pause. "I suppose I could drop by Bridgestone's and—"

"*Timothy*." She *laughed*. In the nicest possible way, he was such a doormat. "It's fine, I was joking. I can go pick up some myself." When it looked like he was going to insist anyway, she stood up and practically pushed him towards the bathroom. "*No*. Go."

He let himself be ushered out of the central room, but paused by the doorway to the stairs, adding as an afterthought, "What's with that whole *jet-black-goth* thing, though? Is she just trying to telegraph how dead inside she is as bluntly as possible?"

Allegra shrugged. "Rich people," was all she had to offer as he went upstairs.

With him gone, she picked up her phone to finish sorting through her notifications with the rest of her breakfast. There was nothing else of note except an email from *Black Standard Advisory*.

She stopped chewing. There was no way that was the name of the organisation.

She already knew the answer before she'd tapped on the message. *"As promised,"* it read. *"Let's be in touch."* There was a PDF of the charity prospectus attached.

Underneath the message was stark branding and the name *Sal Lategan – Chief Marketing Officer (Strategy)*. The Black Standard Advisory logo was dark, bold, and high contrast. Much like Sal herself. In Allegra's opinion, it was all far too much, though she supposed some psychological study or marketing department somewhere had decided this sort of over-the-top branding worked on someone. It turned Allegra off the brand quite powerfully—then again, people who lived in their cars while their ex-husbands house-sat for shelter probably weren't Black Standard Advisory's target demographic.

Anyway, she hated it. Timothy was going to have a lot to say about it, too. She forwarded it to him and was rewarded a minute or so later by hearing a muffled voice yell, "You've got to be kidding me!" down the hall.

She chuckled as she finished the last salmon on her plate and opened the prospectus.

It had the same branding as the email, which did at least make it easy to read. There were no real surprises in it; they wanted someone experienced to survey the area and produce a map outlining where the kids and other participants were allowed to tread. Any highly dangerous locations were to be roped off or otherwise marked on the map and on-site, and they wanted her to brief the educators beforehand and attend on the day in case anything happened. It looked like St John was going to have an ambulance there, too.

The usual terms and conditions were attached on the back. She skimmed them, understood very little, found nothing that appeared to say either *you will personally be liable if anyone gets hurt* or *you need to purchase your own insurance*. That was enough for her. She spent a few minutes Googling the Homeward Foundation, watched some of their material with laughing children hugging each other, then signed the contract and forwarded it back to Sal.

The response almost made her gag. *"Fast. I like it. We're going to work well together."*

Her finger hovered over the 'reply' button to shoot something probably quite rude back at the woman, but she talked herself out of it. Sal was just a middleman; there was no point in creating drama. Instead, she put her phone pointedly on the bench and picked up a piece of salmon toast.

The screen lit up, and Allegra glanced at it. *"I'm almost disappointed you didn't reply to that."*

Okay, that was fucking it. Salmon-oil fingers or not, Sal was getting an immediate reply. *"I'm going to disappoint you a lot."*

The reply was almost instant. *"Oh, I doubt it."*

Allegra managed to *not* piff her phone across the room. That woman had some fucking nerve—perhaps Allegra was beginning to understand Timothy's immediate dislike of her. She finished her breakfast and cleaned up.

When Timothy appeared back in the central room again with wet hair, a freshly ironed shirt and an open tie hanging around his neck, she said cryptically, "Theoretically speaking, of course, if I killed Goth Lady would you help me hide the body?"

Timothy, who had an actual '*What Would Jesus Do*?' sticker on his Transit, didn't even blink. "Yes." He moved on, looking around the counter and the sink with frank surprise. "Did you already put the plates in the dishwasher?"

"I washed them. And my hands, several times. You know, the stain of corporate sleaze, etc."

He laughed. "Well, I suppose that's two fewer for me to wash today." Then his face lit up. "One of our volunteers managed to source 200 whole chickens from some local place that needed to write them off. We haven't cooked a Sunday roast for people for nearly a year. I think word will spread quickly. It'll be a busy day." He looked delighted by the prospect. "I might be back late."

"I'll leave the porch light on," she said, grinning.

He laughed. "Not that late. I'm not young anymore." He sobered, standing a little awkwardly in front of her, tie half-fastened. "Anyway, Allegra, tyres can be expensive, so if you need some—"

"I don't."

"I know. But if you *do* need any—"

She sighed at him. "Timothy. I don't. I have plenty of money as a result of you letting me leave all my stuff in the spare room. Thank you for that."

He looked uncomfortable. "I just want you to know it would be my pleasure to help you with—"

"It's actually my pleasure to help myself." She stood, patted his chest, then spun him around and passed him his phone and keys from the bench. "Go. *Please*. Before I need to hide *your* body."

Once again, he let himself be pushed forward and out the door. Before he left, though, he shot her one more look of patented Deep Concern. "It's just that I don't want you to feel like you have no option but to accept offers from people like that woman. You know I would always—"

"I know. Bye, Timothy. I'm going to spend all day using your electricity and water, there's no need for you to prostrate yourself financially for me to feel like you've Served Me As You Would Him."

That got a smile out of him. As he climbed into the car, he said by way of goodbye, "I do love you, you know."

"Same. Now fuck off." She opened the gate for him to make a point.

He grinned at that and then backed very slowly and carefully onto the road, driving his white and gold Transit inconspicuously up the same street that jet-black sports car had loudly torn up a short while earlier.

Chapter 5: The Push

Allegra had already started emptying the boot of her car into the washing machine when Control sent her the incident paperwork she should have filled in last night. It was mostly pre-filled—they knew what she was like—and attached with an *Urgent!* exclamation mark, plus a somewhat desperate note that read, *"There's going to be a lot of scrutiny of this, so we suggest completing it as accurately and quickly as possible."* Hanging out her washing and replacing her tyres would have to wait.

Her old work tablet had several notifications she'd been ignoring for days. She cleared them, then got stuck into the stupid document. She did put some effort into it, but her attention started to wane on the fourth or fifth page, and she kept getting annoyed every time she remembered the emails Sal had sent her.

Sitting back on the stool, she picked up her phone to reread them. Maybe in the heat of the moment, she'd skimmed them without the perspective they needed. Maybe Sal was being entirely professional. Collegial, even.

Well, that hypothesis flew out the window immediately after she went through the exchange again. If anything, she was even more annoyed the second time around.

It was the overfamiliarity that irritated her most, she decided. That Sal felt she could be so playful with Allegra immediately after meeting her felt like the same type of personal space violation that showing up at someone's gate at 7am was.

Also, Sal's choice of language, her immediate prod when Allegra didn't reply, and her manner of communicating—especially that constant, intense eye contact? All of it felt to Allegra kind of like...

...No. Allegra shook her head, pushing that thought away. It wasn't flirty. Sal was clearly just your average marketing veteran who had forgotten normal people didn't need the hard sell 24/7.

Allegra did roll that thought around in her head for a few moments, though. She even contemplated messaging Timothy to ask if *he* thought Sal was being flirty, before deciding against it because that would just upset him even more. No. She was not spending that much energy on the whole affair. Sometimes obnoxious people were just obnoxious. Sal had probably been obnoxious as a child and learnt how to hone those skills to perfection as an adult.

Sal was getting her star attendee for the charity that had hired her, and Allegra was getting the opportunity to do something meaningful with her skills. All Allegra needed to do was tolerate Sal for a short period of time, and then she could enjoy being free of her forever.

Putting her phone aside, she finished her paperwork with enough detail for Control not to return-to-sender it with an angry emoji. Anyway, according to the news ticker on the television behind her, Isaiah was going to live, so there probably wasn't going to be *that* much scrutiny of anything. Their insurer was just staffed entirely with people who were naturally anxious and always wanted things done better and yesterday. She signed and submitted it.

Allegra then hung out all her washing, changed her rooftop tent bedding, and won the battle against her self-consciousness to tell the television to turn itself off. Afterwards, it was time to hike to Bayline Tyres with one of the flats, get it patched, lug it back, fit it, then drive in to have the spare replaced. At least, that had been her plan.

What she hadn't factored in was how damn heavy the tyre and wheel were. This was particularly frustrating because she considered herself quite strong, and it hadn't even occurred to her that she might not be strong enough to carry it the full distance. Unfortunately, realising that meant she was now forced to prove to herself that she could. In the end, she threaded some recovery rope through it so she could wear it like a backpack.

She got some very strange looks lugging the thing out of Point Piper, that was for sure. A lot of looks, actually. She presumed people were just judging her for not paying someone else to take the tyre in, until one of her neighbours—she presumed?—pulled over beside her.

Some cashed-up retiree, by the look of it, complete with pearls around her neck. "Timothy's wife, isn't it?" Allegra bristled but didn't correct her. "Nice work saving that Vale boy. Lovely job. Such important work you do. You must come around for dinner one day and tell us all about it. Tell Timothy to give number 5 a bell." With that, she drove off.

Allegra squinted at the car disappearing up the hill for a moment, then kept hiking. Honestly, she'd forgotten what it was like after a television appearance—and that was usually just a few pieces of footage included in a larger segment about floods or fires. It had somehow escaped her that her face had been on the news non-stop all night, and that it might affect her ability to move around freely during the day.

New South Head Road was even worse. The brunch traffic was terrible, so as she lugged the tyre up the Esplanade, everyone parked in traffic had plenty of time to scrutinise her. They might not have looked twice if she'd just been your average middle-aged blonde going for a morning power walk, but with an enormous tyre on her back and her body bent at 45 degrees, people were obviously going to stare. And if they stared long enough, they were going to recognise her.

It was the ninth circle of hell, honestly. People had their phones out and pointed at her. Every few cars, someone would roll down their window and call something about the rescue—all compliments, granted, but all still wholly unwelcome. She forced a smile and nodded anyway, because apparently she'd been raised to be polite even under siege. At one point, two young men burst out of a car stopped at a red light to grab a rushed selfie with her. She could only imagine how sweaty and disgusting she was going to look on their Insta.

"You want a ride?" one of them offered when they were done. "It's no trouble."

Allegra glanced over his shoulder at the car full of affluent youths. Remembering her brush with another of their ilk the night before, she politely declined.

It was a giant relief to head down a side street and slip into the inaptly named Rose Bay Community Garden. It was a massive park with meticulously mown lawns and a private golf course; there was nothing community about it. At least it let her continue her hike far enough away from the road to be anonymous.

Bayline Tyres itself was on a roundabout in Bondi, not far from the park. Allegra would never admit how sore her shoulders were when she finally heaved the wheel off her back and rolled it into the shop.

Recognition twigged on the receptionist's face. She kept it together, though. "Good morning! I gather you'd like some help with that tyre?"

An older, weathered mechanic entering something into a computer with only his index fingers glanced up nearby. He didn't manage the young woman's composure. "Hey, it's the SES lady!" he said, standing immediately. "Allegra-something, wasn't it?"

Allegra froze. Her name was out there now? Amazing. Just amazing. "That's right. I need this patched if possible, and then I'll head back in a little later with another one. Can I just pay for both now?"

The man ignored her question. "Whoa, did you carry that big boy in? Or did you park around the corner or something? You can just drive your car into the shop, if you like."

"Well, I could," she said, clearly but still politely, "if both this wheel and the spare weren't flat. I'll get this patched now, carry it back to my car, and then drive in with the other one."

The receptionist spoke next. "Oh, no, there's no need for that at all, Mrs Sinclair," she said, causing Allegra to sigh internally at the title. "We'd be happy to run you back home and fit the tyres, right, Dad?"

The mechanic put a hand on her shoulder. "Of course. We'll fit new ones, no charge. They probably don't pay you enough for what you do anyway. You know, my cousins had the SES secure their roof after that storm in December. Priceless."

Allegra had been completely ready to argue about payment, but the man was already taking the tyre from her, and the receptionist was already lifting the internal phone to call someone out from the workshop. Moments later, there was a car out the front, and Allegra was being ushered into it and driven back onto the main road.

It all felt—uncomfortable. The family seemed very nice, though, and they were being genuine about it, so refusing felt rude.

"Nice house!" the man commented as they arrived, and Allegra buzzed the gate open.

That made Allegra even more uncomfortable. "Not mine," she said immediately. "A friend is house-sitting, and I'm visiting."

"Nice gig, house-sitting this, then!" They drove up beside her jacked-up car and hopped out. "You from this area?"

"I live out of Sydney these days."

"Oh yeah? Did you move up to the Sunshine Coast like everyone else?"

He was just making small talk as he got to work changing the tyre over, but it was getting a little too personal for Allegra's liking. Given how generous he was being, though, she didn't feel like she could shut him down the way she otherwise would. "No. I just prefer quieter, leafier places."

"Oh, like the Blue Mountains, yeah? I have a school friend out near Katoomba."

There was a long pause; it would be impolite not to respond. "Sometimes."

He didn't understand her for a moment, sitting back on his haunches and frowning good-naturedly up at her. Then he noticed the rooftop tent, the survival gear in her boot, and finally glanced over at the house she was 'just visiting'. He came to completely the wrong conclusion. "You're homeless?" His eyes were as big as saucers.

Behind her, Allegra heard his daughter gasp. She threw up her hands. "No, no—nothing like that! It's a lifestyle choice."

He didn't look like he believed her. "You're being heralded as this great hero, and not even someone like you can afford a house in Sydney!" He tightened the last nut and stood, dusting off his hands. "Well, that's it. I'm doing your other wheels, too. I won't have an actual hero driving around on 15-year-old parts. I'll grab them from the shop and drive them down here this afternoon."

"No, please, it's—"

"Shush!" He silenced her with two dirty hands on her sweaty shoulders in what could only be described as a fatherly gesture. "It's the least we can do. Thank you for everything you do, Mrs Sinclair."

With that, they hopped back in their ute and headed off. Allegra was left in the driveway beside a very dirty, banged-up LandCruiser sporting one sparkling new rim and tyre.

She stood awkwardly in place for a minute or two, digesting what had just happened. Not *terrible*, she conceded. They were just being generous. Still, she felt intensely guilty being seen as the face of the SES and getting freebies when she was on salary, while so many actual volunteers got nothing for their hard work. Yes, she was primary on-call for complex and vertical rescues, and yes, they kept her busy with disaster recovery, mitigation planning, volunteer training, and every other odd job that needed a paid pair of hands—but the volunteers were still the spine of the whole thing. Not some salaried specialist who happened to be on the news.

The whole rescuing Isaiah situation was getting a little out of hand; she'd have to lay low until it had blown over.

As the mechanic had said they wouldn't be back until much later, she stowed all the jacks in the boot and went out to the balcony to feel if her clothing was dry yet. It wasn't. Not even close. The warm sun and breeze off the harbour were no match for how fucking long it took bamboo to dry, which meant she was stuck there until it did. At least Timothy would be happy about that, she supposed.

She checked her phone, 10:19am. Early.

Maybe Aaron would like to—? She shot that thought down quickly. He'd be at church right now, and it was exam season, so afterwards he'd likely be studying. If she invited him somewhere, he might feel pressured to see her even if he didn't want to, because of the rent. She didn't want to put him in that position.

She should at least invite Vanessa, then, even if the likelihood of actually seeing her little sister this weekend was almost nil. Vanessa was the sort of person who made herself very busy and needed to be booked weeks in advance.

There were a couple of other old friends she could check in on, although the middle of the day on Sunday seemed an odd time to catch up with people she normally got drunk with after work. And Timothy would feel a little left out if she caught up with their mutual friend Karl without him.

She had decided to take inventory of the food stocks in her car—maybe she could stock up?—when her phone buzzed. Dangling out of the boot by her waist, she checked it.

It was a TikTok frame of her lugging that fucking tyre along Rose Bay, somehow from a flattering angle. *Huh,* she thought, considering it. She didn't look terrible, despite how sweaty and tussled she was. In fact, it was a decent photo.

She tapped on it, wondering who had sent it. As she did, her phone rang in her hand, and the surprise made her smash her head on the top lip of the boot. Swearing under her breath and rubbing her head, she automatically answered as she slid out of the car.

"Oh, Allegra, you are a *gift*."

There was only one person who sounded that smooth. *Sal?!*

Her reply came through gritted teeth. "I think you'll find I'm a person."

Sal scoffed. "When you're done moralising, let's talk about how we jump on this."

Allegra could hardly fucking believe her ears. "*We*?"

"Yes, 'we'," Sal said easily, not deterred at all by Allegra's tone, "unless you've got 25 years of PR experience scrunched up in that boot somewhere. Let's do lunch, my shout. I'll even make it somewhere you'll actually like."

Allegra actually liked Timothy's cooking. Second to that was whatever she could eat somewhere completely quiet with a beautiful view of an early autumn sunset. She doubted Sal had her number on this one. "No. Put it in an email."

"I'll be there at 12."

That knocked the breath out of Allegra. The fucking nerve of this woman. "I said *no*. If you want to use me, you'll need to do it on my terms."

"See you at 12, Allegra." Sal's smirk was audible. The line went dead.

Allegra lowered the phone very, very slowly, staring out at the street, unblinking, and taking a series of measured breaths. She was not going to smash the phone or scream a string of profanities Timothy would need to apologise to the neighbours for tomorrow. She was just going to shut the door, lock the fucking gate, and send a clear message to this infuriating fuckface of a woman.

Chapter 6: Leverage

The balcony off the back of the Point Piper house was a huge, sweeping terrace with a clear railing—nothing to interrupt the multi-million-dollar view of the harbour. Around the bridge side was an ostentatious water feature Timothy never turned on because he didn't like to waste water, and along the front was a heated infinity lap pool that was also never on because Timothy didn't like to waste electricity.

Allegra wasn't ordinarily at the house long enough to spend much time with any of it, beyond drying all her clothes on the railing and probably horrifying Timothy's neighbours. Given the events of the day so far, though, she switched her sweaty clothes for sunscreen and a rashie and went to dunk herself in the pool.

It was cold. The sun hadn't been out long enough to warm it to any sort of hospitable temperature, but after having her blood boiled by a certain pseudo-goth earlier, it was a pleasant reprieve.

She was on lap 38 when the clock ticked over from 11:59 to 12:00. If Sal was ringing the gate buzzer or standing outside the gate, Allegra was none the wiser. Her ears were underwater, and she was focusing on her breath.

Every time she turned her head to the side, she could see the Sydney Harbour Bridge behind the Opera House through the glass wall of the infinity pool. Not a bad view, really. It just wasn't something she personally found that much value in. All these houses were tiny blocks of land crammed together on narrow coastline, jostling for a glimpse of distant architecture. Everywhere you stood, you could hear traffic, power tools, or—especially in this part of Sydney—construction equipment from wealthy people chucking another floor on or refitting their kitchens and bathrooms. Did people really enjoy this?

Silly question, really, she figured, acutely aware she was in the middle of mansion-and-Lamborghini land.

That made her think of Sal's sports car. It must be 12:15pm already, surely?

Allegra's curiosity got the better of her, and at the end of lap 43, she checked her phone. There were some work emails she'd check later (or never, probably), but otherwise, surprisingly, no notifications. Surely if Sal were here and Allegra wasn't answering the door, she'd text or email, right?

Or—Perhaps Sal had just been teasing her after all?

As irritated as Allegra was by the thought of Sal bluffing to get a rise out of her, the prospect of *not* having to spend an hour or two avoiding that invasive corporate sleaze of a woman was unexpectedly uplifting. She climbed out of the pool and towelled the excess water off her before going inside just to double-check. She'd never downloaded the house app that Timothy had on his phone, which meant she didn't have access to the buzzer log or cameras. She'd need to actually look through the door.

Feeling a little self-conscious, Allegra opened the door just a crack to check if anyone was on the other side of the gate.

The black paint of Sal's car stood out immediately against the white architecture. Sal was leaning casually against it—ankles crossed again—with her phone in her hand and an earpiece in her ear, deep in conversation. She glanced up when she saw movement at the door.

They locked eyes.

Allegra froze, and Sal took the opportunity to grin and give her a twinkle-fingered wave.

Fucking—Allegra saw red and *slammed* the door shut, leaning heavily against it. How the *fuck* did Sal know she would check the door? Why the *fuck* hadn't she messaged or called or emailed when Allegra didn't answer?

Allegra probably would have yelled something in frustration, but she didn't want to give Sal the satisfaction of hearing how upset she was. Marching back outside to the pool, she looked down into it and contemplated just getting back in and continuing her swim. Fuck that woman.

After a few moments of deliberation, she decided she was probably done anyway. She threw on some clean clothes in case she had to call the police. In fact—

Grabbing her phone from the bench, she surged out of the door and right up to the gate. Enough of this nonsense. "If you don't leave this very instant, I'm going to call the police!" She brandished her phone.

Sal blinked at her. Then she said very smoothly to her own phone, "I'm so sorry, Gerard, but I'm going to need to call you back. Yes, I know. Thank you." She hung up and pushed herself to stand upright, approaching the gate at a very leisurely pace. "The police, Allegra?"

Allegra wavered on that, suddenly feeling like that may have been an impulsive overreaction. "*Leave.*"

Sal was speaking very slowly and deliberately. "I'm so dangerous that you need the police to make sure I don't physically harm you, or damage your property, or—"

"I just need you to fucking leave."

"Well, let's talk this through, shall we?" Sal said, ignoring her. "I've visited your house twice for business reasons, and you signed a contract with us today." She paused, allowing that to sink in. "I think the bigger issue is that even if they do attend—which they might, you're a VIP now—someone at the station, or perhaps someone around here," she indicated the many houses around them and the many, many windows facing the street, "will get a little nosy. And police attendance might be more interesting online than the fact the Vale boy is doing better."

Allegra felt a blush rise to her cheeks. "Yes, alright, you've made your point. Now go!"

Sal looked intent on doing no such thing. "I will go once we've talked strategy."

What *the fuck* was this woman on? Did she not—? Allegra grabbed the rungs of the gate and rattled them. "No! Leave! Now, or I'll—"

A car honked, startling her.

Sal turned as well. Behind them was a ute with the Bayline Tyres logo across the doors. It honked cheerfully again, and the driver—that father—pointed to the gate, indicating Allegra should open it.

Sal glanced back at her, an eyebrow cocked. Allegra gave her the dirtiest possible look she could muster. In response, Sal held her hands up in a faux 'don't shoot' motion and backed away from the gate so Allegra could punch in the code. The gate opened agonisingly slowly, finally allowing the Bayline Tyres ute to pull in beside Allegra's LandCruiser.

Doors on either side opened to reveal the father and daughter. "Hello again!" the father said, and then noted Allegra's stormy expression. "Hope we didn't interrupt anything, ha ha!"

Allegra looked directly at Sal. "Nothing at all. Sal was just leaving."

Sal's eyes twinkled, and her grin darkened as if to say, *game on*. "Yes, we were just off to lunch."

"No. She was just leaving by herself."

Sal manufactured a truly pleasant laugh. "Oh, Allegra," she said in that insincere marketing voice Allegra hated. She reached out and momentarily touched Allegra's shoulder in an affectionate gesture that would have had Allegra *break her arm* had they not had company. "I don't mind treating you to lunch. You don't have to be so coy about it. It's the least I can do for you after everything you do for others."

Allegra practically gagged.

Unfortunately, it turned out to be exactly the right thing to say for their company. "Right?" the daughter agreed, helping her father lift a massive sparkling wheel from the tray of their ute. "You've earnt it! You might as well enjoy people wanting to congratulate you!" She beamed at Allegra.

Allegra felt like a caged animal. She managed a shaky smile back at the girl—being rude would seem ungrateful, and that poor girl couldn't possibly be older than Aaron—but the whole situation made her ill. Everyone was in good spirits, and if she continued to push the point with Sal, she was just going to look like a horrible grump to people who were doing her favours.

Sal could smell her hesitation and took the opportunity to walk slowly and deliberately past her through the gate. "Why don't you go and put on something nice, Allegra? We can smooth out our differences over a late lunch." She smiled broadly over her shoulder, knowing she had Allegra backed into a corner over the invitation.

Allegra was entertaining violent thoughts about how she'd remove Sal from her property if they were alone. "I don't think the food cares what I'm wearing, Sal."

"Depends what you're eating, I suppose." She locked eyes with Allegra.

Before Allegra had a chance to process that, Sal broke eye contact and wandered slowly over towards the house, considering it. "If it's a place with a dress code, it's worth not rocking the boat unless you're doing it for a specific purpose."

Allegra was still stuck on her initial answer. Had—had she just—? Allegra was unsure if she'd heard any of that correctly, but infuriated by all of it just the same. "I'm not changing."

"Oh, that's what they all say," Sal said, half-mockingly, as if delivering a punchline. Then she gave Allegra a once-over. "Actually, maybe it's even better that you stay like this. We can talk more once we're there." With that, she sashayed past Allegra towards her car as if a decision had been made. "Come on, let's roll."

Allegra would have fired something sharp back at her—literally, if possible—but the prospect of having what would essentially amount to a domestic in front of the family from Bayline Tyres was not appealing. As it was, she stood in place.

Sal reached the gate, then turned back expectantly.

"You can totally just go," the girl piped up cheerfully from over near the LandCruiser, confirming she'd been furtively watching the whole exchange. "We'll shut the gate when we're done."

Sal gave the girl a warm smile Allegra sensed was entirely disingenuous. "Give this one a raise," Sal said to the father, nodding at his daughter. "She's worth her weight in gold."

He puffed up, totally falling for it. "Isn't she!" He shared a glance with his daughter. "We'll talk about it," he told her pointedly, laughing again and getting back to the tyre.

Sal looked at Allegra with a triumphant smile. Allegra was sickened, honestly, but how on earth could she refuse in a way that wouldn't make her look like the bad guy?

Sal crossed her arms. "Perhaps if we wait long enough, Timothy can join us," she said, pretending to check her phone. "What time does his lunch service finish again...?"

At 1:30pm, Allegra thought, glancing down at her own phone. It was still a while off, but who knew how long it would take them to fit the tyres. She took a breath. She knew immediately what would happen if Timothy came home to find Sal outside the front of the house again, and she wasn't sure she'd be able to stop him causing a scene this time. He'd regret that later and be so angry and upset with himself. In her mind, she could clearly picture the big smile on his face as he'd left for church that morning.

She *seethed*.

Sal was watching her, waiting for it to all set in. "Shall we go, Allegra?" She said it in a way that suggested she knew the answer.

Unfortunately, so did Allegra. She somehow managed to force a sort of warm "Thank you" to the family working on her car, then marched over to Sal's own fucking car.

Sal was holding the door open for her, that cursed smile on her pale face. As Allegra swung down into the low car, she yanked the door from Sal, hoping to pull her off balance.

Unfortunately, Sal had anticipated the movement and let the door fall easily out of her hands. Then she rounded the bonnet. It was so low that all Allegra could see through the windscreen was Sal's hips and thighs swaying backwards and forwards in that tailored suit. She slid in, slipped off her heels, and put on a pair of dark sunglasses over her intense eye makeup.

With the touch of a button, the car's engine began a deep, guttural purr that rang through Allegra's ribcage. It was nothing like the comforting rattle of Allegra's LandCruiser. Sal looked sleek and right at home in those glossy black leather seats; Allegra's knees looked rough and ragged in her khaki cargo pants and worn brown boots. Her damp hair was probably ruining the leather. No part of her belonged in this car; she almost felt kidnapped. "Why on earth are you doing all this to me?"

Sal lifted the handbrake and pulled away from the kerb. Allegra expected her to say something teasing or dismissive, but for once, she dispensed with all that bluster. "Because we don't have time for you to realise in a more organic way how important it is to take advantage of being an of-the-minute media darling."

Allegra had been poised to attack her, so it was—somewhat disarming to hear her being honest. It didn't change the general situation, however. "So, you're going to blackmail and manipulate me instead?"

Sal gave her a tired look over the top of her glasses as she waited to turn onto the main road. "Please. All I did was show up at your house a couple of times. Don't tell me you wouldn't have completely ignored any email or text message I sent you otherwise. After all, who am I to you? You might not even have read the email."

Allegra pressed her lips together for a moment. That did sound like something she would do, but Sal was missing the point. "What you need to understand is that it is absolutely my right to not read your emails, not answer the door, and do things in my own time. You do not have the right to force your deal-of-the-century, or whatever it is you're peddling, on me."

"Perhaps not," Sal observed neutrally. "But in your insistence on enforcing your oh-so important rights, you would have missed an incredible opportunity to make hundreds of thousands of dollars for a charity that has meaning to you."

Allegra scoffed. That seemed a bit far-fetched. "As if my presence is going to make hundreds of thousands of dollars."

Sal shot her a dark, dark smile. "Not yet. But if we play it right, Allegra, you are going to be one very sought-after woman." With that, the car turned sharply onto the highway and surged forward with heart-stopping acceleration, throwing Allegra's stomach into her throat.

Chapter 7: Terms and Conditions

It was unnerving being under the traffic. Allegra was used to her 4WD, and being this close to the road—truck wheels thundering past her window—filled her with more adrenaline than Sal practically taking her hostage already had.

When Allegra refused to be drawn into conversation, Sal put on ABC Drive. Normally Allegra wouldn't have minded, but she reached over and switched it off anyway. Then came Triple J—again, not a terrible choice, but she wasn't about to give Sal the satisfaction of being right about the music she liked—followed by police dispatch radio. That one was pure provocation, so she killed the audio entirely and stared at the road ahead.

Sal looked entertained, but didn't comment. Instead, she wove through traffic at a speed that was obviously illegal, slowing only when they approached fixed speed cameras. Every hard merge and too-close brake light hit the part of Allegra that knew too well what unsafe driving could cost. She kept her eyes fixed ahead and her hands loose in her lap.

They drove much farther east than Allegra expected, climbing into the hills before leaving the motorway and turning up a narrow, leafy road that didn't look remotely like what she'd imagined Sal's idea of lunch would be.

The dappled sunlight through the trees made visibility quite low, and Sal leant forward over the wheel as they pulled into a small, neatly kept carpark beside a couple of more modest vehicles. Allegra was out of the car before Sal had even reached for her shoes or her oddly shaped, probably designer handbag.

The venue itself was barely visible over the top of the hill, nestled amongst towering ghost gums and dense bushland. It looked like a large Federation villa, and was only distinguishable as a business by a gold-leaf sign reading *Treetop Tea Rooms* beside a short flight of stairs. Around them, several different types of birds sang in the trees.

Sal removed her sunglasses, folded them, and tucked one arm into her jacket so the frames hung against her cleavage. She was watching Allegra.

Allegra refused to appear impressed. "Let's get this over and done with."

Still faintly entertained, Sal led Allegra up the stairs to the villa. They were met at the top by an ageing lady in a service apron who had an air of authority about her. "Sal! How lovely to see you again." *Again?* "The balcony, I take it?"

"Yes, please. Thanks, Rita," Sal said with her usual familiarity and allowed them to be shown inside, past two or three patrons, and up to a private balcony. "I'll start with a short black, if that's alright. Something Brazilian, if you have it. Allegra?"

Suddenly, they were both looking at her. "Er, water will suit me."

Looking back at Rita, Sal shrugged. "Well, we can grab a pitcher for the table, anyway. Thanks so much." She then pulled out Allegra's chair for her—oddly chivalrous, given the circumstances. Allegra accepted it, resenting how obedient that felt.

Sal sat opposite her at their small square table against an antique railing. The balcony itself looked down across thick bushland, shaded by ancient gums. One of them was quite close to the house—uncomfortably close, Allegra thought, wearing her SES hat for a moment—but it did give her the pleasant feeling of being right in the scrub. She might have quite liked to walk around the grounds after lunch if not for present company.

Present company had taken out her laptop and was making conversation as she unlocked it. "The couple who own this place have had it in the family since the 1900s," she said, typing as she spoke. "They run it as a boutique bed and breakfast, but they do make excellent home-cooked food with local ingredients. And, of course"—she gestured out at the view—"there is this."

A boutique B&B in the bush hardly seemed Sal's style. "How do you know them?"

Sal's dark smile returned. "Business takes me to a lot of varied places," she said cryptically. Then she turned the screen so Allegra could see it: ABC iview, and her own face on the hospital broadcast, with that plastic Vale kid crying into her shoulder. "Let's talk about the opportunity you have here. Tell me what your goals are, Allegra."

That felt very invasive. Normally, Allegra appreciated directness—just not from her. "I've met most of them."

"But not all of them," Sal observed. "So, what is it? Financial security is a common one. What about any causes you've always wanted to champion?" She sat back, fingers laced across her slender middle. "Tell me your wildest dreams, Allegra. What does your future look like?"

Her immediate future looked like going back to the house and locking the front door. After that, she'd probably have dinner with Timothy, stay another night, and head back out bush to have a look at the coordinates of the area she'd agreed to survey. Beyond that, she wasn't particularly interested. "You've picked the wrong person for this."

Sal didn't look surprised. "Not goals for yourself, then," she said, tilting her head in concession. She was watching Allegra closely. "But what about Aaron?"

That name stopped her cold. "He's not up for discussion."

"I'm not asking you to discuss him—just to tell me what you hope for his future."

Allegra stiffened. The worst mistake parents could make was forcing their own ambitions onto their kids—Allegra would never do that to him. Never. "Aaron's future is his own. My only job is to support him in whatever he chooses," she said, her own conviction surprising her.

Sal studied her, her perfect brow furrowed. "Your parents must really have been something, between you, your sisters..."

And Lachie, Allegra thought, but put the thought of her late brother out of her mind. This wasn't the place. "How do you know about my sisters?"

"Even a first-year marketing student knows to do their research. Of course I backgrounded you."

Unease crept back. "Look, I don't want to talk about my goals, my dreams, or my family. Just tell me what you want."

Sal appeared to relent and switch course. "Very well. The Homeward Foundation event is in two weeks. There are currently seven sponsors, totalling just under $40,000—mostly community sports clubs and a couple of private families. The foundation would like to open a new facility in Sydney as a sort of drop-in house for foster children and foster parents who need support, and that'll be expensive. Much more than 40 grand."

"And you want to use me to drum up sponsorships, too."

Sal nodded once. "And I want to use you to drum up sponsorships, too."

"What's in it for you? How much are you getting paid?"

Sal shook her head once, her sharp bob brushing her pointed chin. "I'm volunteering out of the goodness of my heart," she said, the mirth in her voice making the joke obvious.

Allegra snorted. Whatever heart she had buried beneath all that distracting tailoring was probably as black as her car.

"I'm not doing the charity event for money. I'm doing it because you are an investment I'm willing to gamble on."

Before Sal could elaborate, Rita returned with the pitcher of water and Sal's coffee. Sal lifted the cup from its saucer and inhaled deeply, as if she meant to savour it, then threw the whole thing back like a vodka shot. The movement exposed the clean line of her throat for half a second. She handed the empty cup and saucer back to Rita as if this were routine. "Perfect. Thanks, Rita. We'll need 15 or so minutes before ordering, I think."

Rita placed menus in front of them, then bustled back down the stairs.

Sal politely flipped Allegra's glass, poured her some water, and handed it to her. Allegra was already drinking as Sal said, "I booked you some interviews."

Allegra nearly inhaled it. "You did *what*?"

"The first one is, regrettably, with Sky News," Sal said, pouring her own water. "Terrible viewership, but they have a relationship with the Vales, so I couldn't really prevent them from getting the scoop. They want you in the studio. After that, I've got one with ABC and another with Nine. Tomorrow evening, I've organised for a film crew and a few influencers to be at the hospital to introduce you to the boy you saved. Truly compelling TV."

Allegra forgot the water entirely, floored by the continuing audacity of this woman. "Without asking me?!"

Sal at least had the basic decency to look mildly apologetic. "As I mentioned, there wasn't enough time to consult you. There never is. But—" She talked over Allegra's attempt to interrupt. "You've done media before; you know the drill. A minute or so of small talk about the *harrowing rescue*, and then when they ask what's next for you, you mention the charity event."

Allegra didn't even know what to fucking say anymore. *This woman.* "Am I even allowed to refuse?!"

"Of course. I can't force you."

"That has *not* been my experience of you so far!"

Sal shrugged. "I get it, I'm pushy. But it won't be me you'll be shorting if you don't go along with this, Allegra; it will be the kids. I'm not getting paid."

Allegra made a face. "Yeah, you're doing it out of the goodness of your heart," she mimicked, voice dripping with sarcasm. "How does anyone put up with you?"

Sal laughed, genuinely amused. "Because I'm the best of the best at this. In fact, you'll see how good I am." She leant indulgently forward across the table, fixing Allegra with that intense stare of hers again. "Give me tomorrow, Allegra. Let me show you how this all works. I guarantee I'll have you convinced."

It was the hard sell, Allegra knew that. However, she couldn't argue with how expertly Sal had manoeuvred her so far. It was like a well-oiled machine Sal had run many times, and now it was just Allegra's turn to be caught in the gears.

Well. Allegra was sickened by the woman sitting across from her, but she kept thinking about the Homeward Foundation only making $40,000. *That* was why she was here, not this corporate sleazeball who didn't understand the concept of consent.

"The way you forced me into all of this is unacceptable," she said, meeting Sal's eyes with the same resolve Sal had directed at her a few moments earlier. "It's repellent. Try it again and I will walk out."

"Do I hear a 'but'?" Sal asked, predictably missing the important part of that message.

"But alright. I'll do your TV appearances. It's not for you, though; it's in spite of you. You're the most infuriating person I've ever met."

Sal had relaxed back into the chair, a triumphant smile spreading across her face. "Oh, Allegra, I couldn't care less what you think of me. It doesn't matter. As long as you do what I say, you're going to make exactly the right impression."

That sounded more ominous than Sal had probably intended. At the very worst, though, it was just a two-week commitment; then she'd be done with the charity event and Sal. At least, that was the proposal.

Studying the menu, Allegra kept finding herself distracted by one particular comment: Sal calling her an investment.

Chapter 8: The Agreement

Sal already had a media brief for Allegra, which she handed over during lunch. It was one page: three key points to hit in each interview, and several topics to avoid. Interestingly, it included a few stats about the Homeward Foundation that Allegra hadn't seen on the webpage—namely, that they supported more than a thousand families with kinship care.

'Placement with a grandparent, aunt, or uncle helps retain links to culture and family,' she read, remembering Aaron hiding behind Vanessa during video calls and refusing to look at her. Off screen, she could hear him crying.

"Would you like to practise?" Sal asked, knocking Allegra out of that thought. "I can try to pull you off message, and you can practise steering it back."

Allegra shook her head, folding up the brief and tucking it into her cargos. "I know what to do."

"It's no secret that your son was in care. Will you be able to handle it if they—"

"Yes."

Sal studied her for a moment, then appeared to accept that and nodded once. "Alright. You start with a Vale-friendly station anyway, so it's unlikely they'll put you on the spot. Now, do you mind if I—?" She gestured at her laptop.

In a choice between small talk with the most infuriating woman on the planet and letting that woman work over lunch, there was only one clear winner. It also meant Allegra could focus on her food.

Frustratingly, the food was as good as Sal had promised. Allegra had chosen a roast with crackling, something that in all her years out bush without an oven she'd never managed to get right. This crackling was everything she'd hoped it would be. Meanwhile, Sal distractedly picked at a salad while working. She didn't seem hungry.

Maybe she actually eats souls or something, Allegra thought, and nearly popped a blood vessel trying to hide her laugh.

Eventually, she was bored enough to check her work emails, and that was saying something. One was from the SES media liaison, time-stamped early that morning. Eyebrows raised, Allegra opened it—it was just a brief message telling her not to speak to any cameras until they'd had an opportunity to catch up.

Allegra felt a weight lift off her chest. "Sal," she said, swallowing her mouthful, "looks like I'm going to have to pull out of all of this. SES Media says—"

"I spoke with them late morning," Sal said over her, her attention still on her screen. "You'll have another email."

Allegra lowered her next bite, eyes narrowing, then went back to her inbox to check. As per Sal's advice, there was another email confirming the messaging had been cleared with Sal and that they were happy for Allegra to proceed. The usual warnings about not discussing operations in detail and referring any hairy questions to head office were below that.

Allegra sat back, stunned. This woman thought of everything.

Sal's eyes twinkled. "Did you think I'd give you an off-ramp that wide?"

Allegra shot her a sour look. "Don't you have someone to blackmail or something?" she asked dryly, gesturing at the laptop.

"Always," Sal said easily, and then got back to it.

Allegra made sure to finish her lunch before Sal did so she could excuse herself and spend some time not sitting across from her new business partner. Sal probably presumed she was looking for the toilet and didn't question it, giving Allegra the opportunity to wander around the villa. She quite liked big old houses; they reminded her of her childhood home. There was a handout near the front door with more information about the villa—heritage listed, no surprises there—but it included a handy map of the grounds, which extended all the way down to the main road. At the road, there was a little 'x' denoting a bus stop.

Suddenly, Allegra had an idea. Glancing back upstairs towards where they'd been seated to check she wasn't being followed, she went by the front desk, feeling around her pockets for her wallet.

A man, presumably Rita's husband, looked up from his book. "Oh, there's no need for that," he said, covering the EFTPOS terminal before Allegra could use it. "Sal takes care of bills for her guests."

Allegra pretended to be gracious and smiled thinly at him, hoping his voice hadn't carried upstairs. Just in case it had, she quickly headed out the front door, around the far side of the house, and down a short walking trail marked on the map.

It was only a few hundred metres, so she'd be fine without a hat—for now. But when she reached the road and realised that, because it was Sunday, there'd be no bus for ages, she worried her sunscreen wouldn't last. Oh well, even sunburn was preferable to sitting in a car with Sal for another hour.

Setting off along the verge, she checked her phone for the closest train station and decided she could just walk there. Freedom. A smile settled on her face. She had to talk herself out of breaking into a full run.

As she put distance between herself and that lunch, Allegra felt more and more like herself again.

That was, until a low, black car pulled up beside her.

"Nicely played," an all-too-familiar voice said to her, smile audible. "That's a first for me."

Allegra did not believe that for an instant. "Don't tell me no one's ever walked out on *you* before."

Sal shook her head once. "I told you that you were special," she said, driving at a slow crawl beside her. "We have some more details about tomorrow to cover."

Allegra kept walking. "Email them to me."

"I'd rather make sure you actually hear them."

"Well," Allegra said as condescendingly as she could manage, "we can't always have what we want."

Sal laughed. "You're really going to make me set my speed to 7km per hour all the way to Blaxland?"

Allegra looked directly at her, still smiling, and imitated Sal's answer from earlier. "Well, I can't *force* you."

Sal was watching her with her own genuinely entertained smile, eyes fixed on Allegra over the top of her sunglasses. After several seconds, she pulled her elbow inside and pressed the button to close the window.

"You don't strike me as someone who likes surprises," she said neutrally as the window rolled slowly shut, then brightened. "I, on the other hand, very much enjoy other people being surprised. You can decide whether to read my email based on how much entertainment you'd like to be for me tomorrow."

With the last crack of the tinted window, she winked at Allegra. Then her car surged to 80 in an instant and disappeared smoothly around a tight corner.

Good riddance, Allegra thought—then immediately got annoyed at being cornered into reading whatever fucking information Sal was going to send.

The walk to Blaxland was partly shaded and not unpleasant, and once at the station, she didn't have to wait long for the train. It was mostly empty—Sunday, after all—and she opened her phone to continue reading a biography a friend had recommended, but kept finding herself distracted by lunch.

I suppose Sal thinks she's quite smart, Allegra thought, annoyed to have to admit it was because she *was* smart. Smart, calculating, and completely deliberate about everything she did. It blew Allegra's mind that someone could fully grasp their own behaviour, know its impact on others, and still confidently keep doing it.

Allegra was shaking her head. Clearly Sal was a 'the end justifies the means' person; Allegra could accept that logic on some level. What Allegra couldn't accept was the pleasure she seemed to find in treating their every interaction like a game.

Well, I one-upped her in the end, Allegra thought with satisfaction, settling back in the train seat. Allegra might not have been a game player, but she also wasn't going to let herself be steamrolled by Ms Corporate Goth.

Allegra had lifted her phone to continue reading her book, moving her arm out of the hot sun streaming through the train window, when the whole jet-black thing suddenly struck her as a weird fucking choice for Australia. Okay, Black Standard Advisory branding—Allegra got that. But a full-length black suit approaching summer? Wasn't she very bloody hot every minute of the day? Allegra was sweating in cargos and a t-shirt, and Sal hadn't even taken off her jacket.

Allegra caught herself wondering what Sal was wearing underneath the jacket. Surely it had to be very thin so Sal didn't die of heatstroke when—*she stopped herself right the fuck there*.

We are not *following that train of thought*, she firmly told herself, face scrunched up in self-disgust. *Appalling*.

Not that she could have followed that particular thought train very far, anyway—her actual train arrived at Edgecliff. From there, she picked up a five-dollar sun hat she could wear low around her face—she wasn't sure how much time her face was still spending on people's screens—and just walked the rest of the way to Point Piper.

Timothy's van was in the driveway when she got back, and as a result she didn't see her LandCruiser until she'd walked through the gate.

She nearly blinded herself looking at it. Someone had polished it to a mirror shine, buffed out the worst scratches, and, as far as a 15-year-old 4WD could look brand new off the showroom floor, it did look brand new off the showroom floor. That father and daughter had put a lot of effort into it.

Allegra was standing in front of it, feeling a mixture of gratitude and guilt, when the front door opened. It was Timothy, and he'd already changed into loungewear.

"I won't ask what you've been doing today!" he said with a smile, gesturing at the car. "I think that's the first time you've cleaned that thing in years!"

Allegra grimaced and explained what had happened at Bayline Tyres.

Timothy looked a little impressed. "Well, I suppose there's no harm in people giving you freebies. Generosity is good for the soul. I'm sure they enjoyed it."

They had appeared to, Allegra granted him that. She followed him back inside.

"Would you like some lunch?" he asked as they walked into the central room. "We didn't have any chicken left—I knew that would go quickly!—but I do have a lot of roast vegetables. How hungry are you? I could make us some tuna to go with them."

Allegra stopped for a moment. Uh oh. "Not hungry at all."

Timothy's eyes were on her, completely unassuming. "You've already eaten?"

"Yes," Allegra said simply, and didn't elaborate. It was probably best Timothy knew as little as possible about her dealings with Sal. Ideally, nothing. "Tuna for dinner would be great, though."

He brightened. "You're staying for dinner? Karl would love to see you. I could see if—"

"Just us is fine. I need an early start tomorrow. I have some interviews booked."

"Interviews?" He shook his head, chuckling. "Of course it would be rescuing a billionaire that ends up making you famous..." he said wryly. "Oh well, you deserve to be celebrated a little! Which station is it with? Will you be on television?"

He pulled out a chair for her at the table—a movement that reminded her of Sal doing the same. His smile was so earnest, but...

She looked down at the chair, suddenly feeling crowded. She couldn't do this right now. "I'm sorry, Timothy, I just—"

His smile faded a little; he forced it back on, and back into his voice. "That's fine. You're tired. Go!" He pretended to cheerfully wave her outside. "Go relax. I have some paperwork to do anyway. If you're hungry at any point, there are some leftovers in the fridge."

She watched him head back upstairs towards his office a little too quickly. Screwing up her face for a moment against the tightening in her chest, she pushed the feeling away and went to check on her clothes.

They were finally dry, so she set about sorting through them and putting the ones she wouldn't need for summer away in the walk-in robe in the spare room. Then she sat down on the bed for a moment to rest her legs, and ended up lying back on it.

She was quite sore, and when she ran through the events of the last 24 hours, it made sense: her recoveries weren't what they used to be. She probably should have taken it easy today instead of doing what she'd actually done.

Her mind back on Sal, she felt around in her cargos for her phone to check her email. There was one from Black Standard Advisory.

Fuck. She put the phone beside her on the bed for a few minutes, fighting with herself about reading it. Sal was right: Allegra was not a fan of surprises, which meant she would need to read it at some point this evening to find out what Sal had planned. But did she need to read it *now*?

She groaned and put a wrist over her eyes. She could languish all afternoon wondering what was in it, or she could just rip the damn Band-Aid off and move on with her day.

Retrieving her phone, she opened the email, expecting either several attachments or a wall of text to plough through. There was neither.

"*Good girl*," was the only text, followed by a mobile phone number.

"You've got to be fucking kidding me," she said aloud, and furiously replied, "*I am not calling that.*"

"*Your choice*." It was accompanied by a deeply unwelcome winky face emoji.

Allegra stared at her screen, expecting a follow-up. Nothing came; there was just radio silence. She lay there for several minutes with her jaw clenched, deliberating over what to do. She did not want to give Sal the satisfaction of making her call, but she wanted even less to have Sal there, smugly watching whatever warning she was withholding land in real time. Either way was a dead end.

I could just not show up tomorrow, Allegra thought, tempted by the idea. She could drive out bush to the place she'd agreed to survey and do that instead.

But—then the charity wouldn't be able to open that support centre.

Grabbing a pillow, she buried her face in it and yelled, restrained only by not wanting to alert Timothy to the fact she was angry. It would just worry him.

She picked up her mobile again. *This is for kids like Aaron*, she thought, then swallowed all of her fucking pride in one big gulp and dialled.

Sal picked up immediately, and before she could speak, Allegra said clearly, "Just tell me what you're planning and then leave me alone."

The dark smile was audible in Sal's voice. "But Allegra, I want to know what you're wearing."

Those words made Allegra completely forget what she'd been about to say—and recall that earlier, unwelcome thought about what might be under Sal's jacket.

Before she could recover, Sal continued, "They're going to want you to look the part on television, so I think you should probably wear your SES uniform, the orange jumpsuit if possible—that's the most recognisable one. And everyone likes a woman in uniform."

Did they...? Allegra was still stuck on what she thought Sal had said earlier. "You did that on purpose."

"I did what on purpose?" Sal asked, brushing aside the question. "Anyway, there's no need to do anything with your face or hair because they have people in the studio for that." She chuckled. "Not that you particularly need anything done, of course. We've got a lot of places to be tomorrow, so I'm getting us a driver. That way, we don't need to worry about parking. We'll pick you up on the corner of the New South Head Road at 4am."

Not at the house, Allegra realised, and then realised why.

Allegra could almost hear Sal's smirk. "Aren't you glad I didn't surprise your husband by showing up at 4am at your door?"

Secretly, Allegra was. She didn't dignify that sly fucking question with an answer, though. "He's not my husband."

Sal ignored her correction. "That's your reward for answering your emails. Because I would have had to show up at your door if you didn't know where to be and how to get there. Now, I'd better let you get back to what you were doing."

What she was doing? Allegra looked up at the ceiling from where she lay on the bed, legs over the edge. It was actually—quite a position. She could feel heat in her cheeks. "Goodbye, Sal," she said firmly.

"Bye, Allegra." She always sounded like she was on the brink of laughing. "Nice chat. Let's do it again sometime."

Chapter 9: Media Blitz

Allegra slipped out quietly at 4am, pausing by Timothy's door only long enough to confirm he was still snoring. She felt oddly fine for 4am. Usually, being called out this early meant being dragged out of sleep without warning; this time, she'd turned in at 8pm like a responsible adult. Her shoulders were still sore, but it was nothing that a couple of ibuprofen couldn't handle.

There was essentially no traffic on New South Head Road; a welcome discovery, given she was in her full orange SES jumpsuit and recognisable from space. No one bothered her until a black Mercedes van pulled up.

Before she could reach for the door, the driver—a white man in his 60s or so, dressed in a chauffeur uniform complete with gloves—hurried around the van and decorously slid it open for her. Inside were two rows of leather seats facing each other... and Sal seated on the opposite side, long legs crossed and mobile in hand.

Her suit looked even sharper today, if that were possible: pants pressed into perfect lines that ended in a point at her stilettos, faintly triangular shoulder pads, and a single button drawing the lapels into twin triangles across her middle. It looked like exactly the sort of thing a marketing manager would wear to telegraph how avant-garde and edgy she was.

The hand holding her phone dropped into her lap as she gave Allegra a very slow and obvious once-over. "Good morning."

Fortunately, it was dark enough that she probably missed the blush on Allegra's cheeks. *Indignation*, Allegra promised herself. *Just indignation*. "Do I meet your standards?" she asked, irritated already.

Sal had a lazy smile. "It's not for me," she said, waggling her phone in the air. "It's for your soon-to-be adoring public. Not that I'm not loving the orange jumpsuit, though. Very firewoman."

"Thanks. You look like a Disney villain."

Sal laughed openly. "Well, I'm glad someone like you would *never* judge a book by its cover."

"No, I'd judge you by your actions, which are also giving 'Disney villain'."

Allegra meant it as an insult, obviously. Sal didn't take it as one. "Was it volunteering several weeks of my time for charity that gave you that impression? Or just that you personally find me unpleasant?"

"I doubt I'm the only one."

She chuckled. "You aren't. I believe your husband shares your opinion of me."

Allegra aged 10 years in a second, forgetting she was supposed to be verbally sparring with this woman. "Can you *please* stop referring to him as my husband?"

Sal's eyes narrowed for a moment. Then she lifted her phone, unlocked it, and scrolled. When she found what she was looking for, she held the screen out to Allegra. It was Allegra's Homeward Foundation contract, zoomed in on the 'Mrs' in the salutation field.

There was a good reason for that, but Allegra was *not* going to give this woman the sordid details of why she specifically didn't want to be confused with the other Ms Sinclair. "We *were* married. We're divorced now."

"Yet you still live with him."

Was she for real? "My stuff is there. I stay there when I'm in Sydney—in a separate room. Why does it matter?!"

Sal watched her reaction with genuine interest. "Pragmatically speaking, I suppose it doesn't. I was just curious."

"Then why on earth don't you simply ask me?"

Sal's face was unreadable. "I did just simply ask you."

Allegra had no fucking idea how to take that. Either Sal was deliberately messing with her—most likely—or she genuinely didn't know how to be a normal person. Also, did she just voluntarily tell this woman that she and Timothy didn't share a bed?!

"Look," Allegra said, "I gather we're going to need to tolerate each other's company a lot over the next two weeks, so I'd appreciate it if we could—" She chose her words carefully. "—not antagonise each other."

Sal looked amused. "You just called me a Disney villain," she pointed out.

Allegra exhaled. "Fine, I'm sorry about that," she said for the sake of not being a total hypocrite. She was not sorry.

Sal had that irritatingly triumphant expression again. "Apology accepted," she said, as if she hadn't been just as antagonistic. Then she moved on before Allegra could figure out how to get her to apologise, too. "I gather you haven't eaten?"

Allegra couldn't decide whether Sal meant to imply she was being hangry, or if it was a genuine question. "Why are you asking?"

"Because I need to actually feed you if I want you to retain those very marketable shoulders," she said, her eyes dipping to the shape of them beneath the orange jumpsuit. "Is it too cold for you to get them out? I think they'd look great on camera."

Allegra felt heat crawl up her neck. "I'll wait until I'm about to go on air," she said, crossing her arms tightly across her chest before realising how defensive that looked and hurriedly uncrossing them.

Sal observed her reaction with a knowing smile, then unlocked her phone again. "So, what will it be? Something high in protein, I gather?"

Allegra gave Sal her order, and then took out her own phone to halt conversation as they drove.

They drove mostly in the dark, but the sky was just starting to lighten when they reached Sky News Studios in Macquarie Park and descended into the dark carpark underneath it. The chauffeur delivered them to the studio door and then ushered them out.

A young woman with a headset perched over her very short hair was waiting in the doorway. Sal strode forward and shook her hand. "Sal Lategan. Amy, I take it? We spoke on the phone."

The girl nodded. "That's me," she said, and then they both turned a little to look at Allegra. Amy's smile seemed genuine. "Mrs Sinclair, it's wonderful to meet you in the flesh!" she said, standing aside to hold the door open. "Please come this way. We have breakfast waiting for you in Hair and Makeup."

Allegra glanced at Sal, who indicated for her to go ahead. The corridor was bright, long, and clearly at basement level, with staff already moving through it. Everyone she passed recognised and greeted her—it felt like the twilight zone.

Amy and Sal spoke over her head as they walked; Amy gave Sal the run sheet, outlined the news topics around Allegra's appearance, and double-checked what the hosts were allowed to touch on.

Were allowed to? That was new. No one had ever asked permission in her interviews before. It seemed like the sort of treatment a celebrity would get, not a Bush Search and Rescue op who happened to be in the right place at the right time.

Eventually, she was shown into a room with a long table, mirrors, and lights—exactly what she'd expected when she heard the words 'Hair and Makeup'. The room was empty at this hour, but it was easy to tell which chair was hers: a bowl of toasted muesli and Greek yoghurt had been set out for her, exactly as ordered. It was beautifully prepared, with a selection of fresh berries on top she hadn't asked for but that immediately made her mouth water.

It was very thoughtful. "Your idea?" Allegra asked as Amy settled her at the bench. The girl nodded. "Nice touch. Looks delicious."

Amy looked as if her smile might actually crack her face. "I'll let them know you're ready," she said, a little pink-cheeked as she ducked out.

As Allegra got stuck into her breakfast, Sal wandered over and appeared behind her in the mirror. Against the bright room and white walls, she stood out like a deep shadow. "I think you have a fan for life in that one," she said, nodding towards the door Amy had disappeared through. She was grinning.

Allegra didn't think much of it until she noticed the depth of Sal's grin. It was more mischievous than usual. For a second, she couldn't work out why Amy's delight would amuse her so much—then it clicked. Amy was quite butch. Allegra didn't always notice that immediately, given her profession, but it was probably relevant here.

Allegra dropped the spoonful that she'd been about to put in her mouth. "Oh. You think she's...?"

"Yes," Sal said easily. "At least, judging by what she and her friends have been saying online about that video of you hauling the tyre up New South Head Road."

Allegra shot her a hard look for the snooping, though she wasn't at all surprised to learn about it. It seemed like exactly the sort of thing Sal *would* do. Sal ignored the reprimand, her attention fixed instead on Allegra's reaction to the online comments.

She's trying to figure out if I'm into women, Allegra realised, entertained by the idea. After their phone conversation last night, she had assumed Sal had already clocked her.

The thought had to wait. A knock came at the door, and then two more women bustled in.

They both consulted with Sal about styling while Allegra finished her breakfast, which was odd enough before Sal started giving hair and makeup advice as if her own look wasn't one poisoned apple away from a fairy-tale coup.

The hairstylist introduced herself, touched Allegra's hair, and immediately asked, "Have you been swimming?"

Allegra was then subjected to several long minutes of good-natured lecturing about rinsing her hair after swimming, especially as a natural blonde, while the woman worked it into a loose French braid.

After that, she and Sal conferred over Allegra's head before the hairstylist pulled a few strands loose to make it softer and messier.

"I want you to look like you've just hiked 10km to get to the studio," Sal explained.

"Then you'd better spray me with a litre or two of water," Allegra told her dryly, which ended up being unfortunately close to the truth because her orange jumpsuit was getting quite stuffy under the lights.

Because of Sal's earlier interest, Allegra delayed unzipping the jumpsuit as long as she could. In the end, she only unzipped it and unthreaded her arms when the makeup artist took over, mostly so she wouldn't immediately sweat everything off. Underneath, she had only a black tank top—the jumpsuits were murder in the warmer months—which, as Sal had hoped, showed off her shoulders.

Sal noted the shoulders with a smirk, but didn't comment, too busy supervising Allegra's makeup, scrutinising the colour choices, and swapping out the golds and browns for cooler neutrals. When the makeup artist was done, she stepped aside to show Allegra her face. Her skin appeared visibly healthier, but she hardly looked like she had any makeup on at all.

"That's the point," Sal said, then turned to the makeup artist. "Thanks, that's amazing."

The two stylists left discussing a coffee run.

Sal motioned for Allegra to stand. She did, letting the loose top of her high-vis jumpsuit hang from her belt, and Sal walked slowly around her, apparently scrutinising her appearance. At least, that was clearly the premise. In practice, Sal's eyes felt far heavier than any casual once-over needed to be.

This close, on level ground, Allegra realised Sal was two or three inches shorter than her, even in stilettos. For some reason, that was a surprise—Allegra had imagined she'd be taller.

Imagined her? Allegra scoffed at herself, pushing that thought aside.

"Very nice," was Sal's final assessment. She stood back and lifted her phone. "Say cheese."

"Do not take a photo of me," Allegra said, but stood still for her anyway.

"I'm only going to use it to show the other studios what I want them to do with you," she said with a cheeky smile. "I promise." She locked eyes with Allegra for a moment, leaving Allegra to guess what other uses Sal might have for a photo of her.

Amy returned shortly to escort them upstairs and into the studio, walking them onto the floor between live segments and explaining where Allegra should sit and look. Then she went to have a word with one of the floor managers.

Standing there in the studio, with the set and hosts in front of her, made it suddenly real. Shit, she realised, I'm going to be live on television. That got her adrenaline going enough that she had to start breath-counting.

Sal clearly noticed and sidled up to her. "You'll be great," she whispered. "I've watched your previous interviews. Just focus on the points in the brief."

Allegra did not need a pep talk from this woman. "I'm fine."

"Uh huh," Sal said, "and I'm blonde."

Amy returned with a woman who was clearly more senior. "Okay, we'll get you on set, Mrs Sinclair," the woman said, ushering her onto the stage, where the two hosts—a man and a woman—were chatting and sipping coffee while the news rolled in the background.

As Allegra stepped up onto the makeshift stage, immediately warmed by the lights, the two hosts stood to shake her hand and introduce themselves. *Steve*, Allegra repeated to herself several times, trying to make it stick. *Yasmin*. "Just 'Allegra' is fine," she managed, before the floor manager's voice cut across them.

"15 seconds!"

The hosts immediately sat, hurriedly taking another mouthful from their cups, fixing their hair, and smoothing their clothes. Allegra copied them and sat, though she didn't really have anything to smooth.

From her seat under the bright lights, the studio floor seemed very dark. It felt like just the three of them in the room, and that was oddly comforting.

A flashing light in the corner of her vision counted down 4, 3, 2, 1, LIVE.

The hosts sprang to life. "Welcome back, everyone—boy, have we got a special guest with us this morning!" Steve announced, his voice every bit as fake as his perfect teeth. "Allegra Sinclair, local hero, here with us to talk about her daring rescue of Isaiah Vale and bush safety! Welcome, Allegra!"

Here we go, she thought, and forced a warm smile. "Thank you so much for having me. It's great to be able to talk about a topic very close to my heart: bush safety. As we've just learnt, it's so important to take precautions so you can get home safely to the people who love you."

From there, Allegra didn't remember much of the conversation; it was all an adrenaline-filled blur. They gently probed her for details of the rescue, and she gave a brief account of what happened, focusing mostly on her concern for Isaiah. When they asked what advice she'd give people going hiking over the long weekend, she ran through the basics of bush safety: don't hike or camp alone if you can avoid it—although she was an enormous hypocrite on that front—wear appropriate clothing, and bring the right gear.

After that topic wrapped up, Yasmin, who'd been smiling and laughing pleasantly through most of the conversation, interrupted Steve. "Sorry, Steve," she said, leaning towards Allegra. "I'm so sorry. I've got to say it: your arms look amazing. Any workout tips for women who'd like to get arms like yours?"

Allegra was a little taken aback—her arms were nothing like they'd been in her 20s, when she was actually working out—but went with it anyway. "Join the SES, ladies," she said to the camera in good humour, which the hosts loved. Eventually, they convinced her to flex. She did, reluctantly, and after they'd laughed, complimented her, and made far too much of it, everyone settled back into their chairs.

"So, Allegra," Yasmin began in a softer voice. "I hear bush safety isn't the only thing you're passionate about. There's another cause that's close to your heart, isn't there?"

Allegra had mentally rehearsed this part many times. "Yes. I'm doing safety work for a charity fundraiser that's coming up in just under two weeks—the Homeward Foundation. It's an incredible organisation that supports nearly 1000 families caring for children who can't be with their parents." Her throat tightened. She took a steady breath and forced out the rest. "Children like my son, who was in care with my sister while I was posted overseas doing disaster relief work."

Yasmin shook her head. "That must have been such a difficult experience."

Allegra knew that prompt would get her if she didn't move through it quickly. "It was. My sister stepped up to care for him, but she didn't have any support. That's why the Homeward Foundation is so important—they build community not only for the children, but for the people caring for them, so they have someone to turn to when things are tough." She'd written the lines herself, but they still sat heavily in her mouth. "It's really because of my sister that I was able to build the skills and experience I needed to rescue Isaiah. So, if any of your viewers would like to support the Homeward Foundation, I'd be really grateful."

"Sounds like an incredible cause," Steve said sombrely, then looked to the camera. "The details for the Homeward Foundation are up on our website, and after today, I think we'll need to add recruitment details for the SES, too." He smiled. "Thanks so much for coming in, Allegra." His tone changed as he swivelled towards the camera. "Next up," he said, reminding

Allegra of the type of audience they'd just beamed her out to, "are non-stick cooking sprays really raising your cancer risk? Sky Doctor has some advice for you."

The *LIVE* sign faded back to a digital clock counting backwards from 3:45, and the floor manager yelled, "We're clear!" Immediately, conversation murmured across the studio floor as the lights brightened.

Allegra exchanged goodbyes with the hosts as she was ushered back down to where Sal and Amy were standing.

Sal was smiling and nodding in silent approval. To Allegra's frustration, her immediate reaction to that was to feel proud of herself instead of what she *should* have felt: indifferent to the assessment of this incredibly annoying woman.

"Great work!" Amy told Allegra, a little pink-cheeked. None of that made it into her voice, however. "I'd invite you to relax in our green room and decompress, but Ms Lategan says she has you on a tight schedule today, so I'm happy to walk you back out to your car, if you like." She ushered them out of the studio, past a chorus of various people congratulating her on the rescue and thanking her for her service.

It was a relief to be in the well-lit hallway and away from the bustle. One down, Allegra thought, taking a few deep breaths and shaking out her tense muscles.

"Thanks so much for making this really smooth," Sal was saying to Amy as she held the door open. "Absolute clockwork." Amy smiled and stole a little glance towards Allegra.

Sal didn't miss it, either, and Allegra could almost see her brain ticking. "Look," Sal said to Amy, "I know it's against policy, but would you like a selfie with Allegra? I'm happy to shoot Sky comms an email and say I okayed it. You'll need to get their permission to post it on socials, though."

Amy practically inflated, then immediately tried to conceal her excitement. "Yeah, is that okay?" She looked hopefully at Allegra.

With those puppy eyes, there was a zero percent chance Allegra was going to refuse. "That's okay," she said, stepping alongside the girl. "Here."

Amy nearly dropped her phone getting it out, then held it above them—no mean feat given how much taller Allegra was.

As they posed, Sal motioned from the corner of Allegra's vision for her to put an arm around Amy. Allegra draped it across the girl's shoulders, and Amy went quite pink in the screen preview. She took a few different shots, presumably to pick the best one.

"Thanks for breakfast," Allegra said to Amy as she stepped away.

Amy had run out of words and just smiled from ear to ear as Allegra and Sal climbed back into the van and fastened themselves in.

"You handled that well," Sal observed, unreadable. After a few moments, she laughed. "I stand by my previous assessment. You are an absolute gift. There are at least three parts of that interview I guarantee will be clipped for TikTok within hours. The SES is going to be tempted to make you their mascot."

"You sound surprised," Allegra said flatly.

Sal was grinning. "Look, I have watched your previous interviews. I was reasonably confident you'd do fine, or I would have pressed you to practice with me. But it's one thing to assess someone as 'probably competent'; it's another to see them absolutely eat up an interview like that." She paused, holding eye contact. "Especially when that person has only shown you the grumpiest, most reactionary side of them."

It was the tiny twinge of guilt that made Allegra the angriest. "You bring out the best in me. What can I say?"

Sal ignored her sarcasm. "Anyway, that flex and the invitation to join the SES?" She shook her head again. "You are going to have women *all over you*."

Lucky me, Allegra thought. She wasn't especially enamoured with the idea; she'd never struggled to find a bed to share when she wanted one, anyway. Still, she kept her face neutral, refusing to give Sal the satisfaction of confirming whatever assessment she'd made of Allegra's sexuality.

Sal was watching her thoughtfully, and then, without warning, asked directly, "Do you know you like women, Allegra?"

For a second, Allegra was too stunned to answer. Then the phrasing caught up with her. "Do I know if I—why wouldn't I know?!"

Sal was perfectly calm. She opened her hands, then relaced her fingers. "Some people avoid addressing things they'd rather not think about, so I thought I would check, since you specifically asked me to address all my questions to you directly." Her eyes were alight with amusement.

"Well, you're about 20 years too late for that to be news to me," Allegra told her, surprised at how flustered she was.

Sal's smile deepened. "Great. Can we be on the record with it? Do you have a label you use?"

"I'm bi," she said, and was about to say she didn't care who knew about it, but before the words left her mouth, she remembered Aaron. She stopped herself. "I don't really want my son to be bombarded with frank discussions about his mother's sexuality, to be honest. That's not fair on him."

Sal nodded, accepting that. "I hate to say it, but even today that *does* mean you may be slightly more palatable to particular audiences, anyway. And a bigger audience means more reach and opportunities." Looking quite pleased about that prospect, she turned her attention to the mobile that seemed perpetually attached to her hand.

The conversation had apparently ended, but Allegra's thoughts were still scattered like startled birds. She felt raked over and scrutinised, as if all her wounds had been examined and not redressed. And yet the woman across from her seemed perfectly content to leave Allegra exposed while she remained buttoned up to the throat.

Allegra hated it. "Do you have a label *you* use, Sal?" she asked pointedly, aware how antagonising she sounded.

Sal looked up, entertained. "Oh, Allegra, I think you can probably guess the answer to that one," she said darkly, and gave Allegra another slow, languorous once-over. It was disarming in a way Allegra hadn't felt since she was much younger; she sank back into the leather seat as Sal's eyes lingered on every part of her. Then they travelled back up and settled on Allegra's. There was no invitation in them at all. It felt like a challenge. "Well," she said. "What am I?"

Allegra had to find her breath. "Are you always this unprofessional?"

Sal's smile barely moved. "No."

You are not going to get me to say it aloud, Allegra thought, mentally adding 'lesbian' to 'corporate goth'. Instead, she said, "Sal, what you are is extremely manipulative."

Sal looked taken aback, then *laughed*. "That's going on all my forms under 'sexuality' from now on."

Out of breath and out of fight, Allegra sat back and let the van take her wherever they were headed.

Chapter 10: Pressure Point

The worst part about knowing Sal was a lesbian was that Allegra kept accidentally remembering it. She would be scrolling through her phone, trying to avoid the news, and Sal would get her attention somehow. Sal recrossed her legs; Allegra remembered the slow, lingering once-over. Sal made a quick phone call; Allegra's eyes kept dipping to her lips and realising they'd kissed other women. At one point, Sal undid the button of her blazer and Allegra immediately put a moratorium on her thoughts so as not to respond to that. It was maddening.

It was also ridiculous—she'd spent her life around women in perfect shape, and women far more her type. There was no reason Sal should occupy any mental real estate at all. Allegra opted to chalk the whole thing up to Sal's constant manipulation.

Well, whatever was going on with Sal, Allegra was thankful for the small mercy of not having to make small talk with her on the way to the ABC studios. It was rush hour around Central, and even though city foot traffic had supposedly halved since COVID, every pedestrian crossing was still swimming with people in suits, so progress into town was slow.

The van's tinted windows gave Allegra the rare luxury of people-watching as a passenger. She quickly noticed that every woman seemed to be wearing those asymmetric, off-the-shoulder work tops—apparently the latest trend. The sight made her itch to slide open the van door and straighten everyone's sleeves so they didn't look as if they were about to fall off, which conveniently distracted her from the legs only inches from her own.

The driver delivered them to the back door of the ABC where they were met once again by another woman with a headset. She gave Allegra a very professional greeting and then turned immediately to Sal.

So, not gay, Allegra realised as she was escorted inside, half-smiling about that.

They were having another conversation about no-go topics while Sal ran her eyes over a document on a tablet she'd been handed. She stopped at one of the dot points, tapping it with a short but manicured nail Allegra forbade herself from making any further observations about. "'Family'," Sal quoted, glancing over her shoulder towards Allegra. "Are you comfortable discussing your family?"

Allegra considered that for a moment. “Not Simone.”

Sal watched her briefly—it wasn’t clear whether she was interested in that answer or waiting to see if Allegra would say anything else—and then looked back at the woman. “There’s your answer.” The woman nodded and fired the info off to the station.

Where the Sky TV studio had been huge and bustling, this one was cosy and relaxed: three small rooms divided by glass, like the radio equivalent of a fish tank, but somehow more human than Sky’s circus. In one room, two women lounged in front of a control panel, facing the host through the glass. The host was in her early fifties or so, leaning forward on her elbows while she spoke into the mic. What Allegra noticed was her warm smile and real teeth. She liked her immediately.

Their escort waved through the glass at the producers who stood to let her in, leaving Sal and Allegra in the small waiting room.

Sal picked up one of the magazines on the table between them, examining the front. “Can I interest you in a Cosmo from...” Her eyes searched the cover. “June, 2017?” She held the magazine up. The first thing Allegra saw on the cover was the unfortunate headline: *‘Come Again? 10 things to say during sex’*.

She narrowed her eyes, ignoring that story. “Thanks, but I’ve already reached my quota for lectures about my hair care routine today.”

Sal laughed at that and turned the magazine back over to flip through it herself. “I quite like these for entirely the wrong reason. Little microcosms of conformity, packaged in pretty colours and bold fonts,” she reflected, saying the first interesting thing Allegra had heard her say. Then she spoiled it by adding, “Nice glossy pictures, though,” and holding up an ad for ‘the invisible bra’.

Allegra suddenly felt self-conscious about the inbuilt support in her tank top.

She was still trying to work out whether Sal had chosen that advert by coincidence, or whether she was slyly informing Allegra she knew about the lack of bra, when the LIVE light switched off and the glass door opened, revealing one of the producers.

“Welcome!” she said, specifically to Allegra. “Come in and meet Sue.”

As they entered the studio, Sue stood and rounded the table to meet her. She had soft hands and the rapt attention of someone who was really listening. “Allegra! So wonderful to meet you. I think I interviewed your ex-husband a few years back, and he had such wonderful things to say about you.”

Allegra was pleasantly surprised anyone would remember those details years later. "After we separated, I hope."

Sue chuckled and showed Allegra to the desk opposite her, adjusting the height of the mic. "Yes. Maybe we'll talk a little bit about that today, if it comes up?"

Allegra pursed her lips. "It's not out of the question."

Sue noticed her hesitation. "You're welcome to brush off anything that doesn't work for you, anything at all. Just move the topic on. I did read the notes—we also won't talk about your other sister."

'Other sister' suggested Sue knew rather a lot about her already. Allegra felt some trepidation about that, but if Timothy had given a good interview with her, it was probably best not to worry.

Sue's gaze drifted past Allegra. "Sal," she said, greeting Allegra's silent shadow and bringing her into the light as she clasped hands with her in a very familiar way. "You're looking even sharper than usual."

Sal was grinning. "Thanks. You look exactly the same."

That must have been a compliment, because Sue appreciated it. "I have new lines since COVID," she said, pulling at her forehead. "Look. Tom made me promise no Botox, so I'm destined to look like a deflated balloon. Anyway." She went back to her desk. "Would either of you like a coffee? We have a barista downstairs and producers who think they're admin assistants."

Allegra and Sal both ordered coffee, and said producers cheerfully took care of it. Once the coffee was delivered and Sal had stepped back into the glass observation deck with the other women, Allegra found herself alone with Sue. It wasn't unpleasant. Headset aside, the aroma of coffee made it feel like having brunch with a friend.

Sue's eyes were on the clock beside them as it counted down, and then her voice played in Allegra's headset. "You're listening to ABC Mornings with Sue McLellan-Steele." She read off a few future discussions, then looked up at Allegra. "But right now, I'll let you guess who I have with me in the studio. Unless you were offline and off grid over the weekend, you'll have seen her face from the chance rescue of media magnate scion Isaiah Vale: the illustrious Allegra Sinclair. But what you probably don't know about her is that she's actually led a very interesting life. We're going to have a chat about some of that next up. But first, the traffic."

They were briefly offline. "Illustrious?" Allegra asked her. "Infamous, perhaps."

“I stand by my description,” Sue said with a firm smile, and then brought them on air again. “Allegra! Such a pleasure to have you.”

“Thanks, Sue. It’s genuinely nice to be here,” she said honestly, and let Sue guide the conversation.

As Allegra had suspected, Sue had done her research. They started with Allegra’s current role in the SES and how she had happened upon Isaiah, but Sue didn’t linger on the obvious hooks: the rescue, bush safety, or Allegra’s muscles. She was more interested in Allegra’s experience as a woman and mother working in rescue and disaster recovery, and went right back to her overseas deployments, drawing out anecdotes Allegra hadn’t thought about in years.

It was enjoyable. Even framed by the memory of being stuck overseas and horribly missing her son, there was something faintly nostalgic about it.

Because of Sue’s sincerity, Allegra had let herself be carried along by the conversation. She hadn’t noticed where it was leading until it reached something she hadn’t been expecting. “So—here’s perhaps a more difficult question. Why this career? And why drop out of university to do it?”

Allegra’s eyes snapped up. Sue already knew; there was no other explanation.

Allegra looked across at Sal, who had been lounging casually in the background with her arms crossed. When Sal saw her expression, she straightened.

It wasn’t that Allegra didn’t want to answer. It was just that saying his name felt like hauling cargo through quicksand. “There was an accident,” she managed instead. “And my priorities changed.”

Everyone’s eyes were on her. She could feel her pulse quicken.

Sue was monitoring her reaction, trying to decide whether to press or not. “It must have been an awful accident. Was it yours?”

Sue knew it wasn’t hers. Allegra could lie, deflect, or ruin what had so far been a wonderful interview with a reporter she’d connected with. Sue had given her permission to move the topic on at the beginning, but—

No. It was too late for that. The quickest way out was through. She opened her mouth, her lips forming a name she hadn’t said in a long time. “Lachlan. My brother.” She made a face, correcting herself. “My late brother.”

Through the glass, she could see Sal say something to the producers. One of them nodded and reached towards the dump button.

Allegra shook her head at them. Sue understood it for what it was—tacit permission—and gently prompted her, "Was it his death that changed your priorities?"

Not just his death: his disappearance. Days and days of driving around showing people his picture, of yelling at the police to actually fucking do something, of prying her treacherous fucking eyes open as she leant over the steering wheel after 36 hours without sleep, begging her body to last a little longer, because what if the next street she turned down was the one where she found him in the gutter?

Say something, she reminded herself. "Yeah," she managed. She could still hear her own voice—so young—lecturing Lachlan for going out on a final exam night while Mum and Dad were away. He'd ignored her, flashing her what she now knew as Aaron's smile, and promised to bring her back Maccas the following morning.

The last time she'd seen him, he was pulling out of their driveway in Mum's car. The next time she saw that car, it was being dragged out of a ravine, her baby brother's dried blood on the twisted windscreen.

She didn't say that. She repeated the facts just like the police press conference had: six days missing. Hundreds of square kilometres raked over until they'd finally found him. She told a very abridged version of the story—no one needed to know the level of detail indelibly carved into her memory—how she'd quit university immediately and joined the SES.

Sue let the silence stretch between them; ambient static was audible in Allegra's headset because of it.

"And now, with Isaiah," Sue said gently, "another family gets the ending yours didn't."

Allegra hadn't really connected those dots; not consciously. Doing so choked her like hands curling around her throat. She fought them—she was good at that—and managed, "That everyone who's waiting for someone should have," but it was all she could accomplish. She felt her muscles tighten and pull her shut like a slammed door.

Sal made a large wind-up motion to Sue, who was already on it. "Such an awful tragedy in a family's past," Sue said gently, "and such a powerful reminder of what timely search and rescue can mean. Allegra, thank you so much for sharing that with us."

I forgot to mention the charity, Allegra realised only as they came off air, and that drove the door even further shut. Her whole reason for being there, and she hadn't managed one line? She bit her lip, standing. Her body was so stiff that her knees shook.

Sue noticed and came over to her, her worry completely sincere. She put a hand on Allegra's arm. "I hope that wasn't too much," she said, clearly meaning it. "I wanted people to really hear what saving Isaiah would mean to you."

Allegra could have done without hearing it herself. In fact, she could have gone her whole life without making that connection. She nodded, trying both to force a smile and shrug off her stiffness. Neither was very successful.

A pair of warm hands took her shoulders. From the gentle grip, Allegra would have presumed it was one of the producers; the shock of discovering it was *Sal* nearly cured her paralysis. Shouldn't those hands be cold?

"Great work, but we've got a busy day ahead!" Sal said, all business. "Absolute master interviewer as always, Sue. Bit of a tone change from Sky News."

"Best compliment anyone's paid me," Sue said dryly, then looked back at Allegra, giving her arm a rub. "We have access to a debriefing service, if you need it."

Rather than let Sue go any further, Sal physically began to move Allegra out of the room. "Can you email me those details?" she asked over her shoulder. "We've really got to head off. Nine wants her at 10am. Thanks again."

She'd been marched out of the building and into the van before she felt as if she'd taken a single breath. It was a blur.

A water bottle was placed in her hand. It was disposable; Timothy would hate that. Then, directly in her line of sight, Sal extended her phone. "Here, I want you to see this." TikTok was open.

Allegra took the phone mechanically. Once she had it, though, she only held it.

"Keep my phone, then," Sal said with a shrug as she buckled herself in. When she spoke again, that playful note was back in her voice. "I know sooner or later you're going to be tempted to snoop through my gallery anyway."

Was she fucking kidd—*right now, of all fucking times?* Allegra looked up at her, feeling nothing but intense disgust, and was faced with a knowing smile.

Sal nodded at the phone. "Watch."

Allegra contemplated throwing the phone—with how stiff she was, she'd probably just put her shoulder out—but instead held eye contact with Sal, locked it, and placed the phone on the seat beside her.

When Sal went to retrieve it, though, Allegra couldn't help moving it just out of reach.

"Really?" Sal asked, sounding at least slightly entertained. She sat back, smoothed her hair and unbuttoned her blazer again. "Oh, well. It'll give us a great opportunity to talk to each other, I suppose."

She already had that triumphant twinkle in her eyes before Allegra handed the phone back. "A fate worse than death," Allegra said, her throat so dry the words scraped. Then she registered the word *death* and attempted to swallow some of the water.

Sal observed her at length. For a few moments, Allegra was worried she would try to bring up what had happened—in fact, she was bracing for it—but when Sal spoke, she simply said, "I'm going to guess you're not the type of person who knows what a video stitch is."

Surprised by the topic change, it took Allegra a full second to be insulted by Sal's assumption, which was unfortunately true. "I gather you're about to impart that wisdom."

"Mmm," Sal said, nodding once. "It's a type of video where you take a few seconds of someone else's video and attach your reaction to it." She showed Allegra her screen again. "There are dozens of stitches of Sky's clip of you flexing, and it's only been up for two hours."

Allegra stared at her for a moment, still spinning; only Sal would treat viral fame as a trauma debrief.

She accepted the phone anyway and tapped on one of the thumbnails. It was a short—very edited—video of her flexing and then saying, 'Join the SES, ladies,' to the camera. The video then cut to a young woman looking up from her phone with a blank expression. Then she sprang up and ran at full pelt in her PJs and Uggs to the local SES headquarters and beat on the front door.

The second video used the same clip again, cutting to another girl looking up from her phone, eyes wide. Immediately, she rushed to her cupboard, wrenched out a hiking backpack, got smothered in a waterfall of stored crap, and began frantically stuffing it full of clothes.

There were several more just like that one, almost all of them women performing frenetic actions that suggested they'd been compelled to join the SES by the sight of Allegra's arms.

By the time she'd watched the last one, she realised she was grinning.

"It's a good thing you like women," Sal commented, "because you're a hit with them."

"They're all very young," Allegra pointed out.

"The ones on TikTok are. The older ones won't post videos, but they will get out their wallets for the Homeward Foundation, or whatever other cause you tell them to support."

Mentioning the Homeward Foundation dragged Allegra back to the ABC interview. "I didn't say anything about the charity in there." She felt that familiar knife-twist in her chest.

Sal waved that concern away. "Sue will mention it for you, and you'll have plenty more opportunities. We should probably start talking about what Nine wants to focus on."

"Is that where we're going?"

"Eventually. We have two or three hours first," Sal said, as if she hadn't just bustled Allegra out of the studio by citing it. "I thought we could have an early lunch."

Allegra wasn't hungry at all; even drinking the water was a challenge. Sal noticed her expression. "I gather you have a better idea."

Allegra laughed once, humourlessly. "I suppose driving me into the wilderness and just leaving me there is out of the question."

Sal snorted. "Didn't I just hear you lecturing Sydney about all the reasons that would be a poor decision, bush safety-wise?"

At this point, Allegra didn't care if it was. She shrugged.

Sal crossed her arms, reminding Allegra about that unbuttoned blazer. "What about that is appealing to you? Being alone?"

"And beautiful trees, the sky above me, and not being trapped in a tiny van with—" Feeling a bit exposed by that line of conversation, Allegra stopped.

Sal's brain was already ticking. "I bet you're the type of person who prefers to sweat things out." She pursed her lips. "Well, I can't do vast natural wilderness this close to your next bookings—not even with a chopper—but is a treadmill okay? And a set of free weights?"

Allegra was stuck on the casual mention of *a chopper*, like someone might consider taking an Uber. "I'm not sure what you're suggesting."

Sal's resolve solidified. She unbuckled herself and leant towards Allegra, close enough that Allegra's breath caught. Fortunately, it was quickly clear Sal was only reaching for the driver intercom, even if her knee was pressed into the leather seat right beside Allegra's thigh.

"There's been a change of plans," Sal said into the intercom, looking sideways at Allegra. "Back home to The Rocks, please."

Chapter 11: Hospitality

When Sal said she lived in The Rocks, Allegra pictured a quaint little century terrace beside a boutique pub or a warehouse art gallery—something fashionable and convenient. She certainly didn't picture an almost brutalist new build inside a hollowed-out factory with a lift directly accessible from Sal's private carpark.

The building was at least 30 floors, but the lift only had one button. Amused by Allegra's surprise, Sal pressed it. "I gather you've never visited a penthouse before."

"You live in a penthouse," Allegra said flatly, disgusted with herself for not suspecting it.

"Mmm," Sal said neutrally as they began to ascend. "That's why it has a private lift."

Said lift had four walls of mirrors, tessellating their reflections at every angle. Combined with the speed of the lift, the space felt surreal and otherworldly. Feeling a bit giddy because of it—and already out of sorts because of Lachlan—Allegra fished her phone out rather than stare into infinity for the whole ride up.

Immediately, she wished she hadn't: three missed calls from Timothy and a text. *"I heard the interview. Are you still at the studio? I'll come and get you. Please don't make any decisions right now."*

Allegra sighed audibly at it. *Oh, please, I'm not 23 anymore,* she thought. She was well past doing anything stupid; he should know that by now. She dismissed the message.

Another notification popped up, this time from—Vanessa? *"CALL ME IMMEDIATELY!!!"* That was more mystifying because Vanessa didn't listen to ABC radio, so either Timothy had enlisted her to help get Allegra's attention (not out of the question, but not something he'd done before), or, worse, she'd been secretly watching Sky News. That possibility was unfortunately far more likely.

Well, whatever it was, she wasn't calling them immediately. She angrily locked her phone, slid it back into her pocket, and looked up into the mirror. Sal was watching her in it. By her smirk, Allegra figured she'd guessed who one of the messages was from.

"Now, just imagine if he knew where you were right now..." Sal said in a musical voice.

The lift dinged. Sal swept an arm out, inviting Allegra ahead of her. As Allegra passed, Sal's eyes dipped to her body.

The atrium was sprawling and towering, with one wall facing the harbour in a flat expanse of windows and blue, cloudless sky. One side of the room led to a broad terrace with palm trees on it—30 storeys above the ground!—while the other had a suspended staircase that split in the middle and curled up in two directions to two different levels.

There were about three pieces of furniture in total: two couches facing each other that looked more like abstract sculptures than somewhere you'd want to put your feet up, and a table between them. There was not a shred of evidence an actual human called this place home.

"You *live* here?"

Sal was clearly finding Allegra's reaction to ostentatious wealth highly entertaining. "Were you expecting a studio under the bridge?"

Allegra decided not to play into it. "I was expecting black."

That surprised Sal; she laughed openly, and it echoed off the walls. "I thought about it," she said, as if Allegra's comment had been genuine. "But the architect brought several of his colleagues to talk me out of it, and they were very convincing."

The architect? His colleagues? *Sal had helped design this place*? Allegra wandered into the centre of the room, eyebrows raised. This place must be… tens of millions of dollars. At least. She looked back towards Sal. "Black Standard Advisory must pay you a fortune."

Sal laughed once, more darkly. "They don't. But they will." Something about that comment prickled Allegra's skin. She tried to read Sal's face, but couldn't.

Sal didn't elaborate either; she simply indicated a hallway beside the lift. "The gym and guest facilities are that way. I'll be in my office," she said, walking towards the stairwell, her heels clicking on the marble floor. "You can come and find me when you're done decompressing."

Sal climbed the stairs slowly and deliberately, each unhurried step showcasing the tailoring on the seat of her pants. Her fingers trailed lightly over the banister. She'd only made it up one flight when she stopped and looked back over her shoulder—right at Allegra.

Allegra suddenly realised she'd been staring.

As Allegra's cheeks turned a hot red, Sal theatrically feigned scandal. "Allegra!" she said. "And I'm not even wearing a skirt."

Horrified at herself, Allegra shut her jaw and hightailed it down the hallway Sal had indicated.

What do you think you're doing? she berated herself on the way, passing several abstract art pieces whose cost probably could have paid off an ordinary person's mortgage. *Do you want her to know she gets to you?*

Does it really matter if she knows? another part of her chimed in. *Two consenting adults finding each other attractive isn't a crisis.*

If that's what this was, there wouldn't be an issue, Allegra told that voice, still a bit incredulous that she'd found Sal worth staring at. But this wasn't just two adults finding each other attractive. Sal was trying to get a rise out of her, and Allegra was giving her one. Repeatedly.

The trouble was, Sal seemed to have cheat codes for everything that knocked Allegra off balance, and Allegra had no idea how to counter that. She'd never met anyone who could so casually yet thoroughly short-circuit her brain.

By the time Allegra made it to the gym, her head was a jumbled mess of cotton wool and adrenaline. She hardly got through the door before casting off her high-vis jumpsuit in a puddle on the floor, climbing onto the treadmill in her bike shorts and tank top, and switching the damn thing on. The sweet oblivion of physical exhaustion couldn't come fast enough.

Sal's treadmill was a premium model, which meant it glided up to 15 km/h without so much as a whine. Allegra's body was less premium—especially these days—and punished her for not warming up with various jolts of pain. She ignored them.

When her throat started to burn from how hard she was breathing, she began to wonder how fast Sal's treadmill topped out. She tested it: 17. 18. 19... It was only when the screen wouldn't allow her to push beyond 20 km/h that she felt triumphant at reaching the limit and let herself slow back down to 12.

Once she was jogging at a more moderate pace, there was unfortunately enough oxygen available for her brain to start tormenting her again.

Specifically, about an odd decorating choice: someone had filled an architectural void in the corner of the gym with a large, comfortable-looking leather armchair facing the equipment.

Combined with the fact she'd been caught watching Sal a few minutes earlier, the chair cursed Allegra with the mental image of Sal reclined there, drink in hand, legs crossed, her eyes resting indulgently on Allegra's body as she worked out.

Disgusted with herself, she dismissed the image and left the treadmill to inspect the free weights. So much for pretending to be indifferent to Sal's flirting—she couldn't even pretend it to *herself*.

The weights were so shiny that at first Allegra thought they might not have been used at all. It wasn't out of the question that someone who lived in a place like this would put equipment in a gym and never touch it. That was what she presumed, anyway, until she started loading up the bar and noticed a chip on the 10-kilo plate and scuff lines on the inside of the 20s. The scuffs were unexpected. If Sal was using multiple 20s, that suggested some real strength.

Either that or she has guests that use the 20s, she realised, remembering Sal's interest in her shoulders. Perhaps Sal just liked her women built, and those women had been in here using her weights.

What woman could possibly put up with someone like Sal long enough to scuff her equipment, though? As soon as she thought that, she remembered that just about everyone they'd run into who knew Sal seemed, annoyingly, to really like her.

That was confusing. It was confusing for two reasons: if Sal was capable of behaving in a likeable manner, why was she singling Allegra out for mind-games? And, secondly, couldn't people see through what was surely an act?

After a few attempts at squats, Allegra gave up on the weights. Her glutes could have taken more punishment, but her shoulders were still sore from yesterday, which made lifting anything above her waist difficult and painful. She was probably done anyway.

She showered in the fully equipped guest ensuite without entertaining any thoughts at all about the fact she was naked in Sal's lair. Then she towelled herself off and spent a few minutes drying her underwear and tank top with the hairdryer, rather than using it for its intended purpose.

Dressed again, it was only when Allegra wandered back out into the atrium, sore but refreshed and adrenaline-free, that it really landed: Sal had brought her here to give her space to come down after the interview, and after all that stuff with Lachie.

She stopped in place for a moment. *That is rather a nice thing to do,* she had to admit. Then she immediately wondered if it was self-serving. Presumably Sal wanted her to do well in the interviews, and taking care of her was just another way of managing the outcome.

There was another, much more sinister option: maybe Sal had brought Allegra here purely to mess with her, knowing the effect her ridiculous house had on people.

Or maybe she is actually interested in seducing you after all, a sneaky voice suggested.

Allegra responded to that one with an eyeroll as she continued to the stairwell. That was the least likely of any of the possibilities.

The stairs were shallow and wide, and Allegra followed the same path she'd been caught watching Sal take. She wasn't sure what she expected up top, but she found a full corridor of doors along another gallery hallway. It wasn't clear where any of them led.

She felt like she was on a game show, presented with mystery doors and an ethical dilemma.

The situation had evidently been engineered to give Allegra the ability to snoop with the plausible deniability of looking for Sal's office. And damn, was it tempting. Finding that woman's soft underbelly tucked away somewhere in her cupboards was extremely appealing. She probably had framed photos of family and friends, or a room full of souvenirs, or even a revealing selection of items on a bedside table. It was extremely difficult not to start opening doors and hunting through the rooms one by one.

She didn't, though. Mustering all her willpower, she simply walked along the corridor until she heard Sal's voice drifting through one of the doors.

She did lean in to listen, though.

"That is unbelievably good timing, actually," Sal said warmly—she was suspiciously good at sounding friendly when she wanted to. "Wednesday suits us much better, and we can meet somewhere outdoors. What's the weather going to be like...?" There was a pause. "28 and sunny. Perfect. Maybe late morning? Invite a couple of influencers, too, whoever you think is right."

Allegra felt odd about barging in, even though Sal had essentially instructed her to, so she knocked.

"Ah, here's the heroine herself," Sal said in the voice Allegra had come to associate with her speaking to people who weren't Allegra. Then she called, "Come in—I'm on a video call."

She entered and spotted herself appearing on Sal's huge monitor. A man in his mid-thirties or so was on the screen, wearing a headset and a meticulously coifed moustache and beard. Studio staff? Sal was leaning back in her office chair quite comfortably, though, which suggested a much more casual relationship. Sal probably wouldn't sit like that on a call with someone she was trying to impress.

"Well, hello," the man greeted Allegra in a cheeky voice. He sounded very camp. "Allegra Sinclair, it is a pleasure to finally meet you." He seemed to remember they were on a video call. "So to speak."

Sal grinned at that, twisting a little in her chair towards Allegra and indicating the screen. "Gerard, my assistant," she said. "He's been fielding calls all day about you."

"*And* making them," he added.

Allegra didn't want to be rude, so she smiled politely. He seemed friendly enough. "Nice to meet you—thanks for all your work."

Sal's eyes had been idly resting on Allegra when something occurred to her. She sat up straight. "Gerard, are you alone in the office?"

He looked surprised, then gave a furtive tilt of his head to indicate someone was beside him. "Honey, I *wish*." It was clearly just how he spoke, but it was still jarring to hear anyone refer to Sal as 'Honey'.

Sal was unaffected. "I'll phone you later," she said shortly, rolling her chair forward and reaching for the trackpad. "Book Wednesday."

He agreed, and Sal ended the call.

Behind the call, Sal's Outlook calendar was open, with dozens of tightly packed appointments booked from dawn to dusk over seven long days. "Sorry to cut that short," she said. "You have wet hair and you're in my house—I think we'll keep the circle of people who see that image very, very small." She didn't elaborate. Instead, she ran her eyes over the appointments, closed the app, and returned to that slightly sultry tone of voice Allegra was more accustomed to hearing. "Now. Was my bedroom interesting?"

Of course she was back to that. The whiplash was jarring. "I actually didn't look around," Allegra said, feeling quite smug about it.

Sal spun her chair around to face Allegra, interested in that answer. "Why not? You had the opportunity. Clearly, I would have let you." She paused. "Actually, maybe that's my error. I should have just told you *not* to snoop." There was a mischievous glint in her eyes. "Aren't you curious?"

"No," Allegra lied.

Sal had that knowing smile again. "It must have been hard to resist."

Allegra had intended to only think a snarky response, but the voices telling her to challenge Sal more won out. "You know what's hard to resist? *Throttling* you every time you open your mouth to tease me."

Sal laughed, slowly standing from her chair and walking past Allegra just a little too closely on her way to the door. When she spoke, it was in the very lowest register of her voice. "Why resist? Maybe I'm into that."

The sound was unfortunately very sensual. Allegra had been about to fire something back at Sal, but the words were immediately gone. As a result, she ended up following Sal meekly down the hallway, as if that had been the plan all along.

In a way, she was. At the end of the corridor, Sal opened a door to the master bedroom. It was another unnecessarily large room, mostly bare except for a king-size bed with a grey geometric-print doona still pulled back on one side. A half-drunk glass of water sat on the bedside table.

"I'm so sorry, I wasn't expecting company," Sal pretended to confess, as if her penthouse was completely trashed rather than showing the bare minimum signs of life. "There. Does that satisfy your curiosity?" Her eyes were resting on Allegra's.

The way Sal was looking at her quickened Allegra's pulse again. "Did you seriously lead me down here just to show me your bedroom?"

"Well, and to invite you to join me in it. We have time." A smile grew on Sal's lips. "What do you say?"

Allegra didn't for a second think that was a genuine invitation—Sal had that same look of challenge on her face as she had in the car—but Allegra's body immediately responded with an emphatic *yes*. Her breath caught in her throat, and she found herself looking down at Sal's curves, seconds away from wrenching the woman against her, throwing her backwards on that huge ridiculous bed, and devouring her.

Instead, it took all her willpower to simply say dryly, "Nice offer, but I've just had a shower."

Sal laughed—a low, slightly dangerous sound. She let the bedroom door fall closed and headed down the hallway at a more measured pace. "You're very likeable," she said openly, as if giving a snap assessment of a new work colleague. "Grumpy, flighty, but very likeable."

Allegra had absolutely no idea what to make of any of that. "Thanks! As I previously mentioned, you're not."

She looked over her shoulder briefly. "And yet..." She laughed to herself again, then completely switched register. "Anyway, we should probably get lunch and discuss what Nine wants." Allegra was a mixture of relieved and disappointed to hear it.

Sal led Allegra outside onto the terrace off the atrium, offering her a seat at the long table in the shade of one of the palm trees. Even this far up, there was only a gentle breeze, and with the weather already heating up, that made it very pleasant.

"What do you feel like?"

Allegra snapped to attention. That was absolutely the wrong question to ask someone she'd jokingly just offered sex to, because Allegra's body had a variety of opinions about what it would like at that moment. The sun already felt nice on the small amount of skin she currently had exposed, and the table was warm. Allegra pushed all of those thoughts aside and simply shrugged as disinterestedly as she could.

Sal absolutely saw through it. She only smiled to herself. "I'll choose, then." She sat neatly opposite Allegra, on the part of the table in deep shadow, retrieving her sunglasses from her pocket and flicking them open with a single wrist shake. It was such a summery day, and Allegra could not for the life of her figure out why anyone would be so committed to a full black suit this close to summer in Sydney.

And more to the point, Allegra thought, why am I so attracted to someone like that?

"Alright," Sal began, looking away from her phone and placing it on the table in front of her. "Nine's briefing is much more superficial: they want you to talk about the rescue and do another bush safety lesson. They're less tabloidy—or like to think they are—so I doubt they're going to slobber all over you like Sky did. It's radio again, so there's no need to do hair and makeup, but since you're going to be on camera this evening and I know some of the staff there, I sweet-talked them into slotting you in anyway. We'll go there a little earlier than scheduled."

"You sweet-talked them?"

Sal arched her eyebrows. "Mmm. I can be very persuasive when I want to be."

"You blackmailed them, you mean," Allegra accused her.

Sal grinned and looked over her glasses at Allegra. "I asked them nicely," she reassured her, retrieving her phone again. "I promise I save all my very best blackmail just for you."

Allegra was beginning to seriously wonder if that was the case, because it seemed like everyone else Sal spoke to thought the sun shone out of her. It was exasperating.

When their lunch was delivered, it was by a timid Uber Eats cyclist who looked like he'd wandered into the dragon's den. Since Allegra was facing the atrium, she watched him arrive in the lift clutching the bag, look around nervously until he spotted them, and then gingerly approach the terrace door.

Sal only looked up when he opened it. "On the table, thanks," she said, patting the surface before going back to her phone. He placed the bag where indicated, then gave Allegra a scared look and froze as he recognised her.

Poor kid. She smiled as supportively as she could. "Thanks so much."

He just blinked, muttered something unintelligible, and scuttled off.

"I think they're supposed to take a photo to confirm delivery," Sal said, grinning briefly up at Allegra. "You must have spooked him."

"I'm not the one dressed like Morticia Addams," Allegra pointed out, standing to investigate what Sal had ordered. To be honest, she was surprised it was Uber Eats. She held up the bag for a moment to inspect it. "Don't people like you usually have private chefs?"

Sal shrugged. "When I have company, I hire someone."

"Like family things?" Allegra wondered aloud, looking down the long table at which they were seated. She must have a big family.

That elicited a response from Sal. "Family," she said, delivering the word like a slur. "No. Work events, when I'm entertaining prospective clients..." She looked up. "Or my girlfriend..."

Allegra felt the word like a punch in the stomach; her hands tightened on the Uber Eats bag, which audibly scrunched. Sal was watching her.

"...on the very rare occasion I have one, that is."

Allegra exhaled at length, giving Sal a look.

Sal was enjoying it, even if she didn't comment as much. "Staff require management. When I'm at home, I generally want to be alone." She discarded her phone again and joined Allegra in eating lunch.

Afterwards, Sal touched up her own makeup and then led Allegra down to the basement carpark again where the driver was waiting to take them to Nine.

It was becoming a little routine, Allegra thought; an escort waiting by the door, Sal checking the run sheet with them on the way through to Hair and Makeup.

The only notable difference was that, once they were in Hair and Makeup, the stylist greeted Sal with a shallow hug and an air kiss to both cheeks. "Sal!" she said in some variety of European accent, "Lovely to see you, as always. This is our girl?" They both looked at Allegra.

"That's the one," Sal said with a wry smile, and then showed her the photo she'd taken at Sky studios as a reference. The stylist got to work, copying both the hair *and* the makeup and then spinning Allegra's chair to Sal to present the finished product.

Sal nodded in approval. "Thanks so much for fitting us in," she said warmly, touching the stylist's arm in a professional manner. "You're a lifesaver." The woman waved her hand to indicate it was nothing and gave her another hug on the way out.

Allegra felt like she was through the looking glass. Sal guessed why, and while they were being escorted up, she leant in towards Allegra to whisper, "Guess I'm likeable after all."

Allegra scoffed at her, remembering that she'd made sure Allegra observed her flattering the mechanics changing her tyres, as well. Sal was just supremely good at *pretending* to be likeable, and for some reason everyone was falling for it. "Do *you* even like *her*?"

Sal gave a little facial shrug, slowing their pace to fall a little behind their escort so he couldn't hear their quiet conversation. "Does it matter?"

Allegra looked directly at her. "Yes."

Sal studied Allegra's expression. "So I should be rude to people who I don't actively like?"

Allegra gave her a tired look. "Sal, that is *not* what I mean."

"It is, though. Everyone who is capable of ordinary social interaction is friendly and polite to people they don't necessarily like. I'm no different," Sal said, even though she had specifically demonstrated to Allegra how very fabricated it was to her. "Did *you* like the Uber Eats guy?"

"That's not the same," Allegra told her. "Your penthouse was scaring him. I wanted to be reassuring."

"But did you *like* him?" Sal said theatrically, imitating Allegra with a grin. Allegra surprised herself by giving Sal what could only be described as an affectionate shove with her eyeroll. It must have encouraged her, because Sal said, "Or is what you really want to know whether I'm pretending to like *you*?"

Allegra's breath caught. She forced air through it, though, refusing to be suckered. "Are you even capable of truly liking people?"

Sal spent a few moments gazing across at her, a vague smile on her face. "Apparently."

God. Allegra fought the butterflies in her stomach. *She's messing with you, Allegra,* a voice warned. *You have no reason to believe she'd be treating you differently than anyone else.*

That was true, she didn't. But against her better judgement, she couldn't help but find herself asking: what if she meant it?

The idea silenced her. They walked in tandem, following the escort up to the studio.

It was similar to ABC's studio—but had a more boutique than cosy feel—and there was only one producer, a man, seated in the control booth. The host was a man as well, significantly younger than her and Sal. Those things shouldn't have made a difference to Allegra, but they did. She was a bit disappointed.

They weren't live, so the producer waved them into the booth. Again, Allegra was treated to another performance. "Adrian," Sal greeted him, air-kissing beside his cheek—apparently that was the culture at this studio. "So nice to see you again."

He returned the greeting, standing and extending his hand to Allegra. "Allegra, great to have you here."

She shook it. "It's a pleasure to be here."

He and Sal exchanged a few comments, and then while he was speaking to the escort, Sal leaned into Allegra and whispered, "Is it *really* a pleasure to be here?"

Allegra sighed at her, but before she could fire something back at Sal, she was ushered into the studio and seated opposite the young host.

He was agreeable enough; he didn't have Sue's warmth, but at least he didn't have the manufactured feel of the Sky News hosts. He also must have had a very narrow brief because he seemed genuinely interested only in the rescue and bush safety. It was a relief, because Allegra didn't think she could emotionally withstand another foray into her past today.

While Allegra was answering various questions people were texting in about hiking, off-road driving and general safety, a movement in the booth caught her attention.

Sal fanned herself with her hand, making a comment to the producer, and then undid the single button of her blazer. Once she was sure Allegra was watching, she slowly slipped it off her shoulders.

Allegra's eyes had drifted to Sal's body—her sleeveless boatneck was made of fabric that shimmered in the light as it caught the curves of her breasts—but as soon as her arms were visible, that thought vanished.

Sal had *tattoos*.

They were geometric, starting on the crest of her shoulders before disappearing beneath her top, then continuing all the way down the outside of either arm to her wrists like single lines of ancient text. Together with the pale skin, dark hair, and smoky eye makeup, they made her cut an imposing figure through the window. She looked stunning—in the true sense of the word.

"...Allegra?"

Eyes wide, Allegra looked back at the host. Shit, what had she been talking about?! "Sorry, not sure where I went there!" she said, trying to laugh it off. In the booth, Sal was smirking. "Perhaps I should have another go at that question."

Allegra managed to ignore the booth for the rest of the interview; she even remembered to get in a few lines about the Homeward Foundation. She only paid Sal any attention again after she'd shaken hands with the host and producer and was being led out to the car.

Sal had already put her jacket back on. "Do you like my tattoos?" she whispered, already knowing the answer.

Allegra wasn't going to play. "They're why you're always so over-dressed, aren't they?"

Sal inclined her head, glancing up at the escort to check he was far enough away not to hear. "Not everyone is amenable to them. I have to pick the right company."

Allegra remembered her parents' reaction when they'd seen her own, and how 20 years ago work used to insist she wear long sleeves in particular countries so they didn't show. Hers were just faded black tendrils that resembled the curl of vines, too—there was nothing particularly unorthodox about them. They didn't have the sharply alternative vibe Sal's had. Sal's were an odd choice for someone in such an intensely corporate position, Allegra thought, wondering about that while trying not to look at her.

As they got back into the van, Allegra didn't have the opportunity to give Sal's tattoos the level of thought she would have liked. As they buckled up and both looked down at their phones, Allegra's lit up like a Christmas tree, ringing silently. Vanessa's name and portrait appeared on the screen.

She would have thought it was excellent timing if she couldn't see *12 missed calls* and a message: "*Answer your phone for once, woman*!!"

While she was waiting for it to stop ringing, Sal glanced at it, and then up at her. She didn't say anything, and Allegra couldn't read her. "Are you judging me for ignoring my sister?"

Sal was completely serious. "Definitely not."

Allegra felt judged anyway, so when the phone stopped ringing, she spent a few seconds dismissing all the notifications (especially the ones from Timothy, who was threatening to drive around central Sydney looking for her), and considered her options.

Timothy would want to *talk about how she felt*, and she was done talking about Lachie. There was nothing else to say and she didn't want to rehash any of it.

Vanessa was a wildcard, though; over the years, she had on occasion cried in Allegra's arms about various things—usually when her fashionable and obnoxious friends were unavailable or had caused the problem—but whether she'd want Allegra to do anything other than be present and cried on was uncertain. Allegra tabbed through the messages; she didn't *seem* upset? When she was upset she'd usually just make some guilt-trippy comment like, 'not even my own sister returns my calls' or similar. Perhaps it was just a coincidence and unrelated to the interview.

What other things did they have in common that Allegra would need to—wait, what if it was about Aaron?! That was the thought that sealed the deal.

Glancing up at Sal, she accepted that realistically, she wasn't going to be able to do this out of her earshot, so she'd just have to deal with the fallout of Sal hearing whatever it was. Then she tapped 'return call' and pulled the phone against her ear.

Sal observed her as the phone rang, completely unreadable.

Chapter 12: Unfinished Business

Vanessa didn't even wait for Allegra to say hello. "Took you long enough!" she said through the receiver. "Why are you like this?"

"Vanessa *calling* me? I assumed it was a scam." Across from her, Sal's poker face cracked into a smirk.

"Oh, fuck off, you know how busy I am," Vanessa said as if it wasn't deliberate. "I was watching Sky—"

"You were watching *Sky*?"

"Well, know thy enemy and all that," Vanessa said a little defensively, as if they were her enemies and not people she secretly agreed with. "Anyway, I can't believe you chose the Homeward Foundation! I nearly started crying right there in the kitchen."

Oh. Allegra made a face; she couldn't take credit for that. "It wasn't me, my PR rep—"

"Oh, please, can you take a compliment for once in your life? I heard what you said; I've never felt so fucking seen. I mean, obviously I'm a bit sad you have to say nice things about me to, like, all of Australia instead of to my actual face, but given your extreme allergy to being vulnerable in any way I'll take it. I want to see you tomorrow."

Allegra looked across at Sal. "You need me tomorrow, don't you?" She hoped the intensity of her expression relayed the answer she wanted Sal to give.

Sal received the message, but before she could reply, Vanessa repeated, "You *need* me tomorrow, don't you?" Her tone was thick with the expectation of juicy gossip. "Who's that? Someone new?"

That made Sal cackle. Allegra sighed at her and said to Vanessa, "No, just PR managing the interviews."

"Oh. I mean, I guess Timothy will be happy." She paused. "He's been calling me, by the way. I let it go to voicemail."

Allegra exhaled heavily. "You were about to arrange to meet me."

"Oh yeah. I'm pretty busy with the boys..." Her excuse for never crossing the bridge. "Do you think you could come to me? Maybe we could go somewhere nice for lunch!" Wherever it was would have absolutely no parking and be packed with people, but Allegra figured she shouldn't turn down an opportunity to see Vanessa when she decided she was available.

She agreed to let Vanessa choose the place and text her the address, and then hung up.

Sal looked up from her own phone. "Do you need an excuse to get out of that?" There wasn't even a hint of her usual playfulness in her voice.

Allegra groaned, jamming her eyes shut for a second. "Probably not. I *should* see her..."

Sal looked sceptical but didn't argue. "Will 11am to 2pm be enough?"

With Vanessa, 45 minutes was likely to be enough, but Allegra didn't bother giving Sal that level of detail and just nodded. Sal put it into her calendar and then moved on. "We need to talk about this evening, anyway, because it's going to be quite different from the other three bookings. The professional camera team there will be ours, and there will be three influencers filming with their own equipment. Unfortunately, Isaiah's siblings also consider themselves influencers, and we want to endear ourselves to that family, so," she made a face, "there will be a lot of cameras."

Allegra was getting rather used to that idea, although the thought of it exhausted her. "Okay," she said, hearing how tired she sounded. "Tell me what I need to know."

Sal could do better than just tell her: Gerard had put together a brief that included headshots of the influencers and some information about their content and focus, plus some links to their channels and specific videos he thought were relevant.

The three chosen were an odd bunch. One of them Allegra recognised as having done a reaction video to her Sky News bicep curl: Frogsized-femme, 'Froggy', a 22-year-old woman who did lesbian content, light-hearted political rants and some comedy. The next was a 25-year-old pop-culture commentator who had millions of views on all his videos: CertifiedHimboTakes, 'Tye'. The third was a strange choice: a man who mostly did deep-dives on YouTube under the channel name Lost in Austin. His name was, predictably, Austin. His last three videos covered YouTube drama, politics, and the rise of fascism.

Allegra looked up about five minutes into the last video, eyes wide. "Am I going to wake up in a week's time to a *Sinclair exposé*?"

Sal's amusement returned. "He's a strategic choice for the brand," she reassured Allegra. "It's not really you he's interested in. We *will* need to have a chat about what to say to him beforehand, though."

Gerard had already done some notes on potential discussion points with each of them, as well as what they would likely be looking out for.

Notably, he also provided some details about what *not* to talk about with any of them.

Sal also had some advice. "I know how you and your ex-husband feel about the one-percenters," Sal said, using a far vaguer and more euphemistic term than Allegra would have, "but you're going to need to keep your opinions about wealth and billionaires to yourself. You're courting people with a lot of money and a lot of power: do well, and they'll be pouring money into your charities by the bucketload; do poorly, and you'll be plastered across every channel for a very different reason tomorrow."

Allegra swallowed. That was quite a stark warning. "Understood."

Sal nodded once. "Good. I just need you to remember that there is no such thing as 'off the record' around influencers. They will report on everything: what you say, how you say it, and what they think you meant."

Allegra sat back, letting the Lost in Austin video roll for another few minutes while she paid absolutely no attention to it. "You're putting a lot of trust in me," she realised aloud.

Sal looked up from her phone. "I am," she acknowledged simply. Then, a mischievous smile grew on her lips. "If I had any concerns about your self-control, I might even be worried."

With the seriousness of previous discussion, Sal's return to flirtatiousness was somewhat reassuring.

Sal had organised dinner in a private room at a restaurant in the city, which she explained was so they could speak openly. Allegra *was* a little surprised to be taken in through the back door, though. "Force of habit," Sal said dismissively. "I work with big clients, they like their privacy."

Dinner itself was beautifully presented on enormous, pristine plates. Sal didn't finish hers (Allegra finished it for her), and then they went over the brief one more time.

"I'm going to drop you in the deep end when I get there," Sal warned her. "Media handlers generate friction with influencers. You can text me if you have any questions."

Sal wasn't exaggerating. They pulled up alongside the rear entrance of Westmead Hospital. There were other cars with drivers parked along the laneway there; two of them were smoking together. Sal gave Allegra a professional once-over, and then nodded. "Alright, off you go. Good luck."

It was odd getting out of the van and walking through the door unaccompanied. This time, security waved her through, and one of the men split off to take her upstairs.

Through familiar corridors, they approached the suite she'd been in before when she was delivering Isaiah's bag. At the door, she felt the familiar surge of adrenaline and tightness in her chest. She had *no* idea what awaited her on the other side as she pushed it open.

In her head, she'd imagined some sort of media circus: influencers filming themselves, and a room chock-a-block full of people. When the door opened, it was to a loose arrangement of people leaning, sitting, or standing as they scrolled through their phones. The noise level was 'library'.

The three influencers were seated together chatting, and the only person doing any sort of filming was Isaiah's plastic brother. 'Beau', wasn't it? They all looked up as she entered.

"Allegra!" Beau called, again theatrically rushing over to her for another hug. Over his shoulder, she could see the three influencers showing various levels of scepticism, from 'hard stare' to 'eyeroll'. His friend was filming him again.

Remembering Gerard's comments about being genuine, she let him hug her and patted his back. She even managed a smile.

Once she was done dealing with *that*, she approached the influencers, unsure what to expect. "Hi," she said, perhaps a little awkwardly. "Thanks for coming."

Eyes narrowed, Tye looked behind her at the guard at the door. "You're here by yourself?"

Allegra nodded, then felt a little self-conscious about that. "Is that—not usual?"

He smiled. "Nah, it's just that, I don't know... I thought you'd have a security detail or something. Or assistants."

"Yeah," Froggy added beside him, pink-cheeked in the same way Amy had been. "BSA talent is normally, like, *swarming* with staff."

Sal hadn't mentioned that. Perhaps she'd forgotten? "Unfortunately it's just me," Allegra said, wryly presenting herself. "I hope that's not going to ruin your videos."

Tye and Froggy looked at each other, grinning. "Are you kidding?" Froggy asked. "Normally you can't even hold your phone up without 12 people telling you not to shoot talent from that angle. Or they want to see all your footage and then they'll just *delete* it without even asking you. This is way better." She softened a bit, looking more bashful. "Like, normally you can't even have a proper conversation with the person." It was sweet.

"Well, I'm afraid conversation is really all I can offer," Allegra said. "Unless you fall over the balcony or something."

Froggy laughed about that, but she was practically batting her eyelashes at Allegra. "Don't tempt me!"

Tye gestured towards the balcony, deadpan. "No, you can totally go for it, Frog. It's only the third floor and the clicks will be worth it."

"Oh my god, Tye, *you* go for it!" she said, shoving him. "I nearly kill myself just by tripping over my shoes—you're the one who does all that extreme stuff."

Allegra found herself playing along. "It's okay," she said, and then paused for a moment, noticing Austin watching them, looking a little left out. "Let's just throw *him* over."

Austin's eyes widened. "Dude, no, I swear to god, I'll donate at every SES drive!" he said, laughing and backing off as Tye went to grab him.

"What's the matter, Austin, you don't want to be revived by Rescue Guns, is that it?" Tye asked, trying to grab his middle.

"Rescue Guns! Oh my god, I love it!" Froggy had her phone out. "Beau! Help Tye lift him up!"

Allegra found herself rather enjoying their mischief. She had been standing to one side of the shenanigans, laughing, when she realised there were a number of cameras pointed at her. She wasn't sure what to do about that; should she be this cheerful when she was visiting an inpatient?

Before she could make a call on that one, Isaiah's door opened a crack. It was a doctor. "You can come in now, if you like. But let's keep it calmer."

The kids all cleared their throats and made a big show of being all calm and serious, and they filed towards the door.

Inside was a larger room than Allegra had expected; a VIP suite, no doubt. Two haughty 50-or-so-year-olds stood away from the far side of the bed—his parents, Allegra assumed—partly blocked by a large, bored-looking man in a suit, whose job apparently was to look large and bored on camera and obscure the parents.

Isaiah himself was still tightly wrapped up in casts and bandages. He was awake, though, and those blue eyes were just like Aaron's. He was smiling at her—a far cry from the unconscious and bloodied body she'd patched up on the rockface.

She slowly approached him. Not able to help herself, she found her eyes checking that broken leg (now set), then looking up towards where he'd smashed his head (in a helmet—he must have broken it). She ended up on his blue eyes again: eyes that were now focused on her and not rolling back in his head.

When he spoke, his voice came out in a rasp. "Sorry," he said, sounding so, so young. "I just got the tube out so my throat is a bit meh." He laughed awkwardly, finishing in a cough.

"You don't need to say anything," Allegra told him.

"Yeah, I do, though," he said, reaching out and putting his hand over hers on the bed rail. She looked down at it. His wrist and two of his fingers were taped. "Because I'd be dead, wouldn't I?"

You would, Allegra thought. She knew what happened when help arrived too late. She looked across at his mother, who was teary-eyed. "I'm glad that was the road I turned down."

Isaiah's mother turned away for a moment, bending to retrieve a *huge* bouquet of native Australian flowers. She was probably supposed to ceremoniously present them to Allegra, but she was on the verge of tears. Mutely, she gave them to the guard who passed them across the bed.

Allegra accepted them—they were genuinely beautiful and something she may have even chosen for herself—but was more concerned about his mother than the flowers.

She looked like someone who wouldn't have been out of place in the Gilded Age, and her face had *definitely* seen more than one set of needles. Her gold necklace alone could have funded Timothy's charity for a year. But for a moment, Allegra imagined the situation reversed: *Aaron* in that bed, and herself meeting the woman who'd saved him. The thought was unbearable. "I'm glad he's alive," Allegra told her, meaning it.

His mother nodded desperately, and then in an instant she rushed around the bed, dodging the guard and all the observers, and wrapped her arms around Allegra. *"Thank you,"* she whispered into Allegra's shoulder. The weight of it struck Allegra to her core. For a moment, she wasn't hugging a billionaire who probably helped ruin the planet—she was hugging a mother who'd nearly lost her son.

It was a while before she pulled away. She'd been going to speak again when fucking Beau said, "Okay, Mum, it's my turn!" and comedically pretended to be about to pry his mum off Allegra so he could hug her.

Allegra and his mother made eye contact. She had made her point to Allegra and let the moment pass.

"Fuck off, Beau, I haven't even hugged her yet!" Isaiah called from the bed. There was humour in it.

"You've got two broken arms, you loser!" Beau told him. "And you already *got* CPR from her!"

Allegra made a neutral noise. "No one got CPR. He was still breathing when I arrived on site."

"Oh no!" Isaiah began, pretending to cough dramatically. "Oh no, I can't breathe suddenly!"

"Oh, *stop it*," the mother said to both of them. She was smiling. "Leave her alone, you two."

While the brothers were playfully bickering, catering arrived. No one except Allegra seemed surprised by that; if anything, they appeared to be expecting it. Perhaps it was just something that happened at staged events like this?

The room acquired the atmosphere of a particularly chill house party; people were eating and chatting to each other. Isaiah was clearly the star of it—thank goodness—but Allegra was periodically pulled from conversation to conversation by people wanting to involve her in things.

By the time the food was eaten, Allegra had arm-wrestled Tye (and lost horribly, because he was hiding some sizable muscles under his t-shirt), bench-pressed Froggy while she shrieked and proposed marriage, and had a long chat with Austin about climate change and the changes she'd observed in the bush over her lifetime. He didn't film any of it, which was baffling. She still wasn't sure why he was there, but he was a bright young man and clearly very invested in the natural environment, and Allegra always had time for people like that.

Beau and Isaiah grew on her. They were typical rich young idiots, but they did genuinely appear to love each other, and while their father disappeared quickly into the evening, their mother, Cecilie, hung around.

Allegra learnt she was a Vale-in-law with a middle-class upbringing in Scandinavia. Allegra would have liked to hear more about that, but once Cecilie learnt she was staying in Point Piper, the conversation quickly became more uncomfortable: they also lived in Point Piper, and were keen to invite her to lunch while she was in Sydney.

Allegra realised she was probably going to need to accept any invitation offered. She was wondering if Gerard could be persuaded to do a brief for her beforehand when Cecilie sobered somewhat. "Allegra," she said, in a tone that meant business. "Sal mentioned to me that you're fundraising for a charity at the moment."

Allegra brightened. "Oh, yes! The Homeward Foundation. It's an incredible organisation, they—"

She raised a hand, good-naturedly silencing Allegra. "You don't need to give me the pitch," she said. "How much do they need?"

Allegra closed her mouth. She realised all of a sudden that she had no idea what the target was. "As much as possible," she said, feeling self-conscious that she didn't know the exact answer. "They want to purchase a property to provide services and support for the kids and families somewhere in central Sydney."

Cecilie nodded once, giving Allegra a cool smile that made her feel nervous. All previous traces of warmth were gone. "We'll be in touch," she said, and then wandered off to get a refill of her drink.

Allegra watched her for a few moments, mentally berating herself for not knowing the answer to a simple question. Why had it not occurred to her to ask Sal what the fundraising goal was?

I hope I haven't blown it, she thought, making a face at herself and slipping out past the security guard into the corridor for a breather. She felt as if it had been going so well up until that point. What a rookie move. Timothy could probably have winged a question like that; he was so good at getting pledges from donors. At times like this, Allegra felt like she should just focus on disaster recovery.

I should probably say something to Sal, she realised, and took her phone out to message her. Perhaps Sal would know how to rescue the situation somehow.

"Go and say goodbye to everyone," was Sal's reply. *"Smile, take some selfies, and come back to the car."*

Allegra's heart dropped. So she *had* blown it. She followed Sal's instructions, getting some last snaps with the people there and spending a few moments checking on Isaiah. He and his siblings were watching something on his phone and didn't pay much attention to her. *Just like Aaron,* she thought, remembering walking past him sitting at the PlayStation. It was a comforting comparison.

She escaped with her massive bouquet of Australian native flowers, unable to appreciate how nice the boronia and black wattle smelt because of the knot in her stomach.

The black van was parked up the laneway a little away from the convoy of cars. Sal was somewhat camouflaged as she leant a shoulder on it, slender ankles crossed. Her pale face was lit by her phone, which was the only reason Allegra saw her look up as she approached. Allegra felt a jolt of adrenaline. What if Sal was angry?

She didn't *seem* that way, though. The opposite: she nodded at the bouquet once Allegra was in earshot. "Have you been cheating on me, Allegra?"

"Yes, I've been getting advice from other PR reps," she said flatly, stopping in front of Sal and watching her carefully.

"If you'd like to bring someone else in, let's have a conversation," Sal said, that glimmer of mischief in her eyes again. "I'm not completely against outsourcing." She handed Allegra her phone without explanation.

Slightly more at ease because of Sal's playfulness, Allegra accepted it; it was unlocked and in her Outlook app. An email exchange was already open—her eyes darted down to the signature. The exchange was between Sal and some consulting firm; she didn't recognise it. "What's this...?" she asked aloud, reading the rest.

The first email was from Sal, time-stamped only 10 minutes ago, well after Allegra had been instructed to leave. *"Hi Callum, we're finishing the evening. Have you had the opportunity to speak with Cece yet?"*

The reply was no more than three minutes old. *"Sal,"* it began, *"just had a call from Cece a moment ago. She needs to speak with her accountants about it, but has made it clear that they're planning to donate a property in either Darlinghurst or Surry Hills to Homeward. They have a few to choose from, so it'll mainly be a discussion about tax implications—not if it'll go ahead or not. They'll present the keys at the fundraiser, so we should probably have a chat this week about who's going to manage what."*

Allegra took a moment to digest that. 'Cece' was clearly Cecilie. Donate *an entire property*?

She looked up, eyes wide. "A house in *Darlinghurst or Surry Hills*?"

Sal had a triumphant smile. "Not just a pretty face, are you?"

Allegra was too spun to pay any attention to that. "Did I read that right?" she asked, looking back down at the phone to go over it again just in case.

"Mmm," Sal said, gently taking her phone back from Allegra instead of letting her reread the exchange for a third time. There was something slightly predatory about Sal's expression, like she'd captured prey she was about to devour. "I don't often have high expectations of people," she said. "I did, for you. And you still somehow *exceeded* them in a single day." She regarded Allegra as if she were appreciating fine art. "You are an *incredible* woman."

Allegra would ordinarily have felt uneasy about an observation of that nature, but she had completely run out of words; a house in Darlinghurst would be *millions*. Had she just managed to obtain a pledge of that much? Timothy used to celebrate pledges in the thousands, and somehow, she'd managed to fluke *millions*. She'd fluked millions *and* saved a life and a family.

It was surreal. None of it had sunk in yet. She felt like there wasn't enough space in her head for it to.

Sal seemed to understand that. Rather than drill her on it, she preened, victorious. "Well," she began, "now that you've seen my work, may I have a little acknowledgement of the methods you were so quick to insult, please?"

Allegra was snapped out of her haze. "What exactly do you want me to say?" she asked, deeply suspicious.

"'You did the right thing forcing me to engage, Sal.'" This was clearly a moment she'd rehearsed in her mind.

Allegra hated it, but she had a point, and there was no arguing with how perfectly Sal had angled her towards the money for Homeward. She took a breath, giving Sal a tired look. "Fine. You did the right thing forcing me to engage, Sal."

"Thank you," Sal said ceremoniously. "I live to serve." Allegra regarded her with extreme scepticism. Sal laughed about that expression. "Alright," she said, correcting herself. "I live to demonstrate my genius." Allegra didn't think that was likely to be the whole truth either, but Sal clearly wasn't going to spill at this point, so she left it.

Clearly emboldened by being told she was right, Sal stepped in a little closer to Allegra again, as close as she could while Allegra was holding the bouquet. Fingertips brushed Allegra's forearm. "Would you like to come and have a drink with me to celebrate, Allegra?"

Yes, Allegra thought immediately, against her better judgement. Searching Sal's eyes, Allegra suspected at least the offer of a drink was serious; it was hard to tell if Sal intended it to lead where fingertips on Allegra's arm suggested it might. Based on Sal's previous flirtations, Allegra had no reason to believe it would, and yet, she wondered...

"Have a drink where, exactly?"

Sal's smile deepened. "Well," she began, "I know some very intimate little bars." She let Allegra consider that for a moment. "Or we could raid my wine cellar for something appropriately celebratory and enjoy it in my outdoor spa." Something about the way she was speaking suggested a third option. "Or, if you think Timothy's asleep already..." There was a dark, dark smile on her face.

Allegra gave her a look at the last one; no fucking way. Not in what was essentially his house.

Honestly, she was actually quite tired, but she felt that going home to bed now would be an enormous wasted opportunity to actually celebrate something. The high she felt after a successful rescue was oddly dissociating; this high felt different. It felt good. Her body didn't shake, and her mind was clear. It was something she should be popping bottles over: fully funding a charity's wildest dream. And she hadn't done it by herself—as much as this infuriating woman was a thorn in her side, it was through her engineering that it had happened.

That warranted a drink, didn't it? "I haven't been to a bar in a while."

"Is that so." Sal delivered it like a judgement, looking at Allegra with interest. Allegra knew what she was thinking when she said, "It's been a while since you had a drink with someone?"

Allegra frowned and shook her head. "I had a drink with someone on Saturday." Sal didn't need to know it was Timothy, and she didn't need to know that nothing happened between them.

Sal guessed anyway. "I'm sure he was spectacular company."

Allegra shot her a look. She honestly wasn't sure who was more irritating; both of them had their moments. At least with Timothy, Allegra knew what his motivations were. "It was genuinely just a drink, and it is genuinely just a drink I want to have tonight," she said, ignoring a chorus of various body parts excited about the opportunity to contradict her.

"Sure it is," Sal said, regarding her with that sinister competitive edge Allegra only saw when she was flirting. "Let's go have just a drink together, Allegra."

Sal stepped away from her, gave her a sideways glance laden with intent, and let Allegra get into the van ahead of her.

Sal's little hole-in-the-wall bar was, predictably, in The Rocks. It was between a warehouse and some sort of brick storage facility under the bridge, down an alleyway lined with colourful-lidded bins. They didn't smell, so Allegra wondered if they were just part of the décor.

The entrance was just a residential door—although it did have a neon sign on it saying 'The Ropewalk'—and to get to the bar they had to walk down a very tight hallway into a larger but still narrow bar. It was clearly a converted townhouse, but the age of the building and the maritime-cyberpunk fusion of old ship parts and neon lighting on the bare brick walls delivered that niche boutique bar feel. There was, of course, a very edgy-looking man with a mohawk and leather pants pouring drinks.

Other patrons were already occupying three of the four booths on the wall, but the coloured lighting had Allegra confident she wouldn't be recognised. The green lighting in particular made her orange jumpsuit a dull tan colour.

They approached the bar. The bartender gave them a big smile. "What can I get you?"

Allegra spoke first. "Stone & Wood, if you have it." He nodded.

Sal chuckled. "Beer. Of course." She was speaking to the bartender but looking at Allegra as she said, "Make that two." As the bartender passed them across the counter, she asked Allegra, "You don't want to drink something a little more... celebratory?" They took the last empty booth, sitting opposite each other. "You just obtained a pledge of easily three million dollars."

Allegra found herself shaking her head in disbelief again. It was crazy. However, it wasn't strictly true that she'd done it alone, so Sal's comment felt a bit like flattery. "Technically, we obtained a pledge of easily three million dollars."

Sal tested the beer and grimaced. Resigned to her fate, she had another sip. "I didn't abseil down the side of a cliff to rescue someone whose family is on the Forbes billionaire list, and then subsequently charm that person's mother out of a house."

Allegra raised an eyebrow. "Yeah, sure, you did absolutely nothing."

"Alright." Sal inclined her head in concession. "I set up the chessboard for you—you still needed to make all the plays." Sal was looking her over again, with the same air of approval as before. "We make quite the team, don't we?"

Allegra wasn't sure how she felt about that. "I gather you have more planned for me after the Homeward Foundation event?"

Sal laughed—a low, dangerous sound. "Oh, Allegra. Yes." She drank deeply from her beer, finishing it. Tapping the bottle back on the table, she looked back across at Allegra. "You are beautiful and eloquent, and there is a down-to-earth quality about you people will be inclined to trust. Of course I have plans for that."

Allegra felt a little uncomfortable. "I need you to understand I'm not going to do anything that people can't trust."

Sal smiled. "Yes," she said. "I believe that." Rather than elaborate, she nodded at Allegra's beer. "Drink up. Let's have round two."

Allegra eyed her. "You're trying to get me drunk."

Sal nodded once, that maddening smile on her face. "Aren't we here to celebrate?" She stood and rounded the table to the side Allegra was on, standing over her and staring intently down at her.

Allegra wasn't sure what that intent was, and for a moment she thought Sal might be about to unceremoniously straddle her. Her eyes dipped to Sal's hips.

Sal saw where she was looking and prompted her with a smirk, "Your drink, Allegra. Finish it."

Shit. Cheeks hot again, Allegra downed the rest and handed Sal the bottle. Sal took it, eyes lingering on hers for a moment as she went to get them another round.

When the second round arrived, it was another Stone & Wood. Sal held it out to Allegra so their fingers touched as she took it, and then looked back at her own with more than a hint of distaste. "I hope you realise I'm doing this for you."

"Such a sacrifice, forcing yourself to drink beer," Allegra scoffed, taking another sip of hers. "Although we should probably stick to beer." She noted the difference in their respective sizes. "How do you hold your drink?"

Sal pressed her lips together. "Poorly, after three or four."

"And you're expecting to get me drunk first?"

"I'm sure I'm in safe hands, Allegra. You know where I live." Her eyebrows flicked up for a moment. "Maybe you could even carry me home."

Allegra gave her a tired look, leant forward, and plucked the beer out of her hands. "Let's avoid that," she said, drinking Sal's beer for her.

Sal watched her down it with a dark smile. "My hero."

When Allegra had finished it and put the bottle aside to focus on her own, Sal leant back in the booth to observe her. "Do you read much?"

It felt like a loaded question. Allegra gave her a critical look. "Yes, actually," she said after she'd swallowed. "Why, did you expect me not to?"

Sal shook her head dispassionately. "The opposite. As I mentioned, you're quite eloquent, and I recall Sue mentioning you were originally at university. I thought you might." She crossed her arms. "What are you reading at the moment?"

Allegra gave her the rundown of the biography her friend had recommended. She was halfway through it; enjoyable enough, not a masterpiece. She was fond of biographies, so it had been an easy read so far.

Sal made a note of it in her phone while she was speaking.

It didn't seem to be the sort of thing someone would bother doing for show. "You're going to read it?"

Sal nodded. "If you liked it."

Allegra finished the last mouthful of beer. "It doesn't strike you as fairly unlikely we'll enjoy the same things?"

Sal was watching her. "You can learn a lot about someone by the books they enjoy."

"Fine," Allegra said, putting her empty bottle aside. "What books do you enjoy?"

"Anything about the occult," Sal said immediately, eyes twinkling. "You know, virgin sacrifices, blood rituals, profane symbols..." Allegra did not for a single second believe she was serious, but just in case there was any doubt there at all, she added, "You know, villain things."

The alcohol must have been kicking in, because she found herself gently shoving Sal's leg with her own under the table. "Terrible," she said of the joke.

Sal was grinning as she extended her leg back where it had been. It meant one of her legs was between Allegra's, resting against the inside of her calf.

To disguise how electric Allegra was finding just that simple touch, she managed, "What do you actually read?"

Sal shrugged. "Literature, I suppose. Although I wouldn't describe myself as committed to any one genre." She looked up at Allegra, holding eye contact. "Depends on what interests me."

The way she delivered that line made Allegra even more aware of the fact their legs were resting against each other.

Sal looked down towards where their legs were under the table for a moment, and then back up at Allegra.

Then, not breaking eye contact, she slid her hand across the table and slipped it over Allegra's. Her thumb rubbed a faint circle on the back of Allegra's hand; her fingertips lightly traced the veins there.

Allegra realised she was holding her breath. She probably should have stopped Sal, but she didn't. Was she tipsy already?

Sal's fingertips made it to Allegra's forearm, where her tattoos started. Sal considered them for what felt like an eternity, tracing the shape of them, and then looked up along Allegra's arms to where they finished on her shoulders. "Do you have more?"

Allegra took a tiny breath. "Yes."

"Show me." A smile grew on Sal's lips.

She shook her head in a small movement. "Not here."

"Show me where they are, then."

Against her better judgement—honestly, against any better part of her—Allegra took Sal's hand and put it on the outside of her thigh, helping it trace over where she knew the tattoos were under the jumpsuit.

She wasn't sure what she expected; her brain had stopped functioning. But when she saw Sal's lips part and her eyes grow heavy-lidded, that turned her on more than anything Sal could have said to her.

Whatever else she is, she's attracted to me, Allegra realised, enjoying the thought of Sal getting caught in her own games.

Before she was tempted to take Sal's hand and put it somewhere far less defensible, she released it and let Sal sit back.

Sal watched her, still a little breathless. She reached up and unfastened the single button of her blazer, and then very slowly and very deliberately slipped it off her tattooed shoulders again. She folded it and placed it beside her on the table, leaning back against the padded backrest of the booth, the fabric of her shimmering top falling over her breasts so Allegra could clearly see their outline. Under the table, Allegra could feel the fine toe of Sal's heel gently brush one of her ankles.

"I have lots of tattoos," Sal told her, voice low. "Give me your hand."

This woman was something else. Allegra was acutely aware she was exactly where Sal wanted her, and while she wasn't helpless at all—she could simply get up and leave at any point—she had no desire to. None at all. Leaving was not where her desire was pointing, and if she wasn't in danger of making a terrible decision on the cusp of what could turn into a lucrative opportunity to fund all of the charities that so desperately needed money, she might have done it.

Plus—there was no guarantee Sal would go through with it. She hadn't intended to before; Allegra had seen that. She could imagine a situation where she reached for Sal, or tried to kiss her, or accepted her invitation home, where Sal would laugh it off, triumphant, and then walk out knowing she'd got the best of Allegra.

She could look at her, though, couldn't she? She could take in every detail of those lips, those tattooed arms, her breasts, her hips—the crease of fabric between her thighs and her waist, and where that led.

Sal was dangling her body like a carrot in front of Allegra, wondering if she'd be tempted to take it. Allegra wondered if Sal guessed just how very close she was to taking the risk. "Let's tone it down," she managed to tell

Sal, despite every fucking fibre in her body screaming for her to rail that woman.

Sal smiled faintly, enjoying Allegra's reaction to her. "Time for more drinks, don't you think?"

"I'll get them," Allegra said, getting up. Anything to avoid sitting there and being edged into the grave.

"Sit," Sal told her, pushing her down with a grin.

Allegra couldn't hear what Sal asked the bartender, but he loaded up a tray and gave it to her. Allegra's eyes went to her heels. She'd probably be fine, she'd had one beer, but if her legs were shaking as much as Allegra's after that... brief foray... maybe she should offer to help?

She stood, reaching towards the tray. Sal didn't let go of it. Instead, she walked Allegra back against the table until she was half-sitting on it, then stepped closer, close enough that one leg slipped naturally between Allegra's knees, and placed the tray beside them.

On the tray were four shots, a saltshaker, and four slices of lime.

Oh god. "Tequila slammers? Are you kidding?"

Sal was grinning. "I'm not," she said, and then looked back to Allegra. With her sitting against the table edge, their eyes were level. And close. "How would you like to do this, Allegra?"

I'd like to pull those hips against me and kiss those smirking lips, Allegra thought, but simply said, "I know how slammers work, I was 21 once, too."

Sal bent her arm up, bringing her wrist close to her face. "We can start like this," she said. Then she licked a firm, slow line across her wrist with the flat of her tongue, watching Allegra for every excruciating millisecond of it. Dimly, Allegra was aware of her lifting the saltshaker and passing it to her other hand to shake over her skin; they were close enough that stray granules fell on Allegra's chest and into her top. Sal licked her wrist again afterwards, more slowly. Then she lifted the shot to her lips and drank, and chased it with one of the slices of lime.

Allegra was glad she was sitting down.

"Your turn, Allegra."

Feeling the buzz of the beer already, Allegra lifted her own wrist to her mouth, dragging her tongue against it and enjoying Sal's breath catching.

This close to Sal's chest, Allegra could see how quickly it was rising and falling as she licked the salt from her own wrist and finished the slammer.

Sal recovered. "Let's switch this up," she said, slipping her fingers through Allegra's to lace them together and bringing Allegra's forearm up level with her chin. "This time, I'm taking the salt off your wrist."

Eye-to-eye, Sal drew her tongue across Allegra's wrist. It lit Allegra's skin on fire. She felt it in her chest, her groin, her thighs—everywhere that tongue belonged. Sal licked her lips experimentally afterwards. "Tastes like your beer," she said at the lowest register of her voice. "Maybe the taste will grow on me, after all."

After she shook salt onto Allegra's wrist, she picked up a slice of lime and placed it backwards in Allegra's mouth. Allegra let her. God.

Sal then licked up the salt on Allegra's forearm and threw the tequila back.

Then she looked back at Allegra. Slowly... very slowly... she leant her mouth towards Allegra's. Allegra could smell her perfume and the bitter malt of beer on her warm breath. Their lips were inches apart as Sal bit the lime and pulled it out of Allegra's mouth.

There was a brief moment of merciful reprieve as Sal discarded the rind and placed the lime backwards between her own teeth, presenting her wrist.

Allegra held it close to her face. Her skin was so pale the veins through it gave it a bluish tinge, and when she extended her tongue to wet Sal's skin, she was surprised by how soft it was. Soft and warm. Sal was watching her progress far too intently. Knowing she was turning another woman on, even if it was this woman, was inescapably hot.

She shook salt on it and then licked it all off, threw back the shot, and then looked at the lime in Sal's mouth.

Instead of craning her neck towards Sal, Allegra impulsively put a hand on either side of Sal's jaw and pulled her in instead, as if she were going to very firmly kiss her. The shock rattled Sal out of her ordinary perfect composure, and she stiffened and inhaled sharply. *Got you*, Allegra thought, stopping just before their lips met and simply taking the lime out of her mouth. She let her hands fall.

That had more of an effect on Sal than anything Allegra had done so far. Even without Allegra holding her jaw, Sal didn't move away. Their bodies were so close. Their noses were nearly touching. Knees mixed, Allegra could have pulled their hips firmly together and brought her thigh against Sal's groin. God, she wanted to. The thought of Sal sitting heavily on one of her thighs with those smoky bedroom eyes closing and that mouth opening...

Sal's fingers were toying with Allegra's hair. "Come upstairs with me," she whispered into Allegra's ear. "Let's finish this."

Allegra felt like she was in the sixth circle of hell; nothing had ever tempted her like this. That tongue... Allegra felt in her bones that Sal would be unbelievable in bed, and every separate part of Allegra's body was begging her to go and confirm that.

She had to battle through five drinks and raging hormones to find some semblance of rational thought. There wasn't much there: only the memory of telling herself she shouldn't go through with this, and the warning about Sal's intentions. Sal seemed like the sort of person to constantly remind someone of their surrender, and Allegra wasn't interested in giving someone that sort of power over her.

No—Allegra could walk away from this. She could do it. At least until she understood what Sal had in store for her.

She licked her lips. "I—think we should tone it down, like I said before."

She half expected Sal to drop the act and just step away from her, unaffected. That didn't happen, though. When Sal stepped away from her, it was with pink cheeks and unsteady legs.

She smoothed her shimmering top down, wetting her own lips before she spoke. "We should do this again," she said a little breathlessly. "Maybe every time you make me look good."

That alone was enough to confirm Allegra's decision to say no. God, that was close. She sat there for a moment, spinning. "I don't think it's a good idea for us to stay here and keep drinking," she managed.

Sal didn't protest. Instead, she took a moment to regain her composure, taking a few deep breaths and reaching for her jacket. "You going to walk me home as a consolation prize?" she asked as she slipped it back on.

Allegra considered saying no (what if they ended up making out in an alleyway somewhere?), but Sal was a little drunk, and Allegra didn't like the idea of her walking home alone through Sydney at night. Despite all that corporate armour, she was slender and pretty; someone might consider her an easy target. Allegra mutely agreed to accompany her.

Sal led her outside through the narrow hallway again. Allegra's body was doing reasonably well with the fifth drink, but she felt airy and disconnected, and remembered little of their walk up Harrington Street to Sal's building.

When they reached the lift, Allegra watched Sal punch in the code and press the call button.

While they were waiting for it, Sal was smiling. "People don't usually say no to me." She gave Allegra another appraising look. "I wonder how long it will last."

"I'm no pushover, Sal," Allegra found herself saying.

There was admiration in Sal's smile. "I know." The lift doors opened and Sal stepped inside. "Have fun with your sister tomorrow. Leave your phone on—I'll let you know what happens next."

They watched each other until the doors slid shut.

Chapter 13: Midday Catch-Up

The gate intercom woke Allegra.

It was late enough that the sun was streaming in through the open blinds, something that on almost any other morning in her life she would have loved. Not today. Today, she felt sticky, sweaty, and she had a throbbing headache. *After only five drinks*, Allegra reflected, thinking about how much she used to drink in her twenties. She fought the urge to just turn over and go back to sleep.

Perhaps she would have, except Timothy was speaking to someone at the front door, and then there was a gentle knock on hers. "Food," he said softly, presumably placing it at her door. She heard his footsteps head down the hallway.

Food? Who would get her—

Oh. Her stomach fluttered.

That realisation got her out of bed. She retrieved the innocuous Uber Eats bag labelled only 'Allegra', and sat carefully on the edge of the bed to open it with interest.

There was no note inside and nothing on the receipt to suggest Sal had sent it—she appreciated that. Timothy wasn't nosy in the same way that her sisters were, but it was safer to have nothing there, just in case.

Inside was something calling itself a 'mushroom & basil frittata with whey protein', a large sports drink *'chock full of electrolytes!'*, and a box of Panadol. That made her chuckle. She popped two out of the blister pack straight away and washed them down with the sports drink.

She was eating her frittata with one hand and feeling around the bed for her phone with the other—intending to say thanks—when it really hit her what had happened last night.

I nearly slept with her, she realised, freezing mid-search.

Bit by bit, memories of the night before floated to the surface of her fuzzy brain. Sal's fingertips on her arm, Sal's tongue dragging across her wrist, and then seeing Sal step back and realising they were both on the cusp of properly violating some professional boundaries—not that those had so far meant that much to Sal. Allegra couldn't truthfully say crossing them had been a problem for her, either.

Given how ready she'd been to kiss those lips and tear off those clothes, it was an absolute miracle Allegra had managed to extricate herself. The last thing she needed was to end up sleeping with and giving ammunition to someone whose primary motive was *definitely* just using her somehow—probably for a pay cheque.

She looked down at her frittata. There was no real explanation for the Uber Eats order, though. It was simply a nice gesture that meant Sal was thinking about her.

Careful, Allegra, she told herself, finding her phone still in her jumpsuit pocket on 7% battery. Ignoring her own advice, she ended up texting, *"Thanks."*

The response was immediate. *"How's the head? ;)"*

She smiled briefly and immediately threw her warning to herself out the window. *"Awful. What was I thinking?"*

"Thinking didn't appear to be high on our to-do list last night." Allegra sat in place holding her phone for a few seconds, presuming that message wasn't the last. She was right. *"I can't say I have any regrets, though."*

Even as she was tapping out the text, Allegra knew she was making a mistake. *"I don't either."*

There was a good two-minute pause.

"Well. Perhaps one regret."

Allegra's response to that was to want to visit her straight away. *Watch out*, she warned herself. *You remember what she said about rewarding you for making her look good*?

Allegra managed to pry the phone away from her fingers before they could betray her any further. She plugged it in, finished her frittata, and threw on a light robe to go do something about her headache.

Timothy was seated at the counter in front of the familiar large bouquet of Australian natives, holding a cup of coffee and waiting for her like she was a teenager who'd come home late.

She gave him a look and half-shut her head in the freezer.

"You've been drinking again."

Allegra exhaled in a cloud of steam. "With other people," she said flatly, her voice muffled by the freezer door. "In celebration. Not in—anything else."

When her head was sufficiently cold and she'd worked up enough energy to submit herself to Timothy's patented Concern, she stood back and let the freezer close.

What she found when she turned around was worse: his *guilt*. "I knew I should have come to get you," he told her, shaking his head at himself. "It was awful the way that reporter ambushed you about your brother."

Allegra's headache was rapidly getting worse. "Timothy," she said impassively, too hungover to reenact a speedrun of their divorce. "I did the most incredible thing yesterday. That's what I want to focus on."

She gave him the very short version of what had happened with the Vales and the Homeward Foundation, while he listened with his shaggy eyebrows in his hairline. *"A house in Darlinghurst?"*

"Or Surry Hills," she said, still unable to believe it.

Timothy took a moment, too, shaking his head. "Well," he said, "that explains the giant bouquet that was delivered by a black van last night." He looked down at the flowers between them. There was an unopened card addressed to Allegra in beautiful cursive. "I thought it might be from a fan."

"That's from Cecilie Vale. They live at number 14."

He paused, processing that. "They live at—are you *kidding* me?" He got his phone out to check Google Maps, and then they both went out the front door to look uphill.

"The blue house," she repeated, using Cecilie's description. A few houses up the street loomed the rear of an *enormous* multistorey mansion facing Sydney. "That must be it."

"If I'd have known that was a *Vale* house..." he said, delivering the name like a slur.

It made Allegra grin. "It's not too late. How's your pitch shoulder these days? That's almost Molotov cocktail-lobbing distance."

He shot her a frown. "Please don't confuse me with your sister," he said, and then wandered back inside, mumbling to himself, "Maybe there are other options."

Following him, Allegra groaned. "Do I have to do hourly sweeps of their mailbox for your God pamphlets?"

Timothy didn't contradict her. "I'm just saying," he told her, "perhaps they could find a cause that's more fulfilling than destroying the planet and democracy." He looked her up and down. "Well, it's good to see you in one piece. That's worth being a little late to work for." For a moment, she thought he was going to plant a kiss on her forehead. He restrained himself. "Congratulations on that donation," he said instead, and then went to finish his coffee.

While he was draining his mug, Allegra put the bouquet in a vase. After peeling off the wrapping paper, she plucked out the card to inspect it. The handwriting was beautiful.

"Mrs Sinclair,

No words can adequately express my gratitude for what you did for my son. I hope you will allow us the privilege of thanking you properly.

It would mean a great deal to my family if you would join us as an honoured guest at our annual Impact Foundation Benefactors' Gala next Saturday evening.

Please consider this a standing invitation for yourself and a guest of your choosing.

With sincere thanks,

Cece."

Timothy had been reading over her shoulder. "A benefactors gala." He sounded very impressed, which was in sharp contrast to Allegra's reaction: annoyance that she would probably need to attend. "Every wealthy philanthropist in Sydney will be there. Possibly some from other places, too."

That gave Allegra pause. Perhaps there was more she could do for Homeward?

Timothy was having the same thought. "Just think of what *Light of the Redeemer Mission* could do with even a fraction of the money you got last night."

As soon as he said that, she realised she was going to have to fucking take him to it, and she wanted to go even less. She might have considered declining the invitation outright, but Sal's warnings about the Vales, money, and power rang in her ears. It would probably be impolite to refuse, especially after they'd pledged an entire house.

She felt slightly anxious at the thought of attending a fancy gala without Sal there to manage the terrain, though, even if Timothy had almost certainly been to them before. Anxious, and a bit disappointed. What would Sal wear to something like that?

"I'm going to have to get a dress, too," Allegra realised aloud, exponentially more tired at the thought of it.

"You can hire one," Timothy offered. "That's the sustainable option—I'll hire a suit, too. We can go and get fitted tomorrow night, perhaps. Do you have any more interviews today?" She shrugged. "Well, good luck if you do. Can't wait to see what the radio has to say about Allegra Sinclair this morning." He shot her a grin and headed off.

After he'd gone, Allegra sat staring at the invitation.

Better tell Sal, she thought, and went to get her phone to snap a picture of it. *"Timothy saw this so I'm going to need to take him. He runs a charity, after all."*

"I'm sure you'll have a wonderful time with him ;)"

Allegra sincerely doubted that. She would have a barely tolerable time with him. He would be uptight because of how he felt about billionaires despite needing to make nice with them for money, and *everyone* was going to presume they were still married, which he would love, and Allegra would *not* love.

"Has he been to an event like this before?"

"I presume so. Fundraising is something he's very across."

"I'll leave you in his capable hands then ;)"

That is the worst possible thing that could happen, Allegra thought, looking down at her battered phone. Having a quiet shadow that understood how everything worked and told her what she needed to be aware of had been oddly comforting.

"Do you want me there too, Allegra?"

She drew a sharp breath. That was a no-brainer. *"Yes."*

"I'll see you there, then."

Allegra let that breath out slowly. Perhaps she'd enjoy it after all. *"Are we doing anything today?"*

"Not yet. I'm waiting to see what hits socials about last night to decide our next move. You can relax—but don't relax too much. Just imagine someone is always filming you and behave accordingly."

Not a very comforting thought, really, especially given that she'd agreed to meet Vanessa in public later. She went to have a shower and get ready.

Driving her extremely shiny old car made her feel unexpectedly self-conscious because it turned heads. It was also decked out in off-road kit and rescue gear and didn't have tinted windows, so unfortunately she was in the situation of having people waving at her at traffic lights and honking at other times.

Imagine people are filming you, she thought, smiling and waving back at the people in other cars. She was very happy to *finally* find a park for her enormous car in Mosman, flip her very blond, very recognisable plait up inside a Bunnings sunhat, and go to find Vanessa.

Mosman itself was a suburb that took itself far too fucking seriously. Each street was lined with both leafy European trees and expensive European cars, and the main shopping strip contained a combination of quaint little cafes that couldn't possibly be making any money (some kept housewife's hobby, no doubt) and luxury boutiques with eye-watering price tags.

Vanessa didn't live *in* Mosman—the Sinclairs' childhood home was in the next suburb—but she routinely gave her address to people as Mosman anyway, and somehow her mail always arrived.

Allegra arrived at the café to find her sister on time for once. Vanessa rushed over in her fashionable pants and linen blouse to give her a big hug.

"Allegra!" she said as she released her, pulling off her Bunnings sunhat and giving it a judgemental look as she smoothed Allegra's plait down. "Why would you hide your beautiful hair?"

Vanessa herself had genetic-lottery-winning platinum blond hair, and it was something she'd been intensely proud of as soon as she'd been old enough to learn how she could use it. Allegra's was sandier and more pedestrian. "I was hoping to avoid being recognised."

"Bit of a moot point when you've got those out," Vanessa said, looking down at Allegra's tattooed arms. She wasn't wrong. "You look so lovely, though! That old, ruined painter-jeans look is so in right now, it's perfect for you. And you're everywhere! It's so exciting. I can finally be proud of being your sister again!"

It was going to be a *long* 45 minutes. "I'm always ecstatic to be yours," Allegra said with zero enthusiasm, following Vanessa inside the café. Several heads turned.

Vanessa loved it. "Do you think they think I'm your date?" she whispered while they stood at the counter choosing their lunch from the board.

Allegra doubted it; Vanessa may have been paler, slighter, and more delicately featured than Allegra, but there was no way anyone would mistake them for anything but relatives. "I think your reputation as the most eligible widow in Mosman is safe."

Vanessa laughed prettily about that and hugged Allegra around the middle in the same way she used to do when they were kids. "Let's sit out the back, shall we?" she said, nodding at a door at the end of the café. "I know you prefer outside."

The courtyard was small but leafy and shaded from the midday sun. There was also no one else out there yet, which put Allegra immediately at ease as she sat down, briefly checking for any word from Sal as she placed her phone on the table beside her.

While they were waiting for their lunch, Allegra gave Vanessa the abridged version of what had happened at the hospital.

"Holy shit, you're getting cosy with the *Vales*?" Vanessa asked incredulously, interrupting her story. "Just wait until Timothy finds out."

"He's forgiven me about it because we were invited to some fundraising dinner where he knows he'll be able to schmooze donations for *Light of the Redeemer Mi—"*

"Like a foundation gala?!"

How did everyone on earth seem to know what these things were except Allegra?! "Yes, one of those."

Vanessa sat back in her chair, shaking her head. "Just wait until I tell my friends," she said with wide eyes. "Those are a *huge* deal. You're playing with the big boys now." She paused, an impish grin appearing on her lips. "There will probably be single rich people there."

Allegra exhaled. "*Vanessa*."

"No, I'm totally serious, think about it: you'll be beautiful, well-dressed, famous, and—"

"There with Timothy," Allegra pointed out. "I'll give them your number."

Vanessa laughed again. "*Please* do," she said. "Someone's got to pay my boys' school fees when their scholarship runs out!"

That seemed Vanessa's cue to start her monologue about how her twins were doing. Allegra didn't stop her; she was very excited to recount their budding sporting prowess ("Oscar got selected for the under-17s regionals!"), and they were on the cusp of starting year 11, an important academic year—which, by extension, meant it was important for Vanessa. They'd been her world since her husband had been killed in a workplace accident a decade ago, and it seemed needlessly cruel not to allow her every possible ounce of joy it gave her to gush about them. She'd brought them—*and* Aaron—up almost by herself, burying herself in the children as a cloak against her grief.

Allegra half-listened to her, imagining what it might have been like if she'd had somewhere to take them all to play in Darlinghurst or Surry Hills.

There was a lull in the conversation as their food was brought out; Allegra found herself staring down at her steak while Vanessa fussed with the bits of her food she didn't like. Now seemed as good a time as any. "How is he?"

Vanessa sighed at her. "You know you can call your son, right? Look." She reached across the small outdoor table and turned Allegra's battered phone over so she could see the screen. "There's *this* thing. You can use it to contact people."

"He'll call me if he wants to."

Vanessa looked highly sceptical. "At least message him."

Allegra didn't even pick up her phone. "He's got exams. I don't want him to be distracted by needing to deal with his mother."

"'*Deal with his'*—Allegra! He doesn't have to *deal* with you!"

Tell that to everyone listening to ABC Mornings yesterday, Allegra thought. "I pay his rent, I give him grocery money. He'd feel obligated to make time for me even when he doesn't have it. I'm not going to do that to him."

Vanessa looked like she was on the brink of losing it. "Allegra. Oh my god. I'm going to *strangle* you."

Allegra rolled her eyes. Of course *Vanessa* wouldn't understand. "Kids get really stressed and distracted around exam time, Vanessa—*you* of all people should know that!—and I'm not going to be the reason he—"

"That's it," Vanessa said, holding up her hands. "I'm literally going to kill you. Give me that knife. I'm going to put you out of your misery." She reached across the table for Allegra's steak knife.

Allegra caught her hand. "Fine! I'll call him after his exams," she said, mostly to placate her sister, because he'd probably want to relax with his friends afterwards. "I'll take him to dinner or something."

Vanessa watched her through very narrowed eyes as she sat back and picked up her own knife and fork. "I'm going to check with him that you did."

Allegra glanced at her phone before she turned it over—no notifications. She made a face and got stuck into her steak.

She was halfway through it and listening mutely to Vanessa's latest middle-class complaint ("They're putting social housing behind us, in that block where the childcare centre used to be, these *tiny* little units. Right up against our fence, too!") when her eyes drifted back towards her phone.

Unfortunately, Vanessa being Vanessa, she noticed instantly. "You can just turn your notifications off, you know." At Allegra's blank expression, she elaborated, "If you're getting lots of notifications from Facebook and TikTok and all that because everyone's mentioning you, you can just turn them off if you don't..." She trailed off, considering Allegra's non-response. "That's not what you're expecting."

"I'm waiting to see what PR wants me to do next."

Vanessa scoffed. "No, you're not." She sounded pretty damn sure of herself.

"Excuse me?"

"That's not it," she said. "You would pay *no attention* to some random PR person, because with work stuff, you ignore it forever unless it's an emergency call-out. Your coworkers used to call *me* to get you to reply to emails—remember that time with your super form?" she said, pointing at Allegra with her own knife. "There have only ever been two things that get an instant response from you: saving someone's life or getting yourself laid. Those are the only two options." She sat back, confident in her assessment. "So, you *are* seeing someone."

Allegra felt her cheeks heat up. "I hate to break it to you, Vanessa, but you're actually wrong—it *is* the PR rep's message I'm waiting for."

Vanessa's eyes dropped to Allegra's cheeks. "So what you're telling me is that you have a crush on your PR rep?"

Allegra exhaled at length. It was impossible to keep anything from her sisters. "I don't know what to say to that."

Vanessa did. "Man or woman?" she said, popping a cherry tomato in her mouth and squishing it as she grinned at Allegra.

"*Neither.*"

Vanessa took that entirely the wrong way, and her eyebrows went up. "Okay, that was insensitive of me, wasn't it? What are *they* like? I mean, if they're a they, I guess they're pretty alternative? Were they a woman before? No, wait, is that rude? That's rude, isn't it?"

She didn't mean it maliciously; that was the problem. Allegra shook her head, incredulous. She had no words, because where did someone even start with a question like that? *Vanessa.*

"I suppose it doesn't matter. What does matter: you have it *bad* for them."

There was no way out of this type of interrogation with her sisters: it would keep going until she either relented and spilled everything, or died. She closed her eyes for a moment. "I'm just attracted to her, that's all. It's not going to lead anywhere."

"Oooh, a *lady*," Vanessa observed, leaning forward gleefully on her elbows. Her eyes dropped to Allegra's phone. Before Allegra could stop her, Vanessa's hand darted forward and grabbed it.

"*Vanessa*!" She stood up and leant across the table, but Vanessa was much stronger than she looked and evaded her grasp, twisting away from her in the seat and trying to unlock the phone.

Unfortunately, Vanessa knew her passcode and entered it while fending her off. "God, Allegra, your phone is *trashed*. How many times have you dropped it?"

Allegra ignored her question. "There is nothing interesting on there."

"Then why are you trying to get it back?"

"Fine," Allegra said, straightening and sitting back down. "Go for it. As I said: there's nothing interesting on there."

Vanessa swivelled back around to face the table again, scrolling through Allegra's phone triumphantly while Allegra sat back and accepted her cursed, cursed fate. She hadn't been worried at all about what Vanessa might find, until she remembered—

Vanessa froze mid-scroll like someone had hit pause. "Hello..." she said at length, apparently finding something very juicy. Her eyes snapped back up to Allegra. "Who's *Sal*?"

Fuck. "My PR rep."

One of Vanessa's pointed little eyebrows arched as she read theatrically, "'*Thinking didn't appear to be high on our to-do list last night*'." She let Allegra reach forward and snatch her phone back, having achieved her goal.

Allegra put it as far out of Vanessa's reach as she could. "We didn't sleep together."

"Sounds a lot like you did."

Allegra was reminded exactly why she could never keep a single fucking secret from either of her sisters at any point in her entire life, ever. "Things got a bit heated, but we called it off before it went anywhere serious."

"And now you're waiting for her to text you," Vanessa finished, looking very self-satisfied. "What does she look like? I want to see who's stolen my sister's heart..." She was being glib. Food completely forgotten, Vanessa already had her own phone out. "What's 'Sal' short for, anyway?" she asked. "And what's her surname? Let's Google her."

Since Allegra had no choice but to surrender completely, she spelt Sal's name out for Vanessa so she could plug it into the search bar and see what came up. There was surprisingly little—other than Sal's LinkedIn. Even Allegra found that odd.

"Maybe it's not her real name?" Vanessa suggested. "It is a bit weird, after all."

Allegra doubted that, but didn't have another explanation. She didn't need to offer one as Vanessa was already scouring Sal's LinkedIn—which also lacked a photo of her. "*Black Standard Advisory*," she read, her tone thick with disapproval. "What on earth is that name? Is it a race thing?" Before Allegra could say she also doubted *that*, Vanessa was on Google sleuthing for more information. Whatever she read surprised her. "The *Black* family?" she said, as if Allegra was supposed to know who that was. "It's run by the *Black* family?!"

"...I gather they're important?" Allegra said, making a go-on gesture.

Vanessa looked at her like she'd grown another head. "I know you spend all your time in the wilderness but even *you* have a phone," she said. "*Yes,* they're important. They're billionaires. They own half of New South Wales. Big in property development and all that. Do you think she's one of them?!"

Allegra remembered Sal's penthouse. It was beginning to make more sense how she could afford that. "I'm not sure."

Vanessa had already come to her own conclusion. "Okay," she said, putting her phone down beside her plate and lacing her fingers. "There are no photos of her anywhere, but I guess it doesn't matter what you look like when you're a billionaire. We're in agreement you'll be marrying her, right?"

Vanessa. "What I'm going to be doing with her is following her advice on handling the media attention so I can funnel more money into charities that need it, like Homeward."

"*And* sleeping with her. And then marrying her. Or at least being a sugar baby or something." Vanessa considered that. "Actually, that would probably be better for you because you'll still *have your freedom* or whatever it is that makes you go bush for weeks. Also, you could just not tell Timothy."

At least they both agreed on the last part, Allegra decided, feeling years drain from her life every time Vanessa said anything else on the topic of Sal. "Can I finish my lunch now?"

"You may," Vanessa said graciously, unlacing her fingers and working on her own food.

When they were done and Allegra thought the torment might finally be over, Vanessa was being all cuddly with her as they paid, which suggested she hadn't finished with Allegra just yet. "Let's go shopping! We can do something normal for a change."

Allegra tapped her phone against the EFTPOS machine, regarding Vanessa critically. "Shopping for what?"

"Does it matter? We can just look around. Maybe you'll see something you like."

"You can't fit much in a LandCruiser," she pointed out, letting Vanessa link arms with her and lead her out.

"Then perhaps you should think about moving into something much bigger," she said. "Like your billionaire PR lady's mansion, wherever it is."

Vanessa was probably fishing for some information about that, but Allegra didn't offer it, or the fact she'd been there already. "I'm happy with my current arrangement."

Vanessa sighed at her, shaking her head and leading her through a string of boutiques of various sizes and genres, touching leather handbags, draping far too expensive and fragile clothes on herself and Allegra, and eliciting Allegra's opinion on various homewares.

The only thing of note to Allegra about any of the shops was how very attentive and helpful the staff were. No one embarrassed themselves by rushing up and asking for selfies or yelling out at her in the street as they'd done southside. However, no one could do enough to help her, either. *They're probably used to public figures in these places*, she realised. *I'm no big deal.*

The pretend anonymity made the whole process of shopping for nothing—something Allegra would happily have replaced with almost any other activity—slightly more bearable. It made Vanessa happy, though, and it was nice to see her without puffy eyes.

Allegra had been so resigned to shopping for hours that when her phone rang while Vanessa was trying on sunglasses, it startled her.

"Your phone *isn't* on silent?" Vanessa observed, looking extremely smug.

Allegra had a retort ready until she saw who the caller was and drew a sharp breath. Taking long strides out of the shop to try and put some space between her and Vanessa, she answered it. "My nosy bloody sister is right here, just FYI," she said into the receiver, fighting said sister off as she arrived hot on Allegra's heels to try and furtively eavesdrop.

Sal's voice was alight with amusement. "Let's make it a party, then," she said, and hung up.

Allegra and Vanessa looked down at the phone for a moment before it rang in Allegra's hands again, surprising them both. It was a video call.

Allegra might not have answered it—for Sal's sake—if not for one of Vanessa's perfectly manicured fingers shooting up and pushing the slider across. Allegra *shoved her* and she fell away laughing, which meant when Sal's face appeared, she didn't see it straight away.

Sal was at home in her office, by the look of it, seated comfortably in her office chair. She could clearly hear Vanessa laughing. "I gather it's going well, then."

"As well as it can go when you have relatives like mine." Allegra let Vanessa crowd into the frame. Vanessa's pale eyebrows shot up, and she put one hand on the phone under Allegra's to steady it so she could get a proper look at Sal.

"*You're* Sal Lategan?" she asked, just as confirmation. Her eyes were wide.

"The very same," Sal said coolly.

Before Vanessa could embarrass them both, Allegra plucked her phone clear of Vanessa's hands and walked a bit further up the street. Out of frame, Vanessa mouthed 'marry her!' and then, apparently satisfied, stood to watch from a distance.

"You and your sister are quite different, I gather," Sal remarked when she saw Allegra relax.

Allegra looked across at Vanessa standing outside the shop. "That is the nicest thing anyone's ever said to me."

Sal laughed at that. "She's pretty, isn't she?" was Sal's assessment of Vanessa, and there was something open-ended about that statement that made Allegra wary.

"Why do you say that?"

Sal pressed her lips together and shrugged. "It was a neutral observation."

With Sal, nothing was neutral. "She's straight," Allegra said flatly.

Sal was suddenly finding this conversation much more interesting. "They all are," she said as she watched Allegra, "until they're not—"

"If you touch her, I don't care about how much I'm relying on you right now, I *will* hit you," Allegra said very casually, but meant it. "Which will be redundant, because she will hit you herself. She only *looks* fragile."

Sal actually seemed to find Allegra's response *charming*. "And what about your other—"

"Simone would just flat out kill you and deal with the jail time."

"Oh, is that what happened?" Sal asked, clearly prodding about Simone, as if Allegra would actually grace that with an answer.

She was *not* going to be drawn on the subject of why her other sister was on house arrest, even if Sal was almost certainly just teasing. "I gather you called me for a reason other than hitting on my sisters the day after sharing tequila slammers with me?"

Sal laughed openly at that; an oddly genuine sound from her. "Yes, in fact," she said, shifting gears easily in the way she usually did. "Have you seen what Froggy posted?"

"I woke up midmorning with an awful headache that's only got worse as the day's progressed, including during this phone call," Allegra told her to explain why she hadn't. "Is it bad?"

"The opposite, of course, proving once again what a natural you are at media, despite being a terrible grump at all other times. I was calling to say that we're going to need to onboard you into BSA's client management system as fast as possible so we can officially manage your socials."

Allegra didn't have many social media accounts and wasn't bothered by the thought of Sal or her lackeys creating them for her—in fact, they were probably more qualified than she was to run them. She was happy to give Sal information to pre-fill on the form so it was faster to digitally sign.

Sal sent the forms through and was waiting for Allegra's confirmation when Allegra spotted Sal's own signature beside '*Black Standard Advisory*' at the bottom of the email. It reminded her of the impromptu snoop session with Vanessa.

Should she ask...?

In the end, curiosity won. "Sal," she began cautiously, "can I ask you a personal question?"

Sal looked back at the camera with interest. "You can certainly *ask* it," she said, reclining in her chair away from the keyboard. "I'll decide whether or not I answer it based on what it is."

Allegra took a breath. "Are you part of the Black family?"

The question surprised Sal. She considered Allegra for a moment or two, studying her face. Allegra wasn't sure she was going to respond until she did. "That depends on who you ask," she said cryptically. "But yes. In a way."

Allegra was silent for a moment, processing that.

"That question was courtesy of your sister, wasn't it?"

Allegra found herself grimacing. "Is it that obvious?"

Sal nodded slowly. "Pretty *and* smart," she said with a grin. "Maybe I'm representing the wrong Sinclair."

Allegra scoffed. "Well, you're welcome to *that* Sinclair," she said dryly, gesturing back towards where Vanessa was waiting for her. "You want me to get her? You can have her right now. No returns."

Sal looked thoroughly entertained. "That's a very generous offer, but after some consideration, I'm more than satisfied by the one I already have," she said, watching Allegra intently. "Or," she added with that twinkle in her eye again, "at least I suspect I soon will be."

Pfft. "Goodbye," Allegra said pointedly to her, and then hung up. She was smiling.

Vanessa took that as an invitation to sidle up behind Allegra again while she was finding all the places she needed to sign in the document. "I hope that's a marriage contract," she said. "Because if it's not, give her my number. I don't care how weirdly she dresses."

Allegra snorted, still going through the email. "She said you're pretty."

Vanessa gave her a wide-eyed stare for a few seconds. "So, you know that old meme 'would you kiss a girl for a million dollars?'," she said eventually, "turns out I would be prepared to *marry* one for a billion." She put her chin on Allegra's shoulder, watching her complete the document. "She's pretty, too, I suppose. In a bizarre goth way. Why does she do that?"

Allegra shrugged. "It's her schtick, I guess. I just presumed, you know, black clothing, Black Standard Advisory..."

"Black family..." Vanessa continued. "Maybe she's trying to make super sure everyone knows she's a Black. I mean, I would."

Allegra paused for a second, remembering Sal's cryptic answer about whether she was part of the Black family. "I don't think it's that simple, Vanessa."

She'd already moved on. "Black is such a weird colour to want your hair to be, though. What colour do you think her hair is naturally?" she wondered aloud.

Jesus. So many levels. "Vanessa, it's not something I've thought about."

She was grinning. "I thought maybe you might already have seen some evidence." She waggled her eyebrows.

Allegra sighed audibly and shrugged her off. "God, you're as bad as she is, *fuck off*," she hissed, which only made Vanessa laugh and hug her.

As much as Allegra loved her sister, she'd reached her Vanessa tipping point a while ago and needed to say her goodbyes. She hugged her, let her take a selfie of them, and then left her in the fancy glasses shop, escaping back to her car for a much-needed reprieve.

Her Panadol was wearing off. She popped another two and then drove across to the national park at Middle Head—somewhere that the fine, upstanding citizens of Mosman wouldn't be offended by her having a nap in her car.

She'd rolled back her seat and was getting comfortable when her phone dinged.

She glanced at it. *"I see a Vanessa Sinclair had a peek at my LinkedIn profile."*

Allegra nodded to herself. *"When I said my sister was nosy, I meant it in the strongest sense of the word."* She paused before typing more, wondering if she should push her luck about the total lack of details regarding Sal anywhere on the internet. *"And LinkedIn was the only search result."*

"What dirt was she hoping to find on me, exactly?"

Allegra may have thought more carefully about her answer, but the Panadol hadn't touched her headache yet. *"She was just looking for a photo."*

"Please relay my apologies to her, then. I strictly control who has access to my image: you can't misuse or train AI on images that aren't digitised."

Allegra raised her eyebrows. A bit intense—like everything about her—but it tracked with her obsession with total control.

"Why was she looking for a photo of me, Allegra?"

...and *that* tracked with Sal's enjoyment of pushing Allegra off-balance. However, Allegra had just spent the entirety of lunch being systematically tortured for personal information, so handing over anything more was off the table. *"She wants to marry you for your money, and she was hoping to find some idea of what she was getting into before she proposed."*

Allegra wasn't sure what sort of response she expected—probably Sal playing along with the idea of marrying Vaneesa to upset her, probably. The reply surprised her. *"I would never do your sweet little sister the disservice of inviting her into my family."*

Allegra reread that a couple of times, recalling some of the comments Sal had made about them and trying to piece it all together.

Lost in thought, the next message caught her completely off guard. *"You, on the other hand... How do you look in white?"*

Allegra's jaw dropped. She stared at the text, refusing to feel anything and even more irritated that Sal clearly knew she would. *She is messing with you, Allegra*, she furiously told herself. *Do not reply to that. Lock the screen. Put the phone down.*

She obeyed that voice, setting the phone aside and lying back in the reclined driver's seat. How was she supposed to go to sleep now?!

When her phone dinged again, she had to vigorously fight with herself for several seconds not to open the message. In the end, her poor judgement prevailed.

It was a photo. Sal had taken a full-length mirror selfie, wearing sharp heels as she always seemed to, with a severe, modest black top. She wasn't in her usual suit pants, though. Today, she was wearing an asymmetric tailored skirt that looked like someone had draped a very expensive length of fabric around her and fastened it at her waist. As a result, a narrow slit climbed slightly above her knee. She had the defined calves of someone who wore heels every day, and the legs of someone who had never seen a single sunbeam in their life.

"I'm not wearing stockings today," was the message that accompanied it, *"if you felt like giving my stairwell another chance..."*

The skirt barely registered. It was the way Sal was looking directly into the camera that hit her harder than if she'd actually been naked.

The final text read: *"Careful what you do with this picture, Allegra."*

Chapter 14: Field Work

Generally, when Allegra was crammed into a small space, it was either a split in the rockface or a stormwater drain. It wasn't usually the kitchen sink cupboard with her arm craned behind a leaking $10,000 dishwasher. Honestly, for that price, it should fix itself.

The position she was in—on her back, legs bent and splayed to support the twist of her body—was exactly the sort of thing Sal would have made a lascivious comment about. Unfortunately, it was just *Timothy* crouched beside her, not Sal.

"I hope there aren't any spiders back there," he commented, holding the torchlight towards the back pipes.

Allegra was happy she didn't have to worry about *snakes* for once. "Can you pass me that?" She held her hand out and accepted the torch from him, holding it behind the appliance.

The leak appeared to be coming from a join in the hose, which looked about 100 in hose-joiner years. The outlet had seen better days, too. "I think I've found the problem," she said, shuffling out of the cupboard and sitting up. "Time for a Bunnings trip."

Timothy jumped up, then promptly winced because of his knees. "I'll go," he said, rubbing them. "Can you write down what I need to get?"

Allegra did better than that: she put the items in his Bunnings cart online.

"Do you need anything for yourself?" he asked just before he ducked out. "Any supplies for your car, etc?"

Allegra considered that. "I suppose I can always use another burn kit," she decided. "Especially as we get towards summer. I'm forever using my hydrogel on tourists getting sunburnt."

As he went to collect everything, Allegra was trying to shuffle the dishwasher out of its nest in the cupboard so she could access and replace the hoses more easily when her phone dinged.

She presumed it was Timothy with a Bunnings question, so glanced over at it to try and decide if it needed an immediate response. When she saw it was Sal, she nearly dropped the dishwasher on her foot.

She spent a moment grounding herself before she opened it. *Don't do or say anything pathetic,* she instructed herself, even as her brain unhelpfully supplied her with a very clear memory of that *hot* mirror photo from yesterday.

Giving up, she opened it. *"Sorry for the short notice, you're needed on site for the Homeward survey at 11. Comms team will be there. I won't be, which should make the whole thing much less distracting for you. Can't have you missing anything ;)"*

"Oh, fuck off," Allegra said aloud, and texted back, *"No one"—not even you—"is distracting enough for me to risk botching a Phase 1."* If she missed a critical detail, people could die.

"Is that a double-dare, Allegra?"

Everything was just another opportunity for Sal to see how close she could push Allegra to the edge, wasn't it? She shook her head. Since it definitely wasn't an invitation to put people's lives at risk, Allegra ignored her. *"Tell your comms team I'll meet them at the eastern gate."*

The dishwasher would have to wait. She left it shuffled half-out of the kitchen counter and went to get ready for the survey.

It's good she's not coming, Allegra told herself, still faintly irritated by the implication a little light flirting could tempt her to endanger families. After all, she wasn't convinced a woman like Sal had ever encountered a plant that wasn't in a designer pot, let alone hiked for hours through rough terrain.

The thought of Sal attempting it was entertaining. While Allegra was picking out clothes that would both be appropriate on site and look reasonable on camera (since she supposed 'comms team' was likely to involve some sort of camera being pointed at her), she found herself wondering what Sal would look like in something similar. She laughed at the thought. Sal out hiking, *really*? Didn't her people turn to ash in sunlight?

By the time she'd selected her clothes, she realised she'd spent the past 20 minutes thinking of nothing but that woman; thus unfortunately proving she *was* distracting.

Not distracting enough for me to stuff up an event safety report, Allegra promised herself firmly, trying not to imagine how fucking smug she'd be if she knew, and then gave herself a once-over in the mirror.

She ended up selecting hiking cargos and an olive-green tee; Vanessa had commented once that green suited her, and Vanessa tended to be an authority on those things. She picked a midsize daypack for some water, an additional phone battery, and all the tape and paint she was going to need to cram in there. All her sun protection gear was already in the car.

Timothy arrived home as she was leaving. "Call-out?" he asked her, watching her climb into the car.

"Kind of," she said, and *nearly* blurted out 'Sal wants me on site' before she caught herself. "...Homeward wants me to do the survey today for some reason."

He raised his eyebrows. "Good luck, then," he told her. "Don't forget we've got the formalwear fitting tonight."

Ugh. Allegra had forgotten about that. "See you then," she said, and pulled out of the driveway.

It took an hour and a half to get to the location—a private property south of Sydney near the Royal National Park. The road up to the property was asphalt (good for passenger vehicle access, Allegra decided, approving of that), and there was a large cleared-out area near the main gate that could easily function as a carpark in fine weather. Allegra would need to make a note about weather-related use in her report, because it was clay and could easily become a tyre and shoe graveyard if it rained.

There was already a black Falcon parked on the asphalt edge of the space, and two people were sitting in it with the doors open. *Small comms team*, Allegra thought, parking nearby.

As soon as she opened the door of her LandCruiser, she was greeted by the sound of sulphur-crested cockatoos yelling at each other from the canopy, and the smell of eucalyptus being warmed in the late-morning sun. The land around them bordered on rainforest, so the undergrowth was mostly ferns and palms. She knew just by looking at it that the air would be cool and crisp once they were deep inside.

She wished she could just don her daypack and dive straight in—but that wasn't possible. She had a job to do. She sighed and went to meet her temporary coworkers.

They got out of the car: a man and a woman, both of whom looked to be late 20s or early 30s and polished. They had clearly been instructed to wear appropriate clothing, as neither of them was in a suit and both had closed-toe shoes, but even in casual wear they were city kids through and through. Allegra realised she was going to have to babysit them if they wanted to follow her around the property for the survey.

Perhaps they'd just want some shots of her on site and then they'd retreat to the safety of their air-conditioned offices.

She shook their hands in greeting.

"Tom," the bearded man told her, and then gestured at his co-worker, whose main distinguishing feature was a pair of very bold 50s-style cat-eye glasses. "That's Zoe. She's Social Media and I'm on cameras. Basically, I do what she says."

Allegra nodded, and then listened to their brief. Essentially, they'd been instructed to put together some content showing Allegra on site and doing her job. While Zoe was explaining the type of shots they'd need and how she wanted to focus on 'authentic storytelling', Tom backed away, retrieved his enormous camera, and was already filming Allegra listening to his colleague before her speech ended.

"Tom's going to follow you around. Treat it like a normal survey—we might ask you to repeat some tasks or explain what you're checking. Try and forget the camera is there."

Allegra looked over at Tom; his camera looked like something you'd see in a film studio, not like something you'd want to carry around open bushland. "I hope that thing's insured," she said of it. "Because it's easy to trip over even *without* a giant camera on your shoulder."

He laughed. "Believe it or not, I've actually carried it around worse places." He paused. "Although, I did raid Equipment for a spare just in case. It's in the boot."

They got to work. After Allegra let them film her putting all the barrier tape, fluorescent paint, and orange flags in her backpack, she made them all slather themselves in sunscreen. Then, on learning Zoe hadn't actually brought a hat with her, Allegra retrieved a spare from her boot and sternly handed it to her. Zoe laughed about that, and Tom filmed her getting a light-hearted dressing-down from Allegra for her lack of sun safety while she glanced at the camera and grimaced.

Allegra explained the plan: first, she'd send the drone over the area to get a basic understanding of the layout and flag anything obvious they needed to be aware of. Then she'd walk and mark the perimeter, if it wasn't already fenced. After that, she'd go section by section, taping off anything that posed a risk, marking dangerous trees or other hazards, and making notes in her survey app.

"There are a couple of things I'll pay particular attention to," she told the camera. "We're in bushfire season, so I'll need to check the dry fuel load and scout evacuation routes. But we've also had some really nasty rains recently, and they can cause flash flooding and slip hazards. 10 days is too far away to know which scenario is more likely, so I'll need to make two reports: a fine-weather report and a wet-weather report." She showed them two different colours of tape she was going to use for different weather hazards.

Then, she let them film her operating her drone. It wasn't one of the enormous, decked-out SES ones; it was just a smaller one she'd bought privately and then later discovered all sorts of additional uses for.

The property itself was a reasonable choice for an orienteering event: it was only a gentle incline and roughly 100 hectares. While it was mostly thick bushland, there weren't any obvious things that would need attention, either: no water bodies, cliffs or rock overhangs. There was a burnt-out shed on the far side of it that she wanted to go evaluate, but otherwise she estimated she'd probably have the scouting and site assessment for the report finished in a single day. The write-up, she could do later.

Once she'd made a mental note of all the sections she'd need to do some groundwork on, she spent a minute or two just coasting high above the trees and appreciating the birds alighting en masse as she passed. The canopy was thick and untouched; some of these trees would be hundreds of years old.

Tom had been watching with interest while she was operating the drone, so she ended up letting him have a go flying it while Zoe held the camera. He crashed it, as people always did when they were learning, but his horror was palpable as he looked at Allegra for her reaction.

She pretended to be stern for a second—but couldn't hold it for very long because of how upset he looked. She burst out laughing.

He took off his hat and fanned himself with it, exaggerating his relief. "I thought I was about to be fed into the woodchipper by Allegra Sinclair," he said, laughing. "Oh my god. I hope I didn't just destroy your drone."

The drone was fine, as Allegra knew it would be. "I've crashed it into the sea before," she told him, plucking it out of the bush it was lodged in. "If salt water didn't destroy it, a banksia isn't going to."

Zoe handed the camera back to Tom after he'd recovered. "May I have a turn at crashing the drone?" she asked Allegra, deadpan, and then broke out in a smile when Tom made a strangled noise behind her.

The comms team turned out to be less of a hassle than Allegra had expected, despite being bona fide city folk. They were obviously well-acquainted with each other, and they were chatty and amiable with Allegra, too. Both were fit enough to keep up with her as they moved through the ferny undergrowth along the lightly beaten track—although noticeably quieter during the thicker stretches—and both were happy to let Allegra dictate where they were going and when.

Eventually, they stopped for lunch, sitting on the fallen trunk of an old redgum. They'd had their lunch arranged for them by Gerard, and he'd also supplied one for Allegra, which meant that her own slightly stale ham and cheese roll was going to end up as dinner. Inside the lunch boxes were the fanciest bagels she'd ever seen.

"A little different from my usual fare," Allegra commented, finding feta and haloumi in it.

"Hah," Zoe said, showing the other two her lunch box. It had '*absolutely no mayo*' scrawled on the side of it. "Thanks, Gerard!" she said as if he could hear it, and then started eating.

I suppose they've worked together for a long time, Allegra reflected, observing their ease with each other. She suspected they'd behave very differently if Sal were there. "Is Black Standard Advisory a good place to work?"

They glanced at each other to gauge the other's reaction, but they looked relaxed. It apparently wasn't a taboo topic. "I'm happy," Zoe said neutrally, looking across at Tom, who nodded. "I've been working there for 11 years, so it must be okay."

"Yeah, it's fine," Tom agreed, "I've only been working for Dimi for about six months, though, so I guess we'll find out how it's going at annual review time."

That was a surprise to Zoe. "Oh, you're not under Sal anymore?"

He shook his head. "Not officially, although she's always sending me out on jobs anyway. I'd just be sitting around the office helping Corporate with video processing if she didn't, so I guess Dimi doesn't have a problem with it."

Allegra was listening very closely. "Dimi?"

They looked at her in much the same way Vanessa had when she said she didn't know who the Blacks were. "Dimitri Black," Zoe repeated, just to check Allegra definitely didn't know who it was. "He's the CEO."

Allegra grimaced. "I'm sorry, you're going to find I know very little about these things."

Zoe grinned. "That's okay, we know very little about *these* things," she said, gesturing at the bushland around them. "Anyway, yeah, BSA's fine."

Allegra decided to push her luck. "And Sal?"

That made them laugh. They looked at each other again; Tom spoke first. "She'd be good at poker," was his initial assessment. "I remember at first I used to have these nightmares about disappointing her, because she just gives you *nothing*, you know? She's never anything but *so* cool and professional, and she'd sign off on all my footage, but I'd sort of exist in this purgatory of having no idea what she thought of me or my work."

Zoe was nodding. “I hear you on the nightmares thing,” she told him soberly. “When I was in the graduate program, I handed in a couple of videos with some suggested posting strategy, and she looked at it, and then looked at me, and then gave it back to me straight away and asked me to try again. She wasn’t nasty or anything, but I was 22 and straight out of uni so I went out and cried in my car.”

Allegra’s chest felt a little heavy. “That sounds awful.”

Zoe put her hands up. “Oh no, don’t get me wrong, I think everyone just goes through a phase where they’re terrified of her because you just never have any idea what’s going on in her head. Oh!” She thought of something, and snapped her fingers at Tom. “Did you ever attend a pitch with her? She’s like a different person.”

He shook his head. “I heard about it though. Trung said she was smiling and laughing and all that and then when she walked out the door of the meeting room it just all fell away.”

Allegra remembered how easily Sal seemed to switch gears. She didn’t say anything.

Zoe shook her head with a smile. “She can really work people. I guess that’s why she’s CMO.”

Tom scoffed at that. “Be serious, she’s CMO because she’s Dimi’s niece.”

“That’s just a rumour,” Zoe quickly pointed out, glancing anxiously towards Allegra as if she’d suddenly remembered she was there. “People just say that because she gives away *nothing* about her private life so she might as well be. Dimi laughed when he heard what people were saying.”

Tom shrugged. “It guess it doesn’t really matter, anyway,” he decided. “She obviously knows what she’s doing, no matter how she got the job.” He took another bite of his bagel, chewing it thoughtfully before he swallowed. “I’ve got to say, though, Dimi is a relief. He’s really warm.”

“I’ve heard that,” Zoe said neutrally, but didn’t offer any further assessment. She didn’t appear especially interested in comparing the two of them, or in talking more about Sal.

Allegra had so many unanswered questions and wanted very much to listen to them continue to discuss their bosses, but judging by Zoe’s disengagement, now wasn’t the time to push for it. Sal *was* her manager, and they’d been heading into rumour territory—it made sense she’d want to leave it.

What didn’t make sense was that Allegra had known Sal for a few days and already had more insight into her personal life than these two people who’d worked daily with her for years.

It gave Allegra food for thought; what food, she wasn't sure. She ate her actual food in silence after that, listening to the two of them chat lightheartedly to each other before they continued along the perimeter.

All the talk about Sal brought the woman to the front of Allegra's mind again; she reflexively checked her phone, which still showed *Emergency Calls Only*. With the amount of time Sal spent on her own phone, Allegra couldn't even imagine what she'd be like if she were out here with them and couldn't use it—and that was saying nothing about the insects, the spiderwebs, and the thick fern cover. Allegra suspected that if a fern dared touch Sal's face, she'd probably be tempted to coolly bulldoze its entire genus.

Then again, maybe she'd like it? She worked 24/7; maybe not having access to her phone or any creature comforts would be a welcome shock to her system. Allegra loved the difference herself—there was nothing more humbling than sitting in total silence beside a 1000-year-old redgum and feeling your insignificance. Listening to herself, Allegra shook her head. Feeling insignificant didn't really seem like something Sal would enjoy. *Perhaps she'd just hate it here after all*, Allegra thought, and kept pushing through the ferns.

It was mid-afternoon when they reached the burnt-out shed, which jutted out of the earth like some sort of alien spaceship had landed amongst the gum trees. From the shape of the burn and the damage to surrounding bushland (minimal, Allegra thought), She guessed the fire probably started in winter, and inside the structure. From what, she couldn't say; it was steel framed so possibly lightning. Sheds on private property were often places people stored recreation equipment, so it was also possible there was some sort of battery explosion—or a thief setting it alight to hide the fact the equipment had been stolen.

The fire was probably never properly investigated. Many of them weren't, if they didn't cause bushfires and the equipment wasn't that valuable.

Allegra stood back and snapped a few photos of the structure. There was no trace at all of what it had been previously used for; everything had been razed to the ground. Now, it was nothing more than twisted metal.

"Wow," was Zoe's only comment.

"Fire will do that," Allegra said shortly. "Just a few minutes and everything's gone." She ran some safety tape around it so people weren't tempted to explore.

Once they were done there, they continued around the perimeter to check it was all fenced, and Allegra followed all the friendly instructions to let them film her walking along lightly beaten tracks, assessing and tagging zombie trees, and explaining what she was doing at every step of the way.

They reached the last stretch of perimeter track, running parallel to a council road. Allegra was halfway to the gate to assess it for fire truck access when a sign on the far side caught her eye. She hopped the fence to read it.

It was a giant real estate sign with *'SOLD!'* plastered across it.

Her first reaction was to look past the sign at the beautiful wild bushland beyond it and feel a visceral sense of pain at the thought of it being flattened, even if that wasn't necessarily likely. These places tended to be bought up by conservation efforts and councils, sometimes even the state government.

Her second reaction was to feel deeply uneasy. The timing of the sale didn't seem right. Did Sal know about this?

She stood in front of the sign, studying the details of the property and wondering if a Phase 1 Environmental Assessment had already been done by someone else for the sale—if so, she hoped she could get a copy of it. They were similar reports and it would halve her work.

She took her phone out to message Sal, but even this close to the road there was no reception. It would just have to wait to get back to the signal booster on her car. She snapped a photo of the sign, anyway.

It was a short walk back to their original access point, and back to their vehicles.

Tom put his equipment back in the boot, stretching out his neck and groaning. "That'll be my exercise for the year," he said, grimacing as he rubbed his camera shoulder. He then shook hands with Allegra. "Really nice to meet you. It's a breath of fresh air to not be working with a politician." He exhaled at length. "And now back to the office to download all the raw files and give them to Sal before she asks me where they are."

Allegra looked at the clock: 5:30pm already. She didn't comment on it.

Zoe did, though. "Sal wants them *today*?"

Tom shrugged. "That's what she said. Just the raw files, though. Not edits. It'll only take me a few minutes."

"What's she going to do with raw files, though?" Zoe asked somewhat rhetorically, and then shook her head and held up her hands in defeat. "You know what? Okay. That's what she wants," she said, and gave her borrowed sunhat back to Allegra. "Thanks for being the protector of my skin."

Allegra laughed about that. "You'll thank me when you're my age."

"I'll thank you right now because I'm not going home sunburnt," Zoe said, and then they said their goodbyes and hopped back into the car, heading off.

Allegra climbed back into her own car, turning on the auxiliary aircon for a couple of minutes to clear the hot air inside while she checked her notifications.

With Sal's earlier double-dare comment, Allegra half-expected a series of cheeky 'distracting' messages sent throughout the day to arrive now she was in range—but nothing came through. The last message she'd sent was that morning.

A little irritated by her own disappointment, she sat back, gazing at the ferny undergrowth rippling in the wind and thinking about the feedback Sal's staff had about her.

She wasn't sure whether Sal was Dimi's niece—but it seemed likely she was his something, given their conversation yesterday. His something, and his subordinate. She also clearly disliked her family. *Not a happy relationship*, she reflected, immediately wondering what was going on there, and whose fault it was.

Her gut feeling was to want to defend Sal, although that seemed like a mistake. *You've known her for a few days, Allegra*, she pointed out to herself. *You were ready to throttle her initially. Is it really that hard to believe her family might want to do that as well?*

She was more tolerable since they'd gone drinking together, but if she truly was 'a completely different person during a pitch', and 'knew how to work people', who was to say that Allegra wasn't just being worked, too?

Her brain supplied her with a memory of Sal stepping back from her in the bar, breathless and rosy-cheeked. That wasn't the cool, calculating demeanour of someone whose only intention was to exploit her somehow.

Maybe she just really *enjoys her job,* offered a dry voice inside her.

Allegra didn't know what to make of it, but she had a lot to think about.

When her phone dinged, she brightened and immediately checked it.

It was Timothy. She released the breath she'd been holding. "*Ready for the fitting at 7:30? Please be presentable*."

She resented the message, but on looking down at her dusty cargos, she realised how terrible her face and hair would look thanks to the greasy sunscreen and its love of attracting dirt. She couldn't try on formalwear like this. If she was going to be on time to the fitting, she'd need to leave immediately so she could shower first.

She gave the beautiful late afternoon sun and the golden-tipped bushland one last forlorn look before closing her door and buckling herself in.

Time to squish herself into something that would make billionaires throw money at her—or at least impress one of them in particular.

Chapter 15: Under the Table

The dress was burning a hole in the spare room wardrobe, even though it was zipped up in a protective bag and tucked beside all her various hiking gear.

The previous night at the fitters, Allegra had expected not to be very fussy about what they suggested as long as it was comfortable and appropriate. Unfortunately, as they started bringing dresses out for her, she discovered she had opinions about them.

She ended up with a plum-coloured full-length silk dress that gathered in the centre of her torso and fanned out to give her draping full sleeves, a flowing skirt with a slight train, and, perhaps most notably, an uncomfortably low V-neckline that extended below the curve of her breasts. Allegra had resisted at first—did she really want to be walking around like that?—but the fitters had explained that with the full sleeves (as apparently her extremely benign tattoos were still too risqué for polite company), if she didn't have *some* skin on display, the dress would age her up.

As they'd been there for an hour already, Allegra ended up letting the girl talk her into renting the dress so they could go home. Now, she wondered if perhaps she'd made a mistake.

That morning, while Allegra had sat herself at the big dining table in Timothy's central room with all her reporting paraphernalia, the dress was distracting her from her Phase 1 Environmental Constraints Assessment for Homeward.

She'd downloaded all the photos from her phone to her laptop and was planning to use them to prompt her memory. Instead, she was staring blankly at her screen, caught between tentative excitement and dread about this stupid gala the following night.

What would Sal think about that neckline?

Oh, for fuck's sake, Allegra, she told herself, shaking free of all that nonsense. *Focus on your job.*

She went back to the photos, scrolling through them and jotting things on the notepad next to her. The *'SOLD'*-stickered real estate sign appeared on screen.

She sat back, staring at it again. That one *did* actually prompt a message to Sal.

She found the photo on her phone and attached it. *"Did you know about this?"*

Sal didn't reply straight away. Allegra had already selected most of the photos she needed when her phone dinged again. *"Yes—it's part of the reason Homeward got the land for their event. Bit of a long story, but the short of it is that the bank that repossessed it decided making it available for the event fit their corporate responsibility charter."*

Allegra had very little idea what that meant. *"Give me the long story."*

"Pushy ;) It was owned by a family who couldn't afford to reinsure it after there was a fire on the property and it got reclassified as higher bushfire risk as a result. The land price dropped and the bank moved in to protect their interests. The stated reason for lending the event space to Homeward was that it met the objectives of the bank's corporate responsibility charter—but I'm sure you'd like my personal opinion of the matter which is that repossessions can attract unfavourable attention and lending the land to charity is likely to mitigate that."

It read as very polished, like PR. Allegra read each sentence a couple of times, trying to play out the scenario in her mind. It *did* sound logical. If that was the case, though, why didn't it feel right?

She tried to set that thought aside so she could work on the Phase 1, but the discomfort persisted and her mind kept circling back to it. It wasn't unusual for insurance premiums to shoot up after fires, that was true, and the reclassification of the land after a fire was not uncommon either, but...

She pulled up the photo of the twisted, burnt-out shed. It was the greenery around it that made her realise the problem.

The fire *hadn't* caused a bushfire, not even close. It had been contained, self-limiting, despite being nestled in a mix of eucalypt forest and subtropical rainforest.

She hopped onto the NSW government website to check its fire rating, which was the very highest: BAL-FZ (Flame Zone).

"Oh, that's *bullshit,*" Allegra told the screen. Nothing about the property she was on suggested it was at imminent risk of combustion. There was absolutely no way a qualified bushfire assessment specialist could have inspected the property after that fire and re-rated it. Perhaps it was just a tick-and-flick job by some bureaucrat.

Allegra got her phone out. *"That increased fire risk classification is absolute and total nonsense,"* Allegra texted Sal, *"and I am putting that in my report."*

"Could you put it in an email for me, as well? I'll forward it to Homeward to supply to the bank for insurance purposes."

Allegra did as she requested, getting back to the report.

Around midday, her phone dinged. She was wrestling with topographical maps on her geriatric laptop and desperate for the interruption.

"Got some light lunchtime entertainment for you," read Sal's message, *"Froggy and Tye's full videos are up. Enjoy."* Attached were the links.

Well, that sounded better than being told 20 times that she didn't have enough memory resources to continue. Curious, she clicked on Froggy's.

The video popped up—the thumbnail was a very dramatic photo of Froggy with massive heart eyes and the text *'10 Reasons Why I Will Immediately be Marrying Allegra Sinclair'*. Allegra snorted and pressed play.

Froggy was standing in front of a green screen, badly pretending to be a reporter. "Ladies, gays, and theys," she began in a very newsreader voice, "a *national emergency* has occurred. I have just listened to the ABC interview with Allegra Sinclair, and I regret to inform you that I will be marrying her. Immediately. Today. As soon as she texts back."

She turned towards another camera. "Now, before we begin, some of you may be asking, 'Froggy, is this legally binding?' And to that I say: absolutely not. But emotionally? Spiritually? Gay-culturally? Yes. This is a covenant."

She dramatically swivelled back to the main camera, holding up a clipboard which was just the words *'Official Report!!'* scribbled on it with Texta. "I have compiled a comprehensive, peer-reviewed list of the 10 Reasons I Will Be Immediately Marrying Allegra Sinclair, using the scientific method of: her literally bench-pressing me in a hospital corridor and my frontal lobe exiting the chat."

She pointed at herself, deadly serious as the camera slowly zoomed in. "My good gays: I saw God, and God was a jacked SES rescue worker with forearms carved by the heavens and a moral compass so sharp that it stabbed me clean through my tiny lesbian heart."

She dived right into the reasons: "She looks like she would kill a spider for me but also lecture me about habitat displacement."/ "She accidentally created a nationwide lesbian meltdown by existing on television for five minutes."/ "She has that 'I don't know I'm hot' energy that makes lesbians lose structural integrity."

By the end of the video, Froggy looked like she'd been dragged through bushland herself. "This has been Froggy, reporting live from the Lesbian

Affairs Desk. Thank you for joining me for this critical national briefing. Stay safe, stay hydrated, and if you see Allegra Sinclair in the wild... please alert her that I have chosen her as my wife and there's no takebacks."

When the video began to repeat, Allegra stopped it and sat back in her chair, eyes wide. After a few moments, she laughed awkwardly. *What on earth*?!

Honestly, she needed a moment; she was so used to slow media pans of disaster zones, or static direct interviews. She wasn't used to having two hours of content blended on high and delivered into her brain in under four minutes. It was giving her the same processing issues as her old computer.

She was tempted to rewatch but didn't think she had the personal strength. Instead, still spaced out, she texted Sal, *"I didn't realise bench-pressing someone once could cause a national incident."* She laughed uneasily again, thinking about it. *"It probably shouldn't have, she's tiny and nowhere near my limit."*

"I'll let her know she can bring a friend next time," was Sal's reply.

She opened Tye's next. His content was harder for her to follow—he was a pop-culture guy, and Allegra was the opposite of someone who followed pop culture. *'Allegra Sinclair Would Last Longer Than Most Avengers'* treated her recent week like a superhero movie, complete with a scorecard for her stats. It even cut to Tye in the shower, water running dramatically over his shoulders as he fake-sobbed: "I watched one interview—*one*—and now I'm weeping before lunch?? Where is her Oscar? I'll storm the Academy *myself*!"

Allegra had no idea at all what he was referencing but was still very entertained. She double-checked the message to see if there was a link to Lost in Austin; there wasn't. Oh, well. Sal had said he was there for some other reason rather than to post about her, so it made sense.

She flipped over to her message app. It was only when she was trying to decide what she could say to Sal about Tye's video without sounding like she was just looking for an excuse to text her *that she realised she was looking for an excuse to text her.*

Sighing at herself, she pushed aside her discomfort about the videos and tried to get back to the report.

She had it finished towards late afternoon and spent a little while reading through it and making sure all the important details had been included.

It felt odd sending it directly to Homeward, though (normally it would need to go through about three layers of bureaucracy inside the SES), so she ended up being able to text Sal after all. *"You can shoot it to me, if you like,"* was Sal's reply. *"One of our juniors can proofread it."* Allegra took her up on her offer.

Report done, she ended up going to face the dress again. She unzipped it and stood back to consider it.

There was no point in taking it back: there wasn't time for another fitting before the gala tomorrow night and she'd already spent $100 on the special bra and invisible tape. Come on—it was four or five hours max, and the online lesbians would want to see 'Rescue Guns' dressed in it anyway. That thought gave her war flashbacks to Froggy's video and she dropped her head into her hand, *groaning*.

Well, at least this dress would make *someone* happy, in that case. She took her phone out *again* to text Sal. *"Will there be media at the gala?"*

"Yes, but coverage will be soft—auction pieces and arrival shots. You'll draw some attention once they realise you're there."

Allegra sighed at length. *"I suppose I'll need to be photographed with Timothy."*

"If you're arriving with him, yes. He's a very handsome man, perfectly acceptable arm candy."

"Won't it upset the lesbians that I'm bringing him, though?"

This time, there was a much longer pause before Sal answered her. *"Just one of them."*

Allegra let her phone fall, glared at the ceiling, and made an incoherent sound of protest. The way this woman *got* to her. It made her want to know things that absolutely did not matter. She typed *'Are you bringing someone?'* and deleted it. She typed it again and deleted it faster.

Get a grip, Allegra, she ordered herself, shoving the dress deep into the wardrobe and heading to the veranda to 'read', which of course meant staring blankly at the same page while her brain did laps around Sal.

The following evening, Vanessa made a very brave and very heroic journey south across the bridge. Apparently 'help sister get ready for billionaire gala' was enough to mobilise her to drive through suburbs full of Sydney's Most Wanted to get to the safety of Point Piper.

She arrived looking very rattled. "I'm going to need a late afternoon coffee to recover," she advised Allegra and Timothy, and then spent a good five minutes ranting about all the 'maniacs' on the roads as if she wasn't one of them.

While Timothy was getting himself ready and making them some light pre-drinks, Vanessa helped Allegra get the dress on, figure out the special bra, and tape everything down. Then she bundled Allegra into a chair and ordered her around while doing her hair and makeup. Allegra dutifully complied, getting the sense that this might be something she had a lot of practice doing with her friends, since it had been literal *decades* since she'd done this for Allegra.

Vanessa delivered with the fashion assistance, as always. By the time she was done with Allegra, she looked more than just presentable. She blinked at herself in the mirror.

Her much-maligned dress was actually a lovely plum colour on her, especially with the soft, understated colours Vanessa had chosen for her makeup. The French braid Vanessa had sacrificed part of the ozone layer to spray-set looked formal enough for black tie, but still relaxed enough to be Allegra. Most importantly, the deep plunging neckline didn't look like it belonged on someone twirling around a pole. It showed a lot of skin—honestly, probably more cleavage than she'd *ever* shown in public—but with the rest of her body covered, it looked tasteful.

"Breathtaking, as always," Timothy told her from the doorway with their drinks. "Although should you really drink this? Won't it ruin your lipstick?"

Vanessa gave him a critical look. "It's long-wear liquid matte," she told him as if he (or, honestly, Allegra) would have any idea what that meant. "It's set, so you're good to drink as much as you want." She took the glasses from Timothy, clinked them together between her hands, and then gave one to Allegra. "Bottoms up!"

The closer they got to the time they were planning to leave, the more restless Allegra found herself. Timothy had already spent their entire dinner the night before lecturing her on how to behave and what to expect, and although Allegra wasn't a big fan of anything formal, she *had* grown up in an upper middle-class family and wasn't a complete stranger to etiquette. "I'm just horribly out of practice," she confessed as she did a few laps of the central room in her heels to ensure she wasn't going to trip and embarrass herself.

Timothy watched her from the doorway, also looking uncharacteristically polished with his fresh haircut. He *was* handsome, she had to reluctantly admit. It was just a pity he didn't try to find someone who would appreciate his coddling.

He smiled. "Ready to go?"

"No," she said instantly, but followed him out to the car anyway.

While they were driving there, Allegra inspected the little clutch Vanessa had packed for her. Her phone was inside, and she was having last-minute nerves about Timothy and Sal being in the same room.

While he was leaning forward and trying to explain to Vanessa how to approach the Museum of Contemporary Art (and Vanessa was panicking because she was in the wrong lane to turn), Allegra managed to get off a furtive text to Sal. *"He still doesn't know—please be discreet."*

"O ye of little faith…" was the reply.

She exhaled, not exactly *reassured*—this was Sal, after all—but at least knowing they were on the same page.

It was a red-carpet drop-off. Vanessa pulled up into the circular driveway, yanking the handbrake and twisting around to face Allegra with intent. "Okay, I'm going to need you to go in there and find me a rich husband," she instructed Allegra. "Or at least find yourself one. No offence, Timothy."

"None taken," he said, amused. "Although I doubt we're in danger of losing Allegra to anyone in here."

Regrettably, Allegra was not as confident about that. She laughed about it with them anyway and then let Timothy help her out of the car.

There was media, just as Sal had anticipated. While it wasn't the scrum she'd been subjected to outside the hospital, the cameras swivelling towards her made her realise these photos would be *everywhere* tomorrow—and her neckline was *very* low. Wonderful. As if Froggy hadn't already declared her a public menace to lesbians everywhere, now she was going to add 'reckless cleavage' to the charge list.

She smiled as best she could and tried not to drag Timothy along the carpet too fast towards her escape.

Inside, incredibly intricate flower arrangements along the wall led the way to Foundation Hall, a hugely extravagant room with towering ceilings and soft lighting.

The tables were large and circular with 10 seats each—Allegra counted 20 or so of them—and above each table hung an enormous flower bouquet like a floral chandelier. Dozens of people were already inside, and as a result there was the quiet hum of conversation.

Allegra cast her eyes over all the beautiful and glamorous women, searching for a sharp black bob and what she expected to be an equally dark dress—and couldn't see either. Perhaps Sal hadn't arrived yet. Feeling a little deflated, she followed Timothy in.

Along one side of the room was a thin table with various items on it, including a number of silver platters holding a single sheet of information. Allegra and Timothy walked along the table.

"A silent auction," Timothy explained. "You scan the QR code beside the item you'd like and use the app to bid." Some of the descriptions Allegra passed were dinners on yachts, holidays, use of a private celebrity chef for a private dinner and hot air balloon rides. "The bigger ticket items will be auctioned on stage later."

At the end of the table was the seating list. They paused by it to search for their names.

"Table six," Timothy said, squinting a little without his glasses. "Along with... six, seven, *eight* Vales." He was speaking quietly, but his tone told Allegra everything about how he felt about that. She swallowed a laugh.

"Go get that grub money!" Allegra told him with a grin, giving him a gentle shove in the centre of his back towards the table.

As she did so, she spotted a familiar figure standing beside the door they'd come in, half-hidden in the shadow of a giant flower arrangement. Her breath caught.

Sal's dress was a satin death sentence. It was black, high-shine and liquid-draping, cut in a sharp slit shoulder-to-shoulder so it drew a straight horizontal line under her collarbones and then fell in a clean line from shoulder to wrist. It poured down her body in a single slender column, flowing over her breasts, hips and slightly bent knee. So unforgiving was the dress that Allegra could make out the subtle line of the bra she'd chosen and see each breath as she took it. It was the dress of someone who knew *exactly* what to do with their body.

Locking eyes with Allegra, Sal raised her drink in a 'cheers' motion.

Allegra felt like a deer in headlights. She may have stood there staring for an entirely inappropriate amount of time if she hadn't heard Timothy's concern as he called, "Allegra?"

A hand touched her arm, knocking her out of her stupor. "Are you alright?"

Her heart was pounding. "Yes," she said, snapping her attention away from Sal. "Sorry. This is a bit much."

Timothy's face softened. "It is, the first time, isn't it?" He led her over to their table to inspect their seating. Over the crowd, her eyes found Sal's one more time.

At their table, Allegra's place setting had an additional spray of flowers; yellow, orange and the olive greens of Australian bush. It had clearly been specifically designed for her, and Allegra was touched that someone had gone to the trouble of making sure that happened. It was a nice gesture.

Timothy was laughing about his place card that read *Guest of Allegra Sinclair*. "My lot in life," he said wryly.

"Allegra! How lovely to see you again!" She recognised that slight Nordic accent from the hospital and turned towards it. Cecilie Vale walked up to her and took her forearms, pulling her down to kiss the air beside one of her cheeks.

"Thanks so much for inviting us tonight, Cecilie," Allegra said as she straightened. "How's Isaiah?"

"'Cece', please," she told Allegra with a smile. "And doing very well, although he has another surgery on Wednesday, which of course means I won't be sleeping between now and Thursday morning." She looked to Allegra's plus one. "And this must be Timothy! I hear we're practically neighbours!"

Timothy shook her hand briefly. "We are! Number 22," he said, transitioning seamlessly into small talk as he always did, "it was interesting to learn you live in the blue house! We've often walked past it and admired your beautiful roses."

That was *clearly* the right conversation starter, because Cecilie warmed immediately. "Ah, yes, my David Austins!" she said, flushing with pleasure at having them praised. "They're doing so well this year, despite all the rain. We've been trialling a new fertiliser." Timothy, having spent years maintaining his nephew's gardens, was keenly interested in learning about this new method.

With nothing to add, Allegra's attention drifted towards the direction Sal had gone. She was still watching that corner and wondering where Sal had vanished to, when fingertips skimmed lightly along her back.

She didn't need to look to know who had brushed past her—especially when the woman stopped, glanced their way, and seemed to recognise them. Sal pivoted towards the table, appearing pleasantly surprised.

"Well," she said in her smooth marketing voice, "looks like I've found the hottest table in town. Cece! Always a pleasure."

Cecilie took one of Sal's hands and air-kissed her cheek. "Sal! I'm glad we could fit you in," she said, sounding like she meant it.

Sal thanked her and then looked to Allegra and Timothy. Allegra's heart stopped in the moment between when Sal looked at her and when she spoke. "Allegra," she said with courteous detachment, "I believe a congratulations is in order about a certain *incredible* donation..." She trailed off, looking across to Cecilie.

Cecilie was grinning. She held her hand over her lips. "It's not announced yet!" she said, looking delighted. "I don't want it to overshadow the gala!" Sal theatrically pretended to shush up and fall in line. They both laughed about it.

Timothy even managed to sound polite. "Ms Lategan," he acknowledged, with only about half of his usual warmth.

'Ms Lategan' returned his smile and then looked to Allegra again. "Such a lovely dress," she said with completely polished neutrality. There was nothing about her voice, her face, or her body language that could in any way hint she had anything but a distant professional relationship with Allegra. "I do hope you enjoy your evening." Their eyes locked for a moment; Allegra made very certain this time not to get trapped gazing at her.

Nodding politely at the other two, Sal sashayed off in the direction she'd been heading.

Look away, Allegra firmly instructed herself, turning back to her tablemates.

Timothy and Cecilie slipped straight back into their garden chatter, leaving Allegra to reckon with just how extraordinary an actress Sal truly was—and what that meant.

The room slowly filled up; the rest of their table introduced themselves as they sat down. Cecilie's husband sat for a moment, had a sip of champagne, and then rushed outside to take a phone call. The rest of the table were various couples of a similar age to Allegra and Timothy, and the very glamorous brunette beside Allegra ('Miranda', she discovered, glancing at her place card) turned to her and looked delighted. "Oh, wonderful! I was thinking of doing the Kokoda Track next year and I'm sure you're just the person I need to speak to about what to expect."

Allegra had never done the trek herself but *had* been posted for a total of nine months in and around Port Moresby, so did in fact have a number of recommendations for her.

While Miranda was listening intently to her, Allegra felt her clutch gently vibrate. Her heart skipped a beat. "Excuse me a moment," she asked Miranda, and took her phone out, her eyes darting up to confirm Timothy was thick in conversation.

"Please inform her the role of 'stunning brunette with your full attention' is already occupied," it read.

Allegra snorted, shooting back, *"Are you going to be watching me all night?"*

"In that dress, Allegra? I can't stop."

God. With how light her chest suddenly felt, she could barely exhale. She put her phone screen down on the table beside her place setting, smiling at Miranda. "Sorry about that." She swatted the butterflies in her stomach and got back into the trekking discussion.

Before long, staff were circulating with bottles of wine. Allegra briefly excused herself to find out if it might be possible to get something a little simpler.

While she was trying to find a waiter to flag down, an older man who'd clearly already had a few approached her. "Mrs Sinclair!" he said, off to a bad start. "You're looking beautiful tonight. Are you here with someone?"

She considered lying and saying 'my husband', but in the end couldn't bring herself to. "Officially," she said with a smile, and was about to make some excuse to escape but he'd already interrupted her.

"Hah, me too! My wife. Very inconvenient." He gave her an exaggerated wink-wink, nudge-nudge look that was probably supposed to invite assumptions about infidelity and then launched into a whole thing about his wealth that may have impressed someone who was *not* Allegra. She listened politely for a minute or two, trying to figure out exactly why he was bragging to her about his various properties and vacation homes and constant trips overseas, and then it occurred to her he was listing his credentials as a *sugar daddy*.

She froze. Before she could figure out a way to extricate herself from the situation, the problem was already solved for her.

"John!" Sal glided over, laying a careful hand on his arm as if they were old friends. "Impact's chairwoman has *entrusted* me with fetching her a chardonnay before she goes on stage. You're the great wine connoisseur; can you help me pick something appropriate for her?" She gave him the barest hint of puppy eyes.

The combination of Sal's request for help and the fact it came from such a strikingly attractive woman proved to be too much for Allegra's drunk captor. "Of course, Ms Lategan," he said, completely forgetting Allegra. "There are some interesting ones on offer tonight!"

As Sal led him away, she glanced over her shoulder at Allegra and shot her a secret smile.

Allegra stood there for a moment, watching the satin move over her body as she walked. She was at least partly grateful Sal was waiting in the wings to rescue her before the conversation got too awkward, but also deeply uncomfortable by how easily she calibrated herself to every audience.

She watched Sal lead him over to the table where people were selecting wines and engage him in some short conversation before he got distracted. Then, she selected two glasses and spun back towards Allegra.

Suddenly, the air was very thin.

Sal approached her in a clean, predatory line, eyes locked on Allegra as she placed one of the wines into her hand. "Come," she said simply and led them a few paces away to where one of the floral features would obscure them from Allegra's table. She stepped into Allegra, her hair just below Allegra's eyeline, so close their glasses could almost clink.

Standing this close to Sal was more intoxicating than the wine in her hand; the familiar, dangerous scent of her perfume reminded Allegra of the last time she'd inhaled it. Allegra stared down at their glasses rather than risk looking up.

"What do you think of my earrings, Allegra?"

The extent to which this woman had her number... "I'm sure they're lovely."

She took Allegra's hand and gently lifted it to brush a long, shoulder-duster earring. Sal's jaw was warm, and the diamonds were cool and sharp on her fingertips.

"Look at me."

Allegra obeyed her, letting her hand fall. Sal had the same smoky eyes she always did, although perhaps a touch longer lashes than she wore during the day. Her lips were understated and matte, in contrast with the high gloss of her dress. *I wonder if that's 'long-wear liquid matte' or whatever Vanessa said,* Allegra thought as she gazed at them, beyond the point of hiding that was what she was doing.

Sal was smiling about it. "I chose this dress thinking of you," she said quietly, close to her shoulder. "Would you like to feel how soft the fabric is?"

Allegra didn't need to be asked twice. She reached out to a neutral part of Sal's waist to run her fingers along the satin.

It didn't matter that the touch wasn't illicit, it *felt* illicit; the satin was warm from her skin and butter soft. "What are you doing?" she murmured.

"Isn't this why you wanted me here tonight?"

Yes, Allegra thought, her eyes lifting over Sal's head for a moment towards a doorway that led outside to the lawns. It was getting dark, but not dark enough to hide them—she couldn't risk those photos turning up anywhere.

Sal guessed her answer by her silence. "Finish your wine," she said as she stepped away, nodding at Allegra's glass. "Let's see what happens."

She gave Allegra a lingering stare and then turned and left with long, deliberate strides that pulled the dress against her every curve.

Allegra stood for a moment behind the flower arrangement, waiting for her pulse to slow. Somewhere in the back of her mind, Froggy's dramatic voice announced a fresh national emergency.

So we're in agreement you've lost the plot, an inner voice said to her, *that woman has you wrapped around her little finger.* Allegra ignored it. Instead, she took a big gulp of wine and opted to return to the table so she couldn't fantasise about any other spots in the room that might be hidden from Timothy's view.

Shortly after she sat down, the chairwoman Sal had mentioned climbed onto the stage: a stately older woman in a pearl-coloured, pearl-encrusted dress. After a Gadigal man had performed a traditional welcome to country, she thanked him and addressed the room, "Good evening, everyone, and welcome." She had a warm smile, and she gave it to the audience. "It's a privilege to gather with so many friends, partners, and champions of the work we do at the Impact Foundation. Tonight is a celebration of what becomes possible when generosity meets purpose."

She went on to detail a few examples of the results the foundation had achieved during the year across different objectives like poverty and conservation, and then the lights dimmed and a highly produced video played.

Allegra might even have been swept in by it, except she had seen with her own eyes the damage private interests like property developers and mining conglomerates had done to the beautiful country they lived in.

Once the video was over and the chair had given them a run-down of the evening: appetisers, main course, and then the auction before dessert, she invited them to visit the silent auction table and bid generously on the items there. "But most of all, please enjoy your evening, surrounded by people like you who have made our important work possible."

The lights lifted back up. Timothy, never missing an opportunity to start the groundwork for helping the wealthy part with their money, turned to Cecilie. "There was a lot about conservation up there—wonderful cause, of course," he said conversationally. "Could you tell me about Impact's strategic goals for tackling poverty?"

Cecilie nodded slowly. "On a superficial level, yes. However, if you'd like to know any detail, I'm going to need reinforcements! I'm not on any of the committees, but our secretary will be happy to have a chat with you. We're always looking for new delivery partners."

"That would be wonderful," Timothy thanked her, and then stood, rebuttoning his dinner suit. "I'm just going to have a look at the bids on the silent table."

Cecilie probably thought he was intending to *place* a bid, but Allegra guessed he was probably going to gauge the level of generosity he could expect from the patrons seated around him.

Allegra wondered if she should be doing the same for Homeward—how, though?! Timothy made it look so easy!—when a familiar shadow descended on the opposite side of the table, apparently to say hello to another guest seated there.

Sal briefly made eye contact with Allegra to subtly reinforce that her appearance was for Allegra's benefit before greeting one of the Vales and exchanging pleasantries.

It gave Allegra the opportunity to quietly watch her; how the very tip of her sharp bob brushed her shoulders as she talked, how her back curved into her hips, and how her dress showed every tasteful detail of the body underneath it.

At one point, Sal offered the woman she was talking to a refill from a central cooler on the table, and leant forwards towards it, causing the boatneck of her dress to gape enough for Allegra to see down to her breasts. She had a tattoo between them.

She was straightening and furtively watching Allegra for her reaction when her eyes lifted and settled on something beyond Allegra. Her smile cooled.

"Not a fan of that vintage, Ms Sinclair?" a warm voice said beside her.

She looked up; it was an older man with relaxed posture and an unassuming smile. He had grey, wavy hair which had a sort of 'Einstein' look about it—a little bit wild—and invisible-frame glasses that gave him the air of someone quietly very intelligent. He nodded at the wine she was nursing. "You don't like it?"

She looked down at her glass; she'd just had that one gulp earlier. Since Sal could hear everything, she didn't really want to insult the choice. "Oh—it's just not really my thing," she admitted, glancing briefly at Sal in apology.

Sal was still smiling, but there was a faint chill beneath it.

The man held his hand out towards Allegra's wine. "May I?"

Eyebrows raised a little, she handed it to him, unsure what he intended to do with it. He took it from her and smoothly handed it to a passing waiter who paused for further instructions. "Then you don't need to pretend, truly," he told Allegra. "Forget what this stuffy lot here expect of you, what would *you* like to drink?"

Allegra glanced back at the table; all but one of the onlookers were highly entertained by this exchange.

"Erm," she said, uncomfortable and unsure how honest she should be about her lowbrow tastes, "I'm more of a craft-beer person."

The man looked expectantly at the waiter, and the waiter nodded to confirm they had them. "One of those for our beautiful heroine, then." The waiter went to retrieve it.

Cecilie was rolling her eyes at his display. "You're absolutely *terrible,*" she said affectionately, chuckling. She reached over to pat Allegra's hand. "Ignore Dimi, he flirts with every woman with a pulse but he's completely harmless."

Dimi?

Allegra froze, but with everyone's attention on her she couldn't look at Sal without it being obvious.

Dimi laughed good-naturedly at Cecilie's assessment of him. "Anyway, Ms Sinclair," he continued, taking a business card out of his lapel pocket and presenting it very ceremoniously to her, "if you need anything—anything at all—please don't hesitate to ask me personally. I'm here to help." He put a warm hand on her shoulder and looked at Cecilie. "Now. You wanted me to speak with someone?"

"Ah yes," Cecilie said to him, and then gestured at the empty seat. "He's gone to make some bids, though! But if you're done with trying to make off with my special guest," she winked at Allegra, "why don't you keep his seat warm—I heard you're a grandfather now! As of Tuesday, wasn't it?"

Dimi gave Allegra another warm smile and rounded her chair, sitting beside her to tell Cecilie all about the new baby. Everyone else at the table returned to their conversations.

Well, almost everyone. Sal was gone.

Chapter 16: Uncalculated Risk

Sal was nowhere to be seen.

That was unlike her. In an instant, Allegra felt the same cold rush of adrenaline she had when her SES phone rang—absolutely ridiculous of her. No one was in any danger. She straightened anyway, looking around to try and figure out which direction Sal had headed in. Nothing.

Standing, she made a beeline to the seating chart to check which table Sal was on. Sal's place was at table 17, but table 17 had no Sal.

The room had plenty of pockets to conceal people—she'd been grateful for them earlier—but now it meant more places to search and more corners to check. She picked the cleanest route through all of them and continued up the hallway.

Get a grip, Allegra, she was telling herself even as she stuck her head in the Women's to check for Sal there, *she's a grown woman whose boss and potential family member flirted with you, that's all.*

Her instinct told her there was more to it, though, and she was wise enough these days to defer to it.

She wove through the crowds of people to the garden door, which was through a short, dark alcove, and emerged onto the terrace by the lawns, scanning the people out there for a small, dark—

"Hello, Allegra."

Directly behind her.

The shock hit her like a freight train. She spun automatically towards the voice, spotting Sal standing right behind her in the shadow of the open door, smiling.

In contrast to Allegra, Sal looked unreasonably calm. "Searching for someone?"

Guess you didn't need the abseiling gear after all, a dry voice said inside her, feeling a mix of relief and embarrassment. "God, Sal," she said, putting a hand on her hammering chest. "You can't do that to me. You're going to give me a heart attack!"

Sal scoffed. "I'm pretty sure that heart is fine," she said, pushing off the wall. It was the long grin Sal gave her that delivered an additional meaning. "Solid gold, some might say."

Maybe that's the appeal, Allegra thought wryly, taking deep breaths to clear the adrenaline. It wasn't going anywhere. "Fuck. In my line of work, the missing person usually doesn't *sneak up on me*."

Sal inclined her head, grinning. "I'm just keeping you sharp while you're on annual leave."

Sal's smile faded, leaving something cooler in its place as they regarded one another. Allegra recognised it from minutes earlier, just before she'd fled Dimi. It seemed ridiculous not to mention it; they were both acutely aware of why Sal was out here.

Her voice softened. "You left."

Sal watched her a shade too neutrally. Eventually, she nodded once. "I did." For a moment, Allegra thought Sal might explain it. Something *did* waver in her expression; it was gone again as quickly as it appeared. The acknowledgement Sal had just given her—not a deflection, not the brush off—was more than she should have really expected, anyway.

Sal wouldn't let her keep it for long. "You came running so fast. I take it you really missed me." Her smirk crept back.

There was no point in pushing for more information. And there was no point resisting when Sal slipped right back into the familiar pursuit of toying with Allegra, not when Allegra was beyond pretending some part of her didn't enjoy it.

Well, two could play that game. Holding eye contact with Sal, she fired back, "Did you *want* me to miss you?"

Sal's eyebrows lifted for a moment. Looking highly entertained by Allegra's challenge, Sal took another small step in towards her, chin tilted up. "Maybe I did." Her gaze swept over Allegra once—slow, measured, and appreciative. There was something evaluating in it. "You're here, so I suppose you granted my wish. Do I get two more?"

"We'll see." Alright, this was fun.

"Ooh," Sal said. "That's different than your usual 'no', Allegra."

Allegra was starting to feel it every time Sal said her name. "You're very hard to say no to in that dress, Sal."

Sal was openly smiling. Clearly enunciating every syllable, she leant forward and said, "How lucky I am that you aren't even trying to say no tonight," and then stepped back, delighted by the exchange. She gave Allegra's dress another glance, and then moved towards the door. "Shall we make our grand return?" she asked. "Separately, of course."

Sal was right, they couldn't go back in together. Allegra let her go through ahead, purely for optics, and not at all because it provided another uninterrupted view of that ridiculous dress doing its best work.

After it disappeared around the corner, Allegra stood outside for a minute or so, feeling a warm evening breeze on her face and neck and letting the residual adrenaline ebb from her.

Not a bad place to flee, really. She cast a look back at the harbour and its postcard lighting, briefly wondering what Sal would think of returning here later—before admitting if they were here together, they wouldn't be looking at the water.

They also wouldn't have been able to enjoy it for long, because *Timothy* would worry if she were missing.

On cue, he appeared in the doorway. "Allegra?"

Of course. She sighed. "Just getting some air," she said, promising herself it wasn't technically a lie.

He walked out slowly towards her. "Do you want some company?"

Yes, Allegra thought, feeling guilty it wasn't his. She shook her head. "I was actually about to come back in. Good timing."

He offered her his arm. "Allow me, then." She took it, because that seemed to be the convention. He looked down at her as they walked through the alcove inside. "I'm glad you seem alright."

Ugh. "Just gets a bit much inside, sometimes."

He nodded, accepting that. "Well, take a breather when you need to." He directed her a wry smile.

Allegra's brow lifted as she realised the opportunities being allowed to periodically disappear without interruption would afford her. "Thank you, I will." She managed a smile at him, already thinking about stealing some more moments with Sal.

Timothy led them back to the table, where Dimi greeted him with a warm handshake. "Cece tells me you're interested in Impact's strategic goals on poverty alleviation this year?" Timothy nodded. "Happy to share," Dimi said easily, "but why don't we start with your organisation? I'd love to hear what you're focusing on at the moment."

Dimi ended up taking the empty seat next to Cece—her husband was gone *again*—and discussing charities and deliverables and things Allegra wasn't fully across. She listened for a short while (after all, she really should be learning the trade) but much of it went over her head. Her mind and her eyes began to wander.

Sal was seated at her own table across the room—Allegra could pick out that black bob instantly. She was deep in conversation with her tablemates. Two of them were younger women, both gorgeous, one distractingly so. An absurd thing to notice, really. And yet she caught herself noticing it twice, then a third time, and then she forced herself to take a sip of her beer and stop simmering about the existence of attractive women within 10 feet of Sal.

After a few minutes, Sal glanced up and caught Allegra staring straight through the crowd. Their eyes met. Sal's conversation didn't so much as pause, but a slow, private smile curved across her mouth. Nothing broad, nothing someone else would notice. Just enough to tell Allegra that she'd been seen, and that Sal was thoroughly enjoying being watched.

Sal's eyes lingered on hers a little, before she very deliberately turned her body a little more towards the more attractive woman, apparently laughing at something she'd said.

It was too deliberate to be a coincidence, and it was too over the top to not be for show—at least by Allegra's assessment. When Sal glanced back across the room at her to make sure she'd noticed, all but confirming she was teasing Allegra—

An entrée landed in front of Allegra.

She sat back, stunned, as the waiter shook out her napkin and laid it across her lap for her.

She glanced up. Sal was laughing and had her phone out.

A second later, Allegra's phone buzzed. *"Eyes on the road, Allegra."*

She scoffed. *"Stop distracting me, then."*

"No :)"

She looked up. Sal raised an eyebrow at her, and then continued with whatever discussion she'd been having.

I'm going to murder that woman, Allegra thought dryly as she watched Sal's earrings brush back and forth across her shoulders and neck as she spoke. She must have been grumbling too obviously because *Dimi* glanced over at her, and then down at her phone.

Busted, she turned her phone over and focused on her carefully sculpted entrée.

People began eating theirs, commenting appreciatively on the food. Allegra didn't really have much reflection on it. It was food, and barely that.

She *did* glance up to see if Sal was enjoying it; Sal had eaten a single mouthful by the look of her plate, and then stood to have a conversation with someone who wasn't a beautiful woman.

"...isn't that right, Allegra?" Timothy put a respectful hand on hers for a moment.

Allegra looked up, wide-eyed. "If you think it's right, then it probably is," Allegra said sheepishly. "But I'm afraid I wasn't listening."

Cece, Dimi and Timothy all laughed at that. Timothy gave her an affectionate smile and her hand a pat. "Cece was just saying that she gets to see you in action next Sunday, and I was just preparing her to be very impressed."

It took Allegra a moment to catch up. Of course Cece would be presenting the keys at the Homeward orienteering event this coming week, where Allegra was supposed to be acting as WHS officer. That must be what Timothy was referring to. "Well, there's nothing more impressive than someone who's sweating, dirty, and probably nagging everyone to slip, slop, slap."

Cece laughed and looked at Dimi. "See? I told you she's a delight!"

Dimi finished his mouthful. "Yes! She definitely makes an impression." He gave Allegra a warm, grandfatherly smile. "With a bit of shepherding, we'll make quite something of her at BSA." He winked at her.

Allegra wasn't sure how to feel about it. While she got the sense it was genuine, she could only think about Sal's immediate reaction to him appearing, and Tom and Zoe's comments about their professional relationship on site. He was a Black, therefore allegedly Sal's family—the family which she was clear about having a poor relationship with.

Then again, did it have to be anything more than simply that? Allegra and her sister Simone didn't get along, and Simone probably made snide comments about Allegra to people in their periphery. Maybe it was a similar situation here. It was possible.

The three of them descended back into chatter, and as their plates were cleared, Allegra found her eyes lifting towards Sal's table again. She wasn't there.

Bored, Allegra drained the last of her craft beer. Perhaps she could get another before dinner was brought out.

She excused herself, taking her empty bottle over to the bar and handing it to the barkeep. He blinked at it, but an unmistakable voice cut in before he could comment.

"The staff clear the tables." Sal approached the bar beside her, amused. "You don't need to clear them yourself."

God. It was so good to see her. "I'm happy to, though," Allegra told her, still feeling a little silly. "One less bottle they need to clear."

Sal looked from Allegra up to the barkeep for confirmation. He gave her an apologetic look that said 'I'm not getting involved in this discussion' and asked Allegra, "Another Henry's?" She nodded.

"Very diplomatic," Sal said dryly to him, shooting him a sidelong, mock-disapproving glance. Then, grinning, she turned her shoulder against the bar to face Allegra, her smile a little too broad as Allegra received her second beer. "We're drinking again, are we?"

Her pulse picked up just a little. "If you can call beer 'drinking'."

"Well, you could always opt for something harder," Sal pointed out, looking deceptively casual for what she was really saying. "Tequila, for example. The choice is always there, Allegra." She leant in.

Allegra inhaled sharply but didn't stop her, trusting that Sal wouldn't do anything inappropriate. She paused with their faces inches apart, close enough to feel her breath, and Allegra finally saw her eyes clearly: deep, warm brown.

When Sal drew back, she already had one of the pre-filled champagnes in hand. She tapped it lightly to Allegra's beer and took a slow sip, eyes lifting over the flute in a clear invitation: *your move*.

Acutely aware she did not have anything like Sal's charm, Allegra scanned the bar for something—anything—she could use to answer that challenge. Her eyes landed on the cocktail garnishes.

Pushing off the bar, she rounded Sal so their bodies were nearly touching, eyes on each other as she went, and then looked down at the tray. There was lime on it.

She picked a slice up with her fingers, and turned back towards Sal, holding it between them with a grin. If she'd been as bold as Sal, she absolutely would have held it between her teeth for a moment before biting it. She wasn't. It didn't matter.

Sal's smile darkened. She turned towards Allegra and stepped in, looking down at the lime, and then looking up at Allegra as she took it from her. She held it for a moment, and then cast her eyes across the room to the dark alcove leading to the terrace. For one bleak second, she panicked Sal might invite her out there again—because she already knew she'd go.

Sal looked thoughtfully back at Allegra, choosing mischief instead. She lifted the lime to her lips, set it there for a moment, and then bit it. A line of juice escaped her mouth.

She finished it, discarded the rind, and leant in to whisper in Allegra's ear, "We can do it the other way next time." She skimmed Allegra's waist with her fingertips and walked off, throwing a knowing look over her shoulder.

Allegra watched her, trapped. *That evil fucking dress is going to be the end of me,* Allegra realised, feeling well on her way to ruin.

She returned to the table in time for dinner service. Timothy welcomed her back with a smile and an appraising glance to check she was alright, which she didn't protest because if he thought she was ducking out for breathers, it gave her far more freedom.

He, Cece, and Dimi still seemed to be getting along like a house on fire, which spared Allegra the need to entertain him all night. It also gave her the option of following Sal's progress around the room—greeting people, pausing for brief chit-chat, and then moving on to the next group.

It was all theatre, Allegra knew. Sal had made that perfectly clear to her many times. Still, watching her smile and laugh, slipping into the role so effortlessly, made Allegra wonder which version of Sal was the one she'd let get under her skin.

When the main course was served, Allegra realised she'd spent most of the last 10 minutes staring across the room instead of listening. She searched the crowd again even as the plate was placed in front of her.

"Looking for someone, my dear?"

Her eyes snapped back to the table. Dimi was watching her, and there was a knowing smile on his face. Alarmingly, there was a touch of pity in it.

Allegra's shoulders tightened. "Yes," she began, trying to think of a plausible story. "There was a woman I...I thought that..." She didn't need to finish, because she could see he already knew.

He nodded, watched her a little longer, and then got back to his dinner.

Allegra stared at hers, horrified at herself for not being at all discreet about the fact she was clearly staring at Sal, but also *not being able to explain* it. To Dimi, of all people. She hoped it wouldn't affect Sal, somehow; she hoped he wouldn't tell *Timothy*!

She cut a piece of chicken and forced it through her lips and down her throat. That was it, she was going to have to keep her eyes on the table for the rest of dinner, for both their sakes.

She was doing so well at pretending to listen to the three of them while planning her next move away from the table when her phone buzzed. She checked it, smiling because she expected it to be Sal—it was *Vanessa.*

"Hi. How's the rich husband coming along?"

Allegra snorted. No point hiding things from Vanessa; she'd extract the truth by force. *"Difficult to focus on nabbing one of those when someone else extremely distracting is here."*

The reply was almost immediate. *"OH MY GOD IT'S HER ISN'T IT. THE GOTH LADY."*

On point as always. *"Timothy's new best friend caught me staring at her. His new best friend is also her boss." And family member,* Allegra thought, but didn't say. That piece of information wasn't hers to divulge. *"So that's where I'm at right now."*

"Timothy's going to cry. You know that, right."

Allegra grimaced. She didn't want to think about it. *"Vanessa, can I please have one crisis at a time?"*

"Hey, don't blame me, the level of shitstorm you got yourself into is genuinely inspired," was the reply. *"Does she look hot at least?? Is it worth it??"*

Allegra glanced furtively up at Sal, who was tilting her head to listen to someone, elegant neck exposed and unfairly distracting. *"Oh god."*

"Allegra. Babe. If you're not scaling that woman like a cliff by the end of the night I'm revoking your bisexual card."

Allegra exhaled all the air in her lungs and turned her phone over, leaning back in her chair.

Timothy noticed. When he looked quizzically at her, she said, "Vanessa." That was enough. And he *laughed* and explained that to his new best friends—which actually had the benefit of perhaps deflecting from the fact Dimi had caught her staring at Sal earlier. Maybe he would just think she was distracted, after all.

It didn't matter that there wasn't much food, because the 'shitstorm' impacted her appetite. She got *some* into her, at least (she needed something to soak up the beer), but ended up letting the staff take most of her food away with her plate.

When most of the plates were cleared, the room lights lowered.

Dimi stood, grinning at them. "That's me," he said, buttoning his dinner jacket, walking up to the stage and out into the light to remarkably enthusiastic applause.

He chuckled on the podium. "You lot can always be trusted to make a man feel important," he told the room, which answered with an easy wave of laughter. "I do have an important job tonight, though, in my capacity as Secretary of the Impact Foundation Board: to put to bid some very, very exclusive prizes that will no doubt be the crown jewels for whoever secures them. So please, take a moment to get out those fat wallets and surrender yourselves to the delightful sport of bidding against your own children, grandparents, and neighbours. Let's begin the auction."

Allegra watched him speak, somewhat uneasy. Almost everyone in this room clearly loved him. That raised a natural question, but she didn't want to ask it.

Instead, given that it was dark again and everyone's attention was on Dimi (and his attention wasn't on her), she looked over to table 17. Sal's seat was empty.

Allegra cast her eyes around the room, spotting Sal up the back, casually leaning a shoulder against one of the pillars, a champagne in hand, apparently watching the auction.

Apparently, because she was looking right at Allegra.

When they locked eyes, she inclined her head a little to beckon Allegra over, and wandered out of sight.

Allegra drew a sharp, involuntary breath, and stood immediately, working her way unobtrusively through the tables back towards the pillar.

Sal was in the shadow of it, waiting for her with a smile. "I bet that's the fastest you've ever attended a call-out." She was looking up at Allegra from under her lashes.

That look made Allegra want to knock the glass out of Sal's hands and pin her against the pillar. Immediately. "Well, I'd have come faster, but..." She gestured at her feet. "Heels."

Sal glanced appreciatively down at them. "Mmm, I'll manage the delay, then," she said, stepping up to Allegra and reaching out a hand to touch the gathered fabric at the centre of her torso, as if inspecting it. She looked slowly up Allegra's body at her, accentuating how much shorter she was. "I like you in heels."

God, and looking down at her like that alluded to an entirely different sort of interaction. Allegra couldn't hide how heavily that realisation made her breathe, and each breath pushed her torso into Sal's hand. She put an arm out to steady herself against the pillar, trying to find her voice. "I like you in that dress."

Sal's smile broadened. "Yes, I noticed how you can't keep your eyes off me." She looked forward, as if she was examining Allegra's own dress. Her fingertips were still at the gathered fabric; Allegra felt them edge onto the skin just below her cleavage, draw a small circle there, and then probe at the edges of the V that stretched upwards. "I like knowing you're watching *everything I do*." Her fingers were drawing a line higher, agonisingly slowly, towards the curve of her breasts. They were nearly there, nearly feeling their rise, their shape, and—

There was laughter and loud cheering from the floor. Heavy applause followed, and a woman's voice was saying, "Thank you! Thank you!" as she laughed.

Several women were suddenly walking past them to use the Women's between auctions.

Sal and Allegra hurriedly stepped apart, so it looked more like they were two people having a private conversation rather than two people about to maul each other in public.

Sal fiddled with one of her earrings, smiling to herself and waiting for the crowd to settle for the second auction.

It was taking far too long. "Can't we take this elsewhere?" Allegra wondered aloud, wanting Sal's hands on her again as soon as possible. She looked out towards the terrace; unfortunately, she could see smokers on it. Then, she looked at the exit.

Sal shook her head. "You're Cece's guest of honour, and I will not give anyone on my side of the aisle the pleasure of chasing me away," she said, and then gave Allegra a pointed look. "And also, there's Timothy."

That made Allegra groan even louder. "I divorced him *five years ago*. When do I get to be free?"

Sal raised her eyebrows. "It was *you* who warned me to be careful of him." She was right, and that's what was so frustrating. "Anyway, I'm not being discreet because of him—although of course I would respect your wishes. I'm being discreet because I have my own situation to manage."

Allegra immediately thought of Dimi catching her stare. Should she say something to Sal?

Before she could make a decision, a woman roughly their age walked right up to them. "Sal, can I borrow you for a sec?" she said, sounding polished and corporate underneath all that glamorous makeup. "We're having trouble closing Brigand and we want an opinion on what would get one of the abstainers across the line. Their board meets on Monday." She grimaced about the timing.

Sal gave her a tired look about it, too. "Of course, Sharon. I'll be there in just a second," she told her, back in marketing mode. As soon as 'Sharon' had walked off to grab a drink while she waited, Sal turned back to Allegra. "I'm afraid I'm going to need to press pause on our little foray," she said. Then, she added a little furtively, "Apparently Sharon hasn't twigged the Brigand board's all men. Someone built like her could shift a vote without touching the pitch deck." She finished her champagne and smoothed her dress, adding almost idly, "People will give you all sorts of things if you make it enjoyable for them."

That line landed in Allegra's ears like a punch in the chest. As Sal left, Allegra watched her, feeling uneasy. It was ridiculous to worry, though, wasn't it? Sal wasn't sloppy enough to reveal her hand in such a way, so it was wasted energy to worry she was turning that strategy on Allegra.

Uncomfortable and probably looking awkward loitering by herself around a pillar, she moved back towards her table at the end of the second auction.

While she was working her way through the tables, a hand caught her arm.

She looked up—at *Dimi*. She froze.

He had the same sort of concerned look Timothy often did, and he pulled her to the side, looking perhaps a little embarrassed to be doing so.

"Allegra, forgive me," he began, shaking his head. "I hope you don't think me out of step, but I couldn't forgive myself if I didn't say something to you personally. You seem like such a nice girl." Allegra's stomach began to drop. "I've known Sal a long time. I can't recall a time she's..." He considered his words. "...*invested* in someone the way she seems to with you. It's flattering, of course. Just remember, her attention is usually in service of a larger design. She doesn't mean harm, not to you. She simply thinks differently about people than you or I."

Allegra stared at him, the hair on the back of her neck standing on end.

He stood back, still looking a mite embarrassed as he held her hand and patted it. "I hope I've made a mistake and there's no attachment there," he said. "But—well, I made my point. Have a lovely evening. My apologies again." He nodded respectfully at her, and then continued to wherever he was headed.

Allegra stood in place, those words ringing in her ears.

This shouldn't be a surprise to you, Allegra eventually told herself, closing her jaw. After all, she'd been dimly aware that Sal had ulterior motives since their first interaction—Sal had been quite explicit that they existed without ever specifying what they actually were.

Why did Dimi's warning feel like such a shock, then?

She managed to find her way back to her seat, collapsing into it and staring at the floral arrangements in front of her. *Because it feels real when she touches me,* Allegra realised, remembering Sal stepping away from her in the bar, breathless and rosy-cheeked. That wasn't acting. Was it?

She looked up; Sal was on her way back to her table, chatting with Sharon and what appeared to be another colleague. Laughing, talking. Bidding them goodbye and then greeting her tablemates as she sat down. It was social theatre. There was no way of knowing how she felt about any of them, really.

That reminded Allegra of what Zoe and Tom had said about her: how basically everyone who worked with her had a breakdown initially over just not knowing what she thought of them.

Maybe that's my future, Allegra thought wryly, pouring herself a glass of water from the pitcher on the table to do something about her dry mouth. But Sal had given her so much more than 'poker face'. Flashes of clarity. Little crumbs of truth when she asked, about her family, or acknowledging that Dimi had thrown her off balance...

God, and Dimi, where did *he* fit into all of this?

Dessert was served at some point; she gave Timothy hers because she just couldn't face eating.

When their plates were collected, a cover band got up on stage and announced they were taking requests from the '80s and '90s. Clearly that was a hit, because the tables started to empty in favour of the dance floor.

Dimi came over again to grab Cece. "All work and no play..." he said to her, holding his hand out. Delighted, she took his hand and then turned around and grabbed Timothy's, pulling him up.

Then, she looked over at Allegra. "Come on, you too!"

Absolutely not, not even when she was in a *good* mood. She politely shook her head.

Timothy patted Cece's shoulder. "Allegra doesn't dance," he told her. "But if you twist your ankle on the floor, she's your girl."

Thankfully, Cece accepted that and the three of them went and joined a larger circle of older guests shuffling to covers of Madonna.

She was alone again. Ordinarily that would mean... she looked up at table 17. Sal was missing. Since the tables were half-empty now, that was no surprise. Sal did *not* strike her as a dancer, but honestly, what the fuck did she know about that woman, really?

Standing, she went through all the heads on the dance floor to see if she could make out that savage black bob. Not finding it, she stood at her table for a moment.

God. Was this worry justified, or was this just the anxiety people generally felt when they were attracted to someone they didn't know very well? It had been *so long* since Allegra had been seriously interested in anyone specific—for any reason, even just sex—she genuinely couldn't remember.

The adrenaline was too much. She couldn't sit down like this. At least if she walked around she could clear it, and maybe she'd find Sal in the process.

People smiled at her as she passed them (such an odd feeling), and even with the cheerful music in the background, she felt an oppressive sense of impending dread that she couldn't put her finger on.

She'd been fighting the urge to be outside in the fresh air for the entire evening, and after having done an entire circuit of the room and not finding Sal, she gave into it. Maybe some fresh air would sort her head out.

She strode through the dark alcove—and nearly collided with the closed terrace door. She tried the handle, it was already locked for the evening.

"I had the same thought."

Jesus Christ, Sal. She turned around to find Sal standing on the inside of the alcove, deep in shadow. "You are creepy, you know that?"

Sal looked unfazed; she may have even been smiling slightly. "Well, to quote Dolly Parton: 'find out who you are and do it on purpose'."

Who are you, then? It was on the tip of Allegra's tongue, *and what are you doing on purpose*? "So, what, purposefully lurking in shadows is part of your identity now?" She turned and leant against the locked door.

Sal smiled slightly. "I'm observing the room from a safe vantage point where no one can see me, but I can see everyone," she explained, and then turned outward again, leaning a shoulder against the edge of the alcove.

Allegra stood up off the door and went to inspect the view, hovering behind Sal. There were a few pillars in the way of the dance floor, and most of the tables were obscured. "Look, it's not ideal," was her assessment. "For a better static lookout position, you'd want..." She gestured slightly towards the IT and lighting box up the back. "...there. Higher sightline, better angles."

Sal looked back slightly over her shoulder. "Mm. This one has other advantages, though."

The knot of anxiety tightened in Allegra's stomach. Part of her wanted very much to slip back into that easy flirtation, and to let Sal say whatever she wanted to her. She'd probably enjoy it; at least in the moment. She couldn't, though. Something was stuck.

When she didn't respond, Sal half-turned, considering her silence. She then beckoned her closer. "Come and see."

Against her better judgement, she did, standing right behind Sal and following her line of sight. The dance floor was very bright—disco lights were apparently a hit with this crowd—and there was what could only be described as a dad dance circle forming near the stage. Someone had convinced Timothy it was his turn in the centre of it. The result was horrific.

"Question," Sal began innocently, "is that the Lawn Mower or is he having a medical event?"

Allegra's voice was strained. "Watching him is giving *me* a medical event," she admitted, and then they both laughed awkwardly, which was at least slightly a relief.

When Allegra straightened, Sal was smiling broadly over her shoulder. It faded into something with a harder, hotter edge. "So," she said, using her lowest voice again, "would you like to pick up where we left off before dessert?"

Allegra was tempted, especially standing so very close to her. But not anymore. She shook her head.

Sal raised her eyebrows. It was a few seconds before she spoke. "Understood." A far too-polished smile replaced the heat. "I'll try not to take it personally." There was an edge to that which, to Allegra's ear, sounded perhaps even slightly hurt?

God, she didn't want to fucking hope. She'd seen what sort of actress this woman was.

Sal went to take a step forward and away from her, and instinctively Allegra reached out and stopped her with a hand on her arm.

Sal let her and looked back over her shoulder in question.

Taking a deep, steadying breath, Allegra stepped forward against Sal's back and—slowly, slowly enough that Sal could stop her if she wished—she slipped her arms around Sal's waist along that liquid satin, drawing their bodies together and hugging her firmly under her ribs.

Sal stiffened. Allegra was sure she would say something ice cold and then coolly unwrap Allegra's arms. She didn't; she turned her head slightly in a moment of calculation. Then, after a few seconds of holding her breath, she relaxed back against Allegra, exhaling at length, and layered her own arms over Allegra's. Her thumbs gently stroked the back of Allegra's hands.

And then they were standing in each other's arms, cloaked in shadow and facing out towards the hall.

It was *ruinous*. Allegra leant into it anyway—holding her was too much of a relief not to. The faint press of Sal's ribs into her arms as she breathed, slow give of Sal's body as she relaxed completely into Allegra, and her own body, welcoming Sal against it with far too easy a surrender.

She turned her face into Sal's hair, feeling how fine and soft it was against her cheek, and smelling the coconut in whatever hair treatment she'd used before straightening it. It was warm, just like the body against her.

At Allegra's touch, Sal tilted her head to grant her better access, and then suddenly Allegra's nose and mouth were millimetres away from the skin behind Sal's ear. It radiated heat, Allegra could feel it on her lips before they'd even touched her neck. She let them touch eventually, resting there a moment while she managed her breathing.

Under her still lips, she could feel Sal's pulse: much faster than it should be for simply standing. *He's wrong*, Allegra thought, closing her eyes for a moment to focus on that pulse. *This isn't acting*.

That realisation caused her lips to part against Sal's skin and—god, was she doing this? She pressed her mouth to Sal's neck, kissing it.

Sal's reaction was immediate. She inhaled sharply against Allegra's arms, pressing closer in their embrace and then letting a rush of hot breath escape her mouth. One of her arms lifted and snaked up to touch the side of Allegra's head.

The heat of Sal's skin guided Allegra as she kissed slowly down the line of her neck. Sal's breath hitched with each new touch—once, when Allegra grazed a sensitive point, she gave a low, quiet laugh and flashed her a wicked grin. Beneath her hand on Sal's stomach, Allegra could feel the muscles tense and ease with every kiss.

Allegra reached Sal's collarbone, pausing for a moment and watching Sal's chest quickly rise and fall.

The fingers on the side of Allegra's head tightened a little; Sal turned her chin towards Allegra's face, looking up at her. It was a clear signal: *I want to see you*.

In answer, Allegra loosened her arms a little and Sal shifted slowly within them, aided by the glide of satin. Her fingers curled at Allegra's jaw as she turned to face her. Face to face, their eyes met—Sal held her there for a breath, studying her with sharp focus as if deciding whether to proceed, or whether Allegra was ready for what she was about to take.

Then, in one smooth and certain motion, Sal slid both hands to Allegra's jaw and pulled her down into a firm kiss.

Sal's mouth met hers with decisive pressure, and then softened, coaxing her into a deeper kiss with a slow and skilled tilt of her head. Sal kissed like she did everything else—decisively, expertly, with a level of control that promised she was holding more skill in reserve. And god fucking help her, Allegra wanted that 'more'. Allegra's breath broke; she grabbed for Sal's waist, dragging her closer, wanting that heat, that impossible fucking mouth, that satin-wrapped body... Everything else paled against the ache of wanting *more*.

Before Allegra could talk herself out of it, she swung Sal up against the wall. Sal let her; from the sound that emerged from Sal's throat as her back pressed against the cold marble, Sal *liked* it. In fact, her hands slipped from Allegra's jaw around her waist and drew Allegra up against her so she was being ground into the stone behind her.

Allegra could feel Sal's breasts pressed against her front, the blade of Sal's tongue against her lips, and—god—one of Sal's thighs ever so slightly slipping between hers. Anchored by their hips, she was sliding her hands up the sides of that satin dress to Sal's breasts, feeling their outside curves against the palm of her hand—

It was Sal's sharp inward breath at that which caused their lips to part. They locked eyes, their heaving breaths mingling between them...

...suddenly sharing an awareness of exactly where they were.

Out in the hall, the cover band was playing Eurythmics, and people were singing badly to it. They were just around the corner from that, and where Timothy, Dimi, Cece and a whole host of people who Sal knew and who knew Allegra were dancing.

Sal was wide-eyed, her expression mirroring *exactly* what Allegra was thinking: *what the fuck are we doing?!*

She put a firm hand on Allegra's shoulder as a clear 'stop'. Allegra nodded breathlessly and stood off her, taking a couple of steps away and putting her own hand to her chest trying to settle her racing heart.

In contrast to Allegra's pacing, Sal stood perfectly still, perfectly poised, eyes tracking Allegra and a stunned but otherwise unreadable expression on her face. They watched each other silently for a few seconds, rendered completely mute by what had just happened.

Eventually, Sal glanced down and smoothed out her dress. "We should..." she began, and then trailed off, abandoning that sentence. She glanced up at Allegra again—her eyes dipping helplessly to Allegra's lips—and then straightened her back, set her shoulders, and walked out of the alcove as if nothing had happened.

Allegra listened to the click of her heels retreating up the hallway in carefully measured steps.

Fuck, she thought, still a little breathless. Was that a huge mistake?

It certainly hadn't felt like one until a second ago; in fact, if they'd been anywhere other than right here, they'd probably still be going. Allegra wouldn't have stopped her.

Those lips. Those arms around her. God, what a torment that fucking woman was, always, in every way. What was Allegra going to do? Groaning, she put her head in her hands for a moment.

No one would have bothered Allegra if she'd stayed in the alcove, but she couldn't stay put without climbing the walls. She checked her makeup in the glossy terrace signage—silently thanking Vanessa for her industrial-strength lipstick—and then crossed to the bar for another drink. She had no interest in drinking it, but holding a bottle and loitering looked marginally less unhinged than pacing alone in a dark alcove.

The band worked through a run of '80s requests, the crowd dancing and drifting to the bar between songs. When the bar closed and the music slipped into obvious wind-downs, the room started to empty out.

Sal was nowhere through any of it. Allegra kept expecting her to reemerge as if nothing had happened, perhaps throw her a sultry glance across the crowd.

She probably left, Allegra realised, and looked towards the exit herself.

Timothy approached her before long, red-faced and breathless for entirely different reasons than she'd been herself. "What a night!" he said, laughing about it. "Thanks so much for staying and letting me collect so many names. Incredible evening. How are you travelling?"

"I'm not sure," Allegra said honestly, but gave him a smile so he wouldn't worry.

"Not really your scene, I know. Let's go—but you should probably come and say goodbye to Cece first."

Allegra let him lead her over to Cece who had clearly had as good a night as Timothy. She gave them both a hug, invited them over 'at some point in the next week or two, I'll let you know', and then Allegra found herself face-to-face with Dimi.

He still looked worried—perhaps more so. "Have a safe trip home, my dear."

Allegra smiled thinly as Timothy led her off, unsettled. Waiting for their rideshare, she listened to Timothy cheerfully recount his fundraising wins and felt guilty she hadn't even mentioned Homeward all evening. He was so cheerful, though, it was difficult to wallow.

Once they were in the rideshare, Allegra took her phone out of her clutch and checked it, but the only text waiting was from Vanessa.

Allegra sighed and opened it. *"I hope the reason you haven't told me what's going on with goth lady is because you're between her legs right now."*

"Jesus Christ, *Vanessa*!" Allegra said aloud, making Timothy laugh as she furiously replied, *"What is your obsession with my sex life?"*

"Look, if I'm living vicariously through you, I need you getting actual action," Vanessa wrote. Then: *"Also, rich wife etc. So???"*

Allegra exhaled. Shaking her head, she smiled a little and texted back, *"Look. I've got to commend your choice of lipstick. That's all I'm saying tonight."*

"OMG!!!!!!!!!" was the reply, which made Allegra laugh again. *"That was worth staying up for. I'm passing out now but don't think you're not going to give me every single detail next time I see you."*

Allegra laughed about that, but her smile faded a little when she thought of Sal. She wondered who Sal would be texting right now—if she was texting someone.

It was nearly midnight when they were dropped off outside the Point Piper house, and nearly 12:30am when Allegra finally scrubbed all her makeup off, showered, and went to turn in for the night.

There was a text waiting for her from Sal as she got into bed.

"Sleep well, Allegra."

Chapter 17: Family Day

Today's the day, Allegra thought, staring forward at the dark road ahead to avoid looking at anyone else in her car. The Homeward Foundation Orienteering Day. She hoped to fuck nothing would go wrong.

Her car felt much heavier with four people in it. It cornered differently, and the centre of gravity felt higher. Going around the sharp, unfenced bends in the early morning half-light with a large chunk of family inside the car made Allegra hyperaware of every bump in the road. Her knuckles were white on the steering wheel.

Vanessa hadn't looked at any of the road at all. She was angled directly towards Allegra, watching her intensely with the pressure of every question she wanted to ask about the gala building up in her like a shaken can of cola. She couldn't ask anything, though, because her 16-year-old twin boys were in the back, playing some online game on their phones with each other.

That suited Allegra just fine. She wanted to think about her day ahead: the safety briefing, the event itself, and the presentation of keys by Cece to Homeward. Media was going to be there; Sal was not. She tried to mentally rehearse the briefing and found herself, annoyingly, thinking instead about where Sal was. "Oh, please," Gerard had said when Allegra asked about Sal's absence. "You've graduated. She trusts you not to need her hovering."

The brief itself was simple. Focusing was difficult—and not just because of the people in her car.

"Maybe I could text you," Vanessa said shortly to Allegra about all the questions she wanted to ask. She glanced furtively back at her boys.

Allegra gestured at her phone in the centre console, in full view of everyone in the car. "I need to look at the road anyway."

Vanessa was fidgeting. "Maybe I could give you *my* phone, and you could tell me exactly what you got up to with her at—"

"Vanessa. You can wait an hour."

The twins glanced at each other; it was Oscar who spoke. "You don't have to be weird about it 'cause we're here. Everyone already knows she's bi—it's literally all over the internet." Beside him, his brother cackled.

"*Oscar*!" Vanessa began, "She does *not* need to know that."

Allegra exhaled all the air in her lungs. "The apple doesn't fall far from the tree," she commented, giving Vanessa a hard stare.

"I did not tell them that," Vanessa promised her. "I don't tell them anything about what you're up to, they only know what's public." She sat back. "I mean, at least Timothy doesn't use social media."

That got Oscar's interest again. "Oh, he doesn't know?"

"He knows," Allegra said dryly, and to Vanessa: "Aaron *does* use social media."

Oscar snickered. "Yeah, he does."

"Right, that's it," Vanessa said, picking up her travel pillow and reaching around to the back of Allegra's LandCruiser to pretend to beat her children up. "Stop causing trouble!"

So much for planning the day, Allegra thought. It was going to be a long drive.

The sun was up by the time they arrived on site. A truck had beaten them there and staff were already putting up the marquee while volunteers climbed out of their cars in various stages of waking up. There were a lot of thermoses.

"Ooh, do you think they'll have coffee?" was Vanessa's comment as they pulled in.

Allegra did recall reading about a coffee machine. "Not for another couple of hours, probably. Set up, first."

Vanessa grumbled about that, but as soon as Allegra had opened her car door, she zipped around the car, wrenched her out of it, and dragged her out of earshot. "Okay, spill," she said, while Allegra's legs were trying to get used to standing again. "Was it just a peck, or…?"

Allegra sighed at her. "No."

Vanessa grabbed her. "Oh my god," she said, "so you full on pashed her at the gala?! Where? In the toilets?"

Allegra looked up at the sky and begged it to take her. Then, she put her hands on Vanessa's shoulders. "We flirted all night, ended up alone after dinner, and kissed for a minute or two." *Against a wall. Hands everywhere.* She patted Vanessa's shoulders once. "I am not expanding on that." Then, she started walking back towards the car.

Vanessa grabbed her arm and was towed along with her. "'A minute or two', *oh my god*?!" she was saying. "That's a *commitment*. I have conceived children in less time, just saying!"

Allegra stopped walking to direct her a profoundly mortified look, and then continued to her LandCruiser.

Vanessa chased the boys out to go and help with the marquee setup, which was probably good for them—but better for Vanessa, who wanted much more information about everything.

While she was unpacking the satellite phones—accidentally counting them twice—Vanessa sidled up, leant against the side of her still-shiny car, and continued to try and drill her for details. When it became clear Allegra had told her everything she was prepared to about the gala, she moved on. "So," she began innocently, "is my future sister-in-law planning to join us today?"

Allegra paused. "No." She kept packing before Vanessa noticed.

Silly to think she could slip anything past her sister, really. Vanessa's smile faded immediately. "Uh oh," she said, noting Allegra's response. "Why not?"

Allegra shook her head, trying to dismiss the worry. "Clay soil and stilettos don't mix." It was technically true, and likely to be one of the reasons Sal wasn't attending. It wasn't all of them, though. "And she only returned from overseas last night, so..."

Vanessa was squinting at her. "She was overseas?" Allegra nodded. "It must have been, like, directly after the gala?" Allegra shrugged; she wasn't sure about the exact timeline. Vanessa relaxed back against the car. "I mean, that's a personal crisis if I've ever seen one. It's probably how rich people have their crises: they freak out and hop on a private jet."

Allegra chuckled a bit at that; it *had* seemed like that to her, even though Sal had specifically said it wasn't personal.

"Maybe she's freaking out because she's fallen for a normal person." Vanessa was leaning on her hands looking speculatively out at the trees. "Although, are you really a normal person at this point? You're everywhere. Maybe you'll end up being a billionaire, too."

Allegra laughed once. "No. I won't be making much at all. According to Gerard, I'll get a percentage of the social media revenue—or rather, I pay *them* a percentage of my revenue. And, honestly, I doubt it'll be that much. I'm really in it for this." She nodded out at the charity setting up for its event.

"Why wouldn't it be lots? You were doing bush safety spots all week," Vanessa pointed out. "I think *I* can lecture people on bush safety at this point, after listening to them all."

She shrugged. "I don't think that's how it works."

"Okay, so we're sticking with the theory that she's freaking out over falling for a normal person, then, right?"

Allegra had to laugh, but it ended up as a sigh. Honestly, she didn't fucking know. Sal had sent her a total of four texts over the last week, and none of them had settled anything. If it weren't for the fact that Sal had packed her diary full of appointments (all carefully managed by Gerard) she might have worried that their impromptu make-out session had changed Sal's mind about—well, whatever plans Sal had for her.

"Allegra." Vanessa clicked her fingers in front of Allegra's face. "Earth to Allegra?"

She swatted Vanessa's hand away like a mosquito, still stuck on those four messages. She looked down at her phone for a second, considering her options. Maybe Vanessa could make herself useful after all. "Can I show you something?"

Vanessa looked at her like she'd grown another head. "Uh, *yeah*?"

Since the second she said 'messages' Vanessa would snatch her phone anyway, Allegra saved time by unlocking it and just handing it to her. Vanessa immediately tapped 'Sal PR' and read aloud, "'There are things I'm saving to say in person'." She put down the phone, gave Allegra a frankly rapacious look, and said very seriously, "Allegra, you are going to be *destroyed* by this woman."

"If you mean that in the literal sense, I agree with you," Allegra said, grabbing her bag, closing the car door, and then giving Vanessa a once-over. "You didn't bring a hat, did you?"

"I don't mean it in the literal sense," Vanessa told her. "And I'll wear sunscreen."

"You'll wear a hat." Allegra opened the door, reached in to grab her ugliest spare hat as penance, and handed it to Vanessa. "Make sure that's on by 10am."

Grumbling, Vanessa followed her over to where a group of official-looking people in the teal blue Homeward Foundation t-shirts were beginning to congregate. Allegra greeted them and shook several hands (and let the volunteers take several selfies with her), and then herded everyone over to the assembly area for the first briefing.

It was standard. Allegra just needed to go over the safety information about the site, warn them about the usual things—particularly sunburn at this time of year—and then brief them on emergency response and how and when to use the satellite phones. "If you're trying to decide if something is a problem, it already is: call it in," she instructed firmly, waving her own phone. Then, they split off into pairs to go and place the waypoint tokens for the families and kids doing the activity.

Vanessa watched uncharacteristically quietly, and then slunk up to Allegra after she'd finished, giving her a private applause. "That's my sister!" she said with a grin. "I filmed some of that."

"For private use, I'll bet," Allegra said dryly, knowing it would be up on social media within the hour of them hitting 5G reception again.

"Can't I be proud of you?"

Allegra was sure that was part of it. *Part*. "Marquee's up so you're going to have to find something else to do with the boys," she observed, nodding at her LandCruiser.

Said boys were milling around it, probably hoping to get back in. It wasn't out of the question (the auxiliary aircon ran okay on her solar panels), but what was the point of being out in this beautiful eucalypt forest on this beautiful day if not to actually experience it?

Allegra let Vanessa deal with them and walked the main route down into the bushland to double-check all her expectations about the terrain.

The volunteers had already worn a clear path to the first waypoint, fanning out to place all of the different coloured tokens. Allegra checked the geolocation—good—the directions the teams had taken—also good—then scanned the area for shade and sightlines. Everything looked right. It was still cool under the canopy, and would stay that way even at midday. Satisfied, she headed back up the hill.

By the time she reached the top, cars were already pulling into the makeshift carpark. One of them was a familiar Ford Falcon from her first visit. She walked over to find Zoe and Tom in the front seats, wolfing down a late breakfast. She waved, intending to leave them to it, but Zoe rolled down the window.

"Hello again!" she called. "Did Gerard tell you? News Corp and Sky are confirmed for the presentation. They'll probably want to interview you."

He *had* said something to that effect, but it was more of a possibility at that point than a certainty. "Wonderful. I'm sure I'll have a spectacular time," Allegra said dryly, before realising she'd picked up 'spectacular' from Sal.

She parked that thought because some of the early arrivers were families with younger kids, which meant she needed to grab a volunteer to watch the carpark and make sure no one got run over.

The area filled quickly. A few Homeward family workers stopped to greet her—names she recognised from email, including the lead event planner—but they were soon swept up shepherding families under the marquee for sunscreen, hats, and shoe checks. There was an entire car of spare shoes, pants, and hats, and volunteers slipped away to fetch them with practised tact when necessary.

Allegra stood back and watched: children wrestling with hats and each other, laughing with volunteers; parents and carers edging into small talk that loosened into real conversation. Family workers nudged quieter kids together and handed out checklists of birds and plants, asking them to help one another.

None of this had existed for her family.

"Mum?"

Her fingers tightened around the satellite phone on her belt. No, it couldn't—could it? She turned towards the voice.

He was standing a few steps away, not close enough to interrupt, but not far enough to pretend he hadn't been looking for her. Tall—taller than she remembered, which seemed to keep happening—and dressed properly for the bush, boots laced, hat tucked under one arm. He looked like such a man now, indistinguishable from the other professionals buzzing around her. That, more than anything else, hit her hard.

For a moment, she didn't trust herself to speak. "Aaron!" Her legs closed the distance between him to give him a tight hug, and then she held him at arms' length to run her eyes over him again. "How did you get up here?"

"I drove," he said. Then, knowing exactly the reaction it would elicit in her, added, "Really, really carefully. I promise."

She found herself checking him over methodically—force of habit—as if it wasn't obvious he was completely fine and even responsibly dressed.

He noticed. "I wore my sensible shoes," he said with exaggerated pride about his hiking boots. She knew he would have preferred to wear sneakers, but apparently her lectures had finally been absorbed by someone related to her. He sobered. "I hope it's okay I came. I didn't want to, like, I don't know, bother you at work or whatever, but the foundation said it would be okay."

God, she was going to be horribly sentimental in front of all these people, wasn't she? "Your dad's going to kill you for missing Church," was all she could manage, pulling him in again for another tight hug.

"Yeah, but he's constantly lecturing me on forgiveness, so, you know," Aaron said wryly, hugging back. "Also," he was grinning as he stepped away, and unzipped his jacket to reveal the teal-coloured shirt all the volunteers were wearing. "I signed up last week. They gave me shifts straight away because they don't have many men, and the older kids prefer someone who has 'lived experience' or whatever they call it."

The embroidery on his shirt read *Homeward Foundation: Volunteer*, and the logo had a little child's drawing of a family on it. God. Allegra *wasn't* going to cry in front of him or anyone else here, so she pushed aside the big tangle of joy and pride and happy surprise inside her to try and focus on the fucking job she needed to do for the dozens of kids already here. "Have you signed in?"

He shook his head. "Where is it?" Allegra pointed him to the register, and then stood back and tried to manage the knot in her chest so she didn't make a fool of herself.

While she was taking some steady breaths, Vanessa sidled up to her. "He looks good."

Allegra nodded, releasing another breath. "Yeah." Then, it occurred to her that Vanessa was unusually calm. She turned her head sharply, looking her up and down. "Did you organise this?"

Wide-eyed, Vanessa shook her head. "Nope. It's all him," she said, guessing the reason for Allegra's briskness. "I just had my moment of surprise all the way over there." She pointed to where her boys were helping one of the delivery trucks.

Allegra relaxed somewhat, and looked back at Aaron. He'd finished signing in and had entered the fray of children, shaking the Lead's hand. He was then immediately handed a big bottle of sunscreen to start covering children with.

"Well, he been training his entire life for this moment," Vanessa said, grinning. "With the amount *you* made me put on him and the twins."

"Look, you married a redhead," Allegra pointed out. "In Australia. And then you bred with him, selectively breeding the most sunburn-prone children in the entire world, right here under the massive hole in the ozone layer."

"And now we're instilling that fear into the next generation," Vanessa said as they watched Aaron very carefully slather up a pair of fair-skinned kids. "So beautiful." She rested her head faux-sentimentally on Allegra's shoulder, and then patted her arm once. "Anyway, the coffee machine's been assembled. You want one?"

Allegra did, so she let Vanessa go and organise that while she greeted the St John Ambulance crew that had rolled up in their van.

By the time everything had been set up and it hit 10am, Tom had his camera out and was following Allegra around at a polite distance. She'd posed for countless selfies (including with the twins), had two awful coffees, and done a child-friendly safety demonstration to a group that had swollen to well over 100 people.

Allegra watched the kids receive their compasses with rapt excitement, spinning in place and waving them around to watch the pins move. Aaron was spinning a five-or-so-year-old in place as he held the compass, big grin on his face as he watched the dial. She also spotted the twins milling around for the presentation of compasses and then take off with one. God fucking knows what they planned to do with it, that would be some later headache.

Looking around, she was struck by how many different versions of family were present—intact, fractured, improvised. Hers, for one tiny moment, felt oddly complete.

Allegra watched Vanessa *suffering* over the decision about whether or not to intervene over the pilfered compass, and then slung an arm around her and gave her a shallow hug. Vanessa sighed, finishing the last dregs of her coffee as Allegra let her go. "Guess I'd better go and make sure the boys don't do anything nefarious with that," she said tiredly, and headed off towards where they were standing hunched over it.

Tom, who had been standing far enough away to not pick up audio but close enough to get good footage, watched Vanessa pass him and then took the opportunity to approach Allegra while she was alone for once. "Got a moment?" She made a 'hit me with it' gesture. "Can you review some of the footage I've taken and okay it if you're happy?"

Allegra blinked at him. "*Me*?"

He shrugged. "Sal told me to ask. She wants it at the end of the day again, and it's easier to just show it to you as I take it."

Allegra was still frowning at him. Sal wanted *her* to okay it? Well, there was no point in probing for more information (it didn't seem like he had it), so she let him roll through the video he'd taken earlier at 2x speed. He'd caught the moments with Aaron and Vanessa—Vanessa wouldn't mind, but she wasn't so sure about Aaron. "Can I just check with my son?" Tom nodded and stood back to wait.

She briefly apologised to the two children Aaron was playing with, and pulled him a little to the side. "There's media here," she said simply. "They've taken footage of us, and they'll take a lot more of it. Should I ask them to keep you out of it?"

Aaron shrugged. "Nah, it's okay, I don't mind. All that stuff about us has never been a secret, so..."

The simplicity of the response unsettled her. Was he ready for the type of attention he was about to get?

He must have seen her expression. "Mum, it's fine," he told her with more certainty. "The foundation makes all volunteers sign media consent forms, anyway. It's not a surprise. Relax, yeah?" He flashed her a bright smile that had a troubling mix of both Lachie and Timothy in it.

With that, he went back to the kids, leaving Allegra a little off balance. She didn't feel comfortable with people talking about him online, but kids these days were always posting about themselves everywhere, so maybe this *was* genuinely normal for him? She had no real option except to trust him on this, anyway. He wasn't a child anymore.

Heading back over to Tom, she told him, "The footage is fine. You can give it to Sal." He looked relieved and nodded, and then pulled back to continue filming.

The permission request still sat uncomfortably with her. Sal had definitely checked in before, but the contrast with how hard she'd pushed Allegra to agree initially was puzzling.

Looking back over at her family again—Vanessa yelling at her boys, specifically—and thinking *I'm glad Tom's not filming that* made something click. *Maybe that's the point of it,* she thought, watching Vanessa herd her boys away from the camera. They were the only difference between now and every other time Sal had wanted something from her.

...had Sal *known*?

She took her phone out and turned it over in her hands, mulling on her options before actually putting words to her question. *"About the veto power over the footage—you expected my family to be here today, didn't you?"*

She didn't anticipate Sal replying immediately; according to Gerard, she was supposed to be sleeping off jetlag. She wasn't. *"I had a feeling they would, so I thought it would be safer that way,"* she replied in exactly the amount of time it would have taken to tap it out. *"Was I wrong?"*

Allegra exhaled, reflecting on her thoughts just before. *"Frustratingly, never."*

This time there *was* a pause. Just long enough to make Allegra worry about it. *"Careful now, Allegra. You're only encouraging me."*

The combination of seeing her name and being able to imagine Sal saying that in her lowest voice made Allegra heady, and put her right back in that dark alcove with Sal and her dress. God.

It took one of the volunteers coming over to ask her a question to get her off Sal and the alcove wall. "Sorry," she said, refocusing on the event in front of her. "Yes—we can do the photo now. I'm sure the kids are chomping at the bit to get into the scrub."

She was herded under the marquee and slotted in at the back with the kids, their compasses, and the mix of guardians and volunteers. When the Lead called the start, Allegra checked her satellite phone, her kit, and that field volunteers were in position.

The kids burst into motion with their maps and compasses out, spilling into the bush with guardians and volunteers in tow. Allegra watched Aaron get swept along by a pack of boys, feeling a brief, intangible tightening in her chest—then a clipboard was pressed into her hands.

The paper was warm, the plastic cover faintly sticky. She logged the start time, signed beside *no incidents*, and stepped out of the sun into a sliver of shade beneath the marquee.

Vanessa returned alone from wherever she'd been and offered Allegra her water bottle. Because Vanessa was Vanessa, Allegra sniffed it suspiciously before taking a mouthful, which earnt her a shove. She grinned, swallowing. "Thanks. Where are the boys?"

Vanessa gave a long-suffering look that said *I am outnumbered*. "They decided they were going to participate."

Allegra laughed despite herself. "*Why*?"

Vanessa had given up. "Who knows why? Probably because I said they had to give the electric compass back if they didn't—so they decided it was their role in life to torture me and had a volunteer agree to sign them up." She took a long drink from her water bottle as if it *did* contain something a lot harder than water. "They're going to come back with a bomb made out of it, I swear to God. You know Oscar talks to Simone on Facebook now?"

Allegra wasn't surprised. "It was *your* idea to keep them in contact."

"Well, they're her nephews, too. Got to say I prefer them rock-climbing, though."

It was quieter without the crowds at the marquee; just a few guardians and younger children remained, with parents chatting as they rocked babies. The lull gave everyone space to check the schedule and reset.

As lunch was set up, a different kind of van arrived with black-suited professionals inside. It double-parked several Homeward cars and earnt a few sour looks as a result. Allegra already knew who they were for.

Sky News and the *Daily Telegraph* followed. She debated going over—she *was* site manager, after all—but fortunately Zoe stepped in first and took care of the logistics.

While she was checking her watch and wondering what time Cece would arrive, one of the workers gingerly approached her. "Uh, Allegra?" she began, grimacing. "Can I borrow your phone? I locked my keys in my car."

Allegra laughed good-naturedly at that. "Which one's your car?" She pointed; it was an ancient sedan. Allegra relaxed. "You can call roadside assist if you want to, or I can try and help."

The girl's eyebrows went up and she brightened a little. "You can open it?"

Allegra went to her own car and popped her boot, ferreting around in it. "Maybe," she said, holding up a wire coat hanger with a grin, and then went and leant her shoulder up against the driver's side window of the old sedan to create a gap in the door. "Does your car have an alarm?"

"Yes..."

"Well, cover your ears then," she said, and then slid the coat hanger into the gap.

The result was immediate: a piercing wail that echoed around the clearing.

Ears bursting, Allegra hurriedly jiggled the hanger around inside until she felt it give a satisfying 'click', then scrambled out of the way to let the girl inside, pulse racing, already scanning the faces turning towards them, already accepting the attention she'd just invited.

No one seemed like they cared at all. She let out the breath she'd been bracing to shout with.

In a few seconds, the alarm stopped anyway. The girl emerged, red-faced and awkward, and scuttled back to her coworkers to debrief about what had just happened.

Tom had filmed the whole thing. "*Please* tell me we can use that," he said, laughing about it as he wandered over.

"I don't know if Sal's going to want footage of me breaking into someone's car circling the internet." She could imagine Sal's face watching it, though, and for that reason alone she told him to give it to her.

Lunch was laid out on trestle tables and families were already trickling back when a stately car, followed by a discreet single-car entourage, rolled into the lot at about one kilometre per hour, with obvious concern for its suspension on uneven terrain.

Allegra had been enjoying watching the children excitedly hand in waypoint tokens and show off their completed checklists, and so was faintly disappointed to have to break away to meet Cece.

She greeted her with a cheek-height air kiss as Cece stepped out of the car. "How did Isaiah's surgery go?"

Cece brightened, seemingly delighted she'd remembered. "Well. He'll probably have a pin in his leg permanently, but that's a small price." She noted Allegra's hat, vest, and WHS gear. "I suppose I'd better stand under the marquee before I get lectured on sun safety." She winked and headed off to greet the staff, distantly trailed by two black-suited, Kevlar-chested men in shiny black oxfords, who looked absurdly out of place in the bushland.

The next arrival was a familiar old Transit van with *Light of the Redeemer Mission* on the side, pulling into the clearing in a manoeuvre that suggested its suspension had long since made peace with God. *Perfect,* Allegra thought wryly, leaving him to occupy Cece while she scanned the returning families for anything needing attention.

He'd come straight from church and was in a full suit; more than once, volunteers mistook him for Cece's husband. *At least I'm not Mrs Sinclair for once,* Allegra thought, watching for the moment he spotted Aaron.

The reaction was immediate: a double take, a shout, then a fierce hug between the two most important men in her life. Timothy promptly took Aaron to meet Cece, who seemed impressed—by Aaron himself, and by the fact he was volunteering. Even from a distance, Allegra could see the gears turning as Cece began plotting a friendship between Aaron and Isaiah. That idea made her uneasy.

Once the children were back, eating, and sitting cross-legged under the marquee, Homeward staff set the organisation banner along the shaded edge. Camera and sound crews clustered nearby, locked in a silent power struggle over positioning.

Allegra had just pulled out her phone to review her interview brief when the Lead appeared beside her.

"This is very exciting!" she said. "Do you know how much she's giving? It must be a lot for all this."

It hadn't occurred to Allegra that they wouldn't already know. "I'm sure they'll share the details shortly," she said, careful not to spoil the surprise.

As people gathered in front of the makeshift stage, more Homeward cars arrived and senior staff stepped out of them to greet colleagues, Cece, and Allegra. There was a simmering sense of anticipation; Allegra wondered briefly who knew what, and whether she was meant to look surprised. The brief hadn't mentioned. So, when the CEO stepped in front of the banner and the cameras began to roll, Allegra—aware at least one lens was trained on her—settled into her best Sal-brand professional smile.

The CEO welcomed them all and presented Cece, who had her own brand of warm, professional smile but to her credit did look genuinely pleased to be there. She thanked everyone for having her and launched into a speech.

"Homeward works with children who feel alone," she said, and let that ring for a moment to the crowd watching. "When these children are most unsure who will come back for them, Homeward supports extended family to step in and tell them, *you're not on your own anymore*.

"These families receive critical support at the hardest part: the beginning. When everything is uncertain, when systems are difficult to navigate, and when love alone isn't enough without someone standing beside you.

"It is my absolute privilege to play my part in supporting these children," Cece said, beginning to smile again. People shifted, whispering to each other, anticipating what she was going to say next. "And to gift an organisation that supports children in temporary homes a *permanent* home of its own: 4 Carrington Lane, Surry Hills—a renovated warehouse with six offices, two meeting rooms, and a large central space for gathering, just a few streets from Central Station." There was a murmur amongst the staff, who were all looking at each other for confirmation of what they were hearing. "We hope this forever home gives Homeward the stability and resources it needs to continue supporting the most vulnerable among us."

There was a swell of excited applause, and then one of the staff members said loudly, "Oh my god?" and cheered. Her colleagues laughed and joined her, and then everyone started talking excitedly about it.

The CEO thanked Cece, ceremoniously received the keys for the cameras, and then shushed everyone. "I would also like to thank Allegra Sinclair." Allegra snapped to attention. "Allegra didn't just connect us with Cecilie and advocate for this work, she trusted us with her story. She spoke openly about her lived experience, and in doing so helped others feel less alone. That takes courage," she said. "Allegra, we are deeply grateful."

Two of the cameras swivelled towards her while she gave the CEO a warm smile and a polite nod—but it was Aaron who she looked at next, not the cameras. The look of surprise and pride on his face fixed itself indelibly in her memory, a moment she would never forget.

Vanessa and Timothy, too, such pride in their faces as they gave polite applause with everyone else.

It—didn't feel deserved. She'd only done what she'd *always* done: the same safety, rescue, and education work she'd been doing for 20 years. The only difference this time was that her efforts had been focused and guided by someone who knew how all these things worked.

She swallowed. And Sal wasn't even here to appreciate her role in it.

The applause stopped, the CEO thanked everyone and Cece again, and then the media went through their interviews with all the key players including Allegra and two very cheerful and well-supported children. They left shortly after that, and Cece and the more senior staff left with them while the volunteers led the kids in some group games.

Then, one by one, the families trickled out and the clearing started to empty of cars.

Allegra had to be the last person to leave the site, which meant waiting for the field volunteers to go out and collect the beacons and token buckets. She would ordinarily have told them to collect the hazard tape as well—except she didn't know who was purchasing the property. Perhaps they'd appreciate the warnings.

With almost all the volunteers and employees gone and the marquee dismantled, Allegra and her family sat around in the late afternoon shade of the gum trees by the edge of the bushland waiting for the last volunteers to return. Timothy had brought food (of course), and they passed it around while they were waiting to leave.

Vanessa—who had finally been allowed to take off her ugly penance hat—leant back in her deckchair, fanning herself with said hat and eating one of Timothy's wraps. "I'm not saying you peaked today, Allegra, but you definitely peaked today," she told her, still staring up at the sky. "I'm proud of you in a way that makes me deeply uncomfortable."

Oscar groaned at that. The twins had been complaining about wanting to go home since the black-suited men with guns left. "Can we go now finally, or do we have to emotionally process this first? There's no internet up here." Vanessa muttered something about practicing his patience (ironic, coming from her), and then Oscar straight up lobbed a grenade into the conversation. "Oh, by the way, Simone says hi."

Vanessa's hat paused mid-fan. "I thought you said there's no internet up here."

"She messaged me."

Vanessa sat up, not believing him for a second. "Show me," she demanded, leaning over and plucking his phone out of his hands to check. "Okay, she did"

Timothy was unmoved, as he always was. "Well, tell her hello from everyone."

That caused a visceral reaction from Allegra. "God, do *not* tell her that." That would be like handing that woman a loaded gun.

Timothy shrugged, swallowing his cold roast chicken. "There's nothing wrong with being polite."

"She will definitely find a way to use it against you."

"There's still nothing wrong with being polite," Timothy told her mildly, looking across at her for emphasis. "People don't stop being people because they've done terrible things."

"Yes, but Simone never stops being Simone," Allegra countered, wishing he'd trust her on this one.

Vanessa was growing increasingly uncomfortable with the tone of the conversation. "Okay, but can we please not slag her off in front of the kids? She's still our sister."

Oscar looked like this had easily been the highlight of his day. "Hey, don't stop on our account, this is hilarious." He tried to wrestle his phone back from Vanessa, who once again proved being small and full of resolve beat being bigger and anything else.

She locked it, tucked it in her pocket, and leant against the backrest of her deckchair again. "Okay, that's enough. Let's have some healthy boundaries," Vanessa said faux-cheerfully. "Today, I'm being proud of the sister who *didn't* commit heinous crimes. Now can I have another one of those wrap-things?"

Timothy was only too happy to share his *truckloads* of food with everyone, but without his phone Oscar was completely insufferable, and both the twins were nagging them to leave.

"Allegra needs to wait until the volunteers get back," Vanessa told him for the hundredth time, sounding about as tired as she looked.

Something occurred to Timothy. "I don't mind driving everyone back?" he said, "I have to go back anyway, it would be my pleasure." Allegra didn't mind either, because Timothy was perhaps a safer driver than even *she* was.

Oscar threw his hands up. "Thank God! Yes! Take us back to civilisation and internet!"

Vanessa gave Allegra a hug as she packed up her food. "Sorry, you know I love you, but I also love the invention of air-conditioning and soft couches."

Aaron was the last to leave. That last hug was more special to her—he was wearing his teal volunteer shirt and a contented smile. It moved something in her chest; she wasn't sure if it was towards happiness or guilt.

He gave her back one last pat. "I'll text you to let you know when I'm home," he said with a smile, and then climbed into his big, sensible car and pulled carefully out of the clearing.

She stood alone in the centre of it, the dust their vehicles kicked into the air around her turned gold by the late afternoon sunlight.

What a day.

It was incredible to think she'd nearly slammed the door in Sal's face two weeks ago and never had it. She shook her head about that; Sal had known exactly what she was doing.

Given that, it just didn't make sense why Sal hadn't come for it. She should have been there to see all the pieces fall into place. After all that planning, why *wouldn't* she want to see all the families celebrating?

She took her phone out, staring at it for a few moments. *"You should have come, Sal. It went really well and you should have been here to see that."*

"Excellent. I'm glad it went smoothly."

Oh fuck off, Allegra thought about Sal's non-answer, and then got annoyed about it again. Worse, she could hear *Vanessa* in her head admonishing her for not being transparent about her feelings, as if that was ever something Sal would accept in any way.

For the next hour or so, while she did another site walk looking for rubbish, stray equipment, or lost possessions, she considered following Vanessa's advice *despite* the fact Sal would likely deflect—maybe even just telling her, '*I wish you'd come.*' There was no harm in that, was there? When her phone dinged again, she wasn't sure what she expected.

Aaron. *"Home safe. Was really good seeing you all today."* She exhaled, feeling her shoulders relax, and all the earlier annoyance drained out of her like water down a plughole. It was difficult to be frustrated with the person who orchestrated all this.

The last volunteers trudged back with the bucket of beacons, signed out with Allegra, and left soon after.

It left Allegra sitting, water bottle in one hand and phone in the other, in the last remaining deckchair, the echoes of everyone's laughter and voices in her ears as she stared out into the bushland.

It was still warm, but the heat was fading and the light was changing. It filtered through the canopy leaves in warm orange and gold, dappling the ground around her.

There was no reason to leave. The transition from day to night in the bush was always magical, and judging by the sky so far, she was going to be treated to a truly spectacular sunset if she stayed here tonight.

She smiled briefly: there she was, using 'spectacular' again. Sal.

With today checked off, she wondered what Sal's next plans for her were. She'd asked enough times to know Sal wouldn't simply tell her—why was that?—but realised as she watched the tips of the gumtrees slowly turn gold that she actually didn't care what they were. Sal's judgement had gifted her today, and Allegra felt safe to defer to it at this point.

She wondered what it would be like if Sal were here right now with her, watching the beginning of this beautiful sunset.

She caught herself thinking *Sal would like this*, and snorted. No, she wouldn't, not really. And they wouldn't be here together anyway; Sal would have vetoed the whole setup. It was nice to think about, anyway, even if the only place Sal probably wanted to watch the sunset with her was on her rooftop terrace.

If she even wants that, Allegra reminded herself. Kissing someone wasn't necessarily an indication that you wanted anything else.

When Allegra's phone buzzed again, she assumed it would be a comment on the footage which she'd have by now. It was, just not the one she had expected.

"He looks like you."

It was such a mundane observation, but for some reason, that felt like the most intimate thing Sal had ever said to her. She typed out a number of replies she didn't send: *He's everything in this world to me. I would have liked to introduce you two. I don't deserve him.*

In the end, she went with 'safe'. *"Yup, he does look like me: absolutely gorgeous."*

"Mmm. You both look very good on camera." That line made her feel somewhat uneasy, reminding her she still didn't know what Sal had planned for her.

Allegra sat with that discomfort for a minute or so before dismissing it. Sal had given her veto power of the footage specifically because of him, and those weren't the actions of someone who planned to use him without consent, regardless of how good he looked on camera. Whatever Sal was planning, she wasn't treating Aaron as collateral.

That mattered more to Allegra than Sal's slightly unsettling reply did.

She was tired. The day had been too full—of people, of responsibility, of things that mattered—to end on 'slightly unsettling', though. Allegra didn't have the energy for deflection anymore.

"Tell me something real, Sal."

Sal made her wait—as she always did for this sort of answer. It came as the sun started to dip behind the horizon, turning the whole bush a rich, vibrant orange. *"I didn't want to sleep today until I was sure everything went smoothly. I knew it wouldn't just be work to you."*

Allegra looked down at the phone, feeling warmth spread inside her chest from the fact Sal had chosen to properly reply. There was so much in that, but only one real way to reply to it. *"You can sleep now, then."*

"Alright. Good night, Allegra."

She watched the typing indicator vanish, then the screen dim, then the phone lock. For a moment, she didn't move, imagining Sal lying her head against those geometric-print pillows and finally resting.

The bush had shifted around her while she'd been sitting still—the light dimming, the air cooling, and the chirp of cicadas beginning in earnest around her.

The heat lifting had caused a slight breeze; a piece of orange hazard tape caught on the boundary fence fluttered in the wind, catching the last of the light. She made a note to grab it later as she got up, folded her deck chair, and moved back to her LandCruiser.

From there, it was muscle memory for her. She unzipped the hard top, unfolded the poles, and fed them through the canvas with practised efficiency. The fabric of the tent was still warm, and she worked on it without rushing and without thinking too hard. At the end of a long and busy day it was a relief just to trust her body to do the work.

She would have liked a shower, but she hadn't filled the tanks; she'd assumed she'd be driving Vanessa and the boys back to Sydney. By the time she sealed the canvas door against the mosquitoes, her dusty boots and cargos were already off and hanging outside, and her phone was beside her pillow.

The last time she'd been zipped up here was after her last day before annual leave—two weeks ago. Those two weeks felt like two years vacuum-packed into the smallest possible space. *Especially with everything Sal puts in my diary,* Allegra thought wryly, her smile already fading.

She's probably sleeping now, Allegra thought, *finally, after waiting for confirmation it had all gone according to plan.* It seemed extremely relevant to Allegra that the confirmation needed to come from her specifically and not from either of her staff, or from Cece's reps.

And yet, Allegra still felt off balance. Like she was waiting for some additional confirmation that Sal had any sort of feelings for her beyond 'useful asset'. What was she expecting, flashing neon signs and grand declarations? Sal wasn't that sort of person—at least, as far as Allegra could tell.

But she was attentive, and logistically available, and she'd deliberately used those unsettling peoplecraft skills to engineer a situation where the people who loved Allegra got to see the best of her, and Allegra got to use the best of her abilities to benefit others.

Honestly, Allegra had to ask herself what the fuck she was waiting for: Sal's full family tree and a vetted description of what she was *really* like when no one was around?

I can learn those things about her over time, Allegra decided. *I don't need the full picture now to know that from what I've seen, I want more than just this.*

More? Her stomach fluttered, and she drew a halting breath. *God, am I really going to do this*? she asked herself, a smile trying uncertainly to make its way onto her face.

I guess I am, she decided, shaking her head at herself and reaching over to get her phone. *Better ask her now before I lose my nerve.*

She unlocked it, already trying to figure out how she'd even word a request like that to—

There was a push notification from her bank app: *You've received $26,750.00.*

"I've received *what*?!" she asked the phone, her voice snapping like a cut guitar string. Half-sitting up, she tapped the notification and logged in to her app.

There, in black and white, was a cheerful banner that announced:

BLACK STANDARD ADVISORY
EFT credit – Threshold Property Group
+$26,750.00

Chapter 18: The Truth

Allegra read the EFT deposit receipt several times, hoping each time that she'd pick up a detail that explained it. She didn't. As far as she could remember, no one had mentioned a 'Threshold Property Group' to her.

Her first thought was that it must be social media related; after all, she hadn't really done anything else yet.

She checked her official TikTok and Insta. There was reposted content and linked stories, all cleared through BSA—nothing new, nothing that explained the timing or the amount.

Also, her understanding was that most of the money was going to be from views or brand deals, and Gerard had given her until next Wednesday to go through the deals he'd shortlisted. She'd been intending to dedicate some attention to that after the Homeward event and hadn't even opened the email.

Just in case the answer was obvious, she opened it right then to check for anything to do with 'Threshold' or $26,750, but nothing like that jumped out at her.

Better ask Sal, she thought, screenshotting the payment and dropping it into the message thread she'd opened for another purpose. *"Hey, I gather you know what this is?"*

While she was waiting for Sal to reply, she flicked on her signal booster, waited for one shaky bar to appear, and tabbed over to her browser to google this Threshold Property Group.

The top result was a slick, overproduced website of sprawling luxury resorts and hotels, barren of anything resembling detail beneath layers of *curated experiences*, *premium destinations*, and *elevated living*. It was exactly the type of corporation that demolished acres of ancient bushland and pristine natural coastline with zero regard for the hundreds of thousands of years that land had been wild and untouched.

Allegra could not come up with one single reason why a corporation like that would be paying her money. In fact, they seemed like the sort of outfit whose bulldozers she'd lie in front of without a second of hesitation. It left a bad taste in her mouth.

She closed the website, letting the arm holding her phone flop by her side on the foam mattress. Maybe it was all a mistake and Sal would clear it up.

The cicadas began to wind down for the evening, leaving only the quieter chirp of other insects, the wind in the gums, and the occasional crack of cooling timber. She lay there wide awake, checking her phone every few minutes—surprised each time to find nothing.

Apparently Sal *had* taken her advice and gone to sleep for once, which meant she really should, as well.

'Should' was something her brain had little regard for, though. It kept ping-ponging between reflecting on how wonderful it had been to spend time with her family today and share all this beautiful bushland with them—and the payment from a *property developer.*

Likewise, she oscillated between '*just tell Sal you'd like to see where things could go*' and '*do you really want to see what level of deflection that woman is capable of?*'.

It ticked past midnight with no reply and no answers, and that's when she plugged her phone into the solar battery, turned it face down, and made the commitment to try and sleep.

She slept badly; unusual for her out in the hinterlands. She was grateful when pale morning light began to creep through the gauze into the tent.

She rolled onto her back and opened the message app again to look at the timestamp for her message to Sal: *Sent 9:37pm.* No read ticks.

Since she was awake herself, she started her morning routine. There were dregs of water in the tanks—stale, but probably fine for a washcloth. She emptied the last of it into her face washer and got the worst of the dust off her before changing into something clean and stowing her rooftop tent. She had disappointing instant coffee and a misshapen muesli bar, and then sat on the bonnet of her LandCruiser and listened to magpies warbling while she waited for 8am.

At 8am on the dot, Gerard would be at his desk—he *did* say she was welcome to call him with any questions, so she called the second the clock ticked over.

"Well, speak of the devil!" he said cheerfully, sounding camp as ever. "I have some *very* glowing emails about *you* in my inbox this morning."

Allegra grimaced. She *was* happy about yesterday, but she had a more pressing issue to attend to. "It went really well," she acknowledged quickly, and then got straight to the point. "I'm sorry to bother you this early in the morning, but I got a payment yesterday I don't recognise from a 'Threshold Property Group'. I'm wondering if you can let me know what it's for?"

"You never need to apologise, my sweet. Let's have a look," he said, and then she could hear some typing while he spoke. "It wasn't anything to do with brand deals or social media, but Threshold is a big client of ours, so perhaps there's something on the projects system that I can..." His voice trailed off as he read through something that clearly required his concentration.

She waited patiently for a response; she could hear him exhaling at the end of the line and presumed he was checking whatever people checked for these things. The wait was unbearable. "Anything?"

He made a neutral noise. "Now it's my turn to apologise: Threshold's client account is a *Bible*. I think I'll be here until Christmas if I try and read all of this." She heard his chair squeak as he sat back into it. "Anyway, that payment would likely have needed approval at exec level, so I don't actually have visibility on it yet."

Allegra exhaled. "Is Sal still off today?"

"Well, she wasn't in here when I got in, so I'm going to take that as a yes. Your calendar is empty, too, so I'll take that as a double-yes. Get some rest!" he instructed, a hint of playful sternness creeping into his voice. "Apparently, you've given us lots of great footage from yesterday: I can see Zoe and Tom with their heads together in Editing. Relax. Leave the rest to us."

Allegra smiled thinly. "Okay," she said. "Thanks." Then she said goodbye to him and hung up.

The sun was beginning to heat up—warming her skin and making all the tussled undergrowth smell very strongly of eucalyptus. It would have been so nice to just lie out here for a while before the UV kicked in, but given how poorly she'd slept with the same set of problems circling her head, she didn't feel like it would be very restful. Better for her to be in town.

Packing up all her breakfast gear, she hopped in her LandCruiser and headed back towards the highway.

Her phone sat secured in the centre console, screen quiet.

Timothy was already at work when she arrived at Point Piper. She dropped the mail in his office and rattled around the central room, waiting for either Sal to wake up or Gerard to get back to her. She considered going for a run, then remembered she'd barely slept. Attempting a nap seemed more sensible—but all it ended up doing was relocating her restlessness to the guest bedroom.

She checked the read receipt again: still *Sent 9:37pm*.

When her phone finally buzzed, she nearly flung it across the room trying to hurriedly check it. It wasn't a reply from Sal. It was an email remittance advice from BSA that had a PDF attachment with all the details.

Fantastic, she thought, opening it and expecting it to make everything clear.

BLACK STANDARD ADVISORY
Remittance Advice

Payment Date: *24 November 2025*
Recipient: *Allegra Sinclair*
Paid By: *Black Standard Advisory Pty Ltd*
On Behalf Of: *Threshold Property Group*
Invoice Number: *BSA-TPG-11482*
Amount Paid: *AUD $26,750.00*
Payment Method: *EFT*
Transaction Ref: *TPG1126-AW*

Description:
Professional services rendered as per agreement.

If you have any questions regarding this remittance,
please contact Accounts Payable:
accounts@blackstandardadvisory.com
(02) 5550 7020

Allegra ran her eyes over it.

'*Professional services rendered as per agreement*'? That read like a default description provided by the software. The whole thing was essentially just a longform version of the push notification she'd received last night.

Her eyes stopped on *'If you have any questions...'* Well, she did have questions, didn't she? Surely there was nothing wrong with making a phone call.

She tapped in the phone number and put the phone against her ear, listening to the ring.

"Black Standard Advisory Accounts Payable, Chelsea speaking," a young and cheerful voice greeted her.

"Hi," she began, already feeling like she was going over Sal's head for some reason. "It's Allegra Sinclair here, I received a payment last night that I wasn't expecting, and I'm just wondering what you can tell me about it?"

"Oh, sure!" the girl answered. "What's the reference number? It will end with -AW."

Allegra read it out to her and could hear her tapping away at her computer on the other side of the phone. "Could it have been a mistake?"

There was a brief pause while the girl was clearly pulling up all of the details. "Nope, no mistake. Everything looks okay at this end: all the authorities are in place."

"Alright," she said. "Do you know what it's for?"

"Well, it's attached to Threshold Property Group," Chelsea said easily, like they *weren't* a major property developer and Allegra *wasn't* a staunch conservationist. "So, I gather it's something you were doing with them?"

"That's the problem, as far as I'm aware, I haven't done anything with them," Allegra told her. "Which is why I'm so confused. There's really no additional information about this?"

Chelsea took a deep breath and let it out, thinking. "Well, I can check the project details?" There was a mouse click. "If you could just give me a moment, I'll have a look at what authorities there are here..." She paused just as Gerard had, reading through information. "So, this is marked highly sensitive by the exec—oh." She paused, brightening. "Apparently you did an environmental assessment for them?"

Allegra stared forward. "Did I?" she asked, confused. "I did one for the Homeward Foundation..."

"That's what it says it's for: 'Phase 1 Environmental Assessment'. The sign off is exec level, though, I can't see any more than that."

"And that's attached to *Threshold Property Group*?"

"Yeah, it's in their cost centre, so it's definitely from them." She sounded certain about that.

Allegra sat back on the bed, feeling sick. "Okay, thanks for your help."

She sat very still for a moment, frowning at the floor as she tapped her phone against her chin. Her assessment had been for Homeward, and the details were very specifically tailored towards group safety—especially for families with children. Why would *Threshold Property Group* need something like that?

Maybe Homeward would know...? Even as she was googling the phone number, she was wondering if perhaps she was making a mistake. After all, whatever it was had been marked 'highly sensitive'.

Well, they should have told me about whatever it was beforehand, she decided a little resentfully, and called the number.

The receptionist put her straight through to their accountant. "Allegra, lovely to speak to you. I heard about what you did for us!" She sounded so warm. It was comforting. "Now: what can *I* do for *you*?"

"Well..." Allegra began, aware of how she sounded. "I have a very strange question to ask. Do you know anything about my environmental assessment being somehow associated with Threshold Property Group?"

There was a pause. "There are two answers to that," she said, laughing to herself. "The first is that I didn't know anything about that specifically, but I *do* know that Threshold purchased the land we did the event on yesterday, and I only know that because I was curious who bought it and for how much! They only paid 1.5 million for it, which is crazy for that amount of land that close to Sydney."

Allegra was beginning to feel creeping nausea, but she couldn't place it. "Wow," she said, to continue the conversation.

"But the proper answer to your question is that in terms of Homeward, I don't think we had anything to do with that: our contract for use was with the bank who repossessed the property. I looked through the contract myself, because I needed to check what insurance we'd need."

Pushing through her unsteadiness, Allegra tried to focus on what next steps she had; at this point, there was no option but to keep following the trail and seeing where it led. "Do you think I could speak to the rep at the bank you were working with?"

She was quiet a moment, thinking. "I can't think of any reason why not? The bank may have privacy processes, but it seems odd to keep them from someone who was clearly involved. What's your email address? I'll shoot her details to you."

Just in case they didn't have her email address on file, Allegra spelt it out to their accountant and then thanked her and hung up.

She had to sit and wait for the email, which meant sitting with the unsettling feeling that she was missing something—or that she *wasn't* missing something and was instead understanding everything.

She checked her phone *again,* still no fucking reply from Sal. She shook her head. Even when Sal was busy, she was texting people mid-call, mid-walk, mid-sentence. It felt—well, Allegra could feel how it felt in the pit of her stomach.

When the email came through, she found the number of the bank rep—'Jacqui', apparently?—and called it.

"Jacqueline Wilson," the woman answered, sounding very corporate.

Allegra wasn't sure which version of her name to use, so used neither. "Hi, I'm so sorry, it's Allegra—Allegra Sinclair. Do you have a moment to talk?"

"Allegra, what a surprise! I heard about the weekend. Lovely work, we were so happy to be able to contribute." Despite her clipped corporate greeting, she sounded warm in the same way Homeward's accountant had. "And now is fine. How can we help?"

Allegra licked her lips, suddenly unsure of what to ask. "This might be a silly question, but I did a Phase 1 Assessment for Homeward that Threshold Property Group now seems to have. I just spoke with Homeward who says they didn't pass it on—honestly, I'm just confused about it, and the link seems to be the land we used yesterday. Can you help me understand?"

The woman paused. "Okay, I have a confession to make: I know very little about all that. I'm just a community engagement manager—I do have colleagues in settlements but I'm not across all the details. Could I pass you on to one of them? I'm sure they'll be able to clarify it all for you."

"Just a second," Allegra asked her. "'Settlements'?"

"Yes, as far as I'm aware, the settlement for that land went through this morning—we needed to wait until after the Homeward event and after all the required documentation was in place. That's about the limit of my knowledge, though."

Documentation. Allegra felt like she already knew the answer she was about to hear. "Did the documentation for the settlement include a Phase 1 Environmental Assessment, by any chance?"

"I presume so, they're needed for settlement for this sort of land. I know they're quite timely to sort out because consulting groups are usually booked out—my impression is that we weren't expecting settlement for some time. I'm glad we were able to get it off our books."

Allegra could barely breathe. "Okay, thanks," she said, and was about to hang up when something crossed her mind. "Can I ask you a really strange question?"

"Of course."

She took a breath. "Does the name 'Sal Lategan' mean anything to you?"

The woman laughed. "Sal?" she said. "Of course! She's in and out all the time with major clients. She's the one who first connected us with Homeward."

Allegra suddenly felt dizzy. "Thanks so much for your help," she said, and then hung up, feeling sick to her stomach.

There's no *way* Sal would've sold the assessment, would she?! She wasn't even involved in it, beyond coordinating Allegra's movements for it and—offering to let one of the juniors proofread it. No way.

Just—*fuck*, no way.

She took her phone out, opening a messaging window. "*Hi Gerard*," she managed. "*Can I ask which exec's sign off would be needed for that Threshold payment*?"

"*Sal's*," he answered very quickly. "*But don't worry about it, we'll figure out what it's for as soon as she gets in. You relax, okay? xx*"

God, it *was* her. All paths led back to Sal.

She opened the message window for Sal again, looking at that *Sent 9:37pm*.

You don't get to fucking ignore me on this, she thought coldly, and marched out of the bedroom, grabbing her keys from the counter.

Time to pay Ms Lategan a visit.

It was a short drive to The Rocks through terrible stop-start lunchtime traffic, during which Sal *still* didn't reply to the text. Allegra parked across the entrance to Sal's private carpark (whatever), hopped out, and went in the front door to the building. Sal's screening camera and intercom buzzer were separate from the others. She leant on it like an angry car horn.

Then, she stood and waited.

She was about to press it again, for much longer this time, when it crackled. "Allegra? What are you doing here?" Sal sounded like she'd genuinely been asleep, and for a split-second Allegra doubted herself. Then, she remembered everything else and the fact that this woman was a spectacular actress.

"Let me up."

There was a pause. "Alright. Give me a moment to make myself presentable."

Allegra thought Sal had meant a literal moment, and so when the moment stretched out to several minutes while she stood there staring at the intercom and waiting for instructions on how to get up, she found herself getting progressively more and more irritated. Why was she making Allegra wait so long?

She was going to press *again*, when it flashed and Sal's voice came through again. "I've opened the private carpark—the easiest way up is to use the lift in that."

Allegra didn't bother responding. She walked back out the front, down to the gate beside the private carpark, and left her car parked across the entrance to it. The lift took an ungodly amount of fucking time to arrive, and then an ungodly amount of fucking time to get to the penthouse, so when it dinged and Allegra emerged into Sal's central room, she half-expected Sal to have aged visibly in the interim.

Sal was not older. She wasn't even fully dressed. She was in the display kitchen wearing a black summer dressing-gown (there existed such a thing?), hair brushed and light makeup applied—both of which would have taken only one or two minutes. She was measuring coffee for the machine, mug in hand, looking *far* too relaxed.

Allegra marched right up to the central table and got straight to the fucking point. "What's going on with Threshold Property Group?"

Sal paused mid-scoop, eyebrows raised a little. "Well, they're a major developer that specialises in luxury resorts, and one of our clients. I'm not sure what you mean by 'what's going on with them'."

There was absolutely *no way* that was not a calculated deflection—and *making coffee*?! "Oh, come on. You know what I'm talking about. The money."

Sal spent a second watching her, and then put her coffee mug down, turned off the machine, and walked slowly around the counter. "A team below me manages Threshold, so I'd need to check any specific details about them. Personally, I work with high-profile individuals," she reached the table where Allegra was standing and noticed the laptop, closing the screen mid-sentence, decisively, without looking at the screen. "And, just so I know exactly what question you're asking me: what money?"

"High-profile individuals," Allegra echoed, watching the laptop close. She laughed once, bitterly. "And boy, do you work us. What was on that screen, Sal?"

She exhaled. "Where is this going, Allegra?"

"You're *using* me."

"Yes," Sal said easily and without hesitation. "And my understanding was that I was very explicit about that and that it was consensual."

"Oh, you were very clear about what you wanted from me," Allegra fired back. "You just forgot to mention you were offering my work to a *fucking property developer* at the same time."

Sal blinked, appearing to be caught off-guard, and then frowned. She held up a hand like she was placating a wild animal. "Okay. Let's slow this right down, because you've said several things that don't—"

Wild animal, indeed. "*No,*" Allegra cut in. "How about instead of you reframing everything you just fucking tell me what's going on?"

"Well, there are a lot of moving parts to how we're managing you but none of them have to do with Threshold," Sal continued, still keeping with her 'I don't know what you're talking about' ruse, "so if you could be a little more specific as to what exactly you've got a problem with, I can explain—"

"If none of them have to do with Threshold, why did I receive $26,750 into my bank account, paid by BSA on behalf of Threshold?"

Sal paused for too long. "If it happened, it must be an error."

That was the final fucking straw. "*If* it happened? I swear to God, Sal. *It happened.* And it's not an error because I spoke to the accounts payable girl! *You* authorised it! There was even a note saying it was sensitive, so you can't possibly expect me to believe that it's—"

Sal's frown sharpened. "I did no such thing."

Allegra threw her hands out. "Oh my god, now you're *lying* to me, too? I should have fucking—"

"I'm not lying to you, and I'm not going to lie to you," Sal cut her off, voice firm. "Now, if you could please tell me the conversation you had with accounts payable, I can—"

"—you can 'reframe' it to me and explain it to me and position me and continue to have me eating out of your hand?" Allegra's voice was so loud she could now hear it echoing off those ridiculous marble walls. "I told you what happened, and you're just saying it didn't happen. It *happened*!" She put her hands on her hips, really looking at Sal, really looking at this person she'd been on the cusp of asking out. Jesus Christ. "You know, I spent all of yesterday on top of the fucking world at the Homeward event. I felt—" she cut herself off for a moment, swallowing, "like what I do matters. Like *I* mattered. And the whole time, you're just back in the office, cashing in on me."

"What you felt yesterday and what you're accusing me of are not the same thing." Sal was tight as a bowstring, but otherwise completely illegible.

It was *that* which really got to Allegra. Sal wasn't defensive. She wasn't angry she'd been accused of exploiting someone she allegedly had some level of care for. She wasn't giving Allegra *anything* she recognised as natural human response.

How could Allegra have thought Sal *cared*? Even with people *warning* her about Sal? "God, I'm so fucking stupid," she realised, feeling that nausea return. "What the *fuck* was I thinking? Dimi was fucking right about you."

That cut Sal's bowstring. She dropped her arms. *"Dimi?"*

"He told me you don't feel the way about people that normal people do and he was fucking right. We're just *resources* to you."

It was the first real emotion she'd seen on Sal's face. "When did he speak to you?"

"Does it matter? He's right, isn't he? Is this why your family doesn't speak to you, Sal? Because you treat them like assets and resources, and—"

At some point during that sentence Sal had checked out, eyes distant, recognition solidifying in them. "I need to check something," she said absently, spinning and hurrying up the curved staircase.

Some naïve, treacherous part of Allegra was still fucking hoping for some confirmation that she wasn't just a number to Sal. Furious, she followed her.

Upstairs, Sal was already sitting at her computer, copying the code from her authenticator and logging in. Allegra walked up behind her, unsure why she hadn't just left.

Sal opened an accounts program, clicked some menu item, and then started tabbing through what looked like logs.

"What is this going to prove, Sal?" she found herself asking. "Are you trying to buy yourself time to come up with why you had *humanitarian reasons* for selling my environment assessment to a property developer?"

Sal paused, turning back towards Allegra for a moment. "Is that what happened?"

Allegra had to remind herself what a good actress Sal was. "You know what happened, Sal. You personally authorised it."

Sal's eyes sat on her for a second, and then she spun back around and pulled up a different log screen.

Allegra had no idea what to expect from Sal, which was probably why what happened next caught her so completely off guard. Sal stopped scrolling, leant forwards, her eyes tracking back and forth over a particular entry.

After a few seconds, she visibly drew into herself, leaning back, clenching and unclenching her hands and then running a hand through her hair in the sort of broad, unpolished movement Allegra had never seen her make before.

She released a breath and then swivelled back towards Allegra. "Is this what you saw?"

Allegra had no idea how to read anything that was on her screen, and Sal would know that. She gave her a tired look.

"Look." Sal pointed at an entry in the log and then read from it. *"$26,750 – THRESH01 – SL (DELEGATION)"*

Allegra shook her head. "That means nothing to me, I don't—"

Sal drew in and released a very measured breath. "It was *not* approved by me. It was approved *on my behalf* by something called a delegation of authority. That's an authority you give to people when you are not available to approve things that need timely approval. That's your 'exec-level approval'."

It took Allegra a moment. "So what you're telling me is that you're trying to pretend *someone else did it*."

Sal's jaw tightened. "It's right there on the screen, Allegra, I don't—"

"You could tell me anything you want about what's on that screen, and you know it—so it still doesn't prove—"

"Allegra," her brows were converging a little, "the one person who has my delegation is Dimi. There's no one else, not even the Chair. The only person who could have approved that payment is him."

Allegra stood back, giving her a hard look. "So, you're trying to blame *Dimi* now?"

"Why wouldn't it be reasonable to blame the person who actually did it?"

Allegra remembered Dimi's apology and soft words to her—he'd known. "He warned me about you. He warned me you would use me."

Sal sat back. "Of course he did."

"And he's right. Look. I'm in here pouring my fucking heart out and you don't even care that—"

"You don't know what I think and feel, Allegra," she cautioned.

That was the fucking point of this, wasn't it? "So here's what I know. I know how fucking spectacular you are at working people—you showed me that yourself. You've *said* that yourself. And boy did you fucking work me," she realised, still feeling *so stupid* about it. "I know you will do and say whatever is necessary to get what you want, including lying about—"

"I am *not* lying to you."

"You're telling me Dimi did this? *Dimi*?"

"Because that's what happened." Again, Sal gestured at the screen as if that would explain anything.

"Why would he do something like that to someone he says he's known for a long time? He even said he cared about you—or something to that effect."

That earnt her the hardest stare so far. Sal scoffed. "He'd do it because he wants to isolate me."

"Why? Why would he do that?" Allegra could only think of that awful, dorky dad dancing Dimi had been doing with Timothy. "That makes *no* sense. I don't believe you."

Sal watched her, clearly deciding not to answer.

Allegra shook her head. "No. You're blaming him because it keeps this neat. Because if you don't, you have to admit you set me up."

"I'm *not lying* to you." There was something tight and strained about her voice.

It caught on something inside Allegra's chest, but she *wasn't going to fucking let it.* "No. No," she told that feeling *and* Sal. "You don't get to seduce me, and use me, and then pretend this is all something we agreed upon while you lie to my face about—"

"Allegra, that's not what—"

"Then fucking explain it, Sal! Fucking explain it! Explain why someone like Dimi would do something this personal to—"

"Because he's my father, okay?!" It burst from her mouth like a desperate shout; she tried to smother it. "And I'm his biggest mistake."

And then silence.

They stared at each other for a moment, wide-eyed.

Sal took a breath—perhaps about to speak. Nothing came.

It was the unbridled horror on Sal's face that made Allegra realise something was very wrong. Sal's face was *never* that honest.

Allegra could see the muscles in Sal's throat tighten. Then Sal stood. "Out," she said once, more quietly.

When Allegra didn't leave—her knees were locked tight, unresponsive, and her feet planted to the floor—Sal took a step towards her, put a hand in the middle of her torso and *pushed her physically* towards the door in a fumbled, frantic movement that caused Allegra to nearly trip and fall backwards despite how much smaller Sal was.

When she reached the hallway, Sal paused in the doorway—too long—then the door closed in Allegra's face.

Allegra stared at the painted hardwood right in front of her. Her breath clouded it.

After a moment, she stepped back from the door, swallowing.

What had—

She took a long, slow breath, still looking at the door. Her *father*? Jesus.

It didn't—she didn't—Well. She frowned at the door.

That whole 'biggest mistake' part finally explained Sal's cryptic comment about her family tree. This was obviously some huge, aching secret for them. It didn't explain why Dimi would allegedly do something like *this* over her head. Or did it?

'To isolate me', why would he do that, though? It was obviously deeply personal, but—

Allegra took another step away from the door, turning a little away from it, scratching the back of her neck, frowning at a different section of the bespoke architecture.

Could she still be acting? Allegra wondered. *Could it maybe be a lie*?

She was forced to admit it could be—feasibly—but generally when Sal was acting, she had complete control of herself, others, and the room. That didn't describe anything about the past few minutes. It was the opposite of what had just happened.

But—Sal had connected the bank and Homeward. Didn't that mean—but Homeward didn't give the assessment to Threshold—but Sal *had* the assessment and could have given it to them herself—but if she planned that, wouldn't she have created some process so Allegra *had* to give her the assessment so it wasn't just an incidental offer she—maybe she knew Allegra would ask and always expected to offer—?

Allegra's head tracked in circles around everything she'd learnt today. Could she possibly have come to the *wrong* conclusion, or was Sal just annoyed to have been—

Wait. Allegra froze in place. If Sal were trying to hide the fact she'd given the assessment to Threshold, why the fuck would she authorise a payment that would basically broadcast that fact to Allegra? Wouldn't it just have been simpler to never tell her than bother with some elaborate lie?

Allegra knew the answer to that question, and she felt *sick*. That was not Sal's playbook. Sal had been using this event to demonstrate to Allegra how they could work together—why would she *nuke* that by selling her out to a *property developer,* of all things?!

She sank against the far wall until she was sitting on the marble floor.

In the cold light of what had just happened, Sal running off at the gala when Dimi showed up made perfect, solid, crystal-clear sense.

She sat there for fuck knows how long, staring at her hands, staring at her phone—the receipt now said *Read 2:49pm*—staring at that remittance.

Peak hour traffic hummed faintly through the windows in the central room; other than that, the only sound was the hum of the aircon system. No sound at all came out of that office. No phone calls, no typing, nothing.

When the latch clicked and the door finally opened, Allegra rushed to stand on stiff legs.

Sal stood opposite her in the doorway for a moment, still. She had her patented neutral expression again, but there were cracks around the edges: red-rimmed eyes and a tight jaw.

She didn't speak. After a moment's pause, she just continued past Allegra to her bedroom and shut the door behind her. The lock clicked.

Allegra slid down to sit on the hallway floor and stayed there, facing the closed door.

Chapter 19: The Set-Up

Allegra would have been much more comfortable sleeping in the rooftop tent on her car, or even down in Sal's guest bedroom. As the sun set, she considered her options. There was only ever one, really.

She rolled up her jacket and tried to get comfortable on the marble floor outside Sal's bedroom door, reflecting that she'd slept in worse places—though not for *many* years. When she woke at the crack of dawn, her body felt four times its usual weight, and she'd acquired an entirely new kind of neck pain.

Sal took a long time to get ready after her alarm went off. When the door finally opened, she was once again wearing a sharp suit, smoky makeup, and a completely neutral expression. She didn't see Allegra sitting in her hallway straight away—she was fixing an earring—and when she glanced over, her surprise was visible.

She stopped in place for a second, door half-shut behind her.

There were so many things to say that 'Good morning' seemed ridiculous, so Allegra said nothing. She just sat and let Sal register she was there.

Sal did. She finished correcting her earring, swallowed, and continued down the hallway to the curved stairwell. Allegra could hear the echo of her heels clicking as she descended.

She stiffly braced herself against the wall to stand and followed her down.

Sal was grinding coffee beans when Allegra reached the central room, facing away from her and towards the sleek grey splashback of the display kitchen.

From where Allegra was hovering near the table, she could see Sal's reflection looking only down at the machine in front of her. She was unsure how to interpret it. Should she leave? The answer was that she probably should have—last night. She stood there, anyway, listening to the intrusive crunching of the grinder.

When the beans were done, Sal carefully transferred the blend to a crystal canister, and then walked it across from the wall unit to the island bench where her coffee machine and mug were. She paused there for a moment, scooping coffee into the filter.

Allegra watched her, shifting her weight between her feet. Without the grinder, it was *silent.*

Sal turned her back on Allegra once more to go and grab something from a cupboard on the wall unit, and when she placed it with a soft tap on the bench, Allegra realised all at once that it was a second mug.

God. She released a breath she hadn't been aware she'd been holding.

Sal didn't look up. "This will take a minute. You know where my guest bathroom is."

Allegra could only imagine how she looked after a day in the bush, two nights with no shower, and spending the night on a hard marble floor. She'd barely even brushed her hair. "I have clean clothes in my car."

Sal turned towards the enormous stainless-steel fridge. "There's a security fob on my keyring."

Other than Sal's laptop, her keys were the only thing on the table. Allegra grabbed them and headed into the lift. Her LandCruiser was where she'd left it: parked aggressively across Sal's private carpark entrance. She winced. After moving it inside, she took a change of clothes from the boot and headed back upstairs to have that shower.

Once she was clean and changed, she returned barefoot to the central room where Sal was now seated at the head of the table with her laptop open and her coffee beside her. The warm and familiar smell of coffee was an odd contrast to the cold reception Sal was giving her. With some remorse, Allegra conceded it was probably deserved.

Determined not to be stuck in a state of liminal acceptance for the rest of the morning—not fully welcomed but not thrown out—Allegra stood at the other end of the table, hands on the very minimalist chair, and attempted to clear the air. "Sal, about yesterday, I—"

"I did not sell your assessment," Sal cut her firmly off. "I did not authorise it. I did not benefit from it." Sal lifted her eyes to Allegra's for the first time since she'd emerged from her bedroom. It was a relief, even if the expression she was wearing was *not* soft. "But," she began less severely, "regardless, the outcome is still dangerous for you."

Allegra absorbed that. She couldn't even hazard a guess as to why that might be. "Dangerous?"

"Dimi won't be content with just causing friction between us. He will want to neutralise you," Sal told her, as cleanly and coldly as if she were delivering a physics lecture. "Pristine, nature-loving Allegra Sinclair doing consulting work for a corporation that intends to bulldoze a huge patch of wilderness near Sydney will read *very* badly if broken by a journalist. He will leak documents to demonstrate it happened."

That sounded—she swallowed. *Insane*. After yesterday, though, she had to admit she probably wasn't an authority on him. "He would do that?"

"He *will* do that."

It all sounded so much. "How do you know?"

"It's what I would do, in his position."

Allegra *stared* at her. There was no expression on Sal's face at all; it was truly shocking. "You would do something like that to someone?!"

Sal exhaled at her. "I'm putting myself in *his* shoes, Allegra." She tempered a little. "I know how this must sound, and I need to apologise for that. This is another situation where I have to bring you up to speed very quickly, because he will act just as quickly. Timing is everything in PR."

Allegra was gripping the chair like it was a steering wheel. She just—couldn't get past that apologetic, warm man doing such *awful* things to anyone, but particularly not to someone who'd never wronged him. It just didn't connect with her. She had to take it at face value, though, or risk being weaponised against Sal again. It was *so much*. "So he's trying to make it look like I'm involved with a property developer," she managed—that much was straightforward. "To ruin my reputation?"

Sal nodded once. "So what I'm going to do, in anticipation of that—and given that the settlement has already gone through so I can't just withdraw the document—is what he won't expect."

Not having a hope in hell of knowing what to expect either, Allegra listened.

"I'm going to go public immediately with a statement to the effect of 'a mistake was made with this document being transferred between clients and used for an inappropriate purpose', get Homeward to issue an official statement in support of you with a copy of the document attached so people can see it's genuinely not for Threshold." She paused to allow Allegra to catch up. "And I'm also going to get an associate I know from the University of Sydney to examine it and give an expert opinion that it could not appropriately be used for any property development purposes."

"Why would he not expect those things, though? Isn't demonstrating the truth a reasonable defence?"

Sal laughed once, darkly. There was no humour in it. "If only. He will expect me to do nothing because moving proactively *always* looks extremely defensive and self-incriminating, and it opens up BSA *and* Threshold for scrutiny. And neither Threshold *nor* the board will be very happy with me as a result." She considered Allegra's lost expression, clarifying, "Your reputation is more valuable than some temporary discomfort at board level."

Allegra wasn't that keen on Sal making sacrifices for her, if that's what this was. "Why, though?" Sal heard Allegra's question, but hadn't committed to a reply before Allegra spoke again. "No, really, *why*? I'm sure there are 100 other people you could make the same amount of money out of."

"If this were about money, that would be true. But you're not interchangeable, Allegra."

She held a breath. Could it be that Sal—? She shook her head, *sighing* at herself. No. No more fucking wondering what the hell was going on.

"Okay, Sal," she said firmly. "I've allowed myself to be dragged into all of this—and not just professionally—trusting that eventually you would tell me what this *big thing you've got planned for me* is. I trusted you enough to stop asking questions. I knew you were keeping secrets from me, though, which is why the fact you were selling me out to a property developer made so much fucking sense." She was resolute on that point. "If you'd been honest with me, I wouldn't have been so easy for Dimi to trick."

Sal didn't correct her. She looked away briefly, and when she spoke again her voice was much quieter than before. "That's true."

"So, here's where you tell me what the fuck is going on, Sal. What *actually* matters more to you than money?"

Sal side-eyed that last comment and opened her mouth to respond—but stopped herself. Instead, she let it stand, drawing a long, deep breath and then releasing it at length. "I hope you're ready to hear this," she said and then sat back in her chair at the end of the long table. "I plan to overthrow Dimi as CEO of BSA."

The sentence hung in the air, intact and meaningless, waiting for Allegra to catch up.

Allegra's first reaction wasn't just shock—it was a hard and instinctive rejection, like throwing up a rancid meal. *Fuck* being part of some corporate power struggle. "And I suppose your plan is to replace him." She was aware of how she sounded.

Sal didn't even try to defend herself, she just shook her head. "I don't care who replaces him. Anyone will be better than him."

That was—maybe fractionally less awful. *Fractionally*. "And he knows, I take it."

"I'm sure he suspects. He's been trying to prevent it for 25 years."

Allegra's eyebrows shot up. "You've been trying to overthrow him for 25 years?!"

Sal appeared insulted by that. "No. That's just how long I've been working there." Hesitating, she added, "I was hired and contained in the same meeting."

Allegra digested that. After a moment or so, she pulled out the chair she was leaning against and sank down into it. Sal had placed a coffee there for her, but there was zero chance she could get anything down her throat right now. "If you knew that was happening," she asked, "why did you stay working for him?"

Sal watched Allegra in silence as she chose how to answer. She looked away, and then down. "I was naïve. I thought working for BSA would move me out of the periphery of his world." Her eyes stayed fixed on the table between them. "I misjudged what performance actually earns."

"Which is what, exactly?"

"Suspicion. Protectionism." She corrected the position of her own mug slightly. "I think he just expected I'd sit harmlessly on payroll, somewhere close and observable. He didn't expect I'd be any good at my job." She hardened somewhat. "If he'd known me at all, he would have known how much of a mistake that was." Her eyes were distant. It was a few seconds before she spoke again. "Genuinely, I think he considered it a kindness."

That, Allegra believed. He *had* seemed so kind, it was like they were talking about a completely different person. She could not reconcile what she was hearing—or the evidence she'd seen—with the sweet old man who'd seemed to have her best interests at heart on the night she met him. "You know, he tried to do me a favour at the gala by telling me I should watch out for you, that you 'think differently about people' than normal people do."

Sal didn't try to contradict it, but Allegra could see the muscles in her jaw tighten. "I'm sure he believes it," she said shortly. "I'm sure he truly believes that removing me early protects everyone else. The company. His *real* family. You." She looked up at Allegra. "Even if there's a cost to your career."

"So he's pre-emptively 'neutralising me' or whatever awful word you used to protect me in the long term from being fucked up by you," Allegra repeated, and then considered the whole big slab of rancid food she'd just been force-fed. "And now you want to destroy him. I gather you want *my* help with that somehow?"

Once again, Sal's lack of attempt to defend herself felt like a deafening silence. She responded only to Allegra's question. "I have a reputation as a highly efficient and effective employee. But to say people don't trust my motives is an understatement. And without trust, people will see what I'm doing as a petty internal power struggle—boring and ignorable."

It—suddenly began to make sense to Allegra what Sal valued in her. "That's why you're always saying how trustworthy people will find me to be. *That's* why you're cosying up to me."

Sal bristled at her phrasing, but didn't correct her. "You're credible where I am not. You're trusted by people who will never trust me, and you can survive scrutiny that would destroy others." She paused. "Currently."

Allegra felt like she'd aged 10 years in the span of 10 seconds. "Fuck, Sal. People think your motives aren't trustworthy because your motives *aren't* trustworthy." She then grimaced, reflecting on what she'd just heard. "But they're also not... unreasonable." What a mess. "So, you want to make me part of all this bullshit."

"Now you see why I couldn't introduce the idea to you earlier. You'd have rejected me out of hand."

Allegra gave her a hard stare. "I'm pretty close to rejecting you out of hand now," she warned. "What will you do if I say no?"

"I would start again, plan something else. Like I always do." The words were tidy. Too tidy—scrubbed clean of anything she actually felt, just like this whole conversation.

That was exactly the problem. This conversation *should* make someone upset. An ordinary person faced with the imminent loss of someone they likely had feelings for *should* be visibly, audibly upset. But not Sal. Sal never represented how she fucking felt about *any* issue, which was part of the reason Allegra was in this whole mess to begin with. If she hadn't seen hard physical evidence Sal was very upset yesterday, she may not have believed it was possible for her to even *be* upset. Dimi had made a comment about Sal not being human about *other* people—she wasn't even human about herself.

God. She couldn't sit here a second longer. "I need to go for a walk," she announced, nearly knocking the chair down behind her as she stood up.

Sal didn't try and stop her. "You already have my fob," she said neutrally, and when Allegra returned from putting her boots back on, there was a travel coffee cup on the edge of the bench closest to the lift. Easy to grab on the way out.

Allegra looked at it, and then at the rest of the empty room. Sal had already gone upstairs to her office. Allegra considered leaving the coffee—especially after everything else Sal had just forced her to swallow—but her stomach was grumbling and made the decision for her. She ended up drinking it all on the spot and heading out.

The footpaths at Circular Quay were choked with people. It took her longer than it should have to push through them and reach the Botanic Gardens, where the crowds thinned and the air cooled under the sweeping canopies of the Moreton Bay figs. She sat among the buttress roots, hidden and wedged into the hollow of one like a purpose-built chair, and stared out through the leaves towards the bay.

She felt hollowed out. Two days ago, she'd been worrying about Sal in the ordinary way—about chemistry, about whether she was misreading things, about what it would mean if she wasn't. Those questions were still there, intact, but they'd been pushed so far to the edges of her mind that she could barely reach them.

Her thoughts kept ricocheting between Dimi and Sal, blame sliding uselessly back and forth, while Threshold's payment sat in her account waiting to demonstrate to the public that she was some sort of corporate sell-out.

I should just get in my car and drive west, she thought, as if it would make everything go away. The idea fell apart almost immediately because of Sal: what she'd said, and what the last 25 years had done to her. The fact that *this* was where her mind automatically went made Allegra bristle with irritation. Sal had dragged her into this! Allegra hadn't asked to be here.

And yet. Was it ever fair to be angry at someone for asking for help, even when that help put you directly in harm's way? What the fuck did she do for a living, if not that? It wasn't like every time a call came in she ran a moral audit to decide if the caller *deserved* to be saved when everything was already on fire.

Her phone buzzed in her pocket.

As usual, she was tempted to ignore it, and only the errant thought of *What if it's the hospital because someone's been hurt?* made her fish it out of her pocket and check it.

Unknown number. Could be a hospital. She answered it and heard a very unsettling voice. "Allegra! I'm so sorry to bother you. Do you have a moment?" *Dimi.*

Allegra froze, the warm breeze no defence against the cold chill that washed over her. "Of course I have a moment," she managed, suddenly remembering Sal being extremely precise about how little time she had to bring Allegra up to speed. She'd been clinically accurate about that.

"Where are you? Would you like to meet an old man for a late breakfast?"

Shit. "I'm actually not sure what's scheduled for me today, can I ask Gerard?" she said, instead of saying 'Sal'.

"I did have a quick look, you don't have anything until two," he said helpfully. "I'm at Horseshoe, it's at the top of the CBA building. Would you like to join me?"

Alarm bells blared in Allegra's head, but she couldn't think of a polite and inobtrusive reason to decline. "I suppose I could come!" she said cheerfully instead of what she wanted to say. "I'm walking though, so I'll be 15."

"Oh, no rush! I'll order you something while I wait. See you soon."

Allegra dropped the phone from her ear for only half a second before immediately tabbing out and calling Sal. Before Sal could make some dry comment about the fact Allegra was phoning rather than texting her, she said urgently, "Dimi just invited me to go have breakfast with him. How do I get out of this?"

There was a pause. "You don't. Go and see what he has to say. Just make sure you have very, very little to say yourself—especially about me and what you learnt yesterday." She spent a moment in thought, and then added, "He will likely know you called Gerard and accounts payable about the Threshold payment, because our CRM timestamps internal file access."

God, Allegra felt *sick*. She was supposed to eat like this? "Okay," she acknowledged, wishing Sal could work some dark corporate magic and get her out of it instead. She climbed out of her fig root chair and made her way back into Central.

The whole inside of the CBA building was like an industrial shell; all steel poles, glass panels and suspended walkways. The lift to the restaurant was clear on all sides, giving a dizzying trip upwards, and the restaurant on the top floor had the same towering glass windows as Sal's penthouse. Dimi was sitting by one of them, his phone upside down on the table as he enjoyed the view.

Allegra was enjoying the knot in her stomach a lot less. The dread only intensified as she approached his table. "Dimi?"

He turned his head away from the window towards her. "Allegra!" he said, rushing to stand so he could grasp her hand and politely greet her.

"So lovely to see you again! Much more relaxed than in a gown, I see. Please, sit!"

'Relaxed' was not a word she would have chosen to use in this context, but she accepted his invitation anyway. There was already a selection of incredibly decadent-looking and artfully presented breakfast food waiting for her. She selected a ham and cheese croissant and made herself eat it.

"I have a confession to make." As he spoke, Allegra stalled mid-chew and looked up. "I know you were concerned about a large payment you received on Sunday night."

Again, Sal had been right about what he'd lead with. She swallowed her mouthful. "Gerard hasn't gotten back to me on it yet," she said, consoling herself that it was the truth.

He nodded, frowning deeply under his bushy brows as he carefully wiped his hands. "Well. There's been an awful mistake with your documents. I'm so sorry about it. It's embarrassing for BSA, really." He shook his head, lacing his fingers and looking down at them a moment, as if he was about to say something really distasteful. "I hope you won't think too badly of her once I tell you this; she does mean well, and I don't think it was premeditated. But Sal spotted an opportunity to pass them on to a property developer who has just purchased that land, and of course they were delighted to pay for them. The developer is a client we've been trying to strengthen our relationship with for many years, so I think Sal just saw an opportunity to increase business and decided the human cost was worth it."

Allegra didn't have to manufacture a reaction to that, because listening to how easily and comfortably those words flowed from his mouth had her cycling through momentary disbelief (maybe it was *Sal* who was lying to her, after all?), shock and discomfort. She had to say something to acknowledge him, though. "A *property developer*?"

She must have been convincing, because he nodded soberly. "Mmm. Awful business. Very against your ethos, I know."

Allegra pretended to process that while she tried to figure out what the hell to say. What would be a natural reaction to hearing this?

'Nothing' was appropriate, apparently. "I'm happy to transfer your management to another BSA rep, if you like. It would be difficult working with Sal again, knowing what she's done, but please don't let her mistake colour your opinion on the rest of us! There are some lovely people in the wider PR team."

Hearing him say that and remembering Sal's comment on Dimi's desire to isolate her made Allegra have the *opposite* reaction to his offer. She mined some half-truths as a response. "Well, honestly, I've had very little to do with her after the gala. I think she texted me four times at most. It's Gerard, Zoe and Tom I've been working with." She paused. "They weren't involved, were they?"

"Oh, no. Not at all. Sal made a unilateral decision, from what I can deduce."

Allegra feigned relief. "Oh. That's good. I like those three very much." At least that much was true.

Dimi appeared to soften a little, relaxing back into his chair. "I'm glad to hear that. I was—well. I was a little worried after the gala."

Allegra had been, too. "I gather that's why she's keeping her distance."

He nodded. "She understands people very well, she just doesn't really let them in." He reached across the table and put a soft hand over hers. Allegra had to fight the urge to fling it off like a spider. "When Sal offers something—time, protection, even kindness—it's on her terms, and it can be taken back just as cleanly." He patted her hand. "You deserve someone who dangles carrots they're actually prepared to give you."

That—struck at a part of her that she couldn't identify. But it made her *violently* angry, on a visceral and instinctive level. This man saying these things about Sal was *her father*.

He seemed to mistake her tight shoulders and clenched jaw as a natural reaction to hearing romantic rejection; it wasn't. She let him speak anyway. "I'm so sorry, Allegra. Truly. As I said at the gala, you're a lovely girl and fabulous new talent for us. The team think the world of you! I hope you can forgive Sal in your own time and work with us towards some truly inspirational goals."

Most of that, she immediately discarded. But the fundraising comment reminded her of the money *this man* authorised. "I want to pay the money back," she said, surprised by the amount of venom creeping into her voice. "Can I do that? I don't want to take that money."

He laughed—apparently finding that sweet. "Of course you don't want to! Very understandable. There's no need, though. Buy yourself something nice! Or perhaps you could treat Aaron."

Hearing 'Aaron' on his lips *chilled* her. The hair on the back of her neck stood on end. She forced a conciliatory smile and finished her croissant—and then the sausages, and then the eggs benedict, and anything else she could put in her mouth to avoid needing to speak.

She didn't need to stay much longer. She managed to get him to talk about his new grandchild—babies were something she could feign at least *some* interest in—and then excused herself by mumbling something about wanting to go for a run before it got too hot.

She then half-walked, half-jogged uphill all the way to Sal's penthouse, let herself in, and took the stairs two at a time up to the hallway and Sal's office.

Sal was poring over budgets when she entered. At least, that's what was on her main screen; one of the others had gone to sleep. She turned as Allegra burst in.

"How much detail do you want?" Allegra asked, breathless.

Sal observed her. "Every word," she said, "in exactly the manner he said it."

She wasn't the actress Sal was, but she did her best to recount exactly what happened. She paused when she got to his assessment of her, though.

Sal's composure didn't look effortless anymore as she insisted, "Hiding it from me doesn't protect either of us." Allegra took her at her word and continued; Sal remained still except to look away as Allegra finished. She didn't speak immediately. "It's a good idea to pay Threshold back," was her only assessment of the whole exchange. "Are you genuinely prepared to do that?"

Allegra gave her a look. "*Yes*." She then opened her mouth to deliver her own assessment of what happened. Other than 'everything he said felt deeply and uniquely unsettling', the only concrete feeling she could recall was the violent surge of anger she'd felt when he'd been 'helpfully' telling Allegra terrible things about Sal.

Dimi was *Sal's father*. As a parent herself, the idea of isolating or 'neutralising' her own child made her stomach turn. It wasn't just wrong, it was *obscene*. Yet the way Dimi spoke—with practised ease—made it seem routine. It was monstrous. "I thought about punching him," she said. "Even if he is a hundred years old."

Sal's expression slipped for a beat; her wide-eyed shock was so uncharacteristic that it made Allegra *laugh*. Sal smoothed her expression almost at once, but ended up chuckling over it a second later, hand over her mouth. She looked perhaps a little charmed. "One Sinclair on house arrest is probably enough," she observed dryly after she'd recovered. "And I'm not sure it would *help* your reputation just yet."

Allegra's smile took longer to fade—longer than it should have. It was good to see her laughing. It had been a while. "You should just leave, Sal. It can't be good for you."

Sal acknowledged her concern, but dismissed it with a headshake. "It wouldn't solve anything. While *his* reputation is intact, he'd find a way to contain me wherever I am. Just my existence is a threat to his reputation as a fine, upstanding family man." Her expression hardened. "But also, why can't I keep this one thing? I *built* BSA. It's where it is because of me. My entire career has been spent shaping that brand from boutique to ubiquitous."

Allegra listened to her, letting that set in as she shifted her weight between her feet.

Sal observed it, then stood and rounded her desk to retrieve the disused guest chair, placing it beside Allegra without comment.

Tired and sore, Allegra sat, gazing down at the padded armrests—that same geometric pattern Sal had on her bedsheets—and tried to process the last few minutes.

Sal broke the silence. "There is something else," she began soberly, her eyes meeting Allegra's for a few seconds. "I think it's relevant Dimi mentioned Aaron."

Allegra's focus narrowed immediately. She sat up straight. "Why?"

"It could have been incidental, just him being friendly. We can't discount that," Sal said carefully. "But it could also be a signal that he knows Aaron is a key motivator for you." Allegra listened, frown deepening. "If he believes you will act in Aaron's interests, he may offer valuable incentives to sway you," she said. "Unfortunately, the opposite is also true."

Allegra's blood ran cold. "He'll threaten Aaron to stop me doing something he doesn't want."

Sal swallowed. "Indirectly. And probably by befriending him himself and getting *him* to unwittingly apply pressure to you."

Allegra really *was* in danger of punching Dimi if he did any such thing. "To *neutralise* and *isolate* me, I gather." Sal nodded. "Well, I'll warn Aaron."

Sal acknowledged that comment with a bleak smile. "It's hard to warn people about Dimi. He's very likeable and therefore warning people about him tends to have the opposite effect: *you're* the one people end up being cautious of." Her comment carried too much certainty to be purely hypothetical.

Allegra was still unconvinced. She wouldn't leave her son exposed. "There will be a way."

"Yes, but I think it's important to be realistic about the difficulty of what you're proposing."

Allegra's expression tightened. "Aaron is a hard fucking line for me. What can I do for 100% certainty that Dimi stays away from him forever?"

"If he thinks Aaron is your Achilles heel, he's likely calling Timothy right now to tee up some sort of nice family gathering," Sal said easily. "But yes, there is a way you can make sure Aaron doesn't become Dimi's next best friend."

Allegra had a feeling she wasn't going to like it. "Is it never having any contact with you ever again?"

Sal shook her head. "It's to take Dimi up on his offer of being transferred to another rep, and then letting him weaponise *you* against *me*." She paused. "He'd offer favours as part of that: get Aaron a scholarship to a prestigious grad school, or internships with world-class companies. It would be very tempting, and a highly effective way to completely ruin me."

Allegra felt sick. "Sal, that's awful."

Sal was unreadable. "Well, you asked," she said. "But no, there may be no other clean way out. If you stay, he will assess you as a risk and shore up every possible avenue to pressure you just in case he needs leverage. It would mean we would need to act in a very rapid, precise way when the moment presents itself to disgrace him," she said. "And if you leave BSA now, he's friends with Cece and apparently now Timothy—my understanding is that he's preparing a very sizeable funding contract for *Light of the Redeemer Mission* on behalf of Impact as we speak." She let that sit. "I'm not sure it's possible to walk away completely anymore."

Neither of them spoke for a moment.

It was Sal who broke the silence. "It—may not matter to you now, but I was meticulous about this. My paperwork was clean. I never did anything, in his view, that would have marked you as anything other than another useful personality for BSA." She shook her head slowly. "I intended to tell you eventually; *after* you trusted me enough to believe me about him, but *before* there was any cost to you. I don't know how he realised we weren't incidental to each other so quickly. Early enough to warn you about me at the gala."

Allegra's blood ran cold. The gala. She knew exactly when Dimi had worked it out. "Sal," she began, "Dimi caught me staring at you there. More than once."

Sal looked up at her again as something finally slotted into place. "He warned you about me *after* he noticed your interest." Then she added, "He may genuinely think it's just personal."

Allegra's puzzle was much less complete. "Is that good?"

Sal pressed her lips together. "I'm not sure," she said. "I'll need to think about it more. But if he just thinks you have feelings for me, it lowers the risk that he'll decide you're a co-conspirator and dangerous in your own right—because *that* is where the real danger lies."

The irony of those words coming out of lips Allegra had actually kissed was not lost on her. "Sal, I'm not a co-conspirator. And I'm not dangerous in my own right."

Sal took the statement at face value. "We're co-conspiring right now," she pointed out, and then moved on. "Anyway, the reason it may not be such a terrible thing is that my original plan wasn't far off this: that we'd be seen together. Often. Pressers, site visits, lunches between appointments. Enough that it stops reading as incidental." She paused. "And starts reading as intentional."

Wait a second. Did that mean—"You planned to have a *relationship* with me to launder your own reputation?"

Sal hesitated. "I thought about it, but I decided against it," she said simply. "It works just as well if we come across as friends."

This fucking woman. "The thought of *actually* making friends with me didn't cross your mind?"

Sal was unmoved. "Would we be friends, Allegra? In the wild?" She sounded unconvinced. "You and Timothy would sooner guillotine me. You wouldn't have given me the time of day. In fact, you tried very hard not to." Unfortunately, Allegra couldn't argue with her logic. "Anyway, it doesn't matter what we *really* are to each other. You appearing to lend your trust and support to me means when I take measures to remove Dimi, my measures are more likely to read as necessary, just, and appropriate by both the board and the broader public. As I said, you are credible where I am not."

Allegra's hands tightened on the armrests until the padding creaked. How did Sal look so fucking calm? She was basically presenting Allegra with a real-life trolley problem. "I honestly just want Aaron completely safe from being weaponised," she said, given it was the one thing she knew. "And you're telling me the only way to absolutely guarantee that is to ruin you."

Sal's throat bobbed. "That's right." She was very, very still.

Honestly, that she was clearly worried Allegra would do that to her was beyond incomprehensible. Of course not, there was *always* another way in situations like this. All Allegra could think of was those red-rimmed eyes yesterday afternoon and then Dimi demonstrating so kindly and casually exactly why Sal was always alone in this big empty house. Allegra knew herself on this front: she wouldn't walk away from someone pinned in a ravine just because they were—well, whatever the fuck kind of person Sal was. "I'm not going to ruin you, Sal," she said, repelled by the idea. "So, I guess I'm staying to get rid of that monster so we can *all* be safe."

Sal's brows lifted as she met Allegra's eyes; she clearly hadn't expected her to agree. She opened her mouth to say something, but Allegra got in first. "I don't fucking forgive you for dragging us into this, by the way. Even if you were *very careful* or whatever you said about it."

"Then don't," Sal said quietly. "We can do this without you forgiving me."

Allegra shook her head. What the fuck was she doing? "Okay," she said, drumming her hands on the armrests of her chair. "Then I guess we're doing this."

Chapter 20: Without the Mask

"There's something I need to discuss with you." Curled uncomfortably in one of the dining chairs in Sal's atrium, Allegra stared at the message she was composing, wondering if it was too cold. Would it make Aaron think something very serious was wrong? After all, if someone sent *her* that message, she'd think they had cancer. She tried adding a smiley, but that just made it feel like something Timothy would say, and a grinning face made it look like a lottery win disclosure. She deleted the smiley, the whole message, and then grumbled at her empty text field. The words felt heavier than the task warranted.

Maybe... *"I just need to warn you about someone who might approach you"*? Or did that do exactly what Sal warned it would and come off as slightly unhinged once Dimi had charmed him?

Allegra was frowning down at her phone when Sal answered hers. She bristled—a quick, unhelpful flash of *this is your fault*—and then caught herself. As Aaron's mother, she should be glad of the excuse to reach out. She got stuck on that thought and had already forgotten about Sal again by the time she heard her dictating familiar words to whoever was on the line.

"That's the line of the Phase 1 that we really need to be focusing on," Sal was telling whoever her associate at the university was, "'limited to participant safety considerations'. Make sure that your assessment specifically quotes that and the 'participant and family safety' line." She paused. "Yes, 1:30pm. I know it's tight, but I have a meeting soon after that and need to circulate this beforehand."

Allegra listened for a minute or two, but lost interest quickly as they were mostly discussing the wording. There was a pause in the exchange while Sal was on hold and tinny hold music played through the receiver.

Allegra was staring at her messaging app and half-listening to the hold music when Sal spoke—Allegra realised, to her. "What have you got so far?" Allegra looked up. Sal nodded at her phone. "To Aaron."

Of course she'd figured out what Allegra was doing. Allegra pressed her lips together, looking back at her phone. "Nothing, at the moment."

Sal smiled slightly at that. "It's harder than you expect."

Allegra scrunched up her face. Since she'd just heard Sal parse for two minutes the difference in impact between 'release' and 'disclose', she put it to her. "What do *you* suggest, then?"

"I suggest not warning him at all," Sal said simply. "Strengthen your own relationship with him."

Allegra scoffed. "You sound like my sister."

Sal's expression shifted just enough to suggest that if two people were giving the same advice, the problem might not be the advice. "Well, then." She started scrolling through the emails on her laptop with the hand that wasn't holding her phone to her ear.

Allegra sighed, looking back down at that empty message box. "She thinks I should have lunch with him."

That, Sal disagreed with. "That's the kind of thing you do out of politeness, not interest," she said. "Do something more personal."

"More personal?"

"What does he like?" Sal asked. "Tennis? Call of Duty? Go do it with him. People love sharing things they're passionate about."

"Well, he does love his PlayStation." Allegra remembered how she'd never been able to peel him off it when she visited, and then remembered he'd still been in high school then. She sank further into the chair. "Or does he?! God. I have no idea what he loves anymore."

"He was at the Homeward event," Sal pointed out, and Allegra nodded. "Well, maybe you could do some volunteering with him."

Allegra half-smiled at that for another reason: now Sal sounded like *Timothy*. Her smile faded as she considered her options, however. "The whole thing just seems very fake." She imitated herself. "Hey, son, let's go plant some trees together!"

Sal warmed a little at that. "Setting it up can feel fake when you know it's for a specific purpose," she said. "Actually spending time together will feel more real." Her expression and register abruptly changed as she turned her attention back to her phone. "Not at all, Kelly, I was just doing some admin while you were busy," she said in her smooth marketing voice. "What's QA's verdict?"

Allegra sat back, waited for Sal to finish, then made her own call to Vanessa. "I need to talk to you about Aaron."

"One day you're going to call because you want to spend time with your little sister..." Vanessa said with exaggerated tragedy. Allegra could hear the smile in her voice. "Want a late lunch? I'm free until school pickup."

"As much as I'd love a repeat of you going through my phone, I have meetings this afternoon," Allegra said briskly, and got to the point. "I need to know what Aaron is into."

She snorted. "Have you lost his phone number?"

Allegra let that pass. "I'm following *your advice*," she explained. "Has he talked about anything he's into recently?"

Vanessa laughed openly down the phone. "He's 22, Allegra, he sometimes asks me if he can borrow my steam mop. That's about it. He talks to the twins more." She sobered. "Also, just FYI, Timothy called me this morning to check that you're okay because apparently he hasn't heard from you the last two nights, and all your clothes and gear are still at his. I told him you just stayed up in the bush and that he needs to get a new wife."

Allegra rubbed her eyes. "Vanessa..."

Vanessa paused, as if considering whether to let that go. When she spoke again, her voice was thick with mischief. "But you just told me you have meetings."

"Yeah." Allegra wasn't following.

"You didn't stay out bush. At least not last night."

Allegra didn't know how to answer that, so she didn't.

Vanessa sounded triumphant. "You stayed with her, didn't you?"

Oh, for fuck's sake. Allegra glanced up furtively at Sal. It was too late to rush outside with this call, wasn't it? She turned away from the table and cupped her hand to the phone, as if that would help. "It doesn't mean what you think it means."

Vanessa was laughing for a different reason, now. "It does," she declared. "I'm living! Are you going to tell Aaron about his new evil stepmother? Is that what this is about?"

Sal looked appropriately disinterested, which was how Allegra knew she was fucking listening. No smirk. No usual smug comment. That restraint felt recent and deliberate. To Vanessa, Allegra hissed, "I will text you," and then hung up.

She put her phone face-down on the table and her head briefly in her hands. God. She looked up at Sal again—she hadn't moved, but there was a ghost of a grin on her lips. "Don't you start," Allegra warned her. "Not after this morning."

"I said nothing," Sal pointed out far too innocently.

"You never need to say anything," Allegra fired back, and then heaved her aching body out of the chair and retreated onto the terrace for some air before she made it worse.

She probably would have hidden out there until they needed to leave for the 2pm meeting, except the UV was extreme and she wasn't wearing sunscreen. It forced her back inside after barely 15 minutes.

Sal didn't look up from her document. "While we're on the topic of our relationship," she said neutrally as if she wasn't poking the damn bear, "before we leave, we need to discuss how we're going to present to others at the office."

Allegra stopped in the centre of the room. The word 'relationship' gave her a brief jolt to the chest and took her back to lying in the rooftop tent, wondering where things could go between them. She shoved it away. That wasn't what Sal meant. "You mean that we should start acting like we're friends now?"

Sal hummed. "I think the safest approach is for you to act as if you're temporarily upset with me and believe Dimi's version of events," she said, eyes on her laptop. "We should give him no reason to believe we're communicating about work in a way that contradicts his narrative."

Allegra processed that. "I need to be angry with you."

"Not angry. Just—cool."

Allegra walked back over to her seat and her phone. "That won't be difficult to fake after this morning."

Sal paused mid-keystroke. "Well, externalise that feeling." She resumed typing. "I don't suppose you have any business casual in that boot of yours?"

"Uh," Allegra said, looking down at her grey t-shirt and navy cargos. She presented them to Sal.

Sal looked up, considering her for a moment, her eyes briefly mapping Allegra's shoulders, her hips, and her thighs. The look was strictly evaluative, which Allegra reminded herself several times. "Unfortunately, I don't think I'll have anything formal with enough stretch to fit you," was her assessment. "I suppose we're staying on brand for you even in the office, at least for now."

After that, Sal made another couple of phone calls—to senior reporters, Allegra worked out—and the ticking clock meant Sal became more economical. Her tone never shifted, but the conversations tightened: fewer preliminaries, cleaner conclusions, attention held and released with precision. The pressure built until she'd attached everything to an email she'd been composing, checked the links, checked the files, and double-checked the wording with her finger hovering over the mouse button—

and then hit send, breathed out hard through pursed lips, and sat slowly back in her chair.

Sal's eyes lifted to the room again, and she closed her laptop. "Alright," she said, standing gracefully despite now looking like she might be as tired as Allegra. "Let's go."

Allegra glanced at the clock on her phone: *1:31pm*. She raised her eyebrows—Sal finished exactly when she told her university associate she would. And in time for their meeting. She followed Sal downstairs.

The ride in Sal's car was quiet but otherwise familiar. Allegra's old boots and cargos looked sharply out of step with the sleek black leather, and ABC Afternoons played softly through the radio. At the lights, Sal nodded at it. "All yours."

Allegra shook her head and just looked out the window. Choosing music didn't feel like a productive use of what little energy she had, given they were about to head into a meeting where every item on the agenda was a collection of words that together had no meaning to her.

Sal had a dedicated park in the basement, and she pulled into it with practiced ease. She then slipped off her sunglasses and stowed them, climbing elegantly out of her extravagant car. Allegra followed her into the lift.

"Showtime," Sal commented evenly, and straightened as the doors opened to the atrium.

The first thing Allegra noticed was the light; or the lack of it. The Black Standard Advisory headquarters was a building between buildings, and as such it seemed the architects had opted to embrace the lack of light rather than coax slivers of it down from above. Artificial spotlights concentrated on the walkways, reception desk, and lifts, and all the other spaces—lounge areas and the indoor water feature, in particular—were lit mostly from the reflection off smooth walls and dark steel accents. Allegra felt like they were walking into a different time zone as Sal led her towards the lifts.

Remembering 'cool' and 'civil', Allegra followed her two steps behind, and let her face relax into something more moody than 'wow, this place is *intense*'.

It meant her view was of Sal, dressed darkly and sleekly, her heel clicks echoing from the floor as she cut through the atrium.

In the lift, people nodded at Sal and gave them space. It was when she stepped out onto their target floor that the atmosphere shifted. People clocked her immediately and adjusted: conversations lowered, bodies stilled, and badges straightened. They were friendly—no one seemed afraid, exactly—but her presence carried a gravity that hushed the space and pulled it into order.

Gerard was already in the meeting room when they entered, looking even more neat and coifed in person. His laptop was all set up and ready to take minutes, and he spun towards them the moment they entered. "Welcome to BSA, my love," he said warmly to Allegra, and then quickly pivoted to Sal. "Heads up, we're going to have company this meeting." He seemed slightly tenser than usual.

Sal stilled momentarily. "Oh?" She sat opposite Gerard, taking her tablet out and neatly crossing her legs. Allegra chose a seat conspicuously far away from Sal for herself.

"Dimi said he was going to 'pop down' for the meeting," Gerard said with the same sort of lack of inflection Sal favoured. To Allegra, he said, "Looks like you get to meet the big boss today."

Allegra glanced surreptitiously at Sal, unsure how to answer. Sal gave her a fractional nod. "I've met him," Allegra told Gerard, less grimly than she felt it.

That surprised him. "Interesting!" he said, sounding like he meant it. He spoke to Sal again. "Apparently it's because you cleared out a whole section of your calendar."

"Mmm, I had some work to get through," she said easily. "Well, he's most welcome."

Allegra closely watched Gerard for his response to that, but there was none. She, too, found that interesting. She would need to ask Sal later what it meant.

Zoe entered next. She greeted them warmly. "Allegra! This is your first time here, isn't it?" Allegra nodded. "Welcome!" She was dressed more smartly than Allegra had seen her before—dress suit and red heels that matched her cat-eye glasses. She looked more senior and more important than she'd looked in jeans and sneakers.

A series of other people with crisp suits and important-sounding titles followed, swiping in, greeting everyone, and introducing themselves to Allegra. Allegra didn't remember many names, but they had positions like 'Legal and Compliance Lead', 'Editorial Lead', 'Analytics Lead' and a couple of platform specialists. The room was fuller than she'd anticipated given her experience with BSA so far, and she felt very grubby and underdressed. She could have at least brushed her hair again.

They were all talking amongst themselves very briefly—about unrelated matters, other accounts, their weekends, when Zoe raised her voice a little, "Alright, everyone," she began, but before she said anything else, the door opened one last time.

Dimi entered, wearing dress pants and a white shirt with his sleeves rolled up. He looked younger and sharper in it, although nothing could *truly* sharpen his soft smile and fuzzy hair. He waved away Zoe's surprise and attempt to welcome him. "Carry on! I'm just listening." He moved up to the back of the room and sat down behind everyone, in one of the chairs along the side wall. Allegra noticed he had a direct sightline to Sal.

When he caught her eye and gave her a wink and salute, she smiled back and pretended to be charmed. *I'm going to need to have another shower after this*, she thought sourly, turning her attention back to Zoe, who formally welcomed her and thanked her for 'taking time out of her busy day' to sit in with them.

Honestly, though, she needn't have been there. As soon as someone with an impressive title stood beside the projector screen and started talking, Allegra quickly checked out. It would have been impolite not to at least *look* at the screen—at all the charts, dot points, metrics—but, by the third presenter, she spent more time noticing how people periodically checked *Sal's* response to what was being said than following the presentation itself.

The next topic got her attention. "Her strongest engagement comes from LGBTQ+ women and the left, particularly those who identify an interest in environmental issues," the presenter said, matter-of-factly. "They read her as authentic."

Allegra scoffed at that. As if it were a performance choice.

"Are we sure we want to go with that?" one of the platform specialists asked. "We're playing her straight into call-out territory. It's safer to pitch her more broadly at this stage."

What followed was an animated discussion about whether to position Allegra as queer explicitly and risk alienating a sizeable cohort of parent scrollers who found her compelling, or allow the audience to infer, and risk alienating queer-identifying followers by refusing to own it. In particular, everyone had opinions about how she should respond if asked directly, which was framed as a critical risk.

Allegra stole a glance at Sal while 20 people in expensive suits discussed her sexuality; Sal was following the conversation, and at one point interjected—and the room quieted immediately—"Allowing the online debate about her sexuality to extend as long as possible will likely be good for engagement, as Farid demonstrated."

20 minutes later and well after Allegra had reached saturation point about her *own* identity, someone finally turned around to her. "Allegra," he asked, causing her to sit upright again. "Do you have any preference about how we move forward with this?"

"I thought the whole point of this discussion was that I *don't* have a preference," she said a little dryly. There were a few smiles and appropriate chuckles. "But no, I don't. As my entire family reliably tells me, the internet has already decided I'm bi. I don't mind how you 'position' me."

Sal ended that discussion so the agenda could move on, summarising the apparent majority sentiment: "We'll let online speculation continue for now."

The rest of the meeting was dry metrics and discussions of which *type* of content belonged on which platform, and the last item on the agenda was Risk. They'd saved the driest topic for last, and Allegra had already run out of steam trying to keep pace with the discussion about her sexuality. She had nothing left in the tank to hear about *stakeholder perception drift* or *adverse reputational impact and trust erosion.*

From the back of the room—"If I may butt into your meeting for a moment on that point?" Dimi's voice lifted over them, as if he wasn't the CEO and the person who employed them all. He looked across at Sal. "Sal, if there's adverse coverage connected to internal decision-making, it's correct for accountability to sit with you. Let's have clarity on that: are you prepared to take that on?"

She nodded once. "That's appropriate," she said easily, as if it was self-evident.

Dimi echoed her nod and sat back, turning his attention to Zoe again.

Allegra almost missed it; the way he visibly relaxed, how his question was delivered in the dying throes of the meeting. He'd already moved on.

After Zoe closed the meeting, Allegra hazarded a glance back at Gerard. He was already standing, his usual pleasant smile in place, but he didn't look at either her or Sal.

With everyone packing up and Allegra finally able to smell her freedom, Dimi rounded the table towards her. She resisted the urge to stiffen and inhale sharply, instead managing a Gerard-style smile at him.

"I'm so sorry about that," he said, shaking his head sheepishly. "These rooms have such a bad habit of forgetting there's a person attached to the slide. About such a personal topic, too! You handled it well."

She forced her expression to stay warm, careful not to glance over towards Sal like she wanted to. Instead, she looked at his eyes: too small behind his glasses. "I expected it," she said lightly. "It comes with the territory."

Behind her, she noticed Sal slipping out of the room. So, she suspected, did Dimi. Neither of them looked at Sal as Dimi patted Allegra's hand. "Thanks so much for coming in today. I do think it's useful to see how the machinery operates, even if it's horribly boring!" he said. "It helps you understand the gravity of every tiny little thing you say and do online, once you're public." He smiled at her again. "I do hope you're feeling better after this morning. Let's catch up again soon, eh?" Allegra wasn't sure if that was a gesture of politeness or an actual invitation, but since her smile seemed to be a good enough response to it, he released her hand and went to have a word to Zoe.

Finally released into the wild, Allegra exited the room and followed their earlier footsteps through the building as best she could to exit it, figuring Sal would be waiting for her in the carpark.

She was right: Sal was seated in her car with the door open, reading emails on her phone. Anyone looking would think Sal just got something important as she was climbing in.

Allegra swung in herself, feeling much safer with the closed door and tinted windows, even if she was faced with her cargos and boots again. "I need a suit," she observed, thinking of her comfy old t-shirt in that room full of pressed and pointed collars.

Sal grinned briefly at that, glancing at Allegra before she slid her sunglasses on and reversed out of her parking spot. "You certainly stood out."

She was right. Allegra had spent the meeting feeling conspicuous and out of place, while Sal seemed to possess her own gravity. The room subtly adjusted around her. Everyone spoke in her register; everyone looked curated to her aesthetic. Allegra recalled Sal saying she'd *built BSA*—impressive in itself, filling that massive headquarters—and wondered now whether Sal had slotted into a ready-made corporate machine, or whether she'd constructed it around her piece by piece. Either way, it was clearly her natural habitat. She wasn't struggling to survive it as Allegra was: it sustained her.

I asked her why she didn't walk away from this, Allegra realised, imagining what that would cost her. It now made sense that she hadn't—even if the man at the centre of it all *owned* the company.

"Does Dimi want you to leave?" Allegra wondered aloud as they were stuck in traffic.

"No," Sal said. "He wants me contained: profitable, isolated, and without a reputation strong enough to hurt him."

Dimi's comment in the meeting certainly corroborated that, but why undermine her if he *didn't* want her gone? "But he doesn't want people to respect you?"

She gave a low hum, the kind of sound that meant *close, but not quite*. "He wants people to respect my authority—I'm a money spinner, after all—but assume my motives are self-serving."

She absorbed that in silence for a moment. "Well," Allegra said eventually, already having reached her tipping point for words like *leverage, legitimacy, and credibility* today, "he thinks I'm on his side, at least."

To that, Sal said nothing. She watched the road ahead, her mind clearly elsewhere.

Sal's eyes dipped to her watch as they pulled into her carpark, and Allegra presumed that was a gentle suggestion that it was time for her to leave. She felt heavy at the thought of driving somewhere else.

She got out of Sal's car and was halfway to her own when she stopped—exhausted, head full, and distracted. Perhaps to the point of being unsafe. "I actually don't think I'm right to drive," Allegra decided. "Could I leave my car here tonight? I'll just walk."

Sal, already at the lift, turned towards her. "To Point Piper," she clarified, flatly.

She'd done it dozens of times. "Yes."

Sal's eyes narrowed slightly. "Well, I'm not going to chain you up," she said evenly. "But it would be more prudent for you to stay nearby for now, in case the story turns and we need to pivot."

Allegra brightened: that sounded better than an hour's walk in the late afternoon sun. She glanced back at her LandCruiser, briefly considering whether to grab another change of clothes while she was down here. She dismissed it almost immediately. Grabbing clothes would only invite a reading she didn't want, and one Sal would once have been delighted to lean into. Allegra didn't want to test how far Sal's new restraint went. She simply joined her in the lift.

Once upstairs, Sal placed her keys on the corner of the kitchen bench closest to the lift and rounded it towards the fridge. "Would you like some water while we wait?" She opened the fridge, displayed two bottles, one still, one sparkling—and a single unopened bottle of white wine.

Allegra was too thirsty to daintily sip chilled water. "Is tap okay?"

Sal's eyebrows lifted fractionally, but she retrieved a glass anyway. Her movement around the kitchen had the same economy Allegra had watched all day: no wasted steps, no excess motion, everything done once and cleanly. She poured Allegra's water with the same unhurried confidence she'd exuded the whole time they'd been at BSA.

Watching her, Allegra had the quiet, unexpected thought: *Oh. You're the same thing everywhere.* Visiting BSA headquarters felt like downloading a translation app. What had been ridiculously extra yesterday now made perfect sense.

Sal caught her watching and met her eyes for a moment as she passed Allegra on the way to the terrace. "I imagine you'd like to sit outside." She handed Allegra her glass and collected her laptop on the way there.

Allegra downed her water in about five seconds, left her glass on the table in case she needed it again, and followed Sal onto the terrace.

Sal checked her watch, opened her laptop, and took a sip of her water.

Allegra, while exhausted, couldn't sit still. She went to inspect the spa that she recalled Sal mentioning at the very back of the terrace—wooden, octagonal, and nested in rich greenery—and then wandered back past Sal to the railing. From there she paused to look at the horizon and listen to the hum of peak hour traffic below, before turning and crossing the terrace again.

She made another circuit. Then another. Sal's eyes lifted from her phone briefly. Her voice was dry. "Would you like me to time your laps?"

Allegra didn't get a chance to answer, however, because Sal's phone beeped and immediately had her full attention. "It's live."

Allegra sat down opposite her and watched her face, trying to guess what her reaction was to the story—a lost cause. After Sal had read whatever was on her phone, she moved to her laptop and went through a number of others, all with the same intense focus. After several minutes, she spun her laptop around for Allegra. "See for yourself," she said, picking up her phone again. "I need to call Zoe and give her the heads up."

While she was doing that, Allegra read the screen in front of her. *'External Assessment Used Outside Original Scope, Company Says'*, the headline read. In a million years, Allegra could not imagine bothering to click on such a headline, but she did, and what followed was the driest, most technically dense article she'd ever fucking read. She almost gave up and went to scan for her name, except that she felt like Sal might test her comprehension at the end, so she soldiered through it anyway.

Sal finished her phone call and hung up. "What do you think?"

Allegra glanced up at her, making her suffering evident. "I'll let you know if I ever make it to the end," she said, and then read a sentence for the third time to try and extrapolate some meaning from it.

Sal looked very pleased with her response. "That's by design."

As Sal was sitting down again, Allegra finally found her name mentioned neutrally and described as 'the assessor', listed once and then never again. The main focus seemed to be internal process failures and how they would be strengthened as a result of the error.

Allegra slid Sal's laptop back to her. "I now know more about quality assurance than I ever wanted to know."

"And that's not even authored by a business correspondent," Sal said with a grin. "Just wait until you read what *they* produce."

Fortunately, Sal didn't make her read any more articles, though she was combing through them all herself.

Allegra spent some time looking through news websites anyway—and finding nothing, as searching for her name just brought up pages of stories about Isaiah and bush safety—when her phone buzzed. Before it had even finished its cycle, Sal's phone also beeped.

They glanced at each other and then checked their messages. The message was from Zoe, who was apparently doing the exact same thing Sal was but on social media platforms. *"Sal's framing did the trick,"* was the message, with a link to a tweet. It was by Froggy. *"Saw my future wife in the news. Asked about it. Fell asleep immediately as someone tried to explain 'process failures' and 'internal document audits' to me and instead dreamt about the dozens of adorable gaybies we'll definitely have together".*

Allegra wasn't sure whether to be amused, mortified, or both. "I hope she's offering to carry them all."

That coaxed a laugh out of Sal. "Oh, you are definitely doing a collab with that one, it will be priceless." She then paused, reconsidering. "Well. Perhaps not *priceless*." Her grin sharpened.

There you are, Allegra thought, unexpectedly steadied by that grin as Sal got back to media tracking.

The flow of articles—each more boring than the last—finally began to slow, and Allegra had presumed that was it until she clocked Sal suddenly paying extremely close attention to one.

Sal's brow furrowed as she leant into the screen to read something more carefully. As she did so, her frown relaxed. She took another sip of her water, sat back in her chair and released a long, slow breath.

When she noticed Allegra was watching her, she said, "Metro Daily confirmed they received an opposing leak."

Allegra *sort of* understood what that meant. At her expression, Sal turned the laptop around with a highlighted section of text for her. Allegra read aloud. "Editor's note: the outlet was made aware of information suggesting an alternative account, but could not independently verify the claims." It still meant nothing to her. She felt a bit sheepish. "I know you want me to respond to this, but I don't really understand why it's so important."

Sal smiled briefly. "This line means they received a leak about you and Threshold, which means I was right Dimi was going to leak very quickly," Sal explained, suggesting she hadn't been 100% certain he would do it. "This one sentence justifies my decision not to consult the usual channels before moving to neutralise a hostile story. Threshold and the Board will notice it." She let her eyes fall closed for a moment again. "It's my Get Out of Jail Free card," she said, enjoying it briefly before getting on her laptop again to email both the Board and Threshold with it.

Afterwards, Sal closed her laptop and checked her phone as she stood up. "I should call the Chair myself," she said somewhat reluctantly, and took her phone inside to do that.

That left Allegra sitting by herself in the golden late afternoon sunlight, feeling more relaxed than she had for two whole days; since the evening after the Homeward event. Same warm sunlight, same pleasant feeling of suddenly having nothing particularly important to do after her family left to drive home.

Remembering them, she pressed her lips together and looked down at her phone. If Dimi moved quickly, Allegra would need to move just as quickly, unless she wanted to feel even *further* from her son. The greater risk was doing nothing and letting Dimi slip into the quiet space her own words rarely filled.

She would just have to make do. She opened a message to Aaron. "*Was lovely to see you on Sunday. Are you free next weekend? Perhaps we can do something* you're *into this time :)*"

She read it a few times and then sent it before she could second-guess herself. She checked the weather for the next few days out of habit, and was just putting her phone in her pocket when it buzzed in her hand. Her heart lifted. "*Yeah, for sure. Probably Saturday this time, so Dad doesn't murder you for making me miss church two weeks in a row.*"

Allegra still had it open when Sal finally returned from her phone call. Something about her posture had loosened.

Allegra briefly showed her the text—both to demonstrate she'd followed Sal's instructions, and also to let Sal know she'd be busy then. Sal observed it and nodded. "Good girl," she said, clearly entertained.

"So," Allegra asked, putting her phone away. "Now that news thing is finished, do we celebrate, or?"

Sal shook her head. "He moved once already, which means he'll move again," she said, and buttoned her suit jacket. "I'm heading out for food." Instead of immediately turning to leave, though, she paused, still facing Allegra.

It's a question, Allegra realised, one she could choose to ignore. It was for that reason that she didn't. "Want company?"

Sal watched her for a fraction of a second and then nodded.

Allegra fell into step beside her, matching her pace as they headed for the lift.

Chapter 21: The Simplest Explanation

They'd already eaten, but neither of them felt ready to call it a night. A warm breeze threaded through the tall terrace houses and old warehouse conversions in The Rocks, and the neighbourhood had spilled outward to meet it; residents leaning on balconies, café tables edging into the street, couples drifting arm in arm towards dinner. In shop windows, the first signs of Christmas had begun to appear: a wreath here, a strand of lights there.

Sal slowed near the entrance to a small, low-lit arcade. She looked thoughtful for a moment. "There's a women's suit tailor in here, one of the better ones," she offered. "If you're still thinking about corporate wear."

Since they were already there, Allegra didn't see the harm in ducking in to have a look.

The shop was a small boutique at the end of a quiet, Victorian-era arcade. It was one room with a rack of various suits along the back, and a huge and ornate full-length mirror in the centre.

As per usual, the tailor—a sharp woman in her mid-50s—recognised Sal immediately and stood as they entered. "Sal!" she said warmly, approaching her. "Lovely to see you again. And lovely to see that *jacket* again. It's holding up, I gather?"

Sal returned her smile, brushing the lapels of her pointy blazer. "I would expect no less of it, given its origins."

The tailor nodded at it with the quiet satisfaction of an artisan recognising her own work. Her eyes lifted to Allegra, and recognition dawned in them. "And I do believe I know who this is," she said, turning to face her. "Ms Bush Safety herself. Lovely to meet you in person."

Well, it was a welcome change from 'Rescue Guns', at least. "Thank you," Allegra said. "I'm actually here looking for some *alternatives* to 'Bush Safety'." She gestured down at her faded t-shirt and cargos. "These stand out a little in the office. Maybe a suit or something?"

She laughed, but it was kind. "What will you be wearing it to?"

Allegra wasn't 100% certain about that. She looked over to Sal, who had been quietly observing, for guidance.

"Meetings, pressers, possibly some non-black-tie events. We may need a selection."

The tailor nodded once and then looked back to Allegra. "Do you need to move in it?"

"...Yes?" Were there suits people *didn't* need to move in?

"How much?"

Allegra considered that. "Enough that if something turns into an emergency, I can respond without stopping to change."

Sal, who'd relaxed a shoulder against the heavy full-length mirror, smiled slightly at that.

The tailor stepped up to Allegra, considering her. "Can you stand as you normally would?"

Obediently, Allegra stood straighter. The tailor stepped backwards a moment, observing her as a whole, and then her eyes moved between her shoulders, waist and hips. She then grabbed a chair from the edge of the room. "Could you sit in this as you normally would?"

Allegra followed her instructions, only noticing now how her knees relaxed open and how her instinct was to lean her hands on them. It made her faintly self-conscious beside these two elegant, precise women.

"Stand again?" When Allegra did, the tailor stepped in, reaching for the tape from a pouch on her belt. It looked electronic, and beeped as she flicked it on and held it up towards Allegra. "May I?" Allegra nodded, and she took a series of measurements, the tape clicking softly each time.

"Alright," the tailor said, letting the tape fall and stepping away. "How would you like it to read?"

Allegra's blank expression did the talking for her. The tailor smiled kindly again. "Do you want to appear more formal and structured, or relaxed? How would you like people to respond to you in it?"

Allegra looked to Sal for help. Sal was clearly enjoying herself, but there didn't appear to be any malice in it. "Competent. Calm."

The tailor looked back at Allegra and nodded once. "Alright. I'll go grab a few examples and we can discuss them."

Allegra was then left alone and facing herself in the big mirror. Sal was leaning on the side of it, watching her. She had that slightly sly grin.

That, with Sal's pointy suit, made Allegra chuckle. "Was that the part where you usually say you want to read as 'Disney Villain'?"

Sal's grin deepened. "Yes."

The tailor returned promptly with a few different suits in different cuts and colours. There were no edgy, fitted cuts like Sal's: they were all loose, clean lines and nice relaxed fits. Allegra liked them all.

"Would you like to try them on? We can adjust the ones you like. Let me grab a plain shirt and get the change room ready."

Change room? "There's really no need, I'm wearing a sports bra and bike shorts," she said, thinking this wasn't that different from the many, many women's change rooms she'd frequented throughout her life. "Force of habit."

The tailor accepted that and grabbed a shirt for Allegra, trundling over the mobile hanger with her suits on it, ready to go. She then went to make some notes on her computer in the corner.

Allegra hadn't thought anything of changing in front of them—they were women and nothing was going to show, after all—but she should have. With the tailor off to the side and her and Sal facing each other, just lifting her t-shirt over her head was... well, it shouldn't have felt like anything. But it did. Especially given that she was standing there in a sports bra and Sal couldn't have been more fully clothed.

The tailor called, "How's the fit of the shirt?" from her computer as Allegra was buttoning it up.

Sal glanced up, first at the tailor, and then forward at Allegra. Their eyes met and held for a moment.

It's—God, it's still there, she thought, feeling it like a gut-punch. "The shirt's fine," she managed, trying to tear her eyes away from Sal's and look down at the buttons to make sure she was matching them with the right holes. She kept her eyes carefully averted while she considered the suits.

Allegra—with Sal's input—ended up choosing four of them: a very structured cut in navy pinstripe, a softer suit in maroon, a light grey fitted suit chosen for on camera, and a simple black suit that seemed very 'corporate uniform'. That particular one only needed a couple of slight alterations, so the tailor did them on the spot. "So you can wear it now."

Allegra received the jacket from her with its new centre back seam. "What, like wear it out?" Since the tailor was clearly expecting her to slip it back on, she did.

The tailor checked how it sat on her back and waist. "Why not? You can take it for a test drive—I'm here until 8 if you need any adjustments." She stood back, satisfied. "Take the shirt, too. We can sort it out later."

Sal stepped forward when the tailor started adding things up, wallet app open on her phone. As the tailor entered the amount on her computer and checked that it had come up properly on her EFTPOS machine, she asked casually, "If your partner comes back needing adjustments, should I put it on your account?"

Sal, who had been flicking through payment methods in her wallet, paused mid-swipe. Before she could say anything, however, the tailor held the machine at her. "Here."

Sal hesitated, and then tapped her phone to it. "Yes, that's fine."

The word 'partner' hung in the air while the machine confirmed *Approved* and spat out several receipts. Sal glanced at Allegra to assess her reaction.

Honestly? Allegra had spent the last few years being presumed to still be Timothy's wife. This was—oddly, not as irritating. At least it was about someone she was still attracted to. She wondered what it was about them that invited that assumption, though.

Neither of them mentioned it as Allegra put her boots back on and collected the bag with her other clothes in it.

The tailor moved Allegra's suits to a queue of suits beside her sewing station. "I think 2-4 weeks on these—you'll have them by Christmas. How does that sit for you?" Her question was directed at Sal, who was clearly in charge of their logistics.

Sal thought for a moment. "Could we get the structured cut a little faster than that? What sort of timeframe can I reach for?"

The tailor pursed her lips. "For you, I can do five days."

Sal nodded, and to Allegra, she briefly explained, "For unpleasant meetings, should the need arise." Allegra had a feeling that suit was going to end up with some bad associations.

Because Allegra was still wearing her thick hiking boots, she hadn't expected to look or feel very different as they left the building. It was catching her reflection in a window on the way out that gave her a reality check: she looked *polished*. Only the tread of the boots and their wide, heavy nose was visible under the suit pants, so it looked like a deliberate choice. Those, with the sleek but androgynous cut of the black suit, the crisp white shirt and her mop of blond hair pulled up into a bun looked—well. She was making quite a statement.

Beside her, Sal was in her narrowly tailored black everything, pointy shoulders, and sharp stilettos. Allegra could only really describe it as looking fetish-adjacent, especially in this hot weather.

Watching their reflections in each window they passed, it occurred to Allegra that like this, either of them alone would still probably read as queer. But together? She looked away, recalling the tailor's casual assessment of them.

As night fell, there was a mutual, unspoken agreement that the test drive had finished.

Allegra had burnt through her emergency changes of clothes already which meant that the only option was to return to Point Piper where the rest of them were. However, getting into the dusty seat of her LandCruiser in her brand new, likely staggeringly expensive suit was not an option, so rather than just change in the carpark (she'd learnt her lesson on that front), she followed Sal up to her penthouse to change in her guest bedroom.

As they went to split off at the top of the lift, Sal stopped her with a sharp, business-like motion. "Oh, before you go..." She gestured for Allegra to follow her.

Mutely, Allegra did. Sal led her to the curved stairwell, up the stairs, and towards her office. It was when Sal walked straight past her office and approached the bedroom that Allegra's stride caught for a moment and she had to make an active decision whether to follow Sal. She did, not sure what she was hoping Sal's intentions were as Sal led her into the master bedroom, and—to both her disappointment *and* her relief—into the sprawling walk-in robe.

It was only as Sal slid open an *entire drawer full of ties* that Allegra caught the hidden smile on her lips. *You evil fuck*, Allegra thought, shaking her head with her own private smile. She'd known *exactly* what she was doing.

Sal didn't linger on it as she might once have, though. She stood aside to display the ties to her. "I think one of these would complete the picture, but it's up to you."

She gave Sal a look. Ties? "I know what demographic you're trying to pitch *me* at."

Sal inclined her head. "Well, I *am* across what they want, Allegra."

Exaggerating a sigh at her, Allegra stepped forward and considered her options. There were some objectively beautiful ties in there—silk, satin, some wool. In an array of patterns and finishes. She selected a deep blue one; anything else would probably stand out like a flag on her. She looped it around her neck and stepped up to the mirror to tie it. It was something she'd seen Timothy do a thousand times, after all; how hard could it be? But, mirrored and on herself, she couldn't copy his actions.

Sal was observing her with a knowing smile. "Would you like me to—?"

Well, there wasn't much option, was there? Allegra let her arms flop by her sides, and turned her body towards Sal, presenting her stubborn tie.

Sal lifted the ends of it and stepped in. Immediately, her presence was different from the tailor's. More magnetic. Her slight and precise hands flipped the ends over themselves and over each other in neat, tight, practised movements, pulling it sharply—tight at her throat. Allegra's lips parted. She closed them.

When Sal stepped away, she briefly straightened Allegra's lapels and tilted her head, appraising her work. Then, she stepped aside so they could consider her new reflection.

The knot Sal had done wasn't standard, it was some sort of three-sectioned pinwheel type thing that looked like it belonged in a fashion show. That little flex aside, Allegra looked *good*. Important, self-confident. A far cry from 'family gardener'. Perhaps too far? "What will my target demographic think of this?"

A low chuckle. "Oh, Allegra, I think it will be difficult for them to look away," Sal said in *that* voice. The deep, soft one Allegra immediately recognised as dangerous. "Truly a win for engagement. And I think I know just the occasion." There was a twinkle in her eye.

Sal didn't explain what that occasion was, and Allegra didn't trust herself to ask in case Sal used that voice again. It was also not particularly prudent of them to be alone in that walk-in robe for too long, either, so she accepted Sal's gestured offer to help her remove the tie. Sal then rolled it into a little tie-holder box and presented it to Allegra without saying a word. That little smile...

God. Allegra hightailed to the guest room to change back into her day clothes and flee back to Point Piper, stuck between two conflicting feelings: comforted by the return of Sal's composure, and uneasy at how quickly she was drawn back into orbit. She would need to wear this suit extremely sparingly.

Back at Point Piper, Allegra hung the suit at the back of the guest wardrobe. She didn't trust it near the rest of her clothes yet—it felt like tempting fate.

That tie, too, curled up in the little box and *looming* on her dressing table. Honestly, what the fuck was *Sal* doing with so many ties? That woman had definitely never worn a tie in her life. At least not to work.

She was only too happy to pull the door to the guest bedroom safely shut and contain them. From there, her next task was finding Timothy in this giant house and letting him know she was alive.

Despite how late in the evening it was, Timothy was still in his office. She said, "Knock, knock?" at the door, bracing herself for his usual *I was so worried about you* routine.

It didn't come. "Come in." He stopped there.

"I'm alive, by the way," she said wryly, wandering up beside his desk. He had his laptop open to an array of spreadsheets she didn't recognise. "What's up?"

He sighed heavily and sat back, briefly taking off his glasses to rub his eyes. "I did something that even at the time I knew wasn't a good idea," he said, threading them back over his ears and looking down again. "Before the Impact grant money was paid—before they'd signed, even—I offered a few of our casuals who I know struggle with their rent full-time hours."

The smile fell off Allegra's face. "What's happening with the grant money?" Timothy looked up at her, and his expression made her stomach drop.

"Dimi just said they should probably do all the usual reviews before proceeding. He's right, of course. This is the usual process. I just jumped the gun a little because of how well our conversation the other night went."

Allegra felt a growing creep of something dark and corrosive. Timothy did *not* deserve this. "And now the funding is delayed."

"And now the funding is delayed," he repeated. "He said with everything happening around you, it was better to be careful."

That fucking—"He said that?"

Timothy did not look as angry as he should have. Or angry at all, even. "He's right. People will poke around. It's best to be safe."

She looked down at his spreadsheets. "Do you have enough to cover the difference?"

"For a couple of weeks, yes. We have the overdraft as well, but I hate to use it," he said. "I just hope this is all sorted out by Christmas, because I was going to use that surplus for the Christmas lunch." He spent a few moments with his temples resting on his hands, and then pushed himself upright and swivelled his chair to face Allegra. "I'm sorry to spring this on you right as you walk in the door, would you like something to eat?"

Allegra was the one who was sorry. "After all the trouble I'm causing you, I should make *you* dinner," she said grimly, leading him out into the kitchen and doing just that.

She'd already eaten with Sal—not something she was tempted to tell him—but even if she hadn't, she couldn't have managed food now.

Timothy talked about Sunday, about the family, and she nodded along, her attention slipping. The lift she'd felt earlier was gone, the weight of the day settling back onto her stiff shoulders. She excused herself early to text Sal.

It was a relief to sit down on the bed. Rather than just asking where Dimi lived so she could *pay him a visit*, she sent, *"Impact is 'reviewing' Redeemer's funding offer, and he told Timothy it's because of me getting so much attention, they want to be careful."*

Fortunately, Sal wasn't sleeping this time. *"That's a warning. He's paused it to watch how you react."*

Allegra felt a cold sweat wash over her. *"Does that mean he knows I'm on your side?"*

"Not necessarily. But I suspect he's testing whether you'll try to resolve it directly with him."

Testing her? She scoffed. *"Well, how long can he drag this out? Timothy's already extended hours to people. Should I go to Dimi straight away??"*

"No. I need to think about this. Leave it with me." Allegra had already locked her phone and put it in her lap when it buzzed again. *"I'd usually assume this goes without saying, but given what's at stake: there's no point explaining any of this to Timothy or anyone else."* Allegra made a face; she already knew that, but knew why Sal felt compelled to tell her anyway.

Allegra was still full of adrenaline, so despite the fact she felt like a sack of lead, she ended up trying to clear it by hauling a bundle of clean clothes from the laundry into the back of her LandCruiser. If she had lots of spare clothes there, it gave her more freedom to be wherever made sense.

While she was filling up the water tanks, her phone rang. There was only one person who would call her at 10pm while she was on holidays (unless it was a hospital). *Sal* flashed on her screen.

"Apologies for the late call, but I've done enough typing today," Sal said in her ordinary, manageable voice. Allegra set the hose aside as Sal continued. "We've found a prompt use for that suit: you're going to do a collab with Froggy tomorrow. Zoe will pick you up at 9am. I presume Point Piper?"

"Yes," Allegra answered. At least if it was Zoe, they wouldn't have to be careful with logistics.

"Okay, that's all set up." There was a pause. "Typically, we send at least two handlers with clients to private residences. Zoe seems to think it's unnecessary this once, and I'm of the same opinion—although I did suggest she park the car outside and do other work while she's waiting. What's your take?"

Allegra thought back to her previous interaction with Froggy. "I don't think she's going to lock me in a shed, if that's what you're worried about."

Sal had a smile in her voice. "Security *is* a concern, but Froggy lives alone and, in this case, the concern is more about making sure you feel supported and not pressured into filming anything you're uncomfortable with."

Allegra doubted there was any risk there. "I think Froggy would be likely to share your concern, to be honest. She's very sweet."

"Interesting. That's what Zoe said, too." Her tone signalled the matter was settled. "Well, I will defer to your judgement on this one. Let me know if you change your mind." She paused. "Sleep well. We can discuss the other issue tomorrow."

After the day Allegra had slogged through—and after a night spent on a stone floor—sleep was guaranteed. She finished filling the tanks and then ended up falling asleep on top of the doona in her clothes.

When Zoe pulled up outside their house the following morning in one of the black BSA Falcons, Timothy was out loading up his Transit and on his way to work. He waved at her, and she gave a pleasant and cheerful wave back, in contrast to his experience with Sal.

"She looks nice," Timothy observed as Allegra, dressed in a full suit and tie, exited the house.

"People can look a lot of ways and still be anything," Allegra found herself saying a little too quickly—and then realised she wasn't actually talking about Zoe at all.

Timothy had stopped packing and was staring at her, concerned.

She swallowed and got back to his point on Zoe. "But, yes, Zoe is actually genuinely nice. She's the social media person."

Timothy gave her a bit of a searching look on that one, but just said, "Ah," and left it.

As she settled into the far more understated black car, Allegra realised the clock was ticking on Timothy not knowing how often she saw Sal—especially if they were meant to be pretending to be friends.

Froggy lived in Newtown, of course. In one of those old Victorian townhouses: two-storey, narrow, and with a front porch only big enough for a couple of pot plants. There were three redbrick stairs up to her old door, and Froggy was sitting on them, clutching a mug of what smelt like chai, and wearing her anxiety. Her hair was frizzier than usual, her clothing hung asymmetrically off her slender figure, and big, circular glasses made her wide eyes look even wider than they already were.

The gate was literally half a metre high. Allegra just stepped over it rather than bother with the ceremony of opening and closing it. "Hey," she said personably, aware of the immediate imbalance between her sleek full suit and Froggy's mismatched everything.

"Hi," Froggy greeted her, standing as Allegra approached. "Great to see you. I'm just going to go and"—she gestured behind herself and clicked her tongue—"completely reinvent myself as a person so I'm also cool and impressive. Back in a sec."

She jogged up the last stair into the house, presumably to feign coming out cooler and more impressive, but instead the door remained closed and there was this kind of panicked screech from behind it.

Allegra did chuckle to herself—from a place of empathy. The ambient frenetic energy around Froggy this morning inadvertently reminded her of Vanessa. "You left your chai out here," Allegra called, and picked it up. "Perhaps we could discuss a game plan over it? That way you can remind yourself how normal and boring I really am." It didn't take much further encouragement for Froggy to let Allegra in.

The inside of her house hadn't been updated recently, and had that cosy, run-down cottage feel. She had a saucepan of chai on the stove, and a still-wrapped bouquet of native Australian flowers on the kitchen table—for her video, it turned out.

Froggy's idea for the quickest possible sketch ("It has to be longer than a minute, but you don't need to be in much of it") was simple: following the proposal in the last video, Allegra would show up in a suit, bouquet in hand, ready to marry her. Froggy would panic, vanish (the montage of preparation shots was something she would film later), and reappear in a completely unhinged makeshift wedding outfit.

Allegra's only line, to be delivered deadpan and with a big smile, was, 'I was reliably informed that I'm required to marry you now. So, here I am.'

"We only need to get a few shots of you, then," Froggy explained. "I won't need to waste too much of your time."

Allegra privately chuckled about that. "Yeah, wouldn't want to keep me away from my extremely demanding schedule of doing nothing. Catastrophe." At Froggy's blank expression, she clarified, "I'm on leave from the SES until after Christmas, and BSA hasn't started paying me for anything yet. So I'm free."

Froggy raised her eyebrows. "So this is pro bono for you?"

Allegra nodded. "Well, for me. I'm not above hustling for charities."

Froggy processed that, realising aloud, "Oh, yeah, Austin told me about that Homeward house-donation thing. Fucking wild." Froggy frowned at Allegra for a moment, then shook herself out of it. "Okay, well, let's get started."

Froggy had a whole setup—lights, cameras, even clip mics—and got flustered correcting Allegra's mic, apologising far too much for needing to touch her. They shot a few takes, reviewed the footage, and then Froggy bundled the cameras outside. "Are you happy to just, like, chill while I go upstairs and make myself look totally unhinged?"

Allegra was 'happy to just, like, chill'. She sat on the redbrick steps and let the morning sun soak in, her thoughts drifting back to Timothy's funding and how she was supposed to convince Dimi she was harmless enough to reinstate it. A couple wandering past did a double take. Allegra smiled and said good morning, and they returned it, surprised, before dissolving into excited whispers and scuttling around the corner. She kept her expression pleasant until they were gone, and then sighed. She still hadn't adjusted to this.

She was still reflecting on that when Froggy appeared behind her in the doorway and said, "Right." When Allegra stood to face her, she was wearing a bedsheet wrapped around her like a dress, an old lace curtain veil, Dangerfield chunky platforms as shoes, and the most horror-bride makeup Allegra had ever seen. Froggy pretending everything was completely normal was what sold it.

They did a few takes of the closing scene and then sat down on the porch steps again so Froggy could review the footage. Allegra watched with interest over her shoulder.

In the middle of it, Froggy stopped rolling for a moment, looking up with a frown. "Is this super weird for you, or?" she asked directly, clearly venting something that had been bothering her. "Like I've been doing vids and stuff since I was 14. But, I don't know, it's obvious this is totally not your thing, so is it weird to have some girl pretending to be all over you?"

Allegra had to smile; there was that earnestness she'd first seen at the hospital. "I mean, I know it's all mostly for..." She searched for the specific term she'd heard her nephews use about it. "...the bit."

Froggy noticed her attempt at the terminology and did finger guns. "Eeeeey, niiiice," she said in recognition. Then she sobered again. "I don't want you to feel, I don't know, objectified or something."

Allegra's immediate reference was yesterday's meeting where she'd been sitting right there while 20 highly paid executives argued how to best monetise her sexuality. Froggy's awkwardness when she needed to touch Allegra was a stark contrast. "Yeah, you don't need to worry about that at all."

Froggy looked comforted for a moment. Then immediately uncomfortable again. "Fuck," she said, mostly to herself, and then put her face in her hands. "Fucking fuck. Okay." She looked up, serious. "Allegra. I need to tell you something, but I also don't want to get in trouble and called out online, so can you, like, not do anything with this that would make it public?"

Allegra's smile faded. "Okay..."

"So," Froggy began, still looking very conflicted. "Austin was digging into that whole property developer payment thing all night and he came across some really suspicious stuff, and he's going to do a video about it." At Allegra's alarm, she threw her hands up. "Don't worry, he's totally convinced you had nothing to do with it. We all are. But you'll be in the video because you did the assessment, and because Austin says that you're..." She tilted her head from side to side, grimacing. "...secretly involved with an exec at BSA."

Allegra let all that settle, and took a big, conscious sidestep over the inference about Sal. Too-hard basket. "What suspicious stuff did he find? Can I see it?"

Froggy made a face. "He probably wouldn't even let *me* see, let alone give it to me for *you* to see. He also can't find out I told you."

"Okay..." Sal would want to know as much as possible, wouldn't she? "Is there anything else you can tell me about it? Anything at all?"

Froggy shook her head. "He was only looking last night, I don't think he has that much yet. But he has enough to know it's going to be something." She looked upset herself. "I just didn't want you to be blindsided, that's all. Even if it's clear in the vid you were just used and didn't do anything wrong, yourself."

'Used'? But what about *Sal*? "Thanks," she said, meaning it. "I appreciate it."

They sat in silence. Froggy stared at her camera for a good 20 seconds before she finished reviewing her footage. "Well," she said bleakly, "now that I've totally killed the mood, do you want something to drink? I can spike it with something that will make you forget I just told you all that."

Allegra laughed once. "Tempting," she admitted, but shook her head.

They finished up, Froggy took a couple of selfies with her, and then hugged her goodbye.

"Thank you," Allegra told Froggy as she left. Froggy nodded and went back to looking tormented; an odd visual in her wild makeup and makeshift wedding clothes.

Zoe spotted Allegra walking up the road towards her car and put her laptop away as Allegra swung in. "All good?"

Not all good, she thought grimly. She made some excuse about being overwhelmed—something she definitely was—and gave Zoe a brief rundown on Froggy's idea while she was waiting to pull out into traffic on the narrow street.

"Well," Zoe said with a big smile, "looking forward to seeing what Froggy comes up with! She's a trooper." They pulled up to a set of lights. "Back to Point Piper?"

Allegra pressed her lips together. She really needed to speak to Sal ASAP. "Can you drop me off in Central Quay?"

Zoe didn't even give it a second thought. "Sure."

The moment Zoe had dropped her off and the car was out of sight, she had her phone out and was texting Sal. *"I need to talk to you in person."*

Not five seconds later. *"Where are you?"* Allegra shared her location. *"Head to my place, we'll get there at roughly the same time."*

It was a short walk, past a few people who recognised her, and she smiled automatically, thinking of Sal's comment about always being on camera. By the time she reached the carpark gate, a familiar jet-black car was already turning the corner. They entered the carpark together and converged at the lift door.

Sal's attention went straight to her expression, not the suit and tie. "Are you alright?" Allegra nodded. That caused Sal to loosen a little, but as they got into the lift, she still pulled out her phone and put it on Do Not Disturb, slipping it back into her pocket. She looked across at Allegra again, eyes narrowed evaluatively, as if to double-check she *was* really okay and not just stoic.

Once they were upstairs, Sal let her exit the lift first. "Do you need anything? A drink?"

"I'm fine, Sal," Allegra reassured her. "I just—don't know how much I can put in writing. Froggy was fine, nothing happened to me. But she did tell me Lost in Austin locked onto your media release."

Sal stilled, focusing on what she was saying. "Go on."

Allegra tried to recall the exact words. "She said he's looking into 'property developer payment stuff' and he found something suspicious, and she couldn't tell me more than that because he's only just started researching. They don't think I'm guilty, they just wanted to warn me." She hesitated, aware of how this would sound particularly after their discussion yesterday. "But he thinks I'm 'secretly involved with a BSA exec'."

Sal was unreadable. "No word on what our involvement is supposed to mean with regard to the payment?"

She shook her head. "But he's definitely going to do a video on it."

Sal looked away, jaw set as she thought. "His videos will get traction."

Allegra thought of how upset Froggy had looked. "Sal," she said, "I also promised Froggy I wouldn't implicate her. She wasn't supposed to tell me."

Sal looked back at her and drew a long, deep breath. She nodded tightly. The difference between Sal wandering casually through the streets with her last night and standing in front of her taut as a bowstring now was so acutely visible that it made Allegra uncomfortable to see it. "Maybe I should get *you* a drink," she said bleakly. "Maybe we should open that wine."

Sal granted her a brief smile for that. "I need a clear head," she said, a trace of warmth briefly audible. It was gone quickly as she returned to reflecting on what she'd just heard. "Sit. I'm going to think a moment."

Sal went to the kitchen, poured herself a glass of sparkling water and then stood, eyes distant, at the display counter as she slowly drank it. Allegra did as instructed and waited, unsure whether to speak.

Eventually, Sal straightened, discarding her empty glass and approaching the table opposite her. "Thank you for telling me so quickly," she said as she gracefully sat. "It gives us more time to figure out how to respond." She looked at Allegra as if evaluating a new employee. "This is rather a complicated issue so I'm going to need to break it down for you. It will still be quite dense."

"Okay," Allegra said, resigned to accepting she'd have a giant headache by the end of the conversation. She was getting used to them.

"Austin's usual pattern is to drop a short first if it won't spoil the story," Sal said. "It helps him draw in additional sources. So, we can expect that soon—days, probably. Every minute counts."

"The fire and land reclassification are a live issue in their own right," she added, almost dismissively. "But that's not the part that impacts us."

She leaned forward. "Here's what can be inferred at this stage by someone standing on the street and looking in: on Monday, a report is misused in a way that benefits Threshold. On Tuesday, a neatly framed explanation appears across the press. Corporate machinery doesn't normally discover genuine errors this fast, let alone respond publicly within 24 hours." A faint smile touched Sal's mouth. "Of course," she said, with a small, unapologetic flourish, "Austin doesn't know how efficient I am. But that's beside the point. That timing doesn't read as discovery. It reads as preparation."

She sat back, eyes on Allegra. "So the assumption becomes premeditation, with the perfect alibi: a champion of Australian nature at the centre, someone who would never do something like that, so it *must* be a mistake." She paused. "You following?"

"So far," Allegra said, hanging on by her fingernails.

"Alright. As no one would have any idea about what's between Dimi and me, to Austin, BSA is acting as a monolith. And he will presume BSA decided they needed to recruit you, convince you that you're doing the right thing for the right reasons, and get you so emotionally invested that you will *also* believe that the payment was made in error." She waited for Allegra to catch up. "There are many ways to recruit people," she went on. "But the fastest—and safest—is usually the one people are most reluctant to report because it requires admitting they wanted it."

"You seduce them," Allegra said, feeling a twinge of doubt herself.

Sal watched her. "Presumably he then sought to find evidence to that effect. I don't think we can expect to know what his evidence is before the video drops, but we haven't exactly kept all our—exchanges behind closed doors."

Allegra sat with that for a few moments. The most disturbing thing was that it made sense; enough sense that for a second, she found herself glancing at Sal and remembering how hard she'd been pushed at the start, and how quickly that pressure had turned into something intimate.

But then, she'd seen the cracks too, especially where Dimi was involved. Unless Sal was acting?

It was just such a neat, clean story: a story about Sal expertly seducing her for financial gain.

"How much money did Threshold even make from the land?" Allegra wondered aloud.

"They stand to make tens of millions on the development, and your report both settled the land quickly and smoothed the way for an easy bushfire reclassification," Sal answered easily. "So, a lot."

"And how much money does *BSA* make from Threshold?"

Sal was watching her closely. "Also a lot."

Allegra considered that, leaning back in her chair. It *was* a clean story. So clean she kept remembering little details of her interactions with Sal that still felt slightly off.

And yet, Sal was sitting openly in front of her, having this conversation. "It's just, part of me says 'This makes more sense, she's using you', but I know what I saw on Monday. This just feels..." Allegra shook her head. "I don't want to believe it, and I don't even think most of me does, but—"

"You still do." Sal's expression softened slightly. There was resigned understanding in it. "It's a very satisfying explanation, isn't it? It seems self-evident."

Allegra nodded.

"And in PR, that's all that matters," she said. "The truth is complex, messy, and full of nuance. It's hard to digest. Narratives aren't. That's the point."

That was the problem to solve: what clean, self-evident narrative could Sal and Allegra give Austin—and everyone else—that would make that story about corporate grooming fall flat on its face?

It struck her. Not even as a new idea, but as something she had been tripping over for days.

The tailor hadn't hesitated. She hadn't squinted at them, or asked clarifying questions. She'd just reached for 'partner', like it was the most obvious thing in the world.

Froggy, too. She'd said it so easily—"secretly involved with an exec"—like it wasn't a shocking revelation, just something she figured she shouldn't speak openly about.

Even Dimi—Allegra sat up suddenly, remembering his response to her feigning confirmation she had feelings for Sal. He'd relaxed back, hadn't he? Like it was reassuring to find out it was only *that* between them.

That was the clincher. *That* was what could lift some of this pressure off Allegra and everyone around her right now.

The idea solidified in her mind as she considered it. And the more she thought about it, the clearer it became what was actually causing the damage. Not the idea that she and Sal were involved: the idea that it was hidden.

The story required no effort. No special knowledge. Two women, close in age and visibly queer, moving in the same orbit. One powerful and one suddenly visible, of course there was something between them. Of course that was easier to believe than a mess of warring executives weaponising personal relationships—and whatever was really going on between her and Sal.

Secrecy was doing the work. Secrecy was what turned coincidence into intent, speed into planning, care into manipulation. Without secrecy, the grooming narrative collapsed into a far more mundane story of an exec overreaching out of personal care—whatever the truth of Threshold and the fire.

And for the first time since that payment had hit her account, Allegra felt something ease in her chest: *clarity*.

She drew a slow breath. "So," she said, "what if we just give all of them—Austin, Dimi, everyone—a really digestible narrative that they'd easily swallow?"

Sal watched her closely, eyes slightly narrowed.

"Something that makes it look like you overreached out of personal bias—and that we're just spending time together because of course we are."

Sal was following. "Allegra," she said firmly. It was a warning.

"I'm serious, Sal," Allegra told her. "Even *you* said you'd thought about it: what if we just tell everyone it's because we're in a relationship?"

Chapter 22: Rules of Engagement

Sal sat quite still, treating the situation with far more gravity than Allegra thought necessary, given the fact that they had already agreed to pretend to be friends. "I don't think you really understand what you're proposing."

"I do," Allegra told her. "And it's not like half of Sydney doesn't *already* think we're together." She leant forward, elbows on the table. "When I let Dimi believe I was heartbroken because you'd essentially cold-shouldered me after the gala, he relaxed. He obviously thinks this is the lesser of evils."

Sal visibly tightened at 'cold-shouldered' but didn't comment on it. "Look, I'm not going to deny it simplifies our presentation to Dimi somewhat. But in doing so, it's going to cause a whole cascade of other problems." She shifted her weight uncomfortably. "Letting people assume we're together and actively confirming it—which confers multiple additional pressures—are two entirely different things," she said clearly. "And if we *fail* to convince people, it will do the exact opposite of what you're trying to achieve: it will look like BSA deployed a fake relationship to give Threshold political cover. Instead of looking innocent, you will *look complicit*."

Allegra let those words settle. "Okay, so we can't fail."

Sal gave her an incredulous look. "That comment is exactly why I'm concerned you don't yet grasp what failure would cost you." She paused. "And us."

"Then tell me what I'm missing."

Sal leant forward. "You're thinking about Dimi," she said. "But you're not thinking about what it does to your credibility the moment people decide you benefited from proximity to me." She added more quietly, "You're also not thinking about what happens when your family starts asking questions you can't answer without actively lying."

Surely that wasn't necessary. "Look, Timothy isn't heartless and he's not stupid. Perhaps if we explain to him why we need to pretend, and what he could—"

"How good an actor is Timothy?"

Allegra closed her mouth. She remembered their separation; how he hadn't been able to hide his despair in front of Aaron, even when he could see the pain it caused. She slumped a little. "Bad."

Sal had clearly figured as much. "And Dimi has already instrumentalised him. If Timothy doesn't believe you, or if he knows the truth, I *guarantee* Dimi will be able to draw it out of him," she said firmly. "It's an unacceptable risk. Which means lying to him."

Allegra sank back in her chair. Sal was right. "I suppose it's not like I'm being honest with him now anyway," she muttered. "Telling Timothy we're in a relationship is more honest than pretending I hardly know you."

Sal didn't stop there. "There's also the question of whether *you* can perform this convincingly."

Allegra privately wondered what there was to perform. After all, people were already assuming—and they both knew that there was *something* between them. "We're not starting from nothing."

She could feel Sal's eyes on her as she realised something. "You think that will make it *easier*." She set her jaw and stood. "Okay," she said. "I'm going to set up a mock interview like I often do when training clients for media. If it's going to be that easy, show me."

Sal went upstairs and then emerged from her office with a large DSLR, tripod, and stand. She set up the camera facing the two-seater—instructing Allegra to sit on one side of it so she could adjust the frame—and then set up her laptop on a stand at eye level. She tabbed through a list of files and chose one. A video of a mock interviewer popped up on screen, dressed like a daytime TV host.

Sal took the remote over to the couch and made herself comfortable on the other side, slightly facing Allegra with her legs crossed towards her. She gave her a sober look. "I hope you're ready for this." She pressed a button on the remote with a pronounced click, rolling the video.

In her peripheral vision, Allegra noted Sal visibly relaxing. In the flipped LCD of the video camera, Sal was flashing a warm, friendly smile at the 'host' as she thanked them for coming. "Thanks for having us, Debbie," Sal said in her marketing voice. "It's great to be here again." Allegra smiled too, aware she was expected to.

"So," 'Debbie' began. "How did you two meet?"

Immediately, Allegra realised they hadn't sorted out details. She managed to maintain her smile as Sal stepped in to rescue her. "Through work, actually," she said easily. "I was under the impression all I was doing was scouting new talent. And then I met her." She looked across at Allegra and delivered the warmest, most indulgent smile. Unbidden, Allegra felt her own smile deepen in response to it.

After a moment of silence, Allegra realised that in order for this to look and feel real, she also needed to participate, and Sal was waiting for that. "She certainly made an impression, that's for sure."

Sal cued the next question with a click. "Who made the first move?"

That, Allegra felt qualified to answer. "I did," she said. "At a formal event. She looked incredible."

Sal, watching her, added as if it was delicious gossip. "To be fair, I had been *heavily* indicating all evening that it was welcome..."

That... wasn't exactly what had happened. Allegra could still remember the shock on Sal's face. She pushed that thought aside.

Click. "What makes this relationship different?"

Sal fielded this one. "*We're* so different. She likes *dirt*."

Allegra scoffed. "Well, I wouldn't say I *like* dirt. It's a necessary evil."

Sal shook her head. "It's an entirely unnecessary one," she said, and then gestured at Allegra as if she were talking to a real host. "She'll come home absolutely covered in it, looking like she's had the time of her life. I practically need to hose her down in the carpark."

"Sal needs to get out more," Allegra told the laptop in reply. "Don't worry. I'm working on it."

"You can work on it all you like," Sal said, grinning at her, "you're not going to get me out of the air-conditioning."

Allegra was pleasantly surprised how natural that sounded.

Click. "When you're in a crowded room, how do you find each other?"

Allegra immediately thought of the gala. "She's magnetic," she found herself answering. "You can't look away from her, let alone lose her." She looked over at Sal, perhaps a little surprised by the fluency of her answer. Sal returned her gaze with a level of intensity that unsettled Allegra. Allegra was very, very worried about what might come out of Sal's mouth as she opened it to speak. "Well, she's a head above everyone else. I just look up," Sal said, shooting her a wink.

Click. "Do you find it hard to keep your hands to yourselves?"

Already knocked off kilter from the question itself, Allegra felt something on her leg—when she glanced down, the tip of Sal's stiletto was lightly stroking her calf. It was the same thing she'd done at the bar just before their tequila shots. When she looked up, Sal was giving her a private smile. It was—

"Of course I do," Sal said, eyes still locked on Allegra's. Then, Sal leant over, slipped her hand into Allegra's, and lifted it up to her lips as she glanced at the camera. "I mean, look at her. She's beautiful," Sal said, narrating Allegra's thoughts as she slowly kissed the back of Allegra's hand.

Click. "Can we see a little bit of that?" Debbie sounded cheeky, like she was egging them on for a daytime TV audience. The implication was very, very clear.

Sal looked at Allegra with that easy smile on her lips. Allegra's eyes dipped to them, realising she was required to *demonstrate* the relationship, not merely discuss it. People would want proof, not words. She leant forward a little towards Sal, intending to close that distance and—couldn't. The performance corrupted it. And now she'd hesitated—and she realised her smile was gone too, and her grip on Sal's hand was probably—

"Cut," Sal said, relaxing and releasing Allegra's hand. Her face slipped out of the warm, private smile into something cool and neutral. The contact was gone.

Sal stood and moved over to the camera, unclipping it from the tripod, flipping the LCD around, and cuing the video for Allegra. Sal's eyes were on the screen for just a second. She pulled them away. "Review this. I'll give you a minute." She went upstairs, leaving Allegra to review the footage.

Grimacing, Allegra looked back at the camera. The thumbnail for the video was still on the screen: Allegra in her formal suit and tie with Docs, and Sal beside her in a suit that was just a little too unorthodox to read as conventional. The visual itself sold the story: they looked like a matching set.

She tapped play, expecting to see warmth reflected back at her. Instead, what she saw was Sal looking relaxed, smooth, and practised. Allegra, on the other hand, took half a second to respond to questions, often glancing at Sal beforehand.

Their bickering smoothed things out for a moment. Watching it back, she even grinned—until she saw her smile drop on camera.

Allegra hadn't realised how quickly it disappeared from her face when Sal kissed her hand, nor how visibly panicked she'd looked at Debbie's last question. That single second where she was frozen in place felt like eternity. All the while Sal was still, smiling, and completely welcoming.

Lips pressed together, Allegra stopped the video, skipped back to the beginning, and watched it again.

Sal returned after she finished the second rewatch. Allegra was slumped into the backrest of the couch, holding the camera above her head, half-watching a third time. She paused it.

Sal stood at the foot end of the couch, looking down at her. "Do you still want to proceed?"

Allegra exhaled and shut the LCD, sitting up. "Tell me how to fix this."

Sal was still for a moment, eyebrows up—not the response she'd been expecting. She gave Allegra a curious look, then walked over to the three-seater opposite and settled into it. "The primary issue is that you're not acting," Sal said, "and you're expecting not to need to. The reason it looks so natural and easy for me is that I'm not relying on anything else that may be there. I'm acting."

Allegra digested that. "Okay."

Sal continued. "The rest is just a timing issue. As soon as you try to check consent in the moment, that lag shows."

"I feel like consent is a pretty important part of touch," Allegra said, voice dry.

"That's why this all needs to be decided in advance, in detail, across contexts and in an array of situations," Sal said. She rose smoothly to her feet and corrected the line of her blazer. "That level of planning will need to wait for evening, however. I've been out of the office for a few days and there was the procedural equivalent of farm animals wandering around the office this morning when I arrived."

Before she moved away, though, she spent a few seconds examining Allegra.

"I know what I need to do, Sal," Allegra told her. "And I still think this is the simplest way to manage our most important problems. You made your point. I'll work on it."

Sal watched her for another couple of seconds and then nodded once. "Alright," she said, stepping across to where her laptop was and switching it off. "I'll get Gerard to email you a link to the entire catalogue of media training videos. The only module that matters is the one on personal relationships. You can practise how you will respond to them." She motioned for Allegra to pass her the camera, and then immediately deleted the video. "I'll do a couple more with you tonight." She fitted the camera back into the tripod. "Only film on this, not on your phone." Allegra nodded. "And if your sister goes through your phone at regular intervals we should consider if disappearing messages are the way to go."

It was a stark reminder of what was at stake and why they were going to these lengths. "When do we tell Dimi?"

Sal thought for a moment. "The board is holding an emergency meeting on Friday evening about the media release," she eventually said. "Dimi and

I have both been summoned for it. That's the ideal time for me to disclose to all of them at once that I'm in a relationship with a client."

Allegra winced. She hadn't thought of that. "Will you get in trouble?"

"Yes," Sal said. "But it can be managed."

Allegra put all that together. "So, I shouldn't speak to him about the Redeemer funding anymore?"

Sal hummed. "You *should*," she corrected her. "It shouldn't look like you're waiting until after the board meeting to initiate contact—it would tip him off that we're coordinating it," she said. "Text him today, but agree to meet up on Sunday. You're busy until then and it's your first availability."

"What should I say?" Allegra wondered aloud. "Hi, I'm worried about the Light of the Redeemer Mission funding and how I'm involved with it being frozen? Can we talk about it?"

Sal gave a small nod. "Perfect."

That made Allegra feel a little better. "When can I tell Timothy?" At Sal's deepening frown, she clarified, "That I'm in a relationship with you."

Sal lightened somewhat. "Also after the board meeting."

Allegra accepted that. Two days: also manageable. "Okay," Allegra said, feeling more certain about what she needed to do. "I'll practise while you're at work."

Sal raised her eyebrows in acknowledgement. "You'll need to."

Fuck off, Allegra thought, scoffing. "I'll surprise you."

"You do frequently," Sal said simply, and then collected her phone, gave Allegra another searching look, and headed back down the lift.

Allegra looked back at the camera. There wasn't much she could do without the catalogue, which meant texting Dimi.

That got her up and out of the couch, rattling around the penthouse atrium for a few minutes before she settled outside to swallow the frog and send the damn message.

Don't overthink it, she told herself, tapping in the wording Sal had okayed but changing the last line to, *"can we meet up on Sunday to discuss it?"*

Like Sal always did, Dimi replied straight away. He gave her message a thumbs up and answered, *"Happy to talk it through, I'll have a look at my calendar and get back to you."*

She exhaled; done. Since she'd already swallowed one frog, she might as well shore up arrangements with Aaron, as well. He was pretty unhelpful with what he wanted to do other than, *"Something outside? Otherwise I never get out."* So, taking Sal up on her suggestion of volunteer work (and figuring Timothy would be delighted about it as well), Allegra did a bit of research and signed them both up for a very Clean Up Australia Day-type program. She texted the details to Aaron.

By the time she'd finished sorting that out, Gerard had emailed her a link and password details for the mock interview catalogue.

She hooked her phone up to the stand and set herself up on the couch with the camera and the remote. Then, she took a steadying breath and started working with Debbie.

Talking to herself felt strange in the empty room, and without Sal she had to answer questions she typically would have deferred to her. It was interesting to hear what came out of her mouth: what her instinct was to say, and then how it felt to say it versus what came across on video.

With repetition, her answers smoothed out. Her posture and timing—consciously performed, but paradoxically closer to how she would move in real life—loosened and became more fluent. The more she leant into the performance, the more natural and relaxed she seemed.

Watching the video back, she found the deliberateness of her performance personally jarring but had to acknowledge that *performed* warmth looked real. Whenever she tried to answer honestly with her whole self, that ease and warmth faded, even when she was being 100% sincere.

When she'd finished with the whole 'personal life – relationships' folder, she was left with nothing to do but a body still irradiated and buzzing with energy. She hung her suit in the guest bedroom and went to burn through the aftereffects in Sal's private gym, set by set.

After she put in some quality time turning her muscles to jelly and was on her way to the guest bathroom, she could hear movement in the atrium. Sal was home. She had a quick shower, put her whole corporate get-up back on, and headed out.

Sal was seated at the table with her laptop open. She'd pulled one of the other chairs up beside hers, and in front of it on the table was a sports drink and a cardboard takeaway box; Allegra could smell the charcoal and vinaigrette as she wandered in. It was a clear invitation to sit beside Sal, so she did.

"Good evening," Sal said as she typed, her formal language undermined by her personable tone. "We have some work to do. I just need to get this email off."

Allegra drank deeply from her drink and inspected the food while she was waiting. It was a BBQ lamb salad with more ingredients than she could easily identify; unusually good for takeaway. She googled the shop—some sort of wellness place nearby. "45 grams of protein," she noted appreciatively, reading the nutrition info.

Sal didn't look up. "There's another 20 in the drink. Zoe mentioned you'd skipped breakfast."

Unless two mugs of chai counted as breakfast, she had. Eyebrows up, Allegra ate it, wondering if Sal would make her present the empty box when she was done.

Once Sal had sent her email, she sat up, circled her shoulders, and then pivoted the laptop so Allegra could also read the screen.

There was a spreadsheet open with categories listed. Allegra chewed her mouthful as she read through them: *incidental public, transitional, corporate,* and it wasn't until she read the text down the side of the chart that ran from *acceptable* through to *do not initiate* that she realised Sal had done a whole sheet for how they were allowed to touch each other in various public situations. It was empty.

Sal gave her a moment to read. "You've seen what happens when things aren't pre-negotiated: sometimes nothing connects." She glanced up at Allegra. "And sometimes, everything does."

She had a point, but *this* level of detail seemed excessive. "Do we really need all those categories?"

"Yes. We'll likely need to add more."

Allegra couldn't imagine Sal not being solidly across the appropriate touch for every circumstance, so it wasn't clear why her input was needed. "Shouldn't you complete it and then let me know what you're comfortable with?"

"Consent requires the input of both parties," Sal said dryly. "And no. You need to be able to behave like yourself, especially around people who know you. Concerns about what I may find tolerable or intolerable are secondary."

That made it sound like *all* touch would be unwelcome to her. "Sal, I'm not comfortable touching you in a way that's only 'tolerable', even if it's nothing I would normally do in the circumstance."

"And I'm not comfortable signalling to others that something is wrong between us," Sal said easily. "I'll manage what's uncomfortable for me. You'll manage knowing that some touches will be uncomfortable." She paused, sitting back and looking at Allegra directly. "Unless you've changed your mind about this."

Allegra gave her a look. Sal smiled slightly and moved the cursor to *incidental public (carparks/airports/restaurants).* "Alright. Let's start here."

The level of minutiae was agonising. Sal wanted to account for everything: *when* a touch could be initiated (while speaking, after speaking, while moving), what topics might prompt it, and what the touch itself could be—an arm. A hand hovering over the small of a back, fingers lacing, arms around shoulders. All the way through to a peck on the lips, or cheek, or temple.

In terms of trying to negotiate everything in a way that would be recognisably Allegra-in-a-relationship to people who knew her, Allegra wasn't certain what would read as 'normal'. She wasn't like Vanessa—her and her late husband had been freely all over each other when they weren't fiercely arguing. She and Timothy had always seemed fairly subdued by comparison.

"I don't think I'm too out there?" Allegra decided aloud. "I'm not a big fan of PDAs, if that's what you're asking."

"I'm asking you if you were seated in a restaurant *beside* someone you were in a relationship with, what would you ordinarily do?"

She certainly wouldn't be critically analysing her body language, that was for sure. "I've never thought about it," Allegra realised. "Probably hold their hand?"

Sal typed that in a box.

Allegra second-guessed herself. "But would I do that *with you*?"

Sal looked up from her screen with a tired expression, finger hovering over the delete key.

"Well, people watching us will take *you* into account as well," Allegra pointed out, "and you don't read like someone who enjoys being freely touched."

"I'm going to need you to focus on what I'm like in public when you answer these questions." At Allegra's frown, she exhaled. She shifted in her chair, expression softening and shoulders loosening until she almost morphed—not into someone else, but into the lighter, easier, more approachable version of herself Allegra recognised from their time in public. Sal fixed her with a disarming smile, toying casually with an earring as she said warmly, "Don't forget this is who you're answering questions about."

Allegra felt uncomfortable. "Sal, that's really creepy."

Sal melted back to neutrality. “So you keep saying,” she acknowledged. “So don’t worry about how *I* read. Let’s just get this finished in a way that feels as true to you as possible.”

After they’d filled in the boxes and agreed on their contents, Allegra scrolled through the sheet glumly. “I’m going to need to study this, aren’t I?”

“I’m afraid so,” Sal told her. “If it helps, I will also need to.”

“Will there be a test?” Allegra said, mostly as a joke as she counted the number of cells they’d filled in.

“Every single day, multiple times a day.”

Oh. Allegra sat back, sighing at the sheet. No chance she could cram this in at the last second and scrape by.

Sal shifted her chair a little closer to Allegra’s. “Let’s do some blocking now,” she instructed. “All of the incidental public and professional engagement moves at least once. You don’t want to be doing any of this for the first time on someone’s iPhone camera.”

They went through the spreadsheet cell by cell, practising all the movements in what started off being rather awkward (from Allegra’s end, at least) and ended up being more relaxed.

It was an odd, clinical way to learn how someone’s body felt. Allegra already had some data; she’d touched Sal before, in ways that sat both inside and outside the scope of the spreadsheet. But the details she lacked—Sal’s sharp shoulders, her knees, the way her fingers fit between Allegra’s—were ones she would have preferred to discover under different circumstances. That was probably the point, Allegra realised, rehearsing C5 as she stood behind Sal. She couldn’t be discovering them for the first time on camera.

As if to prove the point, Allegra glanced towards Sal as she tucked her hair behind her ears and noticed the familiar line of Sal’s neck, the bow of it down into her delicate collarbones. They were in the same position they’d been in the alcove—and she realised she already had her hand on Sal’s slender hip. One tiny step, and their bodies would be together.

Sal drew a breath and turned her head fractionally towards Allegra, chin dipping as if she were about to look up at her—then stopped. She stepped away slightly. “Let’s stick to the spreadsheet,” she said evenly, dictating C10, “A to link arms with S to walk out”.

Whatever Sal had just stopped herself from doing, it clearly hadn’t been nothing. She’d also skipped a few to end that column early. Filing that thought, Allegra followed her directions anyway.

Once they'd worked through the spreadsheet and Allegra had touched Sal in all the agreed, appropriate ways, she felt oddly hollow.

Sal was all business. She stood back. "Alright," she said. "I'll leave my personal laptop unlocked for a couple of days until we're both across this."

She stood up, stretching her back and rubbing her neck. She rarely looked her age, but for a second Allegra could see weight under her eyes. It wasn't lost on her that Sal had essentially been working for sixteen hours straight. "You need a holiday," she said, not joking.

"I can't afford to lose focus," she said dismissively. "I'm too close to the finish line. Anything that disrupts that—even briefly—isn't an option." She began to walk over towards the couches and the camera setup. "Would you mind if I reviewed your practice footage?"

Allegra grimaced. *Oh, God.* "Go for it."

Sal observed that and flipped the LCD on the camera around to watch. Allegra then had to sit by and watch Sal scrutinising every microscopic detail of the videos. She expected Sal would have some sharp comment and braced for it after she finished the third video.

It didn't come. Sal spun the LCD around on the camera and fit it back into the tripod. "Shall we do a couple now, with reference to what we just worked on?"

Huh. Allegra took her hands out of her pockets. "Alright."

She sat back on the couch, watching as Sal selected a video from the catalogue. She reflected on how strange it was that a catalogue even existed at all. "Is pretending to be in a relationship something people frequently need training for?"

Sal guessed why she was asking. "We generally use Debbie with existing couples who are at odds, but who need to look aligned in public," she explained. "People whose authority collapses if their private life looks unstable—conservative politicians and religious leaders in particular." She walked around the camera and settled next to Allegra, remote in hand. "Ready?" Allegra nodded.

Unlike in the first dry run together, Sal hung back. She participated, but Allegra could feel the shift in focus towards her: she was expected to carry the interview. And she did, to an extent. The touches landed where they were meant to, and Sal allowed them. Putting a hand on Sal's knee to accentuate referring to her. Putting an arm around her shoulder to signal 'we'. Kissing her cheek during the question that had tripped her up before. It was only logistical questions that Allegra faltered on—but she'd practised just for this. "Let me check with my calendar," she said, looking across to Sal. Sal grinned at that, appearing amused. "Your calendar?" Sal quoted, still in character. "People are going to talk if you make it seem like I control your movements."

Allegra grinned. "They talk anyway, but now they won't be under the impression that I have any sort of functional memory for appointments."

Sal pretended to shake her head at Allegra as if to say 'hopeless' affectionately. To Debbie, she said, "No, we don't have any plans for Christmas, yet. But I don't expect we'll travel anywhere—we'll probably just have a quiet one."

Sal fielded some of the trickier questions, too; "So when did you *actually* meet?" and "How do you balance work with your relationship?" in such a smooth and easy way. The words just fell out of her mouth in exactly the right tone and order to perfectly paint a picture that wasn't—untrue, exactly. Nothing that came out of Sal's mouth was ever an actual lie. It was just framed expertly to deliver a picture that gave a different impression of the way something had happened.

It was unnerving. It made Allegra realise how little blatant lying was actually required—if you were willing to let people believe what you'd carefully implied.

At the end of the interview, Sal took a deep breath and relaxed out of her public persona. A faint smile remained as she stood to retrieve the camera and sat beside Allegra again.

Sal watched only about half the footage before shutting the LCD and nodding. "Okay," she said with some finality. "Not perfect, but it's coherent. People will read your nerves as sincerity and my steadiness as reassurance. That's workable." Sal glanced at her watch, her eyebrows jumping a little. "It's late," she observed, and then looked up a little slyly towards Allegra. "I'm sure Timothy will be worried about you."

Oh fuck off. Allegra sighed heavily at her.

Sal was grinning. "I'll drive you home."

For once, Allegra didn't have to face her dusty boots and old cargos in contrast with the sleek leather interior of Sal's car. The black suit and black leather blended seamlessly into each other in the streetlights, each swoop of colour they drove past highlighting the delicate patterns in the wool.

Allegra relaxed back into the seat with spreadsheet cell numbers still echoing in her head: A3. B10. E12. Each cell: a context, a touch.

It was a short drive to Point Piper. She and Sal had made the decision to drive up to the front gate; if Timothy saw, he saw. He was going to see even more at some point uncomfortably soon.

Exhaling, Allegra gave Sal a faint smile, unclipped the seatbelt and opened the door.

"I believe you have a couple of bookings tomorrow, but you should come back to mine for a study session afterwards," Sal said. Her eyes stayed on Allegra as she climbed out of the car in her suit and tie. "Wear that again. I need the practice."

She drove off before Allegra had processed what that meant.

Chapter 23: Column C

Gerard had sent through the briefs for Allegra's two bookings by 9am the following morning. She sat in her LandCruiser, eating her breakfast and skimming them with interest.

One was a fluff piece for a Vale rag where they needed a photo of her in high-vis outside the gifted property plus a couple of generic quotes; no sweat. The other was a meeting at an outdoor education NGO—'Northstar Pathways', apparently—that was having problems with their at-risk youth bush camps being cancelled because of insurance issues with the site. Sal had noted specifically that she felt Allegra could provide some guidance about what steps they could take to satisfy their insurer's safety requirements. Allegra thought she probably could, but also noted the engagement was volunteer work. A good fit for her, but odd for BSA.

When she asked Gerard about it, he chuckled, "Not all value is measured in dollars, my dear," he said, and then paused. "Having said that, some *is*. Don't forget to review the brand shortlist I emailed you last week."

Allegra put her forehead on the steering wheel. She couldn't think of anything more painful.

The two engagements went smoothly; the Vale photographer was someone Allegra had worked with before, so the process was quick and pleasant. The NGO appointment was more involved: insurance kept revoking coverage for their camps, and they were desperate for any help they could get to avoid breaching funding agreements. When Allegra offered to help, they were overjoyed and dumped a truckload of documents on a USB for her. She put it in her pocket. The rest of her week involved paperwork, apparently; her *favourite*.

Sal had better make this up to me, she thought dryly, driving back to Point Piper to put on the requisite suit she'd been instructed to wear before heading over to Sal's.

Sal had been vague about the time she was due home ('after work' had little meaning for someone who worked every waking minute), but had made clear to Allegra that she was welcome to come over and use the laptop.

So, Allegra sat down at the table to read through the catalogue of allowable touches, aware on some level that she was treating it with more respect than several actual qualifications she possessed.

Sal returned home late in the afternoon. As she arrived in the atrium, Allegra glanced up from the damn spreadsheet. "Welcome home," Allegra said, and then added very dryly, "Honey."

Sal was already smirking at Allegra's reference to their agreement when she rounded the island bench and saw her properly. She stopped, the smirk turning into something else entirely. It was the same look she'd given Allegra at the gala. "Quite a welcome," Sal commented in a low voice, eyes dipping to Allegra's suit. "You wore it."

When she passed Allegra on her way to drop her briefcase in her office, she walked *entirely* too close to Allegra's back, and more slowly than her ordinary brisk walk. A hand trailed over the back of the chair. "Have you been studying hard?"

Allegra tried to moderate her grin. "Have *you*?"

Sal's own dark grin was audible in her voice as she approached the stairs. "Want to test me?"

Allegra turned in her chair now that it was safe to do so. "Yes." She wasn't sure what had prompted Sal to dial things up again, but she wasn't about to complain.

Sal threw a look behind her as she climbed the stairs with the same deliberateness Allegra had first seen her climb them with. "I have about two hours before I need to prepare for tomorrow night's board meeting." She disappeared into her office and returned down soon after.

She stopped at the head of the table, hands resting on the chair. "How strong are you feeling today, Allegra?"

Not fucking very, Allegra thought, already really enjoying herself. Having said that, she'd manage. Sal had made her position on distractions clear. Instead, she replied, "Hmm..." Her gaze was steady. "What are you suggesting I lift?"

Sal looked entertained. "Your game," she said. "Yesterday, we were both composed and focused. That won't always be the case." She leant on the back of the chair. "There's one particular variable I'd like us both to ensure we're able to overcome to deliver a convincing performance of a settled relationship."

Ah, Allegra realised, *so that's what all this is about*. Like sincerity, real attraction must look different on camera from feigned attraction—otherwise why would Sal go to this extent to test it, now, like this?

"Do you think you're up to it?"

"I am." Allegra paused, remembering their near miss on Column C last night. "Are *you* up to it?"

Sal smiled faintly at that. "Let's see."

She set up the camera, then selected a different set of much more sombre, evening news-style questions.

Allegra went first: her job was to answer the questions without being distracted in any way by Sal, who was allowed to initiate any of the touches from the two corresponding columns. Just having Sal smiling mischievously in her peripheral vision and having *no idea* how she'd be touched, or when, was a distraction in itself before Sal ever laid a finger on her.

The real fun came when it was her turn to distract Sal while *she* was answering questions about quarterly fiscal performance results. Despite the dry subject matter, Sal was an absolute fortress. It was only when they moved to stand and Allegra had access to another column that she was rewarded by a short, unexpected pause mid-sentence as she draped her arms over Sal's shoulders from behind.

Checking her watch, Sal stood up to review the footage with her classic smirk. She offered the camera to Allegra when she was done. "You want to watch us?"

Allegra held eye contact with her. "Maybe later."

Sal's grin deepened. She gave Allegra an appreciative look and fitted the camera back into its stand. "Alright, then. You want to try Column C again?" The near-miss from last night. "Let's record it this time."

Column C (entries and exits) had been bad enough last night—and Sal had been very specifically cool and distant then. Repeating the exercise while Sal turned up the heat was a very special type of torture. An arm around Allegra's waist (C3), holding hands (C1), and then turning towards Allegra (C5). This was where they had faltered.

This time, Sal turned around very slowly and stepped in towards Allegra, throwing a glance up at her for a moment before correcting her jacket. Then she brushed Allegra's lapel flat. And then her arms slipped around Allegra's waist and settled their bodies together in a casual, appropriate hug suitable for a semi-formal event. Sal looked up at Allegra.

Watch your breathing, Allegra told herself, smiling casually down at Sal as if they had done this a hundred times and they were having a light conversation.

Sal said in *that voice*, "You can imagine me recounting an entertaining anecdote, if you like."

Allegra gave an appropriate verbal nod; fighting through how aware she was of Sal's body against her was certainly a glorious challenge. *Casual, entertained expression*, she told her face. She wasn't sure how long she could hold it. "Perhaps you could tell me a *real* anecdote," she suggested, hoping for a distraction. "After all, *you* need the practice, too."

Sal laughed once, at the very base of her throat. "Alright," she said, leaning back so their hips sat together but so she could trace the thread patterns in Allegra's tie with a couple of gentle fingers. "Once I was on a Melbourne to Sydney flight, and the man seated beside me was an anaesthesiologist," she said, somehow able to make that career sound sexy by the way she enunciated it. "Highly educated, well-read, flirty—despite his wedding band. We'd been having a reasonably engaging discussion about health sector trends when the disposable towelettes were distributed. Mint-scented," she said, tightening Allegra's tie just a little, and holding eye contact with Allegra while her hands were on her neck. "Anyway, this man continued to discuss the increasing levels of health department bureaucracy as he slowly ate the entire towelette."

Allegra *genuinely* snorted at that. Although she wondered if she would have found it so funny if Sal *hadn't* been coiled around her and she *hadn't* been as relieved as she was to experience an emotion other than Don't Jump Her. "I think I pictured you in a private jet," she confessed.

Sal laughed, deep and slow. "Perhaps if I had the right surname," she said. "I travel with clients on theirs sometimes, but no. Just business class."

'Just'. Then again, they *were* standing in this extravagant house. "Does Dimi have one?"

"Yes. The Blacks—" a phone started to ring, "have one," Sal finished. She let it ring a couple of times. Then, she exhaled at length, and something drained all the way out of her. Stepping away, back straight, shoulders squared, she switched off the camera and went over to the table to answer her phone. "Gerard."

Gerard. Of course. Allegra stood there empty-armed, front cooling from where another body had been against hers. *We haven't finished*, she wanted to say. But Sal's body language said otherwise. She glanced back once—meeting Allegra's eyes—and hesitated. Then she turned away.

Allegra released a breath. Something drained out of her, too.

"I hope you didn't spend all afternoon on that," Sal was saying into the phone. "He did it to make sure you don't have enough time to help me for tomorrow night."

Sal's atrium was quiet enough that Allegra could hear Gerard through the receiver. "Darling, I did the most incredible half-arsed job you can possibly imagine," he said, "and then I spent the rest of the time on Seek Dot Com."

Sal stilled. "I hope that doesn't mean you found something I should be worried about."

"Everything looks clean," he told her. "No one's pinged HR and the last entry on the Atlas log was before the media release." He paused. "But there's nothing wrong with Seek being obvious when he checks my online activity."

Sal smiled at that. "Alright, then. Just a list of whatever releases you can find that reference the leak plus enough printouts for each member would be great." She thanked him and hung up.

When she turned back to Allegra, she was all business. "That concludes our work for today," she said, locking her phone and casting a glance towards Allegra that didn't hit. "Now back to the grindstone." She headed back upstairs to her office.

Allegra would likely have been welcome to stay and continue with the spreadsheet—at least, that would have been the explanation. She was reasonably confident with it now, however, and there was really nothing else for her to do other than rattle around the penthouse. She opted to leave Sal to her grindstone and head back to Point Piper.

Froggy's video dropped at prime time on Thursday evening: statistically, providing the biggest possible audience. Zoe linked it to both Sal and Allegra with a chef's kiss gif. Allegra watched it just as thousands—maybe millions—of people would, feeling creeping dread at what she was about to get into. Then, there was the question of when Austin's loaded teaser would drop.

The following morning, board meeting D-Day, Allegra didn't have anything booked. What she *did* have was a truckload of paperwork from North Star, which she could look over from anywhere that she could open her laptop. And, while Sal didn't ask for company, Allegra felt very firmly that no one should have to be alone before doing hard things. She headed over there, citing the spreadsheet—but left no room for misunderstanding by wearing cargos and faded everything.

She was buried in insurance paperwork when Sal arrived home from work ahead of the board meeting and greeted her politely. She offered Allegra water and poured one for herself, not drinking it straight away; she just held the glass, eyes unfocused, before taking a measured sip. "Froggy's video is doing numbers," she said briefly. "That gives us a window. I'll have Zoe be in touch." She was already turning away as she spoke, conversation concluded.

Allegra didn't expect to be entertained, so she spent a few seconds looking towards Sal's office, and then got back to the North Star mess.

An hour or so later, Sal came downstairs with her briefcase. Not a hair on that woman was out of place and she was wearing a far more conservative suit than usual, pared back to the point of caution.

She looked nice, but Allegra felt that commenting on it would be the wrong move. "Good luck."

Sal smiled faintly; it was hollow. "I'm well-prepared," she said. "I won't need it." She didn't wait to see if Allegra believed her before she left.

Allegra had no sense of how long the board meeting might run. She kept working, combing through the North Star documents and making notes as the light shifted around her. The deeper she went, the clearer it became that this wasn't something she could solve from a desk.

The lift dinged well after dark—Allegra checked her phone: 10:17pm. She pressed her lips together and looked up as Sal rounded the corner into the atrium. She paused mid-stride when she saw Allegra, but fell back into step again. She looked *exhausted.* Whatever polish she had pre-meeting was gone.

Allegra swallowed. "How did it go?"

Sal stopped briefly to answer her. "As expected," she said. "So, manageable." Rather than elaborating, though, she simply went to pour herself another glass of sparkling water. She stayed put for just a moment longer than necessary after the glass was full.

Allegra remembered Sal very confidently advising her that she was going to get into trouble. *I suppose she did, then,* Allegra thought, noting that she was moving like someone who was conserving fuel.

Rather than engage in any sort of small talk, Sal simply said, "You're welcome to use the guest room," and then disappeared upstairs with her water.

Allegra frowned. Water? No wonder there was less of Sal in the room than usual; she'd be famished. After all, Allegra was and she *hadn't* just prostrated herself before the worst person she knew. Well, if she was going to be out getting food for herself, anyway...

Grabbing her phone, Allegra googled that little wellness place Sal had picked up some protein-enriched whatever from for her last night, and followed the directions to get to it.

The girl behind the counter recognised her as she entered and shot her a big smile. "I gather you'd like something protein-enriched or recovery-related?" she said, her eyes dipping professionally to indicate Allegra's shoulders, which were on display in her tank top.

Allegra smiled at that. "Yes?" she said. "For me, anyway. But I also want something that you'd give to someone who's stressed out and had a really long day." She gestured at the menu board. "I gather being in Sydney CBD you'd have something like that?"

The girl was grinning. "We have something like that, yes," she said. "Allergies to be aware of? Likes or dislikes?"

Allegra hmmed. Sal's main response to food seemed to be disinterest, not caution or pickiness. "We're all good on that front," Allegra decided. "Just something... good quality, I suppose."

The girl nodded once and ran her through the ingredients in something called the 'Balance Bowl'. "How does that sound?"

It sounded exactly like the sort of thing Sal usually ordered. "Great." While the girl was preparing it, she read about it on the menu, reciting with perhaps a little scepticism, "'Anti-Inflammatory'."

The girl observed her tone and grinned, matching it. "Is the recipient particularly inflamed?"

Allegra laughed. "She's pretty inflammatory herself, actually, at times."

"Then she will definitely benefit from the Balance Bowl," she told Allegra, measuring the oil. "And sounds like *you'll* benefit from it, too." She had a playful grin.

Allegra had been smiling along with all of it but hadn't given it much thought until the girl was sealing the bowls and had written 'Allegra' on one of them, unbidden. "And the other one?" she asked, looking up with her pen poised over Sal's bowl.

Allegra stalled. 'Sal' wasn't exactly a generic name, and she was clearly a patron of this place. Given the 'you'll benefit from it, too' comment, Allegra felt like Sal would probably want to be consulted on this one. "It's fine, leave it blank."

The girl nodded, got her to pay, and then slid the bowls across the counter. Allegra transported them carefully back to the penthouse and upstairs, knocking gently on Sal's office door.

Sal was seated stiffly in front of pages and pages of logs, scrolling through them and wearing a simple pair of glasses Allegra hadn't seen her in before. She looked up as Allegra entered.

"Here," Allegra told her, placing the bowl beside her and reciting its ingredients. "And apparently all that is good for tired execs."

Sal was still, looking at the bowl. After a moment, she picked it up to open it and inspect it. "Thank you."

"I presume you're allowed to eat in your own office?"

Sal opened the bowl and put the lid aside. "I would starve if I wasn't."

Allegra grinned briefly at that, and was about to go, when she remembered her conversation with the wellness place girl. "They asked me what name to put on your bowl," she began. Sal, mouth already full, clocked what that meant and glanced at the lid; it was blank. She looked back up as Allegra continued, "What do I tell people about us?"

Sal swallowed her mouthful. "I spoke with Zoe: we're going to deploy a social media piece shortly—directly after Austin drops his short. Demonstrating he's wrong about one thing casts doubt on the whole piece," she said, thinking. "But there's no reason you can't be open with private citizens if they ask. Be vaguer with media until after we've released our video, though."

Allegra took a deep breath and nodded once. "So, I'm in a relationship with Sal Lategan?"

"You're in a relationship with Sal Lategan."

Chapter 24: The Event Horizon

It was a beautiful Saturday morning, and Allegra had no choice but to completely ruin it for both herself and her ex-husband.

She was five metres away from the Point Piper house, separated from the man whose heart she needed to break—again—by a steel LandCruiser door and a wire screen front door. The best part of this situation was that she'd done it before and had some idea what it was going to be like. Unfortunately, that was also the worst part.

Last time, he'd sobbed and begged her. On his knees. *God*.

The sheepskin cover on the steering wheel was going to end up embossing little woollen curls in her forehead if she didn't pick herself the fuck up and just do it. She sat up. "Okay," she announced, grabbed her phone, and got out of the car.

Timothy was in the middle of eating a cooked breakfast, sitting at the dining table in the bright morning sunlight. He stood as she entered, his face lighting up. "Allegra!" *God, he was so happy*. "I just made sausages," he said, heading over to the grill to plate them up. "Just two as usual? I'm heading out shortly, but I can sit with you for a bit. I have some wonderful news!"

Please tell me you're dating someone, Allegra thought grimly to herself. "You do?" She sat opposite his place at the table.

He put the plate down in front of her, almost bursting with joy. "We received an anonymous donation yesterday," he said, going back to the bench to cut her some sourdough. "*$50,000*! Absolutely unbelievable. And what incredible timing."

Allegra paused mid-chew. Very incredible timing. Almost like someone knew exactly how much trouble Redeemer was in at this very moment. "So does that solve all the financial issues the funding freeze caused?"

He scrunched his face a little, but it didn't outlast his smile. "Not really. It does buy us more time, though, and it means the community Christmas lunch will be able to go ahead as well." He put the knife down for a moment, his head held high. "What can I say?" he said, closing his eyes a moment. "He provides. He provides exactly when we need it, through the generosity of strangers. I feel restored."

Allegra briefly closed her eyes for a different reason. *Fuck*.

Timothy had gone back to slicing bread. "Anyway! I gather you're just popping in for clothes before heading out for media and such?"

Allegra hesitated. She could say yes. She could let him continue to feel on top of the world. "Well, not for media. I'm meeting up with Aaron today—we're doing some volunteer work for National Parks NSW."

Unfortunately, that just made him look even more delighted. "That will be good for both of you. Should I pack this instead of giving it to you now?" He indicated the sliced sourdough.

Allegra looked at it. God, it was *so tempting.* She could leave and give him another few hours, or a day, or at most a few days of bliss about that donation.

...only to find out from Aaron, the media, or, worse, *Dimi*, that she was 'dating' Sal. She could not give Dimi the leverage of being the first one to tell him. God, and he'd probably text any second, wouldn't he? *Fuck.* "Actually, I need to discuss something serious with you."

That got his attention. "Oh," he said, sobering immediately. Noting her expression, he left the bread and came to sit with her at the table, giving her his full attention. Sometimes, it was easy to spot the pastor in him.

She swallowed. "You're not going to like it."

He considered that and then nodded. "Alright, I'm ready to hear it."

Are you? "I'm seeing someone."

He hadn't been expecting that, and it took him a moment to digest it.

"It's new—really new. I wanted you to be the first to know because I'm sure it'll be everywhere soon."

She couldn't read him. "Because of the media?" She nodded. He mirrored her nod. "Why is it such a serious issue? Are you safe? Because—"

"Timothy..." She didn't really want to answer that question, because in the purest sense of the word, she *wasn't* safe. He wasn't either. But it wasn't Sal's fault—well, it was, but not directly.

"I had to ask," he said, and gave her a wry smile. It fell quickly off his face. "Are they kind to you?" Allegra nodded. "They respect you?" Allegra nodded again.

"Okay," he said carefully, and then added, "may I ask if it's a woman?"

She flinched. "Yes. It is."

He smiled faintly. "You know that's not the issue for me."

"I know." It was just that he took the whole 'til death do us part' thing literally.

He exhaled. His shoulders were lower than they'd been a moment earlier, but at least he wasn't on his knees. "Well, I appreciate you telling me," he said, looking down at his half-eaten breakfast. "Even if it's—" He swallowed. "Well, I appreciate it." He then turned back to his plate and started silently eating.

He wasn't looking at her. She could leave it there, she realised. Technically, she'd told him, even if he hadn't found out that—

"Well." He smiled slightly. "Receiving the donation beforehand certainly made this easier than it might—"

"It's Sal, Timothy," she said, looking up at him. "Sal Lategan."

He froze. After a moment, he put his fork down. "Sal," he said. "The lady with the black sports car who showed up on our doorstep at *7am* on a Sunday." Allegra took a slow breath, and nodded. "The woman who *you* said was infuriating?"

Allegra opened her mouth, and then closed it again. "Yes."

"*Three weeks ago*."

She made a face. "It's been quite fast," she acknowledged. "We really only hooked up last week, but we've been spending a lot of time together."

He was shaking his head. "You barely said hello to her at the gala!"

Allegra felt her stomach drop. She'd forgotten about that. She hurriedly reached for that 'reframing' Sal employed so she didn't need to say 'I was hiding her from you'. "I wasn't 100% certain what I was feeling at that point," she managed, honestly. "I didn't want to hurt you."

Timothy was *staring* at her like she'd told him she wanted to become an executive herself. He looked entirely unconvinced—for a moment, she thought, about the relationship. "I'm not sure how to feel about this, Allegra." He looked worried. "You're telling me it's serious already?"

Allegra nodded. She wasn't even convincing *herself*, even though at this point specifically she was telling the truth: whatever they had going *was* serious, in a way.

He pressed his lips together for a moment, and then shook his head. "That level of wealth is *dangerous*, Allegra, and you do not have the money to protect yourself from it if anything goes wrong," he said. "I think you're going to get hurt." He looked at her quite sternly for a moment, and then snapped back to his food and very deliberately began eating it again.

Allegra sat there, hearing those words echo in her ears and having nothing to say to them. He was right, that level of wealth *was* dangerous.

When he finished eating, he sat back, drew a deep breath, and said, "I think I need to prune the roses again today. They're out of control with all this hot weather." And continued along that line of chatter—clearing their plates—before putting the sourdough into some Tupperware, adding the leftover sausages, and then packing everything into a small Esky. He placed it on the bench, presumably for her and Aaron.

He hardly looked at her the whole time he was talking, filling the space with chatter. Gone was that open smile, that simple joy. She'd ruined it. She'd poisoned that $50,000—and it hadn't even been the wrong thing to do.

Rather than torture them both by hanging around much longer, she took the Esky, loaded it into her LandCruiser, and went to go pick up their son.

Aaron was waiting outside his block of flats wearing a full outfit of extremely sensible hiking clothes. She smiled a little as she pulled up to the kerb, and he swung his surprisingly large body into the car. "Hey."

"Hey," she said, thinking that she would like to hug him if she hadn't been obstructing traffic. She pulled out and immediately got stuck in a line of cars waiting for a green light a couple of blocks ahead. "Oh, yeah," she said dryly. "We're in Parramatta."

Aaron grinned about that. "Oh no," he said in pretend panic. "We'll be late for the rubbish."

She chuckled at that; she'd forgotten how extremely chill he was about everything in comparison to her and Timothy. He didn't get that from Vanessa, either. As they edged out of Sydney towards Royal National Park, she found herself wondering how he'd turned out that way.

Everyone in Sydney apparently had the same idea they had: hit the national parks on the first mild day in early December. Allegra was lucky Aaron already knew all the important Australian swear words—something he *definitely* got from Vanessa—or he might have picked up a few more from Allegra before they arrived.

The carpark was full. Fortunately, that wasn't something she needed to worry about out bush with her SES-kitted 4WD. She didn't really like to exploit that too often, but since they'd be hauling bags far enough already, she decided it would be okay to park on the verge.

They spent a few minutes slathering themselves in the most industrial-strength sunscreen known to man, collected all their bags and gloves and rubbish collection sticks, and headed towards the mouth of the trail.

They hadn't even left the carpark before someone shouted, "Allegra!" at her. She turned to smile and had a phone shoved in her face. Off to a great start. "Can I have a pic with you?" the girl asked, already taking it.

Don't forget you're always on camera, Allegra thought, reminding herself of Sal's words, and smiled warmly at the phone. Then, the same girl took video of her and Aaron walking up towards the track.

With her back to the camera, Allegra gave Aaron an exasperated glance. Unbelievable.

Aaron looked like he was having a great time. "That's pretty full-on," he said about the whole thing, grinning.

The main track was pretty crowded; fortunately, they branched off early into one of the wild, inland tracks which hid the ocean but surrounded them with dense brush and gnarled Old Man Banksias. The wind came in hard off the headland. It blew grit into their eyes and pushed rubbish from the cliffside tourist areas inland, and made holding onto their rubbish bags a full-time chore. It was a relief when the land rose either side of them and they ended up on a more sheltered path.

By this point, they already had two bags each. Even though her bags were full of wrappers, empty plastic bottles and takeaway boxes, they were already quite heavy. Allegra didn't worry about how much they would need to carry until they descended into an inland creek where a huge amount of junk had washed in from the beach. It was slimy, smelly, *and* heavy.

"We've got our work cut out for us," Allegra observed, turning back to Aaron, who was already retrieving another garbage bag out of his daypack. She'd briefly worried about him carrying it—stupid, really. His arms and shoulders were much thicker than they had been a year ago. "Looks like you're getting good rubbish-carrying arms." She grinned at him.

He brightened. Clearly they were a point of pride for him. "Well, no way am I letting my mum be more jacked than I am."

She laughed frankly at that; she hadn't even thought about it. They cleared the rubbish in the creek and headed back up the hill again, hauling the extra bag of wet refuse. Aaron was still riding high on the compliment.

She observed him, feeling uneasy. It reminded her of arriving at Point Piper to Timothy nearly dancing in the kitchen. She swallowed; gossip travelled fast. "I do need to tell you something," she said, before the internet did.

He'd been admiring the view of the sea that was now appearing over the side of the hill, and looked back at her. "Hmm?"

How did you even tell your adult child this stuff? "I'm seeing someone," she said simply. "Her name's Sal."

His eyebrows went up. "'Sal'?" he repeated, like he might have heard the name wrong. Allegra nodded. He looked amused by that. "Okay. Well, have fun and be safe, I guess." He looked back towards the sea.

And that was that, apparently. Allegra supposed it made sense; after all, who wanted to know about their parents' supposed sex life?

She tried to draw him into conversation as they worked. Wasn't that how people got closer? She tried a few different topics, each of them he had polite and friendly answers about, but nothing moved him until she got onto uni—especially his exams.

"I feel confident about Social Policy," he said. "Honestly, I think I aced that exam. The questions were all ones on the prep and one of them was that whole housing reform issue that came up midyear, so it was literally a function of finding a way to just quote everything verbatim into the paper. If I don't get close to full marks for that one, someone's got it in for me." He paused. "Whether or not I'm a shoo-in for Macquarie postgrad will depend on how I do on Biz Law."

Business Law, Allegra thought, remembering it. "You'll be fine, I'm sure."

He looked at her again. "Dad said you did pretty well on all your legal subjects?"

Allegra nodded. "Yes. Before I dropped out." She didn't want to sook about that, though, because she didn't really regret it. She put a heavy hand on his shoulder with a grin. "So, I plan on living the rest of my life through *you* now."

He scoffed. "Says the woman who literally saves people for a living and who's on the news constantly, getting billionaires to donate entire houses to charity."

They intersected with the main path towards Wedding Cake Rock. Right on cue, a bunch of other Gen Zs recognised Allegra and started whispering to each other. She smiled at them, waved at their phones which were definitely recording (but at least not shoved in her face), and kept walking, laden by bags.

Once they'd completed their track, they doubled back and returned along the main route—gloriously flat and clear, the whole stretch of it—towards the carpark.

Allegra felt like she should probably be talking more with her son, but she'd run out of things to say, and Aaron himself seemed completely content to just walk and work. It wasn't tense exactly. It didn't feel strained. It just didn't feel... close, not in the way she wanted it to. It was an odd way to feel about someone she could not possibly have loved more than she did.

They were nearly back at the carpark when her phone dinged with a text message. *Don't be Timothy*, she thought, placing her bags out of the wind and pulling off a glove to check the notification. It wasn't Timothy.

It was Dimi.

Her breath caught. *"Cece asked me to finalise lunch at her place tomorrow. She's expecting you, Aaron, Timothy, and Sal."*

Allegra stared at it. She then scrolled up a little in case she was missing a message. What the fuck? What lunch?

Aaron noticed her expression. "All good?"

She looked up from her phone. "Did you know about some sort of lunch at Cecilie Vale's house tomorrow?"

Recognition dawned on his face. "Oh yeah," he said. "Dad mentioned she might organise something for after church, but it wasn't locked in then. Guess it is now." He considered her question. "You're coming too?"

"Yes," Allegra said, looking back at the message. "And Sal, apparently."

He raised eyebrows at that, but didn't comment on why. He didn't need to; they both knew how Timothy would feel about it. "Alright."

The inclusion of Sal made it feel quite unlikely the lunch was entirely Cece's idea. Allegra forwarded the message to Sal with *"???"* and tucked her phone in her pocket so she could finish transporting the bags back to the LandCruiser.

They rolled the disgusting wet bags in a tarp and strapped them next to the spare on the outside of her car. The rest went into the back seat. Aaron cranked the window all the way down when he got inside.

Allegra laughed. "It's not that bad," she said, thinking of times she'd transported roadkill or medical waste. "It's part of the *experience*."

"Well, my experience is that I'm no longer interested in whatever Dad packed in that Esky," he told Allegra, looking slightly ill. About 20 minutes into their drive home, Allegra noticed him lift it onto his knees and start going through it anyway. She never ate while driving, so had to wait until after they'd dropped off the bags at the tip and thoroughly washed their everything before cramming a banger and sourdough in. Timothy had even packed fruit for them. She ate it, feeling terrible.

Sal texted her while she was driving Aaron back to his flat. The notification came up on screen, plus an intro that read, *"I'll be home by 9, you can let yourself into my..."* Her phone was in the centre console, and Aaron glanced at it as it buzzed, noted the badge and the preview, and then quietly chuckled to himself.

Allegra swiped to dismiss it. "*What*."

"I just witnessed my *mother* getting a booty call."

She sighed. He had *definitely* spent too much time living with Vanessa. "That is *not* what that is," she said, pulling up to the kerb by his flat. "Go have a shower. You stink."

"It's part of the *experience*," he told her, echoing the way she'd said it with a grin as he got out of the car. "Bye, Mum." He paused. "See you tomorrow, I guess?"

Tomorrow. "Yes," she said, and like it wasn't obvious, "wear something really nice."

He saluted her and headed back towards his building.

Allegra sat there in the car for longer than she needed to, her palm resting on the handbrake as she watched him walk inside. Her chest felt tight.

Watching him disappear through the double doors, she had—suddenly, irrationally—the awful sense that this was the last ordinary moment she'd share with him. It was strange and disorienting, like déjà vu; like seeing Lachie close the front door behind him for the last time all over again.

She stared at the building for a moment, and then pulled out onto the road again, unsettled. The image stayed with her as she drove.

It didn't feel any different without Aaron, she realised as she turned out onto Parramatta Road. She didn't feel the absence of him, or any yearning to still be in his presence—not the way she had when he was much smaller. The absence of that pull felt like a hole; and looking at him felt like visiting a house she'd lived in years ago that was no longer hers. She recognised it, she was allowed in. But it wasn't home anymore.

It wasn't like anything had even been wrong with today; it had been nice. She'd enjoyed spending time with him. But when she thought about Sal's recommendation that she improve her relationship with him, *how*? How did she bridge a divide carved out by years of being gone, doing disaster recovery and bush rescue work?

She had no fucking idea, and the fear was that something else would fill the hole that she'd left.

She had no answers when she arrived at Sal's. Sal had said she could let herself into the penthouse, so she did. She had that shower she'd told Aaron to have (thankfully Sal didn't need to smell her after *that* job) and changed into fresh clothes. Then, she spent ages lying supine on Sal's three-seater, trawling Google for every reputable article she could find about bonding with adult children.

Sal came home after dark. She changed into flats by the lift, and walked slowly into the central room, placing her keys and phone on the island bench. She leant there for a moment.

Allegra sat up, some distance from her. She could see the exhaustion even from there. "How was the marathon?" she asked with a gentle grin.

Sal glanced at her, scoffing gently. "Dinner was fine," she said in reply, and then watched Allegra carefully as she added, "She looked beautiful. Red suits her."

Allegra's lips parted involuntarily. "Oh, you were—"

"Just my legal counsel," Sal finished in explanation, slipping into a deep, mischievous grin.

Allegra exhaled in a hiss, giving her a hard look. "Fuck you." She flopped back on the couch.

Still grinning, Sal came over to sit on the two-seater opposite, crossing her legs. "I see you also survived the day."

Allegra had a pillow over her face. She mumbled something into it and then lay there a moment before putting it aside and sitting up. They did need to talk about Dimi. "Forget about today," she said. "What about this lunch tomorrow? We need to go, don't we?"

Sal noted the pivot, paused, and then followed her with it, nodding. "It would be a snub to Cece for us not to," she confirmed. "Which is precisely the reason he set it up like this. You give Vales what they want, always."

That answered Allegra's other question. "So it *was* him?" Sal nodded. "Aaron said Cece's been suggesting it for a while."

"And he would have picked up on that and seen it as a *brilliant opportunity* for him to further his own goals," Sal said, distaste audible. "And get us all sitting around the same table at once for a lovely family lunch."

Allegra shook her head, making a face. "It's flat-out cruelty to invite both Timothy and you," she decided. Then she added, already anticipating Sal's assessment, "And yes, I know he'll justify it to himself as making everyone suffer for two hours just to spare us the horror of knowing you a second longer than that."

"I wouldn't have put it quite so poetically, but yes."

Allegra leant into the spine of the couch, considering what it meant the lunch was going to look like. "His goal is to break us up, then."

"One of them," Sal agreed. "I gather from your comment that Timothy would probably also like that."

He didn't say that, but Allegra doubted she was wrong. She exhaled. "He thinks I'm going to get hurt."

Sal pressed her lips together. "Then *my* goal for the lunch will be changing his mind," she said evenly. Allegra waited for her to elaborate, but she didn't.

Allegra left it. "You said Dimi has more goals?"

"Yes," she said. "I think he will also be checking to see what I've told you about him." She uncrossed her legs and leant forward on them for emphasis. "It is *crucial* you treat him with warmth, respect, and nothing else. He must not suspect."

Well, Allegra figured, she'd done it once before. She could do it again. "I understand," she told Sal. "And I gather another goal is assessing me for whatever he thinks he needs to reinstitute Redeemer funding?" Sal made an affirmative noise. "Do you think if I do well, he will?"

To that, Sal had nothing. "I don't know."

Mentioning *Light of the Redeemer Mission* funding reminded Allegra of the striking coincidence this morning. "Lucky they got that $50k donation, isn't it?" she said pointedly.

Sal gave no acknowledgement she'd heard Allegra. "I don't know if we can expect the funding to go ahead simply by ticking all of Dimi's boxes. We may need to apply incentive to other Impact Foundation board members." Allegra could see from her expression that her brain was already ticking on that one.

"Well, I've got to try anyway," Allegra told her. "That's what's most important to me right now. I've caused Timothy enough stress this weekend. I need to get his funding moving."

Sal looked at her thoughtfully. "You do realise that the way to do that is to make yourself look harmless? Meaning he's got to question your competence and therefore usefulness to me?"

Allegra wasn't following exactly. "So I just have to be really blonde, or?"

"In front of Timothy, Cece"—she paused—"and Aaron."

That pause meant that she knew exactly how Allegra would hear it: competence was all she had going for her as a parent at this point. She looked away. *That fucker*, she thought, wishing Dimi could just be ousted and gone already. "He really stacked this lunch, didn't he?"

Sal opened her mouth to respond, and then closed it again and took a breath. "There's more," she said evenly. "His 'real' daughter and new granddaughter are coming."

Allegra looked up. "Just for icing on the cake?"

Sal shrugged.

Allegra shook her head. Some men should just be punched. “Monster. I want to kill him.”

Sal remained impassive. “And yet, you’re going to have to charm him, perform a settled and healthy relationship with me, and be the sweetest, blondest, most harmless version of yourself possible,” she said. “Otherwise Timothy may never get his funding, and Dimi may escalate pressure on you—and that’s likely to involve other people you love.”

Allegra thought again of the distance she’d felt with Aaron earlier; how exposed it suddenly seemed. Dimi wouldn’t leave a gap like that alone. “Then that’s what I’ll have to do.”

Sal didn’t look even faintly reassured by her confidence. “And what *I* will have to do is put you somewhere I can’t shield you,” she said. “And trust you not to give him a clean shot at both of us.”

Chapter 25: A Nice Family Lunch

Parked in Timothy's driveway, the LandCruiser smelt like Maccas rubbish and wet cardboard.

Sal had insisted Allegra drive them into Point Piper for the lunch in case either Dimi or Timothy saw them arrive—it was apparently unacceptable for them to show up in Sal's sports car. Allegra preferred to drive anyway, but the timing wasn't ideal. She hadn't even had time to vacuum it.

Sal appeared calm and composed, but the fact that she hadn't teased Allegra about the smell of the car suggested she was otherwise. Her breathing was too slow and too even—measured, not relaxed. She noticed Allegra looking at her. "Watch your micro-expressions," she warned, as if they were already being watched.

Allegra scoffed. They'd been practising those for days. "You still don't trust me."

"If I didn't trust you, we wouldn't be here," Sal said as she opened the door. "I just need you to be thinking about what's on your face at all times." She slid out of the car.

Allegra met her around the other side at the gate. Her dark palette stood out against the white fence, even though she'd switched her structured black blazer for a floaty navy blouse and her sharp stilettos for flat slingbacks. As usual, it suited her—if it weren't going to be 30-something today. "Won't you be hot?"

"It's silk," Sal said, like that settled it, and then her eyes dipped to Allegra's outfit. She was wearing her white shirt with the sleeves rolled up, the hem tucked into her newest pair of jeans, and a tan leather belt. "Fine," Sal decided, and slipped their hands together (spreadsheet cell C1) as they stepped out onto the street to walk uphill to Cece's.

Walking hand-in-hand with Sal felt unremarkable and domestic; too normal for what they were approaching. One of Allegra's neighbours greeted them politely on his way out for a walk. They responded in unison, and then both very carefully pretended that hadn't happened. Before Allegra had any time to process that, they were at Cece's.

She'd asked them to enter through the garden, and that gate was unlocked. It opened to a spacious entertainment area with polished white concrete, a broad pergola, and room for dozens of people. Beyond the entertainment area was a narrow strip of sprawling gardens—roses, all perfectly tended—that led up to what could only be described as a blue spaceship rather than a house.

A large square table had been set up under the awning and out of the direct sun, and a small collection of people were already gathered around it. Allegra didn't realise how tense she was until she noticed Dimi wasn't here yet. She released a breath. Then she saw Timothy.

He turned his head towards them as they entered, whatever he was talking about briefly dying on his lips as he saw Sal and Allegra hand in hand. He forced himself to finish whatever he'd been saying to Cece.

Opposite him, Cece and her husband sat back in the shade as a staff member poured chilled water. Nearby, their children—young adults, really—were gathered around Isaiah's wheelchair, watching a phone. Aaron had pulled a chair up beside him. He looked up as Allegra entered, his eyes moving from her to Sal. He seemed faintly surprised but smiled at Allegra anyway, glancing briefly at Timothy.

As Sal and Allegra approached the table, Beau's phone popped up, angled at them.

Cece swallowed her water and put a hand up to catch his attention. "No videos at lunch. Put that down!" she told him sternly. As he grumbled about it, she said to Allegra and Sal, "I'm so sorry, he knows better."

Sal smiled and shook her head, dismissing it as they sat down together on one edge of the table.

Isaiah was smirking at Beau—for a moment, Allegra thought Beau might actually hit him. Isaiah did look much better, but the bandages, casts, and cranial helmet made it clear he wasn't ready for even a playful shove.

Allegra was worrying about that when she noticed Aaron glance up at Timothy again. Beside her, Sal was turning towards him with a warm, practised smile. "Good to see you again, Timothy," she began in a softer voice than Allegra had heard before. "I owe you a better introduction than the last one." She held her hand out.

Timothy paused just a fraction before accepting and shaking it.

A couple of the other kids glanced up; if they'd noticed the tension while half-listening, Cece and her husband certainly had. Allegra should probably smooth it over. "She was scouting me," she explained to them, and then added, "proactively."

"The marketing exec in me," Sal acknowledged, looking apologetically at Timothy. "Not my best showing. This meeting is under much nicer conditions." She cast her eyes out over Cece's roses. "Speaking of which, Cece, your garden is *beautiful*."

Cece's eyes lit up. She was only too happy to accept the compliment.

Before Sal sat back, she found Aaron—tall, blond, and impossible to miss—and smiled when she caught his eye. "Aaron," she said briefly. "It's good to finally meet you."

All manners, Aaron smiled back. "You, too." He glanced immediately at Timothy, then at Allegra, and then, hesitantly, back at the phone they were all watching.

Noting everyone's attention, Cece took the opportunity to introduce her kids—Beau and Isaiah, whom Allegra already knew, and their younger sister Astrid.

When Cece introduced Sal to her kids, she added, "Sal grew up with Helen Black, Sophia's mother."

Watch your expression, Allegra hurriedly told herself; Sal grew up in a Black household? Not just orbiting elites, but *in their household*? She swallowed. Across from her, Timothy shifted uncomfortably in his chair.

Oblivious, Cece introduced her husband Julian to Allegra, and then Sal and Julian exchanged brief small talk about a business merger Allegra had never heard of.

Her eyes drifted over to the children talking animatedly about whatever they were watching. She didn't give much thought to why they were getting along so well, until she noticed Astrid self-consciously smoothing her hair and checking her makeup while he was angled away from her. That made her smile.

Allegra went back to half-listening to the business chatter, weighing up taking Sal's hand so she looked at least slightly connected to the conversation. Timothy was sitting by himself across from them, though, stiff and not his usual social self. She decided not to touch Sal. In the end it didn't matter, though, because Sal referred to her in conversation and took her hand anyway. Their interlaced fingers rested between the arms of their chairs, tucked neatly under the table.

Allegra was quietly worrying about its impact on Timothy when Sal's hand tightened on hers.

The gate clicked. From Sal's reaction, Allegra could tell who it was.

"Sorry I'm late!" Dimi's warm voice called as he pushed the gate open with one hand, cradling a very small, very pink baby in the other. A much younger woman followed him in—presumably his daughter, the baby's mother. Nothing about her suggested 'new mother': she didn't look tired or frazzled, and she was immaculately dressed. She didn't *look* like Sal, per se—but there was something familiar about her. Allegra couldn't put her finger on it.

"In my defence, I have the best possible excuse for being late," Dimi was announcing as he approached the table, looking down at the tiny little creature in his arms. "Everyone, I'd like you to meet Matilda Grace, the newest, sweetest Black."

Cece was sold. She jumped up immediately to go and dote on her as the mother stood back with a smile. "Technically, she's a Whitcombe," she told Dimi.

Dimi scoffed. "She's a Black! Look at those beautiful blue eyes..." he said as he passed the baby to Cece.

Allegra remembered Sal's brown eyes. She squeezed her hand.

At their linked hands, Allegra remembered she was here to perform. "Nice to see you again, Dimi," she said with her warmest grin. "You weren't wrong—she's beautiful. Congratulations." Allegra moved her eyes briefly to Dimi's daughter.

Dimi looked briefly a little bashful. "Goodness me! Where are my manners? Allegra! This is Prue, my daughter. Prue, Allegra Sinclair." Prue came forward to shake Allegra's hand with a big smile. She seemed warm. Then, so did Dimi.

"Prue," Timothy acknowledged across from Allegra, giving her a nod and a smile.

They knew each other? Allegra's eyebrows would have shot up if Sal's comment about watching what was on her face wasn't still ringing in her ears.

Beside her, and in her line of sight to Dimi, Sal warmly addressed Prue. "She's even more beautiful in person. Congratulations."

"Oh—your gift," Prue said, as if suddenly remembering, "Jack wanted to tell you it was the *exact* same edition his grandmother used to read to him, so even though it's for Tilly, I think it's going to end up in *our* library."

Sal stood for a moment to share a brief hug with her. One arm, polite, somewhat limited. She slipped her hand back into Allegra's as she sat down again.

"I'd let you hold her, but..." Prue said, and then threw a look over her shoulder; Cece had taken possession of the child and didn't look ready to give her up.

Sal chuckled. "I'm happy to wait my turn."

Beside her, Timothy was watching Sal in assessment.

The kids had barely even looked up as Dimi and his family entered—that suggested to Allegra that they might be quite familiar with him.

They all settled down at the table—Dimi took a seat directly opposite Sal and Allegra—as the staff took everyone's drink orders and arranged to bring out the meat for Julian to BBQ. Allegra hadn't even given her order when a craft beer was placed in front of her. It was the same one she'd had at the gala.

She blinked at it and then looked up. Dimi, who had been quietly watching her, smiled and leant forward, lacing his hands on the table.

He's going to talk to me, Allegra realised. He inclined his head towards Sal, his question warm and casual. "How did you decide it was worth another go? What convinced you?" He waited until everyone was looking at them before adding. "I'm curious."

Timothy was listening; everyone was. Her throat tightened. Any light, easy answer—any shrug, any "I don't know," any hint that she'd simply gone along with it—would land wrong. It would make it sound like Sal had manipulated her. Timothy couldn't hear that; *Aaron* couldn't hear that. That wasn't the Allegra they knew. Her plan of being blonde and harmless was dead in the water.

Sal's hand tightened on hers; she would just have to be vague. "It felt worth another conversation," Allegra said. "And I didn't see a reason not to have it." She hesitated, remembering how naturally their bickering had read. "Even if she's pushy as hell."

Sal didn't miss a beat. "Sorry. Occupational hazard."

"Well, let's get some work-life boundaries going," Allegra said lightly to her as if it was something they discussed often. Then, to the table, she said, "Because she works 24/7, she forgets she doesn't need to sell herself to someone who's already agreed to dinner. I'm not a client."

"Technically, you *are* our client, my dear," Dimi said in a tone light enough to suggest he was simply joining in on the fun, but it caught Allegra on the jaw. Sal squeezed her hand under the table as Dimi continued. "And when professional boundaries blur, misunderstandings happen. I'm sure you'll eventually work out what it means to be Sal's plus one." He held Allegra's gaze for a moment.

Allegra was too busy trying to look unbothered to notice why Sal's hand shifted, until she realised Prue was addressing Sal. "Speaking of plus ones, are you two coming to Helen's for Christmas this year?"

Sal made a neutral noise. "I'm not sure of our movements yet."

Prue laughed at that. "Very diplomatic," she said, giving Sal a long-suffering look. "I can't believe she thinks everyone's going to travel up to Byron on Christmas day. Like none of us have any other family?"

Dimi had been listening. "It's an hour and a half," he chimed in, probably referring to flight time. "It will make her happy if the whole extended family is there."

Prue continued complaining about it. When Dimi looked across at Sal, his eyes rested on her momentarily. "You're most welcome to join us if you need a lift up, Sal. Helen would be happy to have you two as well."

Allegra remembered Sal's comment about the Black family jet.

Sal smiled at the offer. "Thank you. That would make things smoother. I'm genuinely not sure what our plans are yet, though." She looked deliberately at Allegra. Allegra gave a noncommittal shrug, playing along, aware of Dimi's intent gaze still on them.

Sal was very, very still beside her.

"Well. I'll stop banging on about it, I promise," Dimi said, his quiet voice still somehow cutting across all the talk at the table, "but it is very nice to see you finally settled, Sal. Such a shame your parents never got to see it. They'd be so happy." Despite addressing Sal, he was watching Allegra.

Sal's hand was briefly tight on hers, restricting movement. The message was clear: be careful how you respond to this.

The way Sal herself actually responded was a warm, easy smile and a glance across at Allegra. Allegra mirrored it—convincingly, she hoped—and made a split-second decision to lift Sal's hand to her mouth and plant a kiss on the back of it.

There was a sort of 'aww' from Cece, her husband, and Prue, hopefully not at the expense of Timothy. Aaron, clearly thinking the same, looked immediately to his father. Timothy was just out of Allegra's line of sight, but she could feel his stillness. She didn't look. Dimi did.

Sal's hand was tight in hers—just as well, because otherwise Allegra would already have turned to Timothy. Even in her peripheral vision, she could see the hunch of his shoulders, the wavering line of his brow. She understood, vaguely, that acknowledging him would give Dimi something. She didn't know what. She just knew she couldn't risk it.

She was managing—until Aaron looked at her. His eyes touched hers, and then he looked back at Timothy. He frowned.

Something tightened inside her. Aaron was *not* going to see her callously ignoring Timothy, whatever the fuck was going on here. She turned her head towards Timothy to acknowledge him.

The worst thing was that she could see gratitude in his eyes that she'd thought of him. He appreciated it. Aaron's brow loosened, too. Comforted, he looked back at the phone.

Dimi looked between Aaron and Timothy, something twigging for him. Rather than look at Allegra again, he relaxed back to listen to whatever Cece was talking about. The moment had passed.

Allegra had no time to dwell on it, though, because all the meat was unwrapped and ready to be cooked. "That's me," said Julian with a grin, and hopped up to go and grill it.

Timothy and Aaron nearly spoke over each in offers to help—something which made the table laugh. "I'll go, Dad," Aaron said, and went over to assist.

That had Cece looking askance at her own non-offering children. Beau and Isaiah glanced at each other and groaned. "Do you need any more help, Dad?" Beau called, clearly expecting the response he got which was a dismissive handwave. Beau gestured at the BBQ. "Dad said he doesn't need help," he told Cece, but his real meaning was 'I told you so'.

Cece leant back in her chair, jogging Tilly a little and shaking her head. "Tell me your secrets," she said tiredly to Timothy.

That made Timothy grin slightly. "Well, I could," he said. "But I hear evangelising is now considered impolite."

Cece sighed. "You hear that, kids?" she said, almost certainly joking. "I'm sending you to church next Sunday." They all glanced at her, and each other, and then ignored her.

Well, except Beau who said, "Okay, Mum," with about as much sincerity as he'd shown when he offered to help with the BBQ.

Beside Allegra, Sal had been quiet, idly toying with one of her earrings as she listened. After a moment, she sat forward. "Does your church need volunteers, Timothy?"

Timothy looked genuinely surprised at both the fact she was speaking to him and that she in particular would ask any sort of question about a church. "Always," he said automatically. "But my charity's where they're always most useful. Preparing and distributing food takes a lot of manpower."

Sal nodded once, ignoring Dimi's eyes on her as she looked over at Cece.

Cece understood immediately what she was suggesting. She stroked Tilly's head, thoughtful. "Volunteer work would be good for this lot," she said of them. "And it wouldn't be bad for their resumes, either." There was a collective eyeroll about that from the kids.

It was Aaron calling from the BBQ, "Pretty sure my dad will let you film it if you *do* help Redeemer, Beau," that had the boys taking it more seriously.

Allegra was impressed. So was Sal. It was a neutral topic, so glancing at each other in acknowledgment was safe. Beyond Sal, Timothy was watching Aaron with a mixture of intense pride and something that looked dangerously like hope—probably at the thought of doing his part for the planet and democracy by converting the next generation of billionaire Vales.

After a moment, he returned to reality, straightened, and looked at Sal. Swallowing, he managed a smile at her. He knew what she'd just done. The smile she returned to him was warm but brief—as if to acknowledge his thanks but not revel in it. She looked back towards Prue and Cece, who'd picked up their conversation again.

That was when Allegra realised how much Sal had just neatly accomplished. Dimi watched the whole exchange, his eyes heavy on Sal.

The conversation broke when Julian announced the meat was done. It wasn't—staff stepped in to rescue it—but Julian, apparently satisfied he'd done his part, dropped back into his seat beside Cece and Tilly. Plates were set, salads passed, meat served.

It was good; Allegra barely noticed. Cece and Prue drifted into talk about childcare and nannies, a level of support so far removed from Allegra's own early motherhood—she'd barely survived it, literally—that it left her wondering, briefly, how different things might have been. She didn't follow the thought where it led.

As their plates were collected and they all settled back in their chairs, Cece sighed, looking down at Tilly. "I suppose I should stop commandeering the baby," she said reluctantly, and then looked across at Sal and Allegra.

Allegra stiffened; hopefully not visibly. She wouldn't be able to say no in front of everyone in a neutral way, would she? Especially not after discussing babies at breakfast with Dimi the other morning.

Sal could clearly feel Allegra's reaction through their laced fingers, and stroked the back of her hand with a thumb briefly before sitting forward and freeing her hands. "If you wouldn't mind lending her to me for a moment, Cece," she said warmly. "I'd love to hold her."

Cece looked faintly surprised. "Well," she said, smiling, "that's... nice to see." She stood to transfer the baby directly into Sal's arms.

Sal settled back down with Tilly, with the same apparent ease Dimi had. Allegra knew enough about Sal at this point to recognise it was *performed* ease, but it still struck her as odd. Tilly in her little pink and white onesie was an unexpected interruption in Sal's dark, sharp geometry.

She figured she shouldn't abandon Sal here; especially since Sal was clearly doing this for her. She shuffled her chair against Sal's so she could reach over and run a palm over that warm, soft little velvet head. Such a tiny, helpless little creature to be responsible for such an uncomfortable reaction in her.

Allegra had been lost in thought—the way the light used to fall on Aaron's bassinet—when Cece's voice got her attention. "It does make you think, doesn't it? About timing." She was watching the 'couple' wistfully.

Allegra had barely managed to conceal a reaction to that when Dimi, who'd been watching, also spoke up from across the table. "Susan used to be friends with a very well-known IVF doctor," he said—from context, Allegra presumed Susan to be his late wife. "If you two are ever looking for a consultation, I could arrange something discreet."

Jesus. Just the thought of being pregnant again caused Allegra's blood to run cold. Too many memories. She glanced over at Aaron, whose eyes were visible over the top of Beau's phone. He was listening.

Sal smiled at Dimi's offer. "Very kind," she said, appearing to be genuinely grateful. "We'll take you up on that if we ever need one—presently, we're still at the 'working out how to share calendars' stage."

Cece tilted her head. "Well, I'm just saying it's nice to have possibilities." She looked across at her kids.

Beau and Isaiah shared a tired look. "Come on, Aaron," Beau said pointedly. "Let's go inside before Mum starts asking us about grandkids." They headed indoors together. Aaron paused just long enough to glance back at Timothy and Allegra before following them inside.

Dimi clearly intended to close out the previous conversation himself. "You're right, Sal—it's probably wise to be sure before making any irreversible decisions," he said thoughtfully, glancing briefly at Prue before his eyes settled on Sal. "Children notice when they aren't wanted."

Sal was close enough for Allegra to feel her freeze momentarily. Sal didn't let it show.

Dimi's eyes then moved to Allegra. Allegra nodded absently as if Dimi had said something general and appropriate, slipping her hand beside Sal's arm, careful not to disturb Tilly. Sal didn't respond.

Instead, she mirrored Allegra's nod at Dimi. "Very true," she told him warmly; Allegra wondered how much effort it took for that to sound effortless. "Anyway." She sat up. "Thanks for letting us borrow her for a moment, Cece! It's much appreciated." She smiled briefly at Prue and transferred Tilly back to Cece. She then stood back, appearing completely relaxed. "I'm just going to duck inside for a moment."

Cece nodded and then looked up at one of her staff. "Could you assist Sal?"

Allegra watched Sal be shown inside.

"Something wrong, my dear?"

That *fucker*. She managed her tone and reached for the most harmless answer. "I suppose I'd never thought about having more kids," she said, as if confessing. "I'm still trying to get the first one right." She paused. "Although he seems to have managed that without me."

Timothy, silent and withdrawn through that whole conversation, warmed briefly. "He's great."

Dimi's eyes moved between them. "He's clearly special to you, that's for certain."

Between how that line set her hair on end and the sharpness of Sal's absence, there was no chance she could stay here and be menaced alone. She needed to check on Sal. The second the girl who'd shown Sal inside reappeared, Allegra glanced at Cece and indicated her. "Mind if I—?" Cece nodded.

Allegra hopped up and allowed herself to be led inside a very large, empty entertainment room with a postcard view of the Harbour Bridge and Opera House. Pretty, but not what she was looking for.

They passed a display kitchen on the way towards what Allegra presumed were the guest facilities; a glass-door fridge was clearly intended for guests to help themselves. Allegra stopped in place, spying some drinks. "Would it be alright if I grabbed one of those?"

The girl nodded. She went to the fridge and retrieved a glass bottle of sparkling water, handing it to Allegra. They continued on until they reached the Women's. "Would you like me to wait here?"

Allegra shook her head and patted her pocket. "Don't worry, I always pack a compass. I'll find my way out." She grinned.

The girl looked entertained, nodded, and then headed back down the corridor to the garden.

Allegra went in. Cece's house was built for entertaining: the Women's was like a small, upmarket commercial facility, with flowers, hand towels, and three separate stalls. Sal was leaning heavily on the opulent handbasin in front of them, staring at herself in the mirror.

She looked up as Allegra entered. Her eyes dipped to the door. Allegra guessed why. "There's no one there."

Sal nodded, took a deep breath, and then looked back at the mirror. Thankfully, her eye makeup was still perfect. Despite that, Allegra's impulse was to hug her; after all, that's what she would have most wanted.

Sal, though? Probably not. Instead, Allegra approached her and put the bottle of sparkling water on the countertop.

Sal looked at it for a moment before she registered what it was and why Allegra had brought it. Allegra was rewarded with an actual smile, however brief. "Thank you," Sal said, taking a sip from it.

As Sal tilted her head back to drink, the line of her neck was very visible and very close. Allegra had to catch herself before she made a mistake. *Leave now*, she told herself, *you being a comfort cuddler doesn't make Sal one.*

Backing away respectfully, Allegra waited outside in the hallway—there was even a chair nearby—until a few minutes later when Sal emerged. She was once again wearing her smooth public persona.

She paused on seeing Allegra waiting for her in the hallway. "Of course," she said dryly. She offered Allegra a hand up. "That's a display chair, by the way. You're not supposed to sit in it." Once Allegra was standing, Sal laced fingers with hers.

It's just C1, Allegra told herself. "Have you tried telling me not to do something?"

Sal shot her a smirk and led her towards the garden. "Touché." As she looked at her, though, her grin faded. "You're not doing badly, by the way," she commented of the lunch, "given all the traps."

At the reminder of them, Allegra pressed her lips tightly together. "He is being *so cruel* to you."

Sal looked impassive. "It's not cruelty. He's checking what you know." Allegra stopped in place for a second, processing that. Somehow, that made it *worse*. Sal tugged her hand, promising, "We can talk more later."

Allegra nodded. Their grip on each other's hands tightened as they walked outside and approached the entertainment area again.

All eyes were on them as they sat down; Allegra was most concerned about Timothy and Dimi's.

"Welcome back," Cece told them, noting their smiles and their linked hands. She clearly found it charming. "I was just commiserating about the fact my daughter wants to go to *Melbourne* University. Apparently, she's not a fan of sunshine or knowing what season it is."

Sal smoothed out her top. "Perhaps she's a fan of good coffee instead," she suggested. "Melbourne is excellent. Two of my best employees graduated from there." Allegra didn't miss the 'my' instead of 'our'. Neither did Dimi.

Cece exhaled. "I suppose I should be happy she even cares about university," she said at length. "Neither of my boys do. Neither of them would have passed a single subject if we didn't heavily incentivise them to."

"We're lucky in that regard, too," Timothy acknowledged. "We never needed to sit on Aaron about studying. He *wanted* to do well. He still does."

Dimi—who had Tilly again—had been sitting back in his chair, his eyes moving between speakers. When Timothy mentioned Aaron, he leant forward a little, looking thoughtful. "Aaron's studying Arts/Law at Macquarie University, isn't he? Third year?"

Allegra's stomach tightened. Had Timothy told him—?

"That's right," Timothy agreed, looking briefly surprised he knew as well.

Dimi was speaking to Timothy, not Allegra. "And he's looking at postgraduate study, I gather?"

"Yes," Timothy said. "A Master of Laws."

Dimi sat back, giving the matter consideration as everyone watched him. "I may come in handy, here," he said at last. "I hold a lot of sway with the admissions board at Macquarie—a number of old friends are on it."

Allegra felt a chill run down her spine. Sal's hand tightened in hers.

His voice was quiet, and his tone was mild. "Perhaps I could change their mind, if it should come to that."

While the floor dropped out from under Allegra, Timothy's eyebrows lifted in hope. "You would do that?" Dimi nodded. Timothy sat back, a little stunned. "I mean, it's a kind offer, but I'm not sure how I feel about that *ethically*—"

Dimi handwaved him. "Oh, no, it's not about asking anyone to do anything unethical. It's about making sure professors' own biases—whatever they may be—don't get in the way of the *correct* decision being made." He was still looking at Timothy.

Timothy wasn't hearing this the way Allegra was. Allegra could only hear it one way: Dimi had found the lock and pocketed the key. *Aaron's been working so hard*, she thought, remembering how he'd lit up talking about his subjects and how well he'd done.

Trying to manage her breathing, Allegra glanced over at Cece and Jules. They both looked relaxed, sipping their wine. Cece even spoke up. "Can you speak to Melbourne and make sure Astrid *doesn't* get admitted?" she joked, laughing. Meanwhile, Allegra could barely breathe.

Dimi looked over at Cece, releasing Timothy. "I stay away from that place as much as possible, I'm sorry," he said with a chuckle, and then nodded at Sal. "Not even the coffee could keep me there!"

Right then, he looked over at Allegra and locked eyes with her.

She knew she needed to perform.

She needed to feign the same gratitude Timothy had expressed. She managed a tentative smile at him—it wavered. Hopefully, he thought it was because she was struggling with the ethics of influencing admissions, and not because the only thing she could hear was: *I'm going to prevent your son from achieving the one thing he's desperate for.*

The conversation devolved into whatever it devolved into; Allegra couldn't follow it. Her pulse hammered in her ears while she remembered how animatedly Aaron had spoken of his exams, and how hopeful he was of getting that postgrad. And—how? How the *fuck* did Dimi know Aaron was going to do a postgrad? And what *year* he was in? Which uni he went to? Just—*how the fuck*?!

Sal's thumb stroked her hand. "Well," she said with finality beside Allegra, "I'm sorry to say we'll need to head off. But this has been lovely, Cece, thanks so much for hosting us." She gave Cece such a warm, open smile, and then looked at Prue. "And so wonderful to meet your daughter, Prue." She nodded at everyone else, and ushered Allegra to stand.

People were saying goodbye to them; Allegra was so shaken she could barely manage social niceties. She forced them—she had to—and then let herself be led out of the garden. She cobbled herself together until they got inside the front door of Timothy's place in Point Piper, but once the door was shut it all fell apart.

She turned towards Sal. "*How does he know*?" Her hands gripped Sal's shoulders. "How the fuck does he know all that about Aaron?"

Sal didn't try to shake Allegra off. She was frowning, instead. "That's a good question," she commented in a very measured voice—and left the thought unfinished.

Allegra couldn't deal with it. She needed the answer. She let go of Sal and made some sort of frustrated noise, walking across the living room to the window and leaning against it for a second. But she couldn't stand still. She couldn't be here, in fact. She walked over to the counter, blocked by the island bench. And then turned, blocked by the table. On her right was a chair, and—she couldn't—she stopped in place, putting a hand on her chest.

And then she saw it: Lachie's blood on the shattered windscreen.

Her breath caught in her throat.

Sal was already there, bracing her. "Look at me, Allegra," she firmly instructed, turning Allegra's face down towards her. "Aaron is a hundred metres away in a plush, safe media room. You can text him right now," she said, reaching into Allegra's pocket and retrieving her phone. She placed it in her hand. "Text him."

Allegra was feeling light-headed, but Sal's hard expression wasn't giving her options. She looked down at her phone, all at once feeling like she didn't know how to work it. It unlocked when she turned it towards her face.

Sal's finger tapped the message app, and then Aaron's icon, and then tapped the text field for her so the keyboard appeared. "You can apologise that you needed to leave without saying goodbye."

Allegra nodded, wiping an unexpected tear away from the corner of one of her eyes. And then tapped out almost verbatim what Sal had said. She showed Sal for approval.

Sal inclined her head. "Perhaps a little more 'mother' and a little less 'robot'," she suggested with a faint smile.

Allegra took a few breaths, made some adjustments, and sent it.

Two seconds later, he replied, *"Text me when you get home ;)"* just like she always said to him.

She smiled briefly at him imitating her and let her hand and the phone flop by her side.

Her heart was still pounding, but at least the light-headedness was subsiding. Thoughts of Dimi and Macquarie and *what the fuck that had even been* kept trying to creep back in—she couldn't let them. Not now. She needed to put that aside or she'd be right back in the ravine.

In a minute, she promised herself, trying to focus on where she was: Point Piper, Sunday afternoon, with sunlight streaming in through the big windows and warming her skin.

And Sal in front of her, waiting patiently for her to return.

When she did, the first thing she felt was a bit embarrassed. "I'm sorry," she said eventually, wiping her eyes again. "Despite what you've seen of me in the last three weeks, I actually don't get flashbacks very often."

Sal just nodded, and then added, "I can hug you, if that would help." While Allegra was recovering from how clinical that sounded, Sal made it worse. "Not my usual preference, but just putting the option out there."

It was so ridiculous that Allegra ended up bursting into laughter and taking her up on the offer—was this woman even human?!—and wrapped her arms around Sal.

Sal was stiff as a board for a moment but soon relaxed, her hands rising to Allegra's back. Allegra's arms were tightly around her shoulders, her cheek resting against Sal's sleek hair. She smelt coconut again.

Having someone there made the difference: it forced her to focus on breathing so she didn't crush Sal. It forced her to focus on little details of her own body: her balance. How stiff her legs were. Even the sound of Sal exhaling against her shoulder. It wasn't long before her pulse stopped hammering in her eardrums.

She could just hear the hum of the air-conditioning system. The moment had passed.

It was over, but she didn't want to pull away. Her pulse settled—and in its wake, something else lingered.

Sal shifted, indicating her intention to step away. Reluctantly, Allegra released her.

They stood there a moment. Sal spoke first. "We can't stay here."

She was right. Timothy would be home any second, and whatever ground Sal may have gained with him by both pushing the Redeemer funding *and* handing him the next generation of Vales to convert, she would instantly lose if he caught them together in his living room. They'd better go. "I'll drive you home."

They climbed wearily into Allegra's LandCruiser again; back into the Maccas fries and wet rubbish smell. Allegra had to spend a second making sure she was focused enough to drive before they pulled out.

They drove in silence for several minutes.

Eventually, Allegra said, "I want to talk about today, but—I need to be in the right headspace for it first."

Sal looked across at her, hearing that and running her eyes over Allegra in assessment. "You should stay at mine tonight." It sounded like a directive.

Allegra was trying to decide how to approach today without setting herself off again, when she was knocked out of her reverie by her phone beeping. Before she even had time to glance at the notification, Sal's phone went off as well.

They glanced at each other. Frowning, Allegra pulled over to the side of the road to check it. Sal had her own phone out.

It was Zoe. *"Sorry to disturb you two on Sunday but this is critically urgent: Lost in Austin just uploaded an absolutely incendiary video, linked below. If you're imagining how bad it could be, you're wrong: it's WORSE. Watch it and then call me immediately."*

Sal looked across at Allegra. The faint lines in her forehead were momentarily visible. "Simply impeccable timing."

Chapter 26: Controlled Burn

The thumbnail for Austin's video was a roaring fire. Allegra was already full of residual adrenaline; she was already teetering on the brink of toppling back into it. The steering wheel felt slick under her palms.

Sal hesitated, brow lowered. "We have a very tight timeframe to respond to this before Dimi becomes aware of it and hamstrings me," she said carefully. "I need to watch this now. Would you like me to get out of the car first?"

Her chest tightened. What if Aaron was in it? "No," she said anyway.

Sal gave her a hard look but accepted her answer. Holding her phone between them, she tapped play.

The video began with footage of a structure on fire. Austin popped up, narrating the process of a fire being discovered, reported, and contained. Crisis over. "Except, that's where the problems began for the Hislop family," Austin's cutout reported beside a burnt-out shed. "A fire doesn't have to destroy a house for it to destroy a family."

Allegra was still half-stuck in an adrenal haze; it took her longer than it would otherwise have for her to recognise the burnt-out structure. It was the one from the property she'd surveyed for the Homeward Foundation event. Her eyebrows shot up.

Austin then reported a series of events: the first people to contact the Hislops *weren't* the police. It was their insurance provider, wanting to make an assessment and skyrocket their premium. Then the bank stepped in and told them the value of their property had dropped below the value of a loan they'd taken against it. Before they knew what had happened, their property—something the family had been camping on for generations—was taken from them.

Austin appeared again, pausing for a moment before saying, "...and sold to Threshold Property Group, a property developer who had been trying to acquire the land from them for *18 months*."

That line made Allegra's blood run cold. She looked across at Sal—had she known about this?

"Threshold were so desperate to get this particular block of land, in fact, that they hired PR firm Black Standard Advisory to try and get the Hislops over the line. It didn't work." He paused. "Interestingly, that perfectly timed fire and its subsequent land reclassification did."

"Now. If only the land *wasn't* as dangerous as the authorities had decided and Threshold could develop it after all?" The screen went black. "And that's where an independent environmental professional enters this story." A picture of Allegra appeared on the screen: a photo of her in her SES jumpsuit with a big, open smile posing in her abseiling gear. "Someone like this doesn't end up in this sort of story by accident. So how did Threshold and BSA get someone like Allegra to agree to do corporate dirty work for them—?"

A candid picture of Sal in her tightly tailored suit walking down a Sydney street appeared. Allegra glanced at Sal beside her.

"Oh. Okay, right," Austin said a bit awkwardly. "I'm sure if someone like *that* approached me from Black Standard Advisory to do a simple land assessment, that would be pretty good incentive on its—" Another picture popped up: the Homeward Foundation Event flyer. "Oh, wow. Yeah, that's a cause Allegra would feel invested in given her history, that's for sure. So doing a safety assessment for an event like this—" he zoomed in on the address on the flyer, "on the property with the terrible fire assessment," he zoomed in on the *'in partnership with Black Standard Advisory'* line, "by the people Threshold paid to get that property into their hands."

His head popped up again. "Yeah. I'm sure it's just a total coincidence, guys."

Allegra sat back a little, feeling uncomfortable. It was the same feeling she'd had following the Threshold payment: it was all too neat. She found herself watching Sal instead of the video. Sal's face was neutral, and her eyes remained on the screen.

"And some coincidences *are* just coincidences. Sometimes it's nothing," Austin continued with a shrug, and then leant forward. "But what if as a result of this coincidence, Sydney's third largest property developer stands to gain tens of millions of dollars at the expense of an ordinary family?"

There was a timelapse of him at his computer going over it all. "Let's follow the money upwards, shall we? Who's the 'inadvertent' beneficiary of this completely random fire? Full investigation coming soon—and don't forget, guys, my inbox is open if you have information relevant to this story or tips for another one."

The video began to loop again. Sal stopped it and sat back, taking a deep breath. "Good," she said grimly. "No surprises at least, thanks to Froggy. We should send her a gift basket."

No surprises? Allegra turned her head to stare at her.

Sal was already putting her phone to her ear. "Are you okay to keep driving?"

Allegra looked forward; she was feeling *many* things right now, but 'not right to drive' wasn't one of them. She turned the key and then waited for a gap to pull into traffic as Zoe's voice said through Sal's handset, "Sal. I'm so sorry. I had *no idea* he was going to do this."

Sal dismissed her apology. "I gather the video's doing numbers?"

"It's Austin, so it is," she confirmed bleakly. "It's charting to crack a million in 9 hours."

A million people, Allegra thought, and felt sick.

"I generated a summary of comments, too," Zoe began.

Sal cut her off. "Allegra is with me."

Zoe paused. "She's seen it too?" Sal made an affirmative noise. The line went silent for a moment; it was very clear that Zoe was responding to both the implication in Austin's video and the fact Sal and Allegra were obviously in the same car together on a Sunday afternoon.

"We're seeing each other," Sal said calmly. "It's fine."

Zoe exhaled at length. "Okay," she said neutrally, and then on consideration, repeated it more warmly. "Okay. Wow, okay, yeah. That may actually make dealing with part of this much easier."

Sal didn't contradict her. "I want Allegra to shoot a candid video reasserting her agency and disconnecting her ethically from this," she said. "I'll work on a script with her on the drive home. But I'm going to need Legal and HR to greenlight it in about 30 minutes. Can you get hold of them?"

Zoe sounded perplexed. "Why would *you* need Legal and HR to approve an optics video?"

"Because I'm dating the client, Zoe, and that's what *the board* says they want me to do." Sal said it coldly, but it seemed clear to Allegra that the icy tone was directed at the board, not at Zoe.

Zoe heard it that way, too. "Frustrating. I'll get them both for you. Speak soon." They said their goodbyes and hung up.

"I've actually already written a script for the video I think you should make," Sal told Allegra. "You can read it and provide your thoughts while I'm in conference with Legal and HR."

It didn't take them long to get to Sal's penthouse. Before Sal went upstairs to put on a sharp suit jacket and set up the conference, she turned to Allegra and looked her up and down with a critical eye. "Where are you at with all this—the lunch, the video?"

It all felt a bit surreal; Allegra was aware she wasn't properly connecting with anything. "Not great, to be honest," she told Sal. "But if you're asking if you can go do your video conference, you can."

Sal narrowed her eyes. "They can wait 10 minutes if you aren't alright."

"What could you do in 10 minutes if I wasn't?" she asked somewhat rhetorically.

Sal wasn't joking, even a little. "Whatever you need."

I need another hug, Allegra thought, although she was already fine. "It's okay, Sal. Go do your conference."

Sal gave her another suspicious look. Her phone rang during it, and she answered, not taking her eyes off Allegra. "Yes."

It was Zoe. "We're good to go in five," she told Sal. "Did you want to brief me first?"

"Did you read the script?" Sal asked her.

"Yes," Zoe said. "It clears Allegra, but I'm a bit concerned it may still frame you as manipulating her, just in the context of a relationship rather than"—she paused, choosing her words—"secretly."

Sal acknowledged that. "The framing will manage that," she promised. "It will present Allegra as the decision-maker of the two of us."

Allegra listened, wondering about this nebulous script that was supposed to do all these things.

Zoe exhaled. "Alright," she said, and then added somewhat cautiously, "Austin will still likely go ahead with his exposé."

"One step at a time, Zoe," Sal said easily. "See you in five." She hung up. To Allegra, she said, "I'll email the script for you to have a look at while I'm upstairs."

Allegra was still stuck on the whole Austin thing. "Did you know he was going to do this?"

Sal had been about to leave and looked back at her, locking her phone. "This, specifically?" she said. "No."

"I mean in general," Allegra elaborated. "Like, why would you get involved with him if you know this is the sort of stuff he produces?"

To that, Sal smiled faintly. "I got involved with him *because* this is the sort of stuff he produces," she said cryptically, and then before Allegra could ask her what she was hoping he'd find, she briefly touched Allegra's arm. "We will speak properly about lunch after all this is dealt with," she promised, and then disappeared upstairs.

Allegra's usual routine upon returning 'home' anywhere was to change into something more comfortable, so now that she had a drawer in Sal's guest room, she did. Then she washed her face, drank from her hands, and went and sat out on the two-seater facing the stairs. Sunlight warmed her hands, and for a moment she was back at that lunch table, with heavy eyes resting on—

Sal appeared at the top of the stairs. Or rather, a storm cloud in the shape of Sal appeared there. She looked *furious*.

Allegra looked up at her against the railing. "Sal?"

"They said no," she said, "they want to meet tomorrow and construct an *institutional* response." Her jaw was set. "They're willing to burn you to protect BSA."

Sal moved coolly down the stairs to the kitchen, placing her jacket gently on the table. She poured herself a glass of water, took a slow and measured sip, and then set it silently on the bench.

"If they want to formalise this, they'd better be sure they want to take me on." She looked up at Allegra. "Because when this blows up," she said coldly, "I get to ask who signed off on stopping me. By name."

Still spaced out, Allegra was a step behind all of it. "I don't get a say?"

Sal's throat was tight and her voice sharp. "Officially, no."

Allegra absorbed that. "So I just get to look like a naïve idiot seduced by some predatory corporate exec in front of millions of people, then."

Sal exhaled at length. "Don't forget who's characterised as the predatory corporate exec here." Sal's voice was bone dry. "But yes. That's what happens when you pay people to manage your public image."

This was *fucking absurd.* Allegra hissed a breath through her teeth. "How is throwing me under the bus to protect BSA supposed to 'manage my public image'?"

Sal opened her mouth to fire something back—and then stopped. She closed her mouth, brow lifting a little. "That is a very good point." She discarded the rest of her water and headed straight back upstairs.

Allegra sat and waited. Light shifted on the walls.

It didn't feel like long before Sal appeared again, brandishing a printout. She brought it down to Allegra and presented it to her. Allegra blinked at her, then looked down at it—it was a copy of her contract. Sal had highlighted a clause in it. It read: *The Agency acknowledges a duty of care to the Client in relation to the management, protection, and representation of the Client's public profile and reputation, and undertakes to act at all times in a manner reasonably calculated to avoid foreseeable reputational harm to the Client arising from the Agency's other contractual commitments, partnerships, or public communications.*

With the headspace she was in, Allegra had to read it a few times before it made sense. "Okay, so BSA isn't allowed to do nothing."

Sal looked thoroughly vindicated. "BSA isn't allowed to do nothing," she repeated, and then said, "And Dimi specifically put *me* in charge of managing reputational fallout on your behalf at our last meeting. That's minuted in black and white. Let those cowards try and say no to me now." She disappeared back upstairs again, calling over her shoulder, "Read the script!"

She was gone longer than before this time. With no brain space to do anything else, Allegra followed her instructions, opening the email with the script in it and reading through it. At first she thought her lack of connection with it might just be because everything felt a little distant just now: the script was fine, it was *Allegra* that was off register. The more she read it, though, the more she accepted that it might be the script. It sounded casual and warm and like something someone would say, but just not... *her*.

She opened a text editor to make some changes to it.

When Sal appeared again, the storm had broken. "Let's get going," she said more neutrally, walking down the stairs like she *hadn't* been about to go through Legal and HR with a scythe. "We need to make my bedroom look lived in."

"I made some changes to the script."

Sal paused mid-step on the stair. "Alright," she said evenly, then continued towards Allegra. "Let me read it." Allegra passed her phone to Sal to read the revised version. Sal ran her eyes over it, her brow relaxing as she did so. "This hits the same notes."

"And it sounds like something I'd come up with myself," Allegra said, following Sal to the bedroom. "Because it is."

Sal's plan was to set-dress her bed, which, despite being someone's genuine bed, looked like it belonged in a display home. To make it look 'realer', she disturbed it, shoved pyjamas under pillows, put a drink bottle on one bedside table and tissues and a book on the other.

However, when Allegra looked at the bed—even as its lived-in version—it was unlike anywhere she could imagine herself feeling completely comfortable. "This doesn't look like me, Sal."

Sal looked across at her for a moment, and then back at the bed, assessing it. "Do you think we should use the guest bedroom instead?"

"I think we should use the rooftop tent on my LandCruiser."

Sal turned and stared at her. Then, considering Allegra beside the master bed, she seemed to reluctantly agree. "It *would* be more authentic," she decided. "Okay," she said, pivoting. "You may need to lend me a t-shirt, though. Because I don't think anyone's going to believe I wear a thousand-dollar silk blouse into a tent."

She ended up choosing one she recognised from a previous photoshoot she'd sent Allegra out on. Allegra was sceptical. "No one will notice that it's mine."

Sal looked at her for a moment and then *laughed*. "Are you a betting woman, Allegra?" The way Sal phrased that made her reluctant to start now, so she shook her head. "Good choice," Sal told her, and then headed down to the carpark with her and watched with interest as she set up the rooftop tent.

The process was comforting. The sound of the zip around the hardtop. The hiss of the hydraulics as she guided the shell open. Slotting the ladder into the sliding edge with a click and leaning her hip against it as she retrieved the aluminium poles from inside. With each pole she fitted into the canvas, she felt herself coming back from that lunch, piece by piece.

Rather than shoot it in a concrete carpark, Allegra would have much preferred to drive out bush somewhere and shoot it properly—somewhere with towering Ribbon Gums, perhaps—but as Sal kept reminding her by checking her watch, they didn't have enough time. It was realistic enough for them both to be inside the tent together with the internal light on; the carpark was dark and it just looked like nighttime.

The video script itself was simple. Allegra would film on the selfie-cam of her own phone ("The worse the quality, the more authentic it looks."), a shot close to her face, showing very little of her body or the background. "There's been a lot of speculation about my private life lately. About who I'm attracted to. About what that must mean for my work. But I'm actually really simple: I care about safety, I care about the natural environment, and I care about the people who are important to me."

Out of frame, Sal made a halting noise. "Pause there for longer next time. Let's go again—single shot."

Allegra followed her instructions on the retake before continuing, "I've been private about it not because I feel like there's anything ugly I need to hide, but because this is my life, you know? It should be mine to decide when I want to share it." The plan was for her to pull the phone back and tilt the camera a little to show Sal was sitting behind her, with a soft and cheeky smile. "There's no deep, dark secret here," Allegra would say to the camera. "Yes, I am." The ambiguity was intentional.

They shot it a few times trying Sal in several different positions for the reveal—in the end, the one that felt the most natural was one where she was close enough for Allegra to grab her for a bit of a sudden hug at the very end, because Sal made a surprised noise about it and accidentally knocked the phone out of Allegra's hand. It made the whole video look very unscripted.

"That's the one," Sal said, rolling it a few times as they lay side-by-side in the tent and reviewed the footage. "That'll do it." She shot it off to Zoe to scrub and edit, gave Allegra back her phone, and then lay there looking up at the sloped canvas roof.

Allegra watched her, reflecting on how odd it felt to have company in here.

"So, this is *your* penthouse," Sal commented with a smile.

"Yup," Allegra said, laughing about it. "The entire top floor of my Land-Cruiser, all for me."

Sal grinned at that, clearly fascinated by the whole thing. "You really choose to live like this?" Her fingers felt around the edge of the inbuilt mattress beside her, testing its thickness. Her eyebrows lifted; it wasn't as thin as she expected. She still looked to Allegra to answer. "You wouldn't live somewhere else, given the option?"

Allegra found it entertaining. "I have the option. I choose this."

"But you sleep in my guest bedroom, even when your car's down here."

Allegra shrugged. "I don't mind staying other places. Especially places with nice bathrooms, hot showers, and air-conditioning." Allegra looked across at her. "I do on occasion even want to visit people."

"How inconvenient for you," Sal said, smile audible. She turned her head on the pillow to look across at Allegra. "Although I must say the company is the key attraction of your penthouse, too."

Allegra's breath caught a moment. They were shoulder to shoulder; she had to be careful not to turn her head at the same time Sal did. Their faces were already close, and after Sal's comment, she didn't trust herself. Especially because the tent was such a comfortable space for her: it reminded her of mountain vistas and the smell of eucalyptus. Being in it felt like being home, even though she was parked in a concrete carpark in central Sydney. After today, it was a feeling she welcomed.

She swallowed. Today.

She sat with that word a moment, feeling around the edges of it, and waiting to see if it triggered another spike of adrenaline.

Sal observed her, letting the silence stretch as long as it needed to.

It was some time before Allegra spoke. "Lunch was—" She exhaled; some things defied description. She tried again. "Even before Dimi got stuck into Aaron, I could barely fucking breathe. Is that what it's always like with him?"

Sal nodded once. "Always."

Allegra shook her head. She couldn't imagine another *lunch* with that monster, let alone any more time than that. And yet Sal saw him five days a week, at minimum. "25 years?"

Sal understood what she meant and shook her head. "My whole life. Although he was..." She chose her words carefully. "...less intense before he decided I'm dangerous."

Her whole life? Allegra couldn't even imagine it. "How does someone even survive that?"

Sal turned her head towards Allegra. "You've seen how," she said, too quietly, and then moved the conversation along. "I think perhaps there's a certain equilibrium there for me now. However, you know the expression about the frog in slowly boiling water?" She paused, reflective. "Introducing another frog made me realise how hot the water really is."

"Yes, well, now my whole family's stuck in the boiling pot."

Allegra could feel Sal freeze. It was a moment before she spoke. "I know," she said simply. "And none of you should be." There was the quiet implication of *just me*.

Allegra heard it. "I'm still angry you dragged us into this, Sal," she said clearly.

Sal was holding her breath. She didn't say anything, and she didn't look at Allegra. She just stared upward at the canvas, waiting for the penny to drop.

She was so very still. Allegra pressed her lips together. "But also, I get it." Sal released her breath and briefly closed her eyes. Allegra watched her do that, feeling a tangle in her chest. "Especially after lunch."

Allegra looked up at the same canvas roof Sal was keeping her eyes trained on. "Anyway, all of this is fucking talk, because we're in the pot now. It's too late to wish it hadn't happened. We need to focus on 'neutralising' Dimi or whatever before he destroys the lives of everyone I care about."

That moved Sal to speak. "It's the only thing I think about, every minute of every day," she said clearly, enunciating every word. "That much, I can promise you."

It was comforting on some level to hear that; Allegra had seen how effective Sal could be when she put her mind to something. She wouldn't be truly comforted, though, until Aaron was safe. "You can spend some of those minutes trying to figure out how he knows so much about Aaron."

Sal acknowledged that. "I'm not sure it's going to take much dedication," she said. "The most likely option is that it's just information someone put into your backgrounding file. Zoe will likely need to pull your whole file on Monday, so I'll get her to sweep it for anything about him."

The possibility that Dimi may have inadvertently come across the information in her file rather than sought it out was at least a relief. "I'd like to know what else is in my file," Allegra told Sal, anyway. "I don't want any more surprises."

Sal considered that. "Alright. It might be jarring to read about yourself in terms of your usefulness and instrumentalisation, though."

Allegra had had worse. "What's new?" she said dryly. It couldn't be more jarring than the meeting where 20 execs all argued about the best way to monetise her sexuality. Or sitting across from Dimi while he casually instrumentalised her son.

Her jaw was tight. Only one thing was clear through all of this: she would fucking *tear shit down* if that monster touched Aaron's life in any way.

"I can't let anything happen to Aaron," she told Sal, listening to the razor edge of conviction in her voice. "I talked myself out of stopping Lachie. I'm not doing that again."

Sal looked across at her, hearing that. She didn't reply, but she didn't move away either. They lay beside each other in silence while Allegra's anger slowly burnt down its wick.

The sounds of Sydney hummed around them: Sunday evening traffic on the Cahill Expressway. People chatting and laughing as they periodically walked past the gate of Sal's private carpark on their way to dinner. Even the buzz of the decrepit old LED light hanging above them.

It got a little stuffy in the tent; there was no breeze down here to blow through it, and two bodies heated it faster than one. Allegra shifted, pulling briefly at her t-shirt to let air into it.

In contrast, Sal lay beside Allegra, unmoving. Her eyes stayed on the sloped canvas above them, her legs beside each other, and her hands laced on her stomach. It seemed very deliberate.

Allegra was sprawled out and a bit restless, taking up much more of the narrow space. Her head was propped up on a wrist under the pillow so she could look down at their legs.

Underneath Allegra's too-big t-shirt, Sal was still wearing her perfectly tailored pants. The absurdity of it struck her as a bit funny. "Do you even own anything comfortable?"

"Everything I own is comfortable."

Allegra shot her a tired look. "Something you could camp in, I mean."

Sal turned her head on the pillow towards Allegra, looking entertained. "Are you inviting me camping, Allegra?"

Despite everything, Allegra found herself smiling at that mental image. "I should," she said aloud. "It would be hilarious."

Sal scoffed. "Don't tell Zoe that idea," she said dryly, without elaborating. She spent a few moments still facing Allegra, studying her, and then carefully sat up so she didn't whack her head on the shell. "Well, this has been simply lovely," she said in a very formal register, "but I'm afraid it's time for me to head back home. Thanks so much for having me." Her eyes were twinkling. "It's been wonderful getting a full tour of the home I've heard so much about."

Allegra felt a sharp ache in her chest—she wanted Sal to stay. It was silly; the tent was stuffy as hell. "Thanks for coming," was all she said. "Let's do this again." She hesitated. "Parked somewhere open, next time."

Sal did *not* look convinced. She threw Allegra a sceptical look as she descended the ladder and disappeared beneath the roofline. Allegra followed her.

Allegra was stowing the tent and zipping it all up again when Sal asked, "Are you hungry?"

Allegra hadn't thought about her stomach since breakfast. It had a lot to report to her when she finally paid attention to it. Food sounded *good*. "You want to go grab something together?"

Sal held her arms out, still wearing Allegra's short-sleeved t-shirt. Her tattoos were showing down her arms.

Allegra scoffed, indicating her own visibly tattooed arms. "What are you saying?"

"Well, *I* have a certain mystique to maintain," she told Allegra with a smile. It faded. "Although I think Zoe, my colleagues and half the internet is going to get a bit of a surprise once that video lands."

In the lift on the way up, they rewatched the video. Sal's tattoos *were* visible, but probably only if someone were specifically looking for them. The quality of the video in the low light made it look like they might be patterns on sleeves. "Looks like your mystique is safe."

"That'll make the next staff meeting marginally less complicated," Sal observed, and then opened Uber Eats. "Feel like anything specific?"

Allegra didn't, so she left food up to Sal and went to switch out her slightly sweaty t-shirt for something clean and dry. She was switching bras too—and holding up an old 2-in-1 tank top to decide if it was too ratty to wear around Sal—when she caught sight of herself in the mirror. In an unfamiliar room and an unfamiliar mirror, it was like looking at herself with new eyes. It was easier to imagine how she might look to someone else; someone specific. Making a snap decision, she left all her bras in the drawer and just pulled on a thin t-shirt.

She wandered out of the guest bedroom to where Sal was leaning a hip against the table, finishing whatever she was ordering them. Sal glanced up at Allegra and then double-took, eyes briefly dipping to Allegra's breasts.

Allegra felt smug. "Watch your micro-expressions," she said beside Sal's ear as she passed behind her on the way to the couches.

Sal lingered on her for a moment longer, unreadable, and then finished the order. "Food will be here in 15," she said neutrally, and then disappeared upstairs.

Allegra had presumed she'd gone up to her office to continue working, as she usually did. Expecting some free time, she opened her library app and committed to finally finishing the book she'd been reading.

Sal was back only a couple of minutes later. She paused theatrically at the top of the stairs, wearing a long black satin slip that could not possibly have resembled her gala dress more if it was designed specifically to mimic it. And no bra.

Allegra was then required either to watch Sal walk down the stairs, or specifically *not* watch Sal walking down the stairs—either way, Sal got the victory she was after. Since she was damned if she didn't anyway, she did. Sal rested her eyes on Allegra the whole way down. Allegra had to curl her fingers into the couch cushions to stay put and keep them to herself.

Sal sat on the opposite couch. "That's better," she said completely impassively, as if simply enjoying the comfort of loungewear. It was her evil fucking smile that indicated how much she was enjoying Allegra's mute reaction to her wardrobe choice.

With her shoulders, her cleavage and half of her back out, there were tattoos on display that Allegra had never seen before; what caught Allegra's attention was the blade of a knife pointing up from underneath her breasts.

"How's the book?" Sal asked, looking far too pleased with herself. Allegra hadn't even glanced down at her phone since Sal had returned.

"You realise that's not loungewear, right."

"You asked if I owned anything comfortable," Sal said easily. "And this is comfortable." She paused. "For me."

"Comfortable *for camping*," Allegra reminded her. "If you wear *that* camping, we may never make it out of the tent."

"Writing my packing list as we speak," Sal said, closing the conversation out by looking down at her phone with a deep smile.

This woman. Allegra sank back into the couch with her phone, grinning ear to ear. Evil fuck.

Sal *did* at least put on a gown to collect the Uber Eats order, delivering Allegra's to her on the couch and then settling opposite her again. Before she ate, though, she said, "The video's out," and then scrolled through some of the reactions. Her eyes narrowed a moment, and then she screenshotted something and annotated it. A second later, Allegra's phone buzzed with a notification. She opened it: it was a screenshot of a list of users who'd liked the video. Sal had circled Aaron's username.

"I guess he approves," Sal commented with a brief smile, and then went back to reading.

Allegra looked down at her screen again, feeling something warm and complicated. *He's safe*, she realised as if that were a revelation, *and also, he's following me.* She saved the screenshot and minimised it, feeling as though she had a brief moment of connection with him. Over a fake video.

She went back to her book. It was only when she got up to dispose of their rubbish that she noticed what Sal was quietly reading: the same book Allegra was, the one she'd told her about at the bar. Allegra recalled her mentioning she would; just a politeness, she'd presumed. Seeing it now, Allegra realised she'd meant it.

Well after sunset, Allegra finally finished the book. She looked up and opened her mouth to announce that—to see Sal had fallen asleep in the corner of the three-seater. She closed her mouth. Right.

She was halfway back from the guest room, doona in her arms, before she really gave much thought to what she was doing. Sal would probably prefer that Allegra pretend it hadn't happened rather than tuck her in.

Well, she can deal with it, Allegra decided, doing it anyway and then standing back.

She looked so small folded up like that, Allegra realised. Asleep, she didn't have that powerful charisma and towering presence that usually hummed around her. She was just a person, and she just looked small, unguarded, and unexpectedly soft.

There was space behind her. Allegra realised she'd probably fit there, if she wanted to. Their breathing could fall in sync as Allegra fell asleep, too.

Allegra almost climbed behind her. Almost. She was so tired.

But there were no columns for this on the spreadsheet. No negotiated, pre-consented moves. She'd have to leave it.

She did the next best thing instead: she settled onto the other side of the three-seater and pulled the other end of the doona over herself, closing her eyes. This would have to do.

Chapter 27: Privileged Information

She wasn't on a mattress. Instead, her face was against a smooth, warm surface. As she lifted her head, the grey leather beside her cheek drifted into focus, and beyond it she recognised the cool grey atrium of Sal's penthouse, lit by the flat morning light.

She yawned and pulled the doona around her shoulders, planning to rest a little longer—it caught on a weight. Sal's calves were over her lap. She must have slipped down during the night to lie on her back.

Allegra turned a little to look over at her, careful not to shift her legs. She was apparently asleep, with one arm behind her head and the other across her middle, her eye makeup smudged and her hair dishevelled. Allegra smiled slightly. The disorder felt intimate.

She let her head rest back against the arm of the couch. She could have stretched, could have adjusted herself more comfortably, but that might shatter whatever fragile equilibrium was here. She stayed exactly where she was.

Yesterday was creeping back into her mind when Sal shifted—and then immediately settled. Allegra hazarded a glance at her, finding Sal still, her eyes closed, and her face relaxed. She laid her head back down again, also closing her eyes, although Sal wouldn't have seen them if she had looked.

Allegra would normally have got up at first light. This morning, she didn't. Neither of them shifted as the sun crept up over the horizon and light inched across the couch. When Sal's alarm went off, it was silenced immediately. The weight over Allegra's lap withdrew.

Only then did Allegra stretch, slowly and deliberately, as if it were still early. As if she hadn't been awake and listening to peak-hour traffic on the expressway outside.

When her eyes cleared, Sal was already on her feet, her robe pulled across her shoulders and phone in hand. She disappeared upstairs before Allegra sat up.

Allegra gathered the doona, still warm from their bodies, and carried it back to the guest room, shaking pins and needles from her legs. She straightened the cushions like they'd never been lying on them and sat down on the couch like they hadn't been sleeping on it.

Her phone was on the coffee table; seeing all the notifications, she nearly fucking left it there. Just in case anyone was hurt, though, she grabbed it to check.

There was an email from Northstar Pathways—she had to pause to remember it was the outdoor education place—inviting her up on-site to inspect it and offer suggestions. The next was Vanessa with a screenshot from the video Sal and Allegra had uploaded and all-caps commentary on it. The last one that mattered was from Timothy.

She opened it cautiously, remembering how lunch had ended. *"I just want to check in after yesterday. I know you hate me asking, but I'd never forgive myself if I didn't. Is everything alright?"*

She pressed her lips together. If she dismissed it or ignored it, he'd take it as evidence she wasn't doing okay—or worse, presume it was something *he* did. She was also aware anything she said about yesterday would likely get back to Dimi. She paused, narrowing her eyes.

Actually, that presented her with a way to manage *Dimi's* response to her freakout.

She tapped her thumbs against the phone for a moment, then typed. *"I'm not okay with getting any personal benefit from knowing Dimi. I don't want him intervening for Aaron—he can get into postgrad himself. I didn't expect to feel this strongly and didn't handle it well. Sorry for running off."*

Timothy bought it. Of course he did. *"I hear you. I feel uncomfortable too. I'll thank Dimi for the kind offer but let him know it's not required."*

Allegra sat back and read over the conversation again, waiting for Sal to return.

When she did, it was in a full Disney villain suit with perfect hair and makeup. "Good morning," she said in her most formal register, but then retrieved two mugs and made them coffee.

Allegra walked her phone over to show her the exchange with Timothy. Sal read it, and then raised her eyebrows and nodded approval. "Anything else of note from yesterday?"

Allegra shook her head. "I'm sure there's a lot of comments on the videos. I'm scared to look."

Sal took a sip from her coffee to test the strength. "You should be," she said, adding a touch more to hers. "That's how to ruin your week. You have professionals managing your accounts for a reason. I will check it." She passed Allegra her mug.

They then sat opposite each other at the table in silence, eyes on their phones.

Now that she had a clear head, Allegra watched Austin's teaser a few times with captions while Sal focused on scrolling, switching tabs, and typing across from her. Nothing else jumped out at her that hadn't yesterday, but the extremely neat and 'coincidental' details of her being onboarded at BSA still sat heavily in her stomach. *Only narratives are neat*, she told herself.

She must have been sighing about it, though, because Sal looked up at her. When Allegra didn't explain herself, Sal didn't ask. Her eyes dipped to her coffee and the empty table beside it and, belatedly, she noted, "There's no food here."

This was something Allegra had already presumed, given that Sal had never been seen inside a pantry at any point, and the only items in the enormous fridge were two different types of water and that perpetually unopened white wine.

"Email Gerard with a list of food or other grocery items you need. He can organise delivery," Sal directed, already looking back at her phone.

Allegra stared at her for a moment, then followed her instructions.

She had been trying to think of what she'd *actually* like to eat (instead of what would just keep inside a LandCruiser) when Sal froze, double-checked something, and then made a noise. "You *did* go volunteering with Aaron."

Allegra looked up from her grocery list. "Yes. That's why the inside of the car smells like wet cardboard."

Sal fit those two details together, and then, eyebrows up, handed her phone to Allegra. It was open on a video someone had taken of Allegra and Aaron on the coastal track, slick with sunscreen and sweat, smiling, and laden with garbage bags. It had 260k likes. Jesus Christ.

Sal accepted her phone back. "The amount of money and planning it would take to get 'candid' footage of a client doing this and seed it with the right accounts to get that much engagement..." She shook her head. "And you do it all for free."

"I didn't plan it, Sal. I was doing exactly what you told me I should do to bond with him."

"I know," Sal said, with faint approval. "Well, I'm sure he'll be Mum's Biggest Fan when thousands of adoring young women start following him." At Allegra's blank expression, she added, "He's tagged."

Allegra froze. Yesterday seemed very heavy, suddenly. Just the thought of Aaron being out there and visible and accessible was... she sucked air through her teeth. Dimi would find some way to use all this, she was sure of it. She needed to get ahead of him. "Can you get my file for me today, please?" Sal nodded, and it settled Allegra a little. "I want to know what Dimi's going to do next."

Sal made a noise. "Well, I have a meeting with him and a whole armada of his staff first up," she said impassively as if it wasn't a genuinely terrifying prospect to any normal person. "So I may have answers earlier than you'll have your file."

Allegra didn't like how that sounded. "I gather he didn't like the video."

Sal remained neutral. "I think that's safe to presume."

"Are you going to get in trouble again?"

"Yes," she said. "But I strictly followed every process required of me, so there won't be much he can do." She paused. "At least, about the video."

While Allegra was still processing that, Sal drained the rest of her coffee and stood, stepping elegantly around the chair. "You should visit me at work today," she told Allegra, almost as an afterthought. "Mid-morning. I want to normalise us. Staff will think the video last night is juicy gossip instead of something ordinary and boring otherwise, and I don't want to walk into rooms full of giggles and whispers for the next month."

She slipped her phone into her blazer pocket, grabbed her keys from the counter, and headed into the lift.

Allegra probably would have hung around in the penthouse longer if hunger hadn't driven her out of it. She bought a toastie at literally the first café she came across, which was an upmarket hole-in-the-wall beside a boutique art gallery, and had designs on eating it in a nice park somewhere. However, it didn't take her long to realise that The Rocks was swarming with people first thing on a Monday morning, and where there were people, there were furtive looks and double takes at her.

Worse: she'd found a few plants beside a bench and had been trying to eat her toastie amongst them in peace when she became aware of drama unfolding around her. A young man was filming her. She pretended not to notice, but it caught the attention of a young woman passing by who seemed determined not to ignore it. "Do you mind?" the woman called to the man. "Can't you see she's trying to eat?"

He turned his phone towards her, still filming. "She's not going to fuck you, babe. Settle."

Allegra realised it would escalate and draw more attention if she didn't quickly intervene. "Guys, I appreciate the interest," she said, lying through her teeth. "Toastie doesn't really go well with 'argument', though, so can we get along?" She tried a tentative smile. People around them were already watching.

The woman flushed, looking a little angry—Allegra worried about that—and the man rolled his eyes and lowered his phone, shaking his head and walking off. Allegra sat there with her half-eaten breakfast, feeling uncomfortable and awkward as people resumed whatever they had been doing.

After she'd managed to force the rest of it down, she texted Sal to find out what 'mid-morning' meant in corporate speak.

She had already decided to forgo a morning walk and just head back to the penthouse where she could be safely anonymous when Sal replied. "*Another 30 should be fine,*" said the message. Allegra stopped in place to read it. "*The tailor should have the other suit ready. Put another 2–3 shirts on my account while you're there—get some colour. Don't look too polished when you walk into the office, sleeves rolled up and no tie is enough. Leave the blazer at home.*"

Be more specific, Allegra thought sarcastically, but figured Sal had a particular read in mind, so doubled back to go visit the tailor.

To her credit, the tailor read the message, nodded, and then brought out some colours for Allegra to try. Sage and grey-blue worked the best, and so when she was back at the penthouse and trying to make the severely structured pants look in any way casual, sage was the only colour that looked even slightly 'Allegra'. She rolled up the sleeves as instructed, undid a couple of buttons, and gave herself a low bun. Then it was time to face BSA HQ.

Because Sal drove every day, Allegra was surprised it barely took 10 minutes to walk there. Security waved her through the gate with half a look, and then she stepped into the lift with a selection of people in sharp suits and promptly forgot which floor Sal's office was on.

Someone reached forward and pressed the button for her with a smile, and once again, she felt very conspicuous. At least she didn't look like she'd crawled directly out of a cave this time.

"Would you like me to take you to Sal?" someone else politely offered when she went to exit the lift. Allegra smiled and shook her head automatically, and then immediately wished she'd accepted.

Sal's floor was as she remembered it, but it was an absolute rabbit warren of desks and offices. Allegra found herself wandering around it, trying to determine where she'd find Sal.

Gerard saw her first and came to collect her. "Hello, there," he said knowingly. "Imagine this: Allegra Sinclair, *lost*."

"Turns out compasses don't work in hell," she told him with a pained look.

He laughed. "Oh, you are *delightful*," he told her. "Sal is this way."

Gerard guided her through rows of staff pretending not to be interested, into a long, dark corridor. Allegra had presumed she was being led towards some sort of office-style executive lair—but they ended up in a meeting room. Sal was in there with several staff, standing behind them as they showed her something on a laptop.

The staff looked up before Sal did, with a long enough gap for them to react to the fact it was Allegra while Sal appeared to be engrossed in the screen.

When she finally looked up, she warmed a tiny fraction of a degree. "Allegra."

She swallowed. There were so many sets of eyes on her. "Hi," she said to Sal, and then, "Hi, everyone else." She had no idea what an appropriate greeting was in this circumstance.

She knew Sal would be entertained by that, but it didn't show on her face. Almost nothing did. "That'll do for today," Sal told the staff there. "Make sure that deck doesn't go out without those changes."

Sal waited until most of them—but not all of them—were gone before she stepped forward, put a warm hand briefly on Allegra's forearm, and then looked her up and down evaluatively. "Have you eaten?" she asked, brushing the front of Allegra's shirt lightly and then stepping right up to her to correct the line of her collar and fasten one of the buttons.

This is a performance, Allegra told herself as she inhaled sharply. It didn't help. "There's always space for more in there." One of the staff who'd definitely not been listening smothered a grin at that as she walked past them on her way out.

She was the last to leave, but Sal didn't step away. Allegra supposed that must be in case anyone walked past the door. Sal *did* soften just a little once they were alone, though. She looked Allegra up and down again. "Civilised," she said, with the ghost of a smirk.

"Do I detect a note of surprise?" Allegra asked her dryly.

Sal shot her a grin and then placed a hand on her lower back for a second to guide her out of the room. "Ready for coffee number two?"

"I was barely ready for number one," Allegra confessed. "You're going to layer another one on that? Do you *have* a nervous system?"

Sal patted her back once. "We'll get you a half-shot."

Sal took what felt like the longest route possible through the maze of offices and desks to the lift, drawing all the detail about Allegra's morning from her and behaving as if she were truly interested in it. By the time they walked out of the building, even *Allegra* was sick of hearing herself speak.

"So how did *your* morning go?" she asked as soon as they were well shot of the office. "I see he didn't subject you to a firing squad."

Sal inclined her head. "Well, the response video is doing what it needed to do," she said, leading Allegra down a side street presumably towards a café. "So perhaps he planned to claim I was too close to source material to make good judgements, but he had to hold his tongue." They paused to wait for a car before crossing. "For now, at least. He didn't say a single word the whole meeting."

The image of Dimi sitting in the back of the room the other day, *watching*, was fresh in Allegra's mind. "So no idea what he's planning next, then."

Sal shook her head. "I gave Zoe instructions with regard to your file," she promised. "She'll have it to me by the end of the day."

Allegra was busy trying to imagine what sort of information she was going to find in it when she felt Sal's fingers thread through hers. *Just C1*, she told herself, feeling immediately buoyed by it, anyway.

"You haven't even asked about the video," Sal observed, interest audible. "With most clients, I would presume that's because they'd already gone through the comments, despite my advice not to." Allegra shook her head to indicate she hadn't, and Sal nodded. "I didn't think so," she said. "Would you like the brief?"

"'The brief'," Allegra repeated, a little wryly. "I probably should."

"Well," Sal began with a smile, imitating a report to her team, "the reception is largely positive with most commentary focusing on people confirming they already suspected you were queer. With regard to Austin's video, a fight broke out in the comments about the suggestion he's implicating you as a knowing participant in the scandal—he's not, of course, but heaven forbid people have any media literacy—and overwhelmingly people are angry at him for outing you." They stopped outside the door to the café to finish their discussion before entering. "There is little comment on the corporate corruption scandal itself, which gives BSA some additional time to formulate a response before the exposé itself drops. And," she said with a little flourish, "it gives *me* additional authority at work because I managed it so quickly." She looked quite pleased with herself.

Allegra spent a few moments with all of that. "Did you know that would happen?"

"That the internet would be far more interested in inter-influencer drama than even a well-framed corporate corruption scandal?" She shrugged. "You can never be 100% certain how things will land, but there are some fairly predictable patterns to exploit."

It sat a bit wrong with Allegra for multiple reasons, but none of them seemed more important than making sure Sal's plans to oust Dimi weren't derailed. "Well, I'm glad my sexuality ended up being valuable to BSA, in the end," she said flatly about the whole affair.

"'Our'," Sal reminded her, with a slightly sharp look.

They stood facing each other in front of the café, hand in hand. With their reflection in the café window and Sal's previous comment, it reminded Allegra that eyes would now be on Sal, too. "How do you feel about it?" she found herself wondering. "People knowing when they look at you—who you are and who you're with?"

Sal shrugged. "What's there to feel?" she asked. "If it contributes to me getting rid of him, it's positive." She studied their reflection. "This was the plan, anyway. I was always going to be more visible."

The plan, Allegra remembered. To launder Sal's reputation. "Is it working? How are people responding to you?"

Sal didn't answer immediately. When she did, she looked across at Allegra, almost curiously. "Warmly." She didn't linger on that thought. "You ready to fry your nervous system yet?" She nodded at the café.

Allegra wasn't, but was following her inside anyway when her line of sight caught on a spread of products in the window. She pulled Sal back out again. There were some rows of reusable coffee mugs displayed for purchase. "Nothing says 'I'm dating an environmentalist' like suddenly using a KeepCup," she observed, grinning at Sal.

Sal did actually look somewhat impressed. "I've created a monster," she said, but let Allegra lead her in and choose her a stainless-steel travel mug with a black rubber band around the centre of it. Sal chose an earthy, ceramic one for Allegra.

Then they walked hand-in-hand with their new coffee mugs back to the BSA HQ and sat in one of the creepy spotlit couches in the foyer so various staff could walk past them and pretend not to notice.

They were just draining their mugs when Allegra's phone buzzed. She slipped it out of her pocket to glance at it—it was *Vanessa*. *"I'm in the city, are you here?"*

Vanessa? On the south side of the bridge? *"Actually I'm in Far North Queensland for the next year. No mobile reception. Oh, well."*

"Nice try," Vanessa fired back. *"I googled that Black Standard place your rich goth lady works in. Are you there?"*

Sal was sitting beside Allegra, reading her screen. "You should introduce us properly," she said with a dark smile.

Allegra sighed out all the air inside her lungs. The two of them were going to end up meeting at some point, after all. It might as well be now. She replied, *"Yes. We're in the foyer."*

"At least there's nothing to convince her of," Sal pointed out as Allegra sank back into the couch and hoped it would swallow her up.

Vanessa must have already been outside because in less than a minute she bustled through the circular doors, squinted at the dim light and cast her eyes around. When she spotted them seated on one of the couches, she brightened and made a beeline for them.

Allegra stood to give her a hug. Vanessa's eyes were alight with excitement about the woman standing coolly beside them. Rather than wait for Allegra to introduce them, Vanessa stuck her hand out. "Sal Lategan, right?" Sal nodded once at her. "Nice to meet you in person! I've heard so much about you."

"Have you," Sal said, amused, giving Allegra a sidelong glance.

Allegra closed her eyes. "Enjoy this brief period of time you get with my sister before *I murder her*."

Sal looked back towards Vanessa. "You'd better give me all the goss quickly, then," she said without missing a single beat. "Tell me everything I need to know about her while she's sharpening the knife."

God, them teaming up was the *last* thing Allegra needed. *"Bye, Sal."*

Sal shared a brief smile with Vanessa, her Disney villain suit and dark makeup a sharp contrast to Allegra's blonde, white linen-wearing sister. "Pleasure to briefly meet you," she said smoothly, shaking Vanessa's hand again. "Enjoy the afterlife."

Vanessa laughed about that, and then Sal pulled Allegra down a little with a tug on her shirt for a slow peck on the lips—spreadsheet cell A5—before taking confident strides through the dark, moody lighting to the lifts, holding her empty coffee mug with elegant fingers.

Vanessa watched her with her jaw open and eyebrows in her hairline. "Holy shit, Allegra," she said, and for a moment Allegra thought she was going to say something normal. But no. "Look at her. I bet she's a *fucking freak* in bed."

She'd said it loud enough for two of Security to hear. They were trying to smother their reactions to it. "I am *begging* you to stop talking for once in your life," Allegra said to Vanessa, gesturing at them.

Vanessa shrugged. "They are definitely thinking the same thing," she said defensively, once again loud enough for them to hear.

Allegra had to physically remove Vanessa from the atrium in order to preserve *some* modicum of dignity.

Once they were outside, Vanessa at least pivoted to something less agonising. "Is this her work, too?" she asked about Allegra's suit. "Very nice! You've been with her for, what, three weeks and she's already domesticated you. You're not even wearing hiking boots!" She linked arms with Allegra and led her to some fashionable restaurant she'd read about in Broadsheet.

Vanessa was keen on revelling in being 'right' about Allegra and Sal all along, and relayed the story of how Oscar actually walked *upstairs* in order to physically show her the video so he could watch her reaction to it. "I'm surprised he didn't make Oliver come with him so he could *film* my reaction," she said, and then leant forward across the table on her elbows. "So, is it true?" she asked, forgetting Allegra couldn't read her mind. "Is she a Black after all?"

Allegra managed her reaction. "No," she said carefully, and then remembered what Cece had openly told her children. "She grew up with Helen Black, though."

It was like a spark in dry grass; Vanessa was already alight with it. "What does that mean?" she asked. "Did they live next door? Did they go to school together?"

Allegra exhaled. "I didn't ask for a chart of her pedigree, Vanessa."

Vanessa's phone was already out to google Helen Black. As Allegra *was* actually interested in the answer, she ended up shuffling her chair over beside Vanessa's to read over her shoulder. She grabbed the phone for a second when Vanessa was scrolling past the Black family tree, looking for any reference to Dimi. She found it—he was Helen's uncle.

She sat back, something fitting into place. That explained Zoe and Tom discussing the rumour about Sal being Dimi's niece. She looked again: Helen's father was Dimi's brother—and her mother was listed as *(1961–2023).*

Vanessa watched her through narrow eyes. "You know something."

Shit. "Yeah," she said. "Just bits and pieces."

Vanessa fixed her with an intense look and gestured for her to continue.

Honestly, even if she *could* say anything, she probably wouldn't. It wasn't hers to share. "Vanessa, I've literally just met her. Give me a few months at least."

Vanessa didn't look convinced. "You've just met her, but you're wearing a suit, hanging out with her at work, *camping* with her already, *and* introducing her to your family," Vanessa pointed out. "Doesn't that warrant being introduced to hers?"

If you only knew, Allegra thought tiredly. "I'll keep you posted on any juicy details she tells me about her home life growing up," Allegra promised Vanessa, safely presuming that topic was one Sal would *never* touch and therefore she'd never have to break her promise.

Vanessa had already moved on anyway, sitting back in her seat and reflecting on what she'd just said. "It is super quick though, don't you think?" she asked Allegra. "Like, I didn't think much of it because you were pregnant with Timothy's baby within like two weeks of hooking up with him so, you know, this is kind of your M.O., but then I saw the Austin video..."

Unprepared, Allegra's expression slipped at 'Austin' before she could catch it. Vanessa noticed and jumped on it immediately. "What's going on?" she asked, brow lowering.

Allegra tried to palm it off. "Sorry—Timothy's a rough topic now because I had to tell him about Sal on Saturday." She thought Vanessa would buy that, and maybe even ask about whether or not he cried.

She didn't. "No, it was about the video."

Well, fuck. "Look, it kind of implied Sal groomed me, so yeah, not an amazing feeling to know everyone has watched it."

Vanessa shrugged, still watching her with those razor-sharp, ice blue eyes. "Well, it is kind of sus, don't you think? The timing?"

Allegra swallowed. "It looks like that."

"That would bother the Allegra I know," Vanessa pointed out.

"It did bother me," Allegra said honestly. "So I confronted her about it. Her explanation made sense, so I left it."

"What was her explanation?"

Allegra was beginning to get irritated. "I'm happy to tell you stuff about *me,* Vee, but I can't tell you things that belong to other people."

Vanessa was like a fucking bloodhound on the scent. "It belongs to you when people start making viral videos accusing you of stuff. It belongs to you if you're getting in trouble for it," she said. "And it obviously bothers you, too, because otherwise you wouldn't be getting shirty about it."

That landed like a punch in Allegra's stomach. "Look, Vanessa, I'm not involved in that whole Threshold-BSA-fire whatever," she said, putting her hands up in a 'stop' signal. "I genuinely know nothing about it beyond the fact that I did a safety assessment for the property that got misused. That's it."

"And you're super sure that your new girlfriend had absolutely nothing to do with it either? The timing was totally coincidental and *not* because she set any of it up?"

Suddenly, Allegra wasn't super sure. "Yes," she said firmly anyway.

Vanessa relaxed somewhat. "Okay," she said. "Alright." She paused, clearly deliberating whether to add something else. "This just really reminds me of when Simone used to call to say everything was okay, but she didn't tell me she was in fucking jail for *months*," she said. "That's the vibe, Allegra."

Menus arrived and conversation pivoted, because Aaron had mentioned the Vales to the twins, which meant that Allegra had to give Vanessa a blow-by-blow of the Nice Family Lunch as if it were actually a nice family lunch. And no matter how much energy Allegra put into really making sure she was skimming off every little bit of tension from it, Vanessa side-eyed her the whole time and decided she was acting weird.

Allegra's *second* Nice Family Lunch in as many days was almost as tense as the first.

It was always a relief to say goodbye to Vanessa—regardless of how much Allegra loved her—and today was no exception. When Vanessa finally hugged her and went to go hop on a ferry, Allegra couldn't retreat to the penthouse fast enough. She was pretty done with everything and everyone, and under any slightly different circumstances, she would have got in the car and just driven *out*. In any direction. Away.

Sal was bringing her file home, though, and she needed to see what was in it so she could figure out what Dimi's next move would be.

Upstairs, there was a card on the centre of the kitchen counter. Allegra lifted it, frowning. "*Your groceries have been delivered by Good Order Pantries*." Allegra looked up and went to check the fridge—it now contained more than just water and wine.

Nothing else in the penthouse was disturbed in any way. Like ghosts had been in and out. That made Allegra a little uneasy. People coming and going silently around her felt intrusive and imposing, even if they were only doing what they were paid for.

Sal returned home from work mid-evening, with dinner. She noted the card on the counter and then set her briefcase and the food on the dining table.

Allegra couldn't have made it over more quickly if she had *run*. When she got there, Sal looked glum.

Allegra studied her face. "I don't like the look of that expression."

Sal unclipped her case and opened it on the table. Her lips were tight. "Zoe swept it," she said, handing Allegra a fat hardcopy file. "There's no additional information in there about Aaron—just basic information I included when I was backgrounding you myself."

Allegra accepted the file, feeling the weight of it like it was a rock settling in her stomach.

"I had Gerard copy your paper file anyway, just in case there was anything else of note in there. Sometimes there's more in the hardcopy file than online." She didn't sound very hopeful.

Allegra processed what Sal had just told her. "So there's nothing about Aaron's university in here." Sal's lips parted for a second, and then she shook her head. Allegra's hand tightened on the file. "So where did Dimi get that information, then?"

Sal was tense. "Well, not from this file," she said, watching her words. "And after Zoe did the sweep, I used our crawling software to see what I could find online just in case there was another simple answer." From Sal's expression, there wasn't. "He could conceivably have determined Aaron was going to Macquarie based on the fact Aaron's been tagged in a few photos by students who are—but there was little other information easily available."

Allegra felt that creeping dread. "Could he just have called around? Or called his friends at Macquarie?"

"He wouldn't," Sal at least sounded certain of that. "Every time you ask favours from someone—especially unethical ones—you create a debt to them. He won't want to create a debt to whoever his friends are at Macquarie unless he's certain there's a return on it."

Allegra could feel her pulse begin to lift. "Could he have followed him?" Sal shook her head. "Well, what, then? Does BSA have some system they can use to check someone's education and qualifications, or something?"

Sal paused for a moment. "Yes," she said carefully. "Gerard checked the access logs for it and HR has just used it for new hires." Her hand rested on the back of a chair but looked anything but restful.

Allegra frowned at it. "Why are you being careful about this?" she just straight up asked her. "What are you trying not to tell me?"

Sal watched her, brow furrowed. "Because there is a likely answer to this," she said. "And you're not going to like it."

"Just fucking tell me, Sal."

Sal looked down, exhaled and nodded once. "It's going to be Atlas," she said, and then wet her lips as she thought. "It's our secure archive room. There's an air-gapped network down there, as well as a networked computer that has some powerful access software on it." She paused. "All of the most sensitive data: high-risk personal information, undisclosed conflicts and liabilities, legacy non-disclosure agreements—" her breath caught, she powered through it, "it's all down there."

Allegra listened, processing that. "Powerful access software," she repeated.

"Obtained at staggeringly high expense," she said. "I'm not across what it does, exactly. I've never used it. I just know that the information it has turned over about some of BSA's biggest competitors and detractors is—" She paused, choosing her words. "Immobilising."

Allegra looked from Sal to the file in her own hands, thick with information about her. Probably useless information. She might as well be holding a ream of blank paper when she now knew where the *real* information was kept.

"So you think Dimi used the Atlas software thing to obtain information about Aaron, and that information is stored down there with it."

Sal nodded. "It's the cleanest explanation," she said. "Not just because the data fusion software would explain how he knows Aaron's university, but the access logs show Dimi entered Atlas on Saturday morning."

Allegra felt her resolve solidify. "Can we go there now?" she asked. "Like, right now? I want to see what he found."

Sal's eyebrows went up. "No!" she said, sounding surprised Allegra even asked. "Access to the software is *strictly* monitored, and access logs are—"

"Fuck logs," Allegra said openly. "You can get in, right?"

Sal narrowed her eyes, drawing back in on herself. "Yes," she confirmed, "but *my* access will be logged just like Dimi's is, and whatever I do in there will be reviewed, and reported, and—"

"Why can Dimi go in there whenever he likes and you can't?"

"Because he's the CEO, Allegra! I'm just his employee! The room is *for* the Chair and the CEO to build—"

Fuck this noise. "He's got information about *my son*, Sal!" Allegra told her, slapping the file on the table. "He doesn't get to just have that! He's basically threatened to use it to ruin Aaron's life if I don't toe the line!"

Sal put her hands up in a placating gesture. "I hear you, and we will find out what it is, and get copies of it," she promised Allegra. "We've just got to be careful about timing, because I could *genuinely lose my job* over this sort of information breach. I need you to understand that." She dropped her arms. "At board level. Not Dimi-level. The board and the exec know the sort of power that software has, and they know what sort of information is stored in that room."

Allegra's hands were clenched, and her breath was moving fast. The fact a file full of—she swallowed—blackmail-adjacent information existed about her and her son and that she was being refused access to it just—she shook her head. Her eyes dipped to Sal's fob beside her on the table.

Sal saw her line of sight and sharpened. She took a step towards Allegra and pointed a finger at her. "Do not *fucking dare*," she said coldly. "Do not even think about it. You using my swipe would burn us both. Listen to me, Allegra: do you genuinely want to stop Dimi from being able to hurt Aaron?" Expression still hard, Allegra nodded fractionally. "Then do not even *think* about doing that."

Allegra exhaled, still watching her. After a moment, she looked away and took a few steps towards the centre of the room so she didn't pick the file up and *fucking throw it*.

Sal gave her space. "We will figure this out," she promised her. "I will not let that file sit there indefinitely. We just need to work out the timing."

Allegra threw a glance at her. Timing? She hissed and looked away. Every second that file sat there with information Dimi knew and Allegra didn't, it was a second longer she had no idea what Dimi's plans were for Aaron.

She didn't need perfect timing. She needed that fucking file.

Chapter 28: 10:00am

Sal's penthouse had five bedrooms, a second prep kitchen, a wine cellar—*and not a single fucking pen that worked*.

Allegra marched down to her LandCruiser and took one from the important junk in her glovebox. Back upstairs, she sat down with the giant and likely useless stack of paper from her BSA backgrounding file, pen ready. If there was even a chance the university detail was in here, maybe it wasn't in Atlas. It was worth a shot.

She hadn't touched her food, so while she was sighing over the printouts and reports, Sal unobtrusively opened the takeaway box, retrieved a fork for her, and placed it all within her reach on the table. Then, she sat down opposite her, opened her laptop, and started typing while ignoring her own food.

"I hope you're working on how we're going to get into Atlas," Allegra said to her, probably more harshly than necessary.

Sal let it go. "I am," she confirmed, adding, "although it will be just me who ends up in there—and accompanied. There is no circumstance in which a client would be allowed in there."

Allegra looked up sharply. "But *my personal information* is in there."

"Yes," Sal said. "Even more reason you wouldn't be allowed. And why I will likely be accompanied."

"Because there's a file on me?"

"No." She didn't elaborate. Allegra filed it away to think about later, looking back at the enormous task before her.

It *was* enormous, and Sal hadn't been wrong about the content. It was mostly dry positioning analyses—how to use her, where she'd be most useful, what value could be extracted. Almost none of it was monetary. So odd, given their earlier meetings. "I get why *you* want to be associated with me, but why would BSA be interested in having me as a client?" Allegra eventually said, sitting back and turning her attention to Sal for a moment.

Sal looked up. "I'm going to need more context."

Allegra gestured at the file. "None of this is about money."

Sal's face relaxed. "Some clients pay us directly," she said. "And others are valuable because they serve a specific function for the clients that pay us directly. For example, someone who can reliably get calls returned by ministers, regulators, or senior bureaucrats. Or an ex-commissioner whose presence at an event confers an air of transparency. Or," she said, eyes on Allegra, "someone who has captured public goodwill and whose ethics would never be questioned."

Allegra sat with that. Eventually, she said, "You realise the problem with recruiting someone for their ethics is that they're not going to support something unethical, right?"

"Yes. It's a delicate balance."

A balance between what and what, Allegra wondered, eyes narrowed. She stared at Sal for a few more seconds and then got back to her file.

She began reading carefully in case Aaron was mentioned in some oblique way, but as she moved deeper into the file she found herself skimming. She would have preferred to read it properly, if she'd had the time—but she didn't. She was tired, and each page was drier than the last. The worst thing about paper files was the lack of a search function. "Why does BSA even keep paper files, anyway?" she wondered aloud, annoyed.

"Audit purposes, mainly," Sal said, eyes still scanning whatever she was looking at. "We keep copies of everything."

Something occurred to Allegra. "Is that the same with Atlas files?"

Sal's eyes snapped up over her screen. "Why do you ask?"

"Just answer me."

Sal searched her face for a moment. "Yes, it's the same with Atlas files," she said carefully. Then, she sat back, expression hard. "I am telling you all this because I trust you *not* to take my fob and access Atlas."

Allegra looked away, jaw tight.

"Allegra. Look at me." She did. Sal's expression was *glacial*. "Promise me you will not use my fob."

Allegra closed her eyes briefly. She knew what the only answer was. "I won't."

Sal released a breath and got back to her screen. After a few seconds of cold silence, she softened. "I know how important this is to you," she said more quietly. "I'm not discounting that at all. But there's a right way and a wrong way to approach this. The wrong way is taking my fob and swiping in without permission."

It's also the quickest and most effective way, Allegra thought. "So you're working on permission?"

Sal nodded. "I'm currently reading the register of other times Atlas was used by the exec and trying to figure out what I could manufacture to get myself in there," she said. "And which exec I could get in there with me, other than Dimi, who'll insist on accompanying me if he knows about it too early."

Dimi? "If he's there you won't be able to look at anything!"

Sal looked grim. "Exactly. There's a lot to consider." She got back to it.

When Allegra was getting to the end of her file, having found very little reference to Aaron, Sal stood from her chair stiffly, making a face as she carefully arched her back and rotated her neck. Allegra watched her slowly walk up the curved staircase, wondering if she was turning in for the night. Instead, she returned a couple of minutes later, to Allegra's relief *not* in satin, but an appropriate pair of summer pyjamas and her robe tied shut. All still black. What was different was that she'd taken off her makeup.

At the last moment, Allegra managed to catch herself and *not* stare. Not because she was one of those women who looked transformed without it, but because she looked so *normal*. Pretty, and normal. With fairly sizeable bags under her eyes. It felt almost indecent to have access to this version of her—and deliberate. Allegra had to consciously manage her own face.

When Sal dropped past the table to collect her laptop on the way to the couch, she held Allegra's eyes just a little too long.

You fuck, Allegra thought when she was finally released, shaking her head to herself. She was faintly smiling when she noticed the untouched takeaway box beside where Sal had been sitting. "You going to actually eat any of your dinner, or is it just for decoration?"

Sal glanced back. "It will be cold."

That sounded exceptionally bizarre to someone who usually lived out of their LandCruiser. "Well, I presume you have a microwave somewhere in this enormous house?" she said dryly. "Do you even know where it is?"

Sal settled down on the couch with the laptop on her knees. "Perhaps you could help me find it." Her bare eyes were alight—and, also, an exceptionally warm brown.

Feeling a mixture of wired and faintly irritated, Allegra located the microwave in a cupboard in the prep kitchen, zapped Sal's food, and then managed to stop herself from dumping the whole box in her lap.

Sal made a hands-empty gesture about the lack of cutlery, giving Allegra a sly grin. Allegra just went over to the table, collected her own used fork, and held it out to her, expression challenging Sal to reject it.

What Sal did was worse. She accepted it and didn't break eye contact as she put it slowly into her mouth.

This woman. "Just remember if I murder you, no one can stop me from using your fob," she warned Sal, going back to the table to resume her hunt for Aaron in the background file.

As she'd expected, it was unfruitful. Aaron existed; there was half a page on care arrangements with Vanessa tied to a possible Homeward alignment. Allegra flicked between those pages, searching for dates. There were none. She wasn't sure that knowing the dates would change anything, but knowing the sequence of events would be comforting, especially given the 'sus' timing of Sal showing up.

But there was nothing on that. Nothing on Aaron, either. She sat back, running a hand through her hair. "You were right," Allegra said reluctantly. "There's nothing else."

When Sal didn't reply, Allegra twisted to look at her. She was asleep again. This time, she'd arranged herself in a comfortable position: she'd put the laptop on the coffee table, closed, and curled up in the corner of the couch. No doona, though. On the table across from Allegra, the fob sat beside Sal's briefcase. Within reach. Allegra stood—then realised she'd stepped towards the couch, not the briefcase.

Allegra's first impulse was to join Sal; it felt like an invitation this time. She took another step—and then stopped. An invitation to *what*, though? There wasn't room behind her. Allegra would have to move her or risk crushing her. *Perhaps it's just like last night*, she decided.

She went and changed into trackies and an old tee, and brought the doona back into the atrium again, spreading it out over Sal and also herself. Then, in tandem at opposite ends of the couch, they slept.

Sal rose early this time. Allegra only woke as her side cooled and the doona shifted; Sal had been against her. She would never know which part of Sal, or how much of her, because Sal was already on her way upstairs by the time Allegra sat up. With no reason to stay, she went to shower as well.

Sal was already sitting in front of her computer at the table when Allegra emerged from the guest bathroom, a lone mug of coffee opposite her. Allegra retrieved her phone and sat at the chair in front of the coffee, gingerly taking a sip. It wasn't as fiercely strong this morning. Sal's coffee, however, looked as intensely black as ever.

Sal had clipped Allegra's file and put it back in the folder. She noticed Allegra's eyes on it. "I gather there was nothing additional in there?" Allegra pressed her lips together and shook her head. Sal made a face. "It was a long shot," she said. "I need to take this back to work—a client file off-site is a security risk." She stood up to put it back into her briefcase, pausing a moment, eyes on Allegra. "You do realise there is breakfast food here now."

Allegra perked up. She'd forgotten about that. She stood up immediately and went to go make herself some toast, hunting around the kitchen for all the bits and pieces she needed.

Sal side-eyed the toaster on the display bench as she got ready to leave, but didn't ask her to move it back into the prep kitchen. "You're welcome to drop by the office again for a morning coffee," she said, as if it were an invitation and not a directive. "After about 10:15, though." She paused, observing Allegra with the Vegemite. "It smells like a worksite kitchenette in here."

Allegra held out a slice towards her. "Want some?"

The look Sal gave her was reward enough. "No thanks," Sal said. "I have my passport if I feel the need to prove I'm Australian." Collecting her briefcase and her fob, she left with enough time to get to the office before 8am.

Allegra took her toast outside on the terrace to eat. Pale gold sunlight skimmed the balustrade and spilled past it onto the concrete. Allegra tested the heat by extending a bare foot off the cold tiles to block it—warm, immediately. The Harbour shimmered in the distance, a little hazy. Haze meant a *hot* day. Convenient that today was an inside-a-building day; sleeping in the LandCruiser during a hot summer was unbearable.

Unbearable like waiting a fucking month for Sal to figure out some BSA-Approved Way to get into Atlas. She took a bite of her toast and was staring at her feet in the sun when her phone rang. Maybe it was Sal with an idea?

She immediately checked it. Timothy. She frowned and answered. "Hi?"

He exhaled. "I wanted to talk to you about the release," he said, clearly presuming she had any idea what he was talking about. "What do you think about it? Should we sign it?"

Allegra narrowed her eyes, looking forwards at the view over the balcony. "A release?" she asked. "What release?" She took another bite of her toast.

Something occurred to him and he groaned. "Oh, of course. No one ever has your current address," he said. "Kirribilli Primary sent us a consent form to release information about us, Aaron, and his schooling."

Allegra stopped chewing. "*Why?*"

Some paper rustled. "Well, there's this standard letter attached which lists a number of reasons: request by the student, therapy and medical, military and government clearance..." He paused. "Did he say anything about this to you?"

"Nothing," she told Timothy, a weight settling in her stomach.

"Do you think it's for Macquarie?" he asked. "It doesn't *say* university applications, but this is just a standard letter."

Allegra felt like she had a very good idea who initiated it. "Don't sign it," she told Timothy firmly. "Let me look into it first."

Timothy paused. "Alright," he said. "That's validating, actually. I thought I was just being an old man, so I'm glad you're worried about it, too."

She said goodbye to him and finished her toast. It was almost certainly fucking Dimi. It *smelt* like him. But 'military clearance'? That... made her think of Simone. The ADF had done all sorts of opaque things after her extradition. It was worth checking first. Maybe they were just looking for references to Simone in Aaron's documents or something.

Simone's name was right down the bottom of her contact list; it had been that long since Allegra had texted her. The last message had a date from the *COVID era* in it. She got straight to the point. *"Do you know anything about an information release request from Kirribilli Primary?"*

Simone made her fucking wait. Like always. *"So good to hear from you, sister."*

Oh, fuck off, Allegra thought, scowling at her phone. *"Can you answer my question please."*

Again, it was 15 fucking minutes before she answered. *"It's interesting you ask me instead of Aaron. What are you worried he's going to say to you?"*

"You know what?" Allegra said aloud to her phone. "Fuck you. I will ask him." She stood up, resisting the urge to *throw* something. Why the fuck did she think Simone of all people would be the right person to ask?! There wasn't a single thing in Allegra's life she hadn't made *worse* by virtue of being exactly who she was.

She stood there wanting to *murder her sister* before forcing herself to exhale. What the fuck could she even *do* about that woman? What was there to do about her? She was who she was, and Allegra didn't have time or energy to waste on her right now.

She put her fuck of a sister out of her mind and got straight to texting Aaron. *"Hey—we received a consent to release info for you from Kirribilli. I gather because we're in it, too. Did you receive one? Do you know what it's for?"*

Thank God her son took after her *other* sister. *"Yeah, I got one this morning. I signed it already because some guy came to my door with it. I just thought it was a Macquarie thing."*

Allegra's stomach dropped. He signed it already?

She sat back, taking a deep breath. *"Someone came to your door with it?"*

"Yeah, kind of like a process server or something. They left copies of the documents which requested academic transcripts etc, so I presumed Macquarie."

After a minute, she closed off the conversation with, *"Okay, if you get any other documents or anything with time pressure, can you just shoot me a text beforehand? The media can be a bit intense, and we should be a little cautious about what goes out."* He thumbs-upped it.

No part of her believed it was Macquarie. At this point, there was only one set of people who'd actually answer her question. She checked the time—8:45am. It was *possible* the office would be staffed. She googled Kirribilli Primary and called them.

No answer. A recorded message informed her they'd be open at 9am.

Rather than sit in place and do nothing, Allegra went back inside, set the treadmill to a brisk walk so she didn't lose the plot, and googled corporate archive rooms. It seemed most were off-site and managed externally; she doubted Atlas was off-site. The fact Sal's fob worked and the way Sal talked about it ('down there') suggested to Allegra it was in the BSA basement, and she'd done enough fire system training and flood rescues with the SES to know it was the sort of thing corporations kept in their basements.

She counted down the minutes until 9am and then called Kirribilli the second it opened. A cheerful voice answered.

"Hi," Allegra said, making an effort to be friendly. "It's Allegra Sinclair," she said, "I received a—"

"Mrs Sinclair!" the lady said, sounding delighted. "Lovely to have you as a former student. I just watched your interview from last week on ABC iview. Such great practical safety information—so appropriate for young audiences. I think we're even thinking of including it in the curriculum next year."

Allegra was grateful and all that, but had other priorities just now. *Be nice*, she told herself. "That's so wonderful," she said, hating herself. "I'm so glad it's useful! I love sharing the Australian bushland with young people." She paused, hopefully long enough. "I'm calling about a slightly different matter, perhaps you can help me," she began. "You see, my family received an information release form for my son. I'm just curious about what it's for."

"Oh!" the lady said. "Well, let me check. We do these all the time. Government and APS jobs require them after all..." Allegra could hear her typing for what felt like an infinite eternity before she finally spoke again. "Here we go: Sinclair, Aaron. The applicant is a law firm by the name of Langford & Pryce. Does that clear things up?"

Not at all, thought Allegra, glumly. "Perhaps," she said anyway. "Is there any other information?"

"Not that I can see," the lady said. "Just an all-record request. Not uncommon."

Allegra thanked her, let her chit-chat a little longer about perhaps getting Allegra out to talk to the children—not out of the question, but definitely not her current to-do list—and then hung up and *immediately* googled them. Corporate Advisory Solicitors.

Already feeling sick, she called Sal. "Sorry to bother you," she began.

Sal made a neutral noise, dismissing that. "You never do unless it's important."

"It is. Do you know who Langford & Pryce is?"

Sal paused. Longer than Allegra expected her to. "Yes," she said. "They're the advisory firm the Blacks use."

Allegra's hand tightened around her phone. "Well, they just requested a full release of all documents from Kirribilli Primary School, where Aaron went," she said, and then explained what had happened since Sal left.

Sal listened and didn't interrupt her, only speaking when she was finished. "I know this may not be very reassuring, but the release isn't required for him to access a lot of that information anyway," she said. "He's done it to get a reaction out of you so he can learn about what you know and what you suspect."

Allegra focused on the important part of that. "*He already has that information*?"

"Most likely. And he likely knows it's damaging in some way which is why he chose to pull it to see whether you suspect he did it."

Allegra's heart was pounding. "God," she said. "How much information does he *have* down there?"

"I don't know," Sal said. "But, like Sunday's lunch, it's important that you don't take the bait and respond to it. Leave it. We'll talk more later this morning."

How was she supposed to leave it? "I'll see you at 10:15," she told Sal and said goodbye.

She stepped off the treadmill and stood in the centre of the room. Overhead, the air-conditioning unit droned—outside, traffic was faintly audible over the sound of her heartbeat. Otherwise, silence.

This is only going to get worse, she realised. The information asymmetry. The testing. He had the luxury of time to sit in his beautiful office wherever the fuck it was and plan what he wanted to do to them next. To contain them.

She'd waited before, a long time ago; calm voices had reassured her everything would be okay. Sal was doing the same. She was going to spend all her free time examining logs and planning routes, making it look pretty and clean. None of it was fucking clean. None of it was fucking right. Sal could afford to play the long game. She couldn't.

If she didn't act now, she was choosing not to act. She was ignoring her gut and letting Lachie walk right out that door again.

Alright, Allegra thought, *time to stop waiting.* She put on her suit. Sal was going to need to come up with a plan—today—or Allegra was going to find a way to get in. If there was an exec access register, each of those execs had a fob.

Allegra put on the suit blazer this time. It was huge, sharp, and structured; it looked imposing. It sent a message.

People responded to her differently on the street, too; fewer selfie requests and less calling out to her. The space people gave her was measurable.

It was 9:45am when she arrived at BSA; too early to go upstairs looking for Sal. She settled on the same couch she and Sal had used yesterday when they met with Vanessa.

Beside her, there was some sort of security briefing underway. Several of them had their heads together, and she couldn't help but overhear what they were saying. "...the main issue is going to be people complaining about the lifts," an older man was saying to an assorted group of less grizzled-looking security officers. "Office folks don't like to use the stairs, so you'll hear about it, especially in a building this high. Just remind them it's important for them to know their limits in case there's a *real* fire."

Allegra's attention sharpened. A fire drill? She kept listening, pretending to scroll through her phone.

"We'll let it roll for five minutes. No point in running it for less time than that, as it will take at least two for the fire wardens on each floor to get everyone up off their chairs," he was saying. "Your job is just to make sure people get out of the stairwells and out the front door. It's hot, expect whinging."

Allegra checked her phone: Tuesday. The first Tuesday of the month, classically a fire drill day, usually at 10am. It was currently 9:47am.

She listened to the rest of the instructions, hazarding a peek at the staff. "The cancel button is in the camera room," the man was explaining. "It's under the switch—you can't miss it, enormous green button, clearly labelled. If for some reason I'm not around to press it, at 10:05am any of you can."

So it is at 10am, Allegra realised. She stared down at her phone. A test alarm would call the lifts down to ground floor, lock them in place for two minutes to make sure people were aware they couldn't be used, but then allow use after that. A test alarm wouldn't disarm doors or external access panels.

A real one would. Emergency staff needed to be able to gain access to every level and every room.

Something crystallised inside her. She checked her phone: 9:51am. There was no harm in going and checking what system they had installed down there; after all, the doors would only disarm for a real alarm if it was a Hermer or a Marion system.

She stood, her knees stiff and muscles tight. She shook them out, smiled at security as they waved her through without much attention, and stepped into an empty lift. She pressed 'B' hoping a fob wasn't needed to even access the floor. The number stayed lit.

The lift opened to a clean and empty corridor lined with Besser bricks and lit with harsh fluorescent lights.

Pulse already picking up, she stepped out of the lift and looked either way—there was no one here. On the ceiling, there were old, painted-over sprinklers and heat sensors that looked like they were last century installations. A long stain low on the wall indicated there was flooding down here at some point. No cameras; she doubted that was an oversight.

And bolted along the exterior of the wall near the ceiling was a bright red Marion cable.

She stared at it. *What are you doing, Allegra*? she asked herself. Without answering, she walked along the wall, past several doors, until she spotted one with a fob access reader on it, glowing faintly red. She walked up to it to examine it: the door was wrapped in steel and lined in rubber, tightly closed all around. Hermetically sealed. She looked down at the fob reader.

The word '*ATLAS*' was embossed on the plastic.

The hair on her arms stood on end. She looked up at the door. *It's all through here,* she thought. She was just metres away from whatever was inside.

She checked her phone: 9:55am.

She stepped away from the door and looked back up at the Marion cable, following it around the corner to a door with a glowing *EXIT* sign—probably to the carpark. The red cable traced off the ceiling in a line down to the manual call point. She walked slowly up to it, looking down at the little red box on the wall. *BREAK GLASS IN CASE OF FIRE,* the box instructed.

There was no need for that. Allegra's fingers felt around the back of the box for the service clips and pulled them, neatly removing the case. The switch was exposed.

She checked the time. 9:56am.

Four minutes, she realised. *If you do this, Allegra, there's no going back.*

Do what, though? If anyone noticed it wasn't run on 'test', they'd assume the system glitched. Old buildings did that. That's *if* they even noticed.

What if someone sees you? she asked herself. All she had to do was look up, no one was around. That's probably why Atlas *was* down here.

9:57am.

She stared at the manual call point switch. *I'm not planning to do anything permanent. I'll just look. Two minutes, that's all. Film it and leave. I can read it later.*

No one would know. No harm done.

9:58am.

She was shivering. It was the way she felt before abseiling backwards off a cliff into the dark. Her muscles *sang*. Every hair on her body rose.

If she didn't do it now, she'd have to wait another *whole month* or more. Who knew how quickly Sal could figure out a way in?

9:59am.

If she *didn't* flick the switch, she was making a choice. She would be stepping aside. Letting him walk out that door again. Forever.

The exposed switch pointed upwards.

Her finger hovered over it.

Her vision greyed.

Muscles braced, she took a deep breath as her phone ticked over to 10:00am.

And flicked the switch down.

Chapter 29: Sensitive Material

Everything was dark. The fire bell above the exit split the air as her eyes adjusted to the emergency lighting.

She needed to move now.

She flipped the switch back to 'off' and replaced the *BREAK IN CASE OF FIRE* box—intact, they'd presume it had malfunctioned—and spun towards the strip lighting. It led down the corridor to Atlas. She took off at a jog, following it.

The fob reader was glowing green. She reached for the handle and the door opened with a *click*. The sound of the fire alarm was muted by the heavy door closing behind her as she slipped in.

Inside, Atlas was lit by dim emergency lighting. Right in front of her was a huge oval table, and behind the table were three computers open on login screens, printers, and a server tower.

The whole other half of the room was taken up by a massive steel compactus. In just the row that was open, there were *hundreds* of dull green files. Maybe thousands. There were full shelves running along the rails; the sheer scale of the archive was dizzying.

She scanned the ceiling for cameras. Finding none, she went straight for the compactus. The power had been cut for emergency mode—she had to move it by hand. Without hydraulics, dragging the shelves apart on the rails took her full bodyweight and all her strength. She was already heaving each breath when she opened section S–U.

Using her phone as a torch, she leafed through file by file until she found *Sinclair, Allegra*. She pulled it out; it was *thick*. She rushed it out to the table, laying it flat to start filming—but the footage was useless. Her phone was old and there was no fucking light.

She carried it over to the strip lighting on the floor. That was better, but she still wasn't getting enough detail to read it in the video.

Shit. She sat back, checking the time: *10:02am*. If they were going to realise the alarm was real, it would be now, when the lifts failed to reactivate.

She looked around. Her eyes fell on the printers: they'd be photocopiers as well. She could try to copy some of this... except they'd keep a record of the file copied and the time it was copied.

Fuck! She looked back down at her file. There was no possible way she could read any of this now. She didn't have time. She was going to have to put it back.

She stood with it, taking a few steps towards the compactus, and then stopped. Was she going to just leave it here? Aaron's smile—*Lachie's* smile—surfaced from the weekend. That could fall in an instant. It had, so many times before.

She set her jaw. She couldn't leave the file here. Unbuttoning her suit, she sucked in her stomach and shoved it into her waistband, wedging it into the crotch of her suit pants. The top, she tucked under her breasts.

She was buttoning her blazer up and moving towards the door when—she stopped.

Sal also needed an escort to enter Atlas. And not for Allegra's sake. Which meant—

Rushing back over to the compactus, she heaved the steel shelves back along the rails again until she reached J–L. As she was tabbing along the files, she noticed a particularly fat one. Discarding the rest, she pulled it out. *Lategan, Sal,* was printed in a peeling and faded label on the front.

She didn't have time to reflect on that, though, because she needed to get it inside her clothes. It was heavy; it dragged on the crotch of her suit pants. She pushed her stomach out against the files to hold them in place and buttoned her blazer over them, hoping they couldn't be seen.

Then, she pulled the door open and slipped back through it. The fob light was still green on the other side. She looked down at it, pausing a moment.

You can still put these back, Allegra told herself. She could put them back and let Sal handle how to get them out. No harm done. There was still time to do this the 'right' way, no one had to know what she'd tried to do.

Aaron, she thought. And she'd come this far. She turned away from the door.

Retracing her steps, she slipped into the stairwell, listening to the torrent of people pouring down. She waited until it thinned and she could no longer hear the ringing of feet on iron stairs before risking a glance up. There was a group of people much further up—too far to see her. She climbed the stairs and exited into the foyer with the people filing outside into the heat.

People were packed together on the pavement. Allegra had to be careful no one knocked her stomach, solid from the files, but otherwise bodies were too close for anyone to notice anything was off about her silhouette.

Of all the things to make smuggling stolen files worse, she hadn't expected it to be people smiling and saying hello. She peeled off as soon as she could and headed down a side street, stepping into a doorway. She searched her pockets, panicking for a second she'd left her phone in Atlas, then found it in her blazer. She texted Sal. *"I need to see you immediately."*

"Meet you at my place in 15." It was a relief—before she realised what she was bringing to the penthouse.

Sal was going to *fucking kill* her.

Too late to pretend I didn't do it, she realised, and took a long way around the BSA building to head back to The Rocks.

Sal's car was in the carpark when Allegra entered it. She was already upstairs. That alone made her heart pound harder than breaking into Atlas had.

She took the lift up, staring at her flushed face and hand bracing her middle in the mirror. The lift door opened to Sal. Her arms were crossed.

As Allegra stepped out of the lift, Sal gave her a once-over to check she was okay, her eyes pausing on Allegra's arm across her torso. "Are you hurt?" she asked, stepping forward.

Allegra stiffened, stepping away. Unfortunately, that just highlighted the shape of her torso.

Sal's eyes dipped to it. "Why are you standing like—" She stopped, her eyes narrowed as she noticed something. "What is that?"

Allegra felt all the blood drain out of her recently flushed face.

Sal clocked something was up instantly. "What have you done?"

Shit. Allegra took a breath, shifting her weight. "That wasn't a fire drill. I manually triggered the fire alarm at 10am."

Sal froze. It was a second before she spoke. "You *what*?"

"Marion systems unlock all doors on a fire alarm." Pinned by Sal's intense stare, she unbuttoned her blazer and lifted her shirt, showing Sal the washed-out green folders.

Sal recognised them immediately and her eyebrows lifted and her mouth opened. She glanced up at Allegra—in horror—and then back at the files. While she was speechless, Allegra took them out of her belt. "I didn't use your fob," she said, as if that was any sort of consolation.

Sal recovered herself. "No," she said coldly, "you triggered a *building-wide fire alarm*." Sal took a step back, her hands raising as if to run through her hair and then falling before they reached her head. "Do you understand how many people will now be *reviewing this moment*?"

"I didn't break the glass," Allegra attempted. "They will presume an equipment malfunction."

Sal was hardly listening to her. "If Dimi finds out it was real—which there is every possibility he will—*he will check Atlas and notice a file missing*." She paused, managing her breathing. "And even if he doesn't, he will notice soon. He was in Atlas on Saturday: he's actively using your file. You've just created a *very* tight countdown."

"We can focus our efforts on figuring out how to get them back inside instead." She wasn't even convincing herself.

Sal was *furious*. Her face hardened. Her hands flexed at her sides as if resisting a clench. "You broke into a room you don't understand and removed leverage you don't know how to use." She paused. "*After* I specifically told you not to."

Allegra looked away. She was right, but the point was moot. "It's done now." She looked down at the files and then slipped Sal's out from underneath hers. The peeling label reading *Lategan, Sal* was curling from the cover as she held it out.

Sal opened her mouth to say something—nasty, Allegra expected—but stopped. Her eyes dropped to the file and didn't leave it. Whatever she'd been about to say died on her tongue. Shooting Allegra an icy look that promised this conversation wasn't over, she took the file and smoothed her name flat, holding it as if it were a cursed artefact. Then she turned and carried it to the table.

Allegra followed more carefully with her own file, sitting opposite Sal.

It took Sal a moment to open her file, fingers lingering on the cover. Before she did, her phone rang. She hissed, silenced it, and flipped it face down. Returning immediately to the file, she opened it. Allegra did the same with hers.

The paper was still warm from her body, and crisp and new like it hadn't been printed long ago. The first page was an ID sheet of Allegra with—*her passport photo*. Unsettling that he had that. There was some information about her service with the SES and her relief work alongside the ADF; nothing she cared about. It didn't take her long to get to information on Aaron.

Kirribilli Primary records, ones she hadn't seen. Not just academic records, but behavioural ones. Details on how disruptive Aaron had been at primary school, how he'd gotten in trouble for punching and screaming at other children. Allegra couldn't remember any of this. She wouldn't put it past Timothy and Vanessa to hide it from her, but it was also possible this all took place while she was drinking. There were so many incident reports that she started counting them, and then gave up. Then she got to the counselling records.

That was so much worse. She read through them in an adrenal haze, following how Aaron said he *hated* it when Allegra and Timothy came back. He wanted them to stay away. How he said he wished Vanessa and Robin—her late husband—were his parents.

After Robin died, there was a referral to Child Protection for social work and grief counselling. Timothy's signature was on it. That, he hadn't told her about.

Details about how tearful Aaron was. How he'd sobbed and told the school chaplain, "I don't think anyone wants me." That line had been highlighted.

On his medical record as a toddler—right after Allegra had first left—the doctor had written 'failure to thrive'.

There were other things in the file. Aaron had assaulted a few people in his early teens—Vanessa's signature was on those reports. There were photos attached of the injuries Aaron had caused. He'd even shoplifted once. There was a police report, with Aaron's mug shot—face relaxed, eyes red from crying.

Allegra sat back, taking a deep breath.

For a moment, she was back at the airport listening to her toddler, her sweet little son, *screaming* and *begging* and *crying* for Mummy not to go as he struggled violently in Vanessa's arms, reaching for Allegra, tears pouring down his chubby little cheeks. Her empty arms ached for him as the International Terminal gate closed behind her.

She'd spent the whole 8 hours of that flight crying.

She put her hand over her mouth. There was nothing more personal or private than this. And Dimi wanted to take this and make it *ugly.* He wanted to tar Aaron and Allegra with it, while he sat back and observed the fallout for 'data' or 'pressure' or whatever the fuck he wanted.

And he could. He could hurt them both with it. And he probably planned to.

There was more in the file—recent details about Aaron including his classes and grades at Macquarie (excellent, Allegra noticed, not that it mattered here). And a warm photo of him with his arms around his twin cousins, beaming.

She sat for a minute with all of it, stuck between the mental image of Aaron punching another child for teasing him about his family, and Dimi reading that line and highlighting it. It was *obscene*.

And there had been *thousands* of files in that room.

She became aware of Sal across from her, still. She'd stopped turning pages; her eyes were unfocused, gazing forward absently at the closed file. She looked up as Allegra registered her. They made eye contact.

Sal took a breath. "Show me."

Allegra felt all at once like that request wasn't fair. But, then again, how did she hope to formulate a response to it if Sal couldn't help? It just—*no.* Not like this. Allegra stuck her hand out. "Show me yours."

Sal sharpened and withdrew her hand. She searched Allegra's eyes, brow furrowed. "I shouldn't," she said coolly. "You've demonstrated how trustworthy you are." After a moment, she inhaled slowly and looked away, briefly closing her eyes. "I'm a fool." She lifted her heavy file with a shaking wrist, and put it in Allegra's hand as Allegra reciprocated.

She received Sal's file, looking down at it. She felt the weight of Sal's disappointment settle on her shoulders.

Sal didn't stay seated opposite. Eyes averted, she took the file upstairs. Allegra heard the office door click shut as she opened Sal's file.

The first page was like Allegra's: a brief. It had a photo of Sal just like Allegra's—old. Sal looked so young, she couldn't have been more than mid-20s. Allegra paused at it: she didn't look so different, really. After it, there were some old performance reviews, work reports. A lease. Then, inside the file was a small document holder with a *Langford & Pryce* logo on the cover.

'DEED OF CONFIDENTIALITY', it read, with a date back in 2004, between *'Dimitri Black (Disclosing Party) and Sally Lategan (Recipient)'*. Allegra read through the recitals and definitions. *'The Disclosing Party denies the existence of any biological relationship between the Disclosing Party and the Recipient (the Allegation),'* it began, *'The Recipient has asserted or may assert that such a biological relationship exists,'* and, finally, *'The parties wish to resolve any dispute or potential dispute arising from the Allegation without admission of liability and without disclosure.'*

It was so long, and outlined in exact, tiny detail what could and couldn't be discussed, with whom, and under what circumstances—Allegra flicked through probably 20 or more pages to that effect—before finally ending on a settlement page. *'In consideration of the Recipient's obligations under* *this Deed, the Disclosing Party agrees to pay the Recipient the sum of AUD $20,000,000 (Settlement Sum).'*

Jesus Christ, Allegra thought, staring at all those zeros. An *insane* amount of money. She looked around her; it explained the penthouse.

'If the Recipient breaches this Deed, the Recipient must immediately repay to the Disclosing Party:

(a) the Settlement Sum;

(b) interest on the Settlement Sum at the rate of 4% per annum, compounded annually, calculated from the date of payment until the date of repayment; and

(c) all Loss suffered or incurred by the Disclosing Party arising out of or in connection with the breach, including (without limitation) any legal costs on a full indemnity basis, investigation costs, enforcement costs, and any damages, liabilities or expenses incurred as a consequence of the breach including any reputational, commercial or operational harm.'

Allegra read over that a few times to understand it. The horror on Sal's face when she'd blurted it out to Allegra suddenly made chilling sense.

After the NDA, there was more documentation to that effect in the file.

A memo from Langford & Pryce assessing 'risk exposure' and recommending a settlement as a cost-minimisation strategy to avoid reputational risk or false claim on inheritance. "*While the evidentiary basis for the alleged biological relationship remains unconvincing, the reputational and operational risk associated with protracted dispute warrants proactive resolution.*" Dated 2003.

A DNA test where the result was 'inconclusive'. Documents about Sal's 'real' parents the Lategans, allegedly a family of reasonable vineyard fortune in South Africa, as well as a maintenance agreement with Peter and Kaye Black in Sydney, Australia for the care of their daughter during the 'turbulence' in South Africa.

There were some handwritten letters, by a young child. Addressed to Mum & Dad. Telling them about what she'd been doing in school and imploring them to visit one day when it was finally safe to.

Next was Sal's financial records. Every year since the turn of the century. Her property acquisitions and sales. Her shares and net wealth. Allegra did peek at the numbers—and felt awful about it—but figured it didn't even fucking matter because if she breached that NDA Dimi would take every cent she had.

At the end of the file was a 'risk assessment and exposure' report, each and every year from the early 2000s. Surveillance photos. Assessments of her friendships and relationships. Assessments of how close she was to various family members. And a recommendation for how 'exposure' could be managed for each.

It was suffocating. Allegra wondered if those lawyers were following *her* around now. Whether they had people taking photos of her and Sal at dinner, or in the car. Making *assessments* about what risk Allegra posed to Dimi's empire.

She closed the file, feeling ill. She could smell the printer ink and old paper—stale. Musty printouts shut in that underground, climate-controlled room for decades, cataloguing every detail of Sal's adult life. A life she'd never owned a second of. The stack of paper in front of Allegra might have looked like a file, but it was a container, sealed tight. A prison that Dimi held the key to.

And he would do the same to Allegra, if she stayed. If they didn't stop him.

Sal didn't come back for nearly an hour. Allegra had thought of getting some air, but it was *shockingly* hot outside. Even the windows were scorching when she tried to lean against them. In the end she just stood facing them, staring towards the huge, close arches of the Sydney Harbour Bridge and the harbour beyond.

The sound of echoing footsteps made her turn—Sal, coming back down with Allegra's file. She didn't look at her. Instead, she went up to the table and collected her own file where Allegra had left it. "These need to go in the safe," she said neutrally, and disappeared down the corridor beside the lift, emerging without them.

Sal was *not* telegraphing that she wanted to talk. She collected her keys from the counter, pausing to face Allegra. "I have work commitments." She finally looked up. When she spoke again, her voice was cool. "Stay here," she directed. "Go *nowhere*. Do *nothing*." She held Allegra in a dark stare, and then exhaled, turning towards the lift. "I need to think." The doors closed behind her.

Allegra stood in the centre of the room, listening to the faint hum of the lift as it delivered Sal to the carpark.

She didn't move straight away. Her muscles felt slightly weak from her earlier adrenaline, and her ribs ached in a line under her breasts from where she'd lodged the files to smuggle them out.

It was too quiet in here without birdsong and the dry hiss of wind through gumtrees. Just stark grey stone around her, bereft of any sign it was someone's home. Not even a pot plant by the windows—nothing that required tending.

Of course there wasn't. It was all lent to Sal on the proviso she perfectly toed the line, never wobbling, never misstepping, for the rest of her life. What point was there in settling into it, in making it hers, her home, where she felt most safe and most free when Dimi was holding it like a sword of Damocles over her head forever?

20 million dollars, and she couldn't even *frown* in front of him. Wealth hadn't bought her safety—only silence.

And now Allegra was standing here in it. The towering penthouse atrium suddenly felt claustrophobic.

That feeling got her moving. Sal had a safe somewhere. Allegra wanted to see it.

Beyond the lift there were only three rooms: a laundry, an empty wine cellar, and a storage room. Allegra went into the storage room, stepping over cleaning supplies and large equipment to find the safe in the corner.

It was large, of course it was. Grey, brushed steel, and mounted into the wall. It had both a touchpad with a fingerprint logo on it and a mechanical number pad that looked new and almost unused. She stared at it—steel once again separating her from her own file. From the highlighted text, *'I don't think anyone wants me'*.

That line was a punch in the stomach. She thought about how her arms, her chest had *ached* to be holding her sweet little boy every second she was apart from him, but how when he was there in front of her and looking up at her with those beautiful blue eyes, she froze. The nights she'd spent holding her phone over her bedroll in all corners of the world, looking at a photo of Aaron. Loving him.

'I don't think anyone wants me'. Dimi had highlighted it, considered it strategically useful, and kept turning the pages.

The ugliness of this private moment being institutional weaponry, the *obscenity* of it, seeped deep into Allegra's bones. But at least now she could see it. She knew which line he would fire. At least now the bullet had a shape.

That made it worth it. Except for Sal.

The memory of Sal's expression as she left drove Allegra out onto the terrace. The oppressive heat drove her back in. She checked her phone, not expecting anything, but just in case. The lift call light stayed dark.

She went and changed out of her suit, but it didn't make her more comfortable. Lunch didn't make her more comfortable. Thinking about how she might apologise made her even *less* comfortable, but there was no point anyway. She could apologise for the method, but not the act. Sal would hear the difference.

Allegra sat on one of the couches, the weight in her gut heavier than the files had been.

Mid-afternoon, when the lift call light finally brightened, Allegra's lungs filled and her muscles tightened. *Fight or flight*, Allegra recognised, hoping she wouldn't need either.

When the lift opened, Allegra could feel the temperature in the room drop. Sal stepped out of the lift, heels clicking on the floor as she moved briskly past Allegra and directly up the stairs without so much as glancing at her. Allegra heard the office door click as it closed.

Allegra sat in place. Perhaps that was it for the evening. Perhaps Sal was going to stonewall her.

While she was processing that, the office door clicked again and Sal appeared in the stairwell, descending in measured steps. She walked across to the table, set her phone on top, and sat at a chair. She laced her fingers and waited.

Allegra swallowed. She pushed herself out of the couch and went and sat opposite her.

Sal didn't speak straight away. When she did, she had that impassive, soulless tone that could have been lifted directly out of a fiscal management briefing. "Security is of the opinion that the status of the alarm was a malfunction. It's logged as such." She looked up at Allegra for a fraction of a second. "As you said it would be."

Allegra couldn't feel too much relief, though, because Sal let another long, cold silence stretch between them. "The more pressing matter is that Dimi is actively using your file. The next time he tries to update it and it's not there, he will know who has it."

Allegra released a breath. "Will he report it?"

"To who?" Sal asked critically. "He won't involve the police—much of the material in that room would not withstand legal or regulatory scrutiny. He won't notify the board, because that room is his responsibility." She shook her head. "His response will be personal."

Allegra digested that, feeling her hair stand on end. "Aaron."

Sal watched her. "Once he knows you took it, he will know you're complicit. He will know what you know about me. And he will act to contain you as he does me." She paused. "I have no idea what that will look like—I've never pushed him that far. But my expectation is that you won't get the carrot. You will get the stick."

At the mention of 'carrot', Allegra remembered all those zeros in that Deed of Confidentiality. *Some carrot*, she thought, as if this was the life Sal would have chosen if she'd known. And it was a loan, not a gift. It was dependent on her good behaviour, *forever*.

"20 million dollars," Allegra found herself saying aloud.

Sal watched her. "45 now, with interest and costs. 60 by the time he's finished with me," she said impassively. "I would need to sell this place."

Allegra cast her eyes upward at the towering atrium. She couldn't imagine Sal in an old city rental.

The extent of containment seemed so ridiculous still, and the amount of money so hypothetical. Over something as pedestrian as having an accidental child—something Allegra had intimate experience of. "Why all this, though?" she asked. "People have accidental kids all the time."

"His brother doesn't know," Sal said neutrally. "And it was his brother's wife."

That just—"How could he *not know*?"

Sal shook her head. "That's a level of detail I'm not entitled to. But you've seen what Dimi's like, so I can believe it."

Allegra sat with that. The scale of the drama around her was incomprehensible. "Surely he didn't need to make it so massive." She shook her head. "All of this. It's crazy."

Sal was cast in stone as she considered that, eyes on her laced fingers. "I knew the scale. I know what he does and what he's like." She looked up—something tight behind her eyes. "But I still wouldn't have acted without asking you. Even if I thought you were wrong." She kept her eyes on Allegra.

Then, she stood. "We will need to move," she said. "Very quickly. We can discuss it tomorrow." It was the middle of the afternoon. "Goodnight," she said as she went up the stairs and the office door clicked shut.

Allegra waited in the atrium all evening. The office door stayed closed.

Chapter 30: Informed Consent

A deafening rattling started without warning. Allegra sat upright on the couch, heart pounding, eyes still clearing, before she registered that Sal was fully dressed in the kitchen, one hand pressed to the obnoxious coffee grinder.

Allegra took a slow, steadying breath, brushing her tangled hair out of her face. When Sal stopped, she asked her, "Was that necessary?"

Sal had her eyes on the coffee cups. "I waited until 7:30." She finished pouring and took one over to Allegra; it was *brutally strong*. Allegra sipped it anyway; she couldn't be bothered making coffee for herself.

Sal sat down with hers at the table. Rather than having a real discussion with Allegra, she unlocked her phone. She was already scrolling as she said, "We need to accelerate our plans to boost my reputation. Who knows how long it will be before I need to move the board."

Sal wasn't seeking comment on that, so Allegra didn't respond. She unwound herself from the doona and moved over to sit across from Sal, ferrying her punitive coffee with her.

Sal wasn't looking at her. "We should have coordinated on Atlas."

"There wasn't enough time. I had just minutes after I realised it might even be possible."

She looked up. "So you settled on *theft* and didn't think to consult me."

Allegra scoffed. It was a bit rich, coming from Sal: someone who didn't bat an eyelid at the arson accusations in Austin's video. "Don't try and pretend you have a problem with felonies."

"Allegra." Sal set her coffee mug down. "The issue for me is the lack of consultation," she said. "How can I be certain you won't do that again?"

Allegra didn't answer. She probably *would* do it again.

"I need you to communicate with me," Sal told her. "That is a *non-negotiable*."

Allegra remembered her 'good, no surprises' assessment of Austin's video, and that was in addition to her keeping Allegra in the dark about her plans for weeks. She fixed Sal with a hard stare. "It's really hard for me to hear that from you specifically, Sal."

Allegra was ready to have it out, but Sal didn't say anything else or push the point. She just got back to her coffee and phone.

Fine, let's not talk about that, Allegra thought resentfully. She had something else to discuss anyway. "I've been thinking about what was in my file." Sal looked up from her phone. "It's clear what Dimi wants to weaponise. I could come forward about it myself to take the sting out of the scandal Dimi wants to create, but it's not really *my* history. It's Aaron's." She turned the coffee cup in her hands. "So, I was planning to ask him if he wants to tell the story in his own words."

Sal sat back, considering that. "If it's not managed carefully, it's going to affect your reputation—we need to avoid that."

"We probably can by being clear I support him to tell it."

Sal spent a few seconds in thought. "Offer him BSA's support," she ended up saying. "And request that we view the video a few hours before he posts it, in case there's anything *we* need to manage as a result." She watched Allegra for a little longer, and then drained the remainder of her coffee in a single mouthful. "Get dressed," she said. "We're going into the office. We'll meet with Zoe first thing. Wear the first suit, sage shirt. No tie."

Sal's cold directions grated on Allegra today in a way they generally didn't, and she had to talk herself down from confronting Sal about it. For now, she followed the instructions and then joined her for the drive to work.

They'd parked when Sal reminded her, "People need to see we're aligned," before getting out and lacing fingers with her on the way to the lift.

Sal didn't keep her hand once they were on her floor, however. She released it, greeting various people and then steering Allegra into a meeting room where Zoe and Gerard were already sitting and politely chatting, sipping tall coffees. They stopped on seeing Sal.

Gerard observed her hard expression. "Oh no. That face. What have we broken?"

"Nothing's broken," Sal said smoothly. "Just some tightening in the schedule after yesterday." She sat, and Allegra sat down beside her. "I've been following the response to Allegra's video. We should do some more joint content."

Zoe stared at Sal, unmoving. Gerard's eyebrows were up.

"Okay," Gerard said slowly, "should I get Short Form for a meeting?"

"Yes, please." Sal turned to Zoe. "I was thinking we could do a series of videos—or perhaps a compilation—of Allegra taking me camping."

Gerard made a short, strangled noise that sounded suspiciously like he'd inhaled his coffee. He smothered it but got immediately back to typing.

Sal stopped what she was doing to coolly regard him. "I gather we're fine, Gerard?"

He looked at her. "Of course. Aside from the visual of you camping, that is."

Zoe picked up on that, brushing aside the ice. "It's a good one, though. It'll get clicks." She was already rolling with it. "'One-percent in a tent'. Or 'Marketing Exec Finally Touches Grass'."

Gerard chimed in. "Marketing Exec Goes Bush." He had a cheeky glint in his eye.

Allegra glanced across at Sal; she was just nodding.

Zoe was clearly sold. "Great," she said. "Do you want sponsors? There's a few I can approach."

"Revenue isn't critical here," Sal said. "I'd rather it not be monetised beyond platform funds at this stage."

Zoe nodded and jotted a couple of things down. "Okay. Anything you two want to avoid in it?"

"Sunburn," Allegra said. Zoe and Gerard smiled at that; Sal didn't. Allegra wasn't sure if that was just Sal at work, or if it had something to do with yesterday.

While they were packing up, something else occurred to Allegra. "Oh!" she said, almost forgetting. "Northstar Pathways—that youth education place—wanted me to go up on site and survey it for them. Perhaps we could combine this somehow?"

The other three glanced at each other. Zoe and Gerard didn't have much of an opinion on it other than 'two birds, one stone', but Sal commented quietly on it as they moved between meeting rooms. "Us being on site together anchors me close to tangible impact," she said. "On the front line, rather than being some nebulous exec in a boardroom. Great idea. Very humanising."

Allegra didn't have much time to process that before they ended up in another meeting room where they were joined shortly by three polished 30-somethings. Allegra learnt they were the team who coordinated short-form video content.

After a dry discussion about trends and targeting, the group of them decided that a compilation would be great. "We'll put together some scripting based on the notes you want to hit," one of them said at the end of the meeting. "But in all likelihood the comedy will be in Sal simply engaging in ordinary camping discomforts. Make sure you get loads of that footage—we'll be able to make something with it."

Mid-morning, they left the meeting room together and headed to the lifts. Allegra's stomach was growling; morning tea sounded great. "Shit," she said, realising she was empty-handed. "I left my coffee cup at your place."

Sal didn't answer. At the lift, she turned to Allegra. "You can pick me up early tomorrow morning. Before peak hour." She adjusted Allegra's collar in front of the staff passing by, smoothed her jacket once, and stepped back.

The lift doors opened, and Allegra stepped inside. Sal remained where she was, watching them close.

When they opened again, it was to a quiet carpark. Allegra walked back to Sal's, collected her car, and drove to Point Piper.

Later in the afternoon, she was packing some photogenic camping gear into her car—her old cast iron billy, a jaffle-maker, and an actual swag she hadn't used in years—when the gate rolled very slowly open and Timothy's Transit rattled in.

He looked delighted as soon as he saw her. Allegra's normally tired reaction to that felt sharper today: she actively disliked it.

Pushing that feeling somewhere, she smiled at his greeting. "Just putting some things in the car," she said by way of explanation. "Got some more camping on the horizon."

"Sounds very hot and full of flies," he told her good-naturedly. "And you never need to explain why you're over. Want some dinner?"

Allegra bristled again. "No thanks, but I might make something for myself later—you're welcome to some of that." She moved along. "Any news on Impact funding?"

Timothy's heavy brow lowered. He shook his head. "Nothing yet, though Cece did send through an email about volunteering opportunities for the kids, so that's nice."

Despite Allegra refusing dinner, Timothy ended up in the kitchen making it anyway. The smell was so enticing that she gave in and accepted a plate. While she had her mouth full, he ambushed her. "So," he began gently, giving her his full attention. "How are you feeling?" He looked concerned.

Honestly, he could not have said anything more repellent to her. Her first impulse was to snap back at him—that was unfair. He was being nice. She swallowed her mouthful. "Great," she lied.

He wasn't convinced. "It's just that when you get ready for a big camp, it's usually because—"

"I'm fine, Timothy."

"But when you left on Sunday you looked—"

"I'm going camping with Sal," she said, probably too bluntly, putting her knife and fork down on the plate. Realising how nasty that sounded when he was just trying to be supportive, she sat back and released a breath. "I didn't want to tell you outright."

He had another mouthful, looking down at his own plate for a moment. "Camping with Sal," he repeated, echoing Zoe and Gerard's reaction.

"We're going to make some more videos."

He processed that. "I did see the one you posted," he confessed. "It wasn't fair of that Austin person to out you. I was unhappy about that." He paused. "Although the rest of his video..."

Allegra stared down at her peas, knowing where this was going.

"It makes me uncomfortable, Allegra," Timothy said. He was shaking his head. "You are so involved with her and it's only been a few weeks. It makes sense people are concerned that there's some ulterior motive—"

"I had sex with you on the night I met you and ended up having your child from it," Allegra told him. "Did you have an ulterior motive?"

They faced off across the dinner table. He softened, frowning deeply again. "I'm just worried about you, that's all."

Allegra closed her eyes, willing herself not to chew him out. She did not need to be *worried about*.

This time, mercifully, *he* moved it along. "Did you find out what that release form was about?"

Allegra had forgotten about that. "Not exactly," she said, grateful to be talking about literally anything other than *how she was feeling*, even if it was this. "But I did contact the school and get a copy of the records myself." He didn't need to know those two things weren't connected. "There's a lot there, Timothy." She really looked at him. "Lots of signatures on lots of paper. Mine isn't anywhere."

Timothy paused, looking up at her. He knew what she meant. "You weren't doing well back then."

"Yes," she said clearly. "I remember." She kept looking at him.

"Given where you were at right after Lachie died, I didn't want to give you any cause to—feel hopeless," he said carefully. "Aaron needed you too much. Your family loved you. *I* loved you."

Jesus, was he really suggesting—"I wouldn't have tried to kill myself over it, Timothy."

He let that sit for a moment, quietly eating his dinner. Eventually, he said, "I made the decisions I made out of love." Apparently, that settled it for him. "And I apologise if they were the wrong ones. I know better now."

Do you? Allegra wondered, thinking about how he'd just *grilled* her about her mental health. Honestly, the topic of *how she was feeling* was fucking exhausting and she just wanted to move on for once. "Anyway," she said after she'd put her knife and fork together. "I think it's possible a news outlet will get hold of some of the Kirribilli records and will do a story on them. I'm planning to ask Aaron if he'd like to tell his story in his own words before that happens."

Timothy looked aghast. "Would they really do that?" Allegra shrugged. He looked disgusted. "Appalling. Absolutely astounding what the media has become. Aaron should certainly have the opportunity to be his own spokesperson about all this." Then he turned *that concerned look* on Allegra again. "There will be some difficult things for you to hear if he does..."

Allegra had had enough. "Thanks for dinner, it was delicious," she said pointedly, taking both their plates over to the dishwasher. Then, she went and shut herself in her LandCruiser.

At least it was slightly less oppressively hot today. Not that being in the Point Piper house wasn't oppressive for *other* reasons; it was such an enormous house to feel suffocated in. She sighed, looking forward at the steering wheel. She really needed to move her stuff out of this place. Maybe she should get a storage unit somewhere or something.

In all of this, she found herself really missing Sal. Even if they were just sitting opposite each other at the table.

Partially because she was stifled by the thought of going back inside, she ended up setting up her rooftop tent and only going inside for a shower once she was sure Timothy was asleep.

Afterwards, lying there and staring across at the harbour through a gap in the houses, she spent a while trying to figure out how to tell Aaron about Kirribilli. She'd cycled through a thousand different iterations before she landed on: *"I think your Kirribilli records, including the counselling records, may end up in the media. We can take the scandal out of the story by breaking the story first. They're your records: if you want to speak for yourself, I'll back you completely. If you don't, I'll handle it. Your call."* She read over it a few times and sent it.

He didn't take long to reply. *"Wow okay so that was what the release was for*?" After a moment, another one came through. *"Damn. Yeah, I'd definitely rather say it myself. Let me have a chat with Dad about it."*

That felt like a punch in the stomach. Dad. She put her phone down and lay with that feeling for a few moments, feeling around the edges of it. Why would Aaron let Allegra handle anything when she never had? When she'd never been given the chance to?

She turned over to go to sleep.

It was always jarring waking to traffic in the rooftop tent; she spent so much time out in the bush with it that cars passing felt intrusive. Not quite as intrusive as a coffee grinder, though.

She waited until after Timothy left (enduring several minutes of him milling between the cars, deliberating whether to wake her before he got in his car and drove away) to go in and make herself some breakfast.

Then she checked the tanks, the battery, the first aid kits, and left to beat peak hour.

Sal was standing on the side of her street *with a suitcase.* She was also wearing thousand-dollar sunglasses, and a black long-sleeve The North Face top and some black high-tech hiking trousers. And the shiniest pair of hiking boots Allegra had ever seen. They looked *oiled*.

As Sal stowed her suitcase and got in, Allegra had to look away to conceal her smile.

Sal took off her sunglasses to a face full of heavy makeup. "Two people comfortable outdoors won't get clicks," she said. "A known bush rescue op with a wealthy executive looking like she's never seen real dirt will."

"But how is that going to make people like you? Won't they think you're arrogant and out of touch?"

"Not if it's funny and I'm clearly happy with being laughed at." Sal looked across at Allegra. "And if someone who clearly loves me finds it endearing."

That word was a shock, even in context. Worse, Sal handed Allegra her ceramic KeepCup. When Allegra took a tentative sip, it was the weaker brew she preferred. Sal was checking her makeup in the visor mirror. "Whatever I think of how we got here, we need to move together now. We can't afford not to."

Allegra put her coffee in the cupholder and pulled out onto the road, still concealing a private smile.

They were out of the city and on the open road before Allegra had any headspace to process anything. Instead of using it for anything useful, she was going around in circles over the fact Aaron wanted to speak with *Dad* before making any decisions, when Sal knocked her out of her reverie by speaking.

"Were the contents of your file what you expected?"

Allegra thought about that for a moment. "The gist of it, yes." She paused. "But it was much more than I knew."

"I thought that may be the case," Sal said. "None of those signatures on the school files were yours."

If even *Sal* noticed that... Allegra set her jaw. "Yeah." Nothing she could do about it now. "What about yours?"

Sal looked away, concealing her expression. "It was *exactly* what I expected." There was bitterness in her voice. "But I didn't know about the annual 'risk' reports and surveillance." She exhaled, neutral again. "Some... exits make more sense now."

Exits, Allegra thought, remembering all the surveillance notes on how to 'manage' everyone who had contact with Sal. It had been shocking to read. She wondered what it had been like for Sal to read Allegra's file.

"I discussed the school stuff with Timothy—after all, he got the release from Kirribilli. I didn't need to explain why I knew the contents."

Sal turned back a little to watch her. "Oh?"

Allegra wondered how to explain it. She also wondered why she was telling Sal. "Decisions 'made in love', or however he put it." Allegra shook her head. "Doesn't matter why he made them. The outcome is the same."

Sal listened to her, but didn't say anything. Allegra remembered something else Timothy had mentioned. She hesitated before raising it; it had been so nice being on the same page as Sal again. "He did say something that Vanessa said. That other people have been saying." She could hear the harder edge in her voice. Sal shifted; she could, too. "And that's that the timing of my onboarding is suspicious. He said it made him uncomfortable." When Sal didn't respond, Allegra pushed the point. "It also makes *me* uncomfortable, Sal."

Sal still didn't give her anything—no reassurance, no explanation. The silence landed like yesterday's lecture about consultation. To Allegra, it felt very deliberate. "Can you just answer that, please?"

"I don't want to slip right back into an argument, Allegra."

"Then answer me."

When Sal hesitated again, something in Allegra snapped. She was done with people hiding things from her; especially someone who had been so quick to lecture her about transparency. "You know, it's really rich of you to insist on prompt and open communication when *you* didn't even tell me what involvement you had with Threshold and that repossessed land before you recruited me." The anger in her voice surprised even her. "What *was* your involvement?"

Sal was watching her carefully. "Are you asking me if I was involved in the circumstances surrounding the fire and the land repossession?"

"That's exactly what I'm asking."

Sal relaxed. "Then no," she said easily. "Not at all. Threshold is a very old client, and Dimi is friends with the CEO. As a general rule, I'm not in any of those meetings."

Allegra considered her reaction. If she relaxed about *that*, what was she tense about beforehand? "But you knew something."

Sal shifted in her seat. "Clearly there's something specific that's troubling you—it would be easier for me to explain where I stand with it if you can articulate it."

Allegra pressed her lips into a line and pulled the car over. This wasn't a conversation she wanted to half-participate in. On the shoulder of the road, handbrake on, Allegra turned to Sal. "It's Austin's video, Sal," she said. "Most of it I had a general sense of, but afterwards you said, 'Good, no surprises'. That whole sequence was a huge surprise to me. Why didn't it surprise you?"

"I was aware of the sequence," Sal said. "I thought you were, too. We had a discussion about it while you were writing the Phase 1."

Allegra remembered that. "You never told me Threshold wanted the land beforehand and stood to benefit from it being repossessed after that fire."

Sal conceded that. "That's fair. I didn't. I'm not sure where I stand on that issue, either," she said. "But no charges have been laid. Our legal advice is that there's no issue with Threshold purchasing it, so that's what we moved forward with."

Allegra narrowed her eyes. "You got legal advice." Sal nodded once. "You don't get legal advice unless you think you need it, which means you *knew* it was dodgy." She paused. "*Before* you got me involved."

Something clicked for Sal. "You think I knowingly exposed you to risk and didn't disclose it to you."

That wasn't exactly how Allegra would have put it. "Yes."

Sal relaxed again. "No," she said. "I—have my suspicions. But things are not always as simple as they seem. So regardless of what would make a very clickable news story about the fire, the sequence was simply convenient for Threshold. We needed to work with that."

Allegra sat with that, trying to figure out why it didn't comfort her. In the end, she realised. "You're a PR firm." A brief frown, then Sal nodded. "Why is a PR firm involved in this?"

"Precisely because it doesn't read well. At all. A fire is lit, causing a land reclassification that delivers land from a family to a property developer. Dimi instructed me to find a charity no one could fault and an assessor no one could accuse to make sure the next assessment of that land was completely untouchable." She gestured at Allegra. "So I did."

That made Allegra's stomach turn. "So I *was* used."

Sal's brow tightened. "I don't understand what you're—"

"To hide corporate corruption. You recruited me to hide that fire and didn't tell me."

"*No*," Sal said slowly and carefully. "First of all, while the timing was convenient, there was no suggestion at that point that it was anything except that. The possibility someone might ask that question was why we needed an unconnected assessment—"

There it was again. Someone deciding she didn't need to be involved in a decision that affected her. "Oh, fuck off with the 'legally, everything is fine' crap, Sal," Allegra told her. "You knew it was dodgy, you *knew* there was the possibility it could go south. It's the reason I was recruited."

Sal sat back, watching her. "My assessment was that there was a very low risk of any adverse effect," she said. "I can show you the documents. You can see why I decided that—"

"*You* decided. *About me.* Without asking me."

Sal studied her for a moment. "Oh," she said eventually. "This is about your Atlas file. And your lack of signatures."

That set Allegra off. "No, this is about everyone around me deciding what information I can handle. Timothy did it. Vanessa did it. You did it," she said firmly. "And now I'm sitting in a car with you after you withheld information I was entitled to at multiple points, while you're fucking telling me *I* need to communicate better!"

Sal gave her a measured look. "What I didn't do was commit an actual felony implicating *and* endangering someone else without their input."

Allegra *seethed.* "No, you just roped me into a property acquisition scandal *and* put me in Dimi's line of fire!"

"Neither of those things had a high likelihood of impacting you, but taking my file out of Atlas is guaranteed to be discovered by—"

"Oh, fuck off, Sal. You know what Dimi's like. I refuse to believe you didn't know it was possible that he'd sink his teeth into me before you had the chance to 'tell me everything and get my buy-in' or whatever it is your plan was to do with me once I was *sufficiently enamoured* with you."

Sal took offence at the last part. She hardened. "I know how it looks. Believe me. But it's not true. Whatever else I did, Allegra, I never misrepresented my personal feelings to you for the purpose of recruitment. The synergies between us were incidental and didn't seem to interfere with anything, so I saw no reason to resist them at all," she said, and then a shadow crossed her face. "Until I did see a reason. Anyway, with regard to Dimi: I will show you, in detail, *every single thing* I did to make sure he could not possibly have found out about us until after I'd achieved your buy-in to help me oust him. I was meticulous. I did my absolute best."

And then he caught me staring at you at the gala, Allegra realised. She pushed that away. "Your absolute best didn't save me. Or Aaron. Or Timothy," she said, and then sat back. "You placed me in a potential land acquisition scandal. You placed my family at risk. And you did both of those things without consulting me."

That hit Sal hard. She withdrew. "You implicated me in a crime, Allegra. If the Atlas files are discovered missing beyond Dimi's internal knowledge, I am finished. I lose my job. I lose the life I've spent 25 years building. *I told you that very clearly.* And you still went ahead and made that decision without consulting me."

"I had minutes to make the decision, Sal!"

"I only had hours." Sal exhaled and wiped her palms on her trousers. "When I 'roped you in', I believed I could make you safe."

Allegra nearly rejected that outright—how could Sal possibly protect her from Dimi? Then again, she had moved quickly over the Threshold payment. And still—that had led to Austin. She sighed. What a fucking headache. No one could solve all that. "You think too highly of your abilities."

Sal gave her a sharp look. "And you're not as morally pure as you think you are," she said. "You're accusing me of being a bad actor when you considered me nothing more than collateral damage on your break-in."

"That was to protect my son."

"Yeah, well, not all of us get the opportunity to have those, Allegra. Instead, every year I was pried apart from anyone I was even seen with. Even Gerard has to pretend he doesn't like me in front of most of the staff." She took a steady breath. "So I acted to protect myself. Not because I'm selfish, or a Disney villain, or whatever you assume when you look at me. Because that's what I have."

Allegra swallowed. "Your circumstances don't entitle you to decide for me."

"My circumstances are what limit my own choices, Allegra," she said. "I'm not warm and sun-kissed and grounded in rescue work. I'm this," she said, gesturing to herself. "I'm cold. I'm corporate. You've seen me manipulate people. You know I can. I know exactly how that reads to you." She watched Allegra. "If someone like me came up to you at the outset and said, 'I'd like you to be involved in a slightly murky situation that I genuinely, *genuinely* don't think will impact you, what do you say?' How do you think you'd respond to that?"

Allegra pressed her lips together. "Whatever I decided, it would've been my right."

Sal exhaled and looked away. "I know. I couldn't afford that."

A silence stretched between them as Allegra watched Sal.

They were back to that same question: if someone needed help, could you fault them for reaching for it, even if it put the responder in danger? Allegra, as a professional responder, should have an answer for that. In the bush, she would. She wouldn't even hesitate. But here?

Fuck it. She released the handbrake and pulled back onto the road.

Sal didn't say anything for the rest of the drive. She sat very still, staring ahead. Nothing about it felt settled.

By late morning, they'd reached the campsite Allegra had chosen deep in the Hunter Valley. It was completely empty at this time of year and in this heat, but surrounded by white and silver grey gums that would look beautiful on camera.

Allegra picked a spot closer to the vegetation and was busy ferrying camping paraphernalia out of her boot into the small clearing while Sal watched silently, leaning against the side of the car (which she seemed unaware would coat her new black clothes in orange dust).

It wasn't that Allegra had been *ignoring* her, exactly, just focused on set-dressing the campsite. She had been distracted enough to be surprised when her arm caught on Sal's outstretched hand and Sal pulled her in. Her hips met Sal's, Sal's fingers gripped briefly at her waist—and then Sal's lips were on hers.

Completely paralysed by the shock of it, Allegra stared forward at Sal's smoky purple eyeshadow, wide-eyed herself. She was too surprised and full of adrenaline from their earlier argument to feel anything from it.

She came to her senses and pulled away a fraction. "What the fuck, Sal?"

Sal said nothing, she was just looking up at Allegra with an expression that suggested she'd acted before consulting herself, too. Her eyes moved between Allegra's, back and forth, as if she were bracing for something.

Allegra *should* probably have pushed herself away. She didn't understand why Sal had kissed her *now* of all times she could possibly have chosen to kiss her—times that would have been far more coherent and welcome. It was the hand tentatively gripping a handful of her t-shirt like a lifeline that destroyed her resolve. *This woman*. "This doesn't fix anything," she warned the evil fuck coiled around her, and then put a hand on either side of her chin and kissed *her* this time, pinning her against the LandCruiser.

Sal was as surprised as she had been—her hands hovered a little before settling back on Allegra's waist. There was none of that finesse Allegra had felt from her in the dark alcove at the gala, either; she was tentative. Searching.

Allegra had been somewhat mechanical about the whole thing—still trying to understand what the fuck was going on—until her boot slipped a little in the dirt as they moved, and she stumbled quite heavily against Sal and the car. Rather than yelping in surprise, Sal *groaned* from somewhere deep in her throat.

That sound went straight to Allegra's groin. *Then* she was kissing lips she remembered from the dark alcove at the gala; grinding up against a woman she'd wanted before she'd even allowed herself to admit it.

...A woman who just an hour ago was freely telling Allegra that she'd sidelined her consent to achieve an objective.

Allegra exhaled in a sigh down Sal's neck. That was true. She also just fucking wanted Sal. She could deal with 'true' after they'd finished whatever this was.

Since she was already leaning heavily against Sal, she let her thigh slip between Sal's and managed to get another deep, low groan out of her. *God*. And Sal wasn't wearing a dress this time, just a long-sleeved top. Allegra's fingers found the edges of it and the warm skin underneath. Silky smooth, just like the satin had been. It rose into goosebumps under her touch as her fingertips climbed Sal's torso. Allegra counted each breath that caught in Sal's throat—which she kissed—as she drew a line upward.

Allegra's fingers moved over the rise and fall of each rib on Sal's chest until they reached Sal's bra. She found her way underneath it, pushed the thin lace upwards, and filled her hands with soft, full breasts. Her own jaw fell slack for a moment—*fuck*. They felt even better than they looked. Sal's breath was hot across Allegra's forehead. Her mouth was open.

Allegra had been kissing down along Sal's neck, thinking vaguely about clothes coming off and skin-on-skin, when she realised there were no hands on her own body. Sal's hands were—still. Still, and resting passively on Allegra's hips.

That felt off.

Sal was handsier than this even when they *weren't* making out; and at the gala, both their hands had been everywhere, grabbing desperately at each other. Here, Sal was receiving. Absorbing.

She's just letting me do this, Allegra realised, noticing her own lips had paused on Sal's neck. It made Allegra feel managed, and that was the opposite of hot.

She fell still as well, but didn't pull away at first. "You're doing this to appease me," she said beside Sal's ear.

Sal was still breathing heavily. "I thought it might help."

That was the death rattle. Sal was going to offer herself up *instead* of closing off their argument. It might have worked; it certainly would have felt good. But it wouldn't solve anything long-term.

Allegra withdrew her hands from inside Sal's clothes and pulled back, saying gently, "No." She left her hips resting against Sal's for a minute. Sal nodded.

They stood against each other for a moment, eyes looking down between them rather than at each other. Sal's hands were still resting on her waist. Allegra took them—just for a moment—and then released them at Sal's side, and stepped away from her.

When she stepped back, the hard late-morning sun hit her face and blinded her; neither of them had put sunscreen on yet. They should get to that quite soon—Sal was so pale. Worse than the twins. They should do hats, too.

While Allegra was busy redoing her ponytail low enough for a hat, Sal corrected her bra and tucked her top back in. As she did that, Allegra got a glimpse of exactly how orange Sal's brand new black clothes were after being pushed up against the LandCruiser.

So did Sal. "There goes the villain aesthetic."

She smothered a laugh. Bad timing. "I'm angry with you," she said evenly after she'd recovered. "Even if your entire back is covered in orange dirt and you're wearing *black* in summer."

Sal smiled knowingly. "You love it."

Fucking. "Fuck you, Sal," Allegra said, meaning it. "Don't be cute with me when you've just admitted you withheld important information from me and would probably do it again *and then* tried to have sex with me to get away with it."

Sal knew exactly the right amount to push. "Fair," she observed. Then, a smirk. "Perhaps you'd like to propose we commit a felony together to make up?"

I'm going to kill her, Allegra thought, giving her a cold, hard stare but unfortunately feeling something other than anger as well. "I just hope there's nothing else you're hiding, Sal," she said, surprising herself with how serious she sounded. "I don't think I can deal with any more secrecy."

Sal sobered, her smirk fading. "There's not."

Despite everything—*everything*—Allegra chose to believe her. "I want to get the drone up first," she told Sal, and then went to retrieve its box from the boot and dumped it in Sal's arms. "Can you unwrap all the bits of that while I set up?"

Sal accepted it without protest, and they both got to work.

Chapter 31: On Record

Dragging the heavier gear into the clearing gave Allegra something practical to think about: weight, balance, and footing. It kept Dimi and Atlas at bay. It kept her from dwelling on her missing signatures in the Kirribilli docs. It also gave her body something different to feel—muscle strain instead of the heat of Sal against the LandCruiser.

After Allegra had finished setting up a bona fide Australian bush camp, there was no more avoiding sunscreen.

"There's sunscreen in my makeup," Sal said, like SPF 15 was going to do anything to protect that porcelain skin in *December*.

"That's nice," Allegra said, and handed her the jumbo-sized SPF 50.

Sal gave her a look. "If you're going to humiliate me, at least film it."

At her request, Allegra filmed Sal before, during, and after she was plastered with greasy Australian-strength sunscreen. Sal examined herself in the front camera of her phone. "Wonderful," she said. "I look like I've been dipped in a vat of oil."

"There's more," Allegra said, accepting the vat of oil back from Sal and putting it back in the car. "Did you bring a hat?"

Sal was watching her suspiciously. "Something tells me I'm going to regret that my answer is 'no'."

Allegra reached over to Sal's phone, which was still angled towards her, and lifted her arms to improve the angle. "Hold it there." When Sal had her public face back on, Allegra tapped record.

Sal followed her instructions. Allegra ferreted around in the boot of her car until she found it: the ugly penance hat, bought purely to terrorise people like Vanessa who were too vain for sun safety. Allegra came up behind Sal and pulled it firmly onto her head. "This is your punishment for not bringing your own hat."

Sal stopped recording and relaxed. "That was good," she commented, and then looked upward at the paisley rim drooping over her face. "I presume you're going to force me to wear this for the rest of the morning."

Allegra's eyes twinkled as she pulled on her own respectable Bunnings hat. "Let's get the drone up," she said, doing just that and getting some sweeping shots of the beautiful bush around them. Then, she flew it back and got a great one of Sal looking sweaty and uncomfortable as she leant against the car and checked her emails.

Smiling at that image, Allegra landed the drone and then thrust the controller into Sal's hands while she was distracted. "Your turn."

Sal narrowed her eyes. "Alright," she said slowly, locking her phone and slipping it into her pocket. "Challenge accepted."

Knowing exactly how this was going to go, Allegra filmed her. Crashing the drone. Swearing while crashing the drone. And, finally, crashing the drone into a nearby tree, where it lodged. "Hmm," Sal said mildly, looking up where it was stuck, several metres off the ground.

Allegra said casually from behind the camera, "Your next challenge is to climb up there and get it." Sal's quick, concerned glance at her to check if she was being serious made the shot.

It was actually Allegra who ended up retrieving the drone. When she reached the drone and waved it at the camera, Sal was smiling—but not at the drone.

Sal wandered over after Allegra was on the ground again, phone stowed. "At least my little accident caused us to get some very compelling footage," she said lightly. "Let's go over the notes from Short Form."

They sat down together—not quite touching—on smooth log benches to read Short Form's notes on Sal's pristine white tablet.

Short Form hadn't been particularly granular about what they wanted, but had reported on the latest trends and the genre of activities and topics they thought would chart well.

"Australian bush-themed first aid," Sal read aloud, and then gave Allegra a sidelong glance. "I'm pleased to report that I'm actually up to date with my first aid certification."

That made Allegra want to ask her if she was up to date for CPR, too. She didn't. "It would make for some funny footage if we pressure immobilised each other." She hadn't expected it to sound like that.

Neither had Sal, who stilled momentarily when Allegra said it. She didn't reply, though, she just looked back at the tablet and scribbled a note in the margin to that effect. They went back to reading.

Well, *Sal* went back to reading. At the implication in 'pressure immobilise each other', Allegra got stuck on the memory of pressing Sal against the LandCruiser with her hips. And maybe Sal had *initiated* that kiss for questionable purposes, but her groan when Allegra slipped a thigh between—

"Sarcastic gratitude log about bush inconveniences," Sal read aloud, bringing Allegra back to reality. She looked amused about that. "Now *that* sounds like something I can contribute to."

While Sal was making notes, Allegra read down a little. *'5-10 assorted shots of physical affection (PG-rated ideally, to be cut into 1-2.5 second segments)'*.

Allegra could tell when Sal finished her notes and read that part, because she went still.

She opened a comment box. "We should probably plan each one of those," she said neutrally, looking up at Allegra. "What do you suggest?"

Those fucking eyes. *I suggest we go back to the car*, Allegra thought immediately. Instead, she said, "Well, if they're wanting a montage, do they want an escalation of the same sort of thing, or—lots of different shots?"

Sal gave the question much longer consideration than it probably required. "Escalations can be cut from the same shot, so we can do a few different shots—perhaps 10 seconds each—and give them plenty to choose from."

"Kissing, or...?" *God.* This was going to sound like a wish list.

"Well," Sal said carefully. "We should start small. Perhaps a touch."

"Where?"

"Somewhere PG-rated."

Allegra looked critically at Sal's body for somewhere suitably PG-rated, discovering that in her current mindset, *nowhere* was PG-rated. "Perhaps your waist? Maybe as I'm walking behind you?"

Something occurred to Sal and she visibly relaxed. "We can pull from the spreadsheet," she realised. "After we're done with everything else."

They made some notes about activities to do and then put the tablet down on the log bench to start its transition from white to orange. As they stood, Sal stopped Allegra for a moment. "The camera will be running," she said. "We should stay in character the whole time so there's less to edit out of the footage afterwards."

Allegra kept out of the way while Sal set up her DSLR so the campfire recess, the log seat, and the LandCruiser parked further away were in the frame. Then, she invited Allegra to sit beside her with a warm, coy little smile that very clearly indicated to Allegra that both the camera and Sal-in-public were 'on'.

Allegra sat beside her, slapped a brisk hand on her thigh and turned to the camera. "Today we're going to demonstrate how to introduce your sheltered corporate girlfriend to the Australian bush."

"Really." The flat tone matched the expression. "'Sheltered corporate girlfriend'."

"Which part of that is wrong?" Allegra asked innocently. She looked back at the camera. "Fine! Today we're going to demonstrate how to introduce your soft boardroom princess to the beautiful Australian—"

"*Allegra*!" She leant over to put her hand over Allegra's mouth. Allegra caught the hand easily.

When she let her go, Sal sat up, straightened her hat, and said to the camera. "I'll be demonstrating how to survive *her*, actually. She's the *real* challenge."

"You do love a challenge." There was a glint in Allegra's eyes.

Sal scoffed. "That is the sole reason I am not currently calling an Uber right now."

After a few more options for video openers—including Sal and Allegra affectionately (and then rudely) introducing each other, and Allegra showing the camera Sal's pristine black front before getting her to turn around and display her dusty orange back—they moved on to activities. The DSLR kept rolling, even though their plan from here was to mostly use their mobile phones.

"I think your adoring fans would like to see you chop wood," Sal suggested, noting that Allegra had brought a few pieces and set them up with an axe just out of the clearing. They headed over there.

After Allegra had split a few logs, Sal showed her the footage she'd taken: it was a total thirst reel.

Allegra then looked appraisingly at Sal. "We should get some thirst content of you, too."

Sal scoffed. "I am not presently appealing to *any* demographic." She indicated her greasy skin and paisley hat.

Allegra's eyes briefly dipped lower. She could think of a demographic. Rather than say it, she nodded sagely. "You're right. Yuck. Let's keep you out of frame."

She was grinning as Sal *swatted* her. "Give me the axe."

Allegra's eyebrows went up, and so did her phone. "You want to chop wood?"

"Sure," Sal said innocently. "That's absolutely what I want to do with the axe."

Taking it, she lined it up with the wood.

"This should be interesting," Allegra said from behind her phone.

Sal shot her a dour look, and then swung the axe in a precise, confident arc. It split the log.

Allegra's eyebrows went up. "Come on, that's not possible," she said, sticking her hand out and feeling Sal's slender arms on film. "What are you hiding in there?"

Sal looked very pleased with herself. "Just the determination not to be outdone by *you*," she said. "Very strong motivator."

"Cute," Allegra said, turning the camera back towards herself. "Anyway, before our stubborn little princess passes out from the heat and the sun, I was thinking we could get her to put up my old tent from—"

The phone fell out of Allegra's hand when Sal shoved her again. It caught Allegra's yelp before it hit the ground.

That prompted Sal to show everyone the state of Allegra's phone, and while Sal was phone-shaming her, she went and retrieved her old tent from the side of the clearing.

"Next challenge," she told Sal and dumped the whole package in her arms.

Sal promptly fell over from the weight of it. The DSLR caught that moment, and the moment afterwards where Allegra, laughing, went to give Sal a hand up and Sal didn't move. Allegra's smile faded. "Sal?" the concern was audible in her voice and she bent down for a moment to check Sal was—

Sal ambushed her and pulled her out of the frame, cackling.

Allegra almost landed on top of her.

Beside her, Sal was holding her breath. They shared a brief, sober glance. Allegra pushed herself up before it could become anything else, brushing gravel from her elbow and offering Sal a hand.

Sal got stuck into the tent, laying it all out and standing over it with the instructions. She frowned at them and flipped the pages a few times, before holding them out theatrically and dictating, "Yellow pole to the red loop end, force, light bending is not." She closed the booklet. "I suspect this may not have been professionally translated," she said, looking back at the tent. "Alright. I will force light bending is not." She worked the rest out herself.

In the end, the tent got pitched. It was passable. Allegra made a big show of fake applause behind the camera.

Sal looked up. Their eyes met, and Sal gave Allegra a cheeky little smile as she unzipped the tent door. "Would you like to inspect my work, Allegra?" The camera was running.

She *could* ask Sal to cut a 'no' out, but... *You want to get in the fucking tent with her*, she told herself. *Get in the tent. Life is short.* Allegra followed her own advice and crawled in.

When Sal crawled in carefully after her and sat cross-legged, they were knee-to-knee. Sal had a sly grin on her face. Allegra's eyes dipped to it for a moment as Sal reached an arm out towards Allegra... and pushed it against the wall of the tent, contorting it. There was probably a hand visible through the tent fabric on the camera as well. She then grabbed one of the poles and wriggled it.

The tent, with them both in it, wriggled.

Allegra had to laugh. "Genius," she commented quietly to Sal, who pretended to brush off her shoulders.

After a few more contortions, it was time to move on. Sal paused briefly to send an email and Allegra went to crawl past her. On her way out, Sal whispered, "Perhaps we can try other ways of contorting it at some point."

That just about guaranteed first aid would be a write-off for Allegra.

They laid out a blanket in front of the DSLR. "You want to go first?" Allegra wondered, trying to decide with about 5% brainpower which way would be funnier.

"This time I'd like to go second," Sal said, holding Allegra's gaze just a little too long. "Lie down."

Jesus. Allegra put the first aid kit on the ground and did as she was told.

Sal knelt beside her, taking a pressure bandage out of the kit and unpacking it. "I hope you're ready to be wrapped up," she told Allegra. She took one of her legs and began a clinical explanation about snake venom... while wrapping a bandage in a slow, deliberate progression upwards.

She reached Allegra's thigh. "I think we're tipping into an M-rating."

Sal had a dark smile. "We can always cut it," she said casually, her hands threading the bandage between Allegra's legs.

Allegra lay there, staring at the sky. They could always cut it. Did that mean they could—

"Congratulations," Sal said. "You're immobilised. Time to call 000 and get a helicopter ride. Good luck! I've got a meeting in about five minutes." She winked at Allegra and stood up, walking out of frame.

When she came back over to unwrap Allegra, Allegra only just managed to talk herself out of pulling Sal on top of her. It would be in frame. "Your turn, Princess," she said when she was free, pushing Sal onto the rug. "Lie down."

Sal grinned at her from the ground. "As much as I'd love you to immobilise me right now, we have a children's outdoor education camp to inspect."

We have a—? Allegra checked her phone: midday. *Fuck*. They *did* have a camp to inspect. She sat back.

"We can come back and film the rest afterwards," Sal suggested, pushing herself to sit. "We have at least 5-10 extra shots we didn't get to." She paused. "We can take our time with those."

Allegra liked the sound of that. Too much, actually. She looked at Sal for a moment longer than she meant to. "That was really fun," Allegra found herself earnestly volunteering. "That could have gone all sorts of ways. But I had a great time." She was smiling.

Sal's eyes widened for just a moment, and she fell still. Almost imperceptibly. Then, Allegra felt her slip their hands together and lace their fingers. "Likewise."

Behind them, the DSLR was still rolling. Allegra had no idea if Sal's move was C1 or something genuine.

Sal squeezed her hand once and dropped it, reaching up past her to turn the DSLR off. She relaxed visibly.

Allegra observed the change. "We should pack up."

Sal climbed up from the rug onto the log bench, settling there. She grinned up at Allegra. "Off you go, then."

Sighing at her, Allegra got to it, aware Sal was sitting it out purely to irritate her. It worked to an extent, except there was something about Sal sitting comfortably and watching her haul heavy things around that was—kind of appealing. She could feel Sal's eyes on her. It left no space for more sobering thoughts.

As they got back into the LandCruiser again, Allegra wet a face washer from one of the tanks and gave it to Sal to do something about what the dust and sunscreen had done to her face.

It was nearly completely black when she was done with it. "Whoops."

Allegra chuckled about that. "Just use sunscreen," she told Sal as she pulled out of the campground onto the highway. "You'll sweat your makeup all off in 20 minutes, anyway."

Sal gave her a flat stare and then went back to applying heavy makeup.

When they arrived at the Northstar Pathways property, Sal's face looked picture-perfect again. For now. They parked in the carpark, where a very youth worker-coded young woman was waiting for them outside a small office.

"Allegra!" She had the sort of bright, cheerful face you'd expect of someone in her profession. She let them in and introduced herself as Sarah.

The office was air-conditioned. Returned to her natural habitat, Sal looked far more comfortable. "You can just leave me in here," she told Allegra as Sarah went to go grab some paperwork.

"You're the one who wanted to look close to the coal face," Allegra pointed out. "That means sweat and dirt."

Sarah returned with a site map and unrolled it on the table, pointing out features, but confessing no one had any idea how to bring the property up to regulation for insurance. Fortunately, Allegra had enough experience to know which issues frequently caused problems. She could have a look.

This property was much smaller than the one she'd needed to survey for Homeward. It only took them 10 minutes to get to the gate that was identified as an 'access hazard'. The issue was ridiculously simple: the heavy gate had a custom-made iron lock. The key was nowhere to be found; emergency vehicles wouldn't be able to get in. Cutting the lock off and fitting a loop chain instead would be a quick, cost-effective solution.

The fire management issue was slightly more cryptic. Allegra didn't think the leaf litter was particularly dense—they were obviously across the need to burn off. The distance between bushland and buildings looked generous enough that Allegra didn't bother to measure it. She was walking around the buildings, trying to figure out if their fire extinguishers were out of date or—

There was a whole wall of firewood neatly stacked against the dorm rooms. Bingo.

"I'm glad I got your reaction to that," Sal said from behind her camera. She glanced up at Allegra and smiled.

"And now I'm going to get your reaction as I tell you this," Allegra said, holding her phone up towards Sal. "You're going to help me carry it all over to the woodshed."

Sal let her phone drop. "Of course I am," she said. "If there's anything I enjoy more than looking terrible, it's physically hurting as well."

They got to work. It only took them 20 or so minutes to clear the side of the dorm, after which Sal's makeup had completely gone to God.

On their way back to the office, Allegra got some footage of Sal looking sweaty, weary, and melted. Sal staged a tired-but-satisfied smile for the camera. It vanished the second Allegra stopped recording, returning only briefly for Sarah's benefit when they reported back to her.

"You've *fixed* it?" Sarah asked, jaw open. "Just like that?" Then, Sal and Allegra found themselves subject to a sudden, overjoyed hug.

"Well, the lock needs to be cut off the gate," Allegra told her, patting her back. "Unfortunately, I'm not in an SES truck, because I'd have the gear to cut it off for you now."

Sarah hugged them several more times, gushing about what it meant to Northstar to have their help, and then took a couple of selfies with them. "Is it okay if I post these on our socials?"

Sal, makeup obliterated, gave Allegra a long-suffering stare, but then answered Sarah with false cheer. "Of course you can!"

Back at the car, Allegra wet another face washer for Sal, and then they were on their way back to the campground.

Sal was sighing heavily about reapplying her makeup *again*.

Honestly, Allegra couldn't imagine why she bothered. "Do you really need it out here?"

"Yes." Sal set the face washer aside and stared down the sunscreen. Exhaling, she squeezed some out and began applying it to her face.

Allegra watched her labour with it for a couple of minutes, and then turned her attention back to the road, when she realised Sal had stopped putting on makeup and was looking at her.

"I should do *your* makeup," Sal said. "For the compilation."

Makeup for anything less formal than a billionaire gala was generally a hard pass for Allegra, but it *would* be quite funny. "Alright."

They went back to the empty campground, set up the DSLR and a few of the props again just to fill the shot.

Then Sal sat Allegra down on one of the smooth logs and stepped between her knees. "Close your eyes."

Allegra did. Sal's fingers moved over her face with slow, deliberate precision—thumbs at her cheekbones, fingertips tracing the line of her jaw, pausing just long enough to steady her chin. It was an unusual type of surrender. Allegra was acutely aware of Sal's warm breath, and the faint brush of her body every time she leaned in.

"Don't look yet," Sal murmured, stepping back. Allegra could hear the scrape of the DSLR tripod being moved closer.

When Sal finally told her to open her eyes, she was handed Sal's mobile to use as a mirror.

The image on screen was a jolt: Sal had given her the same intensely heavy, smoky purple eye makeup she herself had. That depth of tone and colour on Allegra's light palette looked *ridiculous*.

"Amazing, I look so corporate," Allegra said, recording herself examining it in her selfie camera. "Do I feel nothing now, or does that come after contour?"

Behind her, Sal was smiling out of focus, but still in frame. Allegra expected her to fire back something funny, but instead Sal said, "I'm not sure I want you feeling nothing, Allegra."

Oh. Her selfie cam caught her genuine reaction to that. Well, since Sal was apparently going there... "You're in luck then."

Sal reached slowly over Allegra's shoulder—close enough that their cheeks nearly brushed—and turned off the recording. Her smile faded and her eyes dipped to Allegra's. "Let's set up for those 5-10 shots we need."

Allegra sat with that exchange for a moment, butterflies still fluttering. That hadn't felt like performance.

She was still stuck on that log when Sal returned with the tablet and sat beside her. She had the spreadsheet open on it, which would have been more interesting to Allegra if Sal's thigh hadn't been resting against hers.

She tried to focus on the spreadsheet. Most of the moves weren't particularly useful for affectionate compilation content, but they picked a few and stood to film them.

Sal glanced at her and smothered a laugh. "Let's clean your face first," she suggested mildly, and then sat her back down and expertly removed all the makeup. That made for a reasonable first shot.

After filming the chosen spreadsheet cells, they needed some slower shots, so they lingered in a series of relaxed hugs around the campsite—long enough for Allegra to rest her cheek against Sal's head and feel her settle.

It reminded Allegra of that grounding hug after the awful Sunday lunch, and Sal saying, 'Not my usual preference, but just putting the option out there,' like she was offering a discretionary add-on in a service agreement. Allegra chuckled into her hair, her arms draped around her shoulders.

"Share the joke with the class?" Sal's voice was dry.

Allegra was still trying not to laugh. "'Not my usual preference, but just putting the option out there'."

She felt Sal exhale across her arm. She didn't reply straight away. Allegra looked past the top of her head into the bush; shadows were starting to lengthen.

"I meant it, even if it sounded clinical."

Allegra smiled at that. "It worked," she said simply. It was working now, too.

Sal pulled away a little, and then whispered into Allegra's ear, "Let's go into A5," so the camera mic wouldn't pick it up. Her warm breath and low voice gave Allegra goosebumps. A5. A peck goodbye.

Allegra leant in automatically. They'd practiced these, they'd even performed them. She had no reason to doubt the movement, but—when Sal's lips touched hers, she could only remember being pulled into an embrace against the LandCruiser, and that dark alcove at the gala. And, also, the image that had been playing through her mind all day, every single time she looked at Sal.

Sal's lips were beginning to feel familiar; familiar enough that a peck felt—short. Cold. Sal didn't pull back when she should have, either.

There was a moment when they paused, lips resting together.

Sal opened her mouth first. Allegra was sold immediately. She answered without hesitation, slipping her tongue against Sal's at the edge of their lips and drawing her in more firmly. She was acutely aware of Sal's hands after their false start that morning; when one traced up her back, she smiled against Sal's mouth and reached for the camera. Perhaps they were both in a better place this time.

Sal noticed Allegra's hand extend towards the camera and pulled away a little to see what she was doing—and saw her stop recording. Her eyes were fixed on the blank LCD for a moment, brow wavering, hesitating. She exhaled and leant back up to Allegra's lips again.

It felt different when Sal was committing to it. Allegra couldn't stop smiling, cupping that chin, feeling that infuriating mouth and those infuriating lips on hers, feeling the escalating depth, their hands grasping at each other, and—

Sal inhaled sharply, stiffened, and pulled out of the kiss.

She had a firm hand on the centre of Allegra's chest. It was warm, but it also meant Allegra couldn't lean back in. There was a moment where they were eye to eye; Sal's were wide. They dipped to Allegra's lips, lingering there. She took a breath, and then a step away.

And then she was out of Allegra's arms, looking away from her. "I can't—" she began, then abandoned that thought. "I'm not thinking clearly."

While Allegra was standing there, panting, Sal turned her back to Allegra and took a deep gulp from her drink bottle.

It took a moment for Allegra to catch up. She closed her mouth and wet her lips. What had just happened? "Talk to me?"

Sal's head turned a little. "I need a minute."

"Okay," Allegra said. After a pause, she added, "This doesn't have to go anywhere."

Sal twisted enough to give her a sceptical look. "We both know *that* train's not stopping."

Allegra scoffed. "We're not teenagers anymore, Sal. I'm sure we can manage to keep our pants on if—"

"I didn't mean sex," Sal said shortly. She turned away again and finished her water. Allegra saw her chest rise and fall with a long, slow breath. Then, she turned back towards Allegra. She'd brute-forced that earlier panic from her face. "Okay. Let's do some Column Bs," she suggested briskly, as if none of it had happened.

Allegra straightened. She was just going to brush all this off? "Sal," she said. "Come on. We're in this together. Tell me what's—"

"Not right now, Allegra." Her voice was firm, authoritative. Perhaps a little faster than usual. "We have work to do. Let's do it with clear heads."

Allegra squinted at her for a moment. Was she really going to shut this down? *You were thinking clearly enough to kiss me to end an argument*, Allegra thought, frowning at her. *You didn't hesitate when it was useful.*

"No," she told Sal clearly, taking a step back. "If you need a minute, you can have it. I'm going for a walk." She did exactly that before she said something she'd regret to someone who was clearly struggling.

Dry leaves crackled under her boots as she moved along the narrow path away from the camp; on the opposite hill, she disturbed a pair of grey kangaroos. She stopped for a moment to watch them, wondering if Sal had ever had an opportunity to see kangaroos in the wild. Then she wondered if Sal would even care. About this, or anything.

She grimaced; that wasn't fair. It was crystal clear to Allegra that Sal cared—even if she shared none of it. It all felt like another fucking secret.

I wish she'd learn to just bloody talk to me, Allegra thought, watching the ground in front of her as she climbed the hill.

She reached the top of it not much later: a lookout that gave an incredible panorama of rolling hills, gum canopies, and mountains. Standing up there, looking across it, she felt an unfamiliar ache in her gut. There wasn't any sign, anywhere, that other people existed. No voices. No movement. No one to turn to and say, 'Look at that.'

Her pocket buzzed, and relief washed through her as she fished it out, hoping the space had given Sal the opportunity to find words for what had been—

It was Aaron.

Her eyebrows lifted. She opened it. *"Hey. I'm going to give an address at Dad's church Sunday week about the Kirribilli stuff. I'll put up a video before letting people know about it. Thanks for the heads up."*

She was typing out a reply to that when her phone buzzed again. Timothy? *"I offered Aaron the opportunity to give an address before service on the 14th. He would probably like you to be there—although we both know how you feel about church, so I told him you wouldn't want to come. There will be some hard things in it xx"*

Allegra stared at her screen for a moment. Then she locked her phone, put it in her pocket, and looked back at the horizon. She wasn't going to cry.

Those two sitting together, planning what Aaron was going to say without her. For her own good. *Fuck it.*

She looked out across the empty horizon. She wasn't the only person in the world, but at that moment she felt like she was.

And she didn't want to be. Not anymore.

Maybe Sal had taken that minute she needed. Maybe they could talk. She hiked back down the narrow trail to find out.

When she got back to camp, Sal was already moving towards her. After a few steps, something in her face shifted as she took Allegra in, and her pace quickened. By the time they stopped in front of each other, her brow was knit. "Something happened," she observed. "This isn't about earlier, is it?"

Allegra shook her head. "Not entirely." She retrieved her phone and passed it to Sal. "Top two messages."

Sal's eyes stayed on her for a moment, before she turned her attention to Allegra's phone. She read the messages, a tiny frown visible as she closed Timothy's. She handed Allegra's phone back. "Still signing on your behalf, I see."

Allegra exhaled; it was validating to hear that assessment. She nodded.

They stood facing each other for a moment. Sal took a breath. "About before… you tried to talk to me. I didn't let you. That wasn't fair of me." Her mouth stayed open for just a moment—then she closed it and gestured for Allegra to follow her. "I cooked dinner."

She cooked? Allegra's brow relaxed briefly at the mental image. "Uh oh."

Sal gave her a very tentative smile. "Well," she said, "if you can call jaffle-making 'cooking'."

Sal had found the small fridge and two-burner in the back of Allegra's LandCruiser. Allegra almost wished she'd stayed to watch Sal try and figure it all out, because the jaffles that she'd produced were actually passable. She'd also laid out rugs so they could sit in the campfire clearing with the LED lantern ready for after it got dark.

It was endearing. Even if she'd done it to avoid having a proper conversation. Allegra accepted her peace jaffles and went to go sit against the log bench in the clearing with them.

Sal had her own rug against a different log bench. After an indulgent day spent being allowed to touch Sal, the two or so metres between them now felt impossibly vast.

Sal wasn't giving it much attention; she ate her jaffle with one hand and scrolled through her phone with the other. Allegra looked down at her own jaffles and phone, and did likewise.

The silence was oppressive.

"Any book recommendations?" Allegra managed eventually. "I finished mine." *Ours*, she thought, remembering Sal had started reading it, too.

Sal made a thoughtful noise, then stood and came over to Allegra's rug. Allegra's heart lifted; when she sat down, though, it wasn't against Allegra. It was simply beside her. "Here," Sal said, handing over her phone with the eReader app open. "Have a look."

Allegra scrolled through Sal's library, but couldn't focus enough to choose any of the books. Sal was just sitting beside her, waiting patiently. She nodded down at the one currently on the screen. "That one's good."

Not in a state where she had any energy to deliberate, Allegra ended up buying that book on her own reader. She opened it, settled back, and tried to find even a sliver of attention to give it. Her mind was elsewhere.

Sal stayed beside her, her own eReader app open. Silent.

It was better than being alone, but the ache was the same. "You don't have to do this," Allegra found herself saying.

"I know." Sal didn't look up from her book.

They read together for a while; or rather, Allegra reread the same line a hundred times, each time ending up back in her own head.

It was only when she glanced over again at Sal's book to see if she was approaching the end of it that she noticed her page numbers. Sal had flipped the page maybe twice in an hour.

She's sitting with all this too, Allegra realised.

When it was finally cool enough to consider sleeping, Allegra gave Sal another face washer and went to go set up the rooftop tent.

“I dream of a hot shower,” Sal said wistfully, looking at the mixture of red dirt and black eyeshadow on her first pass with the cloth.

“You can have one,” Allegra said, and since she was already sitting on the roof trim, she kicked out the annex that had the shower curtain and pipe on it. “I have two full tanks.”

Allegra showed her how it worked and then left her with it, getting ready for bed and then lying down to wait for her.

Sal returned looking relaxed and barefaced. “You really live here,” she reflected once she’d settled beside Allegra, still as surprised as she had been initially.

Allegra didn’t respond. Wanting her and not being able to say it sat heavy in her throat. She dimmed the overhead LED so only moonlight lit the tent.

They lay there chastely beside each other, after a full day of hands and mouths and near misses. It was almost worse for Allegra than being alone at that lookout. Sal pulling back from her. The memory of how easily their bodies fit together and how abruptly she’d pulled away from it and shut her out and said *nothing*. It all pressed in at once and made her feel—

“This feels like another secret, Sal,” Allegra said into the dark. “When you pull back from me like that and refuse to tell me anything, it feels like you’re hiding *more* things from me.”

Sal’s voice was quiet. “This isn’t about you.”

“It involves me. It affects me. So, talk to me.”

There was a pause. “You’re right,” Sal said more firmly. “I did let it affect you. I’ll take care to make sure it doesn’t in future.”

“Oh, fuck off, Sal,” she said, more gently than she probably could have. “That’s exactly what Timothy does. He decides what I need to know. I’ve had enough people in my life *sheltering me from the impact* of things. What I need them to do is start involving me in the conversation.”

“This is not a situation where I’m overriding your opportunity to parent your son,” Sal said pointedly. “There’s no conversation here. I have things I manage privately, just as we all do.”

“Except you’re not managing them privately,” Allegra shot back, as calmly as she could manage. “You’re starting something with me and then abruptly stopping it, and now you’re pretending it didn’t happen and refusing to talk about it.”

That landed for Sal. Allegra could feel her shift on the foam mattress. “Look, it’s hot,” she said shortly. “I’ve had a long week. I apologise for not managing as well as usual.”

"Managing what as well as usual, Sal? *Me*?"

"*Me*." Sal said that more sharply. "As I said, this isn't about you."

Something occurred to Allegra. "But you know exactly what it is."

Sal opened her mouth. It was a moment before she spoke; for most of it, Allegra wondered if she'd even answer. "Yes."

"Then what is it? Tell me."

A breath. "I don't think it's necessary to—"

"Well, you think wrong. It *is* necessary to." Allegra rolled onto a hip and an elbow, facing Sal's silhouette in the dark. "I'm choosing to be here, Sal. To stay and help you, even though it's not easy. You can fucking choose to be transparent with me about what it is about us that you're managing."

Sal was lying perfectly still, perfectly flat on her back, her chest rising and falling in odd patterns. Each breath was quick, as if she was inhaling to say something, then changing her mind. Whatever she was trying to say was fighting the whole way up her throat.

To Allegra, it felt familiar. Like panic. "What are you so afraid of me knowing that you—"

"*Everything*." The words erupted from Sal's mouth. "And the worst part is you already know it. All of it." Her throat bobbed. "You know enough to completely destroy me."

There was a moment of silence as those words hung between them.

Sal looked across at her, barefaced, open-mouthed, hitching her breath.

After a few seconds, she drew back into herself, looking up at the canvas roof. "And here I am, on the cusp of handing you even more leverage. And I have no idea what happens if I do."

'Leverage' reminded Allegra of the $20,000,000 NDA—now "nearly 60"—and the countdown to when Dimi would discover their Atlas files missing. Allegra's position in the centre of it all suddenly felt very heavy when all she wanted was to protect Aaron and be with Sal.

"Leverage," Allegra repeated, trying to understand that connection. "You mean I'd take that fact that you want me and—use that, somehow?"

Sal closed her eyes for a moment. Her voice was gentle. "No. I know you wouldn't."

"Then why would it bother you that I have it?"

Another hitched breath. "Because it changes the balance."

"The balance between what and what?"

"Between who's more invested."

Allegra made a face. "I'm already pretty damn invested, Sal."

"Well, feelings change." It was almost a whisper, and she was still struggling to say it. "So, say we—do this, and they change. What happens to me?" Her throat was tight. "I need to consider that possibility."

Allegra let that settle. It finally formed a shape, something she could recognise and understand. Something that explained Sal pulling out of the kiss.

Allegra found Sal's hand in the dark and took it. It felt stiff. "That's a lot to carry."

Sal turned her head slowly towards Allegra. In the dark, Allegra could make out Sal's eyes studying her face. "You seem to manage."

Did she mean manage the danger of them getting more involved? "It's worth the risk to me."

Sal exhaled. "You and I have a very different risk tolerance," she observed. There was a quiet resignation in it. "But I think the outcome is going to be the same. As I said, I don't think this train is stopping." Her eyes were still on Allegra.

God. Her stomach fluttered. Despite everything. "I'm really glad it's not," she said, and then realised how that sounded. "I had fun today. When we were just joking around, I mean. We could have more of that."

Sal was unreadable, but her mouth was tight. "Perhaps."

Instead of saying anything else, Sal tentatively turned onto a hip so she was facing Allegra and reached a hand across her stomach. Allegra lay back, and Sal's body followed—hips turning into her, a knee slipping between hers. She settled her head against Allegra's collarbone, still-damp hair brushing her skin, and relaxed there, in the crook of her arm.

It was such a fucking relief to be finally touching Sal that Allegra wrapped her arms tightly around her, hugging her, feeling a smile rise to her lips. She closed her eyes for a moment.

Sal may not have anything else to say, but Allegra did. The words wanted to burst out of her.

She couldn't say them, not now. But she *felt* them: how much she wanted this woman. And she fucking shouldn't, after everything she'd done. She did anyway.

Chapter 32: Breathing Space

Allegra woke to the laughter of kookaburras. Half asleep, she smiled; she'd forgotten how common they were in the Hunter. She listened to them calling together on and off, inhaling deeply and smelling eucalyptus, soil, and—coconut?

That made her open her eyes. Black hair filled her view—Sal's, smelling faintly of her coconut hair product. She was on her side, facing Sal's back; they'd turned during the night. Allegra's arms were still wrapped around her, their bent legs tucked together.

Allegra released a warm breath into Sal's hair and closed her eyes again. This was too nice to waste.

At some point, Sal stirred, shifting her weight and stretching her legs. She froze mid-yawn. The tension woke Allegra, but Sal simply relaxed back against her, head on her arm.

Allegra smiled against her hair. Their bodies fit so well together. "Good morning," she murmured into Sal's hair.

"It is the morning." Sal sounded surprised.

"Mmm, turns out day follows night."

She scoffed, clarifying, "I don't generally sleep through."

Ah. "The sun'll do that."

There was a pause. "Really?" She turned her head a little towards Allegra. Sal's phone came out, and Allegra watched over her shoulder as Sal fact-checked her on Google. "Interesting. You're right." *That* also sounded surprised.

"Shall I schedule peace talks with the sun?"

Sal locked her screen and relaxed back into Allegra again. "Well. Let's not get ahead of ourselves." Allegra could hear the smile in her voice.

She hugged Sal closer to her again; their legs still tangled together under the doona. Sal was right there: coconut scent, warm skin. Right next to her lips. A small move, and she could be kissing it again.

She lingered there a moment, breathing warm air across Sal's neck. Sal didn't pull away.

That settled it. Allegra nuzzled into her, that ethereally soft skin against her nose and lips. Her hand, on Sal's middle, went looking for the same soft skin under Sal's—

Sal's ribs jumped as her breath caught—immediately, she released it. "I see we *are* getting ahead of ourselves." Her voice was dry.

Allegra sighed and withdrew her hand from Sal's top. "Right. Sorry," she said, aware her own voice was also dry. "Where is the line this morning, then?"

Sal laid a hand over Allegra's on her middle. They lay there, against each other. "That's a good question."

Oh. "That you don't know the answer to," Allegra realised aloud.

"Let's just—" She stopped. "Let's not improvise."

"Alright," Allegra said slowly. Was she proposing another spreadsheet? "What's the plan?"

"If we're going—anywhere with this," she said. "It should be deliberate."

It wasn't clear to Allegra if, by 'anywhere', Sal meant physically or emotionally. She got the gist of it, though. "You want to avoid another gala situation."

Sal relaxed immediately. "Yes," she said. "Precisely."

Allegra smiled, despite herself. It reminded her of how Sal's hand had desperately clutched her t-shirt with the same white knuckles she saw on rescue ropes. "Well, I'll let you be deliberate about it, then," she said. "I don't need that, at this point."

Sal rested her head back on Allegra's arm. "Much appreciated."

'Much appreciated?' Allegra smothered another chuckle: this woman was too much. Maybe they should draft a deed of agreement over the terms. Still, it wasn't much to ask, and Allegra didn't have much faith in it lasting. Not at the rate they'd been going.

Which... especially this morning, she was a little disappointed couldn't be faster. She was at a good angle to slip her hand down into Sal's pants; she wondered if they were the same soft lace as her bra had been yesterday. "Want me to make some breakfast?" she said, instead. "I brought peanut butter instead of Vegemite."

Sal made a neutral noise. "Did you bring coffee?"

"It's instant."

"Oh, god," was the response. "Alright. I will be strong."

That meant disentangling herself from Sal. She planted a firm kiss on top of Sal's head, withdrew her arm from under her neck, and sat up.

Sal rolled onto her back and lay there, eyes twinkling. She was between Allegra and the ladder, which meant Allegra would need to climb over her to get it. Sal knew that and grinned up at her.

Oh, so you're fine as long as you can be a little shit about it, Allegra thought, giving her playfully narrowed eyes as she knelt across her. Then, because it was Sal's fucking idea anyway, she put her elbow down on the other side of Sal and, nearly body-to-body, climbed over her much more slowly than she needed to. "Don't want to accidentally bump my head," she said when their noses were almost touching.

Sal was clearly enjoying herself: her lips parted slightly as Allegra's face passed close to hers on the way to the ladder.

Allegra made Sal an instant coffee while she did her makeup and put on *another* completely black hiking ensemble. Then, since the shower annex was already out, Allegra put a change of clothes over the rail and had a quick shower. At least, that was the plan.

"That's a thin curtain," came a smiling comment from nearby as Allegra washed her hair.

Allegra exhaled, looking down her body. Sal was clearly going to push this. Fine. "You know, if you sit on the other side, the sun will be behind it. It will look even thinner."

Over the sound of the water, Allegra heard footsteps pass by the shower annex to the other side. There was a long pause. "You're right." A deck chair unfolded, then creaked as Sal sat in it.

Allegra had to fucking laugh. Unbelievable. *You are freely welcome to join me in here, you know,* she thought. Sal already knew that.

She finished her shower and dressed, and when she stepped out to stow the annex, Sal was reclined comfortably in a nearby deck chair with her coffee and dark sunglasses, grinning.

"Enjoy the show?" Allegra said dryly as she went past Sal to open the boot of the LandCruiser. In response, Sal lifted her coffee mug and toasted her, smiling as she took another indulgent mouthful.

Allegra couldn't do much with her own smile as she put her dirty clothes in the side pocket of her bag, shaking her head. This woman. She was already imagining a situation without Sal's guardrails where they simply stayed upstairs in the tent and entertained each other all morning instead of driving back, when she caught sight of something in Sal's open suitcase.

Amongst the leather purses and pouches and very neatly folded clothes (which contrasted starkly with the mixed gear strewn all over Allegra's boot), there was something shiny and black. Something that didn't look like hiking gear.

Curious, Allegra reached out and lifted the clothes on top of it a little—and recognised the pattern of the lace. It was the satin negligée Sal had threatened to bring camping, the one Allegra said would cause them not to leave the tent if she did.

Allegra stood back a moment. This was absolutely packed on purpose. Which meant Sal was at least *thinking* about going there with Allegra; this wasn't a situation where Sal had anticipated a professional work trip and then their hormones had got the better of them. That was—interesting. It made the decision to construct guardrails feel cruel, in a way. Mostly to herself.

It also meant Allegra now had to contend with two very different memories of Sal: confident in tell-all satin, champagne flute in hand, looking at Allegra like she was about to conquer her... and barefaced, wide-eyed Sal with her gentle touches and desperate voice. The hitch of her breath. The pulse in her throat. The taste of her lips.

Naked beneath this satin negligée.

Allegra closed the boot, leant forward against the car, and rested her head on her forearm. That was it. She was gone. She wanted to *fucking wreck* them both. Lord help her.

She went and poured herself a big mug of terrible coffee and drank it slightly too hot. "Let's get going."

Sal managed to climb elegantly into the passenger seat without being catastrophically violated by Allegra, who instead did a quick walk-around of the camp and car to make sure everything was packed and stowed, then climbed into the driver's seat, eating a muesli bar.

She offered one to Sal, who shook her head. She'd taken the DSLR out. "I need to go over the footage on the way back."

"To make sure there's nothing compromising on it?"

"To make sure it's compromising in the right way," Sal said, resignation audible. "I'll need your phone as well."

It meant Allegra was subjected to the sound of her own voice for nearly two hours on the drive back. It did succeed in turning down the heat in her groin, though, so by the time they pulled into Sal's penthouse, Allegra was in no more danger of jumping Sal than she usually was.

Sal went to change while Allegra transferred food from her on-board fridge—which lasted only as long as her solar battery did—to the giant stainless steel monstrosity in Sal's display kitchen.

Allegra was still doing that when Sal came down the stairs in a sharp suit, looking haute couture and polished again, reminding Allegra of the world she came from.

Sal noticed her expression. "I'm due back at work after lunch," she said, wandering over to the kitchen bench.

Allegra made a face. "Alright."

Sal watched her for a moment, taking a slice of cheese from the pack on the bench. Before she ate it, she asked, "Would you prefer I stay home?" Her eyes were on Allegra.

Two could play that game. "Depends on what you plan to do with me if you do."

Sal's grin deepened. She tore off little pieces of the cheese slice and ate them while she considered Allegra. Finishing the slice, she pushed off the bench and headed for the lift. "Why don't you have a spa while you wait for me?" she asked casually, nodding out towards the terrace. "That'll give me something to think about while I'm at work." From around the corner, she added, "Other than how to get the files back in Atlas."

Allegra stood up from the fridge. Shit. Back to reality. The fridge door fell shut and she stared at her reflection in the stainless steel.

She did end up going to investigate the spa. It was either that or research storage facilities for all her junk still at the Point Piper house, and between facing the fact she'd need to tell Timothy she was moving out or immersing herself in warm water and bubbles, the spa was an easy choice.

The spa was surrounded by enough greenery to soften the transition from rich bushland to polished marble. The only issue with that was that it looked freshly cut, which reminded Allegra that at various mysterious points, strangers freely entered the penthouse. If not for the threat of random service workers showing up, she might have indulged Sal's fantasy of her skinny-dipping in the spa. Instead, she climbed into it in her sports bra and shorts.

The water was still warm from their recent run of hot, dry days. Allegra only lasted a couple of minutes with the bubbles, though; it was more relaxing without them.

She looked up at the light refractions on the ceiling of the spa recess. *Maybe I should just get rid of all my stuff*, she thought, wondering what she actually needed. Owning only what fit in the LandCruiser sounded liberating, but realistically she couldn't fit two seasons of clothes in it. She'd probably need to rent a storage shed... unless Vanessa had space in her garage.

While she was going through the pros and cons of bringing that up with Vanessa, her phone buzzed. She reached out for it.

Sal. *"Can you just confirm for me that Aaron said he's going to post a teaser clip about his church address?"*

Allegra's eyebrows went up. That's not exactly how he'd put it, but, *"Yes?"*

"That sequencing is a concern. We'll discuss it when I get home."

Allegra stared at the screen. Should she warn Aaron not to do it? Sal probably would have said so if she were that worried, though. Perhaps she just had a better idea about how to frame it. Allegra locked her phone and went back to mentally paring back her belongings.

When her phone buzzed again, she reached for it without a second thought, presuming it was Sal—and had a moment of complete disorientation when she saw who it was *actually* from.

Simone. Jesus Christ. What the hell did *she* want? *"You asked about the Kirribilli documents,"* it said. *"I have them, if you're interested."*

Allegra stared at the message and then closed it. Of course she fucking did. She opened a reply field, poised to write something cutting because none of this was her damn business—but closed it again.

Instead of replying (because fuck her), she opened a message to Vanessa. *"Simone has the Kirribilli Primary documents."*

"Yeah, she asked for them."

What in the—"So you just fucking gave them to her??"

Vanessa sent her a shrug emoji. *"She was going to get them from somewhere, you know what she's like. Might as well cut out the middleman."*

Allegra looked up from her screen and exhaled all the breath in her lungs. Giving up, she put her phone back on the side of the spa and sank under the water. That put a lid on asking Vanessa to host her belongings. She'd probably give Simone a guided tour of them the moment she got off house arrest.

When Sal got home from work later in the afternoon, she was so preoccupied that she didn't even notice Allegra's hair was still wet. Hardly looking at her, she skipped the central room and headed down the hallway beside it.

The safe, Allegra thought, sitting straight up on the couch. Was she worried about the Atlas files?

Sal came back out looking concerned, but *less* concerned. She also didn't appear to be going to explain it to Allegra.

That didn't fly anymore. "Did something happen?"

Sal stopped in the centre of the room. She shook her head briefly. "Nothing unusual. I just—wanted to make sure I'd secured them properly."

Allegra frowned. "I wouldn't—"

"Not you," Sal said shortly, and then gave her a pointed look. "This time."

Allegra grimaced. She deserved that. "But you were worried about them."

Sal's lips pressed together. She wandered over to Allegra and perched on the arm of the couch, mind elsewhere. "Mmm," she said without elaborating. "I just—had a feeling." She sat with that a moment, then shook her head and shifted her weight, moving on. "I gave the videos to Short Form."

Not comforted, Allegra let her change the subject anyway. Not explaining a 'just a feeling' didn't seem like a critical omission. "Uh oh."

Sal nodded slowly. "I think I can count on one hand the number of hours I have left as an intimidating member of the exec rather than a 'soft boardroom princess'," she said, enunciating those words. It made Allegra chuckle. Her smile faded as Sal soberly continued, "It is what it is. As long as it gets rid of Dimi, I'll do as many videos as it takes."

'Videos'—that reminded Allegra of Sal's text. "You said something about Aaron's church thing today?"

Sal straightened. "I did." Her frown returned.

"He shouldn't do it?"

"He should," she corrected. "At this stage, anyway. However, I was thinking about the sequencing." She considered her words. "Aaron's bright; I'm not discounting that. But posting a teaser video to advertise an event with greater narrative importance is..." Her frown deepened. "It's professional."

There was only one other optics professional currently in their orbit. Allegra's stomach dropped. "You think Dimi."

"I think it's worth understanding where that decision came from," Sal said carefully. "There is a chance it was accidental."

While Allegra was processing that, Sal's eyes settled on Allegra's hair. She reached out and lifted a lock of it from her shoulders. It was damp. *That* made her give Allegra a knowing smile; she didn't comment on it, though. "Let's go to dinner," she said instead. "We need to discuss our next steps. We don't have much time."

Chapter 33: Sallegra

Finding a restaurant was easy; it was Friday evening, early enough that everything was open but nothing was full. They navigated past shopfronts full of plastic baubles and fake wreaths to end up in a tiny Japanese place whose main commitment to Christmas was a plastic Santa on the front counter. It was empty, loud from the expressway behind it, and staffed by a distracted manager—the perfect place to sit and talk once dinner was done.

The white noise of traffic made thinking easier. Staring at her phone, Allegra tried to figure out how to ask Timothy about the video sequencing for Aaron, since 'Hey, did Dimi tell you to do this?' was probably off the table. Trouble was, she didn't much feel like talking to him.

Beside her, Sal had a glassy expression as she gazed at her own phone. Allegra watched her come to life briefly to check something in her email, make a face, and return to staring blankly.

Her shoulders looked tense. "You're stressed out," Allegra observed.

Sal blinked herself back to reality and nodded once to acknowledge Allegra had spoken.

"Putting the Atlas files back?"

Sal pressed her lips together. "I can work with tight timeframes," she said. "What I'm working with now is *no* timeframes. I have no idea when he'll use Atlas again. That's a problem for me."

Allegra winced. She'd put Sal in that position. "You're still angry with me for that."

Sal shook her head slightly. "That would be a waste of energy. I need all of it to focus on what we do next."

That doesn't mean you're not still angry, Allegra thought, and then looked back at her own phone. She wasn't particularly angry at Sal, either—despite all the excellent reasons she had to be.

And it *did* mean she could think about Atlas: the strip lighting, the compactus with thousands of files. Everything locked up tight in the basement. No foot traffic, and no staff down there.

"Do people know about Atlas?" Allegra wondered aloud. "BSA staff, I mean?"

Sal glanced up. "To an extent," she said. "There's a general knowledge about there being a highly secure archive down there that only the exec and the board can access." She paused. "We have, on occasion, had high-profile individuals on site and they always enter via the guest carpark and rarely come upstairs. I imagine people have joined the dots."

Allegra remembered the corridors. *Oh.* "That's why there's no cameras." Sal nodded. "Are there cameras in the guest carpark?"

Sal looked up sharply at her.

Allegra put her hand briefly on Sal's wrist. "If I get any ideas, the first thing I will do is tell you about them."

Sal's eyes dipped to Allegra's hand, but softened as she looked back up at her. "There are no cameras in the guest carpark—there's no need. VIPs always have security. Confidentiality is paramount."

No cameras in the carpark, and a manual call point right beside the door. "If I trigger another fire alarm, I can be in and out and gone before anyone realises anything is up."

"No. Too obvious. Twice from the same call point would attract attention."

"But if there's nothing missing, there's no crime."

Sal narrowed her eyes. "I'm not comfortable with that level of risk, Allegra. What if someone sees you down there *after* the alarm?"

Allegra didn't answer immediately. She was still picturing the basement: the corridors, the steel door, the guest carpark. There had to be another way in.

Allegra's phone beeped. She looked at it; so did Sal. It was a message.

Fucking—"Simone," she read aloud. "Of course it's fucking her."

Sal sat back, watching her as she opened the message. It was just a photo of a manila folder with Vanessa's handwriting on it. It read '*primary school docs – Aaron*'.

Allegra closed her eyes for a moment. *Leave me alone*, she thought. Since Sal was looking, she showed her the text. Sal's eyes dipped to the label, then rose to the name at the top of the message. "How does she know about those?"

"Before I spoke to you, I hoped the release might have come from the army. They used to ask for this sort of stuff when they were investigating her." Allegra shook her head, remembering her brief conversation with Vanessa. "Vanessa just straight up gave them to her when she asked for them."

Sal mouthed 'ah'. There was a ghost of a smile on her lips. "And I thought that between us, *I* had the complicated family."

Allegra sighed at length. Her family...

Sal wet her lips, thinking. "What do I need to know about Simone?" she asked eventually. "What did she do? I couldn't find anything at all."

Allegra made a noise. "We don't know, her file's sealed," she said. "Whatever she did, though, it seems like the ADF can't figure out what to do with her. She's been on administrative detention for nearly seven years."

Sal looked unconvinced. "Surely you must have *some* idea."

"She's an explosives engineer, so we can guess," Allegra said, and shrugged. "She'd tell us if she wanted to. I think she just likes being enigmatic." She paused. "And fucking insufferable."

Sal took a sip of water, watching Allegra as she did so. "Is she dangerous to us? Would she sabotage what we're trying to do?"

Allegra looked down at the photo on her phone. On the table behind the manila folder, there was a cigarette butt in a glass ashtray. That was deliberate: Simone knew how Allegra felt about smoking. Allegra couldn't roll her eyes far enough back into her head. "I don't know," she said. "Honestly, who the fuck ever knows with Simone."

Sal released a breath. "Someone else to be careful of, then," she said. "Are you going to reply to her messa—"

"No."

Sal smiled slightly at Allegra's quick reply. "Alright then," she said, and gestured at the restaurant counter. "Did you want anything else, or are we done here?"

Allegra shook her head. As they stood and stretched their legs, Sal held her phone out to Allegra. "I want to fix my lipstick. Could you take care of the bill?"

Allegra took the phone. It was unlocked on her wallet app, with a gold and black credit card on top. "I'm sure there are a lot of things I could take care of with this."

Sal laughed once. "If you take off with that, you're stuck with all my notifications," she warned Allegra. "If you think you can handle those, be my guest."

"I can absolutely handle those," Allegra said, and then made sure Sal could see her open the settings and pretend to be about to disable notifications.

Sal shook her head, amused, and then left Allegra alone at the till while she went to the Women's. As the manager was adding up their bill—by hand, their register was broken—Allegra was gazing down at Sal's pristine phone and noticed all the previously dismissed notifications in the settings tab. They were all time-stamped in the last hour: someone sending Sal a file to 'check through', a calendar alert for a report that was due, and a series of requests for invoice approval. She'd snoozed them all to have dinner with Allegra.

Stuck on that, Allegra blankly tapped Sal's phone to the EFTPOS machine when it was presented. She didn't notice Sal return until she felt a hand on her lower back. Sal appeared beside her, leaning on the counter. "What did you decide to buy?"

"This place. You work here now."

Sal tilted her head in pretend concession. "Well. I'm sure my blood pressure will be better."

"I can't promise that," the manager told them, still wrestling with the broken register.

Grinning, the two of them slipped their hands together and laced their fingers on the way out of the restaurant. It was C1, but Sal's little glance up at Allegra from under her lashes wasn't on the spreadsheet. Allegra felt it in her chest. She squeezed Sal's hand as they headed back to the penthouse.

"I have some work to do," Sal said, splitting off as they stepped out of the lift. "I'll be an hour or so. I presume Zoe will post the first camping compilation somewhere between seven and nine—I'll let you know when she has." She headed towards her office.

Allegra stopped in place. "It will be ready *today*?"

Sal turned to look at her. "Mmm." At Allegra's stunned expression, she added, "They've had the videos since this morning."

That still seemed fast. She let it go, giving Sal a wide-eyed look and heading for the penthouse gym. Perhaps exercise would give her some thinking space.

Allegra had zoned out while going for a long run on Sal's space-age treadmill—without any brainwaves about their current situation, unfortunately—when Sal appeared in the doorway. "You're not answering my messages."

Allegra shrugged, pausing the treadmill. Her phone was in the guest bedroom. "I was thinking about Atlas."

That got Sal's attention. "Any ideas?" Allegra shook her head, stepping off the machine and blotting her forehead with a towel. Sal exhaled. "I'm still working on the issue myself." She held her phone out. "The camping compilation dropped."

Allegra accepted Sal's phone again. Her messaging app was open, and the last few messages were between her and Zoe. "*Video's posted*," with a link, *"can I comment on it, or will you write me up?"* That one had a giggle emoji attached to it. Sal's reply was, "*If I wrote staff up for commenting on it, I think I'd be with HR all next week.*" Zoe then replied, "*Yes. Uh. My strongest recommendation is that you don't check Teams right now. Or perhaps ever again.*"

Sal's grimace said it all. "Watch the video."

Allegra did as she was told and tapped on the link. The video was posted to Allegra's Instagram and TikTok as if she'd uploaded it herself, with the caption: '*Hope you folks find her as funny as I do.*' Which was... look, not something Allegra *wouldn't* say, but was clearly written to be as elder millennial cringe as possible.

The video was also... Allegra joined Sal in grimacing. It was about 90 seconds and started strong with the sharp contrast between them and then moved through some of the funnier beats. Allegra had allowed herself to relax and was then blindsided by the physical contact compilation: two middle-aged women from diametrically opposed worlds, completely in love, and unable to keep their hands off each other.

It was one thing to film everything over two to three hours and be dimly aware that only the attention-grabbing parts would be picked; it was quite another to see those parts, scientifically condensed into non-stop second-hand embarrassment for 90 seconds.

Allegra handed Sal's phone back to her, aware that both her face *and* her neck were bright red. "Kill me."

That made Sal smile. "We can die together. How romantic." Her voice was dry as a bone.

God. Allegra took a step back towards the treadmill and leant heavily on it for a moment. Timothy was going to see that. Aaron was going to see that. God, even *Simone* was going to see that.

"Anyway," Sal said, walking past her and taking a seat in the black leather chair in the corner of the gym. "My entire staff will definitely have seen that by the end of the evening." She exhaled, leaning back into the chair. "At least it's Saturday tomorrow. Perhaps the shine of seeing your management in all those compromising positions may have worn off slightly by Monday."

Allegra doubted it. "If this was the SES, that video would come out at every single staff event that involved that manager for their entire career."

Sal looked bleak. "Corporate is no different. Worse, actually: my staff are in PR and Marketing. They will meme it for eternity, in every email, forever." She made a face. "In fact, I guarantee by Monday BSA Teams will have a whole series of new reaction emotes and they will all be stills from that video." She closed her eyes. "At least it'll give them something new to whisper about instead of the Threshold fire."

Allegra watched her. For someone whose picture didn't appear anywhere online a week ago, this was a *big* change. "Are you okay with all this?"

Sal opened her eyes. "I don't have the luxury of worrying about whether I'm 'okay with' it," she said. "This video needed to present me as likeable and authentic. And there's no better way to achieve that than to cheerfully invite people to laugh at your eccentricities."

"That sounds like a 'no'."

"Does it?" Sal asked flatly, and then turned her attention to Allegra, shifting her weight and settling back in the chair as if it were a throne. She then used *that voice* again. "If I say I feel bad, will you comfort me?"

Yes, Allegra thought immediately. She couldn't speak straight away; not with Sal looking at her like that. She swallowed. "That depends on what you want."

"Oh, I think you'd give me whatever I want, Allegra."

God, she was so fucking right. She was also just winding Allegra up. "What do you want, then, Sal?"

Sal considered her a moment with a dark smile across her face, as if she'd been given a menu and asked to select a meal. Eventually, she nodded at the free weights. "A show."

Allegra laughed once. "This is in service of your mental health," she told Sal, and went to load up the bar for some curls. "I don't think I'll be able to focus much on trying to figure out how to get into Atlas like this."

Sal observed her progress. "Good," she said. "Leave the thinking to me this time."

"Yeah?" Allegra said, angling a bicep curl towards her. Sal's eyes rested indulgently on it. "Like this is going to make it any easier for you."

"I'm very good at compartmentalising," she said. Then, eyes still on Allegra's body, she demonstrated by lifting her voice into a more professional register. "We'll wait two or so hours and run reports on the compilation. We can rope a couple of contract influencers in to boost it if needed; got to get the 18-25 demographic."

That seemed very specific, and very unrelated to overthrowing Dimi. "Why them?"

"Several of BSA's private shareholders—including Julian and Cecilie Vale—and three of the board members have children that age."

Allegra's eyebrows went up. That made her think of all the dealings they'd had recently with the Vales. Their families getting acquainted. She gave Sal a hard look. "Why does literally every single thing you do smell like some sort of scheme?"

Sal smiled too sweetly. "I imagine thinking before acting must seem like scheming to someone who's used to doing the exact opposite."

And yet I'm the one who got the Atlas files, Allegra thought, but kept her mouth shut. She didn't want to argue, particularly not when she had a strong suspicion Sal actually *wasn't* travelling as well as she could be. Instead, she focused on giving Sal good angles of all her major muscle groups as she worked them.

Allegra was nearly done when Sal's phone buzzed. She glanced at it, then gave it her full attention and sat forward. "Zoe's already pulling reports of reactions," she said, and then tapped on the message. Her eyes tracked the screen. Clearing her throat, she read aloud what was presumably a comment, "We're calling this Sallegra, right?" She glanced up at Allegra to gauge her reaction.

Allegra made a face. "Why is *your* name first?"

"Brains before brawn," Sal said lightly. Allegra scoffed as Sal read a few more. "'This was next level cringe but unfortunately now I'm emotionally invested'," she read. "'I've discovered a new kind of trope I'm into: corporate vampire x bush bi'." She paused before reading the last one. "These are from Froggy," she said, and read dramatically, "'Allegra! No! Did our vows mean nothing?!', 'this is a hostile corporate takeover of my marriage!'."

Allegra had to laugh at those. Arms shaking a little, she stowed all the free weights. "You should do some videos with her," she suggested to Sal. "Or we should all do one together."

Sal looked up at her, eyes narrowed as she considered that. "That's not a bad idea," she conceded. Then, show over, Sal stood up. "I should probably put on something more comfortable than stilettos and shoulder pads," she said and walked out of the gym, passing far too close to Allegra on the way to the door.

Grinning, Allegra shook her head wryly and then went to have another shower.

On her way into the guest bedroom, she checked her phone. She had a few notifications: two from Sal, several from Zoe, and the last one was from *Timothy*.

Groaning, she tossed her phone back on the bed and went to have that shower. She could face his message after she was clean and comfortable.

Even after she was done, she *still* didn't feel like reading it. She wasn't sure she wanted to know his thoughts on 'Sallegra', now or ever. Still, he *was* the father of her child, and she couldn't ignore him forever.

Sal was already seated on the couch with her laptop as Allegra wandered into the atrium, opening Timothy's message. It was a screenshot of a list of some sort.

Stopping in place, she zoomed in to read the contents. "*Business Law... HD (91).*" It took her a moment to process: these were Aaron's results. Her frown faded as she read down through each of them. "*HD (93). HD (96). Social Policy SC3020... HD (100).*" 100? Did that mean he got *100* for one of his subjects? Perfect marks?

Her chest swelling with pride, she thought back to how animatedly he chatted about university while they'd been out on the cliffs. His big smile. How excited he'd been.

Perfect marks. She was smiling ear to ear about that herself—

Before she realised Timothy was telling her because Aaron had told *him* the results, not her. Timothy was just doing Allegra a courtesy.

She exhaled, looking down at the message. Her smile was gone.

She didn't want to fucking reply to him. She had to, though, because she still hadn't asked him about the 'teaser' video sequencing. Whatever. "*Incredible, he was telling me how well he felt like he did in that exam,*" she said, instead of all the things she wanted to say. "*Hey, just a question: where did the idea of posting a video advertising Aaron's speech come from?*"

She stood and waited for him to reply. "*Well, the idea was to defuse the story, wasn't it? Everyone's on the internet these days, so advertising elsewhere isn't that useful.*" While Allegra was reading over that, another message came through. "*Also, I realise how much of a grub this makes me sound, but I also thought it would be a good way to publicise Redeemer. As you know, money is a concern for us at the moment, so every additional person who knows about us is a help...*"

Allegra released a breath. At least it was *that*. "The video sequencing wasn't Dimi," she said aloud to Sal, wandering over towards her. "Timothy just wanted to publicise Redeemer."

In her peripheral vision, Sal tilted her head a fraction. "Smart."

After a couple of seconds, another message appeared. *"Why? Do you think it's a bad idea?"*

Oh, so now you want my opinion, Allegra thought a little bitterly. *"No, it's a good idea."* She snoozed his notifications. She wasn't in the mood.

Instead, she sank onto the couch next to Sal. She was in the middle of reviewing invoices, by the look of it, but Allegra couldn't resist interrupting her to boast about Aaron's results.

Sal glanced over the phone Allegra held out to her, eyebrows briefly lifting. She nodded, impressed, then gave Allegra a thoughtful look before returning to her laptop.

Allegra sat back and opened a message to Aaron. *"Your dad sent me your results. Amazing! You were clearly right about how well that exam went."*

The phone buzzed in her hand only a few seconds afterwards. It filled her lungs with air. *"Yeah!! Absolutely wild. I can't believe it. I did so well I've been invited to a scholarship information session next week."*

Allegra recalled those. *"You mean those fancy evening events?"* For families, she thought.

"Yeah. Dad and Vanessa are already coming. You're welcome too."

Allegra sat with that for a moment. Of course those two were. Of course they were the family. She couldn't say that. *"Wouldn't miss it! Forward me the details!"*

He did, and she saved them in her calendar. Then she sat there, staring down at those results and wondering if she really deserved to be proud of them when she hadn't contributed. What she *had* deserved was an opportunity to support him to achieve them. Her stomach felt tight.

After a few minutes, she realised Sal had stopped scrolling through spreadsheets and typing. Her eyes were on Allegra.

Before she could say anything, though, her phone buzzed. Then Allegra's did. Glancing at each other and frowning, they checked their messages.

It was Zoe again. *"We have some competition for eyeballs tonight,"* she began. *"Lost in Austin's dropped the full exposé."*

There was a link underneath it that read: *"The Threshold Fire: A Property Deal, a PR Firm, and Some Unanswered Questions."*

Beneath it was the thumbnail: the burnt-out shed against untouched bushland.

Chapter 34: Human Impact

Austin's video was 28 minutes long. Allegra braced herself as she watched it, waiting to see her face on the screen.

She white-knuckled through the introduction. Austin's first comment about Allegra came after 13 agonising minutes: he called her 'bush safety specialist Allegra Sinclair', noting BSA had deployed her to provide services for Homeward and other charities. A photo appeared of her and Sal with the youth worker at Northstar.

He said people like Allegra, seen to be unconnected to corporate scandal, were often used by PR firms to 'sanitise' situations that looked like bad press. He added there was no indication Allegra knew how she'd been used—only that she believed she was helping a charity.

Allegra frowned. That was... alright.

When Sal's face appeared on the screen—a grab from the first video of them—Allegra held her breath, waiting to hear how she'd supposedly been seduced by Sal as part of corporate grooming.

The camera zoomed out, bringing Allegra into frame. Austin suggested the fact that Allegra Sinclair was dating a marketing executive explained the speed with which BSA had moved to protect her after the misuse of the Phase 1 Environmental Assessment. Who *wouldn't* dedicate all their resources to clearing their innocent girlfriend's name? Framed that way, the decision seemed natural—almost defensive—against a more hostile internal leak.

Allegra paused the video, feeling uneasy. "That's a change of tune." She looked across at Sal to interpret it.

Sal had a satisfied smile. "Oh, I think he got *reamed* by all your adoring fans for outing you, thanks to that quick video we shot," she said. "He obviously doesn't believe I'm a bad actor anymore, or he would have doubled down. But he also didn't need to be that kind with the framing."

Austin also commented on the leak Sal had found buried in earlier news coverage. He'd obtained a copy of the whole thing, which he read aloud. "This was a BSA-internal leak, designed to smear Allegra. Who leaked it? Why?"

Allegra and Sal shared a glance, eyebrows up. That was an unexpected connection.

The rest of the video was damning for BSA. Very fucking damning. Austin never made accusations. He never insulted BSA, Threshold, or the bank. Instead, he laid out documents, timelines, land transfers, and asked a series of quiet, pointed questions.

The picture that emerged was unmistakable: land taken from an ordinary Australian family and funnelled, step by step, into the hands of a property developer with a large foreign shareholding—facilitated at every junction by BSA. The crown jewel of the argument was the extremely convenient timing of that suspicious fire.

After that message had landed, Austin pivoted to the Hislop family: a mum and dad in their early 50s, two teenage kids, and their grandmother, who held up a photograph from the 1940s of her and her brother camping on the same patch of land.

The most heartbreaking moment came when the father—Sean Hislop—blamed himself. His landscaping business hadn't been doing well. "If I'd known they'd take the land off us, I would have worked seven days a week to pay that ridiculous insurance premium. I would have driven Ubers or delivered food. I'd have done anything if I'd known." He wasn't looking at Austin. He stared down at his hands, shaking his head.

Allegra's throat tightened. He thought he'd failed his family.

The video ended with Austin leaning back in his office chair. "Maybe it's all coincidence," he said. "But that's an awful lot of good luck for Threshold and Black Standard Advisory."

Behind him, the green screen showed a roaring structure fire.

The video ended. Allegra and Sal sat back, processing it.

Allegra couldn't shake the image of the father hunched over. His life ruined by BSA. She wondered if there was a file on him in Atlas.

"This video may not touch you," Sal said thoughtfully, knocking Allegra out of her head. Sal skipped back to the comments about Allegra and listened to them again. When she spoke this time, it was more confidently. "I think this basically exonerates us both—well, personally. Professionally, this is *huge* exposure for BSA and something that will no doubt become my problem first thing Monday morning." She stood. "I'd better start on the risk outlines."

Oh no, not risk, Allegra thought sarcastically, cueing the video back on Sean Hislop for a second. She handed Sal's phone back so she could log into the BSA executive system upstairs.

Allegra tried to watch the video again on her own phone; it had been a long day, and she ended up falling asleep on the couch. Sal hadn't come down when she woke up around midnight—and the light was still on in her office—so Allegra relocated to the guest bedroom and slept there for the rest of the night.

Despite being up until some ridiculous hour the night before, Sal was awake at the crack of dawn on Saturday, forwarding Allegra reports and links to news outlets picking up the story.

"You're not beating the corporate vampire allegations with this," Allegra messaged her. *"Did you even go to bed last night?"*

There was a gentle knock. Allegra smelt coffee before the door opened to reveal Sal—barefaced, barefoot, and holding two mugs. "Rise and shine," she said smoothly. "It's a workday."

"It's a Saturday," Allegra commented dryly as she sat up in bed and received her coffee.

Sal sat on the edge of the bed. "Every day is a workday when you're trying to overthrow your nemesis," she said mildly. "Did you see ABC?" Allegra shook her head, taking a sip of her coffee. "They put a stub about Austin's video on their website. It doesn't mention us. However, we should probably have a brief discussion about how you'll comment on this if people ask you about it, which I'm sure they will."

Allegra patted the mattress beside her. "Hop in, then, if it's going to be a long one."

Sal paused with the mug at her lips, then lowered it, looking at Allegra with a faint smile.

Even without the makeup and perfect hair, there was a weight to her attention that pinned Allegra in place. Especially with that smile. Allegra had no idea what those lips were going to do next.

For a moment, she thought Sal might place her coffee on the bedside table and climb on top of her. God, she could. If she wanted to.

Eyes still on Allegra, Sal took off her robe; underneath, she was wearing a thin pair of black summer pyjamas, revealing the geometric, ancient text-like tattoos on her upper thighs and all down her arms. She pulled the doona aside and slipped under it, moving close to Allegra.

She was just a few inches away, sitting against the headboard with her coffee. Allegra could feel the heat of her legs under the doona.

Allegra now had to contend with the fact there was only a thin layer of silk over Sal's skin. It clung just enough to leave her nipples plainly visible.

I've touched those, Allegra thought, her eyes tracing the soft curves underneath. ...what had they been talking about? "You were saying about public comment?"

Sal was watching her, smug. She clearly knew exactly what Allegra was thinking. "Well, your family and other strangers may ask you about the video. I think it's important you respond in an authentic but non-incriminating way."

Those lips... "Authentic?" Allegra repeated, trying not to think about them. "Like, 'yeah, this is really fucked up and something here isn't right'?"

Sal chuckled. "You're missing the 'non-incriminating' half of that," she said. "The best way to avoid the facts is to focus on human impact. Something everyone can agree with."

Allegra blinked at her. "You mean, the Hislops?" Sal nodded. "So I say, 'I feel really sorry for that family, particularly the father?'" Sal's nod deepened. Allegra frowned; she didn't like Sal's framing of it. "I do feel that way. It's real."

Sal tilted her head. "Then it's both authentic and non-incriminating," she said. "Perfect."

It may have been perfect, but protecting anyone involved in the acquisition left a bad taste in Allegra's mouth. She tried to drown it with the rest of her coffee.

Sal left shortly afterwards. "I'll likely end up on video calls today. I'd better look the part." She went to have a shower and put on a shirt, and then spent the rest of her day moving between her office and her laptop, checking her phone and occasionally forwarding stories to Allegra.

Austin's story worked its way through second- and third-tier media outlets over the weekend ("Vale media won't cover it—Cece and Julian are private shareholders in BSA") and had reached pop-culture news by Sunday night. Coverage usually included a paragraph about the camping compilation, a link to the video, and a brief note that Allegra had been inadvertently involved.

As a result, the camping compilation video went viral and started spawning memes, remixes, and parodies by other influencers. Even Froggy did a short where she put on heavy Sal-style makeup, melted it on video with a hair dryer, and then cried to the camera for Allegra to come back.

A still from the compilation of Sal—makeup obliterated, staring darkly at the camera—started appearing everywhere with captions like '100% done', 'Got sunburnt. Firing 1000 people tonight', and 'me when I didn't buy the dip'.

Another still showed Allegra relaxed and bright beside a deeply grumpy Sal, captioned 'Someone will die' / 'of fun!'.

Allegra had to interrupt Sal in her office to share that one. Sal snickered. "If only they knew they've got it the wrong way around," she said, eyes twinkling. "Want to post a reply?"

They took a photo of Allegra pretending to be grumpy and irritable and Sal with a cheeky smile and posted that in reply to the original meme. It got so much engagement that Zoe texted to say she had to turn off notifications so she could focus on her reports.

By Sunday evening, Sal had prepared what she described as a 'water-tight' response plan to present to the exec and the board. She sat carefully on the couch opposite Allegra, removing her glasses.

Allegra looked up from her reading app. "Saved BSA, then?" she asked, feeling torn about that.

Sal extended a bare heel out onto the coffee table and crossed her legs at the ankles, leaning back into the embrace of the couch. "Well," she said. "To the best of my capacity. Simply moving the discussion away from BSA would be straightforward. But there's another opportunity here."

Still thinking about the Hislops, Allegra listened. "Oh?"

Sal was smiling. "Threshold has been under Dimi's stewardship. If I can make *just enough* of the scandal stick, it will be very useful for me later," she said, lacing her fingers around her slender middle. "But that *cannot* be legible in the plan, so I've been spending my time trying to calibrate the strategy to cause that outcome without it being too obvious."

That sounded more hopeful. "So BSA could still potentially be held accountable? At least in some way?"

At that, Sal's eyes pivoted to Allegra. She studied her, clearly noting her choice of words. "You mean legally. Legal issues don't stick—they get quietly settled with regulators," she said. "The only thing that ever matters is reputation."

Allegra considered that—but was thinking of Simone, on house arrest for years over a legal issue. "You may be a little biased on that front."

Sal sat forward, considering her—eyes noting her tight shoulders and set jaw. "You want consequences, I can see that," she said gently. "So do I. And following my plan is how we make them land where they belong: on Dimi."

That didn't allay Allegra's unease completely, but she left it. After all, Sal hadn't been involved in the fire. Zoe hadn't been involved in the fire, Gerard hadn't been involved in the fire. Dimi probably had been, somehow.

But then there was Atlas—in the cold, concrete BSA basement behind lock and key. With thousands of files, each of them for someone like Allegra and Sal. Maybe even Sean Hislop.

When Allegra went to bed that night, Sal was predictably still awake and tweaking her strategy. Allegra didn't fall asleep straight away. Her mind was still circling Austin's video.

The following morning, Sal suggested Allegra accompany her to work.

"To normalise 'us'?" Allegra wondered, eating her Vegemite toast right beside Sal so she had to smell it.

Sal ignored her toast. "Maybe I just need backup today," she said dryly. "In case my entire staff come to work with melted dark eye makeup."

Allegra chuckled about that. "I'll protect you," she said valiantly. "Shall I wear my scary suit?"

That got a full smile out of Sal. "Yes," she said, locking eyes with Allegra. Then, she let them trail down her front. "It reminds me how dangerous you are."

That sealed it. Out came the suit and sage shirt, and Allegra accompanied Sal to work looking sharp and imposing.

Security were very engrossed in what they were doing as Sal strode past them. Too engrossed. Allegra spotted a couple of them glancing at each other with smothered grins as she and Sal passed through the turnstiles.

In the lift, people made space for them. Someone said a little too cheerfully, "Morning, Sal!" Sal smiled at her in the most professional possible way, and then glanced up at Allegra. Her expression... Allegra smothered her own laugh.

On her floor, the staff were more open about their curiosity. As she passed through someone called out, "How's the sunburn?" referencing one of the memes.

Apparently unbothered, Sal shot back, "I don't need sunburn to fire you, Jerry. It'll be because you never submit invoices on time."

'Jerry' laughed at that. "They'll be on your desk by 10."

Allegra glanced back as they left to see people already huddling in energetic discussion.

In the hallway, Sal was stopped by two juniors who held a tablet at her. "Sorry, Sal, could you take a look at this timeline?"

Sal paused to glance through it. The junior holding the screen had a perfectly blank, perfectly professional expression. Her work colleague was fucking losing it beside her.

Sal nodded at the girl with the tablet. "Realistic," she said. "You can lock it in." Then she looked at the girl's colleague, who went red and nearly exploded. Sal's eyes lingered on her face a second before she indicated for Allegra to follow her.

They reached a huge corner office with windows facing the harbour and a long, hardwood desk in the centre. There was almost nothing on the table; a laptop dock, a screen, a notepad, and a pen. And, Allegra noticed, a photo frame. With her in it. It was the photo of her in SES gear that Sal had taken at the studio.

Sal saw her line of sight. "That's for realism," she said simply, and then set her briefcase on the table and wandered up to Allegra. "This, on the other hand..." She slipped her hands around Allegra's waist, her eyes lifting slowly up Allegra's body to finally lock with Allegra's.

Oh, boy. "I should wear this suit more often," Allegra managed. Over Sal's shoulder, the big hardwood desk was just a couple of steps behind her. It wouldn't take much to walk—or lift—Sal up against it. And there wasn't much to knock off it.

Following Allegra's eyes, Sal turned and looked behind her. Then she looked back up at Allegra, an eyebrow raised. She pulled her down a little and said in her ear, "I know what you're thinking..."

Allegra opened her mouth and bent to whisper something in Sal's ear when someone cleared their throat loudly in Sal's doorway. Sal froze.

Allegra stood to apologise—and saw white hair, rimless glasses and a too-pleasant smile. Her blood ran cold.

It was Dimi.

Be nice! You need to be nice! She forced a delighted smile onto her face. "Dimi!" she said, stepping away from frozen Sal, pretending to be sheepish. "I'm so sorry. I know this isn't professional. I was just seeing Sal off to work—you two must have a lot of work to do today after the Austin thing."

Dimi waved his hand at her, dismissing her apology. "Oh, that's perfectly fine. I was young once, too!" He chuckled. Allegra felt fucking *sick*. "I do have a lot to do today, though..." He stood aside from the door.

Allegra knew what that meant. She also couldn't do anything to comfort Sal without it making it obvious. "See you at lunch?" she asked, kissing Sal's cheek.

Sal came back to life. "Not sure about lunch," she said, composed again. "I'll text you."

Allegra smiled brightly at her, then at Dimi, and left the office. She'd made it around the corner before she realised Sal's door was still open.

When Sal said, "Dimi," Allegra could hear it. She paused, an ear turned towards Sal's office.

"I gather you've been working hard all weekend on a plan?" Dimi asked. He sounded so fucking normal. Like any other boss. Sal made an affirmative noise, and Allegra heard the crisp click-click of her briefcase springing open. "Thank you," he said, as if receiving something. Paper rustled, and he made an approving noise. "This is very comprehensive. You must have worked all weekend. Poor Allegra."

Allegra bristled. *Shut up, you fucker.*

"Alright," he said. "Well, there's that meeting with Threshold and Legal now." Footsteps. Then a pause. "Oh, do you have somewhere to be as well?"

There was a moment of silence. "The meeting." There was hesitation in Sal's voice.

"Oh!" A pleasant chuckle. "You're not required for that, my dear. Thanks for this, though." He tapped the papers. "I'm sure we'll manage to find *something* useful in it."

"I don't think it would be wise to—"

"Thanks, Sal," he said. "Truly, I'm sure this document will spawn some useful conversation at least." Footsteps approached the door.

Allegra realised she was still standing in the middle of the hallway and ducked into the empty collaboration room beside her, holding her breath as the brisk footsteps passed. She waited until she was sure he was gone before peeking out and stepping back into the hallway.

She looked towards Sal's office. She wanted to go back to Sal. She could wrap her arms around Sal, say she'd heard everything, and *fuck that man.* But—no. Sal wouldn't want any part of that. She wouldn't even have wanted Allegra to overhear it. It was humiliating.

Fighting the instinct to go back anyway, Allegra put one foot in front of the other and headed for the lift, greeting all the too-wide or poorly smothered smiles on the way there.

While she was waiting for the lift, she texted Sal instead. Just to remind her that she had someone on her side. "*I'm going to wander around town. Do you need anything*?"

Allegra was already out on George Street, trying to ignore the phones pointed at her, when Sal replied. "*Thanks—nothing specific. See you later tonight.*"

Allegra stood in place, looking down at her phone. *I'm thinking of you and I want to murder him*, Allegra imagined saying to her. She didn't. She put the phone in her pocket and kept walking.

Perhaps she could buy a present for Sal to cheer her up—but what did you buy someone who could probably afford to purchase a small nation? Allegra wandered around the city, looking for something appropriate.

That evening, when Sal returned home from work, she was distracted. She swapped her stilettos for flats and went upstairs, returning in reading glasses. Not even *her* makeup could cover the bags under her eyes.

"You look like you might need some of this," Allegra said, presenting her haul, artfully arranged on the kitchen counter: several bags of artisan coffee blends from different boutique vendors around Sydney.

Sal stopped in place, eyes a little wide.

She was about to reply when her phone rang. Her face settled back into 'tired', but her eyebrows lifted at the name. Up came the mask. "Sandy!" she said in her smooth marketing voice. "So wonderful to hear from you, how are your girls?" She waited, listening. "Well, I'm glad they both liked the video. Sometimes it's nice to let your hair down. What can I do for you?"

Allegra watched her, trying to figure out who 'Sandy' was. She didn't have to wait long. "It makes sense the board would want to meet," she said neutrally. "After what—" There was a longer pause this time, and something passed over Sal's face. "I'm sorry, Sandy, that's above my head. I'm sure Dimi's completely across the risk of—yes, and the regulators. I'm sure they discussed that today." She closed her eyes, listening, before she finally said, "No, I wasn't." Something 'Sandy' said made Sal look up at Allegra and swallow. "Yes, I think calling Dimi directly is a better move than speaking to me on this one. I'm sorry I don't have your answers this time." She said goodbye and hung up.

Sal didn't speak straight away. She stood by the kitchen counter, unmoving.

Allegra said nothing.

Eventually, Sal reached out and touched one of the new coffee pouches. Her fingers trailed over the name of the roast, then picked it up and moved towards the grinder.

Allegra blocked her and gently accepted the pouch from her. "Sit," she said, going to the grinder herself and unzipping the coffee pouch.

Mutely, Sal went and sat at the table.

It was only then that Allegra realised she had no idea how much coffee to put in the grinder. She decided to be very generous. After all, Sal liked her coffee extremely black.

"I can't cook," Allegra said, pausing the grinder to check its progress and getting grounds everywhere. "I was thinking of trying, though—seems a shame to have this monstrous kitchen and not be cooking awful pasta in it."

Sal smiled slightly at that; it was gone quickly. She let Allegra get to work putting a pot of pasta on the stove, eyes unfocused.

Allegra was draining the pasta before Sal spoke again.

"I've been frozen out."

Allegra looked up from the sink. "Frozen out?"

"I'm not invited to the fallout meetings, or anything about response planning," Sal said. On the next point, her voice had a bitter edge. "Oh, but Dimi will still take my response strategy, pick out the bits that will affect him, and pass the rest off as his own work."

Allegra set the saucepan down. Despite how terrible it was, she couldn't help but feel a small flutter in her chest that Sal had shared it with her. "So what I'm hearing is that you're going to need a lot more cheese in this." She nodded at the pasta.

Sal smiled. Allegra felt that smile deep in her chest. She poured the coffee and ferried it over to Sal. "I'm sorry," she said. "About work. But also about the coffee and the pasta."

Sal glanced up at her, expression softening, and accepted the coffee. She took a measured sip to test it and placed the cup on the table. "It's dreadful," she said. "But extremely on brand for the day I'm having." She took another sip anyway.

Allegra smiled and served them both dinner.

"After you've finished actively poisoning me," Sal said, dutifully eating the cheese-drowned pasta, "I'm going to need to go back to the drawing board." She exhaled. "Again." The word sounded long and tired.

Sal was still at her drawing board the following evening as Allegra got ready for Aaron's scholarship information event. She went upstairs to say goodbye—but also because she thought Sal could use an Allegra-in-a-suit-shaped break.

Sal finished the sentence she was typing and took off her reading glasses. She paused when she saw Allegra.

Her eyes moved over Allegra's body. "Mmm," she said when their eyes met again. "Thank you."

Allegra had to contain her smile. "I'm off."

"Shame. I thought maybe you'd come up here to give me some light evening entertainment."

"If it wasn't Aaron I'd offer to stay instead," Allegra said, meaning it. "I don't know when I'll be back; I'm not sure when it finishes. There's food and drinks afterwards."

Sal nodded, eyes still indulgently resting on Allegra's body. "Would you like me to pick you up?"

Allegra smirked. "Now, or...?"

That got a full grin out of Sal. "I don't think you'd thank me for making you late tonight."

She was right about that. "I don't need a lift, anyway," Allegra said. "I'm driving."

Driving turned out to be a terrible decision. It had been so long since Allegra had anything to do with a university that she'd forgotten how diabolical the parking always was. She ended up needing to download a fucking parking app and pay some exorbitant price for parking anywhere slightly close to the hall where the event was being held.

She was early, as usual—and so was Timothy. He was in a crisp black suit, looking expensive and polished as he waited outside the hall with the milling crowd. He smiled and waved when he saw her.

Sighing, she waved back and walked over to him. He took the measure of her. "You in a suit," he said, eyebrows climbing to his hairline. "I must say, that's a new development."

Allegra gave him a thin smile. "I figured it was more appropriate than high-vis."

He chuckled. "Well, however you're dressed, it's lovely to have you here. Aaron will be delighted." He looked behind Allegra. "Speak of the devil!" he said, brightening.

Allegra turned; Aaron was approaching them, wearing an ironed shirt, suit pants, and Lachie's smile. Allegra held him at arm's length before accepting a big hug from him. "You look ready to deliver the keynote in that," she said with a grin.

He looked delighted by the compliment. "Dad always makes me wear suits for church."

"Well, I suppose I'll see the matching jacket this weekend," Allegra said.

Aaron and Timothy shared a glance.

Allegra's smile fell as she looked between them. "What's up?"

From Aaron's expression, he was going to let his dad field this one. Timothy licked his lips. "Well, after you asked about Aaron doing the video, I wondered if it might not be the best approach," he said. "So I asked Dimi—he manages a PR firm, after all!—and he agreed with you and said he wasn't sure it was a good idea. He thinks we should probably leave the whole thing for now in case it affects your reputation."

Allegra listened to that, stomach dropping. "Don't worry about me!" she said. "This is about Aaron."

"Well, I don't want to do anything that's going to cause people to *hate* you," Aaron chimed in. "You're my mum."

Allegra was trying to figure out how to respond to that when something large landed on her back. "Allegra!" That was Vanessa's voice. "You're here! It's so nice you actually came to something!" Allegra was subjected to a big hug, and then so were the other two.

"Sorry I'm late," she said, like it wasn't her ordinary state of being. "The twins needed to be ferried around. You know how it is." She stood up, brushing off her white pantsuit and pale blue shirt. "Anyway, isn't this place fancy? How exciting!"

As they wandered into the hall, people turned briefly towards them and then to each other in whispers. Unlike George Street, no one had their phones out—at least overtly—and it seemed this crowd was a different calibre from the general public. There were a lot of nice suits and refined parents.

"Everyone's looking at you," Vanessa said in a loud whisper. Loud enough that several people who hadn't been looking turned *to* look.

Allegra glanced at Aaron to gauge his reaction to that. He was grinning. She relaxed a little, receiving her name tag from the front desk and then following her family inside.

They found some seats together in the small auditorium and sat in a line. Aaron had inadvertently ended up seated between Vanessa and Timothy—not beside Allegra. She didn't say anything; they were all adults. It was silly for her to be fussy about seating arrangements.

Aaron had been given a folder with information in it, all beautifully presented. What Allegra noticed was the elegant cursive on the front that said *High Achiever* in gold leaf. She ran her eyes over the text. It did something to her, reading that about her son. He *was* incredible; it was wonderful that people were recognising it.

Aaron himself was holding the folder reverently in two hands while Vanessa felt the thick embossed paper and commented on it.

"Good evening, ladies and gentlemen," a young and smartly dressed man said from the front of the auditorium. The lights dimmed as he thanked them for coming and went through housekeeping for the information session.

Vanessa wasn't done reading the contents of the folder and turned on her torch so she could continue. Allegra put a hand on her wrist. "*Vanessa!*"

"I'm nearly done!" she whispered back, *loudly*, and then proceeded to shake Allegra's hand off and flash the fucking light around like a disco laser. Beside them, Aaron was smothering laughter about the two of them while the keynote speaker was introduced and walked out on stage.

Allegra was trying to decide between wrestling the phone off her or just *letting* her do whatever the fuck she wanted to do and pretending not to know her, when she heard the keynote speaker's voice. "Good evening, everyone! I must say, it's lovely to see so many bright faces."

A chill set in before she registered who it was.

She looked up—the stage lights were bright compared to the dark auditorium and pointed at a figure on the podium. The figure was in silhouette. It was his Einstein hair that Allegra recognised as he stepped forward.

On the stage, smiling broadly, was Dimi.

Chapter 35: Displacement

"Dimi's the keynote?" Timothy whispered, speaking that name with *far* more fondness than it deserved. He flipped through the program.

Allegra looked at her own—the keynote address was simply listed as such. It was only when she turned to the series of headshots on the back that she saw the most generically handsome, bureaucratic, and politician-looking man she'd ever seen. *Keynote: Petr (Peter) Black, CA, FAICD.* He looked like a stock photo.

"Now, I'd like to reassure you that my much more handsome brother *will* be joining us later. Unfortunately, there were some logistical issues with his flight in," Dimi said from the stage. "I told him it would be my absolute pleasure to address Australia's next best and brightest—because that's what you are. You're the future of Australia. And it is our honour to help you succeed in changing the world."

Allegra glanced across at Aaron. He was raptly watching Dimi, clutching his *High Achiever* folder. Even Vanessa had stopped trying to read it and was listening. In fact, when Allegra cast her eyes across the auditorium, there weren't many phones out. All eyes were on Dimi.

Allegra felt nauseous. He was an absolute icon everywhere he went. How on earth was Sal going to oust someone like this?!

"So, while you're seated amongst the peers you will compete with for the scholarship programs," Dimi continued, his voice carrying easily even without the microphone, "each of you has already achieved something incredible: you've stood out from your classmates—thousands of them. You've achieved scores or completed projects that the staff and board consider *exceptional*." He paused, directing a secret smile at the audience. "I had a brief look at some of the results represented here tonight. I think the selection committee is going to have a tough job this year!"

Dimi continued, discussing some of the founders and the achievements of the alumni before turning to the topic of his speech: *From Talent to Impact*. Allegra found herself staring at that animated, friendly face.

At the end of his address, there was loud applause. Dimi nodded once at the audience, lifted his arm in a brief wave, and then shook hands with the MC again as they passed each other. He descended the stairs at the side of the stage and sat near the front, eyes on the speaker.

Allegra's weren't. They kept returning to Dimi. Where he was, what he was doing. His various subtle and appropriate responses to whatever the speaker was saying. His presence had a gravity that drew her eyes and her attention—away from Aaron, the one person who should have had it.

Allegra was still in the pull of it when guests around her turned to each other and a hum of discussion began. People stood, stretching. Others edged past neighbouring seats for the door. Allegra looked down at the program: a 20-minute intermission.

Vanessa was shaking her head. "So many options!" she said, looking at some notes she'd taken on her phone. "It's like a menu of scholarship programs. I don't remember there being this many at uni."

"Do you even remember being at uni?" Aaron asked her with a grin. "How long ago was that again?"

Allegra had barely managed to smile and open her mouth when she saw Dimi stand. He turned. Then he looked over at her, smiled, and waved.

Allegra's mouth fell shut. *Oh my god*, she thought, her stomach tightening. She waved back as cheerfully as she could manage; he could *not* guess she suspected anything about him. She tried to get in character.

He stood right beside her in the aisle, looking across her row of guests. "Allegra!" he said warmly, glancing at her only briefly. "How lovely it is to see your family here. And not a surprise, I must say." He looked pointedly at Aaron, who drew a breath.

Allegra didn't have time to respond before he'd already extended his hand to Vanessa. "And another delightful Sinclair with you today! Dimi Black."

Vanessa could *not* have looked more charmed as she took it. "Vanessa," she said. "I've heard a lot about you!"

Allegra turned her head to look at Vanessa. She'd *what*?

"Oh dear, that doesn't sound good at all," Dimi said sheepishly, but he was clearly joking. He sobered a little. "I just wanted to pop over and say that I ran my eyes over the guest list before writing my keynote—and Aaron," he said. He captured Allegra's son with that smile. "Perfect marks. Incredible." Then, he looked between Timothy and Vanessa. Not at Allegra. "That kind of outcome doesn't happen without someone making it a priority."

Vanessa brightened. "Academic performance is absolutely my priority with my kids," she said, and then put her hand on Aaron's arm. "I mean you, too!" She looked up at Dimi. "I drove him *everywhere* when he started doing well in high school. It's so important to be present and supportive when kids start to show an interest in their education."

Present and supportive, Allegra repeated to herself, feeling those words. All Allegra had done was give everyone money. That didn't mean *nothing*, right? "And to support him financially," she chimed in. "So he doesn't have to work and can focus on his studies."

Dimi glanced at her. "I'm sure that helps," he said pleasantly, returning his attention to the others. "If you needed to be driven everywhere, you must have done a lot of extracurricular activities?"

"I was really into debating in high school," Aaron said, looking quite proud. "Our team did really well! Not all my work, of course. I had some incredible teammates."

"Oh, pfft," Vanessa said to Aaron. "You were the whip! You won so many of those debates."

Allegra needed to be part of this conversation. She *was* part of this conversation. "I used to really enjoy listening to him practice..."

Vanessa turned to frown at her, but then her eyebrows lifted. "Oh, that's right—you were around for a bit then, weren't you?" she said. "When he first started doing well."

Dimi's eyes moved between them as they spoke. They rested on her son again. "If you're a good speaker, there are a lot of doors that will open for you, Aaron," he said. "You could consider the Bar—or even politics, if you're so inclined. It sounds like you have natural talent for it, and definitely the face! People will respond to you."

Aaron had stars in his eyes, Allegra could see them. "I haven't made a decision yet," he said. "For now, I'd like to keep my options open."

"With Law, you can," Dimi said, giving her son his full attention. "And with a Master of Laws *scholarship*..." He shook his head. "Well. That will read *exceptionally* on any resume or application."

The other three were hanging on his every word, but Allegra's smile must not have been perfectly believable; as Aaron looked towards Dimi, his eyes dipped to her and lingered for a moment.

Shit, she thought, beaming broadly at him and feigning excitement. *He'll think I don't want him to succeed!* And if Aaron could tell something was up with her, Dimi definitely would be able to.

She needed to sort her shit out. "I'm so sorry, can I squish past a moment?"

Dimi, hardly looking at her, moved aside to allow her to leave and began to ask Vanessa about her education.

As Allegra moved away, a woman brushed past her and put her hand briefly on Dimi's arm. "Hi, Dimi," she said, air-kissing his cheeks. "I hope Prue and Tilly are doing well. I read about that fire—what a terrible coincidence. Anyway, it'll be forgotten by the next news cycle." He nodded at her in acknowledgement and then turned his attention back to Vanessa.

'It will be forgotten by the next news cycle'... Allegra exited the auditorium, slipping into the foyer and standing out of sight facing the wall. She put a hand on her stomach. All that work Sal had put in to try and make the Threshold fire scandal stick. All the effort Allegra was putting in to try and reconnect with her son.

What the fuck could she do?! If Dimi wanted to lock on to her family in a charm offensive, what tools did she have to counter that?! Aaron looked at him like he was the fucking sun, and Timothy and Vanessa just sat there smiling and encouraging it.

How the *fuck* were she and Sal supposed to do anything about that?

She went to grab a cup from the drinks table, her hand hovering at the wine glasses before choosing one with water in it.

She couldn't handle this alone. Taking a sip of water—useless, what did Sal see in it?—she fished her phone from her pocket and tapped Sal's icon. *"Dimi's here."*

She didn't have long to wait. *"What? Why?"*

"He replaced Peter Black as the keynote. Peter will also be here at some point."

There was a pause. Allegra could almost see Sal sitting in her chair, tapping her thumb against her lip as she thought. *"He's not there because he cares at all about Macquarie."*

Allegra read that comment again, feeling it settle into the pit of her stomach. *"He's here for Aaron."*

"Yes."

Allegra felt her pulse pick up. *"What do I do?"*

"Be friendly. Give him nothing," the reply read. *"Stay with your family."*

Okay. Fuck. Allegra took a big gulp from her water, discarded the glass and headed back into the auditorium towards her seat and...

Dimi was in her chair. Facing her family, engaged in a cheerful, animated discussion with them. There weren't even any seats free around them that Allegra could sit in, and it would seem petulant if she asked for hers back. Hovering nearby would be obvious and awkward.

Instead, she had to stand at the door watching Aaron, his eyes fixed on Dimi and shining with admiration. So excited, so hopeful. So complimented that Dimi was paying him such special attention.

They were all enjoying themselves. No one seemed to notice Allegra had gone.

When the auditorium bell sounded to signal the end of intermission, Vanessa sprang up. Of course she'd choose *now* to get up, when people were supposed to be going back to their seats. Allegra slipped around the door, let Vanessa walk briskly past her, and then followed her into the toilets.

She was just doing her makeup. "There you are!" she said brightly. "We wondered where you'd run off to! Not that it's strange for you to run off, of course."

Allegra let that comment pass without remark. She couldn't give Vanessa any reason to doubt her. "Just a lot of people in a small space," she said with the best smile she could manage. "Plus, my seat was occupied."

Vanessa leant forward to the mirror to touch up her lipstick. "Oh—I told him you wouldn't mind and that you don't really like these sorts of things."

It was true. That was the problem. "Well, whether or not I enjoy them, it's about time I came to them."

Vanessa paused and looked at her in the mirror. "Oh my god, *finally*," she said. "Well. Aaron will be pleased." She smacked her lips together to spread the colour to the edges. "So, how do I look?" she said. "Do I look hot enough to bag a billionaire?"

Vanessa could have *punched* her to less effect. "He's in his sixties!"

Vanessa shrugged. "That's how these things work, isn't it?" She brushed her perfectly straight, perfectly blonde hair so it sat neatly on her collarbones. "I'm not 20 anymore, but that might make me a more respectable choice."

This was—God. Was she *serious*?

Vanessa glanced at her, noting her expression. "Oh, please, like you're the only one who's allowed to date rich people!" she said. "I'll never find someone like Robin again. I might as well be *disgustingly* rich."

When they returned to the auditorium, there was another man standing beside Dimi: taller, even more sharply dressed, and with a sort of crowd-pleasing appearance that made him look like he was ready to hit a campaign trail. Allegra recognised him from the program. Peter Black. At least Dimi was standing now—presumably to greet his brother—and Allegra's seat was free.

As they approached the men, Vanessa's eyes were on Peter. She gave Allegra a look that said, *oooh, there's another one??*

There's another one, Allegra thought grimly. She smiled brightly at 'the other one' in greeting as they passed closely behind Dimi to sit down.

Peter gave her an appropriate smile and a nod, but was thick in discussion with Dimi. Allegra pretended not to be listening over the loud chatter in the auditorium. "Helen told me, 'Make sure Dimi comes to Christmas', so I suppose I'd better do that."

Dimi scoffed. "Cheeky way to remind me I haven't RSVPed! Of course I'll come. I'll bring Prue and Tilly as well."

"That's the way," Peter told him. "Anyhow, thanks for stepping in tonight—good to keep 'Black' engagements nice and tidy. See you on Friday?"

"Oh, you don't need me for that," Dimi said with a chuckle. "You're the trustee, after all!"

He gave a light shrug. "I am, but deciding how much everyone gets is something I should run past them," he said, and then patted Dimi's shoulder again. "Friday, then."

Dimi nodded at him and then turned his attention back to Allegra's family. "Lovely having a chat with you all," he said over the hum of nearby chatter. To Aaron, he said, "I think we'll be seeing much more of each other." He winked.

Aaron *lit up*. Allegra watched him, all the air gone from her lungs. After Dimi had gone, he said to the other three adults, "Do you think that means I'm going to get the scholarship?"

"You haven't even submitted the application!" Timothy reminded him. "He's probably just being nice and implying that he thinks you'll do well."

"Maybe he can put in a good word for you, though!" Vanessa said, squeezing his wrist. "Who knows what he could do!"

Allegra smiled along with them. The rock in her stomach didn't budge.

The information night continued, with an older stately-looking woman discussing several international opportunities in Singapore, New York and London. Dimi disappeared towards the end; Peter was gone from his seat, too.

Maybe they've gone, Allegra thought, relieved until she looked across at Aaron. He was only half-listening, eyes unfocused. He was lost in thought with a smile on his face.

Afterwards, people were invited for drinks and canapés. Timothy apologised that it was well past his bedtime on a work night and headed off. Vanessa told them she had to take the boys to swimming early in the morning and immediately offered to take Aaron home before Allegra could.

She walked behind Vanessa and Aaron on the way out; they were already deep in discussion about which scholarship Aaron should apply for and what to include in the application. Vanessa turned briefly to Allegra as they exited the hall. "Do you think Dimi would look over the application and give us feedback?"

Unfortunately, Allegra knew the answer to that. "He would."

Vanessa brightened. "Amazing, Timothy can ask him before we submit it—maybe Dimi could even write you a reference!"

They were parked in a different lot; Allegra watched them disappear around the corner and into darkness as she stood on the kerb by the hall.

Then she was standing alone. Already losing her son. And she was *trying* this time; she wasn't just letting him leave. But he was. His foot was already halfway out the door—

Her breath caught in her throat. Halfway out the door. Just like Lachie.

Her knees—she stopped on the kerb. They'd buckle under her if she didn't do something. She started breath-counting.

Nearby, there were a series of stately black cars and staff. Beyond them, Peter and Dimi were in casual discussion with several other well-dressed people. Her breath-counting stopped.

Dimi's eyes lifted from the man he was talking to and rested on her.

She was frozen in place. Knees weak. Breath still. He excused himself from the conversation and headed towards her.

Lightheaded, she pushed aside every sensation in her failing body and forced a smile onto her face.

He looked so gentle. "Allegra," he acknowledged her. "So good of you to manage to get here tonight." His eyes met hers. "They've done very well with him. It must be a strange feeling, coming in at this stage."

Whatever breath she had was gone. She forced herself to recover quickly: this was a test. She had to at least *try* not to fail it. "Yeah. It's—yeah. I'm really proud of him. It just feels strange."

He nodded warmly, but his eyes settled on her face. "Of course. Pride can feel complicated when you haven't been part of the day-to-day." He put a hand on her arm—Allegra had to physically restrain herself from violently *shaking it off.* He was looking into her eyes.

Allegra could read nothing in his, not a flicker. Nothing other than warmth and concern. Did he even believe her?

He smiled, patted her arm once, and then headed back over to where the luxury cars were waiting for some of the guests.

Knees be damned, Allegra was out of there. She drove to The Rocks alone, putting on music to try and deal with the adrenaline. It didn't help: she missed a green light and got aggressively honked at.

Sal was waiting for her in the atrium of her penthouse, sitting stiffly at the central table, face drawn. She was in her robe, but there was nothing soft or welcoming about her.

She stood up as soon as the lift doors opened, running her eyes over Allegra as she approached her. Whatever she saw confirmed something. "You're shaking," she observed, and guided Allegra to the table. "Walk me through it."

As Allegra recounted the evening, Sal had her hand on Allegra's arm—but it tightened as the story progressed. Allegra's wrist tingled when Sal withdrew her hand and sat back. She was thinking.

"Did he believe me?" Allegra asked aloud, lost.

Sal glanced at her, frowning. "It's impossible to know," she said, then exhaled. "I suppose we always knew he'd do this."

That was no comfort. Knowing Dimi would do something and the experience of him actually doing it were two entirely different things. "How do we *stop* him doing it?"

Sal's eyes settled on Allegra. "Here's the problem," she said. "If he thinks you're uninvolved with anything I might be doing, it might buy us some time. But either way, he will set things up around you as a threat to me." Her jaw was tight. "There's a good chance he'll do something I've never seen before." Her eyes lifted to Allegra's, unguarded. "I have no idea."

Allegra could feel her pulse pick up again. She was relying on Sal for guidance here. The idea that there may actually be no useful advice to—

Sal's phone beeped. Sal glanced at it, clearly intending the movement to be vanishingly brief. It wasn't. She double-took and held her phone up, focusing on it.

Whatever she saw made the colour drain from her face. Looking up at Allegra, she stood, her chair scraping against the marble floor. "I need to check something." She spun and rushed upstairs.

Allegra followed her, heart pounding.

Sal sat at her computer, taking long and measured breaths as she copied the numbers from her authenticator and clicked into the log system. Leaning towards the screen, Sal's hand made quick, practiced movements with the mouse.

She froze. Her breath caught. She sat back, a hand running through her hair before she forcibly replaced it on the arm of her office chair. She turned towards Allegra.

"Dimi just swiped into Atlas."

Chapter 36: Controlled Conditions

On the screen, the line Sal had highlighted was *21:47:12 | BLACK_D | ATLAS_SECURE_ENTRY | ACCESS GRANTED.*

A chill ran over Allegra's skin. He'd notice the files were gone. "So that's it, then," she said, light-headed. "He's going to take Aaron."

She was back at the auditorium doors, watching Dimi move in on her family. And if that was what he did when he only suspected she knew about him and Sal—what would he do if he was sure? "Will he make them hate me?"

Sal looked up at her, silent. "We can't know what his first move will be."

God. She put a hand on her chest and felt her heart pound underneath it. The way Aaron had looked at Dimi. How easily Dimi had slipped into her chair. The way no one had noticed she'd gone.

He'd slip into the hole she'd left. Her family would fucking invite him. They'd gaze at him and laugh at all his jokes and think to themselves what a kind and sweet and generous—

"Allegra." Sal put a hand on her arm. "We need to discuss how to get ahead of this."

How could they get ahead of something she was already behind on? "Sal, he's already got them. I've been doing everything—what else is there?!"

"You're scared," Sal said. "But that line of thinking only helps him, so you need to step away from it."

"Oh, okay then! I'll just stop worrying that he's *stealing my family*."

"I'm not asking you to stop worrying about it," Sal told her evenly. "I'm asking you to set that worry aside for now so we can talk about what this changes and what it—"

"I'm not like you, Sal," Allegra said, sharper than she meant to. "I can't just switch off how I feel when it stops being convenient." Sal's eyebrows lifted—just slightly. Allegra realised she'd overstepped. She let her hands fall by her sides, jamming her eyes shut for a moment before she spoke. "But alright. Fine. What do we do?"

Sal gave her a long, hard stare. She moved on. "I'm going to think aloud so you can follow me here," she said. "The timing on his entry is a concern. He would have gone directly from the scholarship event to Atlas. Was it something you said? Did he think of something he wanted to check?" She shook her head. "We can't know. But, when he realises the files are gone, he will presume it was me. You, however," she said, "he will probably not automatically think you had anything to do with it."

"But my file is missing, too," Allegra pointed out.

"He's seen enough to know you matter to me," Sal said, glancing sidelong at Allegra, "so he won't assume I can switch that off. He'll assume I took your file to protect you. Taking my own will likely look like an afterthought."

"Okay," Allegra said. "So he'll think there's a chance I still don't know what's in them."

Sal nodded slowly. "For you, nothing should change. Keep acting as though you're oblivious." She paused, looking up at Allegra. "No matter what he says or does."

Allegra swallowed. "Alright."

Sal put her computer to sleep and sat back. "And for me," she said more quietly. "I think work is about to descend to a new circle of hell." She stood from her chair. "I will need to think about how to throw him off the scent of what happened." She walked past Allegra and held the door open for her; an oddly formal gesture given she was barefoot and in her robe. "The atrium's more comfortable than my office."

Allegra followed her downstairs, accepted a decaf, and half-listened as Sal thought aloud—her mind drifting back to Aaron. God, and *fucking Vanessa.* "Vanessa joked about marrying Dimi or Peter."

Sal looked up. Allegra expected her to brush it off. When she didn't, that rock settled back in Allegra's stomach. "She's very pretty," was Sal's deeply unsettling assessment. "I don't think either of them would entertain the idea—they care too much about their reputation. But I can see Dimi letting her believe it might be possible."

Allegra's jaw set. Vanessa would fall for that, hook, line and sinker. "She doesn't deserve that."

Sal sat silent for a moment, then returned her hands to her mug. "Let's try and keep them apart."

Just like I tried to be present this evening, Allegra thought. But—Sal was right, *irritatingly.* She *couldn't* think like that. "Maybe I should text them now," she said. "Say it was nice to see them, or..."

Something shifted in Sal's expression. "Text Dimi."

Allegra stared at her. "*Dimi*?"

"Yes. If you didn't know anything about him, you would have thought he was just being generous and attentive," she pointed out. "He observed you in a mess afterwards—perfect opportunity to thank him for his kind words."

Ugh! "Sal, I want to throw him *off a fucking cliff*."

Sal inclined her head. "A feeling I know well. Swallow it. Text him. And sound a little embarrassed but grateful."

Allegra felt *dirty*. She took out her phone, opened a message and stared at the keyboard. Eventually, she came up with, *"I'm sorry I didn't thank you properly before—like you said, everything's a bit complicated. Thanks so much for spending time with Aaron, though. We all want the best for him."* Sal nodded at the wording, so she sent it.

Then, she set her phone face down on the table and stared at it.

Sal reached across the table, took the phone, and put it on Do Not Disturb. "Trust me on that one," she said, standing up. "You should leave it out here tonight." She moved towards the guest room.

Aware she was being led, Allegra stood to follow her. Her hand hovered over her phone. Grimacing, she collected it and followed Sal.

Sal's eyes rested on the phone as she entered. She looked up at Allegra, her expression cool, and said nothing. Instead, she opened the door to the built-in robe, swinging a mirror out to face Allegra. Still in her suit, Allegra could see the sallow colour under her eyes. It made her look old and tired rather than dashing and sharp.

Sal approached her, hands lifting to the buttons on her blazer and slowly undoing them.

What are you doing? she thought, watching her—until Sal looked up from under her lashes.

Oh, Allegra thought, feeling it. Her chest swelled in a sudden breath.

Sal slowly slipped her hands inside the shoulders of Allegra's blazer, slid it down her arms, caught it, and hung it up. In her reflection, Allegra could see her parted lips and quick breathing. She closed her mouth.

When Sal returned and her hands went to Allegra's tie, Sal locked eyes with her. The sharp pull at her throat was—fuck. Now wasn't the time. Allegra put a hand over Sal's. "I'll do it."

Sal nodded, stepped back, and took the tie to hang with the blazer. She returned with Allegra's favourite old trackies and t-shirt, which had been washed and folded. By someone. Not Sal. Allegra accepted them, uncomfortable in too many ways to name, and left to change in the bathroom.

When she returned, Sal was waiting for her. She'd taken off her robe and was just in her summer pyjamas. On the bed, legs crossed, thigh visible almost to her hip. Tattoos out.

Beside her was Allegra's phone; the screen was still dark.

Sal stood and lay a hand on Allegra's stomach, her thumb circling on the soft t-shirt and then slipping up the side of her body to her neck. Then, she pulled her down into a tentative kiss—and, *God,* Allegra could have relaxed into it. Those lips were so familiar now. Sal's body was warm under the silk fabric of her pyjamas. But her movements were too practised, too smooth. Like she was focusing on them. Her hands were still on Allegra's body, and her eyes stayed closed.

Making a face, Allegra pulled away. "You know I don't want it like this."

Sal's eyes dipped to her lips for a moment and then nodded and stepped away. "Alright," Sal said. "Then we won't." She smoothed her pyjamas a little stiffly. "Would you like me to go back upstairs?"

Despite fucking everything, her response was immediate. "No."

Sal's shoulders loosened slightly. She rounded the bed to the far side, lifted the doona, and climbed in.

Allegra checked her phone—still nothing—set it on the dressing table, switched off the light, and climbed in.

Sal lay down. She inclined her head in an invitation as she turned her body away. Allegra understood, sliding over to her, slipping an arm under her neck and bringing their bodies together. Like this, it was easy to hug her. And she was so warm, and her smaller shoulders fit so well between Allegra's arms. Allegra could smell coconut again. She found herself smiling, letting the stress of the evening and Aaron and Dimi and everything soften into—

Wait. Allegra lifted her head a little. "Are you just doing this to settle me after everything tonight?"

Sal glanced over her shoulder. "You mean, allowing myself to be held?"

"All of this."

Sal paused. "Yes," she said. "I thought it might help."

Allegra leant back a little. "Well, I don't want to do anything you don't want."

"Can't I offer something because *you* want it?"

"It's not—" Allegra stopped. "What about what *you* want?"

"What if what I most want here is for *you* to feel comfortable?"

But what do you *want*? Allegra found herself thinking. "I don't want to have my arms around someone who'd rather be elsewhere."

"You don't."

Allegra frowned. "But you said you're only doing it for me."

"Allegra," Sal said evenly. "If I'm comfortable here, does it matter why?"

It does, she realised, and then felt deeply uneasy. She rolled away from Sal, looking up at the dark ceiling. The cool doona settled on her chest now that Sal wasn't against it.

Sal lay in place, still. Allegra turned her head on the pillow to look at her—at the slope of her neck, and the curve between her shoulder and hip under the doona. Her soft hair. Allegra wanted so much to lie back against her.

Instead, she kept checking her phone periodically until she fell asleep.

She jolted awake—the pressure of an abseiling rope at her hip, her hands hot from skimming the cord. Hair in her face.

When she opened her eyes, she realised it wasn't her own hair; she was in a bed, a plush doona over her and limbs—not all hers—gathered about her, a knee over her hip. Somehow, they'd ended up in each other's arms.

That was—alright, actually. She left the hair where it was, closed her eyes, and went back to sleep.

When she woke up again, Sal was sitting up in bed scrolling through her phone. Robe on.

Allegra looked over at the window; sharp lines of bright light cut around its edges. She checked her phone: *6:46am.* She still had no notifications. "He hasn't texted me back."

Sal looked up, frowned briefly, and then went back to scrolling. "Hmm," was her only comment. "And good morning."

"Good morning. Does that mean he knows it was bullshit?"

Sal's thumb paused mid-scroll as she considered that. "I don't think we can know what it means at this point."

Allegra lay back, staring at the ceiling as yesterday flooded in and settled on her chest.

He'd just—stepped in. Slipped into her seat and been welcomed by all. It was so easy for him. Too easy.

And that's my fucking fault, she thought, remembering the Kirribilli files. No—she stopped herself there. She *hadn't* known. She had been actively prevented from knowing. Perhaps she should have figured it out, but she didn't spend much time around children. She just assumed Vanessa, who did, would handle it. Vanessa made vague statements about calling him or having lunch, but no one had ever sat her down and said, 'He's lost without you.'

If they had... she felt it in her chest. If they had told her. If someone had said, 'He thinks you don't love him,' while she went to sleep every night after saying goodnight to his photo... If Aaron had done anything other than shut himself in his room every time she visited...

And Dimi had taken that empty seat because it was right there waiting for him.

Beside her, Sal exhaled audibly, knocking Allegra out of her thoughts. "Amazing. IT will be open," she murmured, swiping confidently on her phone and then putting it to her ear.

"Hi Jace," she said, sounding as professional as a recorded message. "Just a quick one for you first thing. I'm just looking at audit prep right now and I can't remember: if I wanted a full report from an access log with everyone's credentials, how do I create that?"

Looking at audit prep? Allegra craned her neck to check for a laptop on the bed. There wasn't one.

"Well, I can walk you through it," Allegra could hear the IT tech say, "but if you're busy, I can pull that sort of report very easily from backend. Want me to raise a ticket?"

"Yes, please," Sal said smoothly, and then sat there. After a measured silence, she said, "Actually, no, don't worry about a ticket. I think I've answered my own question. Sometimes it just takes another set of ears. Thanks, Jace." She hung up.

Allegra watched, frowning, as Sal moved from her phone app to email. Then she held the screen open until two emails came through: one with the subject *[[Your Ticket 1209: access log report]]* and another *[[Cancelled: Your Ticket: 1209: access log report]]*.

She locked her phone, and then noticed Allegra's expression. "It's breadcrumbs," she explained. "I think Dimi will presume I've swiped into Atlas and scrubbed myself off the logs somehow. If he finds confirmation I've been paying unusual attention to them, he'll focus on that instead." She let the silence stretch, fingers tightening slightly around her phone. "I don't want to go in today."

When she didn't continue, Allegra turned to face her. "Then don't."

Sal laughed once. "If only," she said. "There's a board meeting this afternoon, probably about the Threshold fire. Stupidly, perhaps, I'm going to prepare for it, even though I almost certainly won't be invited. And there are some other critical meetings that I need to be 100% for. It's going to be a long day."

They sat in silence again, Sal staring at her hands. After a little while, she smiled bleakly. "I suppose at least we can forget about Atlas now."

That—didn't sound right. "Why would we forget about Atlas?"

Sal's brow dipped; the answer was apparently obvious. "If he knows the files are gone, there's no point in wasting energy trying to return them," she said. "I was worried I was going to have to do something exceptionally risky. I'm glad I don't need to."

Allegra propped herself up on an elbow. "You'd figured out a way to get in?"

Sal tilted her head. "Well, *a* way," she said. "Atlas is also used for discreet crisis planning. I could choose a time he'd be unavailable to trigger a comms crisis, invite the VIP in question in for planning, and inform Dimi afterwards."

Staring at Sal, Allegra ran that back slowly. Trigger a crisis while he was—It hit her. "You mean *manufacture* a crisis!"

Sal nodded once. "One I was sure I could manage."

Just—*Absolutely not.* "Why would you do that when I could just pull the fire alarm again?"

Sal smiled at the suggestion. She shook her head. "Too risky."

Allegra made a face. Too risky to whom? "So you would damage some-one's reputation—on purpose—just to avoid me pushing a button?"

Sal was watching her, completely still. "I wouldn't cause irreversible damage, Allegra. They're my clients. I've carefully curated their reputations for years."

Allegra remembered how seriously Sal had taken the threat of her own reputation being tarnished. How Dimi had highlighted Aaron's tearful quote in the Kirribilli files, ready to load it into his gun. God, and Aaron saying last night: 'I don't want people to hate you, you're my mum!'

That was it. "Sal," Allegra said quietly. "What if their children heard the rumours and believed them, even for a second? What if their families, and friends, and—"

"People with a high level of personal wealth have a resilience about reputational fallout that makes them less—"

Was she serious? "People are people, Sal," Allegra cut in. "Cece wasn't magically immune from being terrified her son was going to die just because she has billions of dollars."

Sal's focus narrowed. "You're not comparing apples with apples, Allegra. We're talking about a reputational risk that I would very precisely control within—"

"You can't be guaranteed precise control. There's always a risk. And rather than letting me voluntarily take that risk, you'd force it on one of your clients."

"Yes."

Allegra's stomach dropped. She hadn't expected Sal to say it so plainly. When Sal spoke again, her words were slow and deliberate. "I would rather manage a false leak I could easily disprove than manage the public fallout of you being hauled before the police for an actual break and enter," she said clearly. "And, in case you missed the most important point: none of it turned out to be necessary. I am grateful for that."

Allegra shook her head, staring at Sal. "You would have done it, though."

Sal reached a hand towards her. Allegra withdrew. Sal didn't push; she fixed her with a puzzled expression. "Why are you getting angry over something that didn't even happen?" she asked, not unkindly. "I wouldn't have allowed it to get out of hand."

There it was again. That same wrongness as last night. That belief she could perfectly manage everything. "You can't guarantee that, Sal," Allegra told her. "You were so sure I was safe when you recruited me. You told me repeatedly how careful you'd been, and Dimi *still* nearly got us. He still might."

Sal opened her mouth—and then it closed. She watched Allegra, her throat bobbing.

Allegra could see she'd landed a blow. Sal's wavering filled her with a mix of vindication and unease. Barefaced, all her tattoos out. Completely open about—*God*—the shit she was prepared to do. It was like cradling a blue-ringed octopus.

Allegra couldn't stay here. "I'm going," she said, looking away as she got out of bed. She showered and dressed; Sal was gone by the time she left.

Allegra got in her car and just started driving—it didn't matter where. She ended up on a road north of Sydney, somewhere off the M1. The shoulders of the road pressed inward, collapsing the lanes until there was only room for one car.

Leaning over the wheel to avoid pits in the gravel hidden by dappled light, she slowed to a crawl. She squinted at the road as she replayed their argument.

Fuck. That 'Yes'. 'Yes, I'd hurt someone.' The horror at realising Sal would do that if she deemed it necessary—Allegra grit her teeth. She shook her head. Would Sal *really*, though? Maybe she only thought she was the kind of person who would do that. Or maybe she only *wanted* to be the kind of person who would do that?

Or maybe she'd do it without a second thought, and you're trying to avoid facing the fact you're completely gone for someone who would do awful things, Allegra told herself, feeling slightly ill.

Fuck.

And what was with last night? Allegra thought. *She'll offer up her body to me as a fucking service, but not under any other condition? Not as herself, because she wants me, too*?

Allegra was glancing upwards at the canopy, lost enough to look around for where the sun was but not lost enough to consult Google Maps, when her phone buzzed.

Sal, she thought, feeling a mix of relief and unease. She pulled over. As she reached out to tap the notification, she saw the nameplate.

Dimi Black.

It knocked the breath out of her. Of course. She'd been waiting for a text back from him. Fuck.

Turning the engine off, she lifted her phone off the cradle and unlocked it.

"Oh, don't worry about being a little out of it—comes with the territory. Especially when you're a parent of such an exceptional young man. There's a very bright future there." Allegra was processing that when another came through. *"With the right support, of course. That's where I come in. I'd actually like to invite you, Aaron, Timothy, and your lovely sister Vanessa to dinner tonight. I know it's short notice. If that works for you anyway, just let me know where you are and I'll take care of the rest."*

Chapter 37: The Knife

For a few minutes, Allegra entertained the idea of not telling Sal about dinner. After their argument, something lodged deep in her chest made the idea of going to dinner and leaving Sal in the dark ruinously appealing.

Too ruinously. Allegra had given her word: no more secrets. Not after how Sal's had felt.

And, worse, she knew exactly how it would land for Sal; she wouldn't make a scene. She'd say something sharp and understated, and never detail the impact.

She opened a message. *"Dimi replied finally. He invited me, Aaron, Timothy and VANESSA to dinner tonight."*

Sal's usual quick reply never came. The delay told her everything about how Sal's day was going. She was halfway back to Sydney when her phone beeped; she had to wait another 10 minutes for a fucking exit so she could read it. *"Of course it's today. I'll be in meetings until 10pm."* The next message read, *"Come to the guest carpark. Let me know once you're there."*

Allegra followed her instructions and drove into the guest carpark, pulling in beside a row of sports cars and prestige badges in her dusty old LandCruiser.

She texted Sal and had climbed out of the vehicle to stretch her stiff legs—wondering if Dimi's car was any of the thoroughbreds parked beside hers—when the lift dinged.

Sal appeared as the doors slid open. Despite her perfectly neutral expression, Allegra immediately noticed she looked more drawn than usual. After this morning, the last thing Allegra wanted was to feel sorry for her. Some treacherous part of her softened anyway.

Sal glanced around them as she approached. Allegra shook her head. "We're alone."

Sal nodded, glanced at the newer cars, then led Allegra around the far side of her LandCruiser. "Show me the message?" Allegra passed her phone to Sal, who read from the screen. She gave the phone back and let her hands slowly fall to her sides, eyes unfocused. Allegra didn't miss her wiping her palms on her pants.

Allegra exhaled. "I can't say no, can I?"

Sal shook her head, still not looking at Allegra.

"Fuck. Okay." Allegra looked down at her phone and typed, *"No, tonight's not too soon at all—I'm sure everyone will be delighted. Let me know where and what time."* She showed Sal, whose nod was more of a slow eye-close than anything else. She sent it, feeling gross. "Do you think I could ask him if *you* could come?"

She shook her head. "He knows I can't come today." When she finally looked at Allegra, the whites of her eyes were showing. "He's going to try and take you. He always does."

That expression. God. If Sal had been anyone else, Allegra would have enveloped her in a big hug. Instead, she turned and opened the passenger side door, taking a step up and in so she could reach her water bottle. She shut the door and held it out to Sal.

Sal looked at it, registering what it was. She stood there a moment, frozen, and then looked up at Allegra. The intensity in Sal's—

Allegra felt herself hauled downward and forward by a handful of her t-shirt. Lips met hers—firm, desperate—and she was pulled forward, spun by her cargos and dragged into Sal as she hit the LandCruiser. She groaned as the air was knocked from her lungs.

Sal's hands were behind her neck, her head, then at the fabric at her throat. Between breaths Allegra pulled back, noting the deep creases in Sal's brow, the hunch and draw of her shoulders, her wide-eyed urgency. It was quick, and rough, and uncomfortable—even slightly painful. But it was perfect.

And it was over almost before it started. Sal pulled out from under her, dragging her jet-black suit along the orange dust on the LandCruiser to break free.

Breathless, she looked up at Allegra and smoothed her suit down—the whole side of it, and probably the back, smeared in dust. Brushing it did nothing. Sal either didn't notice or didn't care. She took one step away from Allegra, and then another. "I—" she began. "I'm not—" She stopped. Then she turned and left. Her heels clicked on the concrete, echoing through the carpark as she half-ran towards the lift.

The lift doors closed. The sound of her heels cut off with it.

Alone again, Allegra stood in place.

She recognised all of it—her body knew how it took hold. That thud in her chest. The way her thoughts outran her. The way Sal had reached for her, grabbed at her—and those wide eyes. This wasn't new for Sal. It was bone-deep.

Allegra stood there a moment, listening to the distant sound of traffic. She couldn't go after Sal now, not into BSA. She lifted her phone. *"Come back."*

Sal replied with a screenshot of her calendar, packed until 10pm.

"Be late, Sal. Come back."

"Tonight: remember, you don't know anything. He's just an attentive benefactor. Don't touch your phone during dinner—he'll know. Come home afterwards."

Come home afterwards. Allegra felt that in her *own* bones. And she'd been sitting in her LandCruiser earlier, indulging the thought of not telling her. *Fuck*. She grimaced and then climbed in her car.

She hadn't even cleared the carpark before her phone buzzed. She braked to check it.

Aaron. Her heart jumped. *"Hey, Dimi asked me to pass on the details: Grand Asterre, top floor, 6pm (he said it's all good if you're a bit late)."*

Allegra stared at the message. He'd gone through Aaron. She typed back a short and appropriately excited response for her son's benefit and then headed to The Rocks.

The atrium was huge and empty—as usual. It felt even emptier today. In contrast, her head felt so packed full that nothing moved inside; choosing what to wear felt difficult despite the lack of options. She ended up in the black suit with the sage shirt, running out of time and simply giving up. She paused by the full-length mirror on the way out.

Her lips were still red from Sal's. Her skin still felt hot from the friction, and the echo of Sal's last words crept back in. *Come home afterwards.*

Those words stayed with her as she let Google Maps take her to the Grand Asterre.

It was a towering art-deco building in Potts Point. There was absolutely nowhere to park anywhere near it, and if she were late, she'd give Dimi more time alone with Aaron. She drove into the valet circle.

The valet made no comment about the state of her car—but double-took when he realised who it was. "Your keys, Mrs Sinclair?"

She paused a second before handing them over. Inside, a doorman collected her immediately and escorted her to a private lift. When it opened again, it was to a sprawling, decadent restaurant.

It was a vast room of glass, gold, and mirrored panels that stretched upward, its patterns repeating with unnatural precision. The scale should have felt grand; instead it felt deliberate, as though the space had been designed not just to impress, but to hold you in place. A beautifully gilded cage.

It was empty—except for one table. At that table sat Dimi, Timothy and Aaron. Already in amicable conversation. Servers dressed in neat 1920s-style suits stood unobtrusively around the edges like part of the décor.

She took a breath, put on her game face, and walked forward out of the lift. She knew nothing. He was just an attentive benefactor. If he thought otherwise, she was done.

Dimi's head turned towards her. His eyes settled on her. "Allegra! We've been debating something," he said. "Perhaps you can settle it. Is it ever acceptable to order for someone else without asking them?"

Is it ever acceptable to—God, who was he kidding? "Hi everyone," she said as warmly as she could, smiling particularly at Aaron, and then answered Dimi. "I live out of a LandCruiser," she pointed out, "so I'm probably not the best reference for fine dining protocol."

Timothy and Dimi shared a glance. Dimi laughed about it and turned back to Allegra. "No, no—no abstentions. I'm going to insist on an answer."

Ugh. Allegra had been about to give him one, but as soon as she sat, a waiter descended on her and unfolded a napkin in her lap before she could stop him. Her expression made the other three laugh.

"On second thoughts, perhaps we'll take you at your word," Dimi said a little wryly, turning back to the others. Allegra glanced up; neither of them seemed to have heard the condescension in it. "Now, Aaron, what were you saying before all this?"

She wanted to explain she'd just been surprised by the waiter, but it would sound defensive and it didn't seem to matter to anyone else. They were all relaxed, leaning back in their chairs. Allegra leant back a fraction later than the others.

"Oh, yes—" Aaron said, his focus sharpening. "There's a global environmental sustainability conference in Shanghai in February. China has some really interesting new tech, but what's even *more* interesting is how quickly their regulatory system moves. I was planning on going."

Allegra felt a quiet surge of pride—he'd chosen that, on his own. Her son.

"Their system moves quickly because the decisions are made in very few places," Dimi said, idly running a finger along the lip of his champagne glass as he thought. "Shanghai is an excellent market to be familiar with. There are a few people I might be able to introduce you to—if you'd like to step out of your conference for that, of course."

Aaron lit up. "Of course! That would be amazing."

Allegra watched, uneasy. That had happened very quickly.

Timothy had his arms crossed. "Can you introduce me to anyone who can convince me it's a sensible idea to tag along?" he said dryly. "I'll be relying on him to tell me what I'm supposed to be impressed by."

Oh. It was already settled. *Timothy* was going with him—to an environmental sustainability conference. Allegra felt that in her chest; no one would need to tell *her* who to be impressed by.

Dimi's eyes went briefly to Allegra, but he was speaking to Timothy. "I'm sure he'll just be happy to have you there. It's the kind of environment where it helps to have someone grounded alongside you." He looked back at Timothy.

While she was listening to their travel chatter, the lift dinged. *Vanessa*, Allegra thought, twisting in her chair.

Vanessa appeared in the lift, framed by the doors. Then she slowly sashayed out. She was wearing a (thankfully) appropriate pale blue dress and looked shockingly beautiful. Allegra would probably have admired her if she hadn't been completely aware of exactly why Vanessa had given such attention to her appearance.

"Hello everyone," she said, taking the empty seat beside Dimi as the waiter poured her water and set a napkin in her lap. Her eyes moved around the table. "Oh—Sal's not coming?"

Allegra thought of the carpark. She was about to explain how busy Sal was, when Dimi said, "I thought it might be a bit much for her. This is more of a *family* evening." His eyes settled on Allegra.

Allegra felt the blade and didn't react. "She's got meetings until 10pm," she told Vanessa as casually as possible. "She wouldn't have been able to come anyway."

Vanessa put her clutch on the table beside her. "10pm?" she said. "That's a bit nuts, what on earth could cause—" Her brow lifted. "Oh, that's right! That Threshold fire thing people are blaming BSA for, yes? So awful for that poor family."

The rest of the table shifted, each with some degree of discomfort. To Dimi, it was water off a duck's back. He waved it off. "Yes—Sal's made that her little project. She does like to keep control. Very effective, but there's no need." His shaggy white eyebrows converged. "That situation is very sad. A terrible outcome for that family—we've reached out, of course. People always look to assign blame for these things, but sometimes it really is just an unfortunate set of circumstances." He clapped his hands.

"Well, now that we're all here, let's get some drinks, shall we?" He looked across at the waiters. "Shall we open a Clos d'Ambonnay?"

Allegra had no idea what that meant, but Vanessa's eyes were as wide as saucers. It must have been expensive.

A waiter circulated, pouring everyone a glass. Dimi lifted his. "I have a bit of a confession to make," he said a touch self-consciously. "I do have an ulterior motive today—after all, my company is built on spotting talent. It's somewhat of a sixth sense of mine." He looked across at Aaron with an understated smile. Allegra watched Aaron smile breathily in reflex at the attention. "Aaron. You have a very rare combination of attributes. People like you have options." He lifted his glass, almost as an afterthought. "To the luxury of choice."

Allegra lifted her glass a fraction late and smiled at Aaron. When he looked at her, those big blue eyes hit with the same weight they had when he was a toddler. She held the smile. There was no other option; she couldn't let him think she wasn't excited about his future.

The expensive champagne just tasted like champagne. She didn't particularly like it but had another sip to be polite and then set it down.

Dimi didn't take a big sip either. Vanessa did. "This is *amazing*," she said indulgently, taking another.

"Have as much as you like, my dear," he told her, looking back at Aaron. "So is environmental regulation a special interest of yours?"

Dimi let Aaron talk, asking a question here and there—what subjects he enjoyed, what had held his attention the longest, and what he imagined doing with it. Aaron warmed quickly, leaning forward, more animated with each answer, talking about environmental policy and the kind of work he thought he might want to do. Dimi listened without interruption, his attention steady, as though he were weighing something rather than simply hearing it.

When Aaron finished, he nodded once. "That's a useful instinct," he said. "Policy gives you a strong foundation—but it doesn't have to be where you stay." He glanced briefly at Timothy, then back to Aaron. "People who can understand it and communicate it tend to move quickly. There are a number of directions open to you." He gestured at Aaron's neat appearance. "If you're a confident speaker, it should be public-facing."

Allegra could not have pried Aaron's attention from Dimi with a crowbar. "You mean politics?"

Dimi nodded once. "That's certainly the most obvious option. But there are many others: lobbying, a masthead position in a large, global charity—

" He nodded towards Timothy. "You're in early with some charity experience here. Or, perhaps, even diplomacy." He leant forward. "Where would be the most interesting place in the world for you to live, Aaron?" He glanced briefly at Allegra.

Allegra's stomach bottomed out. Aaron—moving overseas?

There were already stars in Aaron's eyes. "What a question!" he said, a smile spreading across his face. "There are so many places I want to see."

While Allegra was managing her internal conflict about him leaving Australia, a beautifully ornate menu was placed before her.

"Oh!" Vanessa said, finishing her champagne and lifting the menu, delighted.

Like many places Sal had taken her, this menu had no prices—not even for the à la carte. There was a lull as they inspected their options.

"So much to choose from..." Vanessa observed. Allegra watched her glance up at Dimi and subtly adjust her dress. "Dimi, you seem familiar with this place. If you were ordering for me, what would you choose?" That smile. *Vanessa.*

Timothy glanced up, and then across at Allegra. Allegra was acutely aware Dimi always had half an eye on her, so just pretended to be invested in the menu.

Dimi handled the question as if it were no more loaded than a comment on the weather. "Well, for Asterre, it has to be the tasting menu," he said. "The chef here trained in Kyoto—*incredible* fresh produce. Everything is very crisp."

"Sounds delicious," Vanessa said, trying to make eye contact with him.

Dimi politely avoided meeting her gaze, nodding once at the waiter to confirm that order and then looking at his own menu. But not before glancing at Allegra.

Allegra pretended not to notice. But there was no way not to.

After they'd all chosen, Dimi turned back to Aaron, steering him into a long and enthusiastic description of his volunteer work at Redeemer.

Allegra watched him. She'd never heard so many words out of his mouth. Under Dimi's attention, he came alive. The hopeful smile didn't leave his face. For most of his life he'd been somewhat monosyllabic towards Allegra; she'd never been able to draw this excitement from him. Here, he lit up. That was the knife.

The realisation of what this evening actually was settled on top of her.

She wasn't here as a guest—she was here for a demonstration. It wasn't just that Dimi had taken her empty chair: he was offering something she never could. And showing all of them what Aaron could be.

He deserves this, Allegra thought. After everything he'd been through, he deserved the world.

When their entrées arrived—Vanessa got *three*—they were back to the topic of travel.

"Have you ever been anywhere in Africa?" Dimi asked Aaron, inspecting his entrée. "I've been to South Africa a few times."

Allegra's heart jumped, but she treated the mention like any other country. She knew why he'd said it.

"Not yet," Aaron admitted.

"Lovely place," Dimi continued. "Incredible boutique wine labels there—they value old growth. Something Australia should look at more closely." He paused. Allegra was aware he was looking at her. She pretended to be interested in Vanessa's entrées. "That's how we met the Lategans, actually."

That was a jolt to the chest. Allegra immediately knew what this was—a test. And she remembered how desperate she'd been for even a scrap of information about Sal.

She feigned immediate interest. "It is?"

Dimi was watching her. It was all Allegra could do not to visibly sweat. "Mmm," he said. "They ran an event vineyard in Stellenbosch. Very difficult time in South Africa, of course. They were interested in the opportunities their new daughter could have in a stable country like Australia."

Allegra pretended to want to ask more, but to not know how. Fortunately, she was related to Vanessa, who straight up asked, "Oh, so you offered to take her in?"

Dimi smiled at her. "Well, Peter did. He's always had a soft spot for people in a bind—like you, my dear."

Vanessa gave him a coy little smile at the compliment, but it faded as her eyes fell on Allegra, who was still pretending to be interested. "Wait, she *still* hasn't told you anything?"

Everything Vanessa did was deeply embarrassing; this time, Allegra let it pass—it might actually *help* her feign ignorance. "She'll tell me when she's ready."

Dimi's eyes had been moving between them. They rested on Allegra. "She prefers to keep things to herself. Given where she's come from, that's hardly surprising—but she may not be inclined to change that."

Timothy had been watching the whole exchange with concern. "Some people find a sense of community makes a difference with that sort of thing," he chimed in. "Is she free on Sundays?"

Aaron groaned. "Dad."

Timothy inclined his head towards Aaron. "I'm just saying, being surrounded by people who want the best for you and the world is a wonderful place to open up."

God, they were *not* dragging Sal to a fucking church. Allegra cut in. "It's early days. I'm not expecting everything at once."

Dimi put a warm hand on her arm. "Of course," he said gently. "She's very good at keeping things at a level she's comfortable with."

That caught Allegra off guard. While she was processing it, Vanessa joined in on the fun. "God, so is Allegra though," she said openly, her cheeks flushed from the champagne. "She's such a commitment-phobe. She can't even commit to a house—she lives out of her car most of the time."

Allegra couldn't stop herself from glancing over at Aaron—he looked relaxed.

Dimi was watching her. "Mmm," he said lightly. A few small smiles—even from *Timothy*—and the conversation carried on. No one argued the point.

Everyone here believes this about me, she realised. *Of course they do.*

She found herself staring at her half-finished glass of champagne.

Don't, she told herself. Not here. Not now.

Before she could finish talking herself out of it, a shadow fell over her glass. She looked up—her glass was being refilled. Over the bottle, Dimi was smiling warmly at her.

She smiled back and took the glass, pretending to have a sip. She simply wet her lips.

The main courses were delivered with great ceremony—three waiters came bearing enormous white plates. Allegra's was a few slices of wagyu, a smear of something dark and puréed, and vegetables positioned with great care and very little intent to feed anyone. At least the rock in her stomach dulled her appetite.

Vanessa had something different where all the parts of the dish were artfully separated. "What do you think happens if they touch?" she asked Dimi. "Do you think my plate will explode?" She laughed prettily at her own joke, batting her eyelashes at him.

Aaron looked up when she laughed and then glanced across at Allegra. The question was on his face: are we okay with that? She couldn't give her *real* opinion, of course. She rolled her eyes and good-naturedly shook her head; of *course* Vanessa is flirting with him.

He brightened, relaxed, and went back to his meal.

She watched him for a moment, the rock weighing heavily inside her.

"Oh, dear. Craft beer for you again, then?" That voice was close enough to make her flinch. "I really thought I might change your mind with this label."

She looked back—Dimi was standing beside her chair, champagne bottle poised. Her glass was still full. He'd already looked over at the waiters to order it for her.

Shit. He's not going to let this go. "Unfortunately, I need to drive," she said, sounding as regretful as possible.

"I'm very happy to have my driver take you home." Smooth and immediate. No hesitation.

Allegra would rather *swim*. "I appreciate the offer," she said evenly. "Because so many of my possessions are in my car, I prefer to keep it with me." He watched her for just a moment too long.

Vanessa, now far too relaxed, had witnessed the whole exchange. This was about to go badly. "Don't bother," she told Dimi pleasantly, waving a perfectly manicured hand at him. "Allegra's very uptight about cars and driving because of what happened to Lachie."

Dimi glanced back at Allegra in brief assessment, before rounding the table to Vanessa. He filled her glass to the usual level—and then a fraction more. "More for you then, my dear," he said warmly, and then sat down in his chair, picking up where Vanessa had left off. "Lachie?"

Vanessa gave him a coy little smile in thanks for the champagne and then took a large mouthful of it. "Our brother, Lachlan. He died in a car crash when we were all at uni."

Dimi made a show of being taken aback. "Oh—goodness, I'm so sorry." He even looked over apologetically towards Allegra and touched her arm briefly as he sat back down. "I had no idea."

There was a zero percent chance he didn't listen to the interview with ABC Radio. "It's fine. It was a long time ago."

Dimi looked up at her. "These things have a way of creeping back in," he said, turning back to Vanessa. "It must have been so awful."

Allegra watched as Vanessa finished her—third? fourth?—champagne. Dimi refilled it without looking away from her. Allegra's own eyes were on the glass, unable to stop her from taking another sip before she spoke.

"It *was* awful. He'd just pulled an all-nighter after exams and took Mum's car out the next evening. He was missing for days, and the police kept telling us not to worry." She took another sip. "When they finally looked, they found he'd driven off a cliff. And Allegra was in charge while Mum and Dad were overseas, so—"

"*Vanessa*," Allegra said in warning, glancing across at Aaron. "We don't need to—"

"Allegra had to go and identify him."

It hit. For a second, she was back there—the cold, the stainless steel—then she was here again, with everyone watching, uncomfortable. Dimi's line of sight hadn't changed.

Vanessa took another sip, unbothered by the silence. "Anyway, that's the story of why Allegra is a very safe driver," she finished. "Also, why she went off the rails."

Timothy had been shifting uncomfortably in his seat for most of that, but Vanessa's final assessment tipped him into action. "And lucky for all of us that she did!" he said quickly, clapping his hand on Aaron's back. "Or none of us would be here celebrating Aaron."

Dimi had been watching all of it with too-focused attention, his expression carefully troubled. "Well, lucky for Isaiah that she did, too," he said. "And all the other people she's rescued."

Watching it felt like a slow-motion car crash. She couldn't step in without it looking like she was overreacting, or leave without looking rude. And she did *not* want to fucking know what Dimi was going to do with all this information. It wasn't stopping, it was just getting worse. Vanessa was giving him ammunition—bullet by bullet. That gun was going to be pointed at Allegra.

Or Aaron. Or Sal. Or Vanessa herself—or anyone. God.

Dimi asked Timothy something about their overseas deployments, and the conversation moved on. Without Allegra. She was still grasping at threads of it, unable to get a grip before the next person spoke.

Dessert was served: it was *black* ice-cream covered in gold leaf. Dimi looked a little sheepish about it. "I couldn't help myself," he said with a grin.

Vanessa examined it. "Oh, is there charcoal in this?" she asked, not really requiring an answer. "I suppose I'd better have my antidepressants tomorrow morning instead then." She cheerfully tested the black ice-cream. Her cheeks were too pink, and no matter how much she drank, her glass was always topped up.

Allegra was already trying to work out how to intervene without Dimi or Vanessa reading it as anything other than Concerned Sister—when Vanessa drove right back into the topic they'd only just steered her away from. "Anyway," she said to Dimi, not drunk enough to slur her words but drunk enough to give him a lazy smile. "If you think *Allegra's* off the rails, just wait until you hear about our other sister, Simone."

Allegra looked sharply across at Timothy. He nodded.

Dimi's attention didn't falter. "Simone?"

"Okay," Timothy said, standing. "I think it's past my bedtime. This has been so lovely—thanks so much, Dimi. What a wonderful place. Come on, Vanessa."

She was still lucid enough to know exactly what he was doing. "Don't be ridiculous, I'm fine," she said, waving a hand. "Besides," she said, glancing at Dimi. "I was just starting to enjoy myself."

Timothy deferred to Allegra to handle that one. She'd opened her mouth, trying to throw together something Vanessa might listen to, when—

"Don't the twins have swimming first thing in the morning?" Aaron innocently wondered aloud.

Vanessa exhaled. "*Yes*." Bullseye.

That turned out to be what managed to get her out of her chair. Well—that and Timothy; she was perfectly stable seated, but her heels were a little much with all that champagne. Aaron volunteered to help them down to the car.

When Allegra stood to follow them, Dimi put a hand on her arm. "Must you leave so soon?"

A chill ran down her spine. "Well, the main attraction left."

He inclined his head. "Let's get some air." He stood, moving out onto the balcony, hands in his pockets. Her legs stiff, she followed him out.

As the last of the day's sunlight bled from the horizon, the city lights began to glimmer on the dark water of the harbour. There was a warm, gentle breeze; in any other company it would have been a pleasant night. But even at a polite distance behind her, Dimi made the air feel used up.

"Aaron's a delight, isn't he?"

Her lips parted. "He is." She managed a smile. *He's everything*.

She couldn't see him, but the hairs on the back of her neck stood. She could *feel* him. "A young man like that could have a great many options," he said. "Placed in the right circumstances, people will respond to him. Opportunities, introductions—doors opening." His tone stayed light. "The people around him matter more than you expect. You want to be deliberate about who's shaping that trajectory. That includes who's around him." There was a long, heavy pause. "And who's around *you*."

Her breath caught. "You mean Sal."

He came up alongside her, leaning casually on the balustrade. "Well," he said, eyes fixed on her. "It wouldn't take much for someone like Austin to make the connection," Dimi said. "If someone tipped him off—you and Sal an item, and then Aaron, suddenly having doors opened for him by BSA..."

Allegra stared forwards. *If someone tipped him off*. She understood *exactly* what that meant: Dimi would do it. He'd do it *while* offering Aaron everything and then Allegra would look like the one who was destroying Aaron's life—again—even if unintentionally.

It didn't matter what she chose or what she knew at all. He won either way.

"Anyway, as you said, it's early days with you and Sal," Dimi said with a shrug. "You still have the advantage of being able to decide what level of involvement you'd like to have—or to be visible." He brushed something off his jacket. "I'm sure the two of you will come to something sensible."

He doesn't have to know we're together, Allegra immediately thought—and then realised that hiding it would undo everything Sal was planning. Being seen with her was the point.

She was already too late. "You want us to pull back from being so public."

"Well," he said. "I think it would be best for Aaron to be making waves because of who he is. If rumours start circulating that it's being arranged for him, doors start closing."

Over the balcony, a familiar laugh surprised Allegra—Vanessa's. She looked down. Several storeys below, Aaron and Timothy appeared in the valet circle with Vanessa strung between them. She was being her cheerful drunk self as they waited for their car. Aaron and Timothy were humouring her. Laughing, chatting.

They'd had a nice night with Dimi. They were already his.

"Lovely girl, Vanessa," he commented, sounding nothing but kind. "She's been through a lot, hasn't she?"

Allegra stared down at her. "Yes."

"I'm sure knowing Aaron's future has the chance to be secure brings her such relief." His sentence sounded unfinished. Like there was a second half he wasn't saying.

But Sal, Allegra thought, remembering her desperate kiss in the carpark.

But—*Aaron. God.* Allegra looked down at him. Watching his smile as he agreed with whatever Vanessa was saying, listening to his laugh. After an evening spent talking about a bright future with doors thrown open in front of him, he had a warmth and radiance she could feel even from here. He *shone*.

He deserved *everything*. Everything the world had to offer.

Beside her, Dimi smiled faintly. "So, what would you like to do, Allegra?"

Chapter 38: Closed System

Dimi had a gentle smile. His soft white hair moved in the breeze. And still his eyes on her felt like the weight of a firm hand resting on the back of her neck. He was waiting for her answer.

Below them, Aaron was softly teasing Vanessa. She was laughing, holding on to his steady arm. Both unaware Allegra was watching them, and of the choice she needed to make. The impossible fucking choice. "I'll speak to Sal."

Dimi shifted. His eyes didn't. "It will be hard for her," he said. "She may not take it well. Although I'm sure in time, she'll understand that you want to contribute to your son's life in a *positive* way now."

He could have stabbed her in the chest to less effect. "I'm going to go."

He nodded towards the door. "Of course. I know all this is very hard," he said. "Being in the public eye comes with a lot of sacrifices. You're a strong woman, Allegra."

She had fucking nothing to say to that; numb from head to toe, she pushed herself off the railing on shaky legs and headed towards the door inside.

"Oh, I nearly forgot."

She stopped, turning back to face him.

"Here." He took a business card out of his lapel pocket and handed it to her. On the front were his title and the stark, high-contrast lines of the Black Standard Advisory logo; on the back was *'Rosie Hislop'* and a mobile number scribbled in blue biro. "I meant it when I said we want to reach out to the family and offer our condolences. They won't believe it from us, of course," he said. "But if you reach out—someone already impacted by this whole horrible misunderstanding, I'm sure they'll take it better from you." He watched her. She didn't look at him. "Perhaps you will find a way to convince them to accept our offer."

A chill spread across her. "Your offer?"

"Mmm," he said mildly. "We're very sorry they've lost their holiday property, so we've offered them use of ours in Palm Beach whenever they like. Just a little show of goodwill."

Palm Beach? Pristine streets, ornate streetlamps, and manicured hedges? That was nothing like the beautiful wild bushland that had been stolen from them.

"Thanks so much for helping me with this—I want to make sure they understand we're not what they think we are. It's all just a nasty coincidence, but we'd still love to soften the blow." He paused. "If you could give her a call tomorrow, that would be perfect. I have a meeting on Friday with someone I'm considering as a contact for Aaron."

Allegra could see the blade glinting off every word as he spoke. She couldn't stay, and he didn't expect her to.

She fled down to the valet circle, trying not to look too much like she'd seen a ghost. When the valet brought her car around—*detailed*—she climbed into it, drove around the corner, and then parked across a driveway.

She needed to tell Sal. She looked across at her phone and then at the clock: 9:10pm. Sal would be in meetings, but she'd probably want to know if—*no*, Allegra told herself. Sal would hear it as the end of all her plans. And it wasn't. It *couldn't* be.

Rosie's phone number was in her pocket. That phone number was a time-gated ticket to Aaron's future. Tomorrow.

Fuck! She stared forward at her hands on the lambswool steering wheel cover and imagined them closing around Dimi's neck.

But then Aaron would never get his big break; she couldn't even *fantasise* about killing Dimi without worrying about Aaron! She smacked the wheel once with both palms. "*Fuck*!"

Only one thing was clear to her: nothing could affect Aaron. *Nothing*.

She couldn't stay here. She needed to get home.

When she pulled into Sal's carpark, she had no memory of how she got there—her mind had been on Aaron's smart suit and bright smile. And how much he'd *talked,* and kept talking. It was in her head all the way up to the top of the lift. She barely managed to rescue enough brain space to change, remembering all his bubbly chatter about his hopes and dreams for the future.

By the time the lift dinged, Allegra was seated at the atrium table. She had to excavate herself from inside her head: Sal would make sense of this all.

When the lift doors slid open, Allegra heard heels step out onto the marble—and then fall silent for a moment. Then the sharp click continued until Sal appeared in the atrium. She stopped there a moment, her eyes falling on Allegra at the table.

The dust on her suit was gone. Something about her was still off—her step faltered when she saw Allegra, like she'd expected the chair to be empty. She straightened and continued to the table. She sat across the corner from Allegra. "What did he do?"

God. Just having her here—like there was finally someone at the wheel. Allegra reached out for her hand on the table. Sal's eyes glanced momentarily down at it as Allegra spoke. "He's going to give Aaron everything," she said. "But he says it will be bad optics if we're together."

Allegra had expected Sal to hear that and interpret it; perhaps explain what they were going to do, how they should handle it, and what their next move should be.

Sal drew a short, shallow breath and released it. She looked up at Allegra—for too long. Her jaw was tight. "That's what he said."

Allegra nodded, watching the waver of Sal's brow closely.

For a moment Sal said nothing; then her shoulders slumped as she looked away. She nodded once; there was finality in it. "Give me a minute," she said quietly. She pulled her hand out from under Allegra's as she stood.

Does she think that I would—? Allegra caught her arm. "What—?"

Sal looked back at her. There was something ancient and tired about her expression. "You're not going to choose someone you've known for a few weeks over your son, Allegra."

Allegra didn't release her. Dimi did *not* get to dictate this. "No, that's *his* bullshit," she said firmly. "I'm not choosing between you two. Let's figure out what to do!"

"'His bullshit' is what we're all operating under," Sal said calmly. "You're living in a fantasy if you think he hasn't considered all possible exits here. He has." She looked haunted. "I knew this would happen."

"And you still tried anyway, because that's what you do." Allegra didn't release Sal's arm. "And *we* still have to try, because I am not going to choose!"

Sal looked at her. There was no anger; it was like she was reciting the weather. "Allegra. He will ruin your son's life, and he will make it look like your fault."

"*No*," Allegra said. "We won't let him."

Sal half-smiled; there was no warmth in it. It was gone quickly. She closed her eyes for a moment, and then gently but decisively, she peeled Allegra's fingers off her arm and went upstairs.

Allegra sat for a moment, stunned. She felt a hot flash of anger—at Sal. *At everything*. Why was she just giving up?! Sal didn't give up. She pivoted. She positioned. Unless she knew something that meant that—Allegra swallowed, feeling the question form before it crystallised. What if there *isn't* a way out of—? *No*. There had to be.

She put her head in her hands, feeling a deep ache in her chest for Sal. But when she leant into that thought—refusing the suggestion that anyone had the right to pull them apart—her mind landed on Aaron. How a bright spark of hope lit his eyes. How he *gushed* about all the things he wanted to do, animated and shining and joyful. All the things that Dimi would give him—

If she left Sal. If she took Sal's hope, her freedom, her happiness, and threw it over the edge of a—

A cliff. She swallowed, moving away from that thought.

She didn't expect Sal to come back downstairs. And she probably shouldn't go up after her—Sal had asked for space. But right *now*?

Allegra stood on shaky legs and climbed the stairs to Sal's hallway. The light in her office was off; not that Allegra had thought she'd be there this time. Instead, there was a slit of light spilling from underneath Sal's closed bedroom door into the dark hallway.

Allegra walked up to the door and lifted her hand, initially intending to knock. But—if Sal needed some alone time, especially now, wasn't that her prerogative?

While she was standing there, she heard the scrape of a glass being lifted from the bedside table. A swallow, and then another.

There was a loud *clunk* as she set the glass down awkwardly, and then a silence, too quick, like she'd caught herself.

Allegra nearly opened the door right then. "Sal?"

Allegra thought Sal had simply ignored her. She leant her head against the door—and saw two shadows blocking the light beneath it.

She took a breath. Even through the thick door, she could hear Sal's, too.

"Come on, Sal." Her voice was quiet.

She waited for the handle to tilt.

It didn't. The shadows faded, leaving an unbroken sliver of light on the floor.

Allegra exhaled—she felt a hollowness in her chest. And anger. *Fuck you*, she thought to Sal, even though it was probably misplaced.

She went down to the guest room, filled her arms with bedding, and took it back up to Sal's hallway to sleep there for the night.

The following morning, she was awake well before Sal emerged. It was impossible not to be. Her head felt like it was full of ants, ping-ponging between 'fuck him, he can't make me choose' and 'maybe Sal and I can find another way', until the door opened and light spilled into the hallway.

Sal was less surprised this time. She took a few precise, immaculate steps out of her room and looked down at Allegra.

"I brought a pillow," Allegra said from the floor. She tried a smile.

Sal's eyes were distant. She gave Allegra one last look and then headed off down the hallway.

Allegra lay back against the hard marble for a moment, then hauled herself up and carried the bedding back to the guest room.

Sal had a coffee ready for her by the time she sat down at the table. Allegra took a sip; at least Sal was down here today.

In body, anyway. Nothing she would normally recognise about Sal was present, except her neutral expression. Her eyes were unfocused. Her posture small. She *looked* like Sal, but Allegra wanted to both hug her and *shake* her. Where was the Sal she knew when they needed to solve this?

'If you could give her a call tomorrow...' Allegra looked down at the table in front of her; Dimi's business card was still there, with the Hislop phone number on it. *Palm Beach*, Allegra thought, curling her lip. *A free stay at someone else's mansion isn't going to make it up to Sean Hislop*. She remembered how he couldn't look at the camera, and the way his voice had cracked as he spoke.

She pushed the business card across the table to Sal, biro-side up. "Dimi wants me to call her today."

Sal returned for a moment, glancing down at the card. She lifted it, thumb stilling briefly at the name. "Then you should call her today."

Allegra balked at that. "Or I just don't call her. I'm not going to lie to that poor family."

Sal locked eyes with her. There was no malice in her expression, just certainty. "He's not kidding about taking out non-compliance on Aaron. He will do it."

Allegra set her jaw. "Then we don't let him."

Sal's voice was even. "The way we don't let him is by following his instructions."

She drank the last of her coffee in a single mouthful and stood. Just like normal. It was jarring. "You're really going to go into work? After knowing what he pulled last night?" Sal's eyes settled on her briefly. The answer was obvious as she took her mug to the dishwasher.

Allegra remembered her quiet comment yesterday, in bed. "Call in sick, Sal. Just for today."

Sal stood at the bench for a second, the decision already evident on her face. "That won't change anything. I'm going in."

"I'll be here. When you get back."

Sal looked a thousand years old in that moment. "Make sure you call Rosie Hislop," she said, and then headed for the lift.

Allegra had very little intention of doing that. Despite that, after she had a shower, she put the business card in one of her pockets.

The penthouse felt claustrophobic. She ended up in the CBD looking for somewhere to eat breakfast—and decision paralysis had her heading towards the café where she and Sal had had coffee last week. Which led her past BSA.

There were two police cars parked on the kerb. Allegra eyed them as she passed and then looked towards the dark building. There was nothing obvious happening nearby; they must be inside. Through the tinted windows of one of the cars, she could see briefcases. Frowning, she kept walking.

The front counter of the café was busy—it was coffee run o'clock, apparently—but there were tables free in the dining area. Morning news droned in the background as waitresses bussed food around and people chatted cheerfully to each other.

Eyes were on her, even here. People glancing at her, phones furtively angling at her. She couldn't bring herself to wave and smile while she was waiting for service, so she pretended to be really engrossed in her phone.

She had been scrolling her SES work emails—just in case there was something interesting in there—when the word 'Threshold' made her look up.

The TV in the corner showed an old, amateur thumbnail of an Austin video. "...self-styled 'investigative journalist' Lost in Austin appears to claim that all signs point to arson..." The newsreader reported it like the premise was ridiculous. The next image was the Hislops—drunk, in footy gear, laughing in a backyard with unmown grass.

Allegra went cold. She recognised Sean Hislop immediately. *That's* the photo they were using? "You've got to be fucking kidding," she found herself mumbling.

She remembered her meeting at BSA where a whole room of people had been arguing about how best to frame her. Probably some room of BSA execs—minus Sal—had decided how to frame *this* story. Making the Hislops and Austin look like a joke.

And now Dimi wants to use me to convince them it's all okay, she realised, feeling the shape of the business card in the pocket of her cargos. Fucking *nothing* about this was okay.

Around her, people were chatting and laughing. Several sets of coworkers. A mother and a daughter. Two people making eyes at each other over their breakfast. Everything was so ordinary.

And she was sitting here without Sal, about to morally bankrupt herself by doing Dimi's dirty work. She had to do it, though. Dimi's comment about having old friends at Macquarie University weighed heavily on her. And those Shanghai contacts.

"...We have some breaking news to bring you about an ongoing story..." The TV in the corner began, interrupting the usual low-stakes chatter of morning news shows. Allegra glanced up—a nasty car versus tree was on the screen. There were flashing lights all around it; the SES had been there with the jaws of life, by the look of the car.

Seeing the jaws of life and the twisted car stirred something deep within her.

She looked back at her phone.

"...Early this morning at 4:30am, emergency services were called to a serious single-vehicle crash on the Princes Freeway just south of Sydney, where a car left the roadway and struck a tree. Crews worked to free the driver from the vehicle. The driver, a father recently featured in a viral YouTube video..."

Allegra's hearing sharpened and her vision narrowed.

No.

When his photo appeared on screen, she already knew who it was going to be. "...Sean Hislop, whose family is in the centre of an alleged fire and land repossession scandal, has been transported to hospital, where his condition is yet to be confirmed."

Chapter 39: The House Always Wins

Allegra was so focused on the footage of the flashing lights and car wreck that when the waitress placed her breakfast in front of her, she nearly jumped. By the time she looked back up, the breaking news had finished. The hosts moved on with a brief mention of the Threshold fire, "Terrible luck to lose your property and suffer such an awful accident so soon afterwards. Our thoughts go out to the Hislop family," and then moved on to something else.

She looked down at her plate. She could only hear Sean Hislop's broken voice saying, 'If I'd known they were going to take the land off us...' The memory sat too heavily in her stomach for her to eat.

Her SES experience told her exactly what this was. Not speed. Not alcohol. A man alone in the dark, with too much in his head. One impulsive decision, one twist of the wheel—and over the edge.

God. There was no way Dimi expected her to call them now. She took out her phone and let her breakfast go cold while she figured out what to say. *"Just saw the news—let's wait until next week with the Hislops."*

"Awful stuff. Terrible luck to lose your property and suffer such an awful accident so soon afterwards," was the reply. Word for word what the reporter had said. *"Cece told me how comforting it was to have you at the hospital. The Hislops will benefit from your experience today."*

She locked her phone and put it on the table beside her plate. Of course. How could she have expected different?

She managed half a piece of cold toast and then gave up on the rest of it, paid, and left, slipping down an alleyway into a little park nearby. She looked around. Here would do, if she was going to fucking do it. She fished her phone out of her cargos, Rosie's phone number in the other hand.

Am I really going to call a woman whose husband has just had a very serious accident? she asked herself.

Think of Aaron, was her answer. She took a breath and picked up the phone, punching the number in and putting it against her ear. It rang for what felt like an eternity.

"Hello, Rosie speaking." Her voice was cracked, tired. She sounded *young*.

"Rosie," Allegra said automatically. "It's Allegra Sinclair. I know I'm calling you out of the blue—I heard what happened. I'm so sorry."

There was a long pause. "Allegra Sinclair?" Another pause. "If this is another AI call, I swear to god, I'm not in the—"

"No, it's me. I can meet you in person if that would be more reassuring?"

A heavily exhaled breath distorted the audio for a moment. "You know what? Whatever. We're at Westmead. You can come if you want. I don't care anymore."

Allegra stared forwards. That was *not* a woman in her 50s. "I'll drop past and say sorry in person."

"Okay," she said, uncaring. "Bye." The call ended.

Allegra frowned at her phone. She opened YouTube and went to *Lost in Austin*, tapping on the video with the roaring fire and dragging the slider along it until she got to the Hislops. Sean was interviewed, but his wife wasn't, and her name wasn't mentioned. She *did* speak, though, and she wasn't the person on that phone call. It was when the video ran forwards to the two children that her blood ran cold. Two teenagers in school uniforms. The oldest was a girl.

She ran the video back and paused on the girl's face.

Dimi had given her the number of a *teenage girl*. What the *fuck*.

She let the phone drop, her mouth open.

She wouldn't have gone any further if she hadn't promised that poor girl she'd visit the hospital. She'd have torn the card up and fed it piece by piece into that fucker's mailbox—well, okay, probably not. But she would have pushed back harder.

Maybe she still should. She lifted the phone again and opened a message to Dimi, her thumbs hovering over the keyboard to write, *'You're asking me to groom a family via A CHILD after her father's been in an accident?'*

His last message was still on the screen, though. And it was very clear.

She pressed her lips together, staring down at the patchy grass at her feet. She'd just have to make this *not* terrible. Perhaps she could be of comfort to this poor fucking family—and she could do it in a way that would benefit BSA and satisfy Dimi.

She could only fucking try. Jaw set, she headed back to the penthouse to collect her car and drive out to Westmead.

There was media at the hospital again—she expected it this time. She smiled and nodded sombrely at the cameras and headed inside. Reception sent her up to critical care; she knew the way because of Isaiah.

The family wasn't in the VIP suite, though. They were on the general ward. There was an older teenage girl slumped in a hallway chair, staring at her phone, dark brown hair a curtain around her face. Allegra recognised her anyway. She also recognised the closed face, the crossed arms, and the scowl. "Rosie?"

She looked up, surprise breaking her stormy expression. "It *was* you after all."

Allegra didn't even have to force a smile. "Yeah." It faded. "I'm so sorry about your father."

Rosie shrugged. "He's not dead," she said, bluntly. "I'm just out here because me and Mum aren't talking and he can only have two visitors after surgery. But it'll be ages."

Allegra remembered the photos in Austin's video. The four of them, sitting together around a campfire on the Threshold property, smiling and laughing. She shoved that memory aside. "Can I get you something to eat, then?"

Rosie shook her head. "Just say whatever you have to say, condolences or whatever. I need to go and get Dad's stuff out of the car before they tow the wreck somewhere."

Whatever you have to say. Allegra pressed her lips together. The last thing Rosie needed now was some glowing Palm Beach advertisement. "Are you driving up?"

Rosie shook her head. "I mean, I can. But we only had one car, so..."

At least there was *something* she could do here. "Do you want a lift?"

Rosie looked up critically at her. "You're serious?" Allegra nodded. Her expression relaxed slightly. "Well, it beats spending $300 on an Uber, I guess." Then her face crumpled. "But there's fucking cameras everywhere downstairs."

Allegra remembered her most recent visit. "Come with me." She led Rosie down to the back exit where the VIPs always parked. There were two or three black cars there today—but no one in them.

Rosie looked around and smiled slightly. No cameras.

Allegra's heart lifted. "I got a park along the river," she said. "Let's go."

Allegra had forgotten how much her car smelt like Maccas and wet cardboard until they both got into it. "Sorry," she said with a grimace.

Rosie looked briefly entertained. "It's okay," she said. "My dad's a landscape gardener so everything always smells like fertiliser in ours."

It was a smooth trip out. They'd missed peak hour; the traffic was light. Not wanting to cause *another* accident, Allegra focused on the road as the city gave way to bushland.

Orange witches' hats and 'Police Operation Ahead' signs lined the road. Allegra slowed, glancing at Rosie—she was already watching, brow low. A police officer waved them through at the sight of her SES-decked vehicle. She parked behind the Crash Investigation Unit cars and got out.

Ahead, surrounded by police tape, was the twisted wreck of the Hislop car. Grip marks on the driver's side showed it had been pried open by the jaws of life—he'd been trapped inside for some time. That did not bode well. Allegra knew how this went—especially with all the police. They were expecting to need to file something serious, maybe a state coroner's report.

She looked down at Rosie, whose eyes were fixed on the wreck. She placed a firm hand on the girl's shoulder. When Rosie looked up at her, her eyes were haunted.

Police stopped them at the tape. "Mrs Sinclair," the officer greeted her. His eyes went down to the girl.

"Rosie Hislop," Allegra said.

The officer's eyebrows lifted. He nodded slowly. "We can't let you inside—the investigation is mostly done but the petrol tank's perforated."

Hardly an issue this late in the event. "I'm SES," she reminded the officer. "We just need to collect his personal effects from the car, then we'll be on our way."

The officer considered her, smiled tightly, and went over to speak with the supervisor. She saw them glance up. *Then* the supervisor phoned someone.

"What are they doing?" Rosie asked.

Allegra watched them carefully. "Checking with HQ to see if they're allowed to say no to me," she guessed.

In the end, the officer returned and lifted the rope. "Just Mrs Sinclair, I'm afraid," he told them. "Safety protocol. Kit up. You're going to have to clear what you take out of the car with the investigators before you go."

After getting instructions from Rosie, she pulled on tactical gloves and stepped under the tape.

Eyes were on her as she approached the wreck. The Hislop car had been a bottle green ute with a business logo—now twisted beyond recognition with glass, various fluids, and plastic debris spread across the road. It was wrapped around the gum tree like it had melted there, with the trunk encroaching on the cabin.

It was seeing the shattered windscreen that hit her in the chest—there was blood on it. Like in the ravine. She held her breath; not now. Glass and plastic shards crunched under her boots as she approached the wreck.

She fit through the gap in the driver's side, brushing safety glass granules off the seat and feeling around the side of it for his wallet and phone. There was half-dried blood *everywhere*. The smell of it was both deeply sickening and hauntingly familiar.

In the end, his wallet was on what was left of the passenger side, and his phone was nowhere to be found. They might already have taken it if they suspected distraction as a cause of accident. She stood up out of the car, stripping off her blood-covered gloves. The police briefly took the wallet from her to check it, confirmed they had the phone, and then gave her a bag for the gloves.

Allegra nodded and walked back over to Rosie to give her the bagged wallet. She was about to say something, but her eyes fell to Allegra's shirt.

Allegra looked down. It was stained with Sean Hislop's blood. *Shit.* "I'm sorry, I'll change." As Rosie climbed in the passenger seat, Allegra went around the back of her car and switched into a clean t-shirt.

When she got back in the car, Rosie wasn't looking at her. One hand was clutching her father's wallet through the plastic bag. The other was at her mouth. She was looking away from Allegra, towards the wreck. Her cheeks were wet.

Allegra looked forwards at her own hands on the wheel for a moment. She knew that feeling.

"Thank you."

Allegra looked across at her. She was still looking at the wreck.

"You didn't have to do this."

Allegra watched her; as if she could do anything else. While she was trying to decide what to say to Rosie, an intrusive, creeping thought surfaced: *she trusts you now.*

Allegra sat with it for a moment, not wanting to follow it but knowing where it led: what all of this was for. *This is what Dimi wanted,* she realised. *You could do something with this.*

She could feel Dimi's hand resting coolly on the back of her neck. She knew what he would want her to do.

She twisted the key in the ignition instead. *Not now*, she told that thought. *Soon*.

The diversions left the road back into Sydney almost empty. Allegra was stuck between 'do what you need to do' and 'respect this girl's grief' when Rosie's voice broke the silence.

"Your brother died like this, didn't he?"

A sharp breath—"Yes."

She was looking towards Allegra, her voice so small. "What happened after?"

After. It was a blur.

A blur of tears, and shouting, and then silence. Of the tiny cracks that had always been there opening into gaping and untraversable chasms between them all. The beginning of the end. "Everything fell apart."

Rosie turned away sharply, hand to her mouth again. "Everything's already fallen apart," she whispered. "After they took the property, all we do is fight. Mum and Dad hardly talk to each other. She blames him because he took a loan against it for his business, which is doing badly."

Allegra could only listen, but it was like looking in a mirror.

"Mum thinks he was just tired because he doesn't sleep these days," she said. What she said next took effort. She was trying so hard to hold it together. "I think he tried to kill himself."

Allegra looked forwards at the road, swallowing.

"I guess it doesn't matter. Nothing matters. Everything is fucked. I'm supposed to go to uni next year but what's the fucking point?"

Allegra heard that *in her own voice*. She could have said those exact words, after Lachie died. She blinked to clear her eyes. She was driving, she needed to see.

She wants me to give her something, Allegra realised. *Maybe not to tell her everything's okay but—to tell her something. Things matter. Not everything is fucked.*

She wasn't sure she believed it, herself.

And yet.

Something gnawed at her. She couldn't make the shape of it. But there were a *lot* of police at that crash site. Asking questions.

If nothing mattered, no one would be asking those questions. It wouldn't be on the news. There were seeds of—something. Something was here.

Something. "There were police at BSA this morning, too."

That made Rosie look over. "Really?" Allegra nodded. Something flickered in Rosie. "Maybe they'll fucking do something for once."

Allegra wanted to tell her they would, but she remembered Sal's comment about how the law didn't stick to big corps. "I hope so," she said anyway, realising only as the words left her lips *that was the exact fucking opposite of what Dimi wanted her to do*. Her breath caught. What was she doing?!

Rosie was watching her. "Aren't you with one of the execs?"

It was like sliding down a moss-covered slope. She couldn't stop. She almost said, 'Not one that had anything to do with this', but it wasn't strictly true. Sal had done cleanup for it. Maybe it wasn't her fault and maybe she wasn't happy about it, but she played along. Allegra set her jaw. "I can have my own opinions."

Her voice was hard. "Did they do it?"

"I don't know. She doesn't either." *Holy shit. Allegra?!*

"Well, someone fucking did."

Alarm bells were hammering her skull. Some part of her was holding her, *shaking* her. "Yeah."

Rosie looked vindicated. "I hope the police fucking put whoever it was in jail. I hope they *rot* there."

Allegra felt sick. That probably wasn't going to happen. But what could she say to this poor girl who was desperate to hear that something mattered?

"Whoever did this deserves *everything* coming to them."

She dropped Rosie off at the back door of the hospital—and found the girl briefly in her arms. Those big eyes that looked up at her afterwards had a measure of hope in them. A tentative agreement somewhere inside her to wait and see what happened before giving up.

It made Allegra feel *sick*.

Once Rosie was gone, she spun back towards the laneway, hand on her stomach. *What the fuck, Allegra*?!

That was the exact *opposite* of what Dimi had instructed her to do! She took a few steps towards her car on shaky legs. She'd blown it. And soon, he'd find out.

But what was she supposed to do, tell that girl—whose hope was already draining out of her, lost—that BSA was great, actually, and they wanted to give her and her shattered family a free holiday as consolation?

No. There was no other way that could have gone.

That's it, then. She remembered Aaron's joy and excitement. His own eyes lit with hope—gone. He would slam his door in her face just like he used to.

She managed to drive back to the river. She turned the engine off, the cabin facing the swaying gumtrees and rippling water. Behind her, she listened to the rise and fall of conversation as people walked past along the track. She stared forwards, numb.

Aaron. *Do I have time to tell him I love him before he never speaks to me again*? she wondered. *One last hug,* she thought, remembering that big hug he'd given her at the Homeward event. One more. With Lachie, she never got that chance.

Hugs made her think of Sal, but there was no point in texting her. Sal would be horrified by what she'd said and done. She'd tell Allegra that she'd done it, now. She'd tell her to march into that hospital and try to fix that family's perception of BSA.

Allegra wasn't going to do that. She couldn't. Her mouth wouldn't say those words, not even for her own son. She closed her eyes. Dimi had her now. He had all of them.

He sat atop all of it. All that leverage, all of those connections. He stood on stage, charming patrons and the public alike. People smiled at him and kissed his cheeks. Students admired him, *Aaron* admired him. Timothy—a pastor!—deferred to his wiser opinion. Nothing fucking touched him. Nothing at all.

Yet, a small voice said.

She opened her eyes and sat with that for a moment.

Something—a part of her that said no, that's not right.

Her gut. There was something there.

It landed. *I broke into Atlas*, she realised. *Unless I told Sal, she wouldn't have known. If I didn't take the files, Dimi would never have known. I would have slipped in and slipped out of a system designed to completely prevent intrusion.*

Which meant—there might be a way. Something *outside* those closed systems. Away from how they functioned. A different system, on a completely different axis.

Dimi's rules were choose Aaron, or choose Sal. A fork in the road. But what if, instead of choosing a path, she simply stepped off the road?

He will separate us, Allegra realised. *Forever. He will make it clear that I did this, and Aaron will never talk to me again. To him, I will always be the person who ruined his life.*

Something heavy settled in her stomach. It stayed there, lodged.

She could feel exactly what this was going to cost. She couldn't make it smaller, and she couldn't stop the blade from twisting.

But doing nothing didn't mean keeping Aaron in her life—she'd already fucked up. It just meant losing him for nothing.

She watched boats move along the river, people walking along the footpath with their dogs, chatting. Children on bicycles chased by their parents. Allegra felt frozen in time, nursing the ancient hole in her chest.

As the shadows began to lengthen, she returned to the surface. If he was lost too, it should mean something. She would *forge* meaning.

Okay, she thought. *I'm doing this. I'm going to stop him somehow. How am I going to do it?*

There was no point going to Peter or anyone in the Black family. If that were possible, Sal would have done it. And Sal's comments on the law never touching BSA gave Allegra little faith that going to the police would achieve anything.

Dimi was rich. Respected. Frighteningly connected. There was only one thing that touched people like that.

But—he controls the narrative, Allegra countered herself. *He runs a PR firm, this is what he does, he has every fucking lever—look at what he's fucking doing to the Hislops and Austin.*

...But it was still on the news this morning. And people were still talking about it. She looked down at her phone and her YouTube app with Austin's video open: more than *five million views.*

She sat back, letting all that settle.

The story was hitting. That Threshold fire was supposed to be dealt with, cleaned up. Hidden. She'd seen how hard Sal had worked on things like this—*teams* of people worked on crushing this stuff. But the fire was on the morning news. Sean Hislop's accident was on the news. Despite all Dimi's vast resources, it was breaching containment. It was beginning to spread.

Her skin rose in goosebumps. *I can use this. I can do something with this. I can fan these flames.*

Flames.

Even as she thought the word, air fell still in her throat. That fire. Everyone was talking about the 'Threshold' fire. 'A terrible coincidence,' people were saying to him. But... what if she could show it wasn't a coincidence?

She couldn't prove who did it, she couldn't even begin to start. That wasn't her area of expertise. But maybe it didn't need to be.

One fire was a tragic coincidence. But... two?

As the idea crystallised, she was afraid to breathe. *Two fires. Two fires is a pattern. While it's still part of the news cycle. While there are police outside BSA. And—if there needs to be two fires, that second fire needs to go somewhere*. And in her stomach, in her core, deep within her and with every fibre of her being, she knew there was only one place that second fire belonged.

In a highly secure, top-secret archive.

That was something impossible to ignore, while eyes were already on them. Neon flashing lights in the middle of an existing media frenzy.

It was imagining how she'd actually light that fire that snapped her back to reality. She put her hands to her temples. "What the *fuck,* Allegra?!" she asked aloud, horrified with herself. *You want to light a fire*? *In summer*? *You've spent half your life preventing them—what the fuck is wrong with you?*

That creeping voice whispered back: *it's all concrete. That fire won't go anywhere.*

She shook her head—was she seriously thinking about committing grand fucking arson here? A federal crime?!

You've already committed one, she reminded herself, as if break and enter was anything like *lighting a fucking fire in an office building full of people*.

If I get caught, I'll get fired from the SES, she realised. Everything she was. That would be the end of her and Aaron. Sal would definitely never talk to her again.

But if I do nothing I lose Aaron and Sal anyway, she thought. *Don't I at least want a shot at preventing that?*

Her thoughts circled as the shadows lengthened. What if she did nothing? What if she did something *else*? What if she got caught? It was an unsolvable set of questions—every single option ended badly. Choose Aaron: give Dimi control and lose Sal. Choose Sal: Dimi poisons Aaron against her.

And doing nothing? That was the *worst* option. She'd lose both of them *and* any chance of fucking stopping Dimi.

And she'd done nothing before when it mattered. She'd shoved that wrong feeling aside and let her little brother walk right out the door and off a cliff where he'd bled to death *alone*. She never heard his laugh again. Never hugged him again. And everything, *everything* had fallen apart.

She was hovering by that same door now, her palm resting on the handle.

Her phone dinged, snapping her back to the sunset; her heart lifted momentarily—maybe it was Sal.

The name on her phone settled on her shoulders like a crucifix. Dimi. *"I saw you on television outside the hospital. How did you go with Rosie? :)"*

She stared at the message. Something shifted inside her.

She could only think of the hope in Rosie's eyes when she'd mentioned the police. When there was a chance *some* sort of justice might visit Dimi so the world would make sense. Justice would never naturally visit someone like Dimi.

That man dealt in shame, and blackmail, and control. He destroyed *everything* he touched. He'd consume Rosie's family. Allegra's family. And the families of *thousands* of people, each with a neatly labelled file, locked away in that house of horrors.

And he'd keep doing it, if someone didn't stop him. He'd even keep doing it to Allegra if she did nothing.

She let her hand fall into her lap and stared at the sunset.

Sal was wrong. The only way to stop him wasn't to try and outplay him, because the house always fucking won. It was to refuse to play and flip over the table, even if that meant losing her life savings.

That was it. The moment was now—while the news cycle was live.

She couldn't just sit politely and watch as the house took everything.

She was going to burn Atlas to the ground.

Chapter 40: Irreversible

The bright sunset had faded by the time Allegra got back to Sal's penthouse, leaving the atrium washed out and grey. Allegra sat at the dark stone table, cool lights above her, bracing herself for Sal's return.

When Sal finally got home—already wearing her reading glasses—she paused by the counter, still for a moment, noticing something was off with Allegra.

Here we go, Allegra thought, taking a breath to steady herself.

Sal took a moment to categorise what was off, eyes sweeping her. Allegra watched her, unwavering.

Sal hardened as she put her fob on the counter and slowly approached the table. She didn't mince her words. "What have you done?"

Allegra exhaled at length, spine straight against the backrest of the chair. Where did she even begin?

Sal's eyes narrowed momentarily. "You didn't call her."

"I did," Allegra said simply. "Rosie wasn't his wife. She was his teenage daughter."

Sal didn't look at all shaken by that. Her expression tightened, not with shock, but calculation. As if that made her *more* suspicious of Allegra. "What did you do?"

"I met up with her at the hospital, took her out to the crash site, and got Sean Hislop's blood all over my top."

"Allegra," she said very precisely. "That's not what I'm asking. Get to the point."

"Alright," Allegra said slowly. "Dimi wanted me to convince the family to accept the Blacks' Palm Beach property as compensation for everything." She leant forward. "Sal, you need to understand—that family is destroyed by what happened. A beach house isn't going to solve it. That girl doesn't need a holiday, she needs her family back."

Sal looked down at the floor for a moment, steeling herself. The hand she had draped on the back of a nearby chair tightened. "You don't have any control over that, Allegra," she said. "But you're throwing away something you *do* have control over: what happens to *your* family." She paused. "And you still haven't told me what you've done."

Allegra took a breath. "Rosie asked me if the fire was BSA. I didn't say no."

Sal's eyes snapped up. "*What*?"

"I told her I don't know who did it, and you don't either."

Sal *stared* at her for a moment, eyes hard. "You've lost your mind," she said. "You know what he'll do now, don't you?"

Allegra pressed her lips together. She did. And she didn't expect Sal to support her—that wasn't why she'd come. "I'm here because I promised I'd tell you before I do something risky that might affect you," she said evenly. "I'm going to do something risky that might affect you."

"Something riskier than the exact opposite of what Dimi asked you to do?"

"Yes."

Sal fixed her in a direct stare. "What are you planning?"

Allegra leant forward slightly. "I can't prove who lit that first fire, but it's all over the news. I've heard people talking about it—even people who know Dimi personally."

Sal sharpened. "It will blow over, he will make sure of that," she said dismissively, but had already latched onto something else. "Why did you say 'first'?"

"Because it won't blow over if there's another fire."

She knew immediately what Allegra was suggesting, and the colour drained from her face. She took a step back. "Jesus Christ. Is that what you did: light another fire?!"

There was abject horror—Allegra had expected that. She *hadn't* expected Sal to click so quickly. "Not yet," she said, feeling oddly calm. There was no point in hedging it. "But I'm going to set fire to Atlas."

Sal fell still.

For a moment, she stared at Allegra—openly, as if she didn't trust what she'd heard. When it was clear she'd understood correctly, her eyes widened. She shook her head in disbelief. "Are you *out of your mind*?"

Allegra watched her, unmoving.

Sal, in comparison, walked in a tight circle, hands in her hair. "Allegra, are you *fucking insane*?" she asked, taking a step towards her. "Do you even hear yourself? Lighting a fire in an office building—do you even *hear yourself*?"

"Yes," Allegra said. "I know there's a risk I'll get caught, and I'd go to jail for—"

Sal laughed darkly, shaking her head. "Oh, no," she said. "No, jail would be merciful. You'd serve your time and be done. If Dimi figures out how you did it, he won't turn you in. He'll prevent it. He'd *keep* you. You'd be a mouthpiece for him forever—can you imagine what *that* would do to your family?" She paused. "Or what would be left of you afterwards?"

This wasn't hypothetical anymore. "He's destroying my family *now*, Sal. And what he's doing to *Rosie's* family, and you, is completely—"

"Do *not* pretend this is in service of me," Sal interrupted her. "This is not what I want. I want you to banish this fucking *ridiculous* notion immediately and use all that goodwill you fostered today to get Rosie's family to take a holiday in Palm Beach whether you believe it's the best for them or—"

"That is not happening, Sal."

"—or not," Sal said, powering over her as if she hadn't spoken. "I want you to use that very smart head of yours to *really* think about what you're doing here before you do something irreversible."

When that didn't have the intended effect, Sal took a step towards Allegra. "I mean irreversible, Allegra. We're talking about destruction. You of all people should understand what you're saying."

I do, Allegra thought, watching her steadily.

When Allegra didn't respond, she could see a flash of panic on Sal's face. "My staff are in that building, Allegra. My life's work. *Everything* is in there. And you are proposing to *burn it all*?" she asked. "And claim that's *for my benefit*?"

"It's a concrete room, Sal. It's not going to spread beyond—"

"You can't make that sort of statement, Allegra. Neither of us knows what its limits are, and this is not how to test it," she said, her breath fast and shallow. "Do you know what temperature the fire you light will burn to? Because I don't. Do you know what grade the paint, and the steel, and the—"

"You're not going to talk me out of it, Sal."

"*Do you even know how, though*?" Sal asked her, hand landing firmly on the table. "How are you starting the fire? What are you using? Will toxic fumes fill the air vents and circulate around the building or will you—"

"I'm not going to use accelerants," Allegra said, only deciding that as she said it.

"What are you using, then? How are you going to light it in the short length of time you'll have? Have you even thought about it? Or are you still at the 'If I can't have my son, no one can have anything' stage? *How are you starting this fire you're so committed to*?"

Allegra opened her mouth—then stopped. Alright, she *hadn't* got that far. But it was a fire—she knew the types of things that caused fires, even if she didn't know exactly how to—

Sal guessed the answer and laughed once, darkly. "You don't know."

"It's a fire, Sal. I know what—"

"Well, why don't you ask Simone," Sal said sharply, meaning it as an insult. "You can compare notes on how you convinced yourself this was the only option."

...Simone.

Allegra sat up.

Realisation dawned on Sal's face. "Dear God. You're actually going to do that." She looked at Allegra like she'd suddenly transformed into a stranger.

Allegra let that settle. *I guess I am,* she realised.

Sal watched her. "Do you understand the position this will put me in? Especially if you get caught—but even if you don't?" she asked. "It's going to be obvious the fire was deliberately lit. He will suspect me!"

"If my plan works, that won't matter. Everyone will think it was to hide something about the Threshold fire. And you've been iced out of that. *He's* the one who's been doing all of Threshold's—"

"You have no way of steering public sentiment once the fire is lit. *He does.*"

"He can steer it, but he can't control it," Allegra said. "No one can."

"'No one' includes *you,* Allegra." Arms tightly crossed, Sal stilled. She took a few slow and measured breaths, trying to settle herself. There were more lines on Sal's face than Allegra had ever seen. "God. This is *beyond* reckless," she said. "You're going to risk lives, property, and your freedom—*without a guaranteed outcome*. I'm already associated with you. This will end up impacting me somehow. Possibly *worsening* my position with Dimi and the BSA board." She took a breath. "You're ruining *everything* I've worked for!"

Allegra swallowed. "Sal, you want me to sit and wait while you figure out the perfect plan to 'neutralise' him. In decades, that moment hasn't come," her voice was gentler than she expected. "Meanwhile, the Hislops are losing each other. I'm losing my son." *And other people I care about,* she silently added.

Sal heard all that and absorbed it, withdrawing slightly. "The solution is not setting fire to Atlas."

Allegra leant heavily against the backrest of the chair. "I have to try."

A silence stretched between them. Allegra stared down at her hands. Sal stood frozen in front of her, arms still tightly crossed, legs stiffly planted on the ground.

When Allegra thought Sal might soften, might shift a little, and begin to understand why her way would never—

"Get out. Now."

It was like being struck in the chest.

Of course. Sal wasn't built to burn things down. She was built to hold them together. She looked up at Sal; Sal matched her gaze, steady.

After everything. Allegra swallowed. "So that's it, then."

"You've made your choice."

Allegra nodded and stood.

Sal didn't move straight away; Allegra didn't either. They stood facing each other. She could see Sal take a breath like she wanted to speak—she waited. She waited for Sal to offer another option. Another chance. Or even to just fucking kiss her again.

She didn't. She didn't move.

Right. Allegra turned and followed a well-worn track to the guest room. Her bed had been made. Her clothes had been folded; her phone charger coiled neatly on the bedside table.

Before she could think about it, she started emptying her drawers.

The first trip she made down to the LandCruiser was just with armfuls of neatly folded clothes—more than she remembered bringing in. She tossed them into the boot of her car, shoving them back to make sure she'd have room for everything else.

The blood-stained t-shirt was still there, beside her bagged tactical gloves. Her eyes fell on them a moment before she went back up.

The next trip was for the suits and suit shirts—she deliberately pushed memories of wearing them aside. There was no point leaving them here, even if she wouldn't have any use for them on the side of a cliff. Or in jail.

After she'd filled her LandCruiser, she went up to do one last sweep of the guest room.

Like the atrium, it was empty. Grey. No sign anyone lived here; just like it had been when she'd first seen it. A stark room in an Architectural Digest magazine.

The atrium was silent when Allegra went to retrieve her KeepCup from the dishwasher. She cast her eyes upstairs towards Sal's suite; there was a light on at the end of the hall. She was in her bedroom. The door was shut.

And she wasn't coming down to say goodbye.

Oh. Allegra looked back down at the KeepCup, then walked mechanically into the lift, out of it to her car, and put the KeepCup with the rest of her cutlery and a big jumble of clothes. She climbed into the empty cabin.

She waited, though. Just a couple more minutes. In case a message notification popped up on her phone. In case it rang. In case the lift opened and Sal burst out, half-walking, half-jogging over to the car to pull Allegra into another embrace.

But it was just silent and dark. Streetlights filtered through the slats on the door of the carpark.

The realisation settled. *She's not coming.*

Still, Allegra waited another minute or so. Maybe she would.

Nothing but the distant hum of expressway traffic and the metallic clicks of her car adjusting to the new weight in it.

She's going to let me go. She won't even come downstairs.

She had a sudden, intrusive memory of Sal stroking her lapel flat and smiling up at her. That cheeky grin. And a weak coffee always waiting for her in the morning. The smell of coconut. The weight of Sal's head on her arm when they'd fallen asleep together on the couch. Sal's gentle observation of Aaron: 'He looks like you'.

The feeling was so heavy she could hardly breathe. *I would have given her everything,* she realised, throat tight. *I risked everything for her. I'm about to risk everything for her. And she won't risk anything for me. Not even this. Not even*—She let out a short, disbelieving breath. *Not even after everything. She's just going to let me go.*

She closed her eyes, her fingers curling around the soft sheepskin steering wheel cover.

In the end, this was her own fault. She never should have got in that black sports car.

She couldn't stay here. Wiping her eyes with her palm, she took her phone out. *Better just fucking do this.*

Dimi's text was still on her screen—she should reply to it.

Whatever. She dismissed it and opened a text to Simone. *"I'm coming over."*

"I didn't hear the magic word."

Fuck off, Allegra thought, closing her eyes for a moment. *"I'll be there in 30."*

The car door loudly opened, startling her.

Sal climbed into the passenger seat beside her.

Her breath caught. She almost reached for her—and stopped herself.

Sal glanced at her briefly. "My office was searched." She was holding a business card. It had the high-contrast BSA logo on it.

Sal was looking forward, knees pressed together. Her hands gripped them. "Do *not* mistake this for helping you. I will probably actively prevent you from doing it," she said coolly, fastening her seatbelt. "But if you're actually doing this, I'm seeing it first."

Chapter 41: Wildcard

They drove up to Simone's place in silence, turning off the main highway into leafy, narrow roads lined with large semi-rural properties.

She'd been relieved, at first, that Sal had come. That didn't last. Sal may have been with her in body, but she was withdrawn for the whole trip, staring absently out the window. Her phone wasn't even out.

Allegra didn't push; Sal had the right to draw a boundary around what she was planning. Allegra just wished that she wouldn't.

Gravel crunched under Allegra's tyres as they pulled into the driveway and up to the house—or as close as the overgrowth allowed.

Leaf-litter, debris, and a rusted car wreck filled the front garden. A glory vine had grown around the house and died at some point, its dry and brittle skeleton curled around the eaves and crawling up the roof. Gum trees hung over it, filling the gutters with leaves. The whole thing looked like one spark would take it up in minutes.

Sal spoke first. "How much are you going to tell her?"

Allegra probably sounded like Vanessa. "There's no point in trying to hide anything from her. She's going to find out when it's on the news."

Sal looked down at her lap. "I feel uncomfortable about this."

"Stay in the car, then."

She shook her head, looking down at her slender legs.

Allegra glanced at them, aware she might never touch them again because of what she was going to do to Atlas. And because there was no point in pretending they were dating for Dimi's sake anymore. "Are we still going to pretend that..." She didn't know how to phrase it.

"For the sake of continuity, probably yes."

That actually hurt more than a straight answer. "I don't want to pretend anymore," Allegra realised aloud. "Just don't touch me if you don't want to."

Sal was perfectly still. Too still. Allegra's jaw tightened.

"I don't want you to feel falsely reassured if I do," Sal said eventually. "I'm trying to find a way to stop you that doesn't make this *worse*."

All Allegra could focus on was the slight whisper of an implication that Sal *did* want to touch her; not what she should be focusing on when she was about to commit a serious crime. Logically, it would be better without Sal there trying to interfere. But fuck it.

"You can try," Allegra told her, unconvinced she'd manage to. "I want you here."

Sal looked across at her. "Alright."

They got out of Allegra's car; Sal rounded it to her side. *C1*, Allegra thought, her hand itching to reach for Sal's like she normally would. She didn't, and Sal didn't. Both of them avoided looking at the other.

A movement from the porch caught her eye: a figure, leaning back against the house, smoking. Eyes on them.

Allegra was used to her—if anyone ever could be. But with Sal beside her, she felt the impact of it again.

White hair, like Vanessa's, was loose over her shoulders. Shirt buttoned and tucked with military precision into straight-leg jeans, cuffs rolled up over heavy work boots.

When she stepped into the light, two things hit at once: how pretty she still was, and how the white lashes, white brows, and washed-out blue eyes made her look faintly eerie.

She took a slow drag of her cigarette. "You brought company."

Allegra wasn't in the mood for this. "Can we just go inside?"

Simone exhaled, smoke billowing in the streetlights. She wandered back to the door, opening it and spilling bright light onto the porch. Allegra had to walk through the cloud of smoke to follow her.

Simone stood aside and let her walk through, but as Sal followed, Simone stepped in front of her, blocking her passage and sizing her up. "Sal, isn't it?"

Sal smiled in the most pleasant manner possible, giving her a simple nod. Nothing about her invited challenge.

Simone considered her. After a few long seconds, she stepped aside, watching her closely as she said to Allegra, "Trying something different, I see."

Allegra gave her a tired look.

Simone followed them into the living room. It was small, crowded with heavy furniture—an old couch buried under books and schematics, her cracked leather chair, their father's ornate mahogany desk.

A toolbox lay open on it, with slender screwdrivers, cut wire ends, and something gutted from its casing. Allegra tilted her head at it.

It was a *lithium battery,* open right there on the fucking table. Jesus Christ.

"Want something to eat?" Simone asked them, noting where Allegra was looking. "I can get the BBQ going."

"We're not here for that," Allegra said. Simone seemed content to let them stand around awkwardly, so she prompted, "Can we sit?"

Simone—always with that *fucking* ghost of a smirk—gestured at her cluttered couch. "Of course," she said. "Please, make yourselves comfortable."

Allegra needed to remove all the books and schematics before there was room for them to sit. She dumped them unceremoniously on the carpet while Simone watched.

"Must be awkward coming out here. What if your fans see?"

Allegra released a stack of books so they dropped loudly on the floor. "You going to tell them?"

"Maybe," she said, locking eyes with Allegra as she and Sal sat on the freshly cleared couch. "Does Vanessa know you're here?"

Allegra didn't fucking answer that. "Can we skip all this bullshit? I need your help."

Simone grinned. "Yes, I gathered." She sat in her leather armchair facing them, resting an ankle on a knee and her arms on the armrests. "Go on." She gestured at her. "Let's hear it."

Allegra glanced at Sal, who was holding herself very steady. Allegra didn't even manage to get it out straight away. She ignored the alarm bells. "I need to start a fire in a building."

Simone began to smile like Allegra had said something intensely entertaining, then laughed once. "Oh, if Mum could see you now," she said, enjoying that for a moment, before hardening again. "Why?"

Allegra glanced at Sal. Simone clocked it, but looked at Allegra for an answer. Instead, Allegra asked her a question. "Do you know about the Threshold fire?"

Simone looked insulted she'd ask. "*Yes*."

"A second fire will make that look deliberate."

She considered that, fingernails toying with the cracked leather of her chair. She looked from Sal to Allegra in calculation. "At the Black Standard Advisory HQ, I gather?"

Sal's expression was neutral and pleasant, but her body was so stiff and the vein on her temple so swollen that Allegra wondered how long she'd last. Before Simone could notice, Allegra quickly answered, "We don't need to tell you where."

Simone shrugged. "You don't. But you just did." She relaxed into her armchair. "So you want to start a fire at *her* work."

Allegra exhaled at Simone. "Just tell me how."

Simone gave her an appraising look, then turned her attention to Sal. "How are you involved here?"

Sal was caught off guard. Her hesitation was noticeable. "I'm not. At all."

Simone's eyes narrowed. "Interesting. Because the Allegra I know wouldn't do this lightly," she observed. "She meets you, now she's everywhere. On TV. In your bed. Setting fire to your work." She looked back at Allegra. "Are you doing it for her?"

Allegra paused for a fraction of a second.

Long enough for Simone to interpret it. "You are."

"Simone, it's not what you—"

"So, Sal." Simone pivoted her whole body towards her. "Why is my sister lighting it if it's for you?"

For fuck's sake. "Can you *not,* Simone?"

"It's fine," Sal said, holding a hand up towards Allegra. She was very still, her movements careful. "Allegra's the right person for it. I'd make a mistake."

"...but you're not involved," Simone repeated, throwing Sal's earlier comment back at her.

Sal smiled. "Officially, none of us are involved."

Simone smiled back. "Nice save." Then, she added more quietly, "But if this lands on her, there's something you should understand about me." She leant forward. "I'm not afraid of jail."

"Simone." Allegra's voice was hard. "Don't. She's not using me."

"I didn't say she was using you. I said it's for her." Her eyes lingered on Sal before returning to Allegra. "But since you said it, let's go there. A fire gets lit, tied to the Threshold fire, and whoever she's decided should take the fall does. She walks away from it with her hands clean," Simone said. "And you carry that shit for the rest of your life."

"I'm actually doing it for myself as well, Simone."

She scoffed. "Sure you are. You love torturing yourself." Even before Simone said his name, Allegra knew where this was going. It always came back to this—even decades after the crash. "Who would you be if you didn't get to suffer over your perceived wrongdoing?"

Fuck her. "I know 'remorse' isn't in your vocabulary, but sometimes people feel bad about what they've done."

"At least this time you'll be doing something worth torturing yourself over."

"Fuck off, Simone. You weren't there."

"Did you push him out the door, Allegra?" she pressed. "Did you turn the wheel and drive him over the edge?"

"I fucking knew he was tired," Allegra said, her voice louder than she'd expected.

Simone let that hang in the air. She sat back. "I feel remorse if it's warranted," she said flatly. "I just didn't build my whole identity around an imagined role in something tragic." She looked Allegra dead in the fucking eye. "And then make it a child's problem."

That was—

Her mind blanked. Just—gone.

Allegra sat, breathless like she'd been slapped.

She surged to her feet—already moving. She might actually have punched her or strangled her—*something*—if a hand didn't quickly shoot up and grab the raised arm.

"Allegra." Sal's voice was quiet. Calm.

Simone didn't break eye contact and she didn't flinch. She sat, impassive. "Are you done pretending you're a better person than me?" she asked easily. "Can we go back to discussing your crime?"

She didn't want to. She wanted to walk the fuck out, leave this monster to her own devices... but she also wanted to stop Dimi. She let Sal guide her to sit again, numb.

For a second, none of it felt real—the room, Simone, any of it. Just Lachie's smile, Aaron's smile. She brute-forced her focus back to the task at hand.

Simone relaxed into her old, cracked chair, already moving on. "So. Tell me more about this building you want to burn. What's in it?"

Allegra took a breath. She described all the details she could remember about Atlas and BSA HQ. Simone examined her fingernails. If she hadn't been asking the occasional, pointed question, Allegra might have thought she wasn't listening.

"...So I'll probably have a couple of minutes at most to light it so the place gets completely destroyed. Is that possible?"

"Possible?" Simone inclined her head. "Yes. I could rig something that would take down the whole building in a couple of minutes. But I'm afraid it won't look like an accident."

Jesus Christ. That was—Allegra swallowed. "Just the archive."

Simone shrugged. "Then a small, organic fire will do. It connects them, even if it hardly burns anything. You can do that in two minutes."

A small, organic fire. "I can't get caught. If the police find out that—"

"Allegra," Simone said, like she couldn't believe she had to explain this. "You need to understand, the authorities don't give a single fuck. They'll *love* writing it off as an accident, especially if the alternative is investigating someone important in a very powerful organisation." She made a small, dismissive motion with her hand. "Even if you got caught, you'd get a slap on the wrist. Just enough to look like they've done something without making you tempted to spill what you know."

Allegra listened. It didn't sit right. She'd spent her whole life working alongside people who didn't look the other way—not when it mattered. Simone was just biased.

She pushed that thought aside. It wasn't the main thing she was worried about, anyway. "I just don't want anything to happen that would make Aaron find out."

"Guess you'd prefer I don't tell him, either."

Beside her, Sal went very still. Simone's eyes moved to her.

"Then you'd need to tell him you helped me," Allegra pointed out.

Simone was impassive. "I don't care if he knows that."

Something in Sal snapped. She put a hand on Allegra's knee—and left it there a fraction longer than necessary. "Well, that's a lot to consider," she said to Simone, and then looked to Allegra. "Perhaps we'd better think more about this before moving forward." She stood.

Simone was toying with a grin. "A little too much for you, 'Boardroom Princess'?"

Sal opened her mouth and then closed it. She smiled tightly. "I don't want to be part of it."

"You're already part of it," Simone said, flat out. "You think walking away now and pretending you have nothing to do with this makes you clean. It doesn't, and I don't care. So sit down."

Sal was still, but unreadable. "Simply listening to a discussion doesn't make me complicit in anything."

"What do you get out of it if she succeeds? What's her motive here?"

"There is no motive because she *hasn't done it yet*."

Allegra made a noise. "I'm going to, Sal."

Sal stiffened. She looked back at Simone, who was smiling. "You seem pretty comfortable enabling her."

Simone shrugged. "I'm not a fucking coward."

Sal froze, lips parted. She recovered herself much faster than Allegra had. "Well, I suppose that's easier when there's no one left to protect."

Simone sneered. She leant forward. "I burnt what needed burning."

"Dramatic."

"Says the corporate goth," Simone said. "I love your suit, by the way." Her tone suggested otherwise.

"I'd recommend my tailor, but she likes to fit at her shop," Sal said cleanly, without missing a beat. "So, you know..."

"Give me her details. Maybe I'll visit her."

Sal paused. She couldn't tell if Simone was bluffing or not. Simone bent down and lifted the cuffs of her jeans slightly. She wasn't wearing an ankle monitor.

Sal's lips parted. "But aren't you—"

"Yes," she said. "For now. We'll see what happens."

White as a sheet, Sal stood there, assessing her. Simone matched her stare.

"So," Simone said evenly. "I'm sure you'll be careful that nothing lands on my sister." She nodded at the couch. "Now sit down."

Allegra pulled gently on Sal's suit. Outnumbered, Sal sat. She was hardly breathing.

Simone ignored her and got back to the discussion she'd been having with Allegra. "There's a really easy solution to your fire problem," she said. "You said there are servers down there. A tower."

"Yes."

"Those things burn hotter than the sun when their cooling system is jammed," she said. "So jam it. It hasn't been cleaned in ages—it's full of dust. It'll catch. Terrible luck."

Allegra grimaced. "It looked pretty clean in there."

Simone paused, then stood and disappeared into the kitchen, returning with a tiny ziplock bag of something that looked like black cocaine. She handed it to Allegra, who examined it suspiciously.

"Carbon dust," Simone said. "Only use it if you have to, and don't inhale it. Dust from the actual room makes the forensics cleaner."

She went over to her table, grabbed her fat notebook, and drew a diagram of what to jam and where the source of ignition would be. "Put something beside the tower to catch," she said, and then sat again.

Allegra looked down at the drawing and the carbon dust. A heaviness, something like dread, settled in her stomach. She was really going to do this, wasn't she? "Okay."

Sal was watching her, still. At that, she looked away and swallowed.

Simone indicated the notebook. "You done with that?" Allegra nodded. Simone stood and took it from her, tearing the instruction page out and putting the rest of it back on her desk.

Sal's eyes were on the torn page. "What are you going to do with that?"

"I'm thinking sausages," Simone told her mildly. "Or maybe some lamb." She turned back to Allegra. "If we're done here, I think you'd better take this one home and put her in the thunder jacket." She nodded at Sal. She moved towards the door, in case they didn't get the hint.

Allegra and Sal glanced at each other and then stood, following her back to the hallway.

At the door, Sal hesitated. She half-turned to Simone. "Why are you helping us?"

"'Us'," Simone repeated appreciatively, like a proud schoolteacher. "You're getting there." She held the door open for them. "Isn't it enough that I want to help my sister?"

Allegra gave her a worn look on the way past.

Simone smirked and said directly to Sal, "There's nothing else on TV this weekend."

Allegra was already on the porch stairs. "Fuck you, Simone."

"You're most welcome." The door shut. It was dark again.

Simone not bothering to see them off meant they didn't need to leave straight away. There was a lot to process. Sal was strung as tightly as a guitar string, rigid in her seat and staring down at her knees.

Allegra watched her, wondering if she should start the car. When Sal didn't speak, Allegra fastened her seatbelt and put the key in the ignition.

"You said you'd be comfortable triggering another fire alarm."

Allegra let her hand fall away from the key. "Yes," she said. *Much more comfortable than having you endanger any of your clients.*

"It's too dangerous to use the same call point again," she murmured. "It's too close to Atlas. If he makes that connection, he'll realise how the files were taken. He'll suspect you."

Allegra watched her, frowning. "What are you proposing?"

Sal closed her eyes. "Something might get stuck inside a toaster in the staff kitchen."

Allegra pursed her lips. Not a bad idea, but not an option for her. "I wouldn't be able to get down the stairs in time. I'd need someone else to do it."

"Yes."

Allegra's lips parted. "You're offering."

Sal looked down at her lap, hands curling sharply at her knees again. "*No,*" she said immediately. "I don't know what I'm doing. I don't know if I mean that." She looked up at Allegra. "This is insanity. I'm insane for even *considering* it."

God. *Please*, Allegra thought. Because if she did, it would mean that they—*Please.* "How about I go and wait in the guest carpark," she suggested, not wanting to smother that spark. "If the alarm goes off, I'll use it. If it doesn't, I'll just use the same call point as I used before."

Sal relaxed slightly—but only slightly. "Alright," she said. "Do it early. Before there are many people in the building. The doors unlock at 7:45am."

"I'll wait until 8:15am."

Sal's eyes stayed on her hands in her lap; her crisp suit pants oddly smooth against the stained and torn passenger seat of Allegra's Land-Cruiser. "We'll see what happens." She fastened her seatbelt and sat back, eyes out the passenger window again.

Allegra's hand went back to the key. "I'll drop you home," she offered. "Assuming you still want to go home knowing he can just get into your house."

"I've always known that." She didn't elaborate. "Yes. Drop me off."

The drive home was quiet; traffic was light. Allegra's head was full of server tower diagrams, carbon dust, and how Aaron's expression would look if he found out his mum—bush safety veteran, famous search and rescue extraordinaire—had deliberately lit a fire inside a building full of people. Would that be worse than just thinking she was a loser who got in the way of all the opportunities Dimi wanted so much to give him?

Allegra didn't know. There was a good chance she'd find out if she fucked this up.

But if she didn't?

If she didn't, there was a chance they would *all* be free of Dimi.

She clung to that as she pulled up next to Sal's building in The Rocks.

Sal unbuckled and climbed out. The door still open, she straightened her suit.

Allegra watched her, holding her breath, waiting for *something*. For her to say, 'Come on', or 'Come up', or 'Stay'.

When Sal looked back at her, Allegra's heart lifted—just for a moment.

She didn't say anything. She just gave Allegra a long, searching look, her fingertips still resting on the passenger door handle. Then she shut the door.

Chapter 42: On Purpose

7:38am. Allegra was early.

She pulled into the guest carpark under BSA—empty, at this hour. At least it meant she didn't have to worry about scraping Lamborghinis with her giant dusty LandCruiser as she parked. Engine off, she sat to wait.

Sal hadn't texted her. After last night, she hadn't really expected her to. But she'd checked her phone throughout the night, just in case.

She didn't know what that silence meant regarding Sal's potential offer to trigger the alarm, though—*I'll know soon*, she thought, settling back in her seat. 7:41am.

Before long, cars started to pull past her. A BMW. A Lexus. Her LandCruiser stood out. *I'm a client here,* she tried to reassure herself. *I might be recognisable, but no one has any reason to believe I'm about to light a fire in the building.*

She put her hand to her pocket, feeling the outline of the carbon dust zip lock bag.

8:02am. Her phone dinged, startling her. She reached for it automatically—perhaps Sal had—

Zoe. She exhaled, and tapped the notification. *"Hey you two—some fun stuff this morning. Thought you'd enjoy it."* Below were a few links. The first few were short videos about them—still referencing the camping compilation—and the last was a photo of Allegra's LandCruiser with the tent up on Harrington Street and a series of comments like, *"closest thing to the great outdoors you can get in The Rocks", "ngl that setup would go for $1000/week on Rentaroo"*, and *"this is what 'it's complicated' looks like in the Sydney housing market"*.

'It's complicated'. It wasn't complicated. Not to Allegra. *Come through for me today*, she willed Sal, wondering if she'd opened Zoe's message.

8:05am. 10 minutes left. She checked her hair in the visor—tight bun, no stray hairs. Military-grade. *Simone is probably spamming refresh on the RFS Pager now,* she thought. *I should have bought that bitch some popcorn.*

She docked her phone back in the central console, staring at the dark screen. She knew she couldn't bring it in with her. A small voice was saying *what if you need it while you're in there?* Allegra pushed it away. She had a watch. It would have to do.

8:11am. She stared at the clock on her dash. *Maybe she won't do it after all,* Allegra realised. *But she got in the car last night and insisted on seeing Simone with me. That means something, right?*

Yeah, it means she's trying to stop you. Exactly like she said, Allegra told herself. *Maybe you should just believe her. Maybe in a second, you'll be swarmed by cops.*

8:13am. She stared at the dash, watching the numbers tick over.

Sal got in the car last night, Allegra reminded herself. *But then she left you on the street,* another voice reminded her.

Maybe she doesn't want to give me false hope, Allegra countered—then realised what that meant. No alarm.

But would she really let me do this by myself? Even after Simone threatened her? Even if she didn't *care*?

The last digit on the clock ticked to 8:14am. An inevitability settled in the pit of her stomach. She knew how this was going to go. Still. She had until 8:15am, Allegra would wait until—

8:15am.

A sense of clarity settled on her.

She didn't come through for me, Allegra realised, feeling it in her throat. In her chest. That was probably it for them, then—this was Sal's line.

I wonder if Simone will really hurt her if something happens to me, she thought. She didn't want that for Sal. Even if Sal wasn't prepared to follow her where she needed to go. She was too embedded in BSA. She wouldn't do it. Allegra would.

Checking her pockets again—just to be sure—she slid out of the LandCruiser. She couldn't enter without a pass unless the alarm was triggered; she'd have to go through the main building. Last time she'd done that without a suit, she'd stood out—and with luxury cars pulling in, she couldn't get changed here either.

Fuck. At least if she was acting alone, she could spend two minutes changing in the toilets.

She retrieved her suit—pushing aside a memory of Sal's hands on it—and folded it over her arm.

Once inside, she made a beeline to the ground floor toilets and entered alongside a young woman, probably freshly out of uni. Hair in a neat bun, perfect makeup and suit. However, her eyes were far too bright and that smile was far too big. Allegra had a sinking feeling she knew what that meant.

"Oh!" She sounded so young. Like Aaron. "Oh my god—*Allegra*?"

Fuck. "Good morning," Allegra told her with one of Sal's pleasant smiles.

"Oh my god, sorry, I don't want to be weird, I just—hi. Good morning."

"It's fine," Allegra told her, even though it wasn't. She headed towards a stall.

The woman stopped just slightly in her way, smiling hopefully up at her. "Are you here to see Sal?"

Sal... "Sure am," she lied, and then gestured at the suit. "Just need to get changed first."

The woman's eyes dipped to the suit. Something occurred to her. "Oh—you're using the downstairs bathrooms? The executive ones are nicer. That's where we usually take clients."

"I live in the bush," Allegra reminded her. "Having a bathroom at all is a luxury. These will be fine." She tried to get past—the woman didn't move.

"Oh, it's no problem, I can take you up there if you like?" she offered. "They're on 35. It's a *really* nice floor."

And really far from the basement, Allegra thought, looking past her to the stalls. *What the fuck do I do?* The last thing she wanted was to be suspicious—would refusing look suspicious? And who would refuse it to the point of being rude?

Probably not Allegra Sinclair™. Fuck. She'd lose five to seven minutes. Hopefully that was okay; although the more people arrived, the longer it would take to evacuate if the fire spread. Better do this quickly. "Well, since you're offering."

The woman looked like all her Christmases had come at once. She led Allegra out of the toilets and over to the lifts, merrily chatting; Allegra could hardly pay any attention. People were looking at her. People would know she was here.

The girl swiped the lift to unlock it—that was odd. As they stepped in and the door closed, Allegra realised there was only one floor button. "You need to swipe in?"

"Oh yeah, the CEO's suite and some of the other executive offices are up there, so it's secure."

The CEO—*Dimi*. This girl was taking her to Dimi's floor. The lift was already moving. It was too late to slam the *'Open Doors'* button or step out. And it was express.

"So, you just wanted to sleep outdoors last night, I suppose?"

Allegra looked at her blankly. "I'm sorry?"

She looked a little bashful. "The rooftop. It's all over Insta that you slept in it last night."

Allegra was too thrown to even come up with a lie. "I was tired and it was easy."

The girl kept talking. Allegra barely heard her as the lift climbed. "It must be *so cool* to just be home wherever you—"

The lift stopped.

For a moment, Allegra expected the doors to open. For Dimi to be standing there, face-to-face with her, knowing *exactly* what she was about to do. But the floor counter read 28.

Then, the lights shut off. Only a fluorescent strip around the perimeter remained. The lift display screen went blank, and then *'Emergency Mode'* appeared.

The lift was already descending when she heard it—through the speakers, outside the lift—

The fire alarm.

God, she nearly teared up. Sal had done it. She'd done it after all.

The girl's eyebrows were up. "Weird," she said. "We normally do drills on Tuesdays? Maybe someone burnt something."

Maybe something got stuck in the toaster, Allegra thought, glancing at her watch: 8:21am. "Oh well, if it's just an accident, it will be over shortly," she said, her pulse picking up. It would only take security a few minutes to determine if it *was* a false alarm.

When they reached the ground floor, the woman split off from her. "I'm so sorry, can you find your way to the assembly area? I'm going to use the ladies' before they don't let us."

Normally she'd joke about being shown how to respond to a fire alarm. Not now. She managed a thin smile. Alone finally, she ran at full pelt to the carpark.

There was no one in it. She tossed her suit in the car, locked it, and made a beeline for the basement door. When she opened it, the fire alarm hit her—punishing, shrill. She couldn't think about that now.

She checked her watch—8:22am—and let the door fall shut behind her as she ran towards Atlas.

Inside the room was warmer than the corridor. Disoriented by the change in plans and the loud alarm, it took her a second too long to figure out what the fuck to do in this dark, strip-lit hellhole. Okay.

She pulled on latex gloves as she ran to the compactus and grabbed a stack of files, ferrying them over beside the server. She needed to do a couple of trips before there was enough to sustain a fire.

Then came the dust. There wasn't much. She scraped what she could—from files, corners, under the compactus—and checked the tiny handful in the light. Fuck, so little? It would have to do.

As she approached the server tower again, she could feel the heat radiating from it. She looked for the opening mechanism—and realised it was locked. Stomach dropping, she bent down to examine the bolts keeping the case shut: they were soldered. *Shit.*

8:24am. The ignition was at the base, though. Maybe she could—? Carefully protecting the precious dust, she lowered herself onto her side and shuffled behind the server to where the exhaust fans were. There were bigger gaps in the case here to allow airflow—big enough for a woman to get her fingers into it. And a pen.

She fished a pen out of her pocket and followed Simone's instructions to jam the fan.

With her fourth and fifth fingers, she fed the dust through the still fan to the ignition point. It was already hot, and the gloves meant she couldn't pull back quickly. She'd have to be careful.

She lay there on her side, eyes half-closed against the heat, watching the ignition point. Waiting. Waiting for it to be hot enough to catch.

She craned her neck at her watch: 8:25am.

If it was a real kitchen fire—especially with smoke—security would let the firies clear the room. If that was the case, she probably had a good five minutes. But if it was just a manual trigger, security would clear it fast—she was probably already out of time.

Without her phone, she couldn't check dispatch. A little voice in her head was saying *you should leave now before you get caught.*

That voice had a point. She didn't have time to waste. She'd just have to use the carbon dust to guarantee this would work. As her watch ticked to 8:26am, she fished out the zip lock bag Simone had given her and held it to the light. All the dust was still there.

Work your magic, she thought, opening it and trying to figure out how to get it past the fan.

She couldn't pour it there—she couldn't both hold it *and* fit two fingers into the holes. She tried feeding it in bit by bit, but it stuck to her latex gloves.

She was tempted to try blowing it in—but Simone had probably grievously understated how dangerous it was to inhale. She didn't want to make it airborne.

The bag was empty before almost any of it was behind the fan; stuck to her gloves, on the bottom of the case, or—fuck knows where. Somewhere. Not where it needed to be, not doing the magic it was supposed to do. Doing nothing. The fire wasn't starting.

Fuck. She sat up—managing to prevent herself from peeling off her *stupid fucking gloves* and throwing them somewhere.

She looked at her watch: 8:28am. The firies would probably already be here. The window of time she had for a fire to catch *during* the alarm was closing fast.

She was going to get trapped in here, and that was *way* worse than this just not working. She'd just have to try again at the next opportunity.

Her body moved before she did, rolling her upright and driving her towards the door.

As she got there, though, as her hand hovered over the handle—she stopped. Was she really going to walk out this door?

Sal wouldn't give her another chance to get this right. She almost didn't give her *this* chance.

And you won't do it again, either, she knew. *If it doesn't work, Dimi has you trapped. And Aaron. He will keep going—keep pressing*. As long as she had anything to do with Sal. Or maybe forever, if he thought she knew Sal's secret about him.

She remembered that cold feeling of his presence behind her. The hair standing on the back of her neck. Is that what she wanted?

She dropped her hand and turned back towards the room. Everything was hanging on this fire. She just had to keep trying.

8:30am. She rushed over to the compactus and scraped more dust off the files. There was almost nothing there in the first place—let alone any left for a second attempt. She collected it from under the keyboards and inside the printer. Climbed up on the compactus to get it from the top of the power cables. The room was so fucking clean—but what could she do? She rushed back to the server.

The heat around it was getting oppressive. It hurt her face to lie beside the vents and the grate was hot enough to burn as she fed the paltry amount of dust past the fan.

She lay, shoulder on the hot floor, neck straining, staring at the ignition point.

Nothing. The warm smell of hot electronics. Her fingers tingled as she blew on them.

She could see the fucking ignition point—or at least, the piece of metal it was hidden behind. If she could just get her finger—

She froze. Her body was tense, drawn, before she could figure out why it had suddenly—

A tiny sting, sharp in her nostrils. *Smoke*.

Adrenaline flooded her; her body had a hundred memories of thick smoke, orange embers, and stinging eyes. Her legs shook, ready to go. She resisted, lying perfectly still on her side, staring at the ignition point.

She saw it. A tiny flicker that wasn't the server lights.

Oh my God, she thought, and pulled a piece of paper out of the files, rolling it, feeding it in. It caught, orange flame climbing up the roll. She fed another in. Then another. When there was enough burning to hold, she sat back.

Only one more hurdle: unjamming the fan so it looked like an accident. If it was going to blow out, if she hadn't waited enough time—that was it. But she couldn't wait any longer.

She counted down from three and pulled the half-melted pen out.

The reaction was instant: the fire went from a flicker to a *roar* as the fans sucked oxygen right onto it. It licked out of the frame, curling the edges of the files and reaching towards the papers.

Allegra hurriedly crawled away from it, stumbling as she stood. For a second, all she could do was stare at it, open-mouthed. Even a cigarette butt could destroy whole national parks. Whole towns—people's lives. She'd spent her life preventing this very thing. This one was *much* bigger. And she'd lit it on purpose.

I did it for the right reasons, she tried to reassure herself, thinking of Aaron. And Rosie, and Dimi insisting Allegra call and manipulate a child from that poor family.

That poor family.

Wait a minute. Something occurred to her. Dimi had Rosie's number; of course he did. He'd had Aaron's information too. Which meant... She looked at the compactus.

One more thing, she thought, rushing over and dragging the steel shelves with her full bodyweight so she could get to 'H', tabbing through until—

Hislop, Sean.

There *was* one.

She lifted it up, mouth wide open. The final link in the chain. The final piece in what had been done to that family.

Fuck Dimi, she thought, her resolve solidifying. *Fuck him. He will fucking pay for these horrors.*

Closing her mouth tight, she took the file to the front of the board table, near the door and away from the smouldering server, and set it down label up. It would be the first thing the firies saw when they walked in here. And they would recognise that name after it had been *blasted* over the news the past two days.

She looked back at the compactus: all those hundreds, maybe thousands of files. Each one of them a Sean, or an Allegra, or a Sal. Each one had ruined someone's life, torn someone's family apart. She felt something harden inside her. Something *violent*.

Let them burn, she thought. *Let this whole place go up*.

The computer beside the server shorting from the heat reminded her she needed to leave. She took one last look at Atlas and then shut the door tightly behind her.

There was no one in the carpark when she got into her car. They were probably all out the front. In practised, automatic movements, she fastened her belt, turned the key, and exited the carpark.

The bright sunlight hitting her eyes was a shock; it felt surreal. Almost like she'd imagined it and daylight would turn everything normal again. She'd head back home to Sal's, maybe have a shower. Scroll some morning news.

But it wouldn't go back to normal, not now. Not after what she'd done.

And, unexpectedly, she found she *didn't fucking care*. Normal was fear and blackmail and tiptoeing around someone who should be shot from a cannon. Normal was smiling in Aaron's face and covering up the hole in her chest. If 'normal' was letting Dimi slowly eat away at everything she loved, she'd given it exactly what it deserved.

And that—mattered. She'd done something. She'd done something for that girl, for that family. For herself and her own family. For Sal, even if she didn't approve of or appreciate it. And maybe fucking none of it could be fixed now. Maybe it was too late for them.

But it wasn't too late for whoever Dimi's next search query in Atlas would have been. It wasn't too late for those families.

And maybe—Allegra remembered the fire alarm—maybe it wasn't too late for her and Sal. Maybe there was still a chance. *If* this worked.

Two fire engines tore past her on George Street, lights flashing and sirens blaring.

Stuck in traffic, she leant forward and turned her dispatch scanner and radio on. *Here we go*, she thought. *Please don't let this be for nothing.*

Chapter 43: Descent

There was nowhere for her to go anymore, so she drove. She was on the A2 and heading northwest before she heard anything on the dispatch radio that caught her attention.

It was a crackling transmission, probably from a handheld radio. "Comms, Pump 72. At 78 Pitt Street. Called for kitchen fire. But we've got smoke issuing from basement. Investigating."

"Copy, Pump 72. Standing by." The response was clear and smooth.

Another voice, also smooth. "Comms, Pump 91. We're in the area. Available if required."

Eyes still on the road, she leant over and turned up the volume. This was it. She didn't want to miss anything.

She had to wait through several minutes and a few unrelated dispatches to find out what had happened to her fire. Her knuckles were white on the wheel.

She recognised the crackle before he spoke. "Comms, Pump 72. Basement well alight. Two in BA. Assistance message. Require additional pumps. Enter via Hunter Lane."

"Copy, Pump 72. Assistance message received." Allegra felt her hair stand on end. It was starting. Sal would be inside this already, watching this unfold in real time. "Pump 54, en route to Pitt Street, enter via Hunter Lane. ETA four minutes. Continue response, Pump 91."

Three vehicles. It must still be burning. She checked her watch: 20 minutes. That was enough for the fire to get the adjoining computers and printer. Probably not enough for it to fully engulf the archive—yet. The closed sections of the steel compactus would hold longer. What she *really* hoped was that the table hadn't caught. That the Hislop file was still in front of the door, and that the firies could see it—first thing—despite the smoke. Other than the location, the fire itself should read as an accident. The Hislop file was what made it a crime scene.

It was only a couple of minutes before she got her answer. "Comms, Pump 72. We've got suspicious circumstances. Request police to secure scene. Urgent."

"Pump 72, Police notified. Stand by. Patching channels."

A third voice cut in with police sirens screaming in the background. "445 en route to 78 Pitt Street, ETA 2 minutes."

"Pump 91." There was a break in the transmission. An unusual pause. "Confirm address, 78 Pitt Street?"

A chill ran through her. They'd clocked it.

There was going to be a *big* response shortly. Very shortly.

"Address correct, Pump 91: 78 Pitt Street. All incoming units: 36-storey commercial building, basement well alight, operations in progress. Access via Hunter Lane." Pause. "Crowd on Pitt Street—heavy. Approach rear. Media on scene."

She allowed herself a breathy smile. *Here we go.*

If media was there, though, she wasn't going to get any more details on dispatch—they'd be very careful. She pulled over to check her SES portal for information about local tactical channels. She found the inner fireground channel quickly; there was inter-unit chatter already taking place.

A woman's voice. "Back out on Hunter. Rotating BAs for Pitt Street."

"That's BSA, yeah?" A man's voice. He was eating something.

"Yup. Called for a kitchen fire. Basement's the job."

"Water in there?"

"Not water. Contents fire—an archive."

There was a long, heavy pause. "...Right."

Allegra took a few steady breaths. This was *fast*. Too fast to coordinate a PR response. Like the story itself was catching alight. And if media was already there...

She opened the ABC news website: a headline of '*Breaking: Fire at Black Standard Advisory building in Sydney CBD*', and the text, '*Crews called out for not one but two fires in the PR firm Black Standard Advisory headquarters on Pitt Street in what are reported to be possible suspicious circumstances. Police are in attendance, with no casualties reported. More to come as the story unfolds.*'

God, the *wording* of that. She hoped Rosie had seen it. She wondered what Sal thought of it—and whether this was enough.

None of the commercial outlets had anything yet, though; she'd have to wait for them. They'd probably need to make sure their *vested interests* didn't object to coverage.

She put her phone back in the dock and looked out her window to see where she'd gotten to. Richmond. She hadn't been out this way for quite some time. She swallowed; not amazing memories, actually. She should probably grab breakfast somewhere anyway.

But—since she was here, maybe she could—?

She held her breath for a moment.

I could go there, she thought. *Out to that road.*

Making a last-minute decision, she pulled back out onto the road and turned onto the B59. The last road Lachie had ever driven on.

When she passed Kurrajong, the road dropped steeply on one side and rose sharply in a sheer cliff face on the other. It was a straight, well-lit stretch of road. He'd just fallen asleep.

She didn't need a map to tell her where to stop. Her body knew. Her pulse picked up as soon as she saw it: the place she'd stood as the wreck was hauled out of the canyon. Years later, they'd put a safety rail there. Too late for Lachie. She pulled over, put her hazards on, and got out.

On the railing, there was an old, decaying ribbon tied in a bow. It was discoloured like it might once have held flowers, and probably a year or two old.

Vanessa, Allegra thought, as her fingertips touched it.

She looked over the edge of the cliff. It was obscured by tree canopies; she'd never checked how deep it was. Maybe—

She looked back at her car. The casual, low-stakes chatter from the tactical channel drifted out of her open window. She probably shouldn't block the road.

She frowned at herself. She did roadsides all the time and never worried about briefly slowing traffic. She had the gear in her car for it, and there'd be enough space even for trucks.

But—she was by herself and—

She stopped herself right there. Was she fucking serious? She'd *just lit a fucking building on fire* and she was trying to tell herself a simple roadside was too dangerous? She'd be fine.

She reversed her car up to the edge, placed witches' hats, hazard reflectors, and 'Operation Ahead' signs a good length up and down the road. Only one car went past as she was setting up—yelling a cheerful greeting out the window to her.

She put on all her safety gear in practised, automatic movements. Then she clipped into the winch, backed up to the edge, and tested the line.

I should call Control, she thought, *tell them I'm checking something out, just in case.*

In the end, she didn't. They didn't need to know.

She lowered herself over the edge and started her descent. The day was heating up; the rock was hot. Visibility was perfect until she got past the tree canopy—then it was dark, suddenly. And colder.

It was deeper than she expected, and there wasn't a solid rock face at the bottom. It was uneven ground, a mixture of old-growth and new-growth gumtrees, and lush shrubs.

There was no clear impact site. No damaged trees. But she'd reached the base, so the car would have ended up here. On its roof, they said. It was what made his blood cover the windscreen.

She unclipped, anchoring her rope to a tree, and kicked around the leaf litter on the ground. She expected to find shattered plastic or pebbles of safety glass. Maybe even something that was his.

There was nothing. More than 20 years of leaves had fallen. It was just bushland now. There was no sign her brother had died here.

She sat on the damp ground, looking out towards where she could hear trickling water—the stream wasn't visible from where she was. There were birds around her: the chitter and whirr of bowerbirds. Rainbow lorikeets shrieking at each other. Somewhere, a magpie. The click, click of insects. The sound of it carried through the trees. Maybe he'd heard it.

He'd died of haemorrhagic shock, the report said. Not instantly. He could have still been alive the following morning, while she'd been asleep. Maybe he'd listened to all this as he died.

The thought of him perhaps being conscious. Trapped, his life slipping away. No one to tell him how very loved he was. No one to hug him and—

That thought caught. She was stuck at a cold window in the morgue; his face bloody and pale. His beautiful blonde hair matted. They wouldn't let her into the room, not even to touch him. Not to give him one last hug. She hadn't even hugged him goodbye on the night he left; she couldn't remember the last time she did.

But she could remember the first time—her, four years old, in her best dress at the hospital. Mum placing a tiny swaddled baby into her arms and telling her, "You have a little brother now!" She remembered thinking his face was all screwed up.

She almost smiled.

His face had been screwed up when they'd unzipped the bag the last time she'd seen it, too.

She closed her eyes. *God.*

After his death, the school had posted his results anyway. Such incredible marks, Mum had sobbed as she read them. He'd always wanted to go to the same university as Allegra, but he'd privately told her he wanted to study music—he'd been too afraid to tell Mum and Dad. Allegra had always imagined them driving there together. Listening to him play, ferrying him to concerts and recitals. She'd hoped one day she would stand in a packed stadium and hear *thousands* of people screaming her brother's name.

She'd never know.

That was done.

But maybe she'd stand somewhere in a crowd and listen to Aaron.

You don't even know what he wants to do, she reminded herself. *He doesn't even know what he wants to do*. But he could do anything. He could *be* anything, even if she'd done her fucking best to ruin any shot he had at success and happiness.

She swallowed. Simone's words rang in her ears: she'd made her grief a child's problem.

She forced herself to sit with those words. No 'I was just grieving'. No 'I was saving lives'. Not this time.

She'd left him to go save other people. Every time she came back, it was too much—and she left again.

She felt those words settle around 'I don't think anyone wants me', filling her absence and creating a mother-shaped hole in her son's chest. She *had* made it his problem. And it didn't matter how much she'd loved him from afar, or that she'd thought about him every hour of every day. None of that mattered to a child who wanted his mother.

She could blame Dimi for taking the vacant seat beside Aaron, for whispering promises in his ear—and she fucking *did*—but it was a place she'd left vacant. A spot she'd warmed up for him. And if the fire didn't work, he might stay there.

You going to torture yourself over this for two decades as well? she asked herself in Simone's voice. *After all, you're making a habit of doing things worth torturing yourself over*.

And it was tempting. It was tempting to sink back down—into alcohol, deployments she told herself were heroic, disappearing once again from everyone's lives. To tell herself she was a fucking criminal now. A terrible mother. That there was nothing left of her to be proud of except that she could save strangers.

But in her core, she knew that was ruin. If she wanted to lose him forever, that was how. And she didn't want to lose him, too.

She stayed where she was. She wanted her son. Her incredible, amazing son, who she spent every second being proud of.

She caught herself thinking, *even if he's not proud of you*—and stopped. That wasn't—

He'd sent that text message after Isaiah. And the way he'd looked when people recognised her on cleanup. The wonder.

You don't deserve it after what you did to him, a voice whispered.

She stayed there, with that feeling. Maybe it was true: she *did* deserve estrangement, indifference, all the anger he was entitled to throw at her. He was allowed to hate her. He was allowed to not want her. He was allowed to be done. He didn't owe her anything.

And maybe, despite that, he was proud of her.

Maybe he loved her anyway.

And—

Maybe she could accept it. Believe him. Look at that familiar smile and feel such intense grief for her brother alongside such pride for her son.

'Sorry' would never touch what she'd done to Aaron. But maybe she could say it anyway.

It fucking hurt. It twisted in her guts, what she'd done to him. The tiny baby she'd brought into the world and immediately immersed in harrowing grief: she'd hurt him beyond repair. He had wounds that would never heal, even if he moved forward with them.

And if she wanted him—if she wanted to be with him, be present in his life—she couldn't stay crushed under that. The weight of what she'd done to him wasn't going anywhere. It would sit on her shoulders, heavy and permanent. If she wanted to move forward, she would have to learn to carry it.

But not like this. She had to make room for him.

And she knew what needed to give.

Lachie.

It hit her. Like 1000 tonnes, like a truck speeding along the freeway. Lachie's beautiful smile, his laugh, how he used to fall asleep on her when they were children. How all of them—him and her sisters—used to fall asleep on the couch together watching videos when their parents were out. How they all wanted to buy houses in the same street and grow up and find partners and have all their children together. All the dreams they'd had.

Now, all of that was so spectacularly broken. Shattered into a million pieces, scattering all of them to the wind. And she'd stood frozen in time, stuck at the moment of the accident, watching everyone she loved blow away.

Today, something shifted—something ancient. The ice cracked.

She didn't stand there and let it happen, not this time. She did something.

It didn't change what she hadn't done back then. She hadn't stopped Lachie. But whatever role she played, she didn't have to stay trapped underneath it anymore.

She could lift it from her shoulders and place it here, in this valley: how much she'd loved him, the beauty and wonder his life could have been, and the loving family they'd been around him.

And lay him to rest.

So she could be the person she wanted to be for her son.

I wasn't there for you, she said to Aaron, even if he couldn't hear it. *But I can be. I will be.*

She stood, looking out across the beautiful valley, and wiped her eyes. She wanted to tell him.

Turning, she cast one last look around her, listening to the birdsong and quiet trickle of the stream. Then she clipped on, climbed up, and hoisted herself back into the warm sunlight.

She got straight into her car, turning on her signal booster and taking out her phone. He was at the top of her favourites, even if she hardly ever spoke to him. She tapped it and put the ringing phone to her ear.

He answered quickly. "Mum? Is everything okay?"

God, he sounded like her. "Yes," she said. "Are you alone? There's some stuff I want to say to you."

"Uh..." There was a pause. "I guess?"

"Okay," she said, and then immediately lost it. "I—this isn't going to come out right, just—just let me say it."

A pause. "It's okay, I'm listening." God, *now* he sounded like Timothy.

"I wasn't a mother to you." It was sudden—and a shock, even to her. "I never called. I never came to anything. I chose not to deal with myself, and you paid for that. I know you spent years thinking no one really wanted you or loved you." The line was silent, so she kept speaking. "And that's my fault. I kept leaving, over and over again, for months—*years* at a time. Sometimes not even saying goodbye."

Aaron's voice was tight. "I mean, you weren't even here when you were here."

God, that—she took the hit. For him, she let it land. "Yeah." They were both silent for a moment. "And I know you know why. I know your dad and Vanessa told you why I'm such a mess. And—it is because of Lachie. But it's mostly because of me."

She looked out of the car window, over the side of the cliff. It was a tiny hitch of breathing on the other end of the line that caused her to lose it. "But it wasn't true that I never wanted you or loved you. As soon as phone wallpapers were a thing, you were mine. Before that, I had a photo of you I used to keep in my pocket every single day, on every single rescue. I used to say goodnight to it every night in bed." She still had it in the glove box. "I should have said it to you."

"I wish you had."

God, the weight in that. "I wish I had too. I can start."

It was a while before he spoke again. When he did, it was thoughtful. "When I was little, I used to imagine this moment," he said. "For years. I'd lie in bed and imagine you suddenly opening Vanessa's front door, telling me you'd bought a house and you were coming home. You and me and Dad were going to live in it together. That you'd made a mistake and you'd always loved me."

She closed her eyes. She heard that and held it. She wouldn't let it crush her. "It was more than just a mistake."

"Yeah." Again, the line was silent for a little while. "You know, Dad warned me you might never say that to me," he said. "He always said forgiveness can't come from someone else's actions. Forgiveness is something *you* do, inside yourself, so you can be well and move on." He paused. "It's why I forgave you."

I don't deserve it, she thought—and then immediately countered that with: *But he's doing it anyway*. "Thank you."

A silence stretched out between them before more words tumbled out of her mouth. "I want to come with you to Shanghai. To that environmental conference."

It was so unexpected that Aaron burst out laughing for a moment—a relief—and she could hear both that smile and tears in his voice when he said, "Please do. I was going to have to babysit Dad the whole time there. He doesn't care about this stuff, he just worries like you do."

Shanghai. A warmth filled her belly. Thoughts of them exploring the city together between sessions. Maybe some hiking. Learning about him—about the incredible man he'd become.

"I love you," she found herself saying. "I think you're amazing. You can do anything."

Aaron laughed once about that. "Well, I am your son."

That landed like a blow: that he still admired her. Loved her. Even after everything.

They talked a little more—about where she was. About his plans for the evening and weekend. The conversation ran on—honestly, she could have sat there and listened to him talk for the rest of the day. Once he cheered up, he started sounding more animated—like he had the other night. She asked him questions and listened, just loving him. Just thinking the world of him.

At the end, he stopped. "I can't believe this is happening," he said. "Is it real?" He exhaled. "I should have turned recording on so I can listen to it again if I start to feel like maybe it didn't happen."

"If you start to feel that way, you can just call me."

"Yeah," he said, realising that. "I guess I can."

Eventually, he had to go. "I'll send you information about the conference," he said. "Also I'll tell Dad to transfer his ticket to you. It'll make his day."

Allegra could expect a Concerned phone call from him tonight, probably. She exhaled. Manageable. She said goodbye and hung up.

She might have sat there for much longer if she wasn't backed up to a cliff and surrounded by orange witches' hats. She moved her car and then went up and down the road to collect everything, locking them back in the case in her boot.

She stood there for another few minutes, looking out over the beautiful valley.

The fire would likely be out now. The police would be in there, collecting whatever files were left. Hopefully enough to show them what Atlas was, and hopefully at least the Hislop file. Maybe collecting her DNA from somewhere.

They can come and get me, she thought, feeling oddly unbothered.

Of course she didn't want Aaron to find out. But as she stood in the warm sun and gentle breeze, none of that touched her.

It didn't drag at her like a thousand hands, crushing her throat, stealing her breath and anchoring her in place. The whispers had stopped; she *wasn't* frozen. She *hadn't* done nothing today. And that felt—

She took a long breath, the air filling her chest, a smile rising to her face.

Come what may. She would face it.

Chapter 44: Borrowed Time

On the way back in, news of the fire was all over the radio. Allegra cycled between channels, wanting to hear all the angles.

"In breaking news: emergency services have now contained two separate fires at Black Standard Advisory's Sydney headquarters," a cool, professional voice read. "A small kitchen fire and a larger blaze in the building's basement were both brought under control, with no injuries reported. Police say the circumstances are being treated as suspicious and investigations are underway. We'll keep you updated as details emerge."

The next was more sensationalist. "A double fire at Black Standard Advisory's headquarters is raising serious questions this morning, after a basement blaze and a second fire in a kitchen were both extinguished. No injuries, but crews report that the second fire was in a *basement archive*. Very interesting. Stay with us—this one's just getting started."

Allegra was tabbing across channels when a text came through. She pulled over.

Simone. "*Always love seeing my sister's work. The internet's been more interesting than usual this morning.*"

Does she want to get me arrested? Allegra wondered, trying to figure out a reply that would shut her up without looking suspicious, when another message came through. "*So lovely meeting your new girlfriend last night. Hope she won't leave you in the doghouse too long.*" She attached a picture of Allegra's LandCruiser with the tent up on Harrington, which made the first message look like it was about the car, not the fire—and dug straight into the Sal-shaped bruise.

There was no solution to Simone. Allegra pulled back out onto the road.

She'd only driven another couple of kilometres when *another* message came through. Allegra pulled aggressively over, grabbed her phone, and—

Timothy? "*Aaron told me about your conversation with him.*" Allegra exhaled. "*So lovely you're finally apologising to him. I really hope you won't pull out at the last minute and break his heart. I'll need your passport number for the ticket transfer—could you send through a photo of it?*"

Allegra looked up for a moment. Was her new passport in the car? She leant over and rifled through her glove box, and then through the documents in the chair pocket. She had a feeling she'd left it in Point Piper—

which she could get into and out of without seeing Timothy if she went during the workday.

She fastened her seatbelt again and was about to put her phone back in the dock… and didn't. Not straight away.

I should text her, Allegra thought, looking down at Sal's icon in her message history. Before she second-guessed it, she typed it out, "*I want to see you*," and sent it through.

She watched several rows of cars pass. Her phone stayed silent. That was enough time. She turned back out onto the A2.

She drove through North Shore, through the tunnel and out past the CBD; no message. Her phone was still silent when she pulled in the driveway at Point Piper.

It was slightly uncanny being back there, as if no time had passed—and far too much had. She felt disconnected from it. *I really need somewhere else to put all my stuff*, she reminded herself as she went inside to look for her passport.

After she'd turned over the guest bedroom and hadn't fucking found it, she had to face the fact it might actually be in the car, after all. She went outside, popped open the boot, and started sorting through all the junk back there.

"Oh, Allegra, hello!" That was Cece's voice. Shit.

Allegra stepped out of her boot. "Cece."

She was standing at the gate dressed in athletic gear and sneakers; she must have been doing a lap of the point. Now leaning on the gate, smiling at her.

"How's Isaiah?" Allegra wandered up to the gate, aware of how she herself looked.

"Doing well," she said cheerfully. "He's still not out of the wheelchair, though. He's just worried about all the muscle he's losing while the casts are on." Allegra chuckled about that. She nodded at Allegra's field overalls. "Save someone else's son this morning?"

Allegra looked down at them—for a moment, she had a beautiful clear picture of Lachie's smile. She shook her head. "Just felt like scaling a cliff before lunch."

Cece laughed at that. "You're putting my 5km to shame," she said. Then, unexpectedly, she sobered. "Allegra," she said, in a tone that signalled a topic change. "May I ask you a question?"

Allegra had a feeling she was going to need to put her game face on. "Of course."

"Does Sal talk much about BSA?"

Shit. Showtime. *Two neighbours chatting*, she told herself. "Yeah, a little? To the degree she's able to. Work is very important to her, as you know."

Cece nodded in acknowledgement of that, watching her with the same careful attention both Dimi and Sal did when they were trying to read someone. "Do you know what involvement she's had in—this? Threshold, etc?" She gestured towards the Sydney skyline.

Think quickly, Allegra. "Well, Dimi's handling all that stuff at a higher level, so she hasn't really been involved at all—at least so far. She wanted to help."

Cece gave her a long and measured look, the way she had at the hospital. "I see," she said, and then pivoted back to neighbourly chatter. "Anyway, will you be doing this Christmas thing with Timothy and Aaron? At the church."

Allegra was too surprised by the subject change to not respond naturally to that. At her expression, Cece laughed. "Your community service lies elsewhere, I suppose," she said. "I'm not going either. Beau and Astrid are."

"Timothy will be very happy."

She chuckled. "He was. I heard about your son's results; incredible. Lovely boy. Anyway, I need to get back home before my next meeting." She nodded once, waved, and headed back up to her property.

Allegra watched her go and then walked slowly back towards her car.

Her instinctive response to that 'I see' was unease—but Cece had been like that at the hospital, too. Still. Sal would have had a read on it. If she could ask her.

She made herself a sandwich and sat at the kitchen bench, scrolling the news. More information about the fires, some footage of the crowd outside BSA HQ and—

She stopped scrolling. Holy shit. There was a clip on one of the tabloid sites: cameras following Dimi at a jog as he exited the building through Hunter Lane towards a waiting car. He was walking at a brisk but professional pace, trying to avoid acknowledging them, checking something on his phone as he got in. Several people were yelling questions at him as the door closed. "Is this fire connected to the fire at the Hislop property?", "What records were destroyed in that fire, Mr Black?", and, "Is this an attempt to cover something up?"

Allegra sat back, jaw open. Afraid to smile.

She took another bite of her sandwich and, chewing it slowly, opened YouTube, searching for results there. Because she was following Austin, his latest short came up.

"Alright, this is—this is insane timing, but take a look at this." A photo appeared on the screen: Dimi and someone else, clearly on holiday on a massive yacht together. "Dimitri Black, CEO of Black Standard Advisory, and Thomas Andermatt, CEO of Threshold Property Group. Together. On a superyacht." He zoomed in on the hull, then dropped another picture—Thomas smashing a champagne bottle against that hull, a woman beside him. "Hang on, that's the Andermatt family yacht." He appeared in the shot again, eyebrows way up. "Interesting. I'm sure that means nothing."

Thank you, Austin, Allegra thought, signing a silent truce with him.

She was finishing her sandwich and thinking about her passport when she remembered she'd used it for her Working with Children Check; it would probably be in Timothy's office. She went to grab it, found it in his top drawer, and took it back to her phone to snap a photo for him.

There was a message from—her breath caught.

Sal. *"Are you nearby? I can't leave."*

Allegra closed her eyes for a moment and let out a long, slow breath. She felt she could *run* the whole way to wherever Sal was and not stop for air. *"Point Piper. Are you back inside BSA yet?"*

"No—we have a business continuity arrangement with a commercial rental further down Pitt Street. I'll send you the address." A few seconds later, a location card popped up.

"I'll be there soon," Allegra messaged back. Then she had to brute-force herself into a shower and a change of clothes so she didn't smell like smoke, sweat, and bushland when they reunited.

Her suit still smelt faintly of smoke too, courtesy of the clothes she'd tossed on top of it when she changed into her abseiling gear on the B59. She put those particular clothes in the washing machine and doused the suit in Febreze, hanging it out on the balcony to air. Her other suit would need to suffice today.

In the city, she parked somewhere close to the pin Sal had given her and followed it to a large, generic-looking building, where security checked her name, took her photo, and showed her to the lift.

Upstairs was a generic, smooth, unbranded grey office with 20 or 30 sharply dressed, dark-suited professionals. None of them were as dark or as sharp as Sal. Even just laying eyes on her filled Allegra's lungs with air;

she wanted to rush up to her, lift Sal into her arms, and thoroughly kiss her. But she still didn't know what she was allowed to be to Sal.

They were also in an office. Despite everything, when Sal looked up at her—it was for a fraction too long. But otherwise, she remained steady.

Allegra approached her at a carefully measured pace. "Lunch?"

Sal shook her head. "I'm the only exec here," she said. "We have other deadlines and clients who need supporting." She looked up, her eyes drifting towards a pair of men standing off to the side. Within listening distance. She inclined her head towards a corner room and started walking.

Allegra followed her. Sal let her in and shut the door behind her. They were alone.

Sal was there, a few steps away. "Watch your voice," she said quietly. "These walls are paper thin."

Allegra nodded. There were a dozen things she wanted to say to Sal about the fire alarm and what it meant about them. About what happened to them now. She settled on, "You did it." Sal nodded, still not looking at her. "I thought you weren't going to."

Sal laughed once, humourlessly. "So did I."

"What made you change your mind?"

Sal's voice was a little louder for a moment. "Complete insanity," she said dryly, and then dropped her voice again. "And Zoe's text." She glanced up at Allegra. "I should have let you come up last night. But I thought if I left you alone with it, maybe you'd choose a less drastic course of action."

"I'd made a decision."

The look Sal gave her was steady, evaluative. "Let's see if it's the right one." It reminded her of the look Cece had given her earlier.

"I saw Cece this morning."

Sal was suddenly paying very close attention. "How did that go?"

"She asked if you were involved with the Threshold stuff, so I told her that while you'd love to be, it's above your head."

Sal considered that, eyes elsewhere, her fists tightening and loosening even as she stood otherwise still. In the end, she settled on, "Good." High praise from her.

Allegra couldn't help herself. Not standing this close to her. Not with how well it was all going. "I did well," she said quietly. Sal nodded once. Allegra took half a step in. "Good enough to reward?"

Rather than answering, Sal gave her a cool look. "Do you understand what all this does to me if it goes wrong?"

"Why are you still thinking about it going wrong? You've seen the news."

"Because it still might," Sal said sharply. Instead of stepping away, though, she pivoted, her voice dropping again. "We need to get the official version of what happened this morning decided."

She was so tense. Allegra could see the muscles in her throat as she swallowed, the draw of her shoulders. Allegra was suddenly aware of her own hands. Instead of reaching out to Sal and drawing her thumbs across those taut muscles on her shoulders, she took her phone out and showed Sal the messages Simone had sent.

Sal read them, again nodding once. "A fight isn't a bad idea," she said. "The closer you can get to the truth, the better. It also explains why we didn't text each other this morning when we both would have known about the fire."

"One of your staff saw me," Allegra said. "I didn't get her name, probably a junior. I said I was here to see you, so she was taking me upstairs to 35 to get changed when the alarm went off. We were in the lifts."

Sal's eyes tracked the air, thinking of how they could use that. "You were coming to apologise."

Allegra scoffed. "I was definitely coming to accept *your* apology."

Sal smothered a very slight smile at that. "That you were with someone may clear you," she said, and then stepped in even closer. Allegra could smell coconut as she whispered, "The police are getting electrical engineers in to assess the building in case the two fires were a result of some sort of surge," she said, "but their other theory is that the *same* person lit both fires."

Shit. "Does that mean you're in danger of being accused of both?"

"Perhaps," she said. Then, she casually added, "I jammed the toaster in the executive kitchen on 35."

Allegra's eyebrows went way up. Dimi's floor. "Was he there?" Sal nodded. "Does he know you were?"

She smiled slightly. "No. I won't lie about it if the police ask, but I used the incinerator on 35 to dispose of the files that were previously in my safe," she said quietly, still too close. "It won't be logged because I piggybacked on HR's tag while she was going up, so it will take him much longer to find out—if he even does."

Taking the Atlas files up to Dimi's floor to use the incinerator sounded on par with starting a fire in Atlas, in terms of personal risk. More than the toaster. "Would the HR exec say anything?"

Sal shrugged. "To him? Possibly. But also possibly not because she knows he used my delegation to approve that Threshold payment." She didn't elaborate. "At this point, if they do end up deciding it was arson—*if*—all signs point to Dimi. And they will definitely not do anything about him unless they are very, very certain. That would be an extremely expensive prosecution, because he would defend it with the best lawyers money can buy."

Allegra processed that, trying *not* to process how Sal's earrings brushed her neck. "Well, hopefully they do absolutely nothing and let the public decide," she said quietly. "I gather you've been watching?"

Her voice was dry. "Funnily enough, I have."

"Did you see the clip of all the cameras chasing him?"

Sal gave a ghost of a nod. "Don't get cocky. It's not over yet," she said, but then she conceded, "It *is* going faster than I expected it to. I thought he would quash it; he still may. He has a *lot* of connections and a lot of money. I'm sure he's calling his friends on the ABC board now."

"As long as everyone hears about it first. Did you see Austin's short?" She hadn't, so Allegra showed her with the volume right down.

Sal finished it. When she looked at Allegra, it was with the same assessment she'd worn when Allegra was doing well with the Homeward campaign. "The level of risk you're prepared to take on is—not normal," she said quietly. "But this was a clever strategy."

"Then can you *please* relax even just a little bit? Can you enjoy it?" Allegra asked. "We did something amazing—okay, fucked. But amazing. And it's working." She was smiling.

Sal wasn't. "It's only just started." She sighed at length, her shoulders loosening just a little. At the base of her blazer, Allegra felt fingertips brush the fabric. "Why are you so good at distracting me from the things I need to focus on?"

Allegra's smile deepened. "What's the worst that would happen if you didn't think about it for a few minutes?"

"Allegra—" Sal said sharply, and then exhaled and gave up. She closed her eyes briefly and shook her head. "*The worst*? Someone makes the wrong call and we lose control of the narrative."

"In a few minutes?" Allegra asked flatly. She brushed her own fingertips against Sal's. "I think you have a few minutes."

Sal smiled dimly, despite herself. "You're *a rescue operator*," she said, like an accusation. Like Allegra shouldn't be convincing.

Allegra was grinning. "Did the muscles fool you?"

"They're definitely distracting me." Sal locked eyes with her, and then trailed her eyes down to Allegra's lapels, which she straightened appreciatively. "I like this suit on you." She left her hands there.

Through the woollen suit, the backs of Sal's fingers were resting against Allegra's breasts. Without a shadow of doubt, Allegra knew Sal was doing it on purpose. She grinned slightly. "Take it off me."

Sal stilled. She gave Allegra a long, fascinated look. It was a moment before she spoke. "Here?"

"Anywhere."

Again, Sal found that answer interesting. "But we're here. We're not anywhere."

"What can I have here?"

Smiling slightly, Sal gave Allegra a very appraising look about her sudden forwardness. "This is new," she observed. Her eyes dipped from hers to Allegra's lips.

Then, she stepped into Allegra, toe to toe with her, put a hand on her waist and leant up to her ear. When she spoke, Allegra could feel a warm puff of air on her skin for each word. "What do you want?"

"You know what I want."

That low voice. "Mmm, but I want to hear you say it." She pulled away a little, so they were eye to eye—as much as they could be, given how tall Allegra was.

Allegra held eye contact. Sal wasn't going to make her say it—*she* was going to make Sal do something about it.

Sal chuckled at that—low, sexy. Her fingertips dipped very slightly into Allegra's belt; enough to get a hitched breath from her. Then, she leant up and stopped as her lips almost touched Allegra's. "Okay," she murmured, her breath tickling Allegra's skin. "A few minutes it is." She touched her lips to Allegra's.

Allegra held herself still.

Sal's kiss was slow. Deliberate. A measured, controlled rhythm.

Allegra kept her hands to herself at first, then slipped one beneath the back of Sal's jacket. When Sal didn't stop her, she leant in. Her other hand went up to Sal's face. That sharp chin, her thumb on those defined cheekbones. She could feel the texture of Sal's makeup—she remembered Sal without it. She deepened their kiss.

Sal let her, allowing Allegra to draw their bodies together, her hands moving from behind Allegra's neck to either side of her jaw, then settling firmly at her waist. When Allegra opened her eyes briefly, Sal's brow was knit. She was so focused.

I want you, Allegra told her silently, kissing her neck as Sal murmured something into her skin. Allegra didn't catch it; she was already thinking about something else.

There was a meeting table—Allegra pulled slightly away and glanced at it. Sal followed her line of sight and then looked quizzically back. "This is an office," she said pointedly—but her mouth was still at Allegra's neck. "And as nice as this is, we still have the pressing live issue of *arson*."

That word felt like a slap. Allegra forced herself to step away. "Okay." She straightened her blazer.

Sal rebuttoned hers, smoothing her hair. Allegra couldn't read her.

They stood there for a moment. Allegra spoke first. "You can't leave?" Sal shook her head. "Did you have lunch?" she asked. And then, "Or even breakfast?"

Sal briefly grimaced. "Gerard organised sandwiches earlier, but I was in a meeting at the time, and they were all gone by the time I got back."

"I'll get you something."

Sal smiled briefly. "Thanks," she said. "Get Gerard to give you the card."

Allegra wanted to kiss her again before they parted—in the end, she didn't. They just looked at each other, and she left.

Allegra did not, in fact, get Gerard to give her the card. Firstly, because she was a grown woman who could buy her—colleague? partner-in-crime? *partner*?—a meal, and secondly because she needed a few minutes before she could have any sort of manageable conversation.

In fact, she gave the lift a miss and took the stairs to burn off some of the adrenaline still pumping through her—and give herself a legitimate reason to be breathless. Not because Sal had kissed her, despite everything. Not because there was a chance Sal might be locked in for this. That they might actually *be* something to each other.

She got her phone out to find the quickest way to food—there was a text from Timothy.

Oh yeah. She stopped on the kerb and opened it. *"That's all done,"* he said, presumably about the ticket transfer. *"I'm sure they'll send you a confirmation email shortly."* There was a break, another timestamp, and then, *"Have you seen the news?"*

"Yes, I'm down here at the moment—just getting food for Sal."

He took a moment to reply. She waited; he was usually prompt. *"What do you think?"*

Allegra considered her options, deciding to keep it simple. Timothy would likely share his feelings with Aaron. *"I mean, Dimi has been very nice to us, but mostly I'm thinking about what this means for Aaron."*

"Exactly. It complicates things for him."

Allegra read that a couple of times. He wasn't wrong. It *would* complicate things. Even if it worked.

That thought stayed with her while she followed Maps to some kebabs.

She'd been thinking about something wrapped, maybe with leafy salad and protein. The menu was mostly meat, though—Aaron would love this place—but Sal liked her vegetables. She felt too guilty to just walk out and ordered the most salad-like item available.

The server recognised her. "For you?" she asked. Allegra shook her head, and the girl wrote 'Sal' on the box before she turned around to carve the meat. "She'd be having a day."

Allegra laughed. "Yes," she said with gravity.

The girl made a big show of filling up the box to the brim and then taping it shut. She presented it to Allegra. "At least the authorities are taking it seriously."

Allegra hesitated a moment and then added, "They should have the first time." She watched the girl for any surprise, any confusion—nothing. She simply nodded as if Allegra hadn't said anything unusual or unexpected.

Allegra left the shop feeling her heart lift. Ordinary people already thought the fires were connected. Holy shit.

Since her followers would probably want proof of life after the fires, she took a photo of the takeaway box with 'Sal' clearly visible on the lid and decorated CBD streets in the background. She sent it to Zoe with, *"Can you post this with a caption like 'very competent in a crisis, but no survival instincts'?"* Zoe replied with a thumbs up.

Back at the temporary office, it was Gerard who collected her when she arrived. He was wearing an obnoxious Santa hat covered in sequins; Allegra would have *paid* to be present when Sal first saw it.

"Sal's in a meeting," he told Allegra. "A long one. With angry people."

He was clearly just being dramatic, but Allegra still didn't like the sound of that. "Can I get this to her?" She held up the box.

Gerard glanced at it and then frowned deeply. "We have a card for that. Did you keep the receipt?"

"It's fine."

"Nonsense, text me the receipt. I'll reimburse you." He received the takeaway box. "I'll take it to her." He disappeared down a hallway.

Allegra wasn't sure if she was supposed to wait for him to come back or leave, so she waited, hanging a little awkwardly around the temporary reception area.

She didn't have that long to wait. He returned and made a beeline for her. "Here," he said, handing her a piece of folded-up paper, and then stopped and pointed at her, pretending to be stern. "Get me that receipt!" He went back to his table.

Allegra was smiling about that as she opened the piece of paper. There was a note scribbled in Sal's handwriting, but only a number on it. *251293.* She recognised it immediately.

It was the entry code for Sal's penthouse.

Chapter 45: The Cost

Allegra didn't bother heading to Sal's penthouse before 9pm; even that felt conservative after today. She was fully prepared to spend some time waiting around. When she let herself into Sal's carpark, though, Sal's sports car was there.

Her stomach fluttered.

Allegra had been waiting for this moment. After lunch, she'd driven out to North Head to pass the time and watch the media storm from her phone. In between counselling Vanessa and ignoring Simone, she'd tracked the story across multiple outlets and watched it move from *'Fires under control at Black Standard Advisory'* to *'Embattled PR Firm accused of destroying evidence in ongoing investigation of Hislop fire'*. More footage of Dimi. Dimi's photo. TikTokers wearing Einstein wigs and pretending to hide evidence of minor transgressions by setting them on fire. It was... Allegra could hardly breathe. But she was smiling. She could fucking smile about it.

She'd pasted a whole list of her favourites into a document to show Sal—if they even got into that. Perhaps they'd be busy. The videos could wait.

Feeling uncharacteristically self-conscious, Allegra brushed her hair before pulling it back into a loose ponytail. In the lift on the way up, she examined the front of her sharp suit. Then corrected her collar. This was it, wasn't it? She chased away a breathy smile.

The lift doors opened.

It was dark and Sal's penthouse was mood lit. A spotlight over the display kitchen, and another over the couches. Colourful city lights through the tall windows. Music playing softly somewhere; Goldfrapp.

Allegra walked forward into the room. Sal wasn't at the table or the couches. Allegra thought perhaps she'd gone upstairs to her office when she realised the terrace door was open. Frowning a little, she went outside.

Sal was out there, beautiful in a strapless black dress and leaning stiffly against the balcony. Her eyes were cast out towards Sydney, unfocused. This wasn't 'control', this was 'pain'.

Something was wrong.

Allegra made a beeline for her. "Sal?"

Sal's eyes dipped slightly, to the road below. She took a breath.

Allegra approached the railing beside her, leaning a hip on it to face her. "What happened?"

She opened her mouth. It took a moment for her to speak. "The board is holding an emergency meeting tomorrow."

Allegra frowned. "On Saturday?"

She nodded. "Only two people have been summoned: Dimi, and me," she said. "Normally we would receive a brief or at least an agenda, but we've been given nothing. His PA asked Gerard if he knew anything."

Allegra felt uneasy. "What does that mean for you?"

"It means they're going to terminate us."

What on—"*What*?! Why you?!"

She looked across at Allegra. "The most likely explanation is that they think it's *both* our faults," she said. "This whole media storm is my problem, my job to control—and I haven't been controlling it."

That struck something white hot in Allegra's chest. "But he didn't *let* you control it! Can't you just tell them that?"

"I can tell them," she said. "But I'll sound like I'm covering for myself. And he'll—" She stopped. Looked away. "They all know him. They trust him. It's possible that if they need heads to roll to prove to the public they're doing something, mine will do."

Allegra didn't—"*No*," she said. "They trust you, too, don't they? That board member called you just the other—"

"There's another option," Sal said, more quietly. "That they have additional information about the fires. Or Atlas, or—*something* relevant to both of us. They'll hold it for the meeting. Make it impossible to prepare." She shifted her weight. "I'll have to handle it in the room."

Still incensed, it suddenly occurred to Allegra that—Sal wasn't angry. At all. If she was surprised even, it wasn't visible.

When she chose to jam that toaster and help Allegra, she knew this was a possible end. And she still did it.

"This is because of the fire," Allegra realised aloud, feeling sick. "I did this."

Sal glanced up at her. "I don't recall you jamming a toaster."

"But it was me that—"

Sal stopped her with a hand in the air and a headshake. She wasn't going to let Allegra do that.

They stood opposite each other; Sal lost in thought.

Eventually, she pushed away from the railing, eyes on her dress for a moment, then noting Allegra's suit. Something in her shoulders gave; this conversation wasn't what she'd had planned.

Allegra saw it—and left it there. Being here was enough. "When did they tell you?"

"20 minutes ago."

Allegra made a face. It explained her dress. The music. "You don't have to do this." She nodded towards the couches inside. "We can just read."

Sal followed her in, collecting her phone from the table as Allegra settled herself under the spotlight on the couch. She didn't know where Sal was at, but she left space beside her. Just in case.

Sal saw it and hesitated, her eyes moving between the couches. When she walked into the light, though, it was to sit beside Allegra, hip to hip, and to rest back against Allegra's shoulder. Angled away from her a little—so Allegra could curl an arm around that slender waist, if she wanted to.

Sal's hair was just beside Allegra's chin, smelling as wonderful as it always did.

It pulled up flashes: her in the rooftop tent, barefaced and soft. At the campsite, coated with orange dust, makeup half gone. Not this—precise, composed, untouchable. Even when she was inviting it.

Those flashes, those versions never lasted long. Sal always corrected them. Put her edges back on.

This—this polished version—was the one she trusted. The one she built everything on. The one BSA ran on.

If that went tomorrow...

Sal already had her reading app open when Allegra lost the fight, curling her arm around Sal and placing a slow kiss on the top of her head.

Sal went still. Allegra thought maybe she'd crossed a line, but when she peeked down at Sal, her eyes and mouth were jammed shut against something. It wasn't discomfort. Her hand moved over Allegra's on her middle, clutching it. So tightly.

Allegra discarded her phone so she could put her other arm around Sal. "Talk to me," she said softly.

"I'll be fine," she said. Too even.

"Talk to me anyway."

A tiny shake of her head. Not yet.

When she didn't respond, Allegra said, "You're not fine. I wouldn't be fine about losing my job either. It's who I am."

It took her some time. Measured breaths, several false starts. It was after Allegra kissed her temple slowly—no rush—that she drew a breath, paused, and spoke. Such a small voice, barely audible. "This is *all* I am."

Fuck.

Allegra's hug tightened in response.

There's more to you, Allegra longed to say. But it wouldn't comfort her; she clearly didn't believe it. Sal had always been quick to smooth over anything too soft, too human, too visible. If she lost BSA, Allegra could imagine her doing it harder. Disappearing like she had after the gala—when Allegra saw too much. Leaving her outside it.

Maybe tomorrow night Allegra would be back in her rooftop tent again.

She tightened her arm around Sal. "Then I'm here with you," she said. "Until the meeting."

Sal let her phone drop to her thigh, leaning her head back on Allegra's shoulder. Eyes closed, stiff as a board.

When she opened her eyes, she didn't move. "I can't do this," she said, indicating her book. "There's nothing more I can do tonight. I didn't sleep last night—I should try, at least." She exhaled slowly. "I'm sorry."

She stood up from Allegra, spending a moment steadying herself.

Allegra had a moment where she wasn't sure if the apology meant she was being asked to leave. Sal caught it. "Did you bring pyjamas?"

Allegra's shoulders eased a fraction. "My car's downstairs."

Sal nodded once, and turned, heading up the curved staircase. Each of her steps slow. Allegra watched her for a moment, then went to grab her pyjamas.

When she'd changed into them, Sal was in her bedroom. It wasn't even a question to Allegra: she collected the pillow and the doona from the guest bedroom and took them upstairs to Sal's hallway.

She was arranging them on the floor when the bedroom door opened.

Sal was in silhouette against the light: barefaced, just in pyjamas.

Allegra straightened, still holding the pillow.

They looked at each other for a second. Sal didn't say anything; didn't move.

Allegra wasn't sure what Sal intended—if perhaps Sal was about to ask her to sleep downstairs.

Then, quietly, Sal stepped aside. "You don't have to stay out there."

Allegra opened her mouth—

Sal stilled, just a fraction. Enough.

Allegra closed it again. She left the bedding in the hallway and went into the master bedroom.

Sal's bed was king-size and plush; it looked like she only slept on a fraction of it, right beside the nightstand. Allegra lifted the soft doona and slipped under the other side of it. It felt crisp and untouched. Like a display bed.

Sal climbed in on her side. They only had a moment to look at each other before Sal turned off the lamp.

The blackout blinds cut the room off from the city lights, leaving it completely dark. It made the hiss of the sheets when Sal moved beside her more noticeable. Every couple of minutes. Each breath.

They'd slept side-by-side before. Tonight, she felt oddly untethered, not touching Sal. The gap between them on the mattress was palpable. She remembered Sal's expression from the couch: eyes jammed shut, mouth forced closed. No one should go to sleep feeling that way.

She turned her head towards where Sal was. She could reach out? They'd cuddled to sleep before. Woken up together before. Even just a couple of nights ago, Sal had invited Allegra against her, but—

Sal just said she 'can't do it'. Perhaps *this* is part of what she can't do. *Don't read more into this than just the invitation not to sleep on the floor*, she told herself. *Don't take something she can't give right now.*

The doona pulled a little as Sal turned onto her back—and stopped abruptly when she realised she was pulling it. She shifted more carefully underneath it.

Allegra lay there, so aware of how easy it would be to slide across the mattress and roll Sal over so they were spooning. She didn't.

But—what if she was back in the rooftop tomorrow? Maybe it was worth the risk. It was worth at least letting Sal feel she was here.

Moving her hand along the cool sheet, she searched for Sal's under the doona.

She found it—not that she was sure what she'd been expecting. But not to have Sal immediately take it. To clutch it.

Allegra couldn't hear Sal breathing for a moment; then she heard a very slow, very measured breath. Too measured. And then a swallow.

Allegra wasn't sure what she was hearing until she heard a tiny, hitched breath—caught immediately.

Oh no. "Sal..."

Her voice was tight. "It's okay, you can sleep."

That was the last thing on earth she could do now. She pulled on Sal's hand. "Come here? Please?"

Sal was silent a moment, the doona still. Then she released Allegra's hand and slid across the mattress into Allegra's arms. Her head on Allegra's arm, wrists folded under her chin. It meant Allegra could *fiercely* wrap both arms around her. Sal's face was damp against her collarbones.

Allegra pressed her cheek into Sal's hair. This was right. This was where she was supposed to be.

Sal lifted her head off Allegra's shoulder for a moment as she shifted slightly; Allegra wasn't sure what for, until she felt fingertips on her jaw.

Gentle lips touched hers; she tasted salt.

Yes, Allegra felt with every fibre of her being, letting her. Sal's movements were hesitant at first. Slow and intimate. In the dark, everything felt more immediate; there was nothing else to focus on but how she felt. How warm Sal's breath felt when she exhaled across Allegra's chin. How their bodies rested together under the doona.

As Sal moved, a gap of skin opened between her top and shorts under Allegra's arm; Allegra let her hand go to it. Feeling how warm she was. How soft she was.

She was in Sal's bed, kissing her, touching her. She smiled against Sal's lips.

She felt a tiny smile back.

That was—Allegra's breath caught. She moved towards Sal, turning into her, resting some weight on her. She wanted to see her.

She sat back a little. "Can I turn the light on?"

Under her, Sal froze. "I don't—" She stopped. "I don't want you to see me like this."

"I do," Allegra said. "Please."

Sal was silent a moment and then shifted out from underneath Allegra to sit, stretching an arm out above them. Allegra could hear her fingers moving along the wall before the 'click'.

At first, nothing happened—then she heard a hum from the windows, and a line of soft city lights grew across the bed as the blackout blinds lifted.

In the silver light, this close to her, Allegra could see the red around Sal's eyes. Her puffy skin. She reached up with a thumb to gently stroke her cheekbone near it. Sal let her, looking away at first. Down, at the doona. When she did look up—the control was still there. It just wasn't enough.

She didn't look away.

For a second, neither of them moved. Sal exhaled slowly.

When Allegra's hand fell, Sal's lifted to the buttons on her pyjama top. Allegra's breath caught. Sal heard it—glanced up. She knew why. And, eyes on Allegra, undid her buttons anyway, letting her top fall open and off her shoulders.

Her breasts were bare—but the tattoos were what drew Allegra's eyes. Black on pale skin. The curved knife on the centre of her torso—larger than she'd expected—and the full arc of the tattoos that started on her forearms and ended above her breasts. A dozen other tattoos, half-hidden in the low light, of various ages. Evidence of a life Allegra had hardly seen.

She shouldn't have so openly stared, but—she couldn't tear her eyes away. Her own body wouldn't let her.

Sal watched her. Before she lay down again, she reached for the base of Allegra's t-shirt; Allegra helped her pull it over her head and discard it somewhere. Once it was gone, there was just bare skin. Just breasts. "No other tattoos," Allegra said regretfully with a slight smile.

Sal mirrored it and lay down, drawing Allegra over her until she was half-kneeling above her. Then she paused for a moment... and lifted her head to bury her face in Allegra's breasts.

That did something to Allegra she wasn't ready for. It took her a second to recover and she *laughed*. When Sal lay back against the pillow, she had a broad smile. "They can fire me now," she said—but then the smile dropped off her face. So did Allegra's.

Oh. Tomorrow.

Sal's hand snuck up to Allegra's cheek, thumb on her chin, bringing her downward again. As their lips met, Allegra settled their bodies together, skin on skin. It had been so long that she had forgotten how good it felt to move against someone like this. How nice it was to share it with someone you had feelings for.

They stayed a little while like that; Allegra propped on her elbow and knee, hand on Sal's torso, exploring it. Her ribs. Then up to one of her breasts. The shape of it in her palm was familiar; what was new was Sal's body rising to it. Leaning into her hand.

She must like this, Allegra thought, and moved her lips from Sal's mouth, chin, neck—kissing down slowly, evenly to that breast. Feeling the skin against her cheek. Moving her lips and tongue over the whole curve of it. Taking it into her mouth.

A small sound escaped Sal; her head fell back to the pillow, her knees—one bent up—flopped open, towards the mattress. She put a hand to Allegra's temple, her ear, just resting it there, holding her in place.

Oh—that was—Allegra swallowed. God.

She let Sal enjoy it, moving between her breasts, drawing her own knee up so her thigh pressed higher up Sal's legs. Close enough for Sal to sit against it. And she kicked off her own tracksuit pants so she could better enjoy their legs together.

Sal responded to the skin, her legs moving along Allegra's, tilting towards Allegra's stomach. And her hips were there, and arching towards her, so—Allegra dipped her hand to slide between Sal's legs, over the thin silk of her pyjama shorts. It was warm—and already wet.

That—*Fuck*. Allegra felt that land in the same place, herself. Knowing it was working for her.

Sal's hand slipped over hers, holding it there. Guiding the movement. Allegra snuck a peek up at Sal's face to see her watching.

Seeing her, while touching her like this. Parted lips, heavy-lidded eyes.

She wanted to give her more. Shifting her hand a little, she tugged at the waistband of Sal's pyjama shorts. Sal nodded slightly.

Allegra hooked her fingers inside the waistband and pulled both the shorts and the soft lace she could feel underneath down Sal's long legs. Then she sat up a little, pulling the doona away. So she could see her, all of her. Her beautiful, slender body—and how, now, she could see that the tattoos mostly followed its contours. The lines of her ribs. Her breasts. Her hips. Allegra's eyes followed them down to the join of her legs. Smooth and pale. Like the rest. She was so fucking beautiful, all of her.

Allegra shifted between her legs, kissing down her body. Each tattoo, each landmark, until Sal's thighs were over her shoulders. She kissed those, too—each of them. Then she looked up Sal's body, up past the quick rise and fall of her chest to her parted lips. How intently she was watching Allegra.

She didn't look away. Neither did Sal. Eyes on hers, Allegra settled her mouth between Sal's legs.

The reaction was immediate. Sal stiffened under her, head back against her pillow. Breath held, body tight. Allegra didn't realise Sal's hand was on one of her arms until she squeezed it—silent. Her other hand was half-over her mouth.

Allegra had been with people who vocalised, who yelled, but never someone silent. It became a process of understanding her: the more Sal held herself still—taut and drawn—the more she stiffened and tightened and gripped Allegra with white knuckles, the more she felt it. The closer she was.

Allegra had found a rhythm and settled in to memorise how Sal felt under her lips and tongue, how she tasted, and to map every inch of the space between her legs when she felt Sal abruptly shift, withdrawing a little. Firm hands on either side of her face.

She stopped and looked up.

Sal was watching her closely. Her fingers pressed in. Her lips parted, then—"Up here," she said, tugging Allegra upward.

Allegra climbed her body, settling on her side next to Sal. Sal turned into her, a hand touching her jaw. She was still breathing heavily. Their mouths were close again. Close enough that when Sal spoke, Allegra felt her breath. "I want you up here with me," she said, so quietly Allegra hardly heard it. She nodded.

Sal took her hand and guided it back to where her mouth had been a moment ago, showing her how to continue. Allegra did.

Sal exhaled heavily across Allegra's chin. Bringing their lips together for a moment in a loose, approximate kiss—and then hovering there. So close their cheeks and noses sometimes touched. Sal kept bringing her hands up there, too—by Allegra's jaw, by her cheeks. Allegra's world narrowed to that tiny space between them as she kept her close, hand between them, letting her set the pace.

Sal tried to keep it off her face. Allegra could see her doing it—the careful stillness, the set of her mouth, the way she held her breath like she could outlast it. But it slipped through anyway, in small, involuntary ways. Her eyes lost focus for a second, her brows knitting together, her lips parting just enough for her breath to catch one last time.

Allegra was close enough to feel Sal's body rise towards it, tighter, stiffer—and then watched the moment it broke on her face. Her eyes rolling closed, her eyebrows lifting, mouth opening as she sank heavily against Allegra's hand.

Allegra slowed her movements, guiding Sal back down again until she'd settled against Allegra's body.

Sal lay there for a minute or two, still, body soft again. Then, she sought Allegra's lips—slow individual kisses. Resting their cheeks together in between each one. Their eyes met at one point, and held—letting Allegra in. For that, Allegra ended up kissing *her*.

They stayed that way for a time—short enough that Allegra was surprised when it was over, long enough that she'd already imagined spending Christmas together—when Sal propped herself up on an elbow. She leant in towards Allegra and guided her onto her back, putting a knee between hers, and kissing down past her neck and collarbones.

Allegra let her at first; Sal only kissed down as far as her breasts, settling there for a moment, a thumb strumming her nipple. But then she kept kissing, down Allegra's torso.

Allegra stopped her. She didn't want her to feel like this was purely transactional. "You don't have to."

Sal was unmoved. "I want to." She looked ready to press that point. Allegra certainly didn't feel like debating it.

She helped Sal remove her bike shorts and then lay back, feeling Sal trail a line of slow kisses down her front.

The exposure of it—having someone who mattered see her like that—brought a brief flicker of insecurity. There wasn't a hair anywhere on Sal's body. Allegra was... less fussed about grooming. It had never mattered—until now.

It didn't last. Sal was already kissing her quads, reverent, tracing the lines of her thigh tattoos, paying no attention to it.

When Sal finally settled between her legs and kissed her there, Allegra had a moment—just a second—where she couldn't get past that it was Sal. How much she had wanted this—how little she had allowed herself to imagine it. How she didn't need to anymore: she could just open her eyes and look down her body and there she was. So she did.

She searched for Sal's free hand, finding it wrapped around her thigh, and laced their fingers. *C1*, she thought vaguely. And then thinking got harder.

Of course Sal was like this: precise, intentional. Every movement considered—but not distant, not detached. She was paying attention. Allegra could feel it in the way she adjusted, the way she followed, never missing a beat. It was so easy to let her take over. To just... go with it.

So she did. She let Sal guide her.

It came on quietly at first—just a shift in her breathing, a tension she didn't quite recognise until it was already building. Sal didn't miss it. She kept her right there until Allegra couldn't think about anything else. Not the room, not tomorrow—just this. Just her.

Just Sal's mouth on her, her hands on her. Just Sal. And when Sal guided her there and she finally came hard against Sal's mouth, her tongue, those hands—she came with Sal's name on her lips. She breathed it, whispered it—let Sal know she was the only thought in her head.

She stayed as it passed, as it left her there against the mattress.

Just the two of them. Alone in this massive, grey room. Damp with sweat and tangled in each other and the doona.

For a moment, there was nothing missing. Just for tonight.

Sal came back up at some point. Stroked her face. Gently kissed her lips. Climbed inside her arms and settled there; Allegra could feel a faint smile against her shoulder.

They fit. Allegra let her eyes stay closed, holding onto it—the weight of her, the quiet of the room, the way it all felt settled. Like something that could last, if she let herself believe it.

She almost said her name again.

Something else followed it, rising up too easily. Words Allegra realised only as she was about to say them. She drew a breath, opening her mouth.

Sal stilled in her arms—just for a second—and then her hand came up, pressing lightly against Allegra's mouth.

"Not tonight," she said quietly.

Allegra let her have it. She didn't want to be the one to end this.

They finally slept. Allegra woke up to bright morning sunlight, still tangled in Sal. Bare limbs and skin. They were still facing each other, but Sal wasn't curled up under Allegra's chin where she had started last night. Her head was tipped back, forehead nearly at Allegra's lips. One arm under Allegra's neck, the other across her middle. Her eyes closed. Face relaxed.

Allegra let her sleep for now. A final stretch of peace.

Sal woke with her alarm, stirring, eyes fluttering open. Reorienting with a moment of surprise and adjustment when she saw Allegra. They shared a brief smile and a kiss before Sal had to peel herself away to cancel the alarm.

She sat on the edge of the bed, facing away from Allegra in the sunlight—a whole other collection of tattoos now visible. These ones were more curated. The same geometric shapes and symbols, following the shapes of her collarbones. Fanning out down her arms.

Allegra was so engaged with them that it took her a moment to notice the slump of Sal's body; the weight of the day had settled back on her shoulders.

It pulled in Allegra's chest. "Five more minutes?" She slid across the mattress and kissed some sort of occult-looking shape on Sal's shoulder.

Sal looked over it at her, half-smiling. She shook her head, but lifted a hand and threaded it briefly through Allegra's wild bed hair. When she let it fall, her smile went with it. Standing, she walked across the broad marble floor into the ensuite. Allegra could hear the shower.

The cool air-conditioning and the warmth of the sun on her would have been perfect for rolling over and remembering Sal between her thighs, but—board meeting. Sal being terminated, for whatever the fuck reasons they'd decided were justified. She didn't know how these things worked; it sounded like total bullshit. For Sal to be that shaken last night, she knew it was real.

Sal had been out of the shower for some time when Allegra decided to stop lying in bed and thinking in circles. The door to the ensuite was open, so she slipped in.

Sal was facing the mirror in a thin bathrobe, a blow dryer on the stone basin beside her, running a straightener through her hair. Her eyes dipped to Allegra's body as she entered; lingering for perhaps a bit too long, hand and straightener pausing mid-brush. She directed her eyes back to the mirror and her hair, and continued.

Allegra leant back against the cool hardwood of the door. "If it's going to be over, go out with a bang," she said ironically. "Wear something sleeveless. Show them your stripes."

That got a smile out of Sal. She spent a minute or two making the points of her hair on either side of her chin sharp, and then turned her hip on the counter, facing Allegra. Her robe fell open a little, leaving one of her breasts and the knife tattoo on display.

Sal saw where she was looking. "Go on." A slight grin.

"Okay." Allegra wandered up to her and put a hand... on the knife. It was a dam break. A relief. They ended up laughing silently against each other, tangled again. Allegra kissed her a little—she tasted like mint.

When they pulled away again, she looked down at the knife. "What's it for?"

The warmth drained out of Sal's smile. "I watched a documentary once about ceremonial daggers," she said. "This is one of them. The way the man talked about them. With respect, with reverence. He said, 'weapons can be beautiful', 'they're not just things'." She let that hang. "It's what I've been since my conception, so..."

That—Allegra swallowed. She tilted Sal's chin up. She hadn't done her makeup yet; her eyes were still a little puffy from last night. Open for her.

They ended up kissing in the bathroom for a little while. Silently. Hands on each other's cheeks.

Sal pulled away. "I do need to get ready."

Allegra nodded, kissed her once more, and then left her to it.

When she emerged again, it was fully armoured. An appropriately conservative black suit, perfect hair and makeup—a shade less corporate goth than usual.

"If you're not going sleeveless, go full kink," Allegra told her. "Disney villain, the blazer with the triangle shoulder pads. Fuck them."

Sal blinked at her for a moment and then *laughed*. She came over and kissed Allegra where she sat, on the bed. When she spoke, it wasn't with the same humour Allegra had spoken with. "I don't think they'd survive that."

Allegra's smile faded. "Good. Destroy them. And him." And then, because she meant more of that than she should have, added, "And text me when you're done."

Sal's hand was tight on hers. "I don't get to choose who does what," she said, and then left.

Chapter 46: Effective Immediately

The penthouse was eerily quiet after Sal left. On any other day, Allegra would have been content to lie in the early morning sun—especially naked on someone else's bed. Not today.

She sat up, looking down at her bare legs. Sal would be in her car now, driving to the board meeting. Dreading what she'd find when she walked into that room.

She got up and had a shower.

The atrium didn't smell like coffee this morning. The very morning Sal would need to be alert and think clearly. Allegra nearly started making one for her—then realised she had no idea where the meeting was being held. There probably wasn't a way to get Sal a coffee, but Allegra should go there anyway. For afterwards.

She put her suit back on and checked the time: past 9am. The meeting would have started, so no point in asking Sal where it was. She could check Pitt Street.

There were still two police officers outside the BSA building. She pulled over near them to ask if people were allowed in yet—and got a surly head shake. Further down Pitt Street, she parked in a loading zone and checked the temporary office. When she pressed her face against the glass, the reception desk was empty.

She stood back from the door. Perhaps Gerard would know? She texted him on the off-chance he'd reply on a Saturday.

When she moved her car, she missed the turn onto the M1 and ended up on Park Street, funnelled onto New South Head Road before she could correct it. By the next set of lights, her hands were white-knuckled on the steering wheel. She kept checking her notifications. She was distracted, rattled, and already halfway to Point Piper. She could not fucking drive like this.

Perhaps she could go to Point Piper, get her head straight—work out how much junk she had for storage, if nothing else—and come back once Gerard told her where to go.

Allegra had a moment of disorientation when she saw Timothy's van still in the driveway before she remembered it was Saturday.

He was sitting at the table in the kitchen with his laptop and some paperwork. He took his glasses off when he saw her. "Allegra!" He stood. "You've been busy! Come to visit?"

She grimaced. She didn't have the energy, but there was no point in hiding anything anymore. "I'm going to put my stuff in storage. I need to figure out how much there is."

His smile faded. "Ah."

She stood there a moment. She should say something else but—Sal. She just needed to—she was in a rush. She went to the guest room and quickly emptied all the drawers and built-in robes. Definitely more than she could fit in the car. Maybe three loads—at least one container. Okay.

She left everything in piles and straightened, checking her phone. Nothing.

Back in the living room, on her way to the door, she noticed Timothy had angled the chair towards it. Not fucking now. She needed to get back to the city, and—

"Allegra?"

That tone. She stopped in place and turned a bit impatiently towards him.

"Your suit smelt like smoke."

She froze. Beyond him, on the balcony, it was gone from where she'd hung it.

He leaned against the back of the chair, hands laced over his stomach. Watching her.

"It did?"

"You know it did." Not angry, exactly. But something. "You used most of the Febreze and then hung it up outside."

Allegra didn't know how to react, so she did Sal's trick. She just listened.

"I took it to be dry-cleaned."

"Thank you," she said automatically.

He was watching her. "Even now you're not coming clean." There was a smile pulling at his lips—she didn't understand it. Was it wry? "Anyway, I think it was a lovely thing to do. I'm sure she really appreciated it."

She *stared* at him.

He broke into a smile. "I knew it." He leant forward, gesturing towards her with his reading glasses before putting them back on. "I knew you'd come around with her," he told her. "You went to visit Simone."

Jesus fucking Christ. "I did."

"As I always say, all of us are only ever one bad decision away from jail," he told her, looking thoroughly pleased with himself. Which—*God*. "It's truly wonderful to see you going out of your way to heal your relationships with—"

"Timothy, I'm in a rush," she said, cutting him off. She could do without his proselytising right now. She'd taken a few more steps back to the door when he stopped her *again*.

"Oh, by the way." She looked up at him, exhaling audibly through her nose as he asked, "Have you seen Cece in the last few days?"

She frowned. "I had a chat with her yesterday while I was here looking for my passport."

Now he looked troubled. "Did she seem—short to you?"

That sat wrong with Allegra. Timothy, too? So she wasn't the only one getting a strange read on her?

Cece had certainly seemed *something*. But not short, exactly. "No? What did she say to you?"

He considered the question. "She seemed—" He shook his head. "I just worry about the foundation funding."

"But her kids are coming to volunteer at your Christmas lunch."

"Perhaps it's a consolation prize as she knows their presence will attract donations." He exhaled. "After Dimi stepped back a little—" He sighed. "I can't shake the feeling something is wrong."

Neither could Allegra, but she couldn't put her finger on it, not with Cece. She and Dimi were friends, though, probably long-time friends. Allegra felt deeply uneasy. She said goodbye to Timothy and climbed back into her LandCruiser.

No text from Gerard.

She looked up. In the distance, over the gate, she could see the blue spaceship house at the top of the hill.

She sat there for a moment, frowning up at it.

Sal would probably go there, start a conversation with Cece, or her kids, or the staff—and somehow draw an answer out of them.

Allegra wasn't sure she could do that, not like Sal could. *But I saved her son*, Allegra told herself. *Surely I can just ask if something is wrong*? *Surely that warrants an honest answer*?

Since Gerard hadn't replied, she had a few minutes. She climbed out of the car and up the hill to the spaceship house. This time, though, she went to the front gate and pressed the buzzer. A young woman's voice answered—probably too old to be Astrid. "Good morning, Mrs Sinclair."

Allegra winced. "Hi," she said to the voice. "Is Cece home?"

There was a pause. Too long. "I'm sorry, she's not."

"Do you know if she'll be back shortly?"

Immediate. "I'm so sorry, I don't think she will."

"Should I—"

"You can call her PA," the speaker said. "She'll let you know when Mrs Vale is available. Would you like me to provide you with the contact details for her PA?"

Her PA? "Thanks," Allegra said slowly. "I can get them from Sal."

"Great. Have a nice day." The buzzer went silent.

Allegra stared at it for a few seconds, frowning.

That was cold, right? It felt cold.

She turned and walked back to her car, climbing inside. Maybe it was something as simple as a social faux pas? Maybe rich people didn't just drop in on each other, even if they were neighbours? Even if you saved their kids?

Allegra shook her head, and was putting her phone back in the—

A notification. From Gerard. She hurriedly opened it.

It was one line. No darlings, no oh honeys, no jokes—just an address. She copied it to Maps and headed off immediately.

The building was a hotel in Haymarket with conference facilities, but reception wouldn't tell her which floor the board meeting was on. She texted Sal to say she was there anyway, and then went and sat in the small foyer while staff looked uncomfortably like they might, at any second, ask her to leave. Probably because of who she was, they didn't.

She spent nearly an hour waiting, scrolling through videos of people setting things they didn't like on fire—somehow less satisfying this morning—before she heard a familiar sound. Brisk stilettos on marble.

She sat up, turning towards the lifts. Sal.

She couldn't get to her fast enough. Sal looked—off. She was throwing looks sideways at reception, so Allegra pulled her out onto the street. Sal stopped her at the doorway. "I can't go further." She scanned the street, straightened, and swallowed. "I'm not allowed to leave. They just asked me to step out for 20 minutes, so I—" She held up her phone. "And you said you were here."

"Of course," she said, holding Sal's shoulders. "What's happening? Did they—?" She didn't want to say it.

Sal looked down. Then out—and shook her head. "It's still going on," she said. "It's like a trial. When we walked in, they were facing us. I—"

Allegra looked around them, too. It was Saturday; they were near the markets, and there were people everywhere. And heads were turning. Allegra stood in front of Sal to at least block the stares. "Why did they ask you to step out?"

Sal shook her head again. "He's still in there. I suppose they could be—" She stopped. "I don't know."

"Why would they only want to speak to him?"

Sal's eyes met hers. She shook her head. Allegra knew what that meant, and it made her feel sick.

"Cece was there. She had an Atlas file. Hers."

What on—"What?!" The interrogation yesterday. No. "She thinks you're part of it."

Sal reached a hand to the wall; Allegra hadn't noticed she was unsteady. She took Sal's elbows. Sal let her. "Every second. Every second I waited for them to say my name. I don't know what's going to happen."

Allegra wanted to pick her up and carry her away *now*. If this was going to end badly, it could just end now. It wasn't worth what it was doing to her. "I'll stay here," she told Sal. "I'll wait for you. I won't move."

Sal straightened. "I haven't eaten anything since you brought me food yesterday," she said. "Do you think that—"

"I'll get you something," Allegra said. "Something solid, a—"

Sal squeezed her arm. "Just salad. I can't do anything heavy right now."

Allegra nodded, rushed off, found something that was 'just salad', and got it back inside the 20-minute window. Sal was where she left her. Allegra escorted her inside, up to the right floor, and into the recessed area by the lifts, where there were a couple of chairs.

Sal accepted the box from her, sat, and took a breath. "Okay," she said, sounding slightly more collected than she had outside. "I need to eat this quickly. I only have a few minutes."

Allegra watched her empty the dressing on the salad, toss it, and then eat a mouthful—desperate to know more. She didn't want to pressure her.

Sal swallowed quickly. "They interrogated me," she said, between bites. "What I knew about Atlas. What my role had been with the land and the fires. But they'd already decided what they believed." Bite, swallow. "They already have statements from clients who are pulling out. Demanding action. And—all the major shareholders are there, in the meeting."

By the weight Sal gave that fact, Allegra figured that was unusual and important.

"When Dimi got up, he—" She shook her head. "He was so pleasant, so calm. He smiled, joked, said he completely understands why they're so worried, but that he's seen this all before." She stopped, took a tense mouthful, and swallowed. "Cece just sat there, listening to him."

A stately-looking door opened further down the corridor, and a suited woman stepped out and took a few steps down the hallway towards them. She said coolly, "We're ready for you now, Sal, if you'd like to come back in."

Allegra didn't miss the colour drain from Sal's face. She nodded, swallowed hastily, and gave the rest of the salad to Allegra. "All yours." She turned to face the woman—public face on. She would have given Dimi a run for his money on 'pleasant' and 'calm'. "Thanks, Judy." Each step back into the room was deliberate and, to anyone observing, relaxed.

Allegra watched her go. She forced the rest of the salad down, found a bin beside the lifts, and then sat back to wait. She didn't even have the focus to get her phone out.

Why wasn't Sal allowed to leave? Allegra didn't understand it. She also didn't understand why they would make her step out for 20 minutes—unless they were talking *about* her while she wasn't there. Planning what they were going to do with her. With Dimi.

That idea in her head, Allegra couldn't sit still. She stood—paced—sat down. Shifted position. Went to the other end of the hallway—toilets. When she remembered Cece had brought an Atlas file to the meeting—why? Why did she bring—did Dimi maybe—? Was Cece involved with using Atlas somehow, or—?

She shook her head. That didn't make any sense. God, she fucking wished she knew how any of this corporate bullshit worked.

When she heard the door open again, she sat up straight, looking to see if it was—

Cece?

Allegra froze in place, wavering on whether to say hello. After the reception Cece's staff had given her, she wasn't sure what to think.

Cece spotted Allegra by the lift, anyway. Her smile was impeccably polite, but it didn't make it to her eyes. "Waiting for Sal?" Allegra nodded. When Cece passed Allegra in the hallway, she paused beside her. Took a breath. "She'll need you after this." She continued on into the Women's.

That—

No.

Stuck in place, Allegra stayed there until Cece walked back past her and calmly re-entered the room, giving her a brief glimpse of all the people inside.

They were *smiling*. It was obscene. Someone who'd spent half their life—every single waking hour dedicated to—

The door opened again. Allegra turned towards it, taking a breath.

A man. Someone she didn't recognise, in a grey suit with grey hair and regal features. He *smiled* at her on the way past, and on the way back.

She shook her stiff knees out, pacing up and down the back hallway, wondering what stage of the meeting they were at. What it meant. If Sal already—if she already knew. If it had already been done.

When the door opened again, Allegra looked up to see if it was finally her to—

Dimi.

Him. Seeing him felt like being king hit. And he was composed. Calculated. Intently scrolling on his phone.

Without thinking, without breathing, Allegra's body moved and she backed into the Women's, listening to confident footsteps move past her.

She stood with her ear close to the door waiting for the footsteps to return. She could vaguely hear him talking somewhere in another room—*chuckling*?—maybe she should go and eavesdrop—

The door opened.

Sal, right there in her face.

Allegra was so unprepared that she hugged her. Sal didn't push her away, but she was stiff as a board. Allegra released her. "What's going on?!"

Sal didn't speak straight away. She looked dazed—her lips were parted. Her eyes were unfocused. She put a hand on Allegra's arm to acknowledge her and then walked forward to the basins, leaning heavily on them for a moment.

Allegra could only think about what Cece said, even when Sal spoke. "They terminated his contract as CEO effective immediately," she said, as if she couldn't believe it. "But not only that, they have the shareholder numbers to remove him as director in January. If they do that, those minutes will be on public record—" She took a breath. "Or he can resign as director now and it will be recorded as his retirement. He asked if he could have some time to decide, they gave him *30 minutes*, so he's gone to call his lawyer."

Allegra heard that. But it wasn't enough. "And you?" she asked. "What about your contract?"

Sal looked at her—*haunted*. Like she was simply unable to process what had just happened. "They got me up. Allegra, I—" She stopped. "It was—"

Allegra went up to her, right beside her. Put a hand on hers over the basin.

"I stood there in front of them. Like a rifle squad." She looked up.

"They made me caretaker CEO."

Chapter 47: Exposure

Allegra stood there, still.

Caretaker CEO?

"That's temporary?" she managed eventually. Sal nodded. "They won't bring him back after you've cleaned it up?" Sal shook her head. "What if it's someone worse than him? Controlled by him?"

Sal exhaled, still staring at the sink. "All possible. All better options than him."

They stood together at the basin, silent. CEO?

Sal stared down at their hands. "I told them I needed 10 minutes."

"Would you like them? I can go and—"

"No." Sal's fingers curled around hers. "I'm having them."

Oh. Allegra looked down at their hands.

She wasn't fired, Allegra realised. *She wasn't ejected from the only life she knows. Or mine*. Allegra held her breath for a moment.

"I wasn't prepared for this," Sal said eventually. "He wasn't expecting it, either. He's not happy about it."

"Will he retaliate?"

The furrow in Sal's brow deepened. "Probably," she said. "Although he's got limited options now." Allegra saw it in the basin mirror: the ghost of a smile. Disbelief. "You should have seen it, Allegra," she said. "He's *radioactive*. The way Cece spoke to him at the end—I've never heard her so cold. The other shareholders have confirmed Atlas files, too. The police have them at the moment, but they're going to hand them over to regulators. Once that happens, anyone named can access them." She looked across at Allegra. There was hope. "God. This might really be it."

After last night, that hope—she could have wrapped her arms around Sal. "We might have done it?"

"Well, we're not out of the woods, but—" She exhaled; the smile broke containment. "He's out of options. Everyone's distancing themselves. He'll be quietly sidelined or publicly removed from his positions on Monday. Someone's tipped off the press about Atlas, and Cece managed to get them to wait for a press conference." She was still holding Allegra's hand as she spoke, thinking aloud. "We're going to do some planning now." She straightened. "Before that—I wanted 10 minutes."

Allegra found herself smiling again. She took Sal's hand and laced their fingers together.

Sal watched. Then released a small breath. "I have to go back in."

Allegra nodded and opened the door, their hands still linked as they—

Dimi was waiting by the lifts, already facing them.

He made a beeline for them.

Sal's hand tightened in Allegra's. She froze—held herself—but nearly shrank back. Like a child expecting to be struck.

That lit a fire under Allegra.

Even now. *Even now,* he was fucking doing this.

She was already moving—stepping in front of him, blocking his route to Sal—and his view of her. When she spoke, her voice was pleasant. Authoritative. "I'm sorry. She won't be speaking with you."

He stopped. Took a tiny step back, looking up at her. She was taller. And smiling.

"Oh, Allegra," he said. So mildly. "Good to see you here. I just needed to have a quick word with Sal about—"

"Lift's over there." She nodded at it, still smiling.

Behind her, she heard a tiny gasp.

Dimi watched her, recalibrating. He was adjusting to her. That was new.

"If you're worried about the fires and all this media nonsense, you're missing the actual issue," he said, as if he'd diagnosed the problem with her attitude. He tried to take a small step around her. "Sal, we need to—"

Allegra stepped sideways, blocking him.

It was working. He didn't push past her. Instead, he stood up. Straightened his suit. "You're making this worse for her, Allegra."

"*I'm* making this worse for her?"

A light hand on the small of her back. A vote of confidence.

Dimi didn't see it. "I don't know what she's told you, but—"

"*She* didn't need to say one fucking thing to me, Dimi." The words kept coming. "You showed exactly what you are—at the dinner table. On the balcony. In front of my entire family." She looked him dead in the fucking eye, taking a deep breath, putting her polite smile back on. "And we're not doing that anymore."

Dimi watched her. Poised. "I was only trying to make sure Aaron was being looked after. I still am."

Allegra remembered Sal's 'radioactive' comment. "And what exactly could you offer him now, Dimi?"

That landed, she saw it flash across his face. He quickly absorbed it. "I would've thought that boy might still be wanting for a bit of care and attention. It's been in rather short supply."

There it was. "I've seen what your attention does to people," she said. "That is the *last* thing he needs."

A faint smile returned. "You will let Aaron have a say in that, won't you?"

Allegra did not break eye contact. "Ask him."

Dimi's expression faltered momentarily.

She swung the axe. "Lift's still there," she said. "Enjoy your retirement."

He straightened, looking up at her as the moment settled. His expression reset, mask returning. He nodded politely at Allegra, as if to wish her goodbye, and then stepped into the lift.

He watched her as the doors closed.

Allegra stood in place, staring at the doors.

Had she—*really just done that*? Not just blocked him, but placed herself on the board. Her heart was pounding; his stare burnt into her retinas.

But something else had loosened in her. Something had slipped its leash. It had been waiting.

Behind her, Sal hadn't moved. When Allegra turned to her, she was wide-eyed, breathing slow and measured breaths. Shaking her head. "Jesus Christ, Allegra," she said. A flash of panic. "Do you realise what you just did? He knows you're hostile, now. This puts you at so much risk!"

Allegra was unmoved. "I know."

Sal's eyes snapped up at her. It took her a moment to speak. "This isn't a joke. He is *dangerous*."

"Well, so am I."

Sal opened her mouth and—closed it. Her frown eased slightly. "You are," she conceded, giving Allegra a once-over. "Aren't you worried about him *actually* moving in on Aaron?"

Allegra was, but not enough. "I won't give him space," she said easily. "Plus, you said everyone's pulling their support from him, so..." She shrugged.

Sal stepped back a little, taking all of Allegra in. As if being able to see all of her would make the logic behind what she'd done clearer. "This feels dangerously reckless," she decided, eventually. "On one hand, I—" She stopped. "This is reckless."

Allegra softened. "Do you wish I hadn't done it?"

Sal paused. When she exhaled again, it was in a long, heavy breath. "That's not the point."

"It is to me." She stepped in a little. "Because *I* don't regret it. I'd do it again."

"He will use that against you," Sal said quietly. "You've just made that inevitable."

"Then he can try. I'm not going to shape my life around him." She put her hands on Sal's shoulders. "I know what he can do, I've seen it. I just don't want to live like that."

Sal spent a few seconds considering Allegra before her shoulders relaxed a little under Allegra's hands. She exhaled, panic gone. Surprise remained. "You are..." She shook her head, incredulous, leaning heavily on the last word. "*Insane*."

That made Allegra laugh. "Still a surprise to you, apparently."

"Apparently." When Sal looked back up, she had that evaluative quality in her expression again. This time, she didn't push back; but she did slip their hands into C1.

When the boardroom door opened again, Allegra recognised 'Judy' from earlier, looking expectantly at Sal. Sal gave Allegra's hands a squeeze before releasing them and heading back there.

At the door, she paused and looked back. Something in her expression had settled. She held it a moment—and then went inside.

Allegra hadn't even sat back in her chair by the lifts before the door opened again to a stream of people in suits, mid-discussion, shaking hands with those staying inside. One of them was Cece.

She spotted Allegra, gave her a little wave as if to indicate she wanted a word, and then apologised to whoever she was speaking to. She came over and put a hand on Allegra's arm. "I'm so sorry. I hope Sal can forgive me."

Allegra stared at her.

"Dimi has meant *such* a great deal to her. She always spoke so highly of his guidance and mentorship. I think this will deeply affect her. I couldn't sleep last night—there was no other way."

Right. Allegra nodded slowly, not wanting to start laughing in her face. Better just—go with it. "I'm sure she understands the position you were in."

Cece nodded sombrely. "We all feel for her."

The group she'd been with was already drifting towards the lifts; Cece glanced up. "Anyway. My apologies again. I gather I'll see you about—

especially with the kids getting involved with Redeemer." She was reabsorbed into the group of shareholders before Allegra could ask about the Redeemer funding. She made a face. Her phone buzzed.

Sal. *"I'll be here for a while. Go home, I'll meet you there when I'm done."*

Allegra had missed Cece's lift, so she caught the next one, returned to her car and drove back to the penthouse. She paused before going up, though. She didn't feel like rattling around in there all day. It was so nice outside. Surely she should be out in it?

She didn't want to go far—she didn't know how long 'a while' was. There were plenty of streets to walk nearby anyway, full of people doing last-minute Christmas shopping. Stores twinkled, flashed, and blinked. The crowd threaded in and out of them, around café chairs and into parks to enjoy the sun, arms full of bags.

Surrounded by it, Allegra felt both oddly detached and connected. Families buzzed around her; she'd never done that with Aaron or Timothy, or even Vanessa's kids. At a gift shop window, it struck her: she could. She could buy something. Not just send money.

That thought stayed with her even after Sal had texted her to say she was on her way back.

They ended up arriving back at the same time, meeting in the carpark. Allegra's first instinct upon seeing Sal—suppressed immediately—was to rush over and pull her into a full embrace. Sal read it all over her anyway as they met at the lift.

She gave Allegra a once-over, eyes narrowed. *"Stay,"* she said, as if commanding a dog. Then, "I need to give a presser at 5pm—same hotel as this morning. I have a lot of work to do before then. Ideally, you'd join me there."

They stepped into the lift as it arrived. When the doors closed, Allegra asked far too innocently, "Can I join you afterwards?"

Sal looked up from her phone, then sidelong at Allegra. A very faint smile touched her lips. "Later."

The atrium was the same echoing hall it had always been; the strong early afternoon sun shone through the windows and cast sheets of gold across the floor, overlaying the grey. One fell across the three-seater. Allegra had her eye on that spot as she hovered near Sal at the kitchen bench.

Sal put her laptop on it and began scooping coffee beans into the grinder. "There will be an element of Q&A with the presser. I'll be on camera for a while. I'd like you to join me."

Allegra waited for her to finish grinding the beans. "You mean as your partner?"

Sal transferred them into the filter. "Mmm."

Allegra frowned. She felt—Well. "I don't want to pretend, Sal."

"You won't be pretending."

Her chest leapt, unbidden. She caught it. Did Sal mean—? She tried to read her face.

"Allegra." Sal exhaled, and put the coffee down, pushing the grinder an oddly large distance away from them before looking up. "We won't be pretending because this is clearly a relationship."

She'd barely finished the sentence before Allegra was on her—pushing her back against the counter, arms wrapping tight around her. *My partner. God*. She kissed her, one hand sliding up to Sal's cheek.

Sal let her, at first. She even kissed back (after pushing the coffee beans even further away), her fingertips hooked into Allegra's belt. Not for long. "I have 3 hours and 12 minutes to get ready for the presser."

Allegra's lips began to travel down her neck. "Whatever you can do in 3 hours and 12 minutes," she said between presses of her lips, "you can do in 3 hours and 2 minutes."

Sal paused with that thought—perhaps for a fraction too long. "Tempting," she said eventually. "But I'll need all of them."

Allegra reluctantly released her to her coffee and media prep, going to lie in the patch of sun on the couch she'd spied earlier.

As Sal settled at the table, put on her reading glasses and got to work, Allegra kept craning her neck up to check. To confirm she was there. And real. To look at Sal being cool and professional, as if none of it had happened—or because this was what she did when it had.

She lay her head back, letting the sun warm her smiling face. She wanted to text everyone she knew and tell them that she and Sal were together. Trouble was, their answer would be, "Yeah, that's old news."

And this afternoon, she was going to appear at Sal's presser, stand beside her, be her real plus one for whatever she was going to—

She frowned.

Standing beside her, putting her face to it: whatever Sal was going to say.

Hmm. Allegra opened her eyes and stared up at the distant ceiling. "Sal?"

"Yes?" She was still typing.

"What's the topic of your press conference?"

A pause in typing. Then typing. "It's primarily announcing a change in leadership and doing damage control. I'm still discussing with Threshold what that looks like."

And you want me to put my face to it, Allegra realised. She lay there for a few minutes, processing that. She wasn't—sure how she felt, actually. Putting her face to Sal, she could accept. But to BSA? A corporation that had just done some *really* fucking shady shit, and would perhaps continue to?

She sat up and walked silently over to the table. Sal's eyes lifted from behind her laptop, dipping briefly to Allegra's posture, and then back up to her face. Her typing slowed.

It stopped when Allegra spoke. "If you're putting me up there—if you're attaching me to BSA—it's got to be clean. No new Atlas, no corruption, or whatever. You can't just harm people and put my face on it."

Sal heard that without flinching and considered it. "So your condition is that I operate within a standard you're prepared to endorse."

Allegra felt uneasy about how easily she said that. "Yes. No new Hislops."

She pressed her lips together. "Alright," she said, and put her fingers back to the keyboard.

Allegra sat there for a moment, completely disoriented. "Alright?"

Sal paused. "Yes. You want BSA to avoid harm to third parties. I want to avoid financial harm to shareholders. The solution here is to ensure they never conflict," she said. "That's already how I operate."

Allegra made a face at her. "This feels too easy."

Sal took her hands off the keyboard again, this time removing her glasses. "I'll be more explicit," she said. "Dimi could always get away with all the things he did because it was easy for him to clean it up: connections, pressure, whatever it took. I don't have that leverage, and I've always found that level of exposure unacceptable." She let that settle. "So, if you won't be attached to harm, you don't have to be. I can't clean that up—and I don't make moves I can't contain." She put her glasses back on. "So, no new Hislops."

Allegra absorbed that, feeling uncomfortable. She went back to her patch of sun anyway.

Sal was doing that thing again where she tightly rationed her time. Laptop open, phone to her ear, she moved between them easily—typing, pausing, responding, already ahead of whatever was being said to her. Her tone stayed calm and precise. Decisions quick, instructions clear.

It faded so much into the background for Allegra—Sal being Sal—that she only really noticed when it stopped.

She craned her neck up. Sal was watching her. Not gazing, exactly. Just... thinking. After a few seconds, her brow relaxed. Lifted. She got straight back to typing.

Allegra found that a little puzzling, but forgot about it until she heard Sal say her name.

She looked up. Sal was clearly calling her over, so she went and sat down at the table.

Sal turned the laptop to face her. There was an email open on it. Sal's expression was unreadable, but she was watching Allegra closely.

Allegra looked down at it. It was from Threshold's chair.

"Sal," it began. *"Those terms are acceptable as long as we're able to work within those numbers. Our lawyers had already raised the issue of the settlement possibly being open to challenge, so that does make things simpler."* Allegra wasn't sure what any of that meant, so kept reading. *"We agree in principle to the offer to return the property to the Hislops, as long as BSA is willing to provide us those other assurances and waivers as outlined in the below email. See you this afternoon."*

Allegra sat back.

Then she read it again, just to make sure she understood it. "What am I reading?"

"An in-principle agreement between Threshold and BSA."

"To return the land to the Hislops."

Sal looked slightly smug. She nodded.

Allegra stared at her and then read the email again. "You just arranged this?"

Sal pointed to the timestamp: three minutes ago. Allegra looked up at her. "This was your idea."

"I think it's the simplest solution, both legally and reputationally. Of course, it comes at a significant cost to BSA," she said. "But it's containable. And given the media storm around the fires, worth it."

Allegra's immediate response was *Oh, thank God*, and then, *this is it, this is exactly what should happen*. Rosie's tear-streaked face in her car, the slump of Sean Hislop's shoulders in the video. *This* was the right outcome.

But. That wasn't *why* this had happened, was it? It wasn't why Sal had done it. "You didn't do it because it's right."

"But it is right." She was slightly smug. "Will you put your face to that?"

Allegra sat back, wanting to be happy about the land. Instead, she was deeply uncomfortable. "You are fucking evil, you know that?"

Sal had a small, satisfied smile. "I think I'll put your hair in a plait for the cameras," she said, standing. "Want to come and get ready?"

"I want to tell Rosie," Allegra said, instead. "Can I?"

Sal pressed her lips together. "Threshold are going to announce at the presser," she said. "You can tell her to come to it."

Allegra would rather just have fucking told her. She might have anyway—if she didn't think it might interfere with the land actually being handed back. She didn't know much about Threshold, but what she knew she didn't like.

While Sal was redoing her own hair and makeup, Allegra texted Rosie. *"There's going to be a joint BSA/Threshold press conference at five. I think you'll want to hear what they're going to say."* She attached the address of the hotel to it.

"Okay..." was the answer. *I wish I could tell you more,* she thought, then put her phone away. It was an hour. It would be okay.

When Sal emerged, it was still in her extremely boring, very conservative suit.

"That suit is in no way evil enough for the shit you just pulled on me," Allegra noted as she passed by.

Sal smiled. "Unfortunately, it's necessary for me to look somewhat generic for this one," she said. "Now, time to make you look grounded, slightly wild, and sickeningly earnest." She stood back to consider Allegra in the suit. "The other one isn't clean?"

"Smelt like smoke. It's at the dry cleaners."

Sal's eyebrows were up momentarily. "I see." She looked back to Allegra's clothes. "Let's get you in some sort of soft-coloured t-shirt, then. Green, or blue—something 'nature'. You can look like you've just thrown a random blazer over the top of it."

Once Allegra was appropriately dressed, Sal sat her down in the master dressing room and French braided her hair in brisk, practised movements, and then added powder to control the shine of her skin and some mascara. "Good," was her final assessment, before she bustled off to pack up her laptop and notes.

Allegra drove so Sal could finalise her notes and make sure her own team was up to speed before they arrived; she finished early, though, and Christmas shopping traffic was bumper-to-bumper. Sal ended up staring ahead, eyes unfocused again.

Allegra noticed and glanced at her with mild concern when they stopped. Sal shook her head. "Nothing of consequence," she said. Then, after a moment, added, "This morning still feels like a fever dream. I was so sure it was the end for me." She chose her words. "If he went, too—I'd made that outcome acceptable to myself."

They were stopped at a light, so Allegra put a hand over hers on the centre console.

Sal curled her fingers around Allegra's hand and then looked at her. "He'll try to contain you."

"Fuck him."

A small, involuntary smile slipped up onto Sal's face. She didn't comment further, but she did spend some time watching Allegra.

The hotel was bustling when they arrived; media was already setting up. A hundred cannon-like cameras swung around to face them, a hundred voices called out questions over each other. Allegra just focused on holding Sal's hand—and being towed by her, really—inside the venue and the makeshift office there. There were already BSA staff there, but Gerard was the only one she recognised. He gave her a little wide-eyed wave as she hung back, watching the ant farm.

The Threshold chair, Victor Liang, was nothing like Allegra had expected him to be. He wasn't smooth with a predatory corporate smile, or outgoing like Dimi and Peter. More 'accounting partner' than 'executive'; friendly and unassuming. He and Sal shook hands and then immediately started going over a sheet he handed her.

It was *extremely* jarring to think that high-level stewardship decisions made by this very mild, friendly man might have resulted in Sean Hislop driving into a tree and the Hislop family falling apart.

Or... maybe he was like Sal? Someone to the side of those operational decisions—and it was that Thomas CEO person, whoever Austin had mentioned, who was like Dimi?

Either way, it didn't make her feel good. None of this was any good. At least the land was going back to the family it should always have rested with. That was the only part of it she felt like she was there for.

Before they went out into the hall, Sal took Allegra aside to give her a once-over. "You can either stand a step or two behind me and in frame, or to the side of the stage," she said. "Choose somewhere that feels comfortable for you."

Allegra stopped her. "It doesn't matter where I stand if you're going to say—" She wasn't sure how to put it. "I feel uncomfortable about this."

Sal took her phone out of her pocket and gave it to Allegra. It was open on a document. "That's what I'm saying—or thereabouts. I'm confident you won't disapprove of any of it. But you can have a read now and let me know."

It was two pages. The door was already half open.

Sal saw her expression. "They can wait three minutes."

Allegra looked back at the screen and pursed her lips. "You're confident I won't disapprove of any of it." Sal nodded. "Okay." She gave the phone back.

Sal regarded her for a moment—perhaps a fraction longer than necessary. "You're not going to surprise me on stage, are you?"

"I won't if you won't."

Sal smiled very slightly. "Alright, then." She linked hands with Allegra and escorted them out into the room.

It was *full*. More media than had been at the hospital. Everyone was there: every station, channel, and website. Reporters with phones and tablets filled the chairs, and in a horseshoe around them stood every camera team imaginable. There were other miscellaneous people standing around the edges, watching. A hundred phones pointed at them.

As they moved onto the stage, Allegra searched the crowd for Rosie.

She was standing off to the side by the door, looking a mixture of tired and overwhelmed. Allegra immediately felt the urge to hug her. Instead, when their eyes met, she smiled. Rosie didn't smile back. But she didn't look away, either.

Sal was already at the stand, which was *covered* in microphones. The room fell silent.

"As of this morning, I have assumed the role of Acting CEO of Black Standard Advisory. Mr Black has stepped down." She had to pause because there was an *immediate* clicking of cameras, a rumble of surprise, and a convergence as everyone leant forwards. People immediately started furiously typing into their phones or whispering to each other. "Following recent events, including the fires, we have identified issues relating to material held within our archival systems—and we have made the decision to hand the material in full over to the police and regulators to be examined."

Allegra tuned out through some of Sal's further comments about the police and regulators; they were of no consequence to her, and she was fairly certain nothing would come of it. Instead, she watched Rosie. Worried she was tuning out. Watching her look towards the door—was she thinking of leaving?—when there was a pause in Sal's speech.

Sal looked fractionally towards Allegra before she said, "Our focus now is ensuring these issues are resolved without further harm." She looked to the side of the stage. "I'll hand over to Victor Liang, Chairman of Threshold Property Group, to outline the next steps."

She shook hands firmly with Victor as he passed her and then stepped back beside Allegra. Blocked from the cameras by Victor, her fingers brushed against Allegra's.

Victor said a few polished lines about regulators and cooperation, ending that section on, "Now that I've got that dry stuff out of the way, let's talk about what you're really here for." He chuckled. Some of the audience smiled along with him. "Having considered the circumstances in full, Threshold has made the decision to return the property in question to the original owners: the Hislop family."

In the audience, Rosie looked up, eyes wide, then to Allegra to check it was true. Allegra nodded.

"There were failures in how this was handled, and real impact as a result. Returning the property is the first step in putting that right—and in ensuring it does not happen again."

Immediately, people started yelling questions before they were invited; Allegra was dimly aware that Sal was watching her. She could only look at Rosie, standing at the back of the audience and staring up at her, eyes swimming with tears.

Chapter 48: Proximity

Rosie stayed through the Q&A, her attention drifting until a reporter asked whether Allegra had been involved.

Sal glanced across at her with a warm smile—polished, deliberate—and said, "Allegra's been a steady presence through all of this. She has a very clear sense of what matters on the ground, and I value that."

Allegra smiled for the cameras, but her attention was already on Rosie. She couldn't read her. When the Q&A ended, Rosie slipped outside. Allegra followed.

She was standing to the side of the hotel, looking overwhelmed. "You did this, didn't you?"

Allegra grimaced. Factoring in overthrowing Dimi, destroying Atlas, and creating the PR disaster that forced the land back? "Officially BSA and Threshold did it." She hesitated. "But—yes. In a way."

Rosie nodded, looking down at her hands; only her fingertips showed past the ends of her sleeves. "After you helped me get Dad's wallet..." She swallowed. "I mean... people always said they wanted to help. Then they found out it was Threshold and just—didn't. So yeah, I didn't want to hope you'd do anything."

There were a few cameras pointed at them; likely because of Allegra. Allegra stepped in front of them to block Rosie. "The whole thing never should have happened in the first place."

"It did though." Rosie shook her head. "They were at us for like two years, trying to buy the land. Constantly. The police officer we spoke to told us we should just take their offer—right to our face. The lawyer wanted *$200,000* to fight the fire rating. We would've had to sell the house. Then a guy came to our door and served Dad. And that was it, our land was gone," she said quietly. "It was like, these big corporations can just do whatever they want. No one stops them. No one cares."

Allegra could hear the exhaustion in her voice. She committed it to memory. So if BSA ever touched anything like this again, she'd remember Rosie. And her dad. "I hope you guys can—" She stopped. "I don't know. Just... be together. Maybe find your way back to how you were."

Rosie's eyes were already swimming. "Maybe. I hope so."

She came in for a hug again; Allegra accepted, aware of the fucking cameras in the background. She didn't want to leave Rosie with them in case someone figured out who she was. "Do you need a lift home?"

She did. Allegra checked on Sal—still surrounded by media, answering questions and giving statements. She texted her to say she was taking Rosie home and would be back afterwards.

Rosie's home was an old weatherboard in Campbelltown—once well-loved, now in need of repair, hidden among the other ordinary houses. She let Rosie out, watched to make sure she got inside safely, and then drove further up the road to check her messages.

Aaron! She opened it immediately, smiling. *"Saw the news: Dimi, Sal, etc. Don't even know where to start. Whole thing's pretty wild."* A line break. *"Dad went into church this morning. Just... needed to sit there for a bit. I get that."* And another. *"It was good seeing that family get their property back. That felt right. Very you."*

Very me? Allegra sat back. She wanted to take the compliment—especially from him—but wasn't sure she should. Would anyone have thought she'd been involved if she hadn't been on stage with Sal? Had Sal intended it?

She texted him back. *"We'll need to talk about Dimi at some point—in person, though."* He reacted to it with an emoji.

The next text was from Sal. *"Had a word with police and they're going to let me see the basement at BSA. I'll be home late."*

Allegra returned to the penthouse, washed the makeup and corporate sleaze off, ordered some food, and ended up alone with her phone again. She was going through old photos from the Phase 1 Assessment when a text from Zoe came through—at 8:35pm on a Saturday.

"Hi folks. Strong coverage out of the conference. The usual suspects already posting." Attached were some links.

The first was Austin—predictably quick—opening on a shot of Allegra hugging Rosie. "So, don't read too much into this," he said. "But that's Allegra Sinclair, right after stepping off stage where her BSA exec girlfriend helped announce the Hislop property being returned... to the Hislops." He zoomed in on Rosie's face, cutting it beside a still from his earlier video. *"Hugging Rosie Hislop."*

Next up was Froggy. She was sitting at a table with a printed photo of both Sal and Allegra. "Okay, so everyone was messaging me about my beloved wife apparently being seduced and manipulated by Sal Lategan, soulless media corporate from BSA." She looked down at the photos, swapped them, then glanced back up. "Anyway turns out it's the other way around." She put her hand to her mouth like she was yelling. "Hey guys! New type of environmental activism just dropped: date the execs!"

Allegra was grinning. Before she got too entertained, though, she tried to work out if there was a downside. Other than discounting the fact Sal came up with the solution?

For Zoe to be cheerfully circulating it, Sal would have approved the message. So maybe it was fine if people thought it was her—if they thought she had a master plan instead of a collection of fragmented ideas her gut told her would connect. If they thought it had always been her plan to end up here, on Sal's couch, in control.

...instead of living out of her car and deferring the decision about what to do with all the clothes and belongings spread between here, her Land-Cruiser, and Timothy's. She groaned and opened another tab, googling storage units. Time to actually do something about it.

An idea that died in the arse when she realised she'd be paying nearly $1000 for a fucking shed somewhere. What a waste of money; she could almost rent a studio apartment for that. But leaving her stuff with other people wasn't a solution either—regardless of her relationship with them.

Perhaps she *could* cull her possessions down to what would fit in her LandCruiser? Or maybe she should just buy a trailer for it or something?

She hadn't solved it by the time she accidentally fell asleep—only realising hours later, when she woke covered by a doona, that she had.

Sal, she thought, looking up towards the master suite. No light; Sal was asleep.

Allegra toyed with the idea of going up there anyway; slipping into her bed, snaking her arms around her. Sal would probably let her.

Except neither of them would get any sleep that way, and Sal had been missing a lot of it lately. Allegra made herself lie back down. They were together now. She could be with Sal any time—it didn't need to be right after one of the most stressful days of her life, when she actually needed sleep. She turned over and went back to sleep herself.

—and woke to the gravelly roar of the coffee grinder. Jesus Christ. She sat up.

Sal was standing behind the counter, hand on the grinder, smug grin on her face. "Good morning." She looked up at Allegra. That smile.

Allegra wasn't sure what it meant until Sal rounded the counter to hand her a coffee, letting Allegra see all of her.

She was wearing another slightly eccentric suit—cut to perfection, every seam exact, every line controlled. Her hair fell into two sharp points beside her chin. The black satin boatneck softened it; the same neckline she'd worn at the gala. The same earrings, too. And red-soled shoes, like a permanent red carpet. She knew exactly what she was doing.

"Coffee?" she said innocently, handing a mug to Allegra.

Allegra eyed her grin, failing to hide her own. "Anything else on offer?"

Sal perched on the spine of the couch above her. "Well, you didn't submit any new grocery orders to Gerard, so..." She took a sip of her coffee. "I'm afraid the cupboard is bare." Her eyes twinkled. She moved along. "I went into Atlas last night."

Oh, right. That was enough to drag Allegra's mind out of the gutter. "How much was burnt?"

Sal pulled out her phone and showed her the photos. Half the room was gone; the closed sections of the compactus looked intact. The server and computers had melted completely. "Such a terrible tragedy," she said in her PR voice. "They've ruled out an electrical fault and identified the server as the source. We're allowed back in the rest of the building on Monday." She tucked her phone away. "I need to move my things onto 35."

Floor 35. "Dimi's office."

A slight grin. "My office now." She took another sip from her cup, watching Allegra over the rim. "I could use a pair of strong arms to help me carry the boxes—I'm allowed in from 11am." She brushed something from the cushion near Allegra's shoulder. "I was thinking we could have lunch afterwards."

Oh. "A date."

"I booked somewhere *very* fancy for us," Sal said. "I thought you might like to dress up. My tailor texted: she has another suit ready. We could collect it." She paused. "Take it for a test drive."

Allegra was sold. If she was going to suit up at the tailor's, she didn't need to change—but Sal sat her down anyway, braiding her hair again, quick and precise. A touch too careful. A fraction too tight. Fingertips brushing her neck, hands firm in her hair. And every time Allegra looked up, Sal was watching her in the mirror.

The Rocks was already busy when they reached the tailor's; they had to wait for her to finish with another client. When she returned, she brought out two suits—one Allegra recognised, the other new.

"I took the liberty of ordering something extra to complement your repertoire," she said, removing the cover. "None of your suits had a strong formal presence, and I know Sal is always going to those things."

It was black, thick, and structured. The type of suit someone would give an address in. It wasn't—kinky, exactly. Not like Sal's. But there was something about it.

Allegra wasn't convinced—not her style—but put it on to be polite. It was a power suit. It accentuated her height, cutting her into a sharp, fierce line. She didn't feel like she needed to look fierce, really, and had come out to politely decline it—when she saw Sal's reaction.

Sal was idly leafing through dress shirts, her hand pausing mid-motion as her eyes settled on Allegra. A small breath.

"I like it," Allegra heard herself say to the tailor. Then, because she knew how Sal would hear it, she added, "What sort of ties do you have?"

She could feel Sal's eyes on her as she was led over to a drawer to select one. Before the tailor could loop it around her collar—

"Let me."

Sal came over, taking the tie from the tailor and turning towards Allegra. She lifted Allegra's crisp collar, threading the tie around it. Eyes on Allegra's. A tug—just a little too sharp. Her hands moved quickly, efficiently, drawing it taut at Allegra's throat. Then she brushed the collar down and stepped back.

The tailor's eyebrows went up. "A trinity knot." She sounded impressed. "I gather you'd like to wear the suit out?"

Sal's eyes lingered on Allegra before she turned to pay.

Outside, Sal gave her another look—straightening Allegra's lapels, tucking a loose strand of hair behind her ear. In the sunlight, the fabric held a subtle sheen; the buttons caught the light, unmistakably mother-of-pearl.

"How much was this?" Allegra asked, eyebrows up.

"Worth every cent," Sal said, reaching over to take Allegra's hand. Her grip was firm—slightly warm, slightly possessive.

It was too early to head to BSA, and Allegra had a feeling if they went home *before* lunch, they'd never make it back out. It was nice to be out with Sal, anyway. She looked immaculate. Every time Allegra caught their reflection in a window—or felt her hand tighten in the crowd—it hit her again. She was with this woman. Holding her hand.

Dressed as they were, they drew eyes. And phones. Sal glanced back at her, amused. "You want to give them something to record?"

Jesus. "Sure."

Sal stopped her mid-footpath, stepping in close. She brushed Allegra's lapels, fingers sliding up to her tie—then a small, deliberate tug. Allegra bent down towards her, but Sal redirected at the last moment, lips grazing her ear instead. "Let them see you put your hands on my waist." Allegra did as she was told.

For a second, they stayed like that—close enough to feel it, aware of the eyes on them.

Sal stepped away, eyes doing a sweep of Allegra with a knowing smile. They linked hands and kept walking through the decorated streets, dimly aware of the phones.

"I have some engagements I'd like you to join me at tomorrow," Sal said matter-of-factly. "On Tuesday, as well."

Christmas Eve, Allegra thought. "And what, exactly, do you have planned for me?" She was grinning.

"Interviews. Appearances." She flashed a smile at Allegra. "I'll have you exactly where I need you—beside me, looking like that."

"Bold, given the time of year."

Sal looked across at her. A thread of thoughtfulness crept into her expression. "Do you have other plans?"

Christmas plans? Allegra stopped for a second and then kept walking. Vanessa hadn't said anything; she wasn't sure.

"Do you *want* other plans, Allegra?"

The idea of spending all of Christmas Day with Sal—and how that would play out—was *not* unappealing. But... it would be nice to see Aaron. Just not at church. "Aren't you due at Helen Black's, anyway?"

Sal gave her a sideways look. "No one expects me to go to that, least of all Helen," she said. "Although..." She considered Allegra. "It would certainly be quite fun showing up with you. Dressed like that."

"Won't Dimi be there?"

A dark shadow grew across Sal's smile. "Oh, I think not."

Allegra considered that, and then took her phone out to text Vanessa. "*Are we doing something for Christmas this year*?"

After she put her phone away, Sal said, "Keep me informed. I need to know whether you're available to me." A familiar grin.

The police were gone from the front of the BSA building, so Sal swiped them in, through the security gates, and up to her office.

It was almost bare—it looked like it had *already* been emptied. Sal lifted the photo frame of Allegra from the desk, glancing at it before wandering over to the window. The harbour stretched out beyond it.

"How long have you had this office?" Allegra wondered.

"Nearly 20 years." She turned, casting her eyes around it for a moment.

There wasn't much to move. Sal collected a box from admin, set it on the desk, and emptied her drawers into it—item by item, very deliberately. Then, watching Allegra, she tested the weight to make sure it was sufficiently heavy and pushed it across the desk. "Would you?"

Allegra picked it up, sighing at her. "Wouldn't you rather I wore something that showed off the muscles?"

Sal's voice dropped. "We can try that way next time."

Sal walked behind Allegra to the lifts, stepping in front of her only to swipe them up to 35.

When the door opened to 35, the décor was markedly different. Opulent, with grand furniture and intricate finishing. Even the carpet was plusher, and red like the sole of Sal's heels.

Dimi's office was a corner office as well—and palatial. It had a hardwood desk like Sal's, and a separate section with a grand board table. His computer was missing—the screen, too. From the door, Allegra could see his drawers half-open, as if someone had gone through them in a hurry.

It was already empty. He was gone.

Sal stopped by the door—caught for a moment. She wouldn't want Allegra to see it or comment on it.

So Allegra didn't. She grinned instead. "Want me to carry you over the threshold?"

Sal's mouth sank to a smile. "Not this one," she said, and then stepped inside, placed the photo of Allegra on a shelf, and wandered out towards the window. It looked out over the Opera House and Harbour Bridge—a commanding half-panorama of the city.

Allegra put her box on the plush carpet beside the desk and circled her shoulders.

When Sal was done with the view, she turned back. Her eyes swept through the office. "I know this room well."

Allegra looked around it, too: the plush carpet, the heavy furniture. But mostly the empty shelves and vast space.

"It's a beautiful office," Sal said, almost idly. "Mostly for show—he didn't use it that much."

"Seems like overkill for one person," Allegra observed.

"I always thought so." Sal wandered in towards the meeting table, trailing her fingertips over the top of one of the empty chairs. "Such a waste." She moved past Allegra.

Allegra turned to follow her.

"Rooms like this are for receiving people." Sal reached the door and closed it behind her, taking her time with it, touching the ornate panelling. Her hand settled on the doorknob. "Keeping them where you want them."

A smile grew on her lips. "That's actually a key difference between this office and my old one," she said. She looked up at Allegra. "This one has a lock."

She flicked it.

And stayed there for a moment, leaning back against the door. A dark grin grew across her face.

Now it made sense. Jesus Christ. "...In his office?" Allegra asked, half laughing.

Sal nodded slightly, grin alight. She pushed off the door, straightening. In front of Allegra, she switched on that charisma. White teeth. Dark smile. Her eyes travelled up the length of Allegra's new suit.

Her voice dropped low. "That suit is dangerous on you, Allegra."

Sal began her approach. Slowly. "Let me tell you about it," she said. "Structured through the shoulders, clean through the waist." Her eyes dipped to those lines as she stepped right up to her.

Allegra couldn't stop looking at her mouth. How it wrapped so carefully around every word.

Sal tilted her head. "It's restrained. Deliberate," she said, brushing it down. Far too slowly. "Just enough sheen to draw the eye." She lifted her gaze and held Allegra there. "I can't stop looking at you." She paused there, a slow grin on her lips.

Then her eyes dropped again—to Allegra's chest. She slipped her fingers underneath the folded edges of Allegra's lapels. "It's designed to hold its shape, see?" She gave it a firm tug. Allegra's breath caught. "It doesn't fight you. It'll give—up to a point." A slow smile. "But it's not going to keep up with you."

She released Allegra and took a single step back. Eyes meeting hers. "Turn."

Allegra did, just as slowly, returning her eyes forward with a grin.

Sal mirrored it. "Mmm," she said, eyes fixed on Allegra's. "I love watching how it behaves. It just quietly does what it's supposed to do."

God. This fucking woman. "Then it's on the wrong person, isn't it?"

"That's why it's so dangerous on you." She stepped in again. "You want to move, don't you?" Sal's hands traced the smooth fabric on her waist. "You want to bend," she enunciated each word so carefully, "*Grab*. You want to test all of those seams." Eyes on Allegra's, teeth visible at the edge of her smile. "You're going to ruin your brand new suit, aren't you?"

God, Allegra could barely fucking breathe, and Sal wasn't giving her a single inch—her eyes now tracking down her own body. "What about *my* suit?"

Allegra looked at it. Immaculate. Pressed to perfection.

"Feel that." She took Allegra's hands and ran them down both sides of her blazer. Over her breasts. "Softer. More delicate." There was *nothing* soft about her smile, though. "The seams are hand stitched." She took Allegra's fingertips and guided them across her ribcage, over the line of stitches at her waist, and down to her hips. "They'll hold," she said. "If you're *very* gentle." Her hips pressed into Allegra. Not releasing her for even a second. "Are you going to be gentle, Allegra?"

God, those hips. Nothing about that begged gentleness. Everything about it—her voice, her hands, the way she held Allegra there—said the opposite.

And *fucking hell* Allegra wanted to.

She wanted to test it. Push it. See exactly where it would give. Her hands were already there—at Sal's waist, the curve of her hip. A shift, barely anything, and she could—

Sal leant up just a little. Her breath brushed Allegra's ear. "Go on."

That was all it took.

Allegra lifted her clean off the ground and dropped her onto the executive desk behind them—hard enough to pull a sharp breath from her. Sal's hands were already on her, catching her lapels and dragging her in for a firm kiss.

Then Sal's hands were at Allegra's waist, grabbing the suit and pulling her hips against her. The blazer hem bunched at the small of Allegra's back and their bodies collided. Allegra's thighs hit the desk—she'd bruise there. She couldn't care less. Not standing like she was between Sal's open legs.

Those long legs came up around her, sharp heels pressing into the back of her thighs, anchoring her there. Hips tilting against hers. Lips still on hers.

Allegra pushed into her, feeling the fabric of their suits scrunch together, crushed between them. Sal's back arched into her; her fingers found the edge of Sal's blazer and satin top, trying to reach inside.

The blazer was tight. It wouldn't move.

Allegra tried again, harder, forcing her hand up under the satin. The fabric bunched, trapped her wrist, held. The seam pulled tight against her hand.

Sal broke the kiss just long enough to fucking *smirk* at her.

Allegra glanced down at the neat line of buttons, then back up.

Sal didn't say a word. She didn't need to.

Allegra grabbed her lapels and *pulled*.

For a second, it held—Allegra's muscles braced, her hands tight on the fabric, the stitches straining. Then, suddenly, it *burst* open.

Buttons snapped free—clicking against the window, the wall, the shelves.

Sal was still grinning as she pulled Allegra back in, dragging her lips across her jaw. "Oh no," she breathed, right against her ear. "My suit."

Now the blazer was open, Allegra reached for the base of Sal's loose satin top, intending to slip her hands underneath. Sal caught her wrists. "Already?" she said, the smirk in her voice. She pulled back so Allegra could see it. "Impatient."

Allegra met her eyes for a second—then kept moving, ignoring the hold as her hands found their way under the satin.

Not to be so easily defeated, Sal leant sharply back, out of reach. Allegra's hands closed on nothing. She tried again—Sal retreating further until she was stretched out on the desk, propped on her elbows, thoroughly entertained.

Allegra met her eyes as she put one knee onto the desk, between Sal's thighs, and climbed up. Her other knee came down beside her, her blazer bunching at the shoulders and pulling at the waist as she loomed over Sal.

Sal's expression shifted—just slightly. But when she clocked the tangle their legs were in, her grin came back. With a vengeance. Watching Allegra, she drew one leg higher, sliding it up along Allegra's body, slowly and deliberately, until it was over her shoulder. When she relaxed again, the seat of her very expensive suit pants pressed flush against the join of Allegra's.

Right there—Allegra hitched a breath. Exactly the right spot.

Sal saw that. Her brow lifted—*well*?

Eyes on Sal, Allegra twisted a little, settling them together. The fabric of their suits stretched taut between them—thick enough to soften the angles, thin enough to feel her through it. When Allegra began to move against her, the friction of the two suits dragging together was—God. Worth the price tag.

Allegra held the leg over her shoulders, bearing down on the hips under hers. Watching Sal.

Sal didn't move her eyes from Allegra's. It was intense; almost too much. It was hard to focus on how it felt under the weight of that attention.

Sal noticed. She recognised Allegra's hesitation—and there was that fucking smirk again.

Jesus Christ, this woman. *I'm going to wipe that smirk off your face,* Allegra thought. *Fine. Watch this.*

Eyes on Sal's face, she moved. She adjusted the angle, testing different movements and pressures until—Sal's ribs jumped with a hitched breath. Until her jaw fell slack—then corrected. Suddenly, Sal's focus narrowed.

Got you, Allegra thought, fixing the angle and grinding into her.

Sal responded this time—shifting her hips, searching for a position that would unseat Allegra.

Allegra tried to stop her—and failed. Sal was far too fucking sly to not work it out. Her thumbs hooked into Allegra's belt, holding her there, locking them together. So they were both trapped there, crushing their suit pants between them.

Sal was trying to hold it together. She was *good* at it. But not good enough. Eventually, she stopped caring that Allegra had her number. Her hands slipped from Allegra's belt, gripping her hips instead.

For a second—nothing.

Then her breath hitched—sharp, unguarded—her grip tightening hard enough to pull Allegra into her as the composure finally gave way. Her head tipped back, the control she'd been holding so carefully slipping.

And the *sound* she made. Deep in her throat, the same place that low, sensual voice came from. It—went straight to Allegra's core. And then right between her legs.

Watching Sal lose herself underneath Allegra's hips—*God*, it was going to be enough. She was so infuriating and so *hot* and—*fuck*, the fabric between them moved differently now, they were both slick underneath it, it was wet and dragged heavily, firmly, thickly between them as—

Allegra's breath broke, the rhythm she'd been holding faltered, and her hands tightened on Sal's leg as she bore down against her hips—chasing it, pushing it, holding it—riding it out until she sat heavily against Sal's body, still.

And then it was done. Leaving them fitted together in the disarray of twisted suits, bunched fabric, and tousled hair.

For a moment neither of them moved—just the slow draw of breath, Sal's chest rising under the satin, Allegra's weight pressed into her.

Sal opened her eyes, lips parted, breathing heavily. When she saw Allegra looking, she gave her a breathy grin.

Allegra bent down over her to kiss her. "If you don't wipe that evil fucking grin off your face, I'll flip you over and do it myself."

Sal snickered at that, shuffling over a little so Allegra could lie down on the desk beside her. "Ordinarily I'd invite you to try, but—" She glanced down between them. "Our poor suits."

Allegra made a face, feeling the crotch of hers—wet—and then propping herself up to check how it looked. Which was no different to how it looked dry. She lay back, eyebrows up.

Sal was *never* going to lose that fucking smirk. "There are a lot of differences between a $1,500 and a $15,000 suit," she said. "That one's definitely one of my favourites."

$15,000? She gave Sal a wide-eyed look. "We should probably go home and change before lunch," she said. "I don't fancy sitting in this while I'm trying to enjoy food."

"Mmm," Sal agreed, but didn't get up. "Let's just lie here a minute first. On this desk." She turned onto her side towards Allegra with a lazy smile, lifting a hand to trail her fingers along Allegra's torso before settling down on her—head on her shoulder pads, hand draped across her middle, one knee bent over her thighs. Her eyes fell closed, but the smile was still there. It had lost its edge.

That made Allegra smile. Her hand curled up to stroke Sal's hair as she stared up at the ceiling, at the rows of LED downlights. She shifted her weight on the surface beneath her—solid hardwood.

Surreal, almost. "We're on his desk."

"*My* desk now," Sal corrected her. "But yes. His desk."

Allegra found herself entertained by that. She couldn't think of anything more irreverent—aside from burning it. Very fitting. "That carpet looks quite nice," she commented neutrally. "I bet that's comfortable, too."

A low chuckle. "I've always thought the walnut wood meeting table was beautiful," she said. "And underutilised." When Allegra glanced down at her, she was grinning again.

Allegra tilted her chin up so she could kiss that grin. "How long does a caretaker CEO position last, anyway?"

"Long enough to make sure the entire room is well-purposed," she said, then added, "There's also a private bathroom. With a private shower."

They headed into the bathroom to inspect it—Sal hadn't seen it before. It was huge, dark, and luxurious.

"I'm beginning to wonder if perhaps I didn't think big enough when designing my penthouse," Sal said, stopping by the mirror to smooth her hair and check her makeup. She didn't look particularly dishevelled in just her satin top, but after they'd done laps of the room looking for her missing buttons, the buttonless blazer read a little sloppy.

She took it off and folded it over her forearm, considering herself without it. "Let's go."

Allegra raised her eyebrows. Sal's satin top was sleeveless; her tattoos were on display. "You're going to break the internet."

Sal knew. "The board was keen to decouple from recent scandals and for the public to be aware BSA is going in a different direction," she said. "These may actually help."

The tattoos were certainly very loud, especially against pale skin and black clothes. Not exactly conservative—but then again, walking arm in arm with another woman in what was arguably a masculine-cut suit wasn't, either.

From the moment they stepped out onto the street until they'd retreated inside Sal's penthouse carpark, phones were out and pointed at them.

It made it hard to simply enjoy being with Sal—to revel in the sunlight, hold her hand.

Sal tolerated it well—or appeared to—smiling casually, relaxed. But back at the penthouse, when they washed up and changed clothes, she chose something long-sleeved again.

Dressed in fresh suits, they headed to the 'very fancy' restaurant Sal had picked for them.

It was at the top of a high-rise on George Street, their table set beside a window overlooking the Opera House and the glittering harbour beyond it. It was so high, and the day so clear, they could see Manly and North Head on the horizon.

It was beautiful, but in Allegra's opinion the *real* view was the unusually relaxed woman sitting across the table from her. The room was cleverly broken up; the other tables felt distant. It felt intimate.

She only realised she was staring when Sal's eyes lifted from the menu. The smirk. "Harbour's that way," she said, inclining her head towards it as her eyes dropped back to the page.

Allegra ignored it. It was far too entertaining to watch Sal at ease. Not rationing her time or holding her cards as close as she usually did.

Under the table, the tip of a stiletto brushed Allegra's ankle, hooking lightly into her suit pants. Sal gave no indication she'd noticed.

Allegra was grinning about that, thinking about the new suit—and her other suits—and then, unhelpfully, remembering the one at the dry cleaners. Which she'd need to collect at some point. And stick in her car, or—somewhere. She sighed.

Sal noticed it and glanced up.

"I've been trying to figure out what to do with all my stuff," Allegra told her. "It's too much for my LandCruiser. I was thinking storage, but they charge as much as a studio. Absolute waste of money."

Sal shrugged lightly, unmoved. "There's no problem here. I have five bedrooms."

Allegra grimaced. "You kicked me out a few days ago," she pointed out, knowing how it would land—Sal fell still. "I just—I want somewhere that I control. I don't want to just move my things between other people's houses."

Sal recovered herself. Not completely. "So buy somewhere, then."

Allegra sat with that for a moment. It... wouldn't be a terrible place to park her savings.

Sal wasn't looking at her. She opened her mouth a fraction before she spoke. "There's an apartment for sale in my building."

Allegra winced. The CBD was the last place she would ever consider buying. But that wasn't what Sal was saying. "I know what you're offering," she said softly. "But I'm not going to live full-time in the city."

Sal swallowed and moved on, looking up to meet the waiter who arrived and took her order.

Afterwards, they reclined in their chairs, looking out at the Harbour. Sal was uncharacteristically still and quiet.

"I'll still end up back with you," Allegra said. "When I'm in the city."

"I thought you might," she said, looking back out at the view. "I just—" She stopped, straightened. "Buying land is not a terrible investment," she said. "Despite the experience the Hislops had with it."

Rosie. Allegra wondered how she was holding up today—how her mother had taken the news. Her dad. It was going to be a bittersweet Christmas for them.

Allegra checked her phone, half-thinking she and Sal should just do something quiet for Christmas—then remembered she was still waiting on an answer from Vanessa.

She had a notification, but it wasn't from Vanessa.

It was from Simone. "*Hello there, sister,*" it began. "*Guess whose house Christmas is at this year? Your present to me will be bringing your little handler along.*" Allegra sighed at it. "*See you on Wednesday at 4pm.*"

Chapter 49: Making Room

When Allegra and Sal turned into Simone's driveway, there were two enormous red and gold bows on either side of the open gate.

At Sal's slightly narrowed eyes, Allegra said simply, "Vanessa."

When they got to the end of the driveway, Vanessa's impact was even more stark. Simone's vast front yard looked mown and tended, minus one broken-down car wreck, and plus a beautifully decorated long table and a tall, glittering Christmas tree. All managed in essentially two days. Sal looked faintly impressed; there was a question visible on her face as they pulled up beside Vanessa's Range Rover.

Allegra answered it. "She's an event planner."

Sal made an 'ah' shape with her mouth as Allegra turned off the engine, climbed out of her LandCruiser, and looked across the yard towards the house.

Some distance from them, Simone was already at the BBQ with a cigarette in one hand and tongs in the other, surrounded by smoke and partially obscured by flame. It was technically a Total Fire Ban day, which meant no open flames. Simone definitely knew that. Spotting them, she gave Allegra a long smile and a little wave.

Behind her on her half-rotten porch, their nephews had their bright red heads together tinkering with Simone's electrical scrap. Something was sparking.

Somehow, the Christmas decorations made it worse. Vanessa had transformed the yard into something immaculate and ceremonial, which only made Simone and the boys look more feral by contrast—like wildlife had gotten into the display case.

Allegra glanced back at Sal. It was one thing to tell her that her family was a nightmare; it was another to watch the full horror of it unfold in real time while Sal still had every opportunity to get back in the car.

As Sal rounded the LandCruiser, she had already spotted Simone. Allegra watched her give Simone a polite wave, and then keep her pleasant expression in place, as if that helped. It did not. It only made Allegra more aware there was something to be falsely pleasant about.

"I know," she told Sal as they converged. "You don't need the brave face."

Sal shook her head. "There is no possible way this could even approach how bad my last family Christmas was," she said, and then looked down to check the fall of her dress. Black silk, for Christmas. It certainly was a statement—it looked like it should come with pipe-organ entrance music—but she was polished, as always. Beautiful, as always. And, for some reason, here in the prettily decorated pits of hell with Allegra.

She felt suddenly anxious about that. "You're about to see a lot of context."

Sal smiled slightly and looked past her to the too-perfect Christmas diorama. "Shall we advance?" she asked, opening the car boot.

Allegra hauled Sal's gift hamper out, then paused to count through the presents in her head. Vanessa. Simone. The twins. Timothy. Aaron.

Aaron. Her hand went to her pocket, feeling for the hard edge of her phone. Not his wrapped gift. The other one.

Sal noticed her pause on Aaron's gift, then her thousand-yard stare. "I gather you've definitely decided to tell him?"

Allegra nodded. "No point waiting. It's unconditional."

Sal gave Allegra space to carry the big hamper and the present bag into the fray.

That was when Vanessa appeared in the doorway, wearing a glamorous red and white dress, festive jewellery, and holding a half-empty glass of champagne. "Merry Christmas!" she called, rushing towards them. Even Sal had opted for flats—having learnt her lesson about heels and gravel the other night—but Vanessa was wearing heels anyway, and not doing too badly on them despite how flushed she already was. She helped Allegra put the hamper at the end of the beautifully set dining table.

Vanessa had taken out their grandparents' silverware and bone china—which Simone had apparently kept—and laid gold, red, and green Christmas crackers across everyone's plates. There were candles and holly down the centre of the table, and every place setting had a name tag. Simone didn't need one. She'd dragged her leather armchair onto the lawn and put it at the head of the table. Sal's setting was beside hers. At the other end, closer to where Allegra was propping the hamper, there was an extra place. In Vanessa's beautiful cursive and gold pen, the place card read, '*Lachie*'.

Vanessa saw her line of sight. "I know, I know. It's a bit much. He just would have—" She left it there, straightening once the hamper was set and the present bag propped beside it. To Sal, she said, "I gather all this is your doing? There's no way Allegra would be this thoughtful."

Sal only smothered her smile when she was sure Allegra had seen it. "The presents are all Allegra," she said. "I just thought it would be poor form to come empty-handed myself."

"She's right," Simone said from the BBQ. "What's the point of us having a disgustingly wealthy sister-in-law if she's not also extremely generous?"

All the air in Allegra's lungs, gone immediately. "Well, now that we've dropped these off, it's time for us to go," she said with false brightness, and went to turn away.

Unfortunately, Vanessa immediately grabbed her into a hug. "Oh, no you don't. You're ours today." Then she grabbed a briefly startled Sal, too.

After she'd hugged Allegra long enough to make sure she wasn't leaving, she pulled back and turned to Sal, who looked—remarkably composed.

"That's a lovely dress," she said, giving Sal a once-over. "Very dramatic! Who is it?"

"It was custom," she said, and then nodded at Vanessa's dress. "That cut looks Zimmermann to me. Am I close?"

Vanessa looked instantly charmed. "It is!" she said, batting her eyelashes at Sal and then immediately linking arms with her and leading her inside. "Now, what would you like to drink?"

Allegra watched them with mild concern before deciding that if Sal could handle working with Dimi for 25 years, she could handle being alone with Vanessa for a few minutes. She looked down at the hamper. It needed to be unwrapped, so she started on that.

Simone was watching her from the BBQ, more sharply than she needed to, licking her fingers from whatever she'd just touched. "So," she said. "How much of the present situation was *actually* you, and how much was Mrs Funeral Director teaching you how presents work?"

A few hours, Allegra promised herself. *Just a few hours*. "Do you think I'm incapable of buying presents for my family?"

Simone grinned. "Incapable?" she repeated, then shrugged. "I just thought, you know, it might *trigger* you, or—"

"You're unbelievable." Allegra went back to unwrapping the hamper so she wouldn't murder one of her remaining siblings.

When Vanessa and Sal returned—in one piece—Simone stopped Sal as she passed. "So, Sal," she began, and only continued when Allegra was watching. "Did Allegra actually pick those presents out herself, or did you need to intervene to stop her buying us all servo gift cards?"

Sal behaved as if she had been asked a perfectly ordinary question. "I wasn't involved at all."

Allegra straightened, facing Simone. "I fucking told you."

Simone shrugged lightly. "After 20 years of thinking transferring funds counts as showing up, I had to check."

"Why don't you suck my entire dick, Simone."

That made the twins look up from the workbench like they'd heard deeply juicy gossip.

Vanessa looked alarmed. "My boys are right there, Allegra, and they—"

"—probably say worse things to each other, Vanessa," Allegra said, "and are definitely learning worse behaviour from *Simone*."

Before she could say anything else, Sal stepped in front of her. She had a calm, pleasant smile, and pushed something cold and wet into Allegra's hands. Allegra looked down—it was a Stone & Wood Pacific Ale. Sal wrapped Allegra's fingers around the bottle. Her voice was slightly dry. "You're handling this admirably."

Allegra sighed at her. "You're supposed to be on *my* side."

Sal stepped beside Allegra, facing her sisters. "I haven't made a decision yet." She had a slight smile. "I do prefer to be on the *winning* side, so..."

While the rest of her oh-so-dear family laughed at her expense, Allegra looked sideways at Sal and drank deeply from her beer.

"Oh, I like you," Vanessa said to Sal, which would have been a perfectly reasonable response to the joke if she hadn't so obviously meant it.

She may have said something else to make it worse, but the twins came over from the porch looking far too pleased with themselves, carrying some small, constructed thing made from Simone's electrical scrap. Spotting them, Vanessa's smile dropped. She drank the rest of her champagne in one mouthful.

"Simone," Oscar said, in a very loaded tone. "Oliver made something."

Simone looked over from the BBQ, stubbed out her cigarette, and put down her tongs. "Did he now? Show me."

Oliver presented whatever it was: a small gadget made from a spliced commercial adapter, a series of circuits, and two divergent, V-shaped wires. It meant nothing to Allegra, but judging by Simone's interest, it meant something to her.

Simone took it, turned it over, examined the spliced connection, then checked the wires. "A Jacob's Ladder. Classic."

Oliver broke into a grin. "I bet it'll work, too."

Simone glanced at the BBQ. "The lamb shoulder can wait for three minutes," she decided, leading the boys inside, presumably to plug it in. "Let's see if it does."

Vanessa dealt with that by becoming extremely interested in presents. She carried Allegra's bag to the tree on the other side of the lawn and began arranging the gifts beneath it with unnecessary care. When a loud cheer erupted from inside, she flinched, smiled at absolutely no one, and returned to the hamper. "Ooh, fig jam," she attempted, examining it. "Lovely."

Sal took a casual sip from her champagne flute. "It's local," she said. "A little place in the Hunter. They have a B&B there, as well."

Just as Vanessa looked like she might relax a little, the three burst out from the house looking very pleased with themselves. Oliver brought his ladder thing back to the table, placed it above his dinner plate, and announced he was getting himself and his brother a Coke.

Oscar flopped in his seat a short distance from them, and Simone went back to the grill with a broad grin.

Vanessa spent a minute or two unpacking the hamper like nothing had happened.

When it became clear she wasn't going to comment on it, Simone did. "Oliver is quite the little engineer," she began. "Perhaps if you let him visit me more—"

"Please don't turn my sons into criminals, Simone," Vanessa said quickly, eyes on the hamper.

"It's okay, Mum," Oscar said from where he was sprawled across his dining chair. "I'm going to be a rally driver."

Vanessa exhaled. "Of course you are." She collected some condiments from the hamper to take inside. "I need another drink."

Once Vanessa was gone, Sal said neutrally to Oscar, "You're into cars, are you?"

Oscar grinned. It was broad, wicked, and reminiscent of Simone's. "Nah, not really. I just like winding Mum up."

Sal nodded mildly and took another sip of her drink.

Oscar's eyes narrowed a little, though. He was still watching her. "You said that because you've got some mad car, right?"

Sal's grin grew a sharp edge. "I do." She fished her phone out of her pocket, found a photo of it, and stepped up to Oscar to show him.

His eyes bulged. "Holy shit, a Lambo!" At Sal's nod, he looked straight at Allegra. "I bet she *hates* it."

Allegra laughed once. "I do. It's why we're here in my LandCruiser."

Sal looked up over the rim of her flute. "We're here in the LandCruiser because I don't want gravel sandblasting my undercarriage."

"Perfect. I'll remember that every time you threaten to drive."

For someone who didn't care about cars, Oscar was spending a lot of time pinch-zooming on the photo of Sal's. "Can you bring it next time? Our house has a garage—you can visit us and bring it." He gave Sal's phone back.

Sal glanced towards the house; no Vanessa. Sal frowned but continued anyway. "Do you have your learner's?"

"Yeah." Oscar's eyes widened, realising why she'd asked that. "You'll let me drive it?!"

Sal wandered back beside Allegra. "If your mother agrees, we'll choose somewhere controlled and you can try it. No roads. No showing off."

Allegra's eyes dropped briefly to Lachie's table setting. Simone had also been watching the whole exchange while nursing the lamb shoulder. On this, she was silent.

Oscar considered her offer. "Define 'showing off'."

That was enough to move Simone to comment. "Keep it on the road, Oscar. We've had enough funerals." Her eyes lingered on Sal for a moment, moved to Allegra, then dipped back to the grill.

Oscar pulled a face and collapsed back into his chair, already retreating into his phone. Oliver and Vanessa were crossing back from the house when Timothy's Transit rattled up the long driveway, gravel crunching under the tyres. That meant Aaron.

Allegra's hand went to the pocket with her phone in it. She turned towards the van, already smiling. He spotted her as soon as he got out, and—there. That familiar smile. The way his eyes lit up. He looked sharp in his church suit, impossibly grown-up for someone she still half-expected to come running across the yard.

She handed her beer to Sal and went to him, tempted to run across the yard *herself*. He met her halfway and folded her into a hug. It lasted longer than it usually did. "Merry Christmas," she said when he finally let go.

"Merry Christmas, Mum," he echoed, still smiling at her. He didn't step back immediately. He just stayed there, hand on her shoulder, looking at her like there was something he might say if there weren't half a dozen people watching.

He left it, and his eyes moved past her. "Merry Christmas, Sal."

Sal looked surprised for only a moment—and probably only to Allegra—before her smile softened for him.

The moment passed when Vanessa came jogging over in her heels on the gravel, somehow not falling on her face. "Aaron!" she said, giving him a big, easy hug and a kiss on the cheek before moving on to Timothy, who was carrying a present bag. She took it from him and went to distribute the presents under the tree.

Aaron gave Simone a brief hug (with Simone smirking over his shoulder at Allegra), then went to sit with the twins, as easy in their company as he always was. They were brothers, in a way; they'd grown up together.

Timothy touched Allegra's arm on the way past and smiled at Sal before going over to greet Simone.

"Oh, good." Simone watched him approach through the smoke. "The family doormat has arrived."

Timothy didn't look affected at all. "Merry Christmas to you too, Simone," he said, sounding like he meant it. "Would you like me to take over the grill?"

Simone considered that for a second, then handed him the tongs. "Be my guest."

Timothy immediately turned down the ventilation so the BBQ was less fire and brimstone, and more cosy backyard dinner. When the flames settled, he glanced over at Allegra with the faintest smile.

She smiled back, drinking deeply from her beer. One less bushfire started today.

Unfortunately, no longer being in charge of the grill meant Simone was free to drop into her leather chair and preside over the table. "Oliver," she said, looking directly at Allegra, "can you grab me a beer?"

"Can I have one, too?" he asked, standing up.

Both Allegra and Vanessa said simultaneously, "No."

Simone shrugged faux-helplessly at him as he went inside.

As everyone gravitated towards the table, Allegra and Sal glanced at each other and sat down. There was a moment of negotiation about whether they were going to hold hands underneath the table, or—now they could—on top of it. In the end, their linked hands ended up on Sal's crossed knee, simply because Allegra's arms were longer. They smiled briefly at each other.

Oscar looked physically ill. "I get why Mum drinks now."

Simone looked interested in a somewhat academic way. She was looking at Sal when she said, "Does she do this with you often? Pretend she's house-trained?"

Several things happened at once: Vanessa's face tightened, Timothy looked over with Concern from the grill, and Aaron's eyes moved immediately to Allegra. Oscar, alone, looked delighted.

Before Allegra could tell Simone to go fuck herself again, Vanessa cut in. "Simone," she warned, with the brittle brightness of a woman trying to keep one nice thing alive. "Let's just have a nice family Christmas."

Simone completely ignored her, focusing on Sal. This time, Sal was not intimidated—or, at least, didn't appear to be. Her hand tightened slightly in Allegra's. "I don't require her to be house-trained. I know who she is."

"Do you?" Simone asked, leaning forward on her elbows, fingers interlaced. "She's going to run off on you, you know."

Allegra had enough. "*Fuck off,* Simone."

Sal squeezed her hand, calling her off. "I'm patient."

Simone nodded at Timothy. "So was he."

Allegra *bristled*. Sal didn't. "And their marriage lasted more than 15 years."

"And then they got divorced."

Sal briefly lifted their linked hands. "Luckily for me." She smiled at Simone, every bit as sharp and pointed as Simone was being. She didn't break eye contact.

Simone sat back with a faint smile, watching her. Eventually, she observed, "Less anxious today, I see."

"And you are *exactly* the same."

That got a full smile out of Simone. "With teeth like that, you've earnt yourself a good cut of lamb," she said, apparently finished with whatever she'd been doing. She stood and headed back to the grill to take over from Timothy. "My turn." The fire and brimstone returned. Timothy ducked away from it as it flared up.

Vanessa had already finished whatever champagne number she was on. It couldn't be *that* many because she didn't look relaxed at all. She leant forward across the table towards Sal, genuinely embarrassed. "I'm so sorry, she's not usually like that."

"She's always like that," Oscar piped up.

Vanessa sighed at him. "What I mean is that she won't always test you. Eventually she'll just insult you, or—"

"She will insult you, test you, and bait you always and forever," Allegra said shortly. "Because that's what she's like as a person."

Vanessa sat back. "Do you guys mind? I'm trying to comfort my future *sister-in-law*."

Allegra closed her eyes. *Why.*

Sal's thumb moved over the back of Allegra's hand. "Be generous, Allegra. Your poor sister is only trying to comfort your future wife." Allegra opened her eyes specifically to glare at her evil fucking 'future wife'.

Vanessa exhaled. "*Anyway,* what I was *trying* to say is that she doesn't really mean to..." She frowned. Something occurred to her. "Wait, she said 'today'," she realised. "'Less anxious *today*'. Why 'today'?" She looked at Sal. "Do you already know each other?"

Shit. Both their hands tightened. Simone looked up from the grill, unreadable. Allegra and Sal glanced at each other, trying to negotiate who was going to field that, when Timothy spoke first. "Allegra visited Simone just the other night, I presume to introduce Sal to her."

Sal's grip relaxed. Allegra tried not to heave too obvious a sigh of relief. "It was last-minute. I'm sorry I forgot to tell you."

Vanessa *did* look a little hurt, but consoled herself with, "No, it's nice you're thinking of her again. It must be very lonely out here."

From the grill, Simone called, "Being lonely is your thing, Vanessa. Not mine."

Oliver returned with Simone's beer and, politely, drinks for everyone else.

"*Some* evidence I've taught my boys manners, at least," Vanessa said, accepting another flute from his tray.

"What did I miss?" Oliver asked Oscar.

"Just Simone full-on hazing Sal," Oscar told him. Oliver looked genuinely disappointed.

"Don't worry," Sal told him smoothly. "Everyone assures me it will happen constantly. I'm sure next time you'll witness it first-hand."

That restored peace to the table more effectively than Vanessa's desperate campaign for normality had. Delighted, Vanessa tried to preserve it with light conversation. "How do you normally celebrate Christmas, Sal?"

Allegra's hand tightened on Sal's as Sal said, "I don't, usually."

"What, not even as a child?"

Sal shook her head easily. "Not since I was 10 years old."

"My wealthier clients always go completely wild for Christmas," Vanessa said, curious about the difference. "Christmas and weddings. Those are the big ones." Then, instead of leaving Sal to respond on her own terms, she said, "And you grew up with the Blacks, didn't you?"

"Vanessa," Allegra warned, tired already.

Sal appeared unbothered. "I did. And for family occasions, there is an expectation of fuss, that's true," she said, then nothing else.

"Oh," Vanessa said, her voice softening with sympathy, unhelpfully saying the quiet part out loud. "So Christmas was one of those things happening around you, not really... for you."

For fuck's sake. "Give me that glass, Vanessa," Allegra said, standing to reach for it. "You've had enough."

Vanessa was sober enough to dodge her, too interested in Sal to let her go. "We don't normally celebrate Christmas all together, either," she said, as if that was a confession and not extremely obvious. "We did when we were little." She looked at Sal with soft, disastrous interest. "Did you have a normal childhood?"

Beside her, her sons were *losing it*. Even Timothy and Aaron glanced at each other. Allegra sat back again because apparently this was happening, and even in the presence of an actual pastor, God had abandoned her.

Sal gave absolutely no indication that there was anything wrong with the question. "Probably not under any definition of normal, no."

"I mean, like, emotionally not normal, or rich-people not normal?"

"Both, unfortunately," Sal said casually, as if making a comment on the weather. At the grill, Simone made no attempt to hide that she was following the conversation with interest.

"Oh." Vanessa nodded sympathetically, taking a thoughtful sip of champagne. "Is that why you're like this?"

Sal's smile stayed where it was. "You mean a lesbian?" She knew what she was doing.

That was it. The twins were gone. They made vein-bulging attempts at hiding outright laughter right beside Vanessa, who looked deathly serious and horrified at the suggestion she might be homophobic. "No! God, no, I mean—I'm Allegra's sister and she's been with *loads* of—" In a last-minute Christmas gift to Allegra, she stopped there. "No, I just mean the whole..." She gestured at Sal's clothing. "Black thing."

Simone sharpened at the word 'black', tongs freezing on the lamb. It was a moment before they moved again.

"This came much later," Sal assured Vanessa.

Sensing the table had just about reached its quota of extremely loaded personal questions, Timothy cut loudly in. "Speaking of wealthy families," he said pointedly. "Cecilie Vale's kids helped serve lunch with us at Redeemer today."

Thank fucking god. "How did that go?" Allegra was genuinely interested, but far happier that Vanessa was no longer in control of the conversation.

Aaron and Timothy glanced at each other. Aaron answered. "Very well, actually," he said. "I was worried Beau would film everything—some of our parishioners and guests don't like to be filmed. He was surprisingly respectful, and so was Astrid. There were camera crews there, anyway."

At the mention of the camera crews, Allegra looked up at Timothy. "Any word on the funding?"

Timothy made a so-so gesture. "Cece did mention that Impact needs a new secretary because Dimi's stepped down, so there may be further delays. She sounded hopeful that time would make the difference, though. And we'll be on the news tonight, so..."

At Dimi's name, the twins recovered quickly from their laughing fit. "Did he do it, you reckon?" Oscar just straight up asked. "The fires?"

Vanessa looked like she was going to shush Oscar, then changed her mind and turned to Allegra for her answer.

Allegra's first instinct was to look at Sal. She stopped herself a fraction too late; Sal had already found her. One glance. A warning, and an answer. Sal fielded this one. "The police have only just started their investigation," she said easily. "They're not even certain the fires were deliberately lit."

In the background, Simone called, "Hi. Ignition specialist here. They were deliberately lit."

Timothy shifted uncomfortably in his seat. "You can't know that, Simone."

Simone locked eyes with Allegra. "Call it a hunch."

Sal's hand tightened in Allegra's as she said to Oscar, "Dimi has simply decided this level of scandal is beyond what he's interested in managing this late in his career, and has stepped down."

Oscar didn't look like he believed a single word of that. "That is the most party-line crap I've ever heard," he said. "He totally lit those fires. Or, I mean, had someone light them for him. I doubt billionaires go around lighting their own fires."

Timothy looked as stoic as he always did. "Oscar, we don't accuse people of serious crimes unless there is excellent evidence—which, as Sal noted, we don't have at this time."

Simone flipped the lamb shoulder in a tongue of flame. "And don't assume rich people are too good to get their hands dirty."

Sal's hand was still in Allegra's as she got back to the point. "What matters right now is that Dimi is no longer in a position to influence the funding decision."

Aaron had been watching the exchange. At that, he leant forward. "So if he stepped down, does that make the funding more or less likely?"

Timothy made a small, careful gesture with one hand. "Slower, perhaps. But Cece sounded as though she wanted to protect the program from the scandal, not walk away from it."

"Alright, everyone," Simone said from the grill. "Enough speculating who lit what on fire. Food's ready."

Simone brought the lamb shoulder to the table and took her time with the knives. Too much time. The steel whispered against steel before she slowly, deliberately set to carving. When the boys held out their plates, she smiled without looking at them. "Uh-uh-uh." Her gaze settled on Sal, the carving knife still bright in her hand. "Guests first."

Without flinching, Sal presented her plate, holding eye contact with Simone.

Almost without breaking it, Simone passed over the chewy, burnt cuts and chose a big, juicy piece of meat to flop on Sal's plate.

For Allegra, though, it was a chewy, burnt piece. Of course. Fortunately, Sal only ate part of hers, which meant Allegra could eat the rest. "Got to make sure you get your protein," she said with a private smile, sliding it onto Allegra's plate.

Across the table, Oscar's expression went completely dead. Oliver glanced at Oscar. Oscar glanced back. Some silent twin verdict was passed, and they both returned grimly to their dinners.

For a few minutes, dinner settled. Plates moved around the table. Timothy poured water. Vanessa checked that everyone had enough salad, and Simone sat back with her beer while the boys ate with their heads bent together.

Allegra let the noise of it pass over her: cutlery against china, low conversation, the occasional scrape of a chair in the grass. Sal's knee was warm against hers beneath the table. When Allegra looked over, Sal met her eyes and gave the smallest nod. Still here. Still fine.

It was almost peaceful. Then Vanessa reached for the Christmas crackers.

She insisted everyone do it properly, crossing arms around the table so everyone was tangled together. Grinning, Allegra crossed her arms, angled one cracker at Sal, and reached for Timothy's—only to realise the seat beside Aaron was empty. There was no one for him to cross crackers with on that side. Because it was Lachie's.

Aaron noticed, his eyes dipping to the name card, his big open smile fading just a little. When he saw Allegra looking, though, he brightened again and held the cracker out as if there was someone there to pull it.

When the boys on the other side noticed, he said easily, "What? Maybe my uncle would like to pull a cracker with me." He directed that familiar smile—Lachie's smile—at Allegra.

For a second, the whole wound opened in front of her: Lachie's empty chair, Aaron's hand held out towards it, that same smile crossing the years between them. The boy they had lost and the boy Allegra had nearly lost, sitting side by side in the space Vanessa had made for them.

Allegra held it together. Vanessa didn't. "I'm sorry!" she said, looking far too emotional for even this moment, jumping up from her chair like it was something she could fix. "I'm sorry, I forgot not all the chairs were full. I was just thinking it would be really nice for us to do crackers the way we always used to, and I thought—"

Aaron stood to wrap his arms around her. "It's okay, Vanessa," he said in his my-dad-is-a-pastor voice. "I think it's a lovely gesture. Love doesn't stop needing somewhere to go just because someone's gone. And I think—" He looked at the empty chair. "I think he'd be glad you saved him a place."

Well, that well and truly finished Vanessa off. Aaron had to escort her aside to comfort her, hurriedly retrieving her latest half-full champagne flute and passing it to Allegra to pour on the grass.

Sal was being more attentive than usual, her thumb stroking over Allegra's hand, legs crossed inward towards her. She didn't say anything, but she was watching Allegra.

Allegra waved it away. She was alright. But—she remembered those flowers at the crash site.

"I'll be right back," she told Sal, and stood, heading over to Aaron and Vanessa beside the Christmas tree, far enough away that only Vanessa's loudest sobs could be heard.

Allegra put her hands on Vanessa's shoulders, making eye contact with Aaron. *I'll take it from here*, she silently told him. He received the message and ducked off.

Vanessa didn't hug her at first. "Here I was, complaining about *other* people ruining Christmas..." she said self-deprecatingly, looking upwards and circling her fingertips under her eyes to try and rescue her eye makeup. "Sobbing like..." She was a little tipsy; the right word didn't come to her immediately.

"Like a widow?" Allegra offered very gently. "Who'd already lost her brother?"

Vanessa held it for a moment, eyes shut, mouth closed. Not for long. "My whole family," she said immediately. "Everyone. Gone or dead." She looked up at Allegra. With the same big, soulful eyes that she'd had as a child. Hoping.

Allegra had seen that look before. On Vanessa at 19, newly orphaned and still grieving Lachie, looking to Allegra as if someone older might be able to prove there was still a family here.

Heavily pregnant and lost, Allegra hadn't been able to be that person. Not then.

But maybe—"I went out to the crash site the other day," Allegra said. "To visit him. There were flowers there."

Vanessa was watching her. Waiting.

"Yours."

She made a small, helpless gesture, like it was obvious. "Someone has to let him know he's still loved."

And there it was: the whole shape of her, suddenly. The table, the name cards, the crackers. Aaron's birthday cards, and Christmas presents, and phone calls Allegra had missed or made too late. All of it a desperate question longing for someone to answer: for the ships to sail back to harbour, for her family to return home. Because no one else would reach for that. *Someone has to.*

"You always did," Allegra said.

Vanessa's mouth trembled. "I was trying. I know I didn't always get it right. You were—" She swallowed. "You were just—gone. In every possible way."

"I know," Allegra said, quieter. "I know that now."

She turned Vanessa a little to face the table. The Sinclairs. At Aaron, laughing as he put on his cracker crown. Even now, an adult, he was so fucking beautiful. And so happy. "Look at him," she said to Vanessa. "Look at what you did."

Vanessa wasn't looking at anything through her tears. But when she hugged Allegra, her arms were so tight. So still and firm. No longer just reaching.

For a few seconds, Allegra let herself be held there. Not forgiven, exactly. Not fixed. Just finally there.

It was a while before Vanessa pulled away. "You're back at work soon, right?"

Allegra nodded. "Next week."

"Back on the road..." Vanessa said, taking that in. "Are you going to live with Sal when you're on call?"

Allegra shook her head. "Not full-time. But I'm sure I'll spend a lot of time there."

Vanessa drew a hopeful breath. "You can come and live with us," she said immediately. "You could have your old bedroom back."

Allegra smiled; she could never live in that house again. Not after Lachie. Not in her old bedroom, with all that history pressed into the walls, waiting to make her 22 again and useless with grief. Vanessa meant it as shelter, and Allegra knew that. But that house belonged to the version of their family that had shattered, and to all the years Vanessa had spent trying to put it back together.

Allegra couldn't move back into that. But she could build something else. And it reminded her of what she needed to tell Aaron.

She shook her head. "That's a really lovely offer," she said, meaning it. "But I need my own place."

Vanessa laughed miserably. "God, she really did house-train you," she said. "You're going to rent somewhere? Out here, or north? Closer to the depot, I gather?"

"Maybe," Allegra said cryptically, and then gave her one final hug, and moved the topic along. "I need to talk to Aaron about Dimi while everyone's still eating."

Allegra had already counselled Vanessa through most of the fallout on the day it happened, but she still leant in for the scoop. "Do you know any more than Friday?" she asked. "Do you think he did it?"

Allegra shrugged. "Beside the point. Everyone thinks he did, so the effect is the same."

Vanessa took a few seconds to step through that with her tipsy brain. "Good point," she said. "Good thing I didn't marry him after all," she said, then reconsidered. "But honestly, a disgraced billionaire's money still buys as much as a beloved billionaire's money." As Allegra escorted her back to the table, she continued, "Do you think his brother is, like, evil as well, or?"

Allegra handed her off to Timothy. "No more champagne for this one," she told him. He smiled and offered her more salad instead.

She flagged Aaron back over. He clearly presumed it was about Vanessa. "Is she alright?" he asked, glancing back as Allegra pulled him away.

"The usual," she told him. "I actually need to talk to you about Dimi."

"Oh." He straightened, eyebrows lifting. "You do?"

"Has he tried to contact you at all?"

Aaron shook his head. "No. I'm not sure I'd answer if he did."

That was a surprise. Allegra gave him an astonished look. "You wouldn't? Even after all those wonderful things he offered?" That seemed—"Did something happen?"

He gave a small, vague smile and looked down, hands in his suit pockets. "I mean, I thought about it. Obviously I thought about it. It was... a lot." His smile faded. "Meeting all those people. The trips. The introductions. The way he talked about doors opening like it was nothing." He shook his head. "But that was the thing. It was too much."

Allegra listened, silent.

"I kept thinking, why me?" he said. "I know I'm smart, but I'm not some prodigy. And Dad's church is full of people who've lost everything. People with kids who are brilliant, who work harder than I do, who'll never get offered anything like that because no billionaire happens to be interested in their family." He glanced at her. "You and Dad put me through private school. I've had help. So if someone like Dimi is offering me more, there has to be a reason."

Allegra stared at him. "What did you think the reason was?"

"You. Dad. Sal." He shrugged. *"Something.* Whatever's happening there. I don't know exactly what it is, but I'm not an idiot. It didn't feel right." He gave her an apologetic smile. "And, sorry, I know you're not a fan of religious stuff, but—I prayed about it. A lot. And every time, I got the same feeling," he said. "That it was wrong. Like I was being offered something I wasn't meant to take. Especially after what people started saying about Dimi and Threshold. It felt like temptation."

Allegra listened, almost unable to believe what she was hearing. She didn't interrupt him.

"And—I'd already decided to step away from it. I'd already promised God I'd listen, and—" His breath caught. "You called. You called half an hour after I made that promise. And then I knew I'd passed the test."

Allegra hugged him immediately, fighting back tears. He was so *smart*, so much wiser than she'd been at his age, even if his wisdom looked nothing like hers. For the life of her, she couldn't figure out how she'd managed to produce such a man. How all of them had. "I thought you'd hate me."

"I told you I don't."

I know, Allegra thought, just hugging him. She closed her eyes.

She had spent weeks trying to protect him from Dimi, from Sal's world, from old money and powerful men and all the doors that opened too easily.

He didn't need protecting, not like that. Maybe he hadn't for a long time.

That thought hurt, but it freed something inside her. The rescue rope went slack. He was tethered by himself, controlling his own climb. Apparently, on this one, he'd been halfway up the cliff before she'd even found the rope.

She couldn't protect him by hauling him back down to where she could reach him. She didn't need to. But she could still give him somewhere to come back to.

Now. It should be now. "I've got something else to tell you."

He pulled back, looking interested. "You do?"

Her stomach fluttered. "Yeah." She reached for her phone, then had to pause before she could unlock it. Her hand wasn't quite steady.

When the realestate.com.au listing opened, she passed the phone to him without explaining.

Aaron looked down, curious, and began scrolling through the photos. A weatherboard house. Bushland. A deck overlooking the trees. His expression softened with each image, but he was careful with it, careful not to assume too much.

"It's nice," he said eventually. "Very leafy." But there was a question on his face.

"I put in an offer yesterday," she said, "and it's been accepted." When he looked up at her, she continued, "It's near Wentworth Falls—nearly 10 hectares, all thick bushland, with the most amazing view of the Kings Tableland. It's a 90-minute drive from Parramatta, but…" Her throat tightened. "It has three bedrooms."

Something passed over Aaron's face. For a second, she saw her little boy behind those eyes.

"I know it's not exactly what you wanted," she said. "It's not your dad and me back together. It's not all of us in one house. You need to live close to uni, and I'll still be on the road a lot of the time. I know that. But—"

"Mum." He looked back down at the phone. He went back two photos, to the one of the deck looking out over the bush, and stayed there for a few seconds too long. Then he scrolled across to the rooms. "Three bedrooms," he repeated, and looked up at her. For confirmation.

"One for you," she said. "Always. Whether I'm there or not."

His eyes were suddenly too bright for his expression. "You're making me want to switch to an online postgrad."

She touched his cheek. "I'm not letting you change your mind about the scholarship," she said. "The house is going to be there when you're done with your master's."

He nodded, but his eyes dropped back to the phone. To the bedroom photos. To the deck. To the impossible proof that she meant it. "After the phone call the other day, I was standing on my balcony looking out at the river," he said. "And I thought, 'Nothing feels better than this', about what you said." He swallowed. "I was wrong."

He tapped the share icon, sent the listing to himself, and then chuckled. "What I really wish I could do is send that listing to myself as a seven-year-old," he said. "And let him know everything's going to be okay."

They hugged again for a moment—less desperately this time—before Aaron pulled away and wiped his eyes. "I have a favour to ask."

"Good time to ask it. I'd give you anything."

He smiled. "Well, Dimi was going to go through my scholarship application and check it. I thought maybe Sal could? Do you think she'd do that? They said we needed to include a resume, and she must see them all the time..."

Allegra smiled. Sal would definitely do that.

She led Aaron back to the table, hoping—foolishly—that everyone might mind their own fucking business for thirty seconds. That didn't happen. Her sisters had dragged the news about the house out of her before she'd even sat down.

Timothy heard it with the others. He looked at Aaron first, then at Allegra, taking in their red eyes. Whatever crossed his face was brief. When he congratulated her, she could hear he meant it.

After presents, they drifted back to the table while the sun went down. Wrapping paper was shoved under chairs so it wouldn't blow away, and half-empty glasses caught the candlelight. It was exactly the sort of thing Vanessa could not survive without getting emotional, forcing everyone into photos, and dragging Allegra into another hug.

Allegra tolerated it well enough until Vanessa held one arm out to Simone. "You, too."

Simone hardened. "Fuck no."

Vanessa ignored that, hooked an arm around her, and dragged her off the leather throne and into a hug with Allegra. They stared each other down over the top of Vanessa's head.

"You have a lot more wrinkles than last time," Simone observed with a smirk.

"Yeah, that's because I get out more."

Simone gave her a Cheshire Cat grin. "I can fix that for you, if it's a problem."

Vanessa hugged them both tighter, holding the three of them together by force.

It took longer than it should have to leave, partly because Vanessa kept pressing leftovers on them, and partly because no one in this family had ever ended a conversation cleanly in their lives. Aaron hugged Allegra once more beside the car and somehow negotiated a hug with Sal, too, now that he had her email address and permission to send through the scholarship application.

Simone didn't move from her leather armchair; it was dark enough that the candles and her lit cigarette were beginning to glow. She gave them a little half-hand wave as they got in the car, and that was it. Allegra could see her watching them in the rear-view mirror as they pulled out.

Sal was quiet beside her. She leant back in the passenger seat, head turned towards the window, watching Simone's house disappear between the trees. Her mobile was still in her bag. That, more than anything, told Allegra the day had landed somewhere.

Hopefully not somewhere bad. "Worse than your last Black family Christmas?"

Sal smiled briefly. It faded. "No," she said simply.

Which should have been comforting. Allegra turned out onto the road, uncomforted.

"I kept waiting for the ask."

Allegra frowned, eyes on the road. "The ask?"

Sal looked towards Allegra, considering her. Then back at the window. "What I was there for."

"You were there because you're my girlfriend," Allegra said, then grimaced and corrected herself. "Also probably because Simone considers experimenting on people a sacred duty."

Sal reached across the centre console and settled her hand over Allegra's wrist as they drove. She didn't say anything else.

For a while, Allegra let that be enough. Sal's hand, the quiet. The fact that she hadn't reached for her phone. But she kept seeing Simone through the smoke, knife in hand, eyes too sharp. The way she'd stopped for a second when Vanessa had gestured vaguely at Sal and said 'black'.

"I think Simone is onto you."

Sal looked over. "You mean about Dimi?" Allegra nodded. Sal considered it. "Well, she already knows I committed a crime. I'm not sure knowing I'm a Black is worse," she decided. "How do you think she'll use it?"

Allegra watched her headlights bounce off the lines on the road ahead. "She'll use it *on* you," she said. "Because she's smug as fuck and she'll want you to know she knows. But beyond that..." Allegra shrugged. "Maybe not against you."

"How do you think she knows? Because of what we did to Dimi?"

Allegra shook her head. "I mean, I'm sure that helped, but it was Vanessa's line. About you wearing black."

That made Sal *smile* for a moment. Allegra caught it reflected in the dark window as Sal gazed out. Allegra's eyes dipped to Sal's black silk dress—beautiful, but black. On Christmas Day.

When Sal didn't say anything, Allegra did. "I wondered that myself, to be honest."

"Why I dress like this?"

"Yeah."

Sal rested her head back against the seat. "There are 26 pages in that NDA specifying, in excruciating detail, everything I'm forbidden to say or do in case it gives away that I'm a Black," she said, a faint smile visible. "And none of them stipulate what colours I'm allowed to wear."

Allegra looked at her in the dark car, at that small, satisfied grin. Of course Sal had found the one thing no one had thought to forbid and turned it into something no one could miss. Allegra had to smile.

It was completely dark when they arrived home at Sal's penthouse. Normally, Sal would take out her phone immediately and spend the whole lift ride scrolling; this time, she took Allegra's hand and laced their fingers together. "C1," she said, echoing Allegra's thoughts. They both smiled at their reflections in the mirror.

Allegra was just thinking Sal was rather uncharacteristically cheerful when the lift doors opened and she was hit by the smell of eucalyptus.

She looked across at Sal, who looked far too innocent. She gestured at Allegra to exit the lift ahead of her, then followed her out.

There was something different about the atmosphere in the penthouse other than the smell. She couldn't figure it out—was it the light?—until she rounded the hall into the atrium.

It was *filled* with Australian natives in polished concrete planters. They started by the couches and grew in size and scope towards the towering windows. Everything was there. Tall, pale mountain gums several metres high; mid-sized banksias and waratahs. Among them, in shared planters and their own smaller pots, were small, brightly coloured flowers. They'd been expertly arranged to resemble forest growth, with spaces between clusters wide enough to walk through, to sit. Under one of the mountain gums was a hammock, almost hidden in deep shadow. All of it, snuck in while they were at Christmas dinner.

It was incredible. Allegra walked up to them, touching the smooth planters, then the trunk of one of the mountain gums.

Sal wandered up behind her. "I'd say Merry Christmas, but I'll wait until you've seen the bedroom."

Allegra looked back at her. "There's more?"

Sal nodded and led her upstairs.

The master bedroom had been transformed, too. The scent of eucalyptus—so familiar—and beneath it, the heavy, earthy smell of soil and water. The trees up here were smaller and denser, and, with the blinds open, they cast shadows from the silver city lights across the room and the bed.

One of the trees was under the air-conditioning vent; it gently rustled as the slats moved. Like wind through its leaves.

It wasn't quite the bush. It could never be. The glass was too clean, the air too controlled, the city still glittering beyond it. But there were trees now; real ones. Eucalypts, banksias, and soft undergrowth, green and breathing at the centre of Sal's immaculate home.

Allegra stood very still, facing them.

She understood what it meant: *I know you need trees. I know you need air. I know this isn't your natural habitat. I can't become the bush, but I can make room for some of it here.*

Not enough to keep her. Sal knew better than that. But enough to make staying a little easier.

Sal stood behind her. When she spoke, her voice was quiet. "I thought it might make you more comfortable," she said. "When you come to stay with me."

Chapter 50: Home

Allegra had an endless list of things she needed to do now that she finally had a moment at the new house. Now that she wasn't in Shanghai with Aaron, or in Newcastle delivering training, or in Katoomba on a vertical rescue anymore. Instead of doing any of those things, though, she kept getting caught on the timber deck off the living room. Leaning on the railing, staring into the gum trees and dense green scrub spilling down the hill.

At dusk, the valley turned blue and gold beneath the birdsong, and she could hardly believe this beautiful, breathing piece of the mountains belonged to her.

A year ago, even a few months ago, she never would have considered it. All that time, she could have been ducking back here to change over her gear, wash things, make repairs. Breathing in eucalyptus and mountain air instead of traffic fumes.

And coming home to little notes Aaron had left for her on the kitchen bench.

One of them was folded in her pocket now, soft at the creases from how many times she'd taken it out and read it. Her phone was in there with it, heavier than it should have felt.

She took it out for a moment. Froggy's message was three days old, but still open. *"Austin's vid goes live 7pm on Thurs. Don't freak out. Sal's not framed badly."*

Prime time, Allegra thought, closing her phone and putting it back in her pocket. Sal was coming up to watch it with her, and due to arrive soon.

Allegra had been perfectly fine for three weeks. Busy, mostly. Practical. Sensible. Then she'd woken up that morning knowing Sal would be here by sunset, and suddenly every part of her seemed to remember at once: the weight of Sal's hand on her sleeve, the low register of her voice, the precise shape of her grin when she knew she was winning.

What Allegra really should be doing was making the house at least somewhat presentable for Sal's first visit since the pre-purchase inspection: unpacking the dozens of Woolies bags in the living room into her side of the wardrobe, and stowing all the work gear laid out across the floor. But it was so beautiful outside. She'd be out here with Sal soon.

We could watch the sun set together tonight, she thought, looking out towards the horizon. *Our first sunset here.*

She *should* have tidied up the house. Instead, she spent another 10 minutes drinking in the view, checked the roast in the oven, and went to put on a suit to surprise Sal.

She was just facing herself in the mirror, alternating between eating an apple and trying to work out if she could braid her own hair in any useful way, when her phone beeped. She glanced towards it.

Sal! She grabbed it immediately. *"Your gate."*

Allegra straightened. *My gate*? She leant over to the window; Sal was outside the temperamental gate, on the smooth driveway she'd paid to seal, with the sports car behind her. She looked a million dollars in the middle of the bush.

Allegra's first thought—beating everything else in her head—was *she's early!* She hurriedly pulled her hair into a ponytail and rushed outside, only to realise halfway to the gate that Sal had made it in just over an hour.

It should take at least 90 minutes—probably more, in peak hour.

She stopped in place, frowning. "You sped."

Sal's expression moved only slightly—in the wrong direction. "For legal reasons I did not speed."

Allegra sighed at her. *"Sal."*

"Also, my car has an escape hatch, so..." When she saw Allegra glance towards her car to make a split-second assessment of whether that might be true, she gave her a wide, cheeky grin. "I left early."

Pfft. Allegra walked back and leant a hip against her LandCruiser. "For that, you can open the gate yourself," she said, crossing her arms and taking a big bite of her apple.

Sal spent a moment standing there, hoping Allegra was kidding, before heaving a sigh, bending down to the gate pin, and trying to pull it out. And failing to, repeatedly.

Allegra took a few more bites, wondering how dirty she should let Sal's hands get before she intervened.

"You could help," Sal said dryly.

"I could."

Eventually, she did, discarding her apple core and walking up to the gate as Sal straightened. "This feels familiar, somehow," she said with a grin, before leaning down and giving the pin a very practised pull.

As she swung the gate open, Sal wandered back to her car, opening the door. "If we're recreating our first meeting, I seem to remember you wearing less," she said, eyes twinkling as she got in the car.

Allegra had to wait until Sal parked in the garage and climbed out to reply. "Maybe we can recreate it properly later." She was grinning. When Sal looked very interested in that prospect, she added, "I can shut you outside the gate and leave you there again."

Sal pressed her lips together and nodded. "I walked right into that one," she said, giving Allegra a very appreciative once-over. "Mmm. Been attending important meetings out here?"

"Just one," Allegra said, and pulled Sal in by the lapels.

Sal's eyes dropped to her mouth a fraction before Allegra kissed her. There was a brief, satisfying loss of poise—Sal's hand catching at Allegra's sleeve, her breath hitching once—and then she was kissing back, arms snaking up behind Allegra's neck.

Allegra had only intended it to be quick—an opportunity to have Sal in her arms after what felt like *fucking eternity.* It was so good kissing her again, though, that they ended up there for a while, stuck between kisses, smiles, and the now-familiar feeling of touching each other.

She pulled away eventually—she should probably check the roast—but Sal pulled her back in. "I'm not done with you yet."

Allegra ended up ruining that one by laughing. As Sal gave up on her mouth and kissed down her neck, she checked her phone over Sal's shoulder. "What time is it? Maybe we can christen the bed before Austin's video drops."

Sal pulled away to glance at her watch. "6:21pm," she said, then gave the proposal some consideration. "Not long enough to account for a three-week break." She flashed Allegra a cheeky smile and nodded towards the house. "And if I'm not mistaken, I smell dinner."

Allegra grinned, straightening. "You do. It's a brisket."

Sal gave her another slow peck. And another. "I leave you alone for three weeks and you become a homeowner with a roast in the oven."

They retrieved Sal's small suitcase from the sports car and headed inside towards the smell of the nearly-finished roast—and into the chaos.

Sal stopped just inside the door, eyes on the Woolies bags full of still-packed clothes, rescue gear all over the floor, and camping cutlery on the island bench in the kitchen. And not a single scrap of furniture. She looked sideways at Allegra. "Have you ever lived in a house before?" she asked dryly. "You do know how they work, don't you?"

"I have been here for *one day*," Allegra pointed out, edging past her and putting the suitcase beside the island bench. She grabbed a very haggard-looking tea towel to take out the brisket.

While Allegra wrestled it out of the oven, Sal noticed a zip lock bag of shiny new bolts on the counter and lifted it with interest, reading the note aloud. "'For the gate, since apparently everyone has accepted defeat'," she said, and then looked at Allegra.

Allegra exhaled. "Simone."

Sal's eyebrows went up. "How does *she* know about the gate?"

"Aaron told the boys, the boys told Vanessa, and then Vanessa told Simone," she said in a voice as haggard as the tea towel. "There are no secrets in this family."

Sal placed the bag carefully back on the bench, as if a jolt might cause it to explode, and wandered out into the rest of the chaos. Her eyes landed on the coloured rope laid out beside stacks of laminated training sheets. "Homework?"

"Training props," Allegra said, poking a knife into the meat. "For the new vertical rescue volunteers I saw in Newcastle."

Sal bent down and lifted some of the rope. "Wouldn't there be somewhere to store these at the depot?"

"Sure," Allegra said, deciding the brisket was ready. "I could leave them at the depot if I wanted to guarantee they'd get used by someone else and lost."

Sal was inspecting the coloured rescue ropes. "There's something aesthetically pleasing about knots tied on these," she decided, touching them. "They're so thick."

Allegra eyed her as she quickly washed her knife. She was being very deliberate about that particular rope. "Careful," she said. "It'll think you're interested."

"Maybe I *am* interested," Sal said with a little grin, bringing the knotted rope back to the kitchen. "Perhaps it could tell me a little bit about itself." She put it on the kitchen bench and leant expectantly next to it.

Allegra gave her a look. "I've seen your bottom drawer. You could teach *me* knots."

"Not these ones," she said. "I don't use rescue knots."

Allegra put the knife down and dried her hands. "Okay," she said, and pointed to one end. "That's a bowline," she said. "Great for anchoring tent lines and securing loads, easy to tie with one hand during a rescue."

"You can tie it with one hand?" Sal asked, impish.

Allegra ignored her and pointed to the other end. "Figure of eight, threaded," she said. "Secures a climbing harness for vertical rescue."

Allegra's expression dared her to say something about the word 'harness'. She could see Sal was thinking about it.

Then she pointed to the middle. "Alpine butterfly. A secure loop tied in the middle of the rope. Rescue work, mostly—for when the climb's already underway and you need a safe attachment point for someone to clip on." Sal had nothing cheeky to say about that one. In fact, Allegra thought she caught—a smile?

Allegra left it, checked the time, and went around the bench to Sal's suitcase. "Let's put this away before we eat." They headed down the short hall.

The master bedroom was identifiable only because it faced the valley and was marginally bigger than the others. No ensuite; the house only had one bathroom. It already had a cast iron queen-sized bed and an old, ornate wardrobe, though—both from Facebook Marketplace.

The bed was one of Allegra's first purchases. "I figured you wouldn't want to sleep on a bedroll."

Sal opened her suitcase, took out a couple of garment hangers and turned to the wardrobe. One side of it was free. She glanced back at Allegra, who nodded. Sal paused, a little private smile on her face, and hung her suits in there. "I've slept in a tent with you," she reminded Allegra.

"In service of ousting Dimi."

Sal's smile barely moved. "Yes," she said, smoothing one jacket onto its hanger. "That was the official reason."

The line of Sal's suits in her wardrobe suddenly felt more intimate than the bed.

On the way back to the living room, they passed the other bedrooms. Allegra showed Sal Aaron's: already fully furnished and half unpacked. Sal's eyes went to the gold-leafed scholarship presentation certificate on the wall.

She inspected it, smiling. "His application was excellent," she said. "He didn't want to put this up at his place?"

Allegra shook her head. "He said he wanted to share it with us."

Sal hesitated at that, looked again at the certificate, and then followed Allegra down the hall. The third bedroom, a much smaller room, was still empty. Sal wandered into it and up to the window. It looked uphill towards thick scrub; an eastern yellow robin dropped from a low branch into the undergrowth, a quick flare of yellow against the dusk. She turned back to the room, thoughtful.

"Maybe I should put some grey marble down in here," Allegra offered with a grin. "So you don't feel too out of place."

Sal mirrored the grin, but it softened quickly as she looked around the empty room. Not assessing it this time. Not exactly.

Allegra leant a shoulder on the doorframe. "Is there something specific you want to use it for?"

"A third bedroom?" Sal said, thoughtful. "Perhaps."

Whatever Sal was seeing in the empty room, it belonged to a future less empty than the ones she usually let herself imagine. Allegra filed that away to think about later as they headed back to the living room, where Sal could stare judgementally (Allegra felt) at the gap where a couch should be.

Reading her mind, Sal said, "Have you chosen what sort of couch you'd like?"

"Something couch-shaped, probably."

"Excellent, I'll add that to the brief," Sal shot back. "Fabric? Leather?" At Allegra's blank stare, she added, "Or were you just going to defer the decision for as long as possible?"

"I was just going to let Aaron choose, to be honest."

Sal considered that. "Would it bother you if I took him shopping for one?"

That was—Allegra stopped. The image of Sal and Aaron standing together in a furniture shop choosing something for this half-empty room should not have felt as intimate as it did. But it did. It struck her somewhere. "That's fine, if you want to," she managed anyway.

She was heading back to the roast as Sal lifted her phone and started texting—Aaron, she realised. Sal texting Aaron.

As Allegra unfolded her knife and started carving up the brisket, she listened to the tap, tap of Sal's thumbs on her phone. Her son and her partner, discussing furniture for her house.

Sal's conversation with Aaron seemed to finish; she straightened, glanced at her phone, and slid it into her pocket. "6:32pm." She approached the bench, eyes on the roast. "T-minus 28 minutes until Austin's video drops."

Allegra glanced up. "You seem very calm about it."

Sal stole a bean from the edge of the roast and ate it thoughtfully. "I've had a long time to get used to the idea."

Allegra stopped cutting for a moment. "You know what he's posting," she said, sounding more accusatory than she'd intended. "Did Froggy tell you more than she told me?"

Sal shook her head. "I don't know exactly what he's posting. But I've been following his work for 10 years. Give him an anomaly and he'll gnaw through concrete." She took a bite of her bean. "If Froggy says not to freak out, let's take her advice."

Allegra watched her for a couple of seconds, then finished plating up and led them both out onto the deck with the camping chairs and table.

They were facing the approaching sunset and the gold-tinged treetops. The birds were still going; now, the cicadas had joined them. Allegra immediately turned to watch Sal's face. Sal had never seen the view like this before—not in the deepening evening, with the valley turning all these colours and the last light catching in the tops of the gums. Allegra could hardly stand how badly she wanted her to love it.

Sal was just watching her with a vague smile.

Allegra's head slumped to the side. "You can look at me anytime," she said dryly. "Look at that." She gestured outwards.

Sal humoured her, looking at the view and nodding gravely. "Beautiful," she said, in the careful tone of someone praising a child's drawing. "So many trees."

Allegra rolled her eyes and good-naturedly gave up.

Grinning, Sal angled her chair towards Allegra's so their knees rested together, then tried the brisket. Her eyebrows rose. "Not bad. After the rest of the house, I would have accepted 'non-toxic', but this is quite good."

The rest of the house. Allegra scoffed. "Sorry, Princess, but this is how the other half live."

"Out of kitchen boxes, Woolies bags, and surrounded by piles of ropes?" Sal inquired innocently.

Allegra gave her a tired look and swallowed her mouthful. "Too rustic for you?" she teased. "Having buyers' remorse about your feral girlfriend?"

Sal grinned. "It *is* rustic," she said. "But no. It's rather charming."

"Your charming feral girlfriend in her quaint rustic house."

"My charming feral girlfriend in her extremely sharp suit," she said with a smile, and took another bite. They must have looked quite the pair, wearing impossibly polished black corporate suits on a worn wooden deck in the middle of the bush. At least Allegra had Docs on; Sal was still in her stilettos. She didn't look at home here either, not yet. But she *did* look comfortable. "I brought my camping clothes. Just in case."

Allegra sat up. "You want to go camping?" She tried not to sound too excited.

"In case you do," she clarified. "I wanted the option to be there."

That gave Allegra a sudden, vivid image of them going down to the edge of her property near the creek: rock underfoot, water trickling over stone, the smell of moss. Maybe, on a day when there wasn't a total fire ban, they could go down there and pitch a tent together, have a campfire, and watch the bush around them fade into darkness while they fell asleep.

"I think you might like it," she told Sal as they were finishing their dinners.

Sal was only watching her. "I think I would."

When they were done, Allegra took Sal's cutlery inside to put in the sink. Sal followed her, eyes on the floor as she avoided the scattered work gear.

Allegra took the ratty old tea towel and playfully tossed it at Sal. "I cooked, you clean." She hoisted herself up to sit on the island bench. "Presuming you know *how* to wash up."

Sal gave her a sidelong look as she walked past. "I do my coffee mug every day," she pointed out, and then looked at the sink. "Gloves?"

"We raw-dog washing up out here."

Sal exhaled, taking off her blazer, unbuttoning her shirt sleeves, and rolling them up. She even took off her heels and put them out of splash distance. "I'm buying you a dishwasher."

Sal turned on the water, holding her fingers under the flow and waiting for it to warm. For a minute, it was just the two of them in the half-unpacked house: Sal at the cheap sink in her expensive shirt, Allegra on the bench beside the leftovers, and the valley darkening beyond the glass. The domesticity of it was surreal.

She was watching Sal, curious about how relaxed she looked at the sink, when Sal took her watch off. There was something around her wrist. "What's that?"

Sal held it up. It was a thin cuff of Gladwrap.

For a second Allegra thought it was another joke. Some sleek little Sal absurdity. Then she saw the redness around the Gladwrap, the careful way Sal held her wrist, and whatever teasing comment she had been going to make was gone. "Did you get a new tattoo?"

Sal's lips parted a moment. She closed them. "Yes."

Allegra hopped down off the bench. "Show me?"

Sal held her hand out, palm down, for Allegra to unwrap it. She did, careful to preserve the Gladwrap—she wasn't sure she had any more of it in the house.

Underneath was another geometric tattoo—at least, that's what Allegra thought at first. It had the same style and looked like a pipe, or a tube around her wrist, or—she noticed the flecks.

Rescue rope.

"Turn it over," Sal told her.

She did, turning Sal's wrist upwards. On the underside was a larger shape on the rope, highly stylised. As Allegra adjusted to the style, she realised immediately what it was: a knot.

An alpine butterfly knot.

That knot. A secure knot tied in the middle of a rope.

Allegra's voice was quiet. "It's an alpine butterfly."

"It is," she said. Then, after a few moments, she added, "I was hoping you might show me how to tie it." She looked up.

Allegra's lips parted. *Tie a knot.* "What are you asking me?"

There was a tiny, private smile on her lips. "Right now, to show me how to tie this one," she said. "But maybe, in the future..."

It hung there, between them.

Allegra could hardly breathe. "I'll show you," she said, meaning it. "Just ask."

The rescue rope was at the top of her training gear where she'd tossed it earlier. She collected it, untied it, and took it back to the kitchen, stepping slowly in behind Sal by the sink. She slipped her hands over Sal's, guiding the rope into them. On Sal's wrist, the fresh red design matched the rope in their hands.

Sal let her hands be guided under Allegra's, so easily.

Allegra had taught hundreds, perhaps thousands of people this knot. Not like this. Sal's hands were warm, her skin soft. At first Allegra's lips were in her hair, then beside her ear. Sal leant her head back, closing her eyes and letting Allegra move her hands.

The knot didn't get finished. Sal turned in her arms and kissed her, backing her into the sink. The rope fell slack between them, but Allegra kept hold of her wrist, careful and steady, as if the knot had already been tied.

Eventually they pulled apart. Allegra checked the time—6:51pm—and Sal turned to the sink again.

Allegra stopped her. "It's okay," she said, cutting in. "Your new tattoo probably shouldn't—"

"Allegra," she said, gently pushing her aside. "I have the cream with me."

Allegra stood back and watched her, taking some steadying breaths. Looking at the slope of her neck, the curve of her back—that private smile.

I caused that smile, Allegra realised, watching her and thinking about the tattoo. Sal wanted a secure attachment, mid-line. Maybe her first.

It was rescue work, in the end. Not the dramatic kind. Not sirens, not floodwater, not hauling someone bodily out of danger. This quieter thing: recognising when someone couldn't speak or call for help, but still needed a safe point to clip on—and being strong enough, steady enough to take the weight.

For Sal, she already had. And Sal had put it on her skin.

Allegra's eyes stayed on the tattoo. "When did you get it?"

Sal's hands stilled a moment on the plate. "Your first day in Newcastle," she said. "When I couldn't make it to the airport because ASIC ran late, I thought, 'I lasted two weeks, I can wait another few hours'." Then Allegra had been called out, almost immediately, for five successive days. "I went home and saw all the trees..."

She was still again. Eyes forward. Allegra reached out to touch her.

She softened a little under Allegra's hand. "I couldn't sleep. I decided not to try." Allegra slipped her arms all the way around Sal from behind and held her tightly.

"I feel it," Sal said quietly. "When you're not here."

It was a lot, hearing her like this. Sal did not give anyone this much unguarded truth lightly. Allegra didn't want to ask, but she had to. "Is it too much?"

Sal's head shook slightly under Allegra's chin. "I expected you to always be gone. But you're around more often than not," she said. "It does make the 'not' very noticeable." After a moment, she added, more quietly, "I've made several *insane* decisions in my life, Allegra. All very recent. Absence is making one or two of them look reasonable."

Allegra just hugged her. "I missed you in Shanghai," she said. "And since. There were a few nights where I imagined you dropping in on us suddenly. Aaron likes to sleep in—we could have gone to breakfast."

Sal laughed once, gently. "I'd be lying if I said I hadn't thought about it," she said. "I didn't want to intrude on you and Aaron."

You don't, Allegra thought, remembering the furniture shopping request and the warmth it stirred inside her. Sal was standing barefoot in Allegra's half-unpacked life, washing dishes in a house without a couch, with camping clothes in her suitcase and rescue rope freshly inked on her skin. She had come all the way into Allegra's world and, somehow, made herself careful inside it. Allegra rested her cheek against the soft top of Sal's head. "I'm so in love with you," she said, breathing it into Sal's hair.

In response, Sal's wet hands rose to cover Allegra's on her middle.

They stood like that for a long time; too long. Sal shifted. "What time is it?"

Allegra opened her eyes and fished her phone out. "6:58pm," she said. "Shit."

Reluctantly, Allegra let her go. Sal finished the dishes, and then they took her uncracked phone back out to the deck and pulled their chairs right up together so Allegra could put her arm around Sal's shoulders.

Allegra's pulse picked up a little as they sat staring at Austin's YouTube page, waiting for the video to appear. Allegra stole a glance at Sal; she looked unnervingly calm. Far calmer than she had been for Austin's other videos.

"What if it's about the fires?" Allegra asked.

Sal shrugged, uncharacteristically unbothered. Allegra's eyes lingered on her, wondering about that.

When the video appeared on the screen, they both reached for it at once.

It started with a sweeping drone shot of green vineyards: hundreds of neat rows of twisted, old-growth vines. Behind them, cloud-topped mountains rose up on the horizon, and white Cape Dutch farmhouses were tucked in amongst the trees.

The camera angle lowered to reveal Austin standing outside one of the farmhouses, smiling into the lens. "You're probably wondering why I'm in South Africa."

South Africa. Allegra looked across at Sal; her eyes remained on the screen, but she was smiling.

"I'm standing in the Cape Winelands, outside the vineyard where official records say a baby girl was born 43 years ago," he began, gesturing behind him. "But the family who own this place aren't the family named on her paperwork—and they say they've never heard of her." His smile faded, just enough. "So, who created a birth story in South Africa, and why did they need the real one buried?"

Allegra paused the video. Sal's eyes stayed on the frozen frame.

"How the fuck would he even know?" Allegra asked.

Sal shrugged. "I'm a permanent anomaly in a rich, powerful family. Someone was going to wonder about that eventually."

Allegra accepted that. For about half a second. Then she wondered whether Austin had found the thread, or whether someone had placed it where he would pull.

Sal reached up and pressed play again.

Austin held up a sheaf of documents. "I'm going to walk you through how a child was given a false beginning, why that lie held for more than four decades, and who it protected." He paused, giving weight to his final statement. "Today, that baby is an adult—a woman Australia knows as Sal Lategan."

On the screen, Austin kept talking, pulling the first threads loose. Names, dates, documents. The kind of proof Sal had spent her life surrounded by, and the kind that had been used to keep her sealed away from herself for more than 40 years. Beside Allegra, Sal stayed very still, watching the lie begin to come apart in someone else's hands.

When Dimi's face appeared, when Austin named him, something loosened in Sal. Something ancient. Allegra tightened her arm around her, and after a moment, Sal let her head sink back against Allegra's shoulder, eyes falling shut as her truth finally broke its banks.

It was out. Sal's secret was no longer locked behind her ribs or sealed inside signed documents; no longer hers to carry in silence. It had broken into the open under the evening sky, while the valley turned blue and gold around them.

The truth was out, and all the lost children it carried had somewhere, finally, to come home.

About the Author

A. E. Dooland is an Australian author, financial counsellor, wife, and mother. By day, she helps people untangle debt, crisis, and the bureaucratic machinery of modern life; by night, she writes queer fiction about love, identity, and the messy work of being true to yourself.

Her books include *Under My Skin*, *Flesh & Blood*, *Solve for i*, and *Godspeed.* They are available through all major online booksellers and library apps, and on aedooland.com

www.ingramcontent.com/pod-product-compliance
Lightning Source LLC
LaVergne TN
LVHW050909080826
845145LV00001B/22

* 9 7 8 0 9 9 4 1 7 7 9 8 8 *